Mary Anne Everett Green

Calendar of State Papers

Domestic series, of the reign of Charles II. 1664-1665

Mary Anne Everett Green

Calendar of State Papers
Domestic series, of the reign of Charles II. 1664-1665

ISBN/EAN: 9783742830715

Manufactured in Europe, USA, Canada, Australia, Japa

Cover: Foto ©Andreas Hilbeck / pixelio.de

Manufactured and distributed by brebook publishing software
(www.brebook.com)

Mary Anne Everett Green

Calendar of State Papers

CALENDAR

OF

STATE PAPERS,

DOMESTIC SERIES,

OF THE REIGN OF

CHARLES II.

1664-1665,

PRESERVED IN

HER MAJESTY'S PUBLIC RECORD OFFICE.

EDITED BY

MARY ANNE EVERETT GREEN,

Author of "The Lives of the Princesses of England," &c.

UNDER THE DIRECTION OF THE MASTER OF THE ROLLS, AND WITH THE SANCTION OF HER MAJESTY'S SECRETARY OF STATE FOR THE HOME DEPARTMENT.

LONDON:

LONGMAN, GREEN, LONGMAN, ROBERTS, AND GREEN.

1863.

Printed by
Eyre and Spottiswoode, Her Majesty's Printers,
For Her Majesty's Stationery Office.

CONTENTS OF THIS VOLUME.

DOMESTIC PAPERS.

CHARLES II.

Vol. CII. September, 1664.

1664.

Sept. [1?] 1. Account [by Jonas Shish] of works to be done on board the six ships fitting out for Guinea, for stowage of provisions and ammunition. [*Adm. Paper.*]

Sept. 1. 2. Report of the progress of five merchant ships fitting out for Guinea, most of which will be ready in a few days. [*Adm. Paper.*]

Sept. 1. 3. Capt. Walter Wood to the Navy Comrs. Recommends John Driver as surgeon for the Convertine. [*Adm. Paper.*]

Sept. 1. Harwich. 4. Report by Sir Wm. Batten of the state of Harwich yard and of his orders and proceedings there at his late visit, August 30 and 31 and September 1. [*Adm. Paper, two pages.*]

Sept. 2. Pass for William Harvey and Isaiah Ward to France. Minute. [*Ent. Book* 16, *p.* 221.]

Sept. 2. Warrant by the Earl of Bath and Sec. Bennet to Ralph Moss and six others, for several parcels of leather and calves' skins, seized on pretence of authority from them, to be restored to William Panton and Anchor Hancock. [*Ent. Book* 16, *p.* 221.]

Sept. 2. The Hastings, Downs. 5. Capt. Jonathan Waltham to Sec. Bennet. Has arrived from Yarmouth and will sail for Portsmouth, unless he receive orders to the contrary.

Sept. 3. 6. Rich. King to John Horner, York. Wishes him the restoration spoken of in 1651, and 1652, not by sword or bow, but by the word of power and by miracles, as in the times of Elijah and Joshua. Looks for the day of the Son of Man on earth, and exhorts them to stedfastness. Hopes soon to see York. Endorsed "Information from Mr. Mascall."

Sept. 3. Whitehall. 7. Petition of Lieut.-Col. Thos. Duncan, farmer in 1648 of the ferry boats and wine licences at Barton-on-Humber, to the King, for a gratuity for life, according to a report on his former petition; also for a lease for life of the ferry at Kingston-on-Hull, it being let by the mayor of Hull, to the wrong of the farmers of Barton ferry.

VOL. CII.

1664.

With reference thereon to the Duke of Albemarle, recommending that a reformado's place in Hull garrison be conferred on the petitioner, if he think fit; and his report, September 17, that he should be commended to Lord Belasyse, to be mustered in one of the companies of Hull.

Sept. 2. Custom House. 8. Sir John Shaw to Mr. Coventry. Mr. Lowe has a quantity of oars very proper for the King or the Royal Company's service; begs that his offer may be accepted in preference to any other. [*Adm. Paper.*]

Sept. 3. 9. Further report of progress of five merchant ships fitting out for Guinea. [*Adm. Paper.*]

Sept. 3. Portsmouth. 10. John Tippetts to the Navy Comrs. Notice of the Guernsey sailing from Spithead. The calkers await their discharge and the payment of their conduct money, &c. Tender of hard wood. Desires orders for painting the new ship. [*Adm. Paper.*]

Sept. 4. The Augustine, Downs. 11. Capt. Rich. Teate to the Navy Comrs. Damage sustained by his ship in a gale off the North Foreland. [*Adm. Paper.*]

Sept. 4. 12. Measurement of scantlings of elm timber sent by Sir Wm. Warren to Woolwich. [*Adm. Paper.*]

Sept. 5. Victualling Office. 13. Certificate by Thos. Lewis that the pursers of seven of the Guinea ships have cleared former accounts, those of two have not been to sea, and the accounts of the other two are still depending. [*Adm. Paper.*]

[Sept. 5.] Petition of Susan Harby to the King. Her late husband, Clement Harby, being in debt to his brother, Sir Job Harby, assigned his estate over to him in trust, to pay his debts, and to give him the remainder; Sir Job disposing of the estate, the petitioner sued him in Chancery; both parties agreed to submit to the mediation of Counsellor Chaloner Chute, who decided, in 1634, that Sir Job should pay the petitioner 3,950*l.*; this he promised to do from the first moneys assigned to him by His Majesty, but died before the payment, and Elizabeth Harby, his widow, refuses to pay her debt. Begs that the farmers of customs may detain in their hands so much of Sir Job Harby's dividend as will pay the said debt. [*Ent. Book* 18, *pp.* 81–3.]

Sept. 5. The King to the Customs' Comrs. Wishing to accede to the petition of Susan Harby, orders them to detain so much out of the dividend, payable to the executrix of Sir Job Harby, as will discharge the debt which she alleges to be due to her. [*Ent. Book* 17, *p.* 57.]

Sept. 5. Whitehall. Warrant from Sec. Bennet to Sir Herbert Price, Sir Paul Neal, and Sir Robert Murray, attended by Gervase Price, serjeant trumpeter, to visit Foxhall, and inquire from Lord John Somerset on the one part, and the widow of Gasper Calthoffe on the other,

1664. VOL. CII.

relative to the possession of the several rooms, engines, tools, &c., to ascertain what belongs to the Marquis of Worcester, and what to Gaspar Colthoffe. [*Ent Book* 10, p. 220.]

Sept. 5. Warrant from Sec. Bennet to receive James Hamilton into custody, and commit him to the Tower. [*Ent. Book* 10, *p.* 221.]

Sept. 5. Warrant to Sir John Robinson to receive James Hamilton prisoner, for fighting in His Majesty's presence. [*Ent. Book* 10, *p.* 221.]

Sept. 5. Leghorn. 14. Fras. Williamson to his cousin Jos. Williamson. Is still fed with fair promises only by his father. Fears ill dealings from Mr. Sidney, if unable to pay the 50*l.* due for his diet. Could trade at Genoa with a good capital, but if he cannot have it, begs to be sent for home.

Sept. 5. The Francis, Hole Haven. 15. Captain Jonathan Waltham to Wm. Coventry. Requests a speedy supply of victuals. There are 18 vessels now lying in quarantine, all in good health, and more daily expected. [*Adm. Paper.*]

Sept. 5. The Reserve. 16. John Bonner to the Navy Comrs. The Reserve has got well into the Hope. More men are wanted, most of those that brought her having gone to Chatham. [*Adm. Paper.*]

Sept. 5. Olleram. 17. Thos. Corbin to the Navy Comrs. Receipt of 100*l.* Difficulties of conveyance of large timber. A carter was killed by the overthrow of his cart, being struck dead by a piece of timber. Delay in lading the hoy. A strong carriage for great timber and another 100*l.* required. [*Adm. Paper, two pages.*]

Sept. 6. Woolwich. 18. Chris. Pett to the Navy Comrs. Particulars of timber sent to Deptford, or wanted for the new second-rate ship. Calkers required for her. [*Adm. Paper.*]

Sept. 6. 19. Capt. Walter Wood to Mr. Hayter. Desires that John Driver may be appointed surgeon with him on the Henrietta, instead of going on the Convertine. [*Adm. Paper.*]

Sept. 6. Augustine, Spithead. 20. Capt. Rich. Teale to the Navy Comrs. Asks orders about replacing his broken masts and bowsprit. [*Adm. Paper.*]

Sept. 6. 21. Report of the progress of five merchant ships fitting out for Guinea. [*Adm. Paper.*]

Sept. 6. 22. R. L—— to her sister Ellinor Hutton, Cornforth, at Durham. Mrs. Hutton's husband wonders she does not attend to what he writes to her, thinks she must be grown cold in her affections, and is troubled that she does not return. Endorsed "Durham—information from the lord."

Sept. 6. Tuesday. 23. Sir Willm. Killigrew to Sec. Bennet. Sir George Carteret is ready to acknowledge that the writer alone put the pin business into his hands, and the rest of his discourse about delivering 500*l.* a year

VOL. CII.

1664. for the King's service, but wishes nothing to be said to the King till the cannon is cast; though the metal is ready, it is delayed, because the King's money is not paid.

Sept. 6. Order granting the petition of Robt. Fitzhugh and other inhabitants of Chatham, for pardon of Wm. Banks, mariner, and remitting the sentence of transportation against him. [*Ent. Book* 18, *p.* 81.]

[Sept. 6.] 24. Blank warrant for payment of a yearly allowance to M. La Fabvolière.

Sept. 6. Pass for Charles Duncan to France. Minute. [*Ent. Book* 16, *p.* 222.]

Sept. 7. Pass for George Hamilton to transport seven horses to France. Minute. [*Ent. Book* 16, *p.* 222.]

Sept. 7. Pass for John Lord Kingston into Ireland with ten horses, custom free. Minute. [*Ent. Book* 16, *p.* 222.]

Sept. 7. Warrant to the High Sheriff of Dorsetshire to pay to Edward Cheek, of Bruton, co. Somerset, a fine of 50*l.* adjudged against Alex. Weeks, of Shaston, co. Dorset. [*Ent. Book* 16, *p.* 222.]

[Sept. 7.] 25. Order for a warrant to Sir John Denham, surveyor of buildings, to permit Edward Progers, groom of the bedchamber, to take up certain useless pipes of lead lying between the conduit in Bushy Park and the stables at Hampton Court, towards the building of his lodge in the North Park.

[Sept. 7.] 26. Warrant as ordered above.

Sept. 7. Entry of the above warrant. [*Ent. Book* 16, *p.* 222.]

Sept. 7. Warrant for a lease to Sir Thomas Osborne, Bart., of Keeton [Kiveton], Yorkshire, of the estate in Brafferton, forfeited by Ralph Rymer for high treason; with tithes and emoluments of the rectory &c., rent 20*s.*; redeemable on payment of 2,000*l.* [*Ent. Book* 16, *pp.* 223–4.]

Sept. 7. Warrant for a lease to Sir Jordan Crosland of the estate of Brafferton, Yorkshire, belonging to Ralph Rymer attainted of high treason, on his payment to Sir Thomas Osborne of 2,000*l.* for redemption of a lease of the same previously made to him. [*Ent. Book* 16, *pp.* 224–5.]

Sept. 7. Whitehall. Order in Council,—on a report prefixed from the Council for foreign plantations, recommending the erection of an office petitioned for [*see July* 12, 1664,] for registry of all persons going voluntarily to the plantations, as being useful, and prejudicial to none, because the registering is left voluntary,—that a commission be prepared, appointing Roger Whitley to be master of the said office. [*Board of Trade, No.* 124, *pp.* 5, 6.] *Annexing,*

1. *Commission addressed to the Duke of York, as Lord Admiral and Warden of the Cinque Ports, and to the other Officers of the ports, for the erecting of an "office of taking and*

1664. VOL. CII.

registering the consents, agreements, and covenants of such persons, male or female, as shall voluntarily goe or be sent as servants to any of the plantations in America;" certificates of the consent of the party are to be delivered under the seal of the office to the merchant with whom he covenants; also appointing Roger Whitley master of the office, with the fee of 40s. a year, and such allowances as the planters may agree to give him. [*Board of Trade, Vol.* 124, *pp.* 7–10.]

Sep. 7. 27, 28. Copies of the above report and commission. [*Two papers, five pages.*]

Sept. 7. Chatham. 29. Commissioner Peter Pett to Sam. Pepys. The delay of the Harwich boy has prevented provisions being sent to the Downs. Has been with Sir John Mennes on board the Deal ships, and taken care for their quick dispatch. [*Adm. Paper.*] *Encloses,*

29. I. *Philip Barrow and three other Officers of the Yard to the Navy Comrs. Mr. Knipe's hemp is just like that sent from Woolwich.* *September* 7, 1664.

Sept. 7. 30. Account of cables and cordage in store at Chatham. [*Adm. Paper.*]

Sept. 8. Woolwich. 31. Chris. Pett and three other Master Shipwrights to the Navy Comrs. Report of Sir Wm. Warren's Gottenburg masts lately delivered; 11 fall short of their proper dimensions. [*Adm. Paper.*]

Sept. 8. 32. Certificate by Capt. Za. Browne of the entry of Abraham Browne as boatswain, and Rich. Slinn as carpenter of the Good Hope. [*Adm. Paper.*]

Sept. 8. 33. Statement by Sir Phil. Musgrave, concerning Robt. Atkinson. His confessions did not agree with one another. He denied some things which were sworn against him, and named persons as privy to the plot whom he never accused before; one in particular, who he said could discover all in the barony of Kendal that were engaged; but these accusations, being after his condemnation, are of little use. Before his trial, he was insolent, and told his guards nobody could get from him more than he had a mind to say; since his condemnation, he said he had rather be hanged than come to the bar as witness against any man, and confessed sending the paper of advice to the prisoners to obstruct their trials. He professed himself at the gallows a moderate Presbyterian, but feared that drunkenness, defamation, and cozenage might be laid to his charge.

Sept. 8. Downs. 34. Earl of Sandwich to Sec. Bennet. Has arrived at Spithead in obedience to the Duke's commands.

Sept. 9. London. 35. Jo. Seymour to Williamson. Sir Rich. Mauleverer is anxious to know where to meet him with the warrant, being wishful to see it despatched before he goes to Yorkshire. It would have been advantageous to have it before Bartholomew fair, and Stourbridge fair is coming on. Sir Richard will pay all fees when he receives the warrant. [*One and a half pages.*]

Vol. CII.

1664.

Sept. 9. 36. Leonard Williams to Sec. Bennet. Has lately conversed with the persons formerly proclaimed, and finds that the design will go on, whether there be a Dutch war or not; they have a stock of money, but use it warily. They intend to take several houses near the Tower, one near Whitehall, one in Southwark, and two or three in the City; to make their interest, and suddenly fall on the Tower and Whitehall, which they say they can do without difficulty. Major Lee, and Jones, who is said to have written "Mene, Tekel," are amongst them. Will take care to inform of all beforehand, and point out the house where they meet, and where some may be found any night.

Sept. 9. 37. Estimates for building a shed to employ 12 or 24 more spinners in the ropeyard at Woolwich. [*Adm. Paper, one and a half pages.*] *Enclosing,*

37. I. *Plan of the building projected.*

Sept. 10. 38. Report of progress of five merchant ships fitting out for Guinea. [*Adm. Paper.*]

Sept. 10. 39. Report by Sir Wm. Batten of eight ships of the Guinea fleet, also of the five merchant vessels above named. [*Adm. Paper.*]

Sept. 10. Pass for two horses to France for the Earl of St. Alban's. Minute. [*Ent. Book* 16, *p.* 228.]

Sept. 10. Pass for Mons. De St. Clement to Lisbon, Tangiers, and other ports. [*Ent. Book* 16, *p.* 229.]

Sept. 10. London. 40. Sir Anthony Desmarces to [Williamson]. Delivered his letter to Mr. Duke, who says some competitors had been with him before, guided by Roche, Finochelli the Italian, &c., but professed willingness to serve their cause, and thought that with the petition should be a breviat of their just claims, which he wishes to examine before the meeting. Sends a list of the [Royal Fishing] Committee, that he may recommend their joint interest to those able to countenance them. They have leave for Stourbridge fair, but want one for a fortnight at Cambridge and Smithfield.

Sept. 10. Whitehall. 41. Sec. Morice to the Corporation of [Bury St. Edmund's]. The King is much pleased with their duty and respect in complying with his recommendation of John Moore to be town clerk, when the place shall become void.

Sept. 11. Chatham. 42. Commissioner Peter Pett to Sam. Pepys. Delay of the Harwich hoy in fetching provisions for the Downs. The Portland has sailed. Both the commissions for pressing men are employed. [*Adm. Paper.*]

Sept. 12. The Francis, Hole Haven. 43. Captain Jonathan Waltham to Wm. Coventry. Account of damage done to the Francis by one of a fleet of colliers. [*Adm. Paper.*]

Sept. 12. Chatham. 44. Thos. Corbin to the Navy Comrs. Particulars of timber in Sherwood Forest. Has dispatched another vessel's load. [*Adm. Paper.*]

1664. VOL. CII.

Sept. 12. Lydney. 45. Dan. Furzer to the Navy Comrs. The Justices of Herefordshire and Gloucestershire have promised to forward the carriage of timber. Requests warrants for 150 loads. [*Adm. Paper.*]

Sept. 12. Woolwich. 46. Chris. Pett to the Navy Comrs. The timber sent for the mainmast of the new ship proves unsuitable; proposes an exchange with Sir John Denham. [*Adm. Paper.*]

Sept. 12. Deptford. 47. Thos. Harper to Sam. Pepys. Requests a warrant for a new wall or fence, in lieu of one lately burnt down. [*Adm. Paper, damaged.*]

Sept. 12. 48. Names of thirteen persons now in London who go in disguise and under other names, with their pseudonymes. They meet at widow Hogden's house in Petty France, and are contriving to seize the Tower. John Atkinson lodges at Worcester Court. With description [by Sec. Bennet] of Atkinson's person. [*One and a half pages.*]

Sept. 12. Whitehall. 49. Order by the Commissioners [for repair of the Tower],—on report of those deputed to view the Tower wharf,—that the wharf should be kept clear for public use, and the way to and from the City chained at both ends, the key to be kept by the Master of Ordnance; also that as former Lieutenants of the Tower have had benefit by suffering persons not relating to the Tower to use the wharf, the King be requested to recompense the present Lieutenant for the diminution of profit.

Sept. 13. Whitehall. 50. Robt. Lye to Williamson. At the last general court of the Royal Company, the business was to secure 30,000*l.*, to prevent inconvenience should the Dutch overcome any of their fleets. It was at last agreed that any of the company might subscribe as many shares as he thought fit, but none else except under the name of one of the company; that a week should be allowed for subscribing, and a month for paying in, but 1 per cent be granted to those who paid in 10 days, and 2 per cent per month forfeited for delay beyond the month's time limited. The Duke [of York] has taken five shares more, and many others three, two, and one. Prince Rupert, with his companions for the voyage, Hen. Jermyn, Mr. Stanley, and others, had a farewell supper given them last night at Kirke House. The ships are to be fitted out with all speed, and 5,000 men ordered to be pressed for service, even out of merchants' ships. Lord of Arran is this day married to Lady Mary Stuart. [*Two pages.*]

Sept. 13. Warrant from Sec. Bennet to the Magistrates, Custom House Officers, and others of Yarmouth, to permit a vessel from Holland, freighted with cordage, to unload, notwithstanding the general order for quarantine. [*Ent. Book* 16, p. 228.]

Sept. 13. Grant of denization to Anthonis Mow, native of Holland. Minute. [*Ent. Book* 16, p. 228.]

Sept. 13. Warrant authorizing the Victualler of the Navy to impress several artificers and carriages, for the use of the navy. [*Ent. Book* 16, p. 228.]

Vol. CII.

1664.

Sept. 13. Warrant to reprieve William Watson, of Staindrop, sentenced to death, till the next assizes. [*Ent. Book* 16, *p.* 220.]

Sept. 13. Warrant for three quarters' advance of Prince Rupert's pension of 4,000*l.* [*Ent. Book* 16, *p.* 230.]

Sept. 13. Whitehall. 51. Warrant to pay to Rob. Lye 3,600*l.* out of the arrears of the late Earl of Norwich's pension, for the service of the supernumerary yeomen of the Guard, admitted by him.

Sept. 13. Entry of the above. [*Ent. Book* 16, *p.* 230.]

Sept. 13. Warrant from Sec. Bennet to Thomas Price, Anthony Arnold, and John Wagstaff, aldermen of Gloucester, to search the houses of Toby Jordan, bookseller, William Jordan, apothecary, Edward Eckly, and Elizabeth Wallis, for seditious books and papers, and to transmit them to him, detaining in custody those with whom such books are found, or taking security for their appearance. [*Ent. Book* 16, *p.* 231.]

Sept. 13. Warrant from Sec. Bennet to R. L'Estrange to repair to Clapham, and apprehend James Forbes, with such books and papers as relate to public affairs, and bring them before himself. [*Ent. Book* 16, *p.* 231.]

Sept. 13. The King to the Dean and Chapter of Hereford, and to the Custos and Vicars-choral of the College. Grants a dispensation to John Chapman, M.A., to hold the place of Vicar-choral in the college with the parsonage of Abberley. [*Ent. Book* 17, *p.* 58.]

Sept. 13. 52. Report by Sir Wm. Batten of the progress of the vessels and merchant ships fitting out for Guinea. [*Adm. Paper.*]

Sept. 13. St. Helen's. 53. Capt. B. Gilpin to Joseph Knapman, master of the Indian Merchant. Is empowered by the Earl of Sandwich to press mariners out of all merchant ships homeward bound; requests therefore that no wages be paid the four men impressed this morning on board the Indian Merchant, till they are delivered to persons appointed by the Navy Commissioners. [*Adm. Paper.*] *Encloses,*

53. i. *Note of the names of the four seamen pressed out of the Indian Merchant.*

Sept. 14. Portsmouth. 54. John Tippetts and two others to the Navy Comrs. Send an estimate for building a new ropehouse; total, 1,143*l.* [*Adm. Paper.*]

Sept. 14. Woolwich. 55. Estimate by Edw. Rundells and Jas. Matthews for building a new spinning house for 24 spinners; total, 660*l.* 17*s.* [*Adm. Paper.*]

Sept. 14. 56. Nomination, by the owners, of Wm. Bolston as boatswain, and Martin Gray as carpenter, to the John and Katherine. Signed Rich. Dennes. [*Adm. Paper.*]

Sept. 14. London. 57. Sir Anthony Desmarces to Williamson. Has sent him word of what passes in the committee, and prepared a form, which should be obtained from the King, to take away the pretensions of their

1664. VOL. CII.

competitors and enemies; requests him to adjust it, and will present it to Mr. Secretary to get signed, so as to destroy the affair by the root. Begs his aid. The King and Duke go to the chase to-morrow, and will not return till Saturday. [*French.*]

Sept. 14. Carry Mallet, Somersetshire. 58. John Pinne to John Quash, Ilchester. Assures him that his deliverance will be with as much honour as his imprisonment has been with dishonour. Card's wife came crying to Major Colburne, to ask if the preferment he intended for her husband was to bring him to the gallows, and he was forced to stop her mouth with a good sum of money. Hunt is very pliable. Fears none but the Martins. Hears they are steadfast after their falsehood, and wishes them to be comforted. [*Copy.*]

Sept. 14. Prison, London. 59. Remonstrance in reference to the Act to prevent and suppress seditious conventicles,—showing that as the words of the Act confine it to subjects of the realm, all magistrates proceed unadvisedly and incompetently against the subjects of foreign princes. With an appendix to show that if the Quakers' principles be from God, no opposition will prevail. By Albertus Otto Faber, prisoner by the said Act. [*Eight pages, printed.*]

Sept. 14. Whitehall. 60. Order in Council, referring to Lord Ashley, as Chancellor of the Exchequer, the following petition, and his appointment, dated 28th Oct., to hear the business on Monday next. *Annexing,*

60. I. *Petition of Sam. Lamot to the King. Is almost the sole importer of Hamburg and Nuremberg wares; viz., "bears, babies, toyes, and other light commodities"; three years ago, was stopped on pretext that they were painted wares, some being slightly coloured and varnished, and therefore contrary to the statute 3 Edw. IV., but on reference to the then Customs' Commissioners, was allowed to proceed; yet Wm. Dickenson, surveyor of customs, has lately stayed his goods on the like pretext. Requests their release, and a prohibition of such proceedings in future. Sept. 14. Endorsed with Lord Ashley's report in favour of the petition, dated November 4.*

60. II. *Clause in the patent to the Farmers of Customs, permitting the free import of such manufactures as have been brought in for the last 60 years.*

Sept. 14. Patent to Robert Hooke, M.A., Fellow of the Royal Society, &c., for 14 years, to be the sole maker and seller of certain two-wheeled chariots, chaises, and carriages of three descriptions. Minute. [*Ent. Book 14, p. 35.*]

Sept. 14. Whitehall. Declaration continuing to Lady Mary Stuart, daughter and sole heir of James late Duke of Richmond and Lenox, married to Richard Earl of Arran, second son of James, Duke of Ormond, Lord Lieutenant of Ireland, the place of the daughter of a duke, which gives her precedence over all countesses—to be registered in the office of arms. [*Ent. Book 23 p. 232.*]

VOL. CII.

1664.

Sept. 14. Post warrant for Rich. Badley to have two post horses and a guide to Towcester. Minute. [*Ent. Book* 16, *p.* 233.]

Sept. 14. Post warrant for Mr. Dupuy to take seven posthorses for the Duke of York's service to Hartford Bridge and back. With note that on September 15, the King went to Bagshaw to hunt. Minute. [*Ent. Book* 16, *p.* 233.]

Sept. 14. Whitehall. Warrant to pay to Sir George Carteret 57,000*l.*, towards the charge of setting forth eight ships for eight months to Guinea, with 1,285 men; and also four merchant ships, manned with 570 men. [*Ent. Book* 16, *p.* 233.]

Sept. 15. Post warrant for four horses to Lord Fitzharding to Hartfor Bridge. Minute. [*Ent. Book* 16, *p.* 233.]

Sept. 15. Warrant to pay to Sir George Carteret 94,508*l.* 19*s.*, being the pay for 2,500 men to be employed on the fleet in the ensuing year, by estimate of 17 October, 1663. Minute. [*Ent. Book* 16, *p.* 233.]

Sept. 15. The King to the Lord Mayor and Aldermen of York. Requests them to grant the freedom of the city to Sir Henry Belasyse, K.B., who is very desirous for that addition of honour. [*Ent. Book* 17, *p.* 60.]

Sept. 15. Warrant to Lord Admiral the Duke of York to order the Master of the Watermen's Company to press 500 watermen, such as have already served at sea, for the navy, and to use all other extraordinary means to complete the full number of men appointed for the service, by taking them out of merchant ships or otherwise, as he finds necessary. [*Ent. Book* 17, *p.* 61.]

Sept. 15. Dover. 61. F. Wivell to Sir John Mennes. Asks whether to pay the pilot's demand of 3*l.* for bringing the Drake and Hector into harbour. Offers his services as agent to the Commissioners for attending to the fitting and quick dispatch of ships, such a person being formerly employed. [*Adm. Paper.*]

Sept. 15. 62. Report of the progress of five merchant ships fitting out for Guinea. [*Adm. Paper.*]

Sept. 15. Woolwich. 63. Wm. Bodham to Sir Wm. Batten. Sends account of threads in the different sizes of cordage. [*Adm. Paper.*]

Sept. 15. Victualling Office. 64. Denis Gauden to Sam. Pepys. Sends account of the declarations, issues, and remains of victuals, since October 1663. [*Adm. Paper.*]

Sept. 15. Portsmouth. 65. St. J. Steventon to Sir Wm. Penn. The bill of imprest for 300*l.* will leave him 40*l.* out of purse when workmen are paid at the end of the month. The pressed men from Bristol have not yet come. Asks whether they are to be entered on weekly wages as formerly. More money wanted. [*Adm. Paper.*]

Sept. 16. 66. Report of the progress of eight ships fitting out for Guinea. [*Adm. Paper.*]

VOL. CII.

1664.

Sept. 16. Woolwich. 67. Chris. Pett to the Navy Comrs. Requests an order to the storekeeper of Aliceholt for timber delivered. The calkers of the new ship may soon be discharged; proposes to allow them a tide a day extra for the time they wrought under water. [*Adm. Paper.*]

Sept. 16. Chatham. 68. Commissioner Peter Pett to Sam. Pepys. Has ordered two pinnaces for the two new fourth-rate ships dispatching for sea. Nearly 100 watermen pressed at London have arrived; they must be entered on petty-warrant victuals, for they have little money to maintain them, and small credit. Survey of timber. [*Adm. Paper.*]

Sept. 16. Wapping. 69. Sir Wm. Warren to Sam. Pepys. Intreats that Michael Pack, his son-in-law, may go as midshipman in the Royal Exchange. "The Dutch did slay his father with a cannon shot, and he hath some mind now to see if he can have his pennyworths of them for it." [*Adm. Paper.*]

Sept. 16. 70. Articles of agreement between Capt. Chris. Myngs, on the part of the Navy Commissioners, and John Taylor, shipwright, for the building of 2 sloops, for 120*l.* [*Adm. Paper.*]

Sept. 16. 71. News from Sir Nich. Crisp. Capt. Hen. Lowe, an officer of customs, went to Hole Haven, boarded two Dutch ships, and inquired what men-of-war were fitted for sea in those parts. One of the masters said there were, at the Texel and river of Amsterdam, 24 men-of-war and merchantmen, though not fully ready, and that the Leopard, taken from the English in Oliver's time, is to go Admiral for Guinea. The other master reported 24 men-of-war in Goree gate on the 13th instant.

Sept. 17. Warrant from Sec. Bennet to the Justices, Custom House Officers, and others of Yarmouth, to permit the unlading of all cordage brought in the Tulip and Swallow from Holland, notwithstanding the general order for restraint of trade with Holland, and for making quarantine. [*Ent. Book* 16, *p.* 234.]

Sept. 17. Deptford. 72. Jonas Shish to the Navy Comrs. Thinks the furnaces of the merchant ships fitting out for Guinea too small for dressing provisions for the number of men that each ship carries. [*Adm. Paper.*]

Sept. 17. Portsmouth. 73. St. J. Steventon to the Navy Comrs. Has paid and discharged the calkers, who were much troubled not to have 7*s.* 6*d.* a piece conduct money up to London instead of 5*s.* Only 38 of the Bristol pressed men have appeared. Will send the quarter-books by the town coach. [*Adm. Paper.*]

Sept. 17. 74. Jerome Collins to Sam. Pepys. Is appointed by the King's positive orders surgeon to Prince Rupert. Begs that no further steps be taken towards furnishing his medicine chest, until he can bring the Prince's request for a greater proportion of medicines than that mentioned before. [*Adm. Paper.*]

Vol. CII.

1664.

Sept. 17. Chatham. 75. Commissioner Peter Pett to Sam. Pepys. Repairs of ships, &c. [*Adm. Paper.*]

Sept. 17. Portsmouth. 76. Edw. Bond to Sir Wm. Batten. Certifies his delivery of the stores out of the Harwich hoy on board the Earl of Sandwich's fleet, now riding at Spithead. [*Adm. Paper.*]

Sept. 18? 77. Summons from Wm. Tomson, high constable of Middlesex, to Wm. Buckman, of Lincoln's Inn Fields, to appear before Wm. Ryley, Lancaster herald, and Henry Dethick, Rougecroix, deputies of Sir Edw. Bysche, Clarencieux, at the Quest House, Holborn, on September 29 or 30, with his arms and crest, that they may be entered in the Middlesex registry, to prevent his name being returned to the Marshals' Commissioners. [*Printed.*]

Sept. 18? 78. Similar summons to Sir Hen. Gifford, of Lincoln's Inn Fields.

Sept. 18? Clerkenwell. 79. Similar summons to John Smith, of Clerkenwell, to appear at Hickes Hall, St. John's Street, 22nd September.

Sept. 18. The Centurion. 80. Capt. Rob. Moulloy to Wm. Coventry. Arrived at Elsinore, and after landing Squire Coventry there, landed Sir Gilbert Talbot at Elsinburg. The lord ambassador [Carlisle] is waiting at Stockholm.

Sept. 19. Woolwich. 81. Ant. Deane to Sam. Pepys. Sends an account of the marking of the Lord Chancellor's timber at Reading, by Mr. Maston, complained of. Marked 500 loads as warranted, and Mr. Blackbury said he would furnish Mr. Maston from other places. [*Adm. Paper.*]

Sept. 19. Woolwich. 82. Chris. Pett to the Navy Comrs. The bilge-ways must be repaired for the launch of the new ship. Timber wanted. Progress of the Bear and Assurance. [*Adm. Paper.*]

Sept. 19. Woolwich. 83. John Browne to the Navy Comrs. Gives the prices of sacking cloth, as ordered by Sir Wm. Batten, of which he can supply a quantity at 21*s.* and 18*s.* a bolt. [*Adm. Paper.*]

Sept. 20. Wapping. 84. Wm. Wood, Nich. Bradley, and John Thornbush, owners of the Maryland, to the Navy Comrs. Request warrants for the entering of John Langley and Wm. Baldry as carpenter and boatswain to their vessel. [*Adm. Paper.*] *Annexing,*

84. i. *Certificate by John Thornbush of the appointment of John Langley and Wm. Baldry.* *September* 20.

Sept. 20. Portsmouth. 85. John Tippetts to the Navy Comrs. Demand for ships' stores. [*Adm. Paper.*]

Sept. 20. Deptford. 86. Edw. Rundells to Sam. Pepys. Progress of carpenters' work at the ropeyard, Woolwich. Complains of bad practices and embezzlement of stores by Robert Elery, foreman, and Mr. Phillips, under clerk. Being instructed to carry on the work, begs the choice of the men under him. [*Adm. Paper.*]

Sept. 20. Harw. 87. Thos. Wale, shipwright, to the Navy Comrs. Account of ships sent by the Earl of Sandwich to be refitted. Tallow is as high as 46*s.* per cwt. [*Adm. Paper.*]

1664. Vol. CII.

Sept. 20. Augustine, Portsmouth. 88. Capt. Rich. Teate to the Navy Comrs. Will be unladen in two days. Asks what is to be done with the cable and anchor brought for the Pearl. [*Adm. Paper.*]

Sept. 20. Lambeth. 89. Dr. Geo. Stradling to Williamson. Congratulates his recovery. [His kinsman], Rob. Stradling, who formerly sought for a place as Yeoman of the Guards, now wants an allowance out of moneys lately discovered to have belonged to some of the late King's murderers, he having had a hand in the discovery.

Sept. 20. Whitehall. 90. Willm. Godolphin to Williamson. Will for Williamson's interest's sake do what he can for Sir Ant. Desmarces, but thinks they avoid him on that business. Was promised a share by Sir Anthony last year, but heard no more of it. Wishes Williamson better health; if he still complain of sweats and short sleeps, Dr. Quatremaine thinks he should return to town. Sends letters from Tangiers, where things are in good condition. Sir George Downing's letters leave it doubtful whether the Dutch will send to Guinea or not; they see we are in earnest and not to be frightened; preparations go on apace. Hutchinson is dead in Sandown Castle. The Lord Chancellor has been feasting about the country four or five days, at Gorhambury, the Master of the Rolls' house. [*Three pages.*] *Encloses,*

90. i. *Dr. William Quatremaine to Williamson. Fears he is not much improved by his journey; would like him nearer, so as to examine into the impediments to his recovery; if he be not advantaged by change of air, something else should be done.* *September* 20, 1664.

Sept. 20. Warrant from Sec. Bennet to Captain Freeman, governor of Sandown Castle, to deliver to Mrs. Hutchinson the body of her deceased husband, his prisoner, with all trunks and other things belonging to him. [*Ent. Book* 16, *p.* 234.]

Sept. 20. Warrant to Robert Child and William Bowles, masters of the toils, to remove all the red deer and 100 brace of fallow deer from the New Park, near Richmond, to such places as shall be ordered, and to carry to the forests of Windsor and Essex deer to be presented by the Duke of Richmond and Earl of Lincoln; also to receive orders from the Earl of Oxford for disposal of other deer for the King's service. [*Ent. Book* 16, *p.* 239.]

Sept. 21. Warrant for the Courts of Records for the honour of Peverel to be kept in the several halls where the assizes are held, in cos. Nottingham and Derby. [*Ent. Book* 16, *p.* 239.]

Sept. 21? Warrant for a licence to John Seymour to print and publish certain classical and school books for forty-one years, with leave to seize any copies printed by others. [*Ent. Book* 16, *pp.* 240–2.]

Sept. 21. 91. Dr. Willm. Quatremaine to [Williamson]. Medical advice and prescriptions. He should lay aside his asses' milk for a while to make room for other things; does not advise him, though bribed by Mr. Godolphin, to entertain business till he is better. [*Four pages.*]

Vol. CII.

1664.

[Sept. 21.] 92. Petition of Jeane, widow of Rob. Lane, to the King, for relief, her husband being slain in Bishopsgate by Venner; presented a petition last Saturday, but has got no answer.

Sept. 21. Order for erecting a Court of Record for trying small actions not amounting to 5*l.*, at Hackney and Stepney. Minute. [*Domestic Corresp., June* 8, 1661.]

Sept. 21. The King to the Mayor and Aldermen of Newcastle. Has been much satisfied with the integrity and prudence of Sir Thomas Clavering, their present mayor, and exhorts them to care in choosing a person of known loyalty to be mayor at the ensuing election, more than ordinary vigilance being needed on account of the late Northern conspiracy. [*Ent. Book* 17, *p.* 62.]

Sept. 21. [illegible] 93. Wm. Coventry to Denis Gauden. The agent at Dover must furnish the Hampshire with victuals, to make up a proportion for three months. [*Adm. Paper.*]

Sept. 21. Chatham. 94. Commissioner Peter Pett to Sam. Pepys. Particulars of timber. Progress of ships. [*Adm. Paper.*]

Sept. 22. Portsmouth. 95. John Timbrell, anchor smith, to the Navy Comrs. Begs to be allowed to press men for dispatch of work, as there is great haste required; it is difficult to keep the men to their business without restraint. [*Adm. Paper.*]

Sept. 22. Portsmouth. 96. John Tippetts to the Navy Comrs. Particulars of rosin offered by Mr. Richbell. Survey of oars tendered. The Earl of Sandwich has spared 200 seamen to help to rig the Mary. Lignum vitæ is wanted. [*Adm. Paper.*]

Sept. 22. 97. Information by Leonard Williams. The messengers sent to Worcester Place to take Atkinson found Richardson, *alias* Fawcett, but let him go clear, and messengers were immediately sent to Atkinson and others to forewarn them lest they should be snapped; received a notice himself. Richardson could have told what places Atkinson frequents. Had the messengers waited, they had been sure to have him. They suspect a woman that lives there of informing; they intend a small number with pistols to get into the Tower, on pretence of seeing the armory, and then let the rest in, so careful watch must be kept.

Sept. 22. 98. Leonard Williams to Sec. Bennet. Intends to reside in the city, but must not stay too long in a place; hopes for something from the King, his charges being the greater that he cannot undertake any public thing for his own benefit.

Sept. 22. 99. G. Duke to Williamson. Thanks for favours. Some lame and faint propositions have been made to the Royal Fishing Company by Mr. Finochelli; better ones by Sir Ant. Desmarces and his associates, who stand fair for the preference, though Sir Anthony may be outbidden by a third person. Thinks the Duke of York should be applied to personally. An order of the committee of the 12th instant reports to the Duke their wish that all lotteries be suppressed, but thinks the evil of this order may be prevented. The

VOL. CII.

1664.

accounts of the profits of all lotteries are also required, and any proposals for lotteries are to be made in a fortnight, stating fine, rent, and security offered. The weekly gazettes are to publish for people to offer what they can for the fishing, and in time it may come to who will bid most for lotteries. Is anxious to serve him. [*Two pages.*]

Sept. 22. Spithead. 100. Earl of Sandwich to [Sec. Bennet]. Has tried to get men thereabouts, but either for want of intelligent going about the work, or from remissness in the magistrates, gains very few. The Gloucester is gone to Plymouth and the Drake to Weymouth, on the same errand. Has put 300 of the men to help to rig the ships appointed to be fitted in that harbour. Lord Colepepper and his family are expected at Southampton, on their way to the Isle of Wight.

Sept. 23. Whitehall. 101. Warrant to Dan. O'Neale to preserve the game at Hampstead and four miles round. Endorsed with several names and addresses.

[Sept. 23.] 102. Petition of William Creed, an ancient sufferer for the late King, to the King and Council, that Sir Wm. Davenport may be ordered before Council to show cause why he does not pay him a debt of 60*l.*, he not having complied with a former request for his appearance; has been a suitor to the Lord Chamberlain 19 months for leave to proceed against him by law.

Sept. 23. Whitehall. Warrant from Sec. Bennet for delivery of a trunk, portmanteau, and some pieces of linen, arrived from Hamburgh at Hole Haven, and there making quarantine, to the Hon. Simon de Petkum, resident for the King of Denmark. [*Ent. Book* 16, *p.* 233.]

Sept. 23. Warrant to stop all proceedings against Sir John Lenthall, knight marshal of the court and prison of King's Bench, for levying fines amounting to 900*l.*, estreated by the Court of Exchequer, and for not returning several writs of habeas corpus the last Trinity Term; to be continued if he can show cause for stay of further process. [*Ent. Book* 16, *p.* 234.]

Sept. 23. Whitehall. Warrant for a grant to Baptist May and Abraham Cowley, on nomination of the Earl of St. Alban's, of several parcels of ground in Pall Mall described, on rental of 80*l.*, for building thereon a square of 13 or 14 great and good houses; also of the common highway lying between the houses in South Pall Mall Street and St. James' Park wall, on rental of 40*l.*, with proviso of erecting no building thereon that should cause annoyance to the inhabitants. The said grant is made because persons were unwilling to build such great houses on any terms save that of inheritance, and the former leases recapitulated were only for years. [*Ent. Book* 16, *pp.* 235–8.]

Sept. 23. Pass for —— with three horses to France. Minute. [*Ent. Book* 16, *p.* 238.]

Sept. 23. Warrant to the Treasurer of the Chamber to pay to the Serjeant Trumpeter 80*l.*, for furnishing two trumpets, a kettle-drum and a drummer, to attend Prince Rupert to sea. [*Ent. Book* 16, *p.* 238.]

Vol. CII.

1664.
Sept. 22. Warrant to Sir Edward Walker, Garter king-at-arms, to assign an addition to the arms of Sir Henry Bennet, for his fidelity and courage in the cause of the late King. [*Ent. Book* 16, *p.* 244.]

Sept. 23. The King to the Governors of the Charter House. Recommends John Brice to be admitted scholar there, in consideration of the faithful services of his father, the late Capt. John Brice. [*Ent. Book* 17, *p.* 61.]

Sept. 23. Limehouse. 103. Phin. Pett to Sam. Pepys. Thanks for sympathy in his late unhappiness. Begs him to send his two bills by his servant. [*Adm. Paper.*]

Sept. 23. Chatham. 104. Commissioner Peter Pett to Sam. Pepys. Particulars of ships' calkers wanted. [*Adm. Paper.*]

Sept. 23. Chelsea. Ambassador Van Gogh to the States General. The equipage for Guinea is hastening and men are pressed in the North of England, as well as in London, and come in fast; 500 seamen are ordered from Scotland, and it is thought no more will be needed. The drums still beat for men to go to Guinea with Prince Rupert, and many come in, besides a number of reformadoes of good quality. The King has been to Woolwich, to view and hasten the ships; 30,000*l.* was brought in to the Royal Company, sums due by members, but not paid in before. [*Holl. Corresp., September* 23, 1664.]

Sept. 24. Warrant from Sec. Bennet to Sir John Robinson, Lieut. of the Tower, to discharge James Hamilton. [*Ent. Book* 10, *p.* 245.]

Sept. 24. 105. "Mr. Woodbridge's reasons and excuses for himself for not coming to church more than once on the Sunday;" viz., that Mr. Sayer, who takes on him to be the bishop there, does not read the prayer for Christ's Church, according to law; that he cannot tell what law he has transgressed; that he thought the proclamation was only meant for six months, and had expired; that if recusants by going to church once a month escape a fine of 20*l.* per month, he ought to be eased of one of 12*d.* by going on a Sunday night; with replies to each point, and note that Bond, Blake, Peirce, and Milton wished to plead the same excuse. [*Three pages.*]

Sept. 24. 106. Capt. John Willgresse and Capt. Dan. Heling to the Navy Comm. Account of the reproachful words and violence used by the chief mate and crew of a vessel bound for Tangiers, on their requesting them to secure 12 pressed men whilst they got some more. Were forced to leave three or four of the men behind them. [*Adm. Paper.*]

Sept. 24. Woolwich. 107. Chris. Pett to the Navy Comm. Has appointed Thomas Stacey, his foreman, to mark out Sir Wm. Warren's timber; about 50 loads are found merchantable. Calkers may be discharged. Particulars of ships. [*Adm. Paper.*]

Sept. 24. Chatham. 108. Commissioner Peter Pett to Sam. Pepys. Particulars of ships. [*Adm. Paper.*]

VOL. CII.

1664.

Sept. 24. Portsmouth. 109. John Tippetts to the Navy Comrs. The new ropehouse, being intended to be low-built and narrow, would not be convenient for stowing hemp over it; for 260*l.*, a substantial storehouse for 200 tons might be erected. [*Adm. Paper.*]

Sept. 24. Deptford. 110. Capt. Wm. Badiley to the Navy Comrs. The Hawk ketch is ready to take in provisions. Requests men for their stowage. [*Adm. Paper, damaged.*]

Sept. 24. 111. Robt. Maguro to the Navy Comrs. Survey of Mr. Halbert's oak timber. [*Adm. Paper.*] *Encloses*,

111. I. *E. Halbert to the Navy Comrs. Tender of 400 loads of timber, lying within 20 miles of London, at the Thames side.* *September* 20, 1664.

111. II. *Note of an offer made for the said timber, but declined.* *September* 27, 1664.

Sept. 25. Portsmouth. 112. St. J. Steventon to the Navy Comrs. Could only muster 43 men out of 93 pressed, some having gone to the fleet. 204 men from the fleet work closely at ship rigging. The width of the river where the three chains are respectively to be placed is 224, 167, and 122 fathoms. [*Adm. Paper.*]

Sept. 25. Portsmouth. 113. Thos. Lancaster to the Navy Comrs. The pressed men from Bristol are entered on board the Mary. She is ready to take in provisions; a master and mate are required to look after their stowage. Progress of ships worked on by men sent from the Earl of Sandwich. Mooring cables wanted. [*Adm. Paper.*]

Sept. 26. Deptford. 114. Capt. Wm. Badiley to the Navy Comrs. Requests orders touching the launch of the new ship now building at Woolwich; 20 men must be entered on her. The Hawk ketch that carried down the pressed men is returned, and other pressed men are sent aboard. [*Adm. Paper.*]

Sept. 26. Chatham. 115. Commissioner Peter Pett to Mr. Harper, storekeeper at Deptford. He is to send an express to Mr. Coventry or Mr. Pepys of the arrival of the Minion yacht at Deptford, as they have some service for her. [*Adm. Paper.*]

Sept. 26. Warrant from Sec. Bennet to Sir John Robinson, Lieutenant of the Tower, to receive and detain Robert Walters safe prisoner in the Tower. [*Ent. Book* 16, p. 245.]

Sept. 26. Warrant for Thomas Simons, one of the King's chief engravers, to prepare three seals for the King's service, to be delivered to Sir Henry Bennet, according to a draft expressed. [*Ent. Book* 16, p. 247.]

Sept. 27. Warrant from Sec. Bennet for some goods belonging to the Countess of Chesterfield, arrived at Hole Haven from Flushing, to be landed without quarantine, the contagion not being in that town. [*Ent. Book* 16, p. 244.]

VOL. CII.

1664.

Sept. 27. Bawtry. 116. Col. J. Frechville to Sec. Bennet. Will deliver his letters to the Earl of Devonshire, but thinks he and the other gentlemen are already acquainted with the business. Is thankful for the King's undeserved bounty, which will give life and fortune to his service.

Sept. 27. London. 117. James Hickes to Williamson. Rejoices in his recovery. The Wolverhampton postmaster thinks, as Williamson is 16 miles from there and but six from Stilton, his letters should be sent the latter way, for should he remain there all winter, the postmaster fears his salary of 20*l.* a year would be eaten in the charge of sending the letters. Hopes to see him on his return.

Sept. 27. 118. Dr. Wm. Quatremaine to Williamson. Is glad of his improvement. Medical directions.

Sept. 27. Edwinstow, Sherwood. 119. John Russell to the Navy Comrs. Particulars of carriage of timber to Bawtry. A new waggon is made. Asks whether to fell 100 trees more to complete the 1,000. Money wanted. [*Adm. Paper.*]

Sept. 28. Gravesend. 120. Wm. Greenhorp to Sir Wm. Batten. Muster of men on board the merchant ships bound for Guinea; they would have been complete, had not as many run away as would man two of the ships. Some are in London, but the captain and officers are confident of their return. [*Adm. Paper.*] *Encloses*,

120. I. *List of watermen run away from each of ten ships.*

120. II. *Similar list sent to Watermen's Hall; with note by the Navy Commissioners, September 29, that such are to be found out, and their persons disposed of according to the Duke of York's commands.*
Navy Office, September 29, 1664.

Sept. 28. Woolwich. 121. Chris Pett to the Navy Comrs. Repairs of ships. Timber and calkers wanted; also poop lanterns for the new ship. [*Adm. Paper.*]

Sept. 28. 122. Jonas Shish to the Navy Comrs. Repairs needed for the Charity. Endorsed with W. B. [Sir W. Batten's?] expenses in a journey to Portsmouth. [*Adm. Paper.*]

Sept. 28. Chatham. 123. Commissioner Peter Pett to Sam. Pepys. Attempted to buy tallow and candles at Maidstone, but found the country so shy that, though assured of good payment, they refused to have any dealings, Battin of Rochester being utterly undone in serving that commodity before the King came in. Repairs and progress of ships. [*Adm. Paper.*]

Sept. 28. The King to the Master and Fellows of Jesus College, Cambridge. Recommends John North, B.A., of that college, to be one of the two to be presented to the Bishop of Ely, their visitor, for election to the fellowship vacant by death of John Machill, dispensing with

1664. Vol. CII.

his incapacity, if elected, as being of a southern county, because there are not two of their society who by place of birth are capable of nomination. [*Ent. Book* 19, *p.* 23.]

Sept. 28. 124. Roger L'Estrange to Sec. Bennet. Has seized Wallis, *alias* Gardiner, the pretended author of a book sent, and given him over to Butler, a messenger. He will not tell his lodging, or notable discoveries might be made, as he is the agent of the most dangerous factions about town. Is going to search for Forbes, his assistant, at Hackney. After taking Wallis, sent to Col. Frowde to have three persons seized in Gloucestershire, so that he doubts not of having clear proofs.

Sept. 28. 125. Dr. Willm. Quatremaine to Williamson. Is sorry that his health is not stronger. Medical directions.

Sept. 29. 126. Return, by Rich. Sutton and Jacob Tonson, constables, of the names of 47 gentlemen resident in the liberty of High Holborn, parish of St. Andrews, with note of such as are not in town.

[Sept. 29.] 127. List of 10 more gentlemen who have removed from their houses in Holborn.

Sept. 29. 128. Sir John Warre and Edm. Wyndham to Sec. Bennet. The Mayor of Bridgewater lays the fault of the liberty allowed to Col. Bovett, by which he made his escape, on his inferior officers, and they throw it back on the mayor, who allowed him the liberty of the town. Think them all liable, but misled by Bovett's parole that he would continue a true prisoner. The Council should send directions for examining the officers, for they and the mayor, being persons of small estate, would be undone by a long restraint under a messenger.

Sept. 29. 129. Leonard Williams to Sec. Bennet. Is spending his time faithfully in the service. Knows as much of their designs as themselves, and will always have power to prevent them. Sees Atkinson daily. Wants an interview with his honour.

Sept. 29. Reference to Lord Chancellor Clarendon on the petition of several commissioners, owners of lands in Wittersham level, Kent and Sussex, for recommendation to the [Duke of Ormond], Lord Lieutenant of Ireland, of the case between them and the owners of the Upper levels in Wittersham, who are 2,879*l.* in arrears to them, sums decreed by the Lord Keeper, in 1629, to be paid to the petitioners, for damage caused by the turning of the river Rothe through the said level. With a second reference, Oct. 4, empowering the Lord Chancellor to compose the difference between the parties, in order to avoid multiplicity of suits, there being 200 persons concerned therein. [*Ent. Book* 18, *pp.* 86, 91.]

Sept. 29. Whitehall. Order to the Sheriffs of London and Middlesex,—on the petition of Willm. Purcell and Roger Moony, prisoners in Newgate, to be set on board a ship destined for Guinea, being trapanned to become

Vol. CII.

1664.

accessory to a felony—that they be delivered to Hum. Berington, Lieutenant of the King's company of Guards, to be conducted in his Majesty's service to the coast of Africa. [*Ent. Book* 18, *p.* 91.]

Sept. 29. 130. Account of Wm. Lashmore's journeys from Woolwich to London, since July 2nd, 1664. [*Adm. Paper, one and a half pages.*]

Sept. 29. Portsmouth. 131. John Tippetts to the Navy Comrs. Particulars of ships' stores. Progress of the new storehouse and ropehouse; 250*l.* are wanted to complete the masons' and labourers' work. [*Adm. Paper.*]

Sept. 30. The Downs. 132. Capt. Geo. Batts to the Navy Comrs. Lent the Hampshire's stream cable for the use of the Rupert, belonging to the Royal Company. [*Adm. Paper.*]

Sept. 30. Chatham. 133. Commissioner Peter Pett to Sam. Pepys. Repairs of ships. [*Adm. Paper.*]

Sept. 30. Chatham Dock. 134. Phin. Pett and Jos. Lawrence to the Navy Comrs. Report of the rotten state of the Victory. [*Adm. Paper.*]

Sept. 30. 135. Memorial by Sir Edw. Walker that the King having authorized the provincial kings-at-arms to wear medals of his arms, the arms are reversed in some of them. He wishes this gross error to be corrected or referred to the Commissioners for the Earl Marshalship, or for His Majesty not to be offended, if he oppose the entry in the office registers of an act whereby any of the King's arms are reversed.

Sept. 30. Chatsworth. 136. Wm. Earl of Devonshire to Sec. Bennet. Has sent his letter and Calton's examination to Sir Brian Broughton, deputy lieutenant of Staffordshire, desiring him to communicate the business no further than may conduce to the King's service, and to inform him of any further discoveries. Asks if any further light is given by Gladman's examination.

Sept. 30. 137. H. P—— to John Knowles. Received his order for 50*s.* for the Poland brethren. Their countrymen are everywhere imprisoned and expecting banishment. Newgate is so full that they have an infectious malignant fever amongst them, which sends many to their long home; and the magistrates, who think them unfit to breathe their native air when living, bury them as brethren when dead. There is great hope, from a report of Judge Hale, that the proceedings on the Conventicle Act will stop, for at Exeter the Quakers were by his means found not guilty, because no sedition appeared, and the Act is not against religious meetings, but seditious conventicles. The statute would do little hurt, if put in execution by impartial Judges. Quotes Mr. Hale's tract on schism. Their Transylvanian friend is not now wishful to see Oxford; invites him to London to see if the Lord has not better work for him. The plague in Holland has decreased from 1,000 to 800 a week. It has taken away Drusius, who has written short pithy notes on the whole Bible. Will send a treatise of his, "De Regno ecclesiastico." With notes by another hand upon the letter. [*Two pages.*]

Vol. CII.

1664.
Sept.? 138. Petition of Sir Wm. Thompson, governor of the East India Company, to the King, for a convoy to sail in November next, to meet 10 ships on their way from the Indies, which will call at St. Helena in March or April for refreshment, and will be in danger if there should be war with the neighbour nation.

Sept.? 139. Petition of Wm. Creed, tailor of the robes in ordinary to the late King, to the Lord Chamberlain of the Household, to move the King for continuance from Michaelmas, 1660, of the allowance of 40*l.* a year granted him by the late King, to save him from imprisonment and ruin. Has been a great sufferer for loyalty, but since the Restoration his place has been disposed of to another, and his former petition referred to Lord Mansfield, then gentleman of the robes. *Annexing,*

139. I. *Petition of Wm. Creed to the King, for re-admission to his office as Tailor of the Robes, in which he served all the time of the war, and was plundered and his family turned out of doors for loyalty. Waited on Lord Mansfield before His Majesty's landing, as being the sole and eldest survivor in that office. With reference thereon, 22 June, 1660, to Lord Mansfield, master of the robes.*

139. II. *Petition of Wm. Creed to the King, for the customary allowances belonging to his place as Tailor of the Robes in ordinary, that he may not perish in prison for debt. Failed in a petition to Lord Mansfield a year ago for restoration to his place, which is now given to another. With reference thereon, 7th August, 1661, to Lord Chamberlain Manchester; and his report, January 10, 1663, that John New, deceased, had 40l. pension from the wardrobe in the lifetime of David Forest, tailor of the robes; that Creed succeeded Forest, and the place being now disposed of to Thos. Barock, Creed requests the pension formerly paid to New.*

139. III. *Certificate by Dr. Ri. Dukeson, and eight others, to the truth of the petition of Wm. Creed.* July 17, 1660.

139. IV. *Certificate by Wm. Rumbold, clerk of the wardrobe, of the allowance of liveries to John New, according to a warrant prefixed, dated July 2, 1624.*

139. V. *Warrant for allowance of liveries to Wm. Creed, as tailor of the robes in place of David Forest, and for further allowance to him of 12d. a day till the pension paid to John New expire, when it is to revert to William Creed.* [*Copy, three pages, certified by Wm. Rumbold.*] September 28, 1639.

139. VI. *Certificate of the burial of John New, 22 December, 1654, from the register book of St. Lawrence, Jewry.* November 27, 1660.

VOL. CII.

1664.
Sept. ? 140. Petition of the two Clerks of the Cheque and the 40 Messengers of the Chamber in ordinary, to Sec. Bennet, to intercede for their arrears of pay. In spite of two references on petitions, they will be two years and a half in arrears at Christmas, and are obliged to neglect their service, to seek bread for their subsistence.

Sept. ? 141. Petition of the two Clerks of the Cheque and the 40 Messengers of the Chamber in ordinary, to the King, for an effectual order for payment of their arrears, to relieve their perishing families, and stop the clamours of their creditors. Were sufferers in the late times, and have hazarded their lives in apprehension of traitors; will be two years and a half in arrears at Christmas. *Annexing,*

141. I. "*List of all the 40 messengers of His Majesty's chamber in ordinary, with their places of abode in London and Westminster.*"

Sept. ? 142. Petition of Paul Hobson, prisoner in Chepstow Castle, to the King, for liberty, and, if deemed unworthy to remain in England, for leave to pass beyond seas, on sufficient warrant not to return without leave. Has been a prisoner above 13 months, without allowance, and in miserable condition.

Sept. ? 143. Petition of John Collins to the King, for satisfaction for his services in discovering transactions of the late dangerous and horrid plot to Capt. Titus and Mr. Coventry, in which he spent 120*l.*, and exposed his life; believes, by their frequent invitations to him to counsel them, that they are as high as ever in contriving the ruin of His Majesty and the nation.

Sept. ? 144. Memorial of Viscount Andover; entreats that the King would remember his promise to the Queen-Mother, and order him the remainder of his pension, as already granted to the other gentlemen of the bedchamber, notwithstanding the present stay of pensions; being "upon the uttermost confines of starving," for want of the money due to him.

Sept. ? 145. Warrant for a grant to Thos. Earl of Cleveland and Thos. Lord Wentworth, his son, of the custody of a weekly market every Saturday at Ratcliffe Cross, Stepney, and a yearly fair at Mile End Green, with enlargement of his court of pleas in the said manor from 40*s.* to 5*l.* [*Draft, one and a half pages.*]

Sept. Memoranda [by Williamson, from the signet books], of warrants, &c., passed during the month, the uncalendared portions of which are as follow:

Discharge to the merchants between England and the house of Burgundy, of all subsidies, English merchants having the like privileges there.

Vol. CII.

1664.

Grant to Ralph Whitley, in reversion after Thos. Edwards, of the office of Constable of Flint Castle; fee 10*l*., and of the Keepership of the Gaol; fee, 6*l*. 1*s*. 6*d*.

Note that John Stone, the Queen's yeoman of the stirrup, and the yeoman rider of her hobby-horse have each 50*l*. a year diet out of the coffery, and her grooms of the chamber in ordinary 2*s*. 4*d*. each a day.

Grant to [Edw.] Backwell of 1,500*l*., for his pains in receiving and telling the money for Dunkirk.

Note that the Queen's pages have 100*l*. pension, and 20*l*. a year to buy horses.

Note that the yeomen footmen have 40*l*. a year.

Grant to the Navy Victualler of a commission to press bakers, smiths, and coopers, at reasonable rates.

Grant to Lord Gerard and others of their invention of water for iron works.

Confirmation to the Duke of Ormond of the sale to him of More Park, made by Sir Rich. Franklin, to whom it was granted by King James, and release of a rent of 120*l*. formerly reserved on it.

Note that the Marshal's Court, as erected by Charles I., is to extend 12 miles round the court, and to be called "His Majesty's Court of his Palace at Westminster;" that it takes cognizance of pleas personal within the palaces, and 12 miles round, London excepted, the Lord Steward and Knight Marshal being the two Judges, and that it was confirmed under the Great Seal, September 1664.

Note that a clerk of the Privy Council has a fee of 50*l*. for life. [*Domestic Corresp., August* 1664, *No.* 97.]

Sept. 146. Valuation of Peter Blackborow's deals and fir timber delivered at Chatham. [*Adm. Paper.*]

Sept. 147. Report that the patent granted to Mr. Thomas to licence the export of any manufacture, except that in the power of Lord Portland and the Merchant Adventurers, cannot profit him, as none of the manufactures enumerated in his grant are prohibited exports, so that licence is not needed unless he should restrain them, which would obstruct trade, and involve him in costly law suits; but a bill might be brought into Parliament, on petition of dyers, pressers, &c., of drapery, forbidding the export of more undyed and undressed cloths than needed for religious orders, and requiring a licence for those thus exported, which licence may be acceptable to the people, and of use to the party who holds the office. [*One and a half pages.*]

VOL. CII.

1664.
[Sept.] 148. Answer of Rob. Thomas to the petition of the Merchant Adventurers, delivered in to Council, Aug. 24, in which they complain that he charges more than 2s. 8d. on every cloth exported, as prescribed by an order in 1617; this he says he does because that order cannot be produced, and they themselves charge 5s. 4d.; also that he grants licence of export to unfree men; this he says they also did, when they were lessees of his patent; also that he obstructs trade, by threatening to seize such cloths as they ship on their own free licence; in this he offers to submit to any authentic patent, but thinks the law will support him in defending the rights of the patent which he holds at great rent from honourable persons, and requests protection therein. [*One and a quarter pages; see Council Reg.*]

VOL. CIII. OCTOBER, 1664.

1664.
Oct. 1. 1. Examination of Thos. Rawson, journeyman shoemaker in Little Britain. Ralph Wallis lodged in his house, and brought in many books—Magna Charta, Good News from Rome, &c., and said he had made several of them without help. Also,

Examination of Ralph Wallis, *alias* Gardiner. As to religion, is a Christian; lived formerly in Gloucester; wrote the books called "Magna Charta," "Good News from Rome," "More News from Rome, discoursed of between a Poor Man and his Wife," and "The Honour of a Hangman." Also,

Examination of James Forbes. Has been 11 years from Scotland; is a public preacher; formerly lived in Gloucester, and not at Hackney; has not read the books which Mr. L'Estrange found in his study, nor the Sufferers' Catechism, and cannot tell whence he had them. [*One and a half pages.*]

Oct. 1. Rydal. 2. Dan. Fleming to Williamson. Wants advice whether to join with Col. Kirkby in procuring the next lease for the excise in Lancashire. The trained bands, horse and foot, of Cumberland and Westmoreland are to rendezvous at Penrith. There have been sharp encounters lately between Col. Kirkby and some Quakers, who conventicled at Mrs. Fell's house since she was convicted of a præmunire, and show the great obstinacy of the sect.

Oct. 1. Staveley. 3. Col. Frecheville to Sec. Bennet. Has delivered his letters to the Earl of Devonshire, who will be at Derby on the 12th, and wants Gladman's examination. That to Lord Brooke, who is in London, is sent to Sir Brian Broughton and the deputy lieutenants of Staffordshire.

Oct. 1. 4. Capt. Wm. Badiley and two others to the Navy Comrs. Survey of stores on board the East India Merchant; endorsed with a note that it is stored according to contract. [*Adm. Paper.*]

VOL. CIII.

1664.

Oct. 1. 5. Capt. Wm. Badiley and two others to the Navy Comrs. Survey of stores on board the hired ship Good Hope, made at the request of the owners. [*Adm. Paper.*]

Oct. 1. Whitehall. Warrant to Col. Wm. Legg, lieutenant of Ordnance, to deliver to Prince Rupert certain habiliments of war for the present expedition. [*Ent. Book* 20, *p.* 25.] *Annexing,*

I. *Account of stores required for a standing carriage culverin, a petard, and for the use of a firemaster, &c.* [*Ent. Book* 20, *pp.* 28–29.] *October* 3. 1664.

Oct. 1. Licence to Sir John Denham and Sir William Poulteney to build 10 or 12 houses, each to cost not less than 1,000*l.*, on a square of 560 feet of ground, next the Earl of Clarendon's. [*Ent. Book* 16, *p.* 247.]

Oct. 1. Pass for five horses to France for Julian Lane. Minute. [*Ent. Book* 16, *p.* 247.]

Oct. 2. Warrant to Mr. L'Estrange to apprehend Thomas Strange and bring him before Sec. Bennet. Minute. [*Ent. Book* 16, *p.* 245.]

Oct. 3. Pass for six horses for the Marquis of Mompesat. *Ent. Book* 16, *p.* 247.]

Oct. 3. Privy seal for 10,000*l.* to be paid to the privy purse. Minute. [*Ent. Book* 16, *p.* 247.]

Oct. 3. Confirmation by the King of the election of William Pauke to be town clerk of Stamford, co. Lincoln, in place of Rich. Butler, deceased. [*Ent. Book* 16, *p.* 248.]

Oct 3. Sec. Morice to [the Governor of Falmouth?]. The Dutch vessel, the Rainbow of Flushing, returning from the Caribbee Islands, is detained at Falmouth, where it was driven, and neither the men suffered to come on shore nor the vessel to proceed on her voyage, on pretence of the order of Council about ships belonging to the United States. If the allegations made about it be true, the King wishes it to be released. [*Ent. Book* 14, *p.* 35.]

Oct. 3. Commission for —— Hull to be Lieutenant to Capt. Bennet. Minute. [*Ent. Book* 20, *p.* 29.]

Oct. 3. The Henrietta, Hope. 6. Capt. Walter Wood to the Navy Comrs. Has received orders from the Duke of York for the fleet to set sail to-morrow. His carpenter's stores are refused unless the carpenter will give his hand for those received by the former carpenter, which seems unreasonable. [*Adm. Paper.*]

Oct. 3. Sherwood. 7. T. Corbin to the Navy Comrs. Has received 100*l.*, but wants 100*l.* more. Particulars of timber. [*Adm. Paper.*]

Oct. 3. Deptford. 8. Capt. Wm. Badiley and two others to the Navy Comrs. Survey of stores on board the Maryland, bound for Guinea. [*Adm. Paper.*]

VOL. CIII.

1664.

Oct. 4. Chatham. 9. Commissioner Peter Pett to Sam. Pepys. Acknowledges his letter hinting at the probability of a Dutch war. Will send demands for provisions wanted. All the eight ships except the Triumph are ready for victualling. Particulars of timber offered. Small cordage wanted. Arrival of Sir Wm. Penn and Sir Geo. [Ayscough]. [*Adm. Paper.*]

Oct. 4. Warrant for a lease to And. Newport, on rent of one fourth of their value, of the extra-parochial tithes in certain demesne lands in the Forest of Delamere, co. palatine of Chester, of which a lease for 60 years was granted to him and Charles Lord Gerard of Brandon. [*Ent. Book* 17, *pp.* 63-4.]

Oct. 4. Haigh. 10. Sir Roger Bradshaigh to Williamson. Not hearing from him, thinks he must have sent the letters to Col. Kirkby. The receiver of hearth-money for the county is active and prudent in collecting it. A man of 88 years lately undertook to run a race of 14 miles near Preston with one of 68, giving him a mile start; the old man ran stoutly for seven miles, but seeing the other a mile before him, gave it over, though it was thought he would have won had they started together. [*One and a half pages.*]

Oct. 5. 11. Certificate by Sec. Bennet that Wm. Leving is employed by him, and therefore not to be molested or restrained.

Oct. 5. The King to the Corporation of Berwick. Recommends, on certificate of George Duke of Albemarle, Thomas Ellis to be a Freeman of the town, in which he holds houses, &c.; he was faithful in the Restoration. [*Ent. Book* 14, *p.* 36.]

Oct. 5. The King to the Dean and Chapter of Ely. Recommends John Boyn and Abraham Hill for admission as Beadsmen or Almsmen of that cathedral. [*Ent. Book* 14, *p.* 36.]

Oct. 5. Chatham Dock. 12. Wm. Castell, master shipwright, and three others to the Navy Comrs. Survey of the Victory, and estimate of repairs needed; total, 5,970*l.* [*Adm. Paper.*]

Oct. 6. Portsmouth. 13. John Tippetts to the Navy Comrs. Particulars of ships' stores and timber contracted for. The captains of third-rate ships say they had three lanterns allowed at Chatham, and the same is wanted for the Mary. [*Adm. Paper, two pages.*] *Encloses,*

13. I. *Ro. Richbell to John Tippetts. If the Commissioners can make no higher offer for his rosin than last proposed, it must be disposed of elsewhere.*

Southampton, October 3, 1664.

Oct. 6. Portsmouth. 14. Certificate by John Tippetts, that the second payment is due to Sam. Ive for carved work on the new ship. [*Adm. Paper.*]

Oct. 6. Portsmouth. 15. Certificate by John Tippetts, that the second payment is due to Thos. Bulbeck, for joiners' work on the new ship. [*Adm. Paper.*]

VOL. CIII.

1664.

Oct. 6. Woolwich. 16. Wm. Acworth to the Navy Comrs. Account of stores ready to be dispatched to Prince Rupert's Guinea fleet. Train oil required for graving ships. [*Adm. Paper*]

Oct. 6. Deptford. 17. Jonas Shish to the Navy Comrs. The disaster of the ship bearing Mr. Dering's deals is owing more to the indiscretion of the men than the badness of the ship. [*Adm. Paper.*]

Oct. 7. Commission for Sir John Sayer to be captain of a company of foot in Portsmouth garrison. Minute. [*Ent. Book* 20, *p.* 29.]

Oct. 7/17. Chelsea. Ambassador Van Goch to the States General. The English fleet destined for Guinea has put to sea. The King, Duke of York, and many nobles accompanied Prince Rupert to the place whence he is to embark, and returned in very boisterous weather. The men wanting of the full number were taken from General Montague's ships. Men are pressing and ships preparing at Chatham and Portsmouth. [*Holland Corresp., Oct.* 7, 1664.]

Oct. 7. Woolwich. 18. Chris. Pett to the Navy Comrs. The King and Duke of York being lately there, have resolved that the new ship be launched at the next full moon. Requests orders and provisions for her speedy completion and launching. The King ordered her carved works and rails to be gold colour. [*Adm. Paper.*]

Oct. 7. Chatham. 19. Commissioner Peter Pett to Sam. Pepys. Account of ships ready to sail. Particulars of timber tendered and contracted for. [*Adm. Paper.*]

Oct. 7. East India Merchant, Lee Road. 20. Capt. John Willgresse to the Navy Comrs. Requests another appointment for Mr. Overton, surgeon, being already supplied from Surgeons' Hall with John Bushell, who has several patients under his care. [*Adm. Paper.*]

Oct. 7. East India Merchant, Lee Road. 21. Capt John Willgresse to Sam. Pepys. Begs that some of the laws of war and a parcel of tickets be ordered for the India Merchant. Is at his wits' end to fit the ship, having to serve two masters, the King and the owners who make small provisions of men or stores. Has no time given to buy stores for preservation of his health in that torrid zone. [*Adm. Paper.*] *Encloses,*

21. I. *Note by Capt. John Willgresse of further wants: a cook to dress the victuals, cook's stores, compasses, carriage for guns, &c.*

Oct. 7. Edwinstow, Sherwood. 22. John Russell to the Navy Comrs. Desires that his last bill of 100*l.* may be paid to his wife. Will proceed as ordered in cutting as much plank as possible. [*Adm. Paper.*]

Oct. 8. Deptford. 23. Capt. Wm. Hadley to the Navy Comrs. Blocks and hawsers are prepared for the launch of the new second-rate ship at Woolwich. Wants men for carrying on the work, the ordinary being employed in watching the pressed men day and night, and in going to press more. Asks orders for their disposal, and money to pay them. [*Adm. Paper.*]

VOL. CIII.

1664.

Oct. 8. Chatham. 24. Commissioner Peter Pett to Sam. Pepys. The James has so drained the yard of men that the sailing of the other ships will be delayed till next week. [*Adm. Paper.*]

Oct. 8. Royal Exchange. Lee Road. 25. Capt. Giles Shelley to the Navy Comm. Wants colours and various stores for the use of the Royal Exchange. [*Adm. Paper.*]

Oct. 8. Watermen's Hall. 26. Certificate from the Watermen's Company, that John Knight, summoned to be impressed as a seaman, having never been to sea, another was provided in his room. [*Adm. Paper.*]

Oct. 8. Lee Road. 27. Prince Rupert to [Sec. Bennet]. Requests him to inform the King and Duke of York that the spirit of mutiny again entered his parson; he talked till 10 o'clock at night, abusing the captain most horribly. Has strained patience to the utmost with him, because he was recommended by the Archbishop of Canterbury, who should be informed of the whole affair. Has sent for all the captains to endeavour to hasten down to the Downs. Expects Mennes next tide.

Oct. 8. 28. ——— to Williamson. The Prince and his fleet are fallen to the road, but the tides being low, they durst not venture over the flat. A Yarmouth vessel arrived from Rotterdam on the 4th, with order immediately to depart if she could keep the sea, for fear lest, having 70 or 80 tons of cordage on board, she should be stopped. Mr. Coventry and Major Wood have landed at Elsinburg, on their way to Stockholm. Has parted with Mr. L'Estrange, finding him treacherous on plea of friendship.

Oct. 8. Whitehall. Warrant for a grant to Charles Duke of Richmond and Lenox of the farm of the subsidy and alnage of old draperies, for 60 years, with the King's moiety of the forfeitures on cloths exposed for sale unsealed, on his surrender of a former similar grant. [*Ent. Book* 16, *p.* 283.]

Oct. 9. 29. Sir Thos. Strickland to Sec. Bennet. Sends some seals, of which a number have been found in the chest of a person who is suspected, though never in arms. Thinks they were intended for the late plot, or to cut stamps for coining. Did not send him to prison, finding that prisoners, after communicating with friends, never make discoveries; thinks therefore he should be privately examined, and then sent to the Tower at York. Asks directions.

Oct. 10. Warrant for a grant to Charles Duke of Richmond and Lenox of the office of Alnager, Collector, Searcher, and Settler of the King's Subsidy on the New Draperies, with the moiety of the King's forfeitures thereon; with proviso of his paying 1,600*l.* a year out of the profits thereof to Benjamin Weston and William Arskin, for the use of Ludovic Lord Aubigny. [*Ent. Book* 16, *p.* 284.]

Oct. 10. Whitehall. 30. Commission to Paul Bucknam of Lieutenantcy in the foot company to be raised in the garrison of Portsmouth, whereof Sir John Sayer is captain.

Oct. 10. Minute of the above. [*Ent. Book* 20, *p.* 29.]

VOL. CIII.

1664.

Oct. 10. Commission for Henry Branch to be Ensign to Sir John Sayer's company. Minute. [*Ent. Book* 20, *p.* 29.]

Oct. 10. 31. Estimate by Chris. Pett and four others of the charge of fitting up the upper breach over against Blackwall as a mast dock; total, 3,593*l.* [*Adm. Paper, two pages.*]

Oct. 10. Chatham. 32. Commissioner Peter Pett to Sam. Pepys. If seamen cannot be had to sail away the fleet, begs that 200 or 300 watermen may be sent down. Progress of ships. [*Adm. Paper.*]

Oct. 10. Deptford. 33. Chris. Pett and two others to the Navy Comrs. Estimate of repairs for the Charity; total, 757*l.* [*Adm. Paper, two pages.*]

Oct. 10. Chester. 34. Sir Geoffry Shakerley to Williamson. Thanks him for his intelligence, and begs its continuance; the assizes are beginning.

Oct. 10. 35. G. Phillipps to Rob. Lye. Has received Sec. Bennet's commands as to the affair he is employed in, but could not summon confidence to ask for money; has been 1½ years in London, on the King's service, and only received 250*l.* The Duke of Ormond says the King promised him a salary of 300*l.* a year: asks an advance of a quarter's salary of 75*l.*, or his family will be exposed to straits.

Oct. 10. Whitehall. 36. Information of Joseph Holden, goldsmith and engraver, living at Nurton Lane, Clerkenwell. Was sent for on the 6th to the lodging of Lady Hawley, up four pairs of stairs; she showed him two papers, with the King's signet affixed, and asked him whether he could engrave such a seal, with all its parts and dimensions. He, intending to discover it, said he would undertake it if well paid, and she bade him have it done by Saturday.

Oct. 11. 37. Wm. Jennens to the Navy Comrs. Begs help to enable seven seamen, pressed from merchant ships, to obtain payment of their wages. They are in sad condition, and unprovided with all things necessary. [*Adm. Paper.*]

Oct. 11. Portsmouth Ropeyard. 38. Gr. Peachy to the Navy Comrs. The ropehouses not being yet lengthened much hinders the work, as in wet weather not above 36 out of 60 spinners can be employed; requests orders for the alteration. [*Adm. Paper.*]

Oct. 11. Portsmouth. 39. St. John Steventon to Sir Wm. Penn. Receipt of 200*l.*; has paid most of it to workmen for the new ship. Wants more money to meet the great charges for seamen's wages, while the Earl of Sandwich's men are employed in rigging the ships, being nearly 48*l.* a week. Only nine pressed men have appeared from Sussex, and not one fit for service, being millers, sawyers, &c., who never saw a ship before. If the others are no better, the King will be put to great charges for little purpose. [*Adm. Paper.*]

Oct. 11. Downs. 40. Prince Rupert to [Sec. Bennet]. Has received the King and Duke's orders; the ship is quiet without Levit; hopes for another

Vol. CIII.

1664.

[minister] of better temper; has not troubled him much with prayers hitherto. The debt which his brother pretends to be due to him from France is a mere chimera; it was money promised to Prince John Casimir to go back with his army from France, and will never be paid. Remits the whole business to the King, and will willingly embrace his offers. Lord Craven will give any information needed.

Oct. 11. Portsmouth. 41. W. Coventry to Sec. Bennet. The Duke of York sent a small vessel to bring in a Dutch ship from the Isle of Wight, laden with prize goods worth 10,000*l.*, she not having behaved so mannerly as she ought. Nothing will more conduce to the manning of the fleet than the strict observation of the embargo, granting few passes to the contrary, and punishing runaways, of whom a list shall be sent.

Oct. 12. 42. Robt. Smyth to the Navy Comrs. The persons propounded for Wm. Jenifer, purser of the Sapphire, are sufficient security for 300*l.* [*Adm. Paper.*]

Oct. 12. The Hector, Downs. 43. Capt. Hugh Seymour to the Navy Comrs. Requests a supply of cables and a boat. [*Adm. Paper.*]

Oct. 12. Woolwich. 44. Wm. Bodham to Sir Wm. Penn. Reasons why it will not be expedient to build the new ropehouse joined on to the old hemp loft, as proposed. [*Adm. Paper, two pages.*]

Oct. 12. The Dover. 45. Capt. Edw. Spragg to the Navy Comrs. His provisions and officers' stores are not yet sent on board. Cannot give the men's tickets till his purser comes. Desires a pilot. [*Adm. Paper.*]

Oct. 12. Chatham. 46. Commissioner Peter Pett to Sam. Pepys. Amount of work to be performed upon the various ships now in dock. Complains of having so few hands; to use expedition in such a service would require 1,000 men. Of the oars lately sent in, not one of eight is worth anything. [*Adm. Paper.*]

Oct. 12. Warrant for a grant to Henry Hildyard of two new fairs at Kingston-upon-Hull, in the piece of ground called the Manor. [*Ent. Book 16, p. 230; and 21, p. 25.*]

Oct. 12. London. 47. Sir Andrew Riccard, governor of the Levant Company, to Sec. Bennet. Has communicated to the company his intimation that they stand liable to all charges in Turkey, ordinary as well as extraordinary, but they only esteem themselves liable to what relates to the support of their trade, and they beg that the King and the ambassador at Constantinople will lay aside their expectations of extraordinary charge from the company. With note by [Lord Chancellor Clarendon] that this is a foolish answer, and the governor must attend the Council Board.

Oct. 12. Whitehall. 48. Order in Council, referring to the Principal Secretaries of State the petition of Thos. Bickham, late mayor of Bridgewater,

1664. Vol. CIII.

Chris. Poore, and Edm. Dawes, keepers of the prison, who are committed to a messenger's custody as accessory to the escape of Rich. Bovett out of that prison, they protesting their innocence, and offering to try to apprehend him.

Oct. 13. Carlisle. 49. Eras. Towerson to Williamson. Returns his quarter's accounts and congratulates his recovery. Wishes to be joined in commission with Williamson's brother to collect the chimney money in Cumberland. Hears that the present arrangement of the excise is censured, at which Sir Pat. Curwen is troubled.

Oct. 13. Dover. 50. Certificate, by Sir John Lawson, of Luke Slayfield's service as marshal in the fleet in the Mediterranean, from September 20 to October 12, 1664. [*Adm. Paper.*] *Annexing,*

50. i. *Like certificate, from Sir Wm. Berkeley and Sir John Lawson, of his service from January 6 to September 20, 1664. September* 21, 1664.

Oct. 13. Victualling Office. 51. Denis Gauden to the Navy Comrs. Will undertake to victual the ships at Leghorn for the ensuing year at 8½*d.* a man per day. As to English victualling for the year, will, for a farthing on each man's allowance per day, secure the King from any loss that may accrue by victuals provided, in case they should not be called for. [*Adm. Paper.*]

Oct. 13. Woolwich Ropeyard. 52. E. Williams and Peter Russell to Sir Wm. Batten. Certify that Wm. Newsum and Wm. Sherwood have cleansed the tar house, but not refined the tar as they undertook to do. [*Adm. Paper, damaged.*]

Oct. 14. Woolwich. 53. Chris. Pett to the Navy Comrs. Desires 30 or 40 watermen to complete the works of the new ship now ready for launch, and a warrant to the officers of Deptford to assist on the launching day; also such silken colours as are used on those occasions. [*Adm. Paper.*]

Oct. 14. Chatham. 54. Commissioner Peter Pett to the Navy Comrs. Progress and repairs of ships. [*Adm. Paper.*]

Oct. 14. Woolwich. 55. Estimate by Chris. Pett and others of the charge of fitting the Lower Breach over against Blackwall, for keeping 680 masts under water; total, 3,660*l.* [*Adm. Paper, two pages.*] *Annexing,*

55. i. *Plan of the Upper and Lower Breach intended to be so fitted. October* 1664.

Oct. 14. Commission for Geo. Houston to be Ensign to the Duke of York's company of foot in Portsmouth garrison, whereof And. Newport is Captain. Minute. [*Ent. Book* 20, *p.* 30.]

Oct. 14. Warrant for creating Sir Theophilus Biddulph, of Westcombe, co. Kent, a Baronet. Minute. [*Ent. Book* 16, *p.* 249.]

Vol. CIII.

1664.

Oct. 14. Licence for Sir Charles and George Berkeley, sons of George Lord Berkeley, of Berkeley Castle, to go abroad for three years, for better education, with their governors and servants. [*Ent. Book* 16, *p.* 249.]

Oct. 14. Licence for Mrs. Arabella Alleyn and Mrs. Isabella Thompson to travel for three years. Minute. [*Ent. Book* 16, *p.* 249.]

Oct. 14. Pass for four horses to France. Minute. [*Ent. Book* 16, *p.* 250.]

Oct. 14. Pass for Peter Willems Buys with three horses to France. Minute. [*Ent. Book* 16, *p.* 250.]

Oct. 14. Warrant for William Lord Crofts to be gamekeeper within ten miles of Lexham, Suffolk. Minute. [*Ent. Book* 16, *p.* 250.]

Oct. ? 56. Petition of Ezechiah Smith to the King, for relief. Served the late King till the surrender of Newark, and has since diligently prosecuted coiners, some of whom have been condemned, but the charges being great, is too poor to proceed therein. *Annexing*,

56. i. *Evidence against Joseph Clarke, the grand receiver of false coin, to prove that he abetted John Beale, the coiner, in his practices, bought counterfeit coin from him at 11s. for 20s., and tried to bribe off the witnesses against him.*

Oct. 14. Warrant for a grant to Ezechiah Smith of the forfeited goods of John Beale, of Wingfield Plain, co. Berks, executed for treason, in consideration of his pains and charge in prosecuting him. [*Ent. Books* 16, *p.* 250; *and* 21, p. 25.]

Oct. 14. Plymouth. 57. —— to Williamson. A Dutch ship of 300 men, beaten by the English out of Amsterdam, New Netherlands, has arrived at Mount's Bay. A vessel has come from Gambia, which landed 60 men on an island taken by Major Holmes, who thinks the Dutch have lost their interest in those parts.

Oct. 14. 58. Sir Charles Cotterel to Mr. Godolphin. Since the King's return, there have been several envoys extraordinary from the French King, who have been brought to Court without ceremony by the French Ambassador. Did however fetch to Court, in the King's coaches, to their first audience, those who addressed themselves to him, though this was not the custom formerly; but the King ordered it through Lord Crofts, who alleged that he was so treated at the French Court.

Oct. 14. 59. Sir Thos. Gower to Sec. Bennet. The schoolmaster of Newcastle, Thomas *alias* Lawrence, whose examination he is ordered to send up, has never been taken, though carefully sought for; he has been at several meetings of conspirators, and been sent on their errands. Details of his proceedings; his different names. He spoke of great

1663.

VOL. CIII.

assistance for the plot from cos. Derby, Notts, and Lincoln; of great preparations in the middle of England; of persons of quality engaged, &c. There are three witnesses against him. He is a man of great consideration among the conspirators, and can give much light on the design. The party will resolve on nothing till they hear from their agents, Washington and Lamm, in Holland. Sent to Lord Lovelace the examinations of certain persons, and will send that of Major Fenwick. Has incurred the heavy hatred and malice of that party, and some persons, even of those faithful to the King, tell the people they would help them willingly, but cannot, as all the persecution comes from himself. [*Two pages.*]

Oct. 15. Derby. 60. Col. J. Frescheville to Sec. Bennet. Lord Devonshire met the sheriff, almost all the deputy lieutenants, and some justices of the peace at Derby, on the 12th, and spent several days in examining the persons accused by Calton. Particulars of what concerns Staffordshire are sent to Lord Brooke. There was a continuous carrying on of the rebellious design, two years before 12th Oct. 1663. On the ejection of the Presbyterian ministers, it was pretended that the Papists would rise and destroy the godly; then that the Act of Indemnity would be repealed.

Oct. 15. Derby. 61. Col. J. Frescheville to [Sec. Bennet?]. In Calton's confession of what passed between him and Fletcher, the agitator for Staffordshire, there are reflections on Lord Fairfax, omitted in the particulars sent to Lord Brooke; but the Earl of Devonshire will give an exact account of it.

Oct. 15. 62. Fras. Lord Hawley to Sec. Bennet. All is in peace in the country; the fanatics hope for an alteration, in case the war with the Dutch goes on. Requests his favour to the reasonable and modest request enclosed. The petitioners are obliged to leave it to chance, as all undertakers do, whether they shall pay their charges, but they will serve His Majesty, and greatly benefit the country. Begs his honour and Lord Fitzharding to do what was designed for him in his absence. *Encloses,*

62. I. *Petition of Fras. Lord Hawley, Sir Wm. Wyndham, Bart., and Sir John Warre, to the King, for a grant of the land on which the river now comes to Bridgewater, which, running a great compass about Pegnes farm, is incommodious, and the banks being much worn, threatens to drown the country. They offer, if an Act of Parliament be obtained, to make a new cut at their own charge, compensating all persons whose lands are damaged thereby.*

Oct. 15. Reference to the Lord Treasurer and Lord Ashley on the petition of Wm. Prettyman, for the office of Remembrancer of first fruits. [*Ent. Book* 18, *p.* 92.]

Oct. 15. Warrant to the Master of the Great Wardrobe to pay 4,749*l.* 4*s.* 9½*d.* to the Royal tradesmen, servants, &c., for necessaries and allowances for the stables, for the half-year ending Lady Day 1663. [*Docquet.*]

Vol. CIII.

1664.

Oct. 15. Warrant to pay to Lord Fitzharding, keeper of the privy purse, 10,000*l.*, without account. [*Docquet.*]

Oct. 15. Grant to John Seymour of the sole imprinting and selling of various books for 41 years, unless the printing of any such have formerly been granted to others, in which case he is to have the reversion. [*Docquet.*]

Oct. 15. 63. Certificate by Rich. Hodges and Thos. Ayliffe of the fitness of Thos. Driver, master mate in several frigates, to take charge of a fourth-rate frigate. [*Adm. Paper.*]

Oct. 15. 64. Anthony Deane and Robt. Magors to the [Navy Comrs.]. Survey of Sir Wm. Warren's timber at Ditting. [*Adm. Paper.*]

Oct. 15. Portsmouth. 65. John Tippetts to Sir Wm. Penn. Asks what gold may be bestowed upon the new ship, besides the King's arms on the stern. Blocks and spades wanted. Progress of the new storehouse. Purchase of timber. Requests a warrant for land carriage to eight justices mentioned in the margin. Arrival of Prince [Rupert] and his fleet. [*Adm. Paper.*]

Oct. 15. Portsmouth. 66. John Tippetts to the Navy Comrs. To similar effect. [*Adm. Paper.*]

Oct. 15 Ullerton. 67. Thos. Corbin to the Navy Comrs. Has not yet received the 200*l.* ordered. The constables cannot make the sluggish carters come in. The justices have promised to grant strict warrants for conveyance of 400 loads of timber. Requests leave to come up to London, to attend a jury at Westminster. Will leave a servant to attend to the work. The Love boy has arrived. More vessels are wanted to convey away the timber, the shore being so full that there is no knowing where to lay any more. [*Adm. Paper, two pages.*]

Oct. 15. 68. Warrant from the Navy Comrs. to the Storekeeper and Clerk of the Cheque at Deptford, to receive from Mr. Johnson, of Yarmouth, one vessel's lading of Holland cordage; to send to Chatham forthwith 5 tons of Surinam wood, lately received from Mr. Howell, and 10 tuns of oil; to put on board the Augustine 5 tuns of oil for Portsmouth, and to send 5 tuns of the same oil to Woolwich. [*Adm. Paper.*]

Oct. 15. Portsmouth. 69. Capt. Jer. Smith to the Navy Comrs. The Mary is ready to sail. Desires tickets for the discharge of several pitiful fellows sent as pressed men, as soon as he can get better ones. [*Adm. Paper.*]

Oct. 15. Portsmouth Ropeyard. 70. Gregory Peachy to the Navy Comrs. Sends John Smith's tickets. [*Adm. Paper.*]

Oct. 16. Chatham. 71. Commissioner Peter Pett to the Navy Comrs. Returns Col. Reymes's bill certified. Begs that 200 watermen may be

1664. Vol. CIII.

sent down forthwith, to release many of the ancient fishermen unfit for sea, who came without pressing and may be a help another time. [*Adm. Paper.*]

Oct. 17. Durham. 72. Sir Thos. Davidson to Col. H. Ewbancke. Many persons in the north of Yorkshire, informed against by Wm. Watson, may easily be taken; others are skulking up and down, and may be taken if the justices of Yorkshire and Durham set persons to watch their haunts. Waits Mr. Secretary's directions about proceeding on the discoveries of Watson, through whose wife many known to be guilty may be taken, and he could do much more if at liberty.

Oct. 17. 73. Sir Jo. Warre to Sec. Bennet. Hill, who was committed with Bovett, still remains in custody, but the new mayor begs his removal, for Hill threatens to challenge him for false imprisonment. His letter to Amory shows his disaffection, and several loyal persons of Taunton say that his ordinary discourses were so seditious that people feared to be in his company; thinks so dangerous a fellow should not be set at liberty.

Oct. 17. 74. —— —— to [Sec. Bennet]. The party are still providing arms, collecting money, and encouraging their friends in Scotland to act. The six persons formerly named manage the business, with two others intrusted about arms. Can give directions if a search has to be made; they lie at fanatics' houses, in bye places between Moorfields and Wapping, and in Southwark; some may be found at Widow Hogden's in Petty France. Thinks one who is discontented, if he had a handsome opportunity to save himself, would find every particular person named, and witness the whole design, and he will be at Mrs. Stubbs', near Tower Hill, to-morrow; the writer fears he should be suspected if that house were searched, as only he and another know of it; shall be sure to know both time and place if the design proceed; gives the names and *alias* names of several of the plotters. Endorsed with a note from Leeds, dated the 31st instant, that a letter from Wm. Friar, an Anabaptist, to a person concerned in the late plot, and now in York Castle, was opened on suspicion, and the writer says that he lay at Mr. North's in Grub Street, with one Dawson.

Oct. 17. Bridewell, London. 75. Esther Biddle, a quaker, to Fras. Howgill, prisoner for the testimony of Jesus, in Appleby gaol. Looks upon him as a precious pillar in the temple of God. There are many valiant ones in London persevering to the death; thanks for his prayers for them. Ant. Garnett and another of their men are imprisoned for the third time, one is banished and the other likely to be. One lies dead at home; her husband [Thos. Biddle] is a prisoner in the Fleet, but has his liberty. Was herself taken to prison from the Bull and Mouth; Browne pinched her as black as a hat, kicked her son, and struck her on the mouth. Is content with the will of God, and relies on him. All meetings were quiet last Sunday except at the [Bull and] Mouth, where George Whitehead and 50 more were taken. The

VOL. CIII.

1664.

sessions have been held: 28 are to be transported; eight women are committed to Bridewell for 11 or 12 months, and several have not been called. The Lord so confounded them that six [of the jury] were for Friends [Quakers] and six against them. [*One and a quarter pages.*]

Oct. 17. Lydney. 76. Dan. Furzer to Sam. Pepys. Lydney is not so fit a place now for building a new ship as formerly, on account of the growing of the sands, "not known in man's memory before." Recommends Conpill, three miles below, as clear of sand, or Rownan, three miles below Bristol, as convenient to the city for all provisions needed in fitting up a vessel. Particulars of cutting, squaring, and loading timber, and of its quality. Since the great windfall, much has been taken away by the country people. [*Adm. Paper, two pages.*]

Oct. 17. Deptford. 77. Jonas Shish to [the Navy Comrs.]. The first estimate of repairs for the Garland amounted to 183*l.*; the further charge in girdling her will be 124*l.* 18*s.* [*Adm. Paper.*]

Oct. 17. Dover. 78. Thos. Wale, shipwright, to the Navy Comrs. Repairs of ships. [*Adm. Paper.*]

Oct. 18. Portsmouth. 79. John Tippetts to Sir Wm. Penn. According to the press warrant, has despatched Abraham Ansley and Fras. Fletcher, boatswain and carpenter of the Montague, to press men at Bristol. Damage to the Mary. [*Adm. Paper.*]

Oct. 18. Portsmouth. 80. John Tippetts to the Navy Comrs. Repairs of ships. [*Adm. Paper.*]

Oct. 18. Barber Surgeons' Hall. 81. Ralph Thickness and Thos. Hollier, wardens of Surgeons' Hall, to the Navy Comrs. Will do their best, in filling up the bills for surgeons for the fleet now going out to sea, to comply with their recommendations, or the requests of commanders of ships; but complain of abuse from apothecaries getting acquainted with the commanders of ships, and recommending to them surgeons utterly unknown, who promise to fit their chests with them, and who are taken on board without the approbation of the Surgeons' Company. [*Adm. Paper.*]

Oct. 18. Newark. 82. John Russell to the Navy Comrs. Mr. Corbin's services may be dispensed with; all he does is to send his man to Bawtry about once a month, to take account of timber lading. The Justices of Newark have given warrants for 300 loads of timber. [*Adm. Paper.*]

Oct. 18. Plymouth. 83. J. C[larke] to [Williamson]. The Eagle from Gambia took in 100 pressed men, and set sail for Portsmouth. Pressed men are sent in every day, but not in the numbers expected. The King Fernando, one of Prince Rupert's fleet, which lost their company, has put in. Knows not whether the fleet has passed, but hears of 15 sail seen off Torbay.

Oct. 18. 84. Certificate by Ri. Butler, registrar to the Bishop of London, that John Smith, of Rickling, Essex, was admitted, in Aug. last,

VOL. CIII.

1664.

curate to Jonathan Devereux, vicar of Canwedon, Essex, and appeared as such at the Bishop's visitation in Chelmsford church, 10th Sept. last.

Oct. 18. 85. Sir Allan Apsley [master falconer to Sec. Bennet?]. Asks him for charity's sake to procure a warrant for John Baxter, to be Falconer in the room of John Barrow, fee 1s. a day, and another for Chas. Pitcairn, in place of Rob. Kettle. Has had sad reflections caused by this last person, in thinking what a master falconer's son may come to. [*Andrew Pitcairn, father of Charles, was master falconer to Charles I.*]

1664? Oct. 18? 86. Estimate of the daily and weekly pay for the officers of Sir Wm. Killigrew's men, 63*l.* a week, and of the raising and shipping 1,200 men at 1*l.* each; total, 1,263*l.*

1664. Oct. 18. Poole. 87. Willm. Skutt to Williamson. Lord Lieutenant the Duke of Richmond has been very careful and diligent in viewing the bands of Dorsetshire, and ordering all things about his great charge. All is peaceable both on sea and land. Some French vessels and an English one from Rochelle have arrived, and they met with no men-of-war.

Oct. 18. Whitehall. Warrant from Sec. Bennet, for special care to be taken that neither Sir John Warner, his lady, nor any of his family be permitted to pass the seas, without the King's special licence. [*Ent. Book* 16, *p.* 252.]

Oct. 18. Pass for Mons. Gramont to export 16 horses to France. Minute. [*Ent. Book* 16, *p.* 252.]

Oct. 19. Deptford. 88. J. Uthwayt to Sir Wm. Batten. Asks whether the Harwich hoy shall take in certain provisions mentioned for Harwich, which will be far short of a freight for her, or whether they shall be sent in the Rosebush. [*Adm. Paper.*]

Oct. 19. Chatham. 89. Phin. Pett and Jos. Lawrence to [Sam. Pepys]. A hundred shipwrights are wanted for forwarding the repairs of ships ordered. [*Adm. Paper.*]

Oct. 19. Chatham. 90. Commissioner Peter Pett to Sam. Pepys. Repairs of the James. Ships ready to sail. Masts, spars, and other stores wanted. [*Adm. Paper.*]

Oct. 20. Barber Surgeons' Hall. 91. Rich. Reynell, clerk of Surgeons' Hall, to Mr. Hayter. The captain of the Pearl, being removed to the Newcastle, requests leave to take his surgeon with him. Wants bills therefor. [*Adm. Paper.*]

Oct. 20. Deptford. 92. Thos. Harper to Sam. Pepys. Account of oars sent in by Capt. Lowe and others. A steelyard is wanted for weighing the anchors for the new ship at Woolwich; also labourers, anchors, &c. [*Adm. Paper, damaged.*]

VOL. CIII.

1664.

Oct. 20. Chatham. 93. Philip Barrow, storekeeper at Chatham, to the Navy Comrs. Complains of the little help afforded him in the extraordinary business caused by the present hasty expenditure. Fears the service has suffered, and the stores been embezzled. The labourers in the yard are almost tired out with early and late attendance, and small encouragement. [*Adm. Paper.*]

Oct. 20? [Chatham.] 94. Demand by Thos. Tunbridge for six men named, for works detailed now in hand, about the storehouse, docks, &c. [*Adm. Paper.*]

Oct. 21. 95. —— to Sec. Bennet. Has tried to find out the Scottish negotiation, but thinks that there is little in it, and that there had been no previous consultation among considerable persons in Scotland. They speak of general discontent among ministers and people; of talk of a revolution, and exhortations to prisoners. The desperadoes would carry on something, but are utterly destitute of money. Can see no sudden preparations, but if the Hollander strike, the humour may show itself.

Oct. 21. Thornton Bridge. 96. Sir Thos. Strickland to Williamson. Sends a letter for Sir Thos. Clifford. Wishes to be named to Mr. Secretary, about the managing of an affair which needs more persons, as the rumour of a Dutch war grows very hot.

Oct. 21. Ad. 97. Ch. Bennet to Williamson. Asks in whose power it lies to prevent the impressing of the second of two sons of a waterman whom he knows, one of whom is pressed on board Prince Rupert's fleet; if his other son should be taken, it would greatly injure his affairs, he being daily trusted with good estates of merchants.

Oct. 21. Warrant for a commission to several Officers of Ordnance to impress at reasonable prices, utensils and necessaries, artificers, horses, and carriages, for the service of the ordnance; also to punish all who contemptuously withstand their commission. [*Ent. Book* 16, *p.* 234.]

Oct. 21. 98. Wm. Coventry to Thos. Hacker. The Thomas and Rebecca is ordered into the Hope, to follow the directions of the chief officers on board the Royal James, for the impressing and transporting of men, or any other service required. [*Adm. Paper.*]

Oct. 21. Chatham. 99. Commissioner Peter Pett to Sam. Pepys. Sailing of ships. Is greatly perplexed to get able men. Will be glad to see the 200 watermen promised, as most of the pressed men are fitter to keep sheep than to sail in such great ships. [*Adm. Paper.*]

Oct. 21. Chatham. 100. Commissioner Peter Pett to Sam. Pepys. Repairs of the Guernsey. The master shipwright is ready to begin a ship of the third or fourth rate, there being a good quantity of timber in the yard fit for it. [*Adm. Paper.*]

Oct. 22. Woolwich. 101. Certificate by Chris. Pett, that the carved work of the new second-rate ship is well and sufficiently performed by John Ledman, whereby his second payment is due. [*Adm. Paper.*]

Vol. CIII.

1664.

Oct. 22. Woolwich. 102. Chris. Pett to the Navy Comrs. The King being there on Saturday, called for a draft of the stern and galleries of the new ship, and ordered a report to be prepared of what parts would be fit for gilding, which is not yet ready. Requests warrants to the officers at Deptford, to send in all their help on the launching day. [*Adm. Paper.*]

Oct. 22. 103. List by Geo. Stanbridge and John Coulson, press masters, of 20 coopers pressed, 10 sent to sea, 10 yet undisposed of. [*Adm. Paper.*]

Oct. 22. Ollerton. 104. Thos. Corbin to the Navy Comrs. The Love boy is returned with lading. Particulars of carriage of timber at Bawtry, &c. The charge by land and then by water, at 50 feet per load, amounts to about 15s. 6d. a load. Account of the quantity of timber sent to Bawtry and Stockwith. [*Adm. Paper, one and a half pages.*] *Encloses,*

104. I. *Account of timber brought in, and of money advanced to Mr. Corbin.*

Oct. 22. Whitehall. Warrant to Richard Smith, keeper of the aviary, to take up small wild birds for the King, in any place where none justly claims property. [*Ent. Book 14, p. 45.*]

Oct. 22. London. 105. H. P—— to John Knowles, Pershore. Wishes Knowles had been amongst them the two last years; they are on too great an equality to determine things; Mr. Firmin wishes to entertain him, or his old lord, Atkinson, would be glad of his company. Will supply him with books, and thinks that his private studies should profit others, and that his coming would promote the cause of truth. Some Quakers, taken on a third default, were arraigned at the sessions; 16 pleaded not guilty, and the jury brought them in so, though they had met together. Lord Chief Justice Hyde and Judge Kelynge, who were on the bench, were angry, and disputed severally with the jurymen, with threats, and thus drew six of the 12 to their side. The judges would not take it for a verdict, but being Saturday night, dismissed them, binding the six who said "not guilty" in 100*l.* each, to answer for it on Monday at the King's Bench, before the Lord Chief Justice. The rest of the Quakers, 20 or 30, who had not pleaded on Saturday, had sentence passed on them without ever asking whether they would plead, though some cried out that they did not refuse to plead. With notes on the letter by another hand.

Oct. 22. 106. Petition of John Sellock, D.D., to the King, for gift of the Rectory of Clifton-Campville, co. Stafford. With note in his favour by Gilb. Archbishop of Canterbury.

Oct. 22. Middle Temple. 107. Attorney General Palmer to Williamson. Thinks it expedient, for the settling of Wildmore, that Sec. Bennet should sign a draft sent about it, and give a note of his consent.

Oct. 22. Isle of Wight. 108. W. S. [Col. Walter Slingsby] to Henry Muddiman. Prince Rupert sent a small frigate to speak with nine large ships, which

Vol. CIII.

1664.

were making for Spithead, found them to be from Emden, and they returned with the frigate, and are coming into Cowes Road.

Oct. 22. 109. Monsieur de Gramont to [Williamson]. Requests an addition to his passport to enable him to pass his mares. [*French.*]

Oct. 24. 110. Dean Guy Carleton to Sec. Bennet. Sends an account of the trial of John Joplin, of Durham, so called to distinguish him from his confederate, John Joplin, of Foxhole, a most uncontrollable rebel, and the centre of the plot. Many papers discovering the whole plot would have been found in his lodging, had Col. John Tempest, a deputy lieutenant, shown more zeal. Sir Nich. Cole and others of their gang take wine with them into the prison, and make merry with him; and even when the plot was ripe, Joplin was allowed to go out of gaol late at night to meet his fellow conspirators, returning before morning to avoid public notice, and he even had leave to travel to Newcastle and Shields. When the Duke of Buckingham ordered him to be sent to York, Col. Tempest and Rich. Noel, gentleman usher to the Bishop of Durham, tried to bring him back, but were checked by Judge Twysden and the loyal gentlemen there. At the trial the Bishop absented himself from the bench, several of Joplin's bosom friends were on the jury; they refused to postpone the verdict till the King's pleasure could be known, and acquitted him. Wm. Blakeston, of Pittington, a deputy lieutenant, threatened to pull the gowns of some of the Durham prebendaries over their ears, for saying Joplin had too much favour shown him, and the prosecutor, Sam. Davidson, had his life endangered; yet they think Joplin an obstinate villain and dangerous traitor, but they were bribed; Joplin, being treasurer for the plot, could dispose of the moneys. The plot is still on foot, an insurrection not far off, and a massacre feared. A deputy lieutenant said there would be mischief unless Joplin were removed to Jersey, or put into irons to prevent escape, as he carries on his designs all the better for being in prison. He corresponds with Holland, and a woman conveys the letters, which are in cypher. The carriage of this business has encouraged the fanatics, and cast a damp on all the loyal party, to see the King's service postponed to private ends. Sir Nich. Cole and Col. John Tempest have been among the most unfaithful. If those two, Wm. Blakeston, and two others were laid aside from office, it would do much good. [*Two pages.*] *Annexes,*

110. i. *Particulars of Joplin's trial, at Durham assizes, Aug. 10, 1664, in confirmation of the above statements, giving also several examinations which were suppressed at the trial.* [*Two pages.*]

Oct. 24. Norwich. 111. ——— to Henry Muddiman. There has been a press for seamen in all the towns of the country; by the countenances of the men, they seem very willing to be employed. A company of 40 marched through the town, with drums beating and other expressions of joy at their taking water. There would be volunteers enough against the Dutch, if they were to be fought at home and not at Guinea.

VOL. CIII.

1664.

Oct. 24. Carby. 112. Jo. Hatcher to Williamson. Fears his return to labour will injure his health. Offers him a share in a purchase, for 4,000*l*., of a lordship near Lincoln, value 400*l*. a year, which, by inclosure is capable of further improvement, and the reversion, after the death of an old lady of 80, is now to be sold.

Oct. 24. 113. Sir Phil. Musgrave to Williamson. Congratulates his return to Whitehall in health.

[Oct. 24.] 114. Reference on the petition of the Duchess of Albemarle to the Lord Treasurer and Chancellor of the Exchequer, and order meanwhile for stopping the Attorney General's confession to Robinson's plea, and all other proceedings.

[Oct. 24.] Entry of the above reference. [*Ent Book* 18, *p.* 95.]

Oct. 24. Warrant to pay to Abraham Walker and John Turnbull 897*l*. 12*s*., due to them from the late Princess Royal, being part of 10,950*l*. due from the King to her executors, for diamond and pearl pendants bought of them. [*Ent. Book* 16, *p.* 252.]

Oct. 24. Warrant of denization to Signor Brunetti, of Florence. Minute [*Ent. Book* 16, *p.* 258.]

Oct. 24. Warrant for a commission appointing John Lord Berkeley of Stratton, Sir John Duncombe, and Thomas Chicheley, to execute the office of Master of Ordnance, void by death of Sir Wm. Compton. [*Ent. Book* 16, *p.* 256.]

[Oct. 24.] 115. Draft of the above.

Oct. 24. Warrant for a grant to Rich. Perrincheif, D.D., of the prebend in Westminster, void by the death of Dr. Jas. Lambe. [*Ent. Books* 19, *p.* 24; *and* 21, *p.* 147.]

Oct. 24. Warrant for a grant to Wm. Levens, M.A., of St. John's College, Oxford, of the office of Greek Professor at Oxford, void by resignation of Dr. Joseph Crowther. [*Ent. Books* 19, *p.* 24; *and* 21, *p.* 147.]

Oct. 24. The King to the Lord Treasurer. Having special need of a present sum of money for divers important services, he is to pay to Stephen Fox 15,000*l*., remaining in the Tower from the sale of Dunkirk. [*Ent. Book* 17, *p.* 64.]

Oct. 24. Whitehall. The King to the Lord Treasurer. He is to pay to Sir George Carteret, treasurer of the navy, 10,000*l*. out of the Dunkirk money, for victuals, &c., which are too important to wait till the ordinary revenue comes in; this money is to be repaid from the ordinary navy assignments, that the fund of Dunkirk money may remain entire. [*Ent. Book* 17, *p.* 65.]

[Oct. 24.] 116. Draft of the above.

Oct. 24. Woolwich. 117. Chris. Pett to the Navy Comrs. Arrangements for the launch of the new ship; is promised the advice and assistance of

Vol. CIII.

1664.

several builders in the river, and many of the Trinity Masters, for Wednesday. Begs that a dinner, as customary, may be provided for them in Mr. Sheldon's house, as his own may be commanded for the accommodation of the King. Repairs of ships. [*Adm. Paper.*]

Oct. 24. The Henrietta, Spithead. 118. Capt. Walter Wood to the Navy Comrs. Requests an order for victualling the retinue of Prince Rupert, 54 persons, being supernumeraries on board. His number of men, 250, is complete without them. [*Adm. Paper.*]

Oct. 24. Chatham. 119. Commissioner Peter Pett to Sam. Pepys. The Charles and Henry have sailed into the Hope; 100 shipwrights and 20 calkers wanted. [*Adm. Paper.*]

Oct. 25. Portsmouth. 120. Rich. Washington, purser of the Nightingale, to Mr. Hayter. Requests a warrant to appoint Thos. Peachy his deputy. [*Adm. Paper.*] *Encloses,*

120. I. *Wm. Jenifer to Mr. Hayter. Being appointed for the Sapphire, requests the Commissioners to appoint Thos. Peachy deputy purser of the Nightingale.*
October 13, 1664.

Oct. 25. Barber Surgeons' Hall. 121. Rich. Reynell to Mr. Hayter. Requests bills to appoint a new surgeon to the Hound, whose surgeon is removed to the Lion. Will soon have to discharge the men, or to saw planks out of timber for the new ships, which is ill husbandry. [*Adm. Paper.*]

Oct. 25. 122. Capt. Wm. Badiley to the Navy Comrs. Arrangements for mooring the new ship. [*Adm. Paper.*]

Oct. 25. Portsmouth. 123. John Tippetts to the Navy Comrs. Purchase of blocks; repairs of ships. [*Adm. Paper.*]

Oct. 25. York. 124. Sir Thos. Slingsby, Rich. Hutton, and Sir Edw. Brett, [governor of York], to the Duke of Buckingham. Send an examination of George Smith, prisoner in York Castle, who wrote a letter to the disadvantage of Sir Solomon Swale; he acknowledges the letter, but denies the postscript. He is an idle, inconsiderable fellow. *Encloses,*

124. I. *Examination of George Smith, prisoner for debt in York Castle. Was offered his liberty in August, 1663, by Wm. Smithson and John Thackeray, of South Stainley, if he would become a trumpeter in the good old cause. Wrote word of it to Sir Solomon Swale, but thinks his letter miscarried. Is in prison at suit of Smithson and Rob. Pallagne, but does not think the latter is in the plot. Denies that the latter part of the letter shown him is his.*
York Castle, October 24, 1664.

124. II. *George Smith, prisoner at York, to Samuel Bonere, or any loyal magistrate in London. Was threatened by Sir Edw. Brett and others who examined him at York. Refused Smithson, Thackeray, and Hen. Thompson's request*

1664. VOL. CIII.

to be a trumpeter in the cause, if it were to be against the King. They said they should have 30,000 men in 20 days. Wrote word of it to Sir Solomon Swale, the next justice; the steward promised to deliver the letter to his master, but he denies receiving it. Wrote word of it to the Commissioners, but the paper was delivered to Swale, and another paper was drawn up by Swale's directions, to which Sir Edw. Brett got Smith's hand. Thos. Waddill, minister of Burton-Leonard, and Hen. Thompson, near Ripon, correspond with Dr. Richinson, late Dean at Ripon; it is said 20,000 English will invade the country with help from their own traitors. Begs that the truth may be heard. Swale has been bribed to conceal three notorious traitors. He detained the information against Smithson and Thackeray given in by Mr. Stevenson, under gaoler of the castle. [*One and a quarter pages.*]

Oct. 25. 125. Hen. Rumbold to Sec. Bennet. Hearing of the death of Col. Dan. O'Neale, who had a patent for gunpowder for 21 years, begs that he and his brother William may succeed in the management of it, as the profits will only be considerable if well managed. Thinks Sir Rich. Ford will want the patent for himself and Mr. Coventry. Wishes the place of Col. Frowde in the post office, or a Commissioner's place in the prize office.

Oct. 25. Post warrant for Mons. De Choqueaux to go to Portsmouth with three horses. [*Ent. Book* 16, p. 232.]

Oct. 25. Memorandum of a warrant signed for payment of 30,117*l.* 15*s.* 3*d.*, for the wares delivered by the tradesmen for the King's great wardrobe for one year, ending Michaelmas, 1662. [*Ent. Book* 10, *p.* 237.]

[Oct.] 126. The King to the Lord Mayor of London. The security of the trade of the kingdoms rendering some extraordinary provisions in the navy necessary for security, requests a loan of 100,000*l.* from the City for one year and a half, at 5 per cent., on security of an unassigned portion of the revenue, to be explained by Lord Treas. Southampton. Will not repeat this proposal unless the public concern of the nation, and more especially of the City, require it. [*Draft by Sec. Bennet, two pages.*]

Oct. 25. 127. Order in the Common Council of London, on signification of the King's pleasure to be accommodated with a loan of 100,000*l.*, that the said sum be advanced, the court of aldermen and commoners taking care of its advance; and that the lord mayor and aldermen present dutiful thanks to His Majesty for his preventing the new bridge being built over the Thames, between Lambeth and Westminster, which would have much injured the City. [*One and a quarter pages.*]

[Oct.] 128. Speech of the Earl of Manchester to the Common Council of London. The King thanks them for their cheerful loan of 100,000*l.*,

VOL. CIII.

1664.

which will much tend to disappoint bragging attempts and malicious designs. His Majesty will never forget their demonstrations of loyalty and affection, and will not be wanting in his care and kindness to the happiness and advantage of the City.

[Oct. 25.] 129. Order for a warrant to the Exchequer, that all the moneys received by the collectors of hearth money be paid in to Sir Thos. Player, chamberlain of London, until the 100,000*l.*, lent by the City to the King be repaid, with interest thereon at 6 per cent. [*Seven sheets.*]

Oct. 25. 130. Report of Sam. Pepys and [George] Duke,—on a reference from the sub-committee of the Royal fishing, upon the collection ordered to be made for the fishery, throughout England and Ireland,—that it has been made only in 32 counties; that the sum received is 1,076*l.*, but more has been gathered in; and suggesting modes of increasing the collection and securing its better management. [*Copy, three and a half pages.*]

Oct. 25. 131. Estimate by the Navy Commissioners of the expense of providing sea victuals for 20,000 men, for one year; total, 213,333*l.* 6*s.* 8*d.*

Oct. 25. Gainsborough. 132. Willm. Harbord to Williamson. Has put in a caveat on behalf of Sir Wm. Hickman, to a petition of the corporation of Newark, and begs a hearing from the King, before any warrant is granted, as promised by His Majesty to Lord Mansfield.

Oct. 26. Pendennis Castle. 133. George Collins to Williamson. A Scots vessel, arrived from Camphire in Zealand, reports that at Helvoetsluys, 15 men of war are ready to set forth for Guinea, and Van Tromp and Opdam, with 25 sail more, will conduct them through the channel, but that they are somewhat fearful. There are also at Pendennis six or seven vessels of the great French fleet, which came from Rouen, and are bound for Rochelle.

Oct. 26. Montacute. 134. E. Phelipps, junior, to Hen. Muddiman. Has been at Dorchester, where the Duke of Richmond is recreating himself with hunting, and has reviewed all the militia at Blandford, who behave so nobly and civilly as to beget terror in the disaffected, and encourage the loyal.

Oct. 26. Yarmouth. 135. Rich. Bower to Henry Muddiman. Letters from Rotterdam report that an engagement must be expected the first easterly wind; 13 or 14 English vessels have been lost, coming from Bourdeaux with wines; 635 died of the plague at Amsterdam last week. The press goes on hotly along the coast; throngs are mustering up and down the streets, frolicking away their press money, and saying, when their friends try to dissuade them from going, that they could not serve a better master.

Oct. 27. 136. Intelligence [sent to Sec. Bennet] of a meeting of Presbyterian ministers on the 19th, when they consulted whether, on account of the falling off of some of their leading men to the Fifth Monarchists, they should enter into a protestation of adherence to the Presbyterian

1664. VOL. CIII.

way; also of a meeting of Fifth Monarchists with those of Cockaine's church at Cockaine's house, Soper Lane, on the 26th. Houses frequented by Fifth Monarchy men. Wallis's landlord has returned to his house, and bail will be offered for Wallis, that he may publish the pamphlet he had in hand. Ecking the tailor, in Blackfriars, says that Ludlow commonly lies at Harry Cromwell's wife's brother's house, a gentleman of great estate in Cambridgeshire; and that Ludlow was lately in London. [*One and a half pages.*]

Oct. 27. / Nov. 7. Chelsea. Ambassador Van Goch to Lord ——. Prince Rupert's fleet lies wind-bound at Portsmouth; there was discontent about decayed provisions, and about going to Guinea, but the provisions being altered, and some of the refractory punished, all is quiet. The press of men for the ships is beyond all custom; they press the very apprentices and handicraftsmen, and have begun with the shoemakers. [*Holland Corresp., Oct. 27, 1664.*]

Oct. 27. 137. Jeffery Flatson to Edw. Progers. Thanks for favours. A breach being likely between England and Holland, does not wish to live in a nation at hostility with the land of his nativity; but would be glad to come over to England if he may do so securely, demeaning himself peaceably, and may there obtain leave to go to some foreign plantation. Wants his encouragement, and a secretary's pass.

Oct. 27. 138. Offer made to Sec. Bennet, to show how 500*l.* a year, for 20 years successively, may be obtained and disposed of by himself, if he can obtain the King's grant, reserving only 100*l.* a year to Jane, widow of Capt. Sam. Brooke, slain with the Earl of Tiveot at Tangiers, whom His Majesty promised to help. She is the only woman, except the Countess of Tiveot and Madam Knightley, who lost an officer husband on that fatal day; their means were consumed in removing from Dunkirk to Tangiers, and finding housing, &c. there; her case would be without danger of precedent for others to molest the King.

Oct. 27. Navy Office. 139. Warrant from the Navy Commissioners to the Storekeeper and Clerk of the Cheque at Deptford, to make allowance to Robt. Waith for 29 ells of cloth left as a pattern for goods contracted for on Oct. 4. [*Adm. Paper.*]

Oct. 27. Deptford. 140. Thos. Harper to the Navy Comrs. The care of measuring and viewing oars is confided to Mr. Fletcher. The measuring business of the yard is too heavy for one hand to manage. [*Adm. Paper, damaged.*]

Oct. 27. The Downs. 141. Capt. Geo. Batts to the Navy Comrs. The reports concerning Wm. Trotter, pressed out of the Trial at Yarmouth, are untrue. Stephen Pearse, the pilot of the Royal James, is very sick. No tidings of the stream cable lent to the commander of the Rupert. [*Adm. Paper.*]

Oct. 27. Portsmouth. 142. St. J. Steventon to Sam. Pepys. Sends the bond for the purser of the Sapphire. The commanders of the Mary and Fairfax have paid the conduct money of some of the men from Hull, last

1664. Vol. CIII.

they should be discouraged, and demand now to be repaid. Asks how to regulate the affair so as to give satisfaction to all parties. [*Adm. Paper.*] *Encloses,*

142. I. *Account of the numbers of men belonging to and of those mustered on board 12 ships now fitting in Portsmouth harbour.* *October* 27, 1664.

Oct. 27. East India Merchant, Spithead. 143. Capt. John Willgresse to Sam. Pepys. Complains of the conduct of Mr. Overton, his surgeon, in absenting himself on pretence of being ill received on board; having dismissed the former surgeon, they are in great trouble for want of one. [*Adm. Paper.*]

Oct. 28. Woolwich. 144. Chris. Pett to the Navy Comrs. Necessity of speedily repairing the wharf of the double dock, which was taken down for working up the new ship, and clearing it of launching gear, after which some shipwrights can be discharged. Repairs of ships. Ballast wanted. [*Adm. Paper.*]

Oct. 28. Warrant for presentation of John Selleck, D.D., to the Rectory of Clifton-Campville, co. Stafford. Minute. [*Ent. Book* 19, *p.* 25.]

Oct. 28. The King to the Vice Chancellor of Cambridge. Recommends John Mayer to the degree of B.C.L., which his constant adherence to King and church debarred him from taking in the late times. [*Ent. Book* 19, *p.* 25.]

Oct. 28. Licence for John, Henry, and Charles Lawson, with Fras. Lawson their governor, to travel for three years. Minute. [*Ent. Book* 16, *p.* 255.]

Oct. 28. Whitehall. Warrant for a grant to Charles Pickerne [Pitcairn] of the office of Falconer in ordinary, in place of Rob. Ketile, deceased; fee, 2s. a day. [*Ent. Books* 16, *p.* 257; *and* 21, *p.* 27.]

Oct. 28. Grant to John Baxter of the office of Falconer in ordinary; fee, 1s. a day. Minute. [*Ent. Book* 16, *p.* 257.]

Oct. 28. Whitehall. Order for a warrant to deliver 30 tuns of French wine, custom free, to the Conte de Cominges the French ambassador. [*Ent. Book* 16, *p.* 258, *bis.*]

Oct. 28. Warrant for creating John Browne, of Casome [Caversham], co. Oxford, a Baronet. Minute. [*Ent. Book* 16, *p.* 258.]

Oct. 28. Warrant from Sec. Bennet to the Farmers and Officers of Customs at Yarmouth, to permit several quantities of cordage, arrived from Holland, to be unladen, notwithstanding the restraint of trade with Holland. [*Ent. Book* 16, *p.* 259.]

Oct. 28. Whitehall. 145. Order in Council for printing and distributing the King's declaration for encouragement of seamen, and marines. [*Printed.*] *Annexing,*

145. I. *Declaration of the King's satisfaction at the readiness with which seamen come forward in defence of their country and trade, and ordering that seamen, whether serving on the King's ships or on merchantmen, shall receive* 10s.

1664. VOL. CIII.

per ton on all prizes taken by them, 6l. 13s. 4d. for each piece of ordnance, and 10l. a gun for every man-of-war sunk or destroyed; also the pillage of all merchandise upon or above the gun deck. Care is to be taken for the sick and wounded and widows, and medals to be given for eminent service. [*Printed, four pages.*]

Oct. 28. 146. Broadside of the above order and declaration. [*Printed.*]

Oct. 29. Chester Castle. 147. Sir Geoffrey Shakerley to Williamson. Thanks for intelligence. Wm. Rock, a Scotch petty chapman, is committed to the castle for seditious words; he said that had he the power, he would have a gallows at every league's end to hang the English; that he had been once into the kingdom with a great army, and hoped within five years to come with a greater; that he would seat himself in the middle of the kingdom, and fight the Earls of Northumberland, &c.

Oct. 29. Isle of Wight. 148. Col. Walter Slingsby to [Williamson]. Will not fail to transmit intelligence. A Dutch 24-gun ship, off Hurst Castle, after being shot at thrice by the Lily frigate, to compel her to put out her colours and show what countryman she was, did so; the frigate followed her to demand money for the three shots; the captain refused, saying there were 30 men-of-war ready in Holland who would satisfy that; his long boat was seized for the money. Fined some of a conventicle of Quakers, who met against the Act, but they did the same the next Sunday, and several strangers from the main land came to seduce and pervert them. The justices will proceed against the inhabitants of the island; as for the strangers, my lord [Colepeper] will give a very good account of them, having orders to press men for Guinea or the sea service. Col. Norton, late governor of Portsmouth, said in discourse, that he should live to see the kingdom a commonwealth again. [*Two pages.*]

Oct. 29. 149. Wm. Earl of Devonshire to Sec. Bennet. Was at Derby on the 12th, with the deputy lieutenants and justices of peace, and examined those who had been apprehended, and others whom they suspected, for four days; found little more than is known already, save that Calton confessed an intended rising of Presbyterians in Staffordshire; those witnessed against are committed to gaol; those only suspected released on bail. Wonders Calton said so little of that county [Derbyshire], where he was an agitator. The persons concerned are very inconsiderable. Has been intent on the service, and made as full discoveries as possible. [*Two and a half pages.*] *Annexing,*

149. I. *List of six persons committed to gaol, and of four who are bailed.*

Oct. 29. Warrant for a licence to John Earl of Bridgewater to enclose 100 acres more of his land, in addition to 240 acres for which he had a grant in 1661, for enlarging his park about Ashridge, cos. Bucks, and Hertford, and making another; also a confirmation of the licence granted by King James to his grandfather, Lord Chan-

VOL. CIII.

1664.

cellor Ellesmere, to enclose 400 acres of land at Ashridge for a park. [*Ent. Book* 16, *pp.* 259, 260.]

[Oct. 29.] 150. Draft of the preceding.

Oct. 29. Commission for Sir W. Blakeston to be Captain of Lord Hawley's troop. Minute. [*Ent. Book* 20, *p.* 29.]

Oct. 29. Portsmouth. 151. Capt. Thos. Teddeman to Sam. Pepys. Notifies his appointment as commander of the Swiftsure, with leave from the Duke of York to remove 100 men out of the Revenge. Requests tickets for them. Wishes to choose his own master for the Swiftsure. Recommends Geo. Woolfrey to be raised from boatswain to master of the Revenge. [*Adm. Paper.*]

Oct. 30. The Henrietta, Spithead. 152. Captain Walter Wood to the Navy Comrs. Writes at request of Prince Rupert, for an order for victualling 50 supernumeraries on board the Henrietta. Mr. Stanley has died of the small-pox, and his four men leave the ship. [*Adm. Paper.*]

Oct. 30. 153. Prince Rupert to [Sec. Bennet]. Lord Craven will state his brother the Elector [Palatine's] desires. Leaves all to the King. The ships will soon be in better condition to meet an enemy, the merchants' goods being put in good order, and Lord Sandwich's arrival will hasten forth those that are in port. Their late parson plays the devil wherever he goes, raising scandalous reports of them all, and of himself in particular. Hopes the Archbishop of Canterbury will reprove him. [*Two pages.*]

Oct. 30. 154. Inventories of the rigging and other appurtenances of the ships St. Peter, St. John Baptist, Wood Cleaver, Arms of Boswell and Son. Endorsed "An account of all the prizes brought into Dover." [*Adm. Paper.*]

Oct. 30. Pass for Sir John Gage and servants, and five horses, to go beyond seas. Minute. [*Ent. Book* 16, *p.* 264.]

Oct. 30. Cowdry. 155. J. Hatcher to Williamson. Is delighted that he will join him in the business, and thinks they shall have a very good pennyworth. Will view the lands and give him a particular account. Enquires after his health.

[Oct. 30.] 156. Chas. Gifford to Williamson. Importunes his help about the business of Sanford House, which would supply his great necessities; would use it for the general good in taking in land from the sea, whereas Mr. Weld, who pleads a sum promised him by the town of Weymouth, needs no money, and intends it for his private use.

Oct. 31. Isle of Wight. 157. Col. Walter Slingsby to [Williamson]. The Earl of Sandwich came on board the London yesterday, and his flag was put up; he will dine in Prince Rupert's ship to-day. The master of a vessel from Bourdeaux says he left 300 Holland wine ships, with many English and Scotch aboard them; also 23 English on a French frigate, whom he asked if they had noticed the King's proclamation; they replied that they took service there when they could have none in England, but when the voyage was done they would consider of it.

VOL. CIII.

1664.

Oct. 31. 158. Sir Philip Musgrave to Williamson. Will come up at Parliament, but the terrible mountain Stainmore is covered with deep snow, which may stop his coach; dares not venture on horseback.

Oct. 31. Spithead. 159. Earl of Sandwich to Sec. Bennet. Sees little ground for accommodation in De Witt's letter, as they positively demand restoration in Africa and America, which will mean vast sums for reparation of damages; thinks the King's honour is engaged not to accommodate. Mr. Stanley was dead before His Majesty's letter could be delivered to the governor. The preparations are forward, considering the weather; men are still wanted.

Oct. [31 ?] 160. Request by Eliz. Poyer to Mr. Williamson and Mr. Godolphin, to remind Mr. Secretary of her concern, and if it be reported that there is nothing against the desired discharge of some recognizances, of which the King gives her the benefit in payment of her demands, then the form of a warrant for discharge of the parties concerned is needed, His Majesty having consented that the moneys be paid in 10 years, by 300*l.* a year.

Oct. 31. Commission to John Lord Berkeley, Sir John Duncombe, and Thos. Chicheley, authorizing them to execute the office of Master of the Ordnance, void by death of Sir Wm. Compton. [*Domestic Corresp., June* 19, 1660.]

Oct. 31. Dover. 161. Thos. Wale to the Navy Comrs. Repairs of the Paradox; value of new scuppers and other stores expended on her, 13*l.* 7*s.* 5*d.* Would have had her scuppers mended, but for fear of dishonouring the Navy Royal. Recommends canvas scuppers instead of leather, as used 40 years ago, whereby "threepence out of sixpence may be saved." [*Adm. Paper.*]

Oct. 31. [Barber Surgeons' Hall.] 162. Thos. Hollier to Sam. Pepys. Notifies the appointment of Wm. Downs as surgeon to the Resolution. [*Adm. Paper.*]

Oct. 163. Roger Thompson to Sir John Mennes. Reminds him to give in his name to Mr. Coventry, as a person worthy to be entrusted with the command of a ship. [*Adm. Paper.*]

Oct. 164. Capt. Edw. Spragg to Sam. Pepys. Sends tickets for the men taken into the Royal James. Five Barbadoes' vessels have arrived in the Downs. [*Adm. Paper.*]

Oct. 165. List of 100 shipwrights and 20 calkers pressed for service at Chatham, by a warrant from the Duke of York. [*Adm. Paper, two pages.*]

Oct. ? 166. Petition of James Harrison and Chidiock Paulet to the King, for payment of three and a half years' salary as keepers of the privy lodgings and galleries at Whitehall, ever since the Restoration, during which time they have not received a penny.

Oct. Whitehall. 167. Warrant to Lord Chamberlain Manchester to admit Jas. Hamilton, as groom of the bedchamber, in place of Dan. O'Neale, deceased.

VOL. CIII.

1664.
Oct. 7 168. Warrant to seize John Wilcox and his wife, of Leadenhall Street, and Eliz. Ward, and Sarah Keat, her daughter, of Billingsgate. Minute.

Oct. Grant to Sir Theophilus Biddulph of Westcombe, co. Kent, of the dignity of a Baronet, with the usual discharge. [*Docquet.*]

Oct. Memoranda [by Williamson from the signet books] of warrants, grants, &c., passed during the month, the uncalendared portions of which are as follow:—

Licence to [Thos.] Togood to use his engine for draining water out of pits and mines.

Grant of 500*l.* to Mr. Hampden, who went to Russia in 1661, and to the Sound in 1662, in order to receive the Russian Ambassador.

Grant to Mr. Godolphin of the reversion of one of the seven auditorships in the Exchequer.

Note that all debts for plate, chains, &c., are paid to the goldsmith, on certificate from the master of the Jewel House, and that the particulars are registered in the books of the Jewel House.

Note that the Trinity House, Newcastle-on-Tyne, being a Corporation like that of Deptford, has 2*d.* on every ship for the maintenance of lighthouses, 2*d.* for the buoys, and an addition of 6*d.* and 4*d.* to the former duty of pilotage by strangers.

Grant to Sir George Carteret, during the lives of Lord Cornbury and Laurence and Edw. Hyde, and for 31 years after, of the Keepership of two walks and of the lodge in Cranborne chace, and of the office of Bailiff of Clewer.

Grant to Col. Russell and others of the arrears of the grant to the Countess of Peterborough, reserving 800*l.* to the King. [*Domestic Corresp., Aug. 1664, No. 97.*]

Oct. 169. Lease from Sam. Selwood, John Sanders, and Rob. Cheval, all of London, trustees for Eliz., wife of Fras. Deacon, clothmaker, to Jos. Williamson, of the house now occupied by him, in Westharding Street, *alias* New Street, near Fetter Lane, containing a cellar, now made a kitchen, a shop, two chambers, and a garret, which premises are held by Eliz. Deacon from the Goldsmiths' Company; on his payment of 10*l.* fine, and 14*l.* yearly rent. [*Ten Sheets.*]

VOL. CIV. NOVEMBER 1–16, 1664.

Nov. 1. 1. W. Coventry to Williamson. Thinks the man coming from Amsterdam wants discharge, not from the press, but from the quarantine, as Capt. Turner, in the Francis, is employed for the quarantine.

1664. Vol. CIV.

Nov. 1. Portsmouth. 2. John Tippetts to the Navy Commrs. Requests ship stores according to a list under-mentioned. [*Adm. Paper.*]

Nov. 1. 3. Capt. Robt. Turner to Mr. Coventry. The ships in quarantine have all gone, their time having expired. Requests a new boat for the Francis. [*Adm. Paper.*]

Nov. 1. Harwich. 4. John Browne, storekeeper, to the Navy Commrs. Arrival of the Love hoy with timber from Sherwood, and of Sir Wm. Warren's ship, Kingfisher, laden with masts. Wants two men under him, as formerly allowed, to assist in overlooking and dispensing the stores, and looking after the iron work. [*Adm. Paper.*]

Nov. 1. The Harp, Dublin. 5. Capt. Jas. Sharland to the Navy Commrs. Ship's stores wanted. Repairs done to the Harp. [*Adm. Paper.*]

Nov. 1. 6. Capt. Wm. Badiley to the Navy Commrs. Objects to fitting the mainmast of the Dunkirk into the Rosebush, to carry it down to Harwich. Proposes towing it down in the Harwich hoy. [*Adm. Paper, damaged.*]

Nov. 1. 7. Simon Nicholls, deputy master, and Four Fellows of the Trinity House to [the Navy Commrs.]. Send a report of ships belonging to the port of London, which they consider fit for men-of-war, and able to carry 30 guns: viz., 45 now in the river, and 70 at sea. [*Adm. Paper, one and a half pages.*]

Nov. 2. [illegible]. 8. John Russell to the Navy Commrs. Arrival of the Golden Star from Sunderland, to take in a lading of timber. Requests orders as to where it is to be taken. [*Adm. Paper.*]

Nov. 2. Woolwich. 9. Certificate by Chris. Pett, Wm. Sheldon, and Ant. Deane, officers of the yard, recommending Francis Hosier as clerk of the cheque at Harwich, he having served under the clerk of the cheque at Deptford and Woolwich for seven years. [*Adm. Paper.*]

Nov. 2. 10. Thos. Cowley to Mr. Hayter. The man's name inserted in the muster book of the Francis, as captain's servant, is Andrew Smith. [*Adm. Paper.*]

Nov. 2. Downs. 11. Capt. Geo. Batts to the Navy Commrs. Has lent a long boat to the Dover, according to orders; she has been driven back by the weather, and is very badly manned. Wants another. [*Adm. Paper.*]

Nov. 2. Woolwich. 12. Chris. Pett to the Navy Commrs. Requests a warrant for the delivery of masts and yards for the Royal Katherine. Another forge is much wanted, there being but three fires to supply all occasions. [*Adm. Paper.*] *Encloses,*

12. i. *Account by Thomas Harper of masts delivered to Abraham Golston, for the Royal Katherine.* November 1, 1664.

12. ii. *Estimate for rebuilding a small shop for smith's work; carpenter's work, 10l. 16s. 4d., brickwork, 3l. 0s.*

VOL. CIV.

1664.
Nov. 2. 13. *Joshua Greathead to Sir Roger Langley.* The three informers, Joshua Westerman, Wm. Dickinson, and John Eastwood, have been in most of the country betwixt and London, and find great discontent, and hopes of deliverance by the Dutch war, but no plot on foot; wishes protection for the three men, who are poor, and live by their hard labour.

Nov. 2. Crutched Friars, London. 14. John Buckworth to Williamson. Is anxious for his directions what to do with a Turkey carpet, which has been sent for him by the Earl of Winchelsea.

Nov. 2. Isle of Wight. 15. Col. Walter Slingsby to [Williamson]. Understands he is not to correspond with him and the print both, so will write to him alone. The wind being north, people are big with expectation. Men are pressing in every corner to be sent on board.

Nov. 2/12 Padua. 16. Sir John Finch to Lord [Conway]. Remains at Padua rather than at Paris, for convenience of study. Knows not whether his lordship is in Ireland. Assurances of affection. Dr. Baines sends his service. Has sent him a chest of glasses.

Nov. 3. Whitehall. 17. Proclamation ordering all cashiered soldiers of the late usurped powers, who have not a special licence from the Council, to depart from London and Westminster before 20th November, and not to return before 20th May.

Nov. 3. Copy of the above. Printed. [*Proc. Coll., pp.* 171–2.]

[Nov. 3.] 18. Draft of the above. [*One and a half pages.*]

Nov. 3. Commissions for —— Stephens to be Lieutenant, and —— Cowart, Ensign, to Capt. Sheldon's company in Guernsey. Minutes. [*Ent. Book* 20, *p.* 32.]

Nov. 3. Whitehall. Reference to Lord Treas. Southampton on the petition of Sir Thos. Prestwich, Bart., Sir Hen. Bennet, and Dr. Jas. Smith, for a lease for 41 years, on the ancient rent, of several houses, lands, &c., in Middlesex, on a piece of ground called King's Bridleway, which is concealed from the Crown by ill-affected persons, but which they offer to make good at their own cost. [*Ent. Book* 18, *p.* 90.]

Nov. 3. Order for a warrant to Sir John Lawson to distribute 3,500*l.*, value of prize goods from the Golden Fountain, taken by the fleet under his command in the Mediterranean, to such officers and commanders as Lord Admiral the Duke of York shall appoint, in reward for eminent services at sea. [*Ent. Book* 10, *p.* 201.]

Nov. 3. Warrant for Mr. Sheldon to have access to Major Breman. Minute. [*Ent. Book* 16, *p.* 261.]

Nov. 3. The Kent. 19. Capt. Thos. Ewens to the Navy Comrs. Has arrived in Lee Road. Receipt of stores. Men wanted. [*Adm. Paper.*]

VOL. CIV.

1664.

Nov. 3. Chatham Dock. 20. Phin. Pett, master shipwright, to the Navy Comrs. Stores wanted. Asks whether, in the haste of works there, the men are to leave work between 10 and 11 o'clock on Gunpowder Treason Day, according to ancient custom. [*Adm. Paper.*]

Nov. 4. The Plymouth. Bay of Algiers. 21. Capt. Thos. Allin to the Navy Comrs. Account of the capture of five Turkish men-of-war and several store ships. Has been five days at anchor, arguing with the Douane about the exchange of slaves and treaty of peace. The Turks refuse to make any satisfaction for damage sustained by the King or merchants, or for the barbarous usage and death of the consul. After much debate, the Grand Seignior has yielded to the minor articles of the treaty, but nothing can be done in exchange of prisoners, as they are all sold to private men, and cannot be taken from them. Hopes it will please the King to keep this peace, as it is promised by the faith of the Great Turk that it shall be kept by them. Total defeat of the French by the Moors and Turks at Gigery; 400 prisoners taken and 35 brass guns. Capt. Parker of the Nonsuch has been chosen consul. [*Adm. Paper, three pages.*]

Nov. 4. 22. Jonas Shish to the Navy Comrs. Report of the Concord, intended to be hired. [*Adm. Paper.*]

Nov. 4. Harwich. 23. Anthony Deane to the Navy Comrs. Arrival of the Elizabeth. Small stores wanted for her. [*Adm. Paper.*]

Nov. 4. Warrant empowering the Commissioners for the Mastership of Ordnance to take up powder, saltpetre, and all mills and materials for making gunpowder, notwithstanding any previous contract. [*Ent. Book* 16, *p.* 262.]

Nov. 4. Order for a warrant to pay to James Hamilton, groom of the bedchamber, a pension of 500*l.* a year. [*Ent. Book* 10, *p.* 263.]

[Nov. 4.] 24. Draft of the above.

Nov. 4. Warrant for a pardon to John Strother, of Kingshaw, co. Durham, convicted of manslaughter for the death of Ralph Eden, of West Auckland. [*Ent. Book* 16, *p.* 263.]

Nov. 4. Pass for a horse to France for Lord Aubigny. Minute. [*Ent. Book* 16, *p.* 264.]

Nov. 4. Pass for Mons. le Conte de Aldrovandy and Mons. Zacoitti, their servants and horses, to any port beyond seas. Minute. [*Ent. Book* 16, *p.* 264.]

[Nov. 4.] 25. List of three names proposed from each county in England to be pricked for sheriffs, with a cross to the names of the sheriffs actually pricked. [*Three pages.*]

Nov. 5. Order on the petition of Dame Elizabeth, widow of Sir Job Harby, recalling the order of 5th Sept., on petition of Susan Harby, that the

Vol. CIV.

1664.

farmers of customs detain in their hands a part of the dividend due to Sir Job Harby, and ordering the whole to be paid to Elis. Harby. [*Ent. Book* 18, *p.* 97.]

Nov. 5? 26. Petition of John Barker to the Council, for leave to stay in town, although he may be included in the late proclamation, of which he was ignorant when he came, and which forbids all who bore arms under the late powers to continue there after the 20th instant. Is subpœnaed on a cause in the Exchequer, and has several causes in the Arches and other courts, the neglect of which threatens his utter ruin.

Nov. 5. Order for a warrant to advance to Sir George Carteret 243,333*l.* 6*s.* 8*d.*, for sea victuals for a year for 20,000 men. [*Ent. Book* 16, *p.* 265.]

[Nov. 5.] 27. Draft of the above.

Nov. 5. Whitehall. Order for a warrant to pay to Stephen Fox, paymaster of the forces, 1,306*l.* 0*s.* 2*d.*, to be by him issued according to directions from George Duke of Albermarle, for raising a regiment of 1,200 foot, whereof Sir William Killigrew is colonel, being the advance of a week's pay. [*Ent. Book* 16, *p.* 266.]

Nov. 5? 28. Order for a warrant to pay to Sir Wm. Killigrew 1,200*l.*, for raising a foot regiment of 1,200 men for sea service, and 63*l.* in advance for one week's pay to the officers. [*Draft.*]

Nov. 5. 29. Draft of the above.

Nov. 5. Whitehall. Commission to Sir Wm. Killigrew to be Colonel to the Admiral's regiment of foot now to be raised, consisting of six companies of 200 men each; with minute of a like commission for him to be Captain. [*Ent. Book* 20, *p.* 32.]

Nov. 5. Minutes of commissions in the Lord Admiral's regiment as follow:—

Sir Chichester Wray, lieutenant-colonel and captain.
Sir Chas. Littleton, major and captain.
Griffin, Legge, and Dorrell, captains.
Bennet, lieutenant to the colonel.
Rich. Dennis [altered from Moyle], lieutenant to Capt Griffin.
—[*Ent. Book* 20, *p.* 32.]

[Nov. 5.] 30. Notes of several of the above officers, naming also Gardner as lieutenant to Capt. Littleton, and Stone as ensign to the colonel. [*Two pages.*]

Nov. 5. Commission to Col. Willm. Legg and others, to provide all manner of necessaries for the Ordnance Office, and press and take up gunners, artificers, carriages, &c. [*Docquet.*]

Nov. 5. Warrant to pay to Col. Willm. Legg, lieutenant of the Ordnance, 35,033*l.*, for furnishing the navy and stores with ordnance, &c. [*Docquet.*]

VOL. CIV.

1664.

Nov. 5. Warrant to the Great Wardrobe to allow of a yearly livery to John Walthew, groom of the privy chamber, in the place of James Pierce. [*Docquet.*]

Nov. 5. Warrant to order Sir John Lawson to pay from moneys in his hands 3,000*l.* to such sea officers as the Duke of York shall think fit. [*Docquet.*]

Nov. 5. 31. Estimate, signed by the Navy Commissioners, of the charge of all materials and workmanship for building a second-rate ship; total, 9,176*l.*

Nov. 5. 32. Similar estimate for a third-rate ship; total, 6,884*l.*

Nov. 5. Portsmouth. 33. Letter of news. A Dutch ship passing before the Isle of Wight had seven guns fired at it for refusing to strike to the Admiral, and then struck. The King's ships *Lizard* and *Greyhound* have arrived.

Nov. 5. 34. Warrant from the Navy Commissioners to Thos. Staines, plater of Chatham yard, to supply Russia glass, solo, and white plates, according to particulars given. [*Adm. Paper.*]

Nov. 5. Lydney. 35. Dan. Furzer to John Jones, Bristol. The trouble of bringing the timber down to Bristol is saved, by some country gentlemen having bought it for 160*l.* Squire Wintour, the owner of the land, has forbidden the removal of the poles, and claims the house as his, because fastened to the free hold. Begs Jones to come up, that they may both give an account to the Commissioners of his unreasonable demands. [*Adm. Paper.*]

Nov. 5. Deptford. 36. Capt. Wm. Badiley and two others to the Navy Comrs. Survey of the stores of the *John and Margaret*; she is ready to take in provisions.

Nov. 5. Woolwich. 37. J. Sheldon to the Navy Comrs. Forwardness of the *Rosebush* lading from Harwich. [*Adm. Paper, damaged.*]

Nov. 6. Woolwich. 38. Chris. Pett to the Navy Comrs. If the dimensions given in the estimate for second and third rate ships be thought too much, they may be lessened in breadth. [*Adm. Paper.*]

Nov. 6. Harwich. 39. Anthony Deane to the Navy Comrs. Intends building a long boat and pinnace for a fourth-rate ship. The place is convenient for such work. Arrival of timber from Sherwood Forest, which proves good and sound. [*Adm. Paper.*]

Nov. 6. Chatham. 40. Commissioner Peter Pett to Sam. Pepys. Progress of the *Charles.* Stores wanted. [*Adm. Paper.*]

Nov. 6. Durham Castle. 41. Sir Thos. Davidson, sheriff of Durham, to Sir Fras. Cobb, high sheriff of Yorkshire. Being ordered to send John Joplin, prisoner there, to him, wants time and place appointing without a moment's delay. Thinks Yarum the most direct way.

VOL. CIV.

1664.

Nov. 6. 42. Prince Rupert to the King. They of the Guinea fleet are complying, against their own opinion and interest, to serve His Majesty in his own way. Choqueux made a scarification upon him two days ago, and will not let him stir, though promising to have him quite well and whole in a few days; was unable, therefore, to go from ship to ship, but Vice-Admiral Mennes has done so, and none can go beyond his diligence; 100 carpenters and 300 of their best men are now at work on the ships in harbour. Asks orders in case they meet with a fleet of men-of-war, lest an opportunity be slipped. [*Holograph, two pages.*]

Nov. 7. Broadwert. 43. Sir Br. Broughton to Williamson. Acquainted Mr. Secretary with what he thought dangerous, till rebuked by Col. Vernon, who said his addresses were not believed, the Irish messenger whom he named still escaping. Sent to Vernon his scout's letter, saying that the messenger was returned to Ireland, with orders for the Irish to be ready with speed, as 1,300 at sea and 1,300 in England are ready, and orders are expected to come into cos. Warwick, Leicester, and Stafford, next week.

Nov. 7. Isle of Wight. 44. Col. W. Slingsby to [Williamson]. Supposes he has heard from the fleet at Spithead the stubborn Dutchman's carriage, when forced in by foul weather; 12 or 14 great ships have been seen to the south of the island, but without colours. Thinks them Dutch merchantmen, driven thither by weather.

Nov. 7. Portsmouth. 45. Capt. Thos. Teddeman to the Navy Comrs. Has received the 100 tickets for the men changed from the Revenge to the Swiftsure. Hears that Sir John Lawson desires to go in the Swiftsure till the Royal Katherine is ready. Desires that Geo. Woolfroy may be master with him in the Revenge. [*Adm. Paper.*]

Nov. 7/17. Chelsea. Ambassador Van Goch to the Secretary of the States General. The fleet of 60 vessels is almost ready to sail; the Duke of York is to be chief, with the Dukes of Buckingham, Richmond, Monmouth, and Norfolk, the Earls of Peterborough, Oxford, &c. Three companies of the King's Guard have embarked, and many of the militia, infantry, and cavalry, offer voluntarily for the fleet. A regiment of 1,200 men is to be raised, under Sir Wm. Killigrew; 30 more vessels are also preparing, to be reinforced from the garrisons. In order to fill their numbers, there is a general embargo on all shipping, except to the East Indies and the fisheries, and an order published for rewarding the maimed and wounded seamen from the prizes taken. [*Holl. Corresp., Nov. 7, 1664.*]

Nov. 8. Amsterdam. 46. Capt. R. Honeywood to [Sec. Bennet]. The danger of a war with Holland obliges him to seek favour; his engagements there, by marriage and by his command, do not lessen his natural loyalty. Hopes by remaining there to do His Majesty some considerable service, and begs his permission to remain and to keep his troop, which is the chief of his present subsistence; as it is horse, it cannot subject him to be employed in this unhappy occasion. [*Two pages.*]

1664. VOL. CIV.

Nov. 8. 47. List of the King's ships now at sea, or fitting forth, with the names of the commanders; viz.,—on the coast of Ireland 3; in the Straits, 13; attending on Tangiers, 1; convoy to the Newfoundland fishery, 2; at New England, 3; at Jamaica, 2; at Guinea, 3; river of Medway, 1; employed in transportation, 1; at the East Indies, 1; Prince Rupert's fleet, 12; in the Narrow Seas, 24. Also of ships fitting out to sea,—in the Hope, 8; at Chatham, 1; at Woolwich, 2; at Deptford, 5; at Portsmouth, 14; yachts, 7. [*Two pages.*]

Nov. 8. 48. Certificate from the owners of the John and Margaret of their choice of Wm. Lies as boatswain, and E. Gwinn as carpenter. [*Adm. Paper.*]

Nov. 8. The King to the Bishop of London and President and Chapter of St. Paul's. Requests their election of Doctor William Sancroft, dean of York, to that deanery, void by decease of Dr. Barwick. [*Ent. Book* 17, *p.* 66.]

Nov. 8. Whitehall. 49. Warrant to the Duke of York to pay to Sir William Berkeley 1,000*l.* from the fourpences defalcated out of seamen's wages for maintenance of ministers in ships, some of which was unemployed, ministers not being provided. [*Two pages.*]

Nov. 8. Entry of the above. [*Ent. Book* 17, *p.* 67.]

Nov. 8. 50. Like warrant for 2,000*l.* to Sir John Lawson, from the said fourpences. [*Two pages.*]

Nov. 8. Minute of the above. [*Ent. Book* 17, *p.* 67.]

Nov. ? 51. Petition of Charles Gifford to the King, for a grant of Sandford House, an old ruinous house demolished by order, near Weymouth; the stones would be of use to him to enclose a piece of land that lies on the sea-coast near.

Nov. 8. Warrant for a grant to Charles Gifford of the stone and materials of Sandford House near Weymouth, with leave to have workmen, carriages, &c., to take them away. [*Ent. Book* 16, *p.* 266.]

Nov. 8. Pass for Robert Burr to embark four horses for France. Minute. [*Ent. Book* 16, *p.* 267.]

[Nov. 8.] 52. Warrant for a grant of 2,000*l.* to Hen. Killigrew, as the King's free gift, for secret service. [*Draft.*]

Nov. 8. Minute of the above. [*Ent. Book* 16, *p.* 267.]

Nov. 8. Presentation of Peregrine Moore to the Vicarage of Gedney, co. Lincoln. [*Docquet.*]

Nov. 8. Grant to Wm. Levens, M.A., on surrender of Dr. Crowther, of the office of Greek Professor at Oxford; fee, 40*l.* a year, payable by the treasurer of Christ Church. [*Docquet.*]

VOL. CIV.

1664.
Nov. 8.
Southampton House.
53. Lord Treas. Southampton and Lord Ashley to the Justices of Peace for Lancashire. They are to assist by all means possible Mr. Kirkby, appointed collector for the hearth-money, in the opposition which he will probably meet with in the first settlement of it, the just payment of a public revenue being a public service; also to appoint times and places in each hundred when and where appeals on differences may be brought before them.

Nov. 8.
Whitehall.
54. Lord Mayor Sir Anthony Bateman to Sec. Bennet. The Lord Chancellor wants to consult with Bennet about what is to be done with Albertus Otto Faber, a German, taken three months ago at a meeting of Quakers in London, a man of crafty principles, and a great doctor of physic among them, his time of confinement being almost out. Begs him before going to Portsmouth to leave orders with Williamson. [*One and a half pages.*] *Encloses*,

54. I. *Albertus Otto Faber to Sir Ant. Bateman, lord mayor of London. In spite of his sufferings, is unconvinced of offence against King or law. Pleads that the law against conventicles could not affect the meeting at which he was present, it not being held with closed doors, and not composed of seditious persons; also that being for subjects, it is not applicable to himself as an alien.* [*French, three pages.*] *London, August 24, 1664.*

Nov. 8.
Cockpit.
55. Duke of Albemarle to Sec. Bennet. Requests a commission for Lieut. Godfrey Dennis to be Lieutenant to Col. Griffith [Griffin's] company in Sir Willm. Killigrew's regiment, in the place of Mr. Moyle, who cannot go.

Nov 8?
56. Note for addition to the privy seal for a week's pay for the officers, &c., in Sir Wm. Killigrew's regiment, of 63*l.*, and 1,200*l.* for raising and shipping 1,200 men; of 2*l.* 6*s.* 8*d.* for a chaplain's week's pay; 2*l.* 5*s.* 0*d.* for a surgeon and his mate, and 1*l.* 8*s.* for a quartermaster; so that 1,269*l.* will now be required.

Nov. 9.
57. Sentence by Dr. Exton, [Judge of the Admiralty Court], in a cause between the Crown and Rich. Batson, who pronounced himself ready to abide the award of the court without appeal, if Sir Walter Walker on the King's part would do the same, which was done; when Batson was condemned to pay expenses, and a day fixed for the taxation of them, and also for hearing the cause, unless the parties agree in the meantime. [*Latin, one and a half pages.*]

Nov. 9.
Order for a warrant to pay to Sir George Carteret 9,170*l.*, being the charge for building a ship of the second-rate. [*Ent. Book* 16, p. 268.]

Nov. 9.
Minute of the above. [*Ent. Book* 16, p. 271.]

Nov. 9.
Warrant to pay 6,884*l.* to Sir George Carteret, for building a third-rate ship of war. [*Ent. Book* 16, p. 271.]

VOL. CIV.

1664.

Nov. 9. 58. Certificate by Capt. Wm. Badiley, and two others, of the civil deportment, loyalty and fidelity of Geo. Martin. [*Adm. Paper.*] *Annexing,*

58. I. *Certificate by Wm. Martin and three other gunners, that Geo. Martin, of Deptford, is qualified for a gunner in any fifth or sixth rate frigate.* *November* 8, 1664.

Nov. 9. Harwich. 59. Anthony Deane to the Navy Comrs. Can give no account of the quality of Mr. Wood's timber. The ship is unladen. [*Adm. Paper.*]

Nov. 9. Chatham. 60. Commissioner Peter Pett to Sam. Pepys. Mr. Wiles is willing to contract for a supply of scuppers. [*Adm. Paper.*]

Nov. 9. London. 61. Wm. Castell to Sam. Pepys. Offers to deliver a ship's lading of New England masts at Harwich, at the same value as those contracted for last year, adding 100*l.*, which the lading cost more this year than last. [*Adm. Paper.*]

Nov. 9. Woolwich. 62. Chris. Pett to the Navy Comrs. Repairs of ships. Ballast wanted. Proposes an extra allowance to men employed in placing bilge-ways for the launch of the Royal Katharine, on account of their working in the wet and spoiling their tools and clothes. [*Adm. Paper.*]

Nov. 9. The Kent, Lee Road. 63. Capt. Thos. Ewens to the Navy Comrs. Is ready to sail as soon as a pilot can be procured. Has received orders to follow Sir Wm. Penn, and to take in 150 men brought up from Scarborough, Whitby, and Yarmouth, and carry them to Portsmouth. [*Adm. Paper.*]

Nov. 10. The Resolution, Gosport. 64. John Robins to the Navy Comrs. Asks the charge of a frigate in the present expedition; has laid up his own vessel because in the last Dutch war he had a vessel sunk by two Dutch men-of-war: has been 18 years in such a charge in merchant ships. [*Adm. Paper.*]

Nov. 10. Portsmouth. 65. John Tippetts to the Navy Comrs. Particulars of timber in the New Forest, and carriage thereof. Mr. Cole's vessels, laden with plank, are stopped by an embargo. Progress of ships. The Duke of York came to the town last night. [*Adm. Paper.*]

Nov. 10. Deptford. 66. Capt. Wm. Badiley to the Navy Comrs. Recommends Rich. Gray as master of a frigate. Seamen wanted to rig the ships. [*Adm. Paper.*]

Nov. 10. Portsmouth. 67. St. J. Steventon to the Navy Comrs. Asks 150*l.* in addition to the 400*l.* sent, to defray the board wages, conduct money, &c., of the seamen from Prince Rupert and the Earl of Sandwich's fleet, employed in fitting out those ships which are behind: they are ordered 18*d.* a day, which for them all is 6*l.* 15*s.* List of ships already sailed and of those not yet completed. [*Adm. Paper.*]

VOL. CIV.

1664.

Nov. 10. Navy Office. 68. Navy Commrs. to the Officers of Deptford Yard. Request that Sir Wm. Warren's barge lading of knees, lately delivered into the stores, may be laid together to be reviewed. [*Adm. Paper.*]

Nov. 10. Temple. 69. Capt. John Strode to Williamson. Being ordered to Dover by the Duke of York, will send his clerk with a petition in which he begs assistance.

Nov. 10. Whitehall. 70. Commission to John Lord Hawley of Captaincy in the King's own troop, in the regiment of Horse Guards commanded by Aubrey Earl of Oxford.

Nov. Minute of the above, dated November 11. [*Ent. Book* 20, p. 33.]

Nov. 10. Portsmouth. 71. Andrew Newport to Williamson. Sir Phil. Honeywood wishes to remind him of the King's promise to make him Commissioner in the prize office, and will make Williamson an acknowledgment. Has had a wet journey thither with the Duke.

[Nov. 10.] 72. Albertus Otto Faber to the King. Is sorry if he has transgressed by showing that he was not liable according to the Act. Did not wish to offend against government, but thought the magistrates mistook the Act. Is informed that he must leave the kingdom in three days; could not promise to effect this, and therefore considering the winter season, and the difficulty of closing his establishment and settling with his creditors, begs to have the time prolonged till Easter. [*French, two pages.*]

Nov. 11. Whitehall. 73. The King to the Mayor and other Officers of Rye. Orders release of a bark detained in that port, by virtue of the present embargo, which was hired for transportation of horses belonging to Viscount Fitzharding, sent on the King's affairs to Paris. [*Draft.*]

Nov. 11. Haigh. 74. Sir Roger Bradshaigh to Sec. Bennet. Thanks for his correspondence, but gives him a writ of ease whilst Parliament sits. Is coming to London. The death of his noble partner for the county, Mr. Stanley, is much resented by his friends. Has laid a foundation for a worthy person to be chosen in his room.

Nov. 11. Plymouth. 75. Sir Jo. Skelton to Williamson. The convoy has not yet arrived. The Martayne galley from New England gives assurance that Capt. Nicholls has reduced the New Netherlanders. The Elias frigate was cast away on that coast, and 22 persons saved.

Nov. 11. Whitehall. Reference to Lord Treas. Southampton on the petition of the Mayor and Aldermen of Newark-on-Trent for renewal of their former charter, with additions and privileges, as annexed. [*Ent. Book* 18, *p.* 97.]

Nov. 11. 76. Lists of Members of Committees appointed by the Council Board, as follow:—

For affairs of Portugal and Sweden, Aug. 8, 1660.
For Denmark and the Hanse Towns, Sept. 7, 1660.
For the King's coronation, Sept. 20, 1660.

1664. Vol. CIV.

For Jamaica and Algiers, Dec. 5, 1660; and Jamaica alone, July 3, 1661.
For Navy affairs, Nov. 7, 1660.
For Spain, Nov. 14, 1660.
For Netherlands, Nov. 14, 1660.
For the affairs of the Prince of Orange, Feb. 1, 1661.
For magazines and buildings of the Tower of London, Feb. 20, 1661.
For affairs of Ireland, April 2, 1661.
For plantations, July 4, 1660.
For England, May 7, 1661.
For Mint, wool, and wool-fells, April 3, 1661.
For the Elector of Brandenburg, June 7, 1661.
For affairs of Tangiers, June 28, 1661.
For Jamaica, about instructions for government, July 3, 1661.
For Postmasters, July 17, 1661.
For the French Ambassador, Aug. 17, 1661.
For the Guinea trade, and receiving provisions from the Duke of Courland, Nov. 20, 1661.
For Bombay in the East Indies, Dec. 29, 1661.
For disposing of the 60,000*l.* for the poor cavaliers, April 4, 1662.
To treat with the Duke of Mecklenburg's agent, Aug. 8, 1662.
To consider the memorial presented by the agent of Lubec, Sept. 17, 1662.
To examine Sir Augustine Coronel, in answer to the Portuguese ambassador's memorial, Sept. 26, 1662.
Concerning Bedford level, Oct. 24, 1662.
Concerning the office of exchanger, Oct. 31, 1662.
To treat with the ambassadors from the Hanse Towns, Nov. 19, 1662.
For the Royal Adventurers' Company, Nov. 28, 1662.
For Lindsey level, Dec. 5, 1662.
About the Portugal duties, concerning the four Brazil ships, and the agents for the Brazil Company, Dec. 19, 1662.
To administer the Oaths of Allegiance and Supremacy, and of a Privy Councillor to Wm. Archbishop of Canterbury, April 3, 1663.
To inspect the accounts of the Russian Ambassador's entertainment, Aug. 7, 1663.
For the Merchant Adventurers, about the English manufacture and clothing trade, Aug. 14, 1663.
For export of strained cloths, Oct. 21, 1663.
For trade betwixt the English and Dutch East India merchants, Oct. 21, 1663.
To inspect the bag containing the ancient assays of English coin, Oct. 30, 1663.
For prevention of the infection of the pestilence, Nov. 6, 1663.
For the Act of Settlement of Ireland, Nov. 30, 1663.

VOL. CIV.

1664.

Concerning the Royal fishing, between the trading and non-trading fishmongers, March 25, 1664.
For the fishing in Newfoundland, Dec. 2, 1663.
For the Merchant Adventurers, Dec. 4, 1663.
Concerning export of powder and ordnance, Dec. 30, 1663.
Concerning the debt of the Count of Oeses, between Mr. Robinson and Dr. Calladon, Jan. 29, 1664.
Touching the incorporation of the Canary merchants, March 25, 1664.
To examine letters patent granted to the Trinity House concerning the Thames, May 6, 1664.
To hear Hans Kroger's business, May 11, 1664.
Concerning importation of rough or wrought glass plates, July 1, 1664.
For navigable rivers, June 22, 1664.
To examine a proposal about preventing the running away of persons entertained [for the plantations], upon pretence they were spirited, Aug. 10, 1664.
About Mr. Garill's new invention of casting gold and silver ingots, and the officers of the Mint and goldsmiths' and wire drawers' answers, Aug. 17, 1664.
To examine the accounts of the Lord Lieutenants about the 70,000*l.* for the militia, Nov. 11, 1664. [*Fourteen pages.*]

Nov. 11. 77. Sir Augustin Coronel to the King. No coldness on His Majesty's part can make him discontinue his zeal. Wants an order to communicate something important that has come to his knowledge. [*French.*]

Nov. 11. Portsmouth. 78. Duke of York to the King. Refers for details to his letter to Sec. Bennet. Will neglect nothing to advance His Majesty's service. They are taking out all the men from the Guinea ships to put into His Majesty's ships at Spithead, and are working to get out the rest of the ships in harbour. Has been on board the new ship, which is very fine, higher between decks, and the contrivance of her stairs convenienter than the Katherine. Mr. Tippetts will try to have her ready next spring [tide]. Has sent the Lily to Cowes to seize an Amsterdamer worth 10,000*l.* or 20,000*l.* [*Holograph, three pages.*]

Nov. 11. Portsmouth. 79. Duke of York to Sec. Bennet. Finds things forward except men and victuals. The ships will soon be ready, but will have to put to sea with a less proportion of victuals than was intended. Men cannot be supplied there, and unless a ship from the Thames can be sent with supernumerary seamen, either some ships must be left in harbour, or they will be too slenderly manned for good service. Those who being pressed, either do not appear, or run away, must be apprehended and punished, for it is grown so common that pressing men is of little effect except to expend treasure; 200 have left the service within a few days; will send a list of them; their punishment is so important, that if the assizes or sessions be not very near, a commission of Oyer and Terminer should be ordered for their trial. There have been for-

1664. Vol. CIV.

merly such abuses about prizes that great circumspection will be required in appointing persons in all the ports of England to receive them, yet it must be done speedily to prevent embezzlement, and to give dispatch to those ships that bring in prizes, which would otherwise weaken the King's fleet instead of the enemy's. Asks whether he is to issue commissions to private men-of-war, as has been the usual practice. Some fire ships should be provided at Dover, in case the Dutch should come into the Downs with a fleet. Some more of the fifth-rate frigates at Deptford should be set forth, to gather up men in the out-ports, and serve as scouts. [*Two pages.*]

Nov. 11. Minutes of commissions in the Lord Admiral's regiment, as follow :—

Collins, lieutenant to Capt. Dorrell.
Robt. Thompson, ensign to Capt. Dorrell.
—— ——, chaplain to the regiment.
Fras. Noblin, ensign to Sir Chichester Wray.
Phil. Bickerstaffe, ensign to Sir. Wm. Killigrew.
—— Ingram, ensign to Capt. Griffin.
Edw. Talbot, lieutenant to Sir Charles Littleton.
—— Hume, ensign to Capt. Legge.
—— Snelling, ensign to Sir Chas. Littleton.
—— Cole, lieutenant to Legge.
Simon Bonings, surgeon to the regiment.

—[*Ent. Book* 20, *p.* 33.]

Nov. 11. Whitehall. 80. Commission for —— Cole to be Lieutenant to the company of foot in the Admiral's regiment, to be raised under command of Sir Wm. Killigrew, whereof —— Legg is captain.

Nov. 11? 81. Bill of Thos. Holder for 247*l.* 3*s.* 7*d.*, disbursed by him for the King at St. Sebastian's, in Spain.

Nov. 11. Whitehall. Warrant for a grant to Thomas Holder of the prize ships St. Sebastian and Nightingale, with their cargoes, taken from the Dutch about 1650; with authority to recover the same. [*Ent. Book* 10, p. 267.]

Nov. 11. The King to Sir Wm. Humble, high sheriff of Surrey. Recommends John Wickham for the place of Keeper of the White Lion prison, Southwark, which will soon be void by removal of Jas. Hall, for want of care and faithfulness in a place of public trust. [*Ent. Book* 17, p. 68.]

Nov. 82. Draft of the above, dated Nov. 9.

Nov. 12. Whitehall. Warrant to the Duke of York to appoint William Viscount Brouncker one of the Commissioners of the Navy. [*Ent. Book* 14, p. 43.]

Nov. 12. Warrant for delivery of 30 tuns of French wine custom free, for the Coute de Cominges. [*Docquet.*]

VOL. CIV.

1664.
Nov. 12. Warrant to pay to Col. Legg 1,073*l.* 1*s.* 5*d.*, for provision for the garrison of Portsmouth. [*Docquet.*]

Nov. 12. Warrant to Anthony Lord Ashley and Sir John Denham to examine into the state of the funds collected for the Protestants of Piedmont, the King being informed that there is a sum in the hands of certain persons, not yet accounted for. [*Ent. Book* 16, *p.* 271.]

Nov. 12. Warrant to John Sompner to receive Albertus Otto Faber. Minute. [*Ent. Book* 10, *p.* 271.]

Nov. 12. Warrant to Mr. Gifford to deliver Faber to the said Sompner. Minute. [*Ent. Book* 10, *p.* 271.]

Nov. 12. Warrant to the said Sompner to search Faber's house for all papers and writings. Minute. [*Ent. Book* 10, *p.* 271.]

Nov. 12. Post warrant for Charles Dowey to Durham. Minute. [*Ent. Book* 16, *p.* 271.]

Nov. 12. Warrant for release from the present embargo of a vessel employed to convey horses to France for Viscount Fitzharding, who is going on the King's particular affairs to Paris. [*Ent. Book* 16, *p.* 272.]

Nov. 12. 83. Trinity House certificate of the fitness of Wm. Wisloke, of Limehouse, to take charge of any ship to the Westward, or to the Straits. [*Adm. Paper.*]

Nov. 12.
York Castle. 84. George Smith, prisoner in York Castle, to the Lord Chancellor. Begs attention to his former letter. Will not conceal treason, but no testimony against Sir Solomon Swale will pass before the Commissioners at York. Would die rather than sound a trumpet against the King; wishes him more faithful magistrates than Swale and Sir Thos. Gower, who hang some by the neck, some by the purse strings. Is in fear of his life for declaring the truth. With names of nine persons made known to Swale two days before the note was discovered.

Nov. 12.
Portsmouth. 85. Earl of Peterborough to Williamson. The Duke [of York] spent most of the day in visiting the ships, where his appearance was useful in forwarding preparations, and delighted the seamen. The south wind is welcome to the commanders, who expect more ships from the river to put them in readiness. Hears no more of Sir T. Blake's proposition.

Nov. 12.
Portsmouth. 86. T. Ross to Williamson. The south-west wind saves apprehensions of the Dutch coming out before we are ready to beat them back. Yesterday it was east, and brought Capts. Lambert, Jennings, and Spragg from the Downs. The ships, in spite of the officers' diligence, require 10 days' preparation. Mr. Godolphin's neglect has done harm in the wool business for his poor lord [the Duke of Monmouth]. Would give 50*l.* never to have meddled with it, there have been such delays, though the failure would be the

Vol. CIV.

1664.

undertakers' loss, and the success a public advantage. His Grace [the Duke of Monmouth] has lost most of their stock at play; there being no other diversion, the Guinea gold rolls freely. Cannot wish his little lord to be singular and sit by whilst others lose 5*l.* with cheerful satisfaction. His Grace intends to write to the King for money; begs a supply for him. [*Two pages.*]

Nov. 12. 87. H. Davies to ——. Requests him to prepare a deed of settlement, by fine or otherwise, of the royalty of Binton Manor, co. Warwick, enumerating the deeds relating thereto.

Nov. 13. Whitehall. 88. Grant to John Brown, who has set up works in Scotland for refining sugar, of licence to trade with four Scottish ships to the English plantations and colonies, notwithstanding the late Act of Navigation, by which all except English ships are forbidden to trade thither. [*Copy.*]

Nov. 13. Portsmouth. 89. Earl of Sandwich to the Lord Chamberlain (?). Most wardrobe services are performed by their warrants. Asks supplies to render compliance with their directions possible, prevent discontent, and save the King's purse. Asks mediation with the King for a full provision; 20,000*l.* will not carry on the wardrobe. If the tallies given by the Lord Treasurer be not paid, their credit will be blown up. *Encloses,*

89. i. *Estimate [by the Earl of Sandwich] that the yearly expense of the wardrobe is 33,512l. 5s. 9¾d., extras 8,778l. 14s. 7d., which will occur again; that the wardrobe assignments should be increased 600l. a year; that 10,000l. is due to tradesmen, who made their bills low on promise of ready money, and 13,000l. on unpaid tallies last year. He begs assignments on good and current branches of revenue.*

Nov. 13. The King to Lord Treas. Southampton, the Duke of Albemarle, and Sec. Bennet. Declared his intention, when Lord Wentworth's regiment was distributed into garrisons, that it should be kept entire with its field and staff officers; but the quarter-master, chaplain, and surgeon, petition because their pay has been stopped since 3d October, 1663. Requests its continuance, as they have merited well in the service. [*Ent. Book 20, p. 36.*]

Nov. 13. Portsmouth. 90. Earl of Peterborough to Williamson. Asks explanation of a letter received from Prince [Rupert ?]. Cannot be always interrupting the Earl of Sandwich about particulars decided on before the Prince, Lord Ashley, and the whole [African] committee. The change of wind has been very advantageous, giving time for ships to come in and congregate more men; would else have had to sail with 23 or 24 frigates, not proportionable to the merit of the Prince who commands.

Nov. 13. Portsmouth. 91. —— to Mr. Lamb. Two frigates have arrived. The fleet is expected hourly to weigh anchor, and stand for sea, as the Duke has ordered the empty casks ashore, and the decks to be cleared for a fight. The wind is at north-west.

VOL. CIV.

1664.

Nov. 13. 92. Wm. Coventry to Williamson. Hopes those in London will be as diligent to increase the fleet as the Dutch are to augment theirs. They are said to be commanding men on board the 18 ships preparing. If those in the Thames could join the others, they would not doubt to give a good account of Opdam. The victualler should not delay them. The seamen are much rejoiced by the King's declaration for their encouragement.

Nov. 13. 93. Wm. Coventry to [Sec. Bennet]. Hopes the wind will change, and bring the Charles and the other ships out of the river; will not then fear what Opdam can do, though the men are raw, and need a little time at sea. The Ruby and Happy Return have brought some supernumeraries, but 500 more are wanted; 200 are expected from Plymouth, but till some runaways are hanged, the ships cannot be kept well manned. Sends a list of some fit to be made examples of in the several counties where they were pressed, with the names of those who pressed them. The Dutch ship named before is brought in, and two others are stayed at Cowes by virtue of the embargo, the order in Council making no exception for foreigners. The King's pleasure should be known therein, as the end, which is to gather seamen, does not seem to require the stopping of foreigners. Prize officers must be sent speedily to [Portsmouth], Dover, and Deal. Those at Deal should have men in readiness to carry prizes up the river, that the men belonging to the fleet be not scattered. Persons should also be hastened to take care of the sick and wounded. The Duke intends to appoint Erwin captain of the ship hired to go to St. Helena; he is approved by the East India Company, which is important, trade being intermixed with convoy, and they find fault if a commander of the King's ships bring home any little matter privately bought. The Duke has divided the fleet into squadrons, assigning to each a vice and rear admiral; Sir John Lawson and Sir Wm. Berkeley to his own, Meanes and Sansum to Prince Rupert's, Sir George Aiscue [Ayscough] and Teddeman to the Earl of Sandwich. Hopes in a few days to be in much better order, if good men can be got. Will send a list of the squadrons. The Guernsey is damaged by running aground. Rear-Admiral Teddeman, with 4 or 5 ships, has gone to course in the Channel, and if he meet any refractory Dutchmen, will teach them their duty. The King's declaration for encouraging seamen has much revived the men, and added to their courage. [*Four pages.*]

Nov. 13. 94. Wm. Coventry to [Sec. Bennet]. The Kent has not arrived; fears she has no sailing orders; she has more than her number of men, so the fault must be in the captain or victualler. Asks where the Sorlings, Mermaid, and Drake are. Hears that Council has rejected the demand for 700 trees from Waltham Forest. Urges the convenience of that place, as affording good timber. Carriage thence is cheaper and quicker, and shipwrights can easily be got from London to mould the timber in the woods. [*One and a half pages.*]

Vol. CIV.

1664.

Nov. 13. Portsmouth. 95. Duke of York to [Sec. Bennet]. Regrets that, whilst Council has increased the number of ships to be built, it has diminished their force. The Dutch will always be superior in number of ships, many of their merchantmen being equal to the King's fourth-rates, therefore the King should have a few ships to carry greater weight than a greater number of theirs. Lists of the runaways are sent. Hopes their speedy punishment will be cared for. Supernumerary men and stores should be hastened. The stores there are much exhausted by supplying defects in Prince Rupert and the Earl of Sandwich's fleet. With marginal notes of reply that letters with the names of the runaways are sent to the vice-admirals, and to the mayor and justices of peace of Bristol, and that the supplies are in the river, going down.

Nov. 14. 96. Capt. Wm. Badiley to the Navy Comrs. The James ketch is well found, and is now taking in her provisions. [*Adm. Paper.*]

Nov. 14. Lydney. 97. Dan. Furzer to the Navy Comrs. Particulars to be considered in building a new fourth-rate ship. Two cannot be built together, as proposed, owing to the difficulty of procuring so many hands, and the want of suitable timber. Coppill is the best place for building, being nearer the forest and having a good dry beach, ballast at hand, and a creek to launch her in. In one year the ship may be fitted; estimates the cost at 3,100*l.* Requests that more men may be employed when the days lengthen. Account of the sale of offal timber and poles in the yard, bought by some country gentlemen at 160*l.* [*Adm. Paper, three pages.*]

Nov. 14. The Downs. 98. Capt. J. Poynts to Sam. Pepys. Has pressed 140 men into the Maryland, many of whom have run away. Requests the payment of 18*l.*, borrowed from Geo. Peterson to defray the expense of conveying, keeping, and maintaining pressed men. [*Adm. Paper.*]

Nov. 14. Ollerton. 99. Thos. Corbin to the Navy Comrs. Particulars of carriage of timber. Intends making proposals about the wood in Sherwood Forest. [*Adm. Paper, two pages.*]

Nov. 14. Edwinstowe, Sherwood. 100. John Russell to the Navy Comrs. Particulars of timber from Sherwood. Has sent one hoy's load to Harwich. [*Adm. Paper.*]

Nov. 14. Leghorn. 101. Thos. Clutterbuck to the Navy Comrs. Explains the unreasonable pretence of Mr. Gauden in holding him responsible for victualling Capt. Smith's squadron at so much a man, when food was at the dearest, and they came unexpectedly. Desires speedy orders for present dues and future supplies. There is a report from all quarters of a speedy rupture with the Dutch. Hopes "that "proud nation will soon be humbled" and the King's undertakings crowned with success. If Capt. Allin might have orders to play

VOL. CIV.

1664.

his game in their seas, while Ruyter is gone for Guinea, many stout merchant ships would be seized. [*Adm. Paper, two and a half pages.*]

Nov. 14. Leghorn. 102. Thos. Clutterbuck to Mr. Coventry. Requests his interest in procuring the reimbursement of what is due for the victualling of Capt. Smith's squadron. No port in the seas is more convenient than Leghorn for procuring supplies. Ruyter is going for Guinea with 12 ships, leaving only five or six men-of-war in the Mediterranean. Capt. Allin may get possession of them, and many considerable merchant ships also. [*Adm. Paper, one and a half pages.*]

Nov. 14. Chatham. 103. Commissioner Peter Pett to Sam. Pepys. The Triumph has sailed with 70 men from the Kent, and 50 soldiers that came from Hull. Progress of ships. [*Adm. Paper.*]

Nov. 14. Portsmouth. 104. Wm. Coventry to [Sec. Bennet.] Believes nothing short of hanging will secure the pressed men. Lord St. John's news can hardly be believed, but the report will do no harm, for if the Dutch begin so roughly, seamen will be unwilling to go on merchantmen, and so cannot live without going on men-of-war. Hears that Taylor was objected to by the Committee [for Maritime Affairs] as a [Navy] Commissioner; he was chosen without contradiction by Sir John Mennes, Sir John Lawson, and Sir Wm. Penn, and the warrants sent for him and others to the Attorney-General, as was usual in Lord Northumberland's time. Thinks the King will not easily consent to his rejection, as he is a man of great abilities and dispatch, and was formerly laid aside at Chatham, on the Duchess of Albemarle's earnest interposition for another. He is a fanatic, it is true, but all hands will be needed for the work cut out; there is less danger of them in harbour than at sea, and profit will convert most of them. The weather is bad; wonders the Scotchmen have not got to the Hope. The new ship is nearly ready, but has no guns; some spare ones should be sent in some man-of-war. [*Two pages.*]

Nov. 14. Whitehall. Warrant from Sir G. Carteret and Sec. Bennet to Jonathan Waltham, captain of the Sorlings, to sail to Yarmouth and take in the men impressed in the North and brought thither by Capt. Fortescue, with any whom he may be able to press on his way thither, and carry them to Portsmouth, to be distributed in the fleet. [*Ent. Book 10, p. 272.*]

Nov. 14. Warrant for two vessels, the Patience and Vale, bound for Portugal with goods for the immediate use of that King, to be released from the present embargo. [*Ent. Book 16, p. 272.*]

Nov. 14. Whitehall. Warrant for leases to Sir Paul Neal and Sir Herbert Lunsford, of certain lands in Suffolk, discovered by them to belong to the Crown, for which a commission of inquiry was awarded on their former petition, reserving yearly rents as usual. [*Ent. Book 14, pp 44–5.*]

VOL. CIV.

1664.

Nov. 14. Whitehall. Recommendation to the Lord High Chancellor on the petition of Dame Anne, widow of Sir Ralph Bash, for protection, ordering him to summon Sir Rich. Combes and three other persons concerned, and take orders for the just relief of the petitioner and her child. [*Ent. Book* 18, *p.* 98.]

Nov. 14. Order,—on the petition of the Duke of Monmouth for authority to appoint commissioners and agents for the prevention of exportation of wool and woolfells,—that when the King sees what Parliament will do in the bills depending before them, he will concur in anything tending to prevent the abuses named, and will gratify the petitioner as far as may be. [*Ent. Book* 18, *p.* 99.]

Nov. 14. Reference to Lord Treas. Southampton on the petition of Andrew Lawrence, surveyor of the King's gates and bridges, for a privy seal for 475*l.*, for repairs of such as are much decayed. [*Ent. Book* 18, *p.* 99.]

Nov. 14. Warrant to the Ordnance Commissioners to order 50 good firelocks, 10 pairs of bandoleers, 4 cwt. of bullets, and a barrel of powder, to be delivered to Gervase Price, keeper of the private armory at Whitehall, which has been disfurnished for other services. [*Ent. Book* 20, *p.* 34.]

Nov. 14. 105. J. Seymour to Williamson. Has hurt his hand; hears of a messenger sent to him from [Sec. Bennet]; asks if there be any service for him; hopes soon to wait on him.

Nov. 14. 106. Examination of —— Knight, before Sec. Bennet. Received a bill of exchange, directed to M. De Busty, and another for 50*l.*, both counterfeited, from Ashmole or Ashbourne, at Chester, who came over with him from Ireland, where he had been to seek employment under Garret Moore, brother of Lord Moore. Has not seen Granger for two years. Particulars of his and Ashbourne's proceedings on their journey from Ireland, &c. [*Two pages.*]

Nov. 14. 107. Resolution of the Commissioners of Lieutenancy of London to desire Sir Rich. Browne, major general, to move the King to raise a month's tax, at the rate of 70,000*l.* for 1664, to defray the charge of the militia; also to obtain a warrant for issue, for the same purpose, of the sums collected in 1662 and 1663.

Nov. 14. Round House, Love Lane. 108. Willm. Hall to Williamson. The list [of ships] come in is almost the same as the last. The Royal Charles and James and the rest of the fleet have not yet got to the Downs.

Nov. 14. London. 109. Sir Rich. Ford to Williamson. Sends Mr. Gifford, keeper of the Poultry Compter, for orders about Albertus Otto Faber, committed for being at a Quakers' meeting, who cannot by Act of Parliament be longer detained. Wants orders for his lodgings to be searched for papers, and he taken into custody to attend King and Council.

VOL. CIV.

1664.

Nov. 14. Isle of Wight. 110. Col. Walter Slingsby to Williamson. A fleet of nine ships was seen at a distance, hoped to be some of the ships from the Thames or Chatham, but more probably Dutch merchants, who would sink rather than come into harbour, where some are driven against their wills; a ship laden with Bourdeaux wines has been cast away on the island at Yarmouth; 25 brave men-of-war now ride at Spithead. Is on an empty employment, spending 5s. where he gets 1s.; wishes to be kept in mind for preferment. The island must have two companies.

Nov. 15. Hull. 111. Luke Whittington to James Hickes. According to the Lord Admiral's warrant for stay of all ships over sea, four bound for Rotterdam and Amsterdam are stayed; six are ready to sail to London with 80 impressed men, making up 300, the full number charged on the port. The garrison is in good condition, and the country quiet. Asks who is to be postmaster general. Note of ships in harbour.

Nov. 15. Warrant to [the Attorney or Solicitor General] to receive a surrender by the Trinity House of the grant made to them, 18 August, 1663, of the lastage and ballastage of vessels in the Thames, on which controversies have arisen, and to prepare a fresh grant to them, in fuller terms, of the ballastage in the Thames, and all creeks or shores adjoining, from London Bridge to the sea, with power to dig up gravel and store it in wharfs; with proviso of saving the rights of Sir Rob. Killigrew, and Edw. Progers, groom of the bedchamber, to whom a similar grant was made, and of payment of 1,000 marks yearly to Col. Wm. Carlos, for the remainder of a term of 31 years. [*Ent. Book* 16, *pp.* 273–4.]

[Nov. 15.] 112. Draft of the above. [*One and a quarter sheets.*]

Nov. 15. Licence for the St. Fortunato, bound for the Spanish Indies, to be freed from the embargo, at request of the Royal Company. Minute. [*Ent. Book* 10, *p.* 274.]

Nov. 15. Portsmouth. 113. John Tippetts to the Navy Comrs. Mr. Coles' vessel, laden with elm timber, was driven on shore and sunk. Has sent a hoy and long-boat to her assistance. Particulars of timber. Tender of deals. [*Adm. Paper.*]

Nov. 15. 114. Warrant from the Navy Comrs. to Mr. Harper [storekeeper at Deptford], to receive from Mr. Coles certain treenails contracted for by Commissioner Pett; to send up the three red flags and one white, lately delivered by Mr. Michell; and to send up to the Navy Office two of the ablest gunners now in ordinary. Minute. [*Adm. Paper.*] *Annexing,*

114. I. *Names of the said gunners; with note, Nov. 16, that an answer to this letter has been sent to Mr. Pepys.*

Nov 15. 114. Wm. Coventry to [Sec. Bennet]. Particulars of the loss of the Elias, with 120 men; only 21 were saved by the Martin. Sends a list of men pressed by Mr. Trelawney, who never appeared, and

1664. VOL. CIV.

therefore are a sort of runaways, as necessary to be punished as any. There are some runaways in custody of the Marshal of the Admiralty, who should be tried either by Admiralty or common law. Asks whether Capt. Allin's instructions,—which were to seize Dutch men-of-war or the Smyrna fleet, but no lesser matters,—should not be altered, as the King has now ordered at Portsmouth the seizing of all Dutch ships; therefore ships going out of the river should have the same orders. Sends blank commissions; able commanders should be sought for the merchants' ships and King's ships fitting out; it would encourage deserving men if masters or lieutenants in the fleet were preferred; 200 men have come from Plymouth, but many are bad men, and some have the small-pox. Urges the hastening of vessels. The French troops have quitted Gigery, leaving 1,200 men to the mercy of the Moors. Cromwell put his generals in prison when Hispaniola failed; fears the King of France will not stop there. Naval provisions are expected from Hamburg and Gottenburg, which should be secured. [*Three and a quarter pages.*]

Nov. 15. The Dunkirk. 116. Capt. John Kempthorne to Coventry. Has had difficulty in reaching the Downs, the wind being contrary. The Drake has arrived, but not the Royal James. Begs confirmation of Sir Wm. Penn's orders to await his coming in the Downs. [*Copy.*]

Nov. 15. The Harlings. 117. Capt. Jonathan Waltham to Sec. Bennet. Will obey his orders to go for Yarmouth, and thence for Portsmouth.

Nov. 15. 118. Col. Reymes to Sam. Pepys. Begs that Portsmouth may be reserved for his furnishing of Noyals canvas, as being more convenient for the western ships than Chatham or Deptford. Has sent samples of cordage to Portsmouth and Chatham. [*Adm. Paper.*]

Nov. 15. 119. Col. Reymes to the Navy Comrs. Desires payment of his bill for disbursements in pressing seamen within his jurisdiction. [*Adm. Paper.*]

Nov. 15. Cockpit. 120. Duke of Albemarle to Sir John Mennes. Wants hammocks and other necessaries speedily sent down for the use of the officers and 50 soldiers, under command of Lord Wentworth, now on board the Royal Katherine. [*Adm. Paper.*]

Nov. 15. 121. Jonas Shish to the Navy Comrs. Complaints of the smallness of the port holes on the gun deck of the John and Margaret. [*Adm. Paper.*]

Nov. 15. 122. Capt. Pakenton Brooke to Sam. Pepys. Justifies the surgeon of the Eagle from the charge of neglect. [*Adm. Paper.*]

Nov. 16. Woolwich. 123. Chris. Pett. to the Navy Comrs. Timber is wanting for completing the Royal Katherine. [*Adm. Paper.*]

Nov. 16. The Hound, Yarmouth Roads. 124. Capt. John Fortescue to Sam. Pepys. Damage sustained by his ship in her late voyage from Newcastle. Wants to deliver up his eight score of impressed men, 40 or 50 of whom he is to receive from Sir Thos. Meadowe at Yarmouth. [*Adm. Paper.*]

VOL. CIV.

1664.

Nov. 16. 125. Trinity House certificate of the fitness of Robt. Wyles, of Redrith, to take charge of any fifth-rate ship in the service. [*Adm. Paper.*]

Nov. 16. Warrant to the the Ordnance Commissioners to deliver 1,200 firelocks and bandoleers, 24 halberts, and six drums, for the use of the Lord Admiral's regiment. [*Ent. Book* 20, *p.* 34.]

Nov. 16. Warrant to the Ordnance Commissioners to deliver to Sir Chas. Littleton, major of the Admiral's regiment, 1,200 swords, 30 barrels of bullets, and two hogsheads of flints. [*Ent. Book* 20, *p.* 35.]

Nov.? 126. Petition of Sir Edward Ford to the King, for reference to the Lord Treas., Lord Ashley, or others named, of his proposition, which is much to His Majesty and the people's good; but his enemies have so misrepresented it, that he could never obtain a hearing.

Nov. 16. The King to the Attorney General. An order was issued to Sir Edw. Ford and Thos. Togood, to demolish their water-house near the Strand bridge, as its height was inconvenient to Somerset House; but they request licence to erect waterworks elsewhere, or they will be ruined and clamoured against by hundreds of people who have laid pipes and taken leases for a supply of water. They also ask leases of their waterworks at St. Giles'-in-the-Fields and Wapping; the licence requested is to be drawn up, with proviso that the waterworks be built between Temple Bar and Charing Cross, and be not more than 15 feet high, and with lease of these and their other waterworks for 100 years. [*Ent. Book* 16, *pp.* 292-3.]

[Nov. 16.] 127. Draft of the above. [*Two pages.*]

Nov. 16. Licence for Esther Smith to have access to Robert Walters Minuta. [*Ent. Book* 16, *p.* 274.]

Nov. 16. Order for a warrant to pay 3,476*l.* a year to Stephen Fox, for the service of the garrisons at Scilly Island, Trescoe, and St. Mary's Castle, according to the establishment made July 15, 1664. [*Ent. Book* 16, *p.* 275.]

Nov. 16. Whitehall. Warrant for a grant to Thomas Blunt of two yearly fairs to be kept at Orleton, co. Hereford. [*Ent. Books* 16, *p.* 276; *and* 21, *p.* 28.]

Nov. 16. Warrant for a discharge to Col. Wm. Lockhart, sent by the late usurping powers to negotiate with France, for a suit of hangings bearing Cromwell's arms, and some plate bearing those of the Commonwealth, which were disposed of for the negotiation, but for which he is liable to be called to account. [*Ent. Book* 16, *p.* 276.]

[Nov. 16.] 128. Draft of the above.

Nov. 16. Warrant for a grant to Dr. William Quatremaine and Richard Alchorne, of 300 acres of land lately overflowed by the sea, called Gatcomb Haven, near Portsmouth, lately belonging to Mary and

VOL. CIV.

1664.

Wm. Wandesford, which Dr. Quatremaine has been at great expense in gaining and improving; rent, 4*d.* per acre. [*Ent. Book* 16, *p.* 277.]

Nov.? 129. Petition of John Frescheville to the King, for a grant of 2,000*l.* worth of decayed wood, within five years, from Sherwood Forest, the late King being indebted to him in 5,000*l.*

Nov. 16. Order for a warrant to pay to Col. Frescheville 2,000*l.*, as the King's free gift. [*Ent. Book* 16, *p.* 275.]

[Nov. 16.] Minute of the above. [*Ent. Book* 16, *p.* 277.]

Nov. 16. Warrant for discharge of such of the clergy as have compounded for their first fruits between October 5, 1663, and March 26, 1664, from payment of one of the four clergy subsidies, lately granted; issued to take away all doubt, arising from a dubious clause in the Act. [*Ent. Book* 16, *p.* 278.]

Nov. 16. Whitehall. Warrant to the Lord Treasurer to order payment to the Ordnance Commissioners, of 20,000*l.* out of the first moneys that come in of the 100,000*l.* loan last made by the city of London, to be used for supply of powder, munition, &c., in this conjuncture. [*Ent. Book* 17, *p.* 68.]

Nov. 16. Whitehall. 130. Warrant to [the Lord Treasurer] to order the Ordnance Commissioners to issue from the stores to the powder makers all the saltpetre remaining, at 3*l.* 8*s.* per cwt., to be converted to powder for the King's use.

Nov. 16. Entry of the above. [*Ent. Book* 17, *p.* 69.]

Nov. 16. Whitehall. 131. Warrant to admit John Werden, [or Warden], of the Middle Temple, to the office of Clerk or Baron of the Exchequer of the county palatine of Chester, the reversion of which, after Evan Edwards, of Rhual, co. Flint, was granted him May 16, 1661. [*One and a half pages.*]

Nov. 16. Entry of the above. [*Ent. Book* 17, *p.* 69.]

[Nov. 16.] 132. Draft of the above.

Nov. 16. Order for a warrant to pay to Sir Faithful Fortescue 100*l.*, as a free gift, for services during the rebellion, the King wishing to contribute to his pressing wants, so far as the present state of his affairs will suffer. [*Ent. Book* 17, *p.* 70.]

[Nov. 16.] 133. Draft of the above.

Nov. 16. Whitehall. Warrant to pay to Sir George Carteret, 50,000*l.* out of the first moneys of the 100,000*l.* to be lent by the city of London, of which 20,000*l.* is to be for victuals. [*Ent. Book* 17, *p.* 71.]

[Nov. 16.] 134. Draft of the above.

VOL. CIV.

1664
Nov.? 135. Petition of Capt. Richard Carr, engineer, to the King, for present relief and employment; has been eight years prisoner in Spain, and was released at His Majesty's request. Wants to send for his wife and family from America.

Nov. 16. Warrant to pay to Richard Carr 100*l.* of the King's free gift, in compassion for the indigence to which he and his family have been brought by long imprisonments in foreign parts, and to encourage him in his military arts and sciences. [*Ent. Book* 17, *p.* 71.]

[Nov. 16.] 136. Draft of the above.

Nov. 16. 137. The King to the [East India Company?] Recommends John Rendu as a fit person to be employed in one of their factories abroad, his relations having deserved well for long and faithful service.

[Nov. 16.] 138, 139. Two drafts of the above.

Nov. 16. Entry of the above. [*Ent. Book* 17, *p.* 72.]

Nov. 16. London. 140. Albertus Otto Faber to Sec. Bennet. Being placed by his order in custody of John Somper, begs a speedy hearing. Is reduced to great straits by his three months' imprisonment for being at a Quakers' meeting; has lost thereby the little practice that he was gaining for a maintenance. [*French.*]

Nov. 16. Whitney. 141. Thos. Whitney to Sec. Bennet. Sent, as ordered, to apprehend Wm. Sheppard, but he and his son were gone to London, to pay money into the Exchequer. Thinks the charge against him is out of malice, John Watkins having sworn to ruin him or himself.

Nov. 16. Poole. 142. Will. Skutt to Williamson. Thanks for his weekly intelligence. It says that ships for the West Indies are not liable to the present embargo, but no such orders having come down, a Barbadoes ship is stayed in that port. A small Holland man-of-war stopped at Swanage, was allowed to take in water, and went on for Cadiz.

Nov. 16. 143. Account of the distribution of the ships into three squadrons, containing respectively 13, 12, and 12 vessels; with list and notes of 14 ships not distributed.

Nov. 16. 144. Estimate of an establishment for one troop of 100 horse with officers, for the garrison of Tangiers; yearly expense, 5,629*l.* 17*s.* 4*d.*

Nov. 16? 145. Estimate of expense of the Duke of York's regiment of foot, commanded by Sir Wm. Killigrew; yearly charge, 18,148*l.* 8*s.* 8*d.*

Nov. 16. London. 146. News letter [from Hen. Muddiman]. The Lord Mayor and Court of Aldermen have ordered that two of themselves, with the Lord Mayor, shall search every Sunday for conventicles. Mr. Backenham produced at the King's Bench a pardon for striking Mr. Hurlestone in Westminster Hall, but the Court finding exceptions in form, he was bound in 1,000*l.* to appear. Two Algiers

1664. Vol. CIV.

men-of-war have taken an English ship, and have sold it and the goods, but the men are not yet disposed of. Several Nonconformists were brought before the High Commissioners' Court in Edinburgh; one got off by promises of obedience, others are to be proceeded against. In the Earl of Seaforth's bounds, a child is born to an old man of 103, his wife 77. News from Holland, Italy, Germany, and Spain. On the Queen's birthday, there were divertisements in the Banquetting House, Whitehall; a chariot ran several times round the room, forced only by one or two men. The Committee of Trade have agreed to recommend to the King the opening of the trade between England and Scotland. [*Three pages.*]

Nov. 16. 147. Thos. Kendall to Williamson. Asks delivery of the commissions of Capt. George Erwin, who is to command the ship William, that goes as a convoy to the East India ships.

Nov. 16. Portsmouth. 148. [Wm. Coventry to Sec. Bennet]. The Duke leaves Taylor's affair to be determined by the King. He thinks the Commissioners should be persons of ability always resident, armed with sufficient authority over the officers of the dockyards to settle disputes which often obstruct the service, and of ability to manage naval affairs with dispatch. They should be persons who have little to do elsewhere to cause their absence, and should have their residences appointed. He thinks the salary should be 350*l.*, as much as Commissioner Pett has, who does work of the same nature. A guard of soldiers is put on board the Dutch ship, to prevent embezzlement. Five or six frigates are sent to cruise in the Channel, and bring in all they can, or else the Holland outward-bound ships may go clear without convoy. Nothing but hanging will man the fleet. The conductors cannot do it, for if the men find means to run away from shipboard, they cannot be secured for four or five days' journey. The best means would be for small frigates to range the coast and gather them in. [*Three pages.*]

Nov. 16. 149. [Wm. Coventry] to Sec. Bennet. Private. Begs him to assure the King that if he once admit a merchant to sit as a Navy Commissioner, the reputation of that office is lost, and the Exchequer charged deeper than if he had given an order for 40,000*l.* Has seen so much of merchants in the Royal Company, as to be sure that if they get into the navy, they will share in all bargains; besides, an able merchant in good trade cannot leave that and give his whole time to serve the King for 300*l.* a year. Could tell him on what depend the endeavours of Sir Wm. Rider, but has had enough of running a tilt to make things go better than those over whom he has no jurisdiction have a mind to.

Nov. 16. [Royal James.] 150. Sir Wm. Penn to Coventry. Got under sail with difficulty, on account of the weather. The two vessels with Scotchmen have come to them; 106 men were put on board the Henry, and 107 on his ship. Journal of his movements from the 10th to the 16th. [*Copy, three pages.*]

VOL. CV. NOVEMBER 17–30, 1664.

1664.
Nov. 17.
Royal James, Downs.

1. Sir Wm. Penn to [Council ?] In compliance with the Duke of York's orders to seize all vessels belonging to the United Provinces, whether outward or inward bound, has sent four vessels to ply between Dover and Calais and Dieppe. Has seized a Dutch galliot, sent by Opdam to discover what could be done with the English fleet, and to return to him at Helvoetsluys. Has sent her into Dover pier. The Bredа and Diamond have arrived, but no news of the Royal Charles, &c. [*One and a half pages.*]

Nov. 17.
Portsmouth.

2. Wm. Coventry to [Sec. Bennet]. The Duke sends for approval of the Committee [for Maritime Affairs] his letter to Sir Thos. Modyford; he does not think fit to write to the privateers, for they are of all men the most libertine and dissolute, and may make ill use of a letter from the Duke, challenging it as a right to have commands in the King's ships, though the least fit for it. The objection against Taylor as a commissioner for Harwich had not been thought sufficient to exclude a man of his abilities; will be satisfied with any choice the King makes. Commissioner Middleton has arrived. Thinks he will do good service, as he is reported able and diligent. Those that know with what earnestness his Royal Highness entered on this voyage, and how he hastened from London only to be out of importuning against it, will not easily believe him returning. It is certain nothing under Heaven but the King's commands will bring him back again. [*Two pages.*]

Nov. 17.
Portsmouth.

Warrant from Lord Admiral the Duke of York to George Erwin, captain of the William, to take the command of the said ship, obeying directions from himself, or any superior officer in the service. [*Ent. Book* 16, *p.* 383.]

Nov. 17.

3. Proposals for a patent to be granted to a Company of Merchants to trade to the port of Mocha on the Red Sea, under the King's special protection, that port [not being used by the East India Company.

Nov. 17.
Portsmouth.

4. Monsieur Dupuy to Williamson. Has told Mr. Coventry what he ordered. They are waiting a north wind to set sail and bring the Royal Charles and James, which they hope are in the Downs. [*French.*]

Nov. 17.
Whitehall.

Certificate by Sec. Bennet that Francis Brunetty, an Italian, has taken the Oath of Allegiance. [*Ent. Book* 10, *p.* 270.]

Nov. 17.
Portsmouth.

5. T. Ross to Williamson. Is troubled about [the wool business]. [*See Nov.* 12.] Sec. Nicholas suggested it. Has stayed three months for the order, and wants to clear himself to the poor men that he did not juggle with them as others have done. All are now well equipped; the winds have greatly befriended them; the Duke of York is indefatigable, and the men cheerful. The enclosed have made a poor young Duke [Monmouth] sigh and sweat, not being used to write; the letter to the King is in answer to a very kind one from him yesterday.

VOL. CV.

1664.

Nov. 17. Cockpit. 6. Sir Willm. Clarke to Williamson. The Duke [of Albemarle] wants an order for 70 muskets and bandoleers, 30 pikes, 100 swords, 1 drum, and 2 halberts, for Capt. Sheldon's company.

Nov. 17. Grant to William Clayton of the office of Musician in ordinary on the treble hautboy; wages and livery, 66l. 2s. 6d. a year. [*Docquet.*]

Nov. 17. Grant to James Hamilton, groom of the bedchamber, of a pension of 500l. a year. [*Docquet.*]

Nov. 17. Whitehall. The King to the Ordnance Comrs. The contract made with the late Dan. O'Neale, for making and repairing gunpowder, has been resigned by his widow, the Countess of Chesterfield. Intends to suppress the office of powder maker, and commit the management of it to them, and therefore authorizes them to conclude contracts for supply and repair of powder, engaging to ratify the same. [*Ent. Book* 20, *p.* 30.]

[Nov. 17.] 7. Draft of the above.

Nov. 17. Edinburgh. 8. Proclamation by the Council of Scotland, that as divers ministers ousted by law still repair to the towns, in contempt of the Acts of Parliament and Council, and debauch the subjects from their duty and obedience, a macer go to the Market Cross of Edinburgh, and order all such to depart the town within 48 hours, unless they obtain licence from Council or their Bishop to remain on some lawful business, on penalty of being seized, imprisoned, and punished, as movers of sedition. [*Printed.*]

Nov. 17. Navy Office. 9. Warrant from the Navy Commissioners to the Storekeeper and Clerk of the Cheque at Deptford, to give directions for building three long boats, two pinnaces, and one jollywat. [*Adm. Paper.*]

Nov. 17. Dover. 10. Thos. Wale, shipwright, to the Navy Comrs. Arrival of a Holland "hoyer" of 90 tons burthen, captured by Capt. Batts; the governor of the castle sent the serjeant of the Admiralty to take an invoice of it and the goods, &c. Squire Gauden begins to slaughter beefs at the newly erected place. The merchants bate little of 50s. a cwt. for tallow. [*Adm. Paper.*]

Nov. 18. Woolwich. 11. Chris. Pett to the Navy Comrs. The particular estimate required for the second, third, and fourth rate ships, mentioning the quantity and price of all materials, and charge of all sorts of workmanship, cannot be made under five or six days. The King has ordered drafts of a second and fourth rate ship. Mr. Gosage's tender of broom. [*Adm. Paper.*] *Encloses,*

11. I. *Chris. Pett and Jonas Shish to the Navy Comrs. Think the building of second, third, and fourth rate ships will be worth 11l., 8l. 10s., and 7l. per ton respectively, and 8l. for a ketch.* *Woolwich, Nov.* 17, 1664.

Nov. 18. London. 12. News letter [by H. Muddiman?]. A committee is appointed for maritime affairs; 5,000 more seamen are to be levied, ships built

VOL. CV.

1664.

or fitted out, accounts brought of merchant ships bearing demi-culverins, cannon cast, &c. The fleet is detained by winds, but daily expected at Portsmouth; the decks are cleared for fight. The navy is in three squadrons:—the 1st of 13 ships, commanded by the Duke of York, with Sir John Lawson vice-admiral and Sir Wm. Berkeley rear-admiral; the 2nd, Prince Rupert, Capt. Allin, and Capt. Sansum; the 3rd, the Earl of Sandwich, Sir George Aiskew [Ayscough], and Capt. Teddeman; this is beside other ships. Several Yarmouth herring fishers have voluntarily gone into the navy service. A vessel coming daily from Rotterdam thither has brought the infection, and several have died of it. [*Three pages, partial duplicate of the letter of Nov. 16.*]

Nov. 18. 13. Earl of Peterborough to Williamson. There is a general impatience for the ships which may bring them in sight of their neighbours, and men are very intent on their business. Is sorry to see the protection designed for Guinea made the subject of raillery; would be glad at least to save the moneys he lent.

Nov. 18. 14. Certificate by Rich. Ogden, that the presence of Walter Brocket, of Kingston-upon-Hull, is needed in a suit which he has in the Court of Exchequer against Edw. Thorold.

Nov. 18. Garsdale, Yorkshire. 15. Abraham Nelson to Sec. Bennet. Begs him to present the enclosed to the King. *Encloses*,

15. I. *Abraham Nelson to the King. Is anxious to preserve him from bloody schismatics and heretics. Wrote to prove that the times of his banishment were the times of Antichrist prophesied about. Knowing that the general pardon would not be accepted, wrote to the House of Commons, to advise a standing army of horse, of old cavaliers; this was proposed, but laid aside. The people will never be quiet till some such course is taken. There are 140 Nonconformist ministers in that county, and many more Anabaptists, Millenarians, and Quakers, who think they should be as much tolerated as the Papists who were not guilty of the late war. If they and their favourers were numbered, they would exceed two parts of the common people, and many of the nobility and gentry are connected with them. It would cost little more to pay a standing army, than foot companies when called up for exercise; it would employ the poorer cavaliers, who are much persecuted, and who would be glad of Oliver's law, forbidding arrests on Sundays; it is hard for them to lie in gaol for debt. Urges His Majesty to read his grandfather's book, and not trust a Puritan more than a Highlander or Border thief; and hopes he may be the means of reconciling the churches of England and Rome, chiefly divided by that hot spirit of John Wickliffe of Oxford, and thus of expelling Antichrist from his dominions. They [the Nonconformists, &c.] cheat in the hearth-money,*

1664. VOL. CV.

and take everything done in Church or State in the worst sense they can invent; they are wary in speaking, to keep themselves from the halter, but they hatch disobedience in the hearers. They know that being so numerous, His Majesty cannot force them to conformity by banishment or death, without putting the kingdom in danger; but by a competent force in the field, they might be brought to their allegiance, or punished with death or banishment for their incorrigible obstinacy. [*Three pages.*]

Gorsdale, Nov. 17.

Nov. 18. Whitehall. Proclamation ordering all cashiered soldiers of the late usurped powers, who have not a special licence from the Lord General, one of the Secretaries of State, or three or more of the Privy Council, to leave town by Nov. 20, and not to return before May 20 next. [*Printed. Proc. Coll., pp.* 173–4; *the same as that of Nov.* 3.]

[Nov. 18.] 16. Draft of the above. [*One and a quarter pages.*]

Nov. 18? 17. John Every to [Williamson]. Requests a pass to London for Peter Bowes, an honest person, who regrets having served the Parliament against the King. On account of the proclamation, he knows not how to procure a pass from the authorized persons. Endorsed with Every's address, in Channel Row.

Nov. 19. Portsmouth. 18. Wm. Coventry to Sec. Bennet. Thinks the fleet so nearly manned that it may now be completed from privateers. Regrets the dissensions at Tangiers. The direction only to secure those who have taken press money till they give security to appear, is not rigorous enough; they will hope not to be looked after or found, especially if pressed out of their own country, and the difficulty of examining the subscription of the bonds is very great; many port bonds in the Custom House are forgotten and passed by; nothing but the rigour of punishment and example will do the business. The rulers of the watermen will be remiss in apprehending the servants and sons of their fellows, as has been already proved; a warrant from the Lord Chief Justice would be of more terror than all that the watermen can do. The Elizabeth, being of 40 guns, is too good to send to Harwich for pressed men, and should join the fleet. The Eagle would do better, and might be manned with London watermen, on promise not to be pressed farther than to carry the ship down to Harwich. Believes the Scotchmen at Yarmouth may be found on merchantmen, where they have run for great wages. The Committee [for Maritime Affairs] free strangers' ships from embargo; asks if the Council, by whom the embargo was laid, consents. The Duke has sent Lord Colepeper to stay Dutch ships, on pretence that they have stayed a ship of masts belonging to the King. Fears the bad weather may damage some of the ships. Thinks by the list of ships in the Downs, that the embargo has been ill kept at Gravesend; inquiries should be made, for very few passes have been granted except for fish ships. Commissioner Middleton hesitates to act,

VOL. CV.

1664.

hearing that his patent is stopped; begs its dispatch, as he will be likely to do good; he is informing himself of the methods of the place. Has received no dispatch from him [Sec. Bennet], but one from Sir George Downing by mistake. Notes that two ketches are ordered to be built, but the King has bespoken the purchase of one. Thinks hiring a cheaper and quicker way. [*Begun on the 18th, five pages.*]

Nov. 19. Isle of Wight. 19. Col. Walter Slingsby to [Williamson]. Hen. Miller, boatswain of the Elias, has been there, and given particulars of taking the New Netherlands. The Elias foundered 140 leagues from shore on the coast of New England, and 100 men were drowned.

Nov. 19. London. 20. H. P—— to John Knowles, Pershore. Hopes to see him this month; he shall return if the work of the Gospel require it. The Quakers sent to banishment from Hertford and shipped for Barbadoes have returned, the master certifying that from the disasters which befell him, he thought it unlawful to transport them without their consent. The jurymen who would not find a verdict against them are to be tried at Guildhall. With postscript by T. Firmin, that he has provided Knowles an upper room, bed, stool, candle, and a good fire shall not be wanting, and that he lives in Lombard Street, opposite the George Inn.

Nov.? 21. Petition of Anna Le Grand, widow, to the King, for a particular order for payment of her pension, now two years in arrear, for want of which she is ready to perish.

Nov. 19. 22. Anna Le Grand to Sec. Bennet. Is in great distress, obliged to beg or pawn; begs him to hasten the signing of an order for her pension; would rather be buried alive than live in this lingering condition. *Annexing*,

22. I. *Form of a warrant to pay to Anna Le Grand a year and a half arrears due on her pension, for relief of her present urgent condition.* *Whitehall, Nov.* 16, 1664.

Nov. 19. Edinburgh. 23. R. M[ein] to Hen. Muddiman. A proclamation is issued, ordering non-conforming ministers to obey the last Act of Parliament, which forbids their coming within five miles of any borough, unless they have business at law compelling their attendance, when they may petition for a special licence. This was issued because many are believed to be lurking about the town, and labouring to seduce the people.

Nov. 19. Beaumaris. 24. Sir Brian Broughton to Williamson. Sends his scout's letter. They fear their design may be discovered, because Col. Careless told his wife to sell off his stock and hasten to London. Downes and Fletcher are said to be at sea. *Encloses*,

24. I. *Wa. Collins to Sir Brian Broughton. The Irish and north country do not like rise speedily, because of the*

1664. VOL. CV.

season. Holland thinks them burdensome, because horses from a foreign nation, which is to help them, have come over there, and want some harbour to winter in.

Nov. 19, 1664.

[Nov. 19.] Royal Charles, Saturday. 25. Prince Rupert to Sec. Bennet. The Charles and all the other river ships came up last night, and the Duke [of York] went on board the same night. The wind is west, so the fleet is fast again. There are there 43 of the bravest ships ever seen. Is just going on board Sir Wm. Berkeley, and will do as he wrote word he should.

Nov. 19. 26. Thos. Kendall to Williamson. Requests delivery of the commissions of Shilling Terry, who is to be Lieutenant of the William, and John Eden of the John and Margaret, both East India ships.

Nov. 19. Commission for John Eden to be Lieutenant of the John and Margaret, under command of Capt. Chappell. Minute. [*Ent. Book* 16, *p.* 383.]

Nov. 19. Commission to Shilling Terry to be Lieutenant of the William, under command of Capt. Erwin. Minute. [*Ent. Book* 16, *p.* 353.]

Nov. 19. 27. Bond of Walter Brocket, of Kingston-upon-Hull, and two others, in 300*l.*, for his not abetting nor concealing any design against government, and appearing within six days on summons.

Nov. 19. 28. Earl of Sandwich to [Sec. Bennet]. Begs his assistance in the affairs of the great wardrobe. Thinks the Duke of Albemarle and Lord Chamberlain have spoken to him about it. Fervently desires to serve the King, but cannot, unless furnished with materials proportionable to what is required. [*Two pages.*]

Nov. 19. Woolwich. 29. Estimate by Chris. Pett and Jonas Shish of materials and workmanship for building a fourth-rate ship; total, 4,234*l.* 10*s.* [*Adm. Paper.*]

Nov. 19. Woolwich. 30. Estimate by Chris. Pett and Jonas Shish for building a ketch of 100 tons burthen; total, 508*l.* 10*s.* [*Adm. Paper.*]

Nov. 19. Ollerton, Sherwood. 31. Thos Corbin to the Navy Comrs. Complains of delay in waiting the leisure of the "base, cross-grained watermen" employed in the carriage of timber. The justices' warrants for 300 carriages have sent in the carters very fast. Commends Capt. Greene's diligence. Will bring up the accounts shortly. [*Adm. Paper.*] *Encloses,*

31. I. *Note of the lading of the Golden Star; 77 loads of timber.*

Nov. 19. Dover. 32. Thos. Wale to the Navy Comrs. A pink of 140 tons, laden with sugars, is captured by the Colchester; being leaky, her goods will be landed at once. The Earl of Sandwich has appointed two pilots for carrying in and out the navy ships. No others should be allowed, in order to prevent casualties and embezzlements. [*Adm. Paper.*]

VOL. CV.

1664.
Nov. 19. The Kent, Downs. 33. Capt. Thos. Ewens to the Navy Comrs. Has arrived in the Downs, having accompanied the Royal Charles, &c., through the King's Channel. [*Adm. Paper.*]

Nov. 20. Dover Castle. 34. Capt. John Strode, Lieutenant of Dover Castle, to the Navy Comrs. Sends rolls of the pressed men. His serjeant has impressed 17 able seamen. There are many fit for service, but the magistrates will not do their duty. Those impressed east of Rye were sent to Chatham; those west, to Portsmouth. Capts. Heling and Batts have sent in three Dutch vessels; knows not what to do with the seamen, having no provisions for them, yet "live they must." [*Adm. Paper.*]

Nov. 20. Portsmouth. 35. W. Coventry to Williamson. Thanks for his letters and news.

Nov. 20. 36. W. Coventry to [Sec. Bennet]. Returns his letters, which the Duke had not time to read before. [*Unfinished.*]

Nov. 20. 37. Account of 32 conventicles held in and about London, since Oct. 26, 1664. [*One and a half pages.*]

1664? Nov. 20. Somerset House. 38. Earl of St. Alban's to Sec. Bennet. The papers he named relate to a debt for arms owing by the late King to Marthias, a French merchant, now solicited by Pestalozzi. They contain the accounts and obligations to pay them.

1664. Nov. 21. Licence to Edw. Bolt to stay in town, according to the power given to Sec. [Bennet] by the proclamation of 18th November Minute. [*Ent. Book* 16, *p.* 270.]

Nov. 21. Licence from Sec. Bennet to Walter Brocket, of Kingston-on-Hull, to stay in town, having delivered bond, &c. Minute. [*Ent. Book* 16, *p.* 279.]

Nov. 21. Like licence to John Barber; noted "Mr. Seymour." Minute. [*Ent. Book* 16, *p.* 279.]

Nov. 21. Warrant to the Ordnance Commissioners to deliver two blankets per man for the use of the Guards under Lord Wentworth, on board the Royal Katherine, now at Woolwich, and the Triumph in the Hope. [*Ent. Book* 16, *p.* 279.]

Nov. 21. Christ's College, Cambridge. 39. Dr. John Carr to Williamson. Asks if any attempts have lately been made to invalidate any of the King's letters granted to some of his college, particularly himself. Dr. Sparrow, master of Queen's, is now Vice-Chancellor, and is coming to visit the college. Presumes he will not interfere with their grants, being himself obliged to the King in that respect. Begs dispatch of a business for one of the Fellows.

Nov. 21. 40. Certificate by Edm. Green, and 18 others, of the good conduct, loyalty, and sufferings of Wm. Sheppard, mercer, of Kington, co. Hereford, and that he was never a cherisher of sects, but adhered to

1664. VOL. CV.

the Church of England; also deposition of Fras. Allen and of Thos. Phillipps, of Builth, co. Brecon, that John Watkins threatened mischief to Wm. Sheppard, on account of some differences between them. [*Copies.*] *Annexing,*

40. I. *Statement of the case between Wm. Sheppard and John Watkins, sen., drover of Gladestry, co. Radnor, that Sheppard, being a deputy receiver of the 18 months' assessment, lent between 300l. and 400l. to Watkins and his sons, and then summoning them for repayment, they denied the debt. Sheppard thereupon commenced a suit against them, to escape which Watkins falsely accused him, before Sec. Bennet, of speaking words against the King and government.*

Nov. 21. 41. List of ships now in the Downs, being 12 of the King's ships and 25 merchantmen; with names of the masters and places of destination of the latter. Wind S.W.

Nov. 21. 42. Thos. Kendall to Sam. Pepys. Entreats an order to Capt. Leonard Webber, commander of the Dorcas, [an East India Company's ship,] which goes before the other ships, to wear a jack, so as to keep the ships together; also, a protection for 17 of her men. [*Adm. Paper.*]

Nov. 21. Portsmouth. 43. Sir Wm. Berkeley to Sam. Pepys. The turning over of men into the Resolution has taken up all the tickets; 100 more are wanted. [*Adm. Paper.*]

Nov. 21. Harwich. 44. John Browne to Sir Wm. Batten. Particulars of contracts for blocks and sackcloth. [*Adm. Paper.*]

Nov. 21. Harwich. 45. Anthony Deane to Sam. Pepys. Excuses his delay in sending the new ship's accounts. Compass timber wanted; there is some which has lain for years at Woolwich. [*Adm. Paper.*]

Nov. 21. Harwich. 46. Anthony Deane to Sir Wm. Batten. To similar effect. Tender of plank by Mr. Robinson of Walderswick. [*Adm. Paper.*]

Nov. 22. 47. Capt. George Erwin to the Navy Comrs. Certifies the fitness of Wm. Bagg for the office of Gunner. [*Adm. Paper.*]

Nov. 22. Portsmouth. 48. St. J. Stevenson to Sam. Pepys. Notice of ships still left in harbour. Promises a speedy account of disbursements. [*Adm. Paper.*]

Nov. 22. 49. Jonas Shish to the Navy Comrs. Proposes the launch of the Paul. [*Adm. Paper, damaged.*]

Nov. 22. Portsmouth. 50. Wm. Coventry to Sec. Bennet. Does not trouble the Duke, who is often abroad, for his signature, when there are only matters of fact to be related, or hints of things to be given, which are fitter for rejection or debate when presented by him than by the Duke. The Mary has brought only 100 very poor men from Plymouth.

Vol. CV.

1664.

Sir Chas. Littleton's soldiers have arrived, but without arms, so that they cannot be improved in the use of them. The Duke hopes other soldiers will bring their arms, when marched for embarking Some are sightly men and will do good service when used to be sea, and it seems likely that the Dutch will give breathing time. Sends for approval short instructions for Capt. Allin, to be forwarded by Lord Ambassador Fanshaw. Hopes the report is false of the plague being in Yarmouth, as it may afford numbers of good seamen. The Duke has sent to Cowes a vessel lately come from Amsterdam, sometimes pretending to be Venetian, sometimes Genoese; asks directions in such cases; if suspicious be totally rejected, no prizes will be found in the sea. The Duke has ordered 6d. reward to any person who shall bring in a soldier or sailor absent without ticket of leave. Whilst the sea is clear, guns should be sent up to increase the number of those in the Straits' fleet, which will soon be returning. Thinks seamen may be obtained from Guernsey or Jersey, and thus French and Flanders seamen engaged on the King's side, who will else be taken by the Dutch. The Duke holds a daily council of the flag officers. Hearing that one of the King's ships, bound for Tangiers, is detained in Torbay, he sent an order to the commander to seize and bring to Plymouth divers Dutch ships riding there; having begun, it is better to reckon for a great deal than for a little. Hopes the Lord Treasurer's orders are coming for his officers to take charge of prizes in all the ports. [*Three and a half pages. Endorsed "Read at the Committee."*]

Nov.? 51. Petition of Henry Earl of Peterborough to the King, for a letter to Trinity College, Cambridge, to procure him the reversion of the rectory and parsonage of Hatchden, co. Bedford, of which his ancestors have long been tenants, but Farrer, his servant, whom he employed during the troubles to renew his lease, renewed it for himself.

Nov. 22. The King to the Master, &c. of Trinity College, Cambridge. During the late troubles, Mr. Farrer, solicitor of the affairs of the Countess-Dowager of Peterborough, obtained for her a lease of the rectory of Hatchden, co. Bedford, to the injury of the present Earl, then beyond the seas on account of his loyalty; as this lease is now expiring, requests that it may be renewed in favour of the Earl. [*Ent. Book 17, p. 73.*]

[Nov. 22.] 52. Draft of the above.

Nov. 22. 53. Wm. Knight to Sec. Bennet. Begs him to prevent any disgraceful infliction which the rigour of a city jury may pass on him. Having given a perfect account of the transaction which has rendered him a captive, hopes he will regard him as candidly as possible.

Nov. 22? 54. Petition of Wm. Knight to Sec. Bennet, for remission of any sentence of disgrace, if the prosecution should be severe. Made the most ample and satisfactory confession to him that he could, and now finds that that alone will be made use of to his prejudice.

Vol. CV.

1664.

Nov. 22. Whitehall. 55. Warrant to the Navy Commissioners to order 25 blankets to be sent on board the Royal Katherine, at Woolwich, and the same number on board the Triumph in the Hope, for the use of 50 soldiers of the King's regiment on board each ship; with draft of a clause, ordering as many blankets as needful to allow two for each soldier, to be certified by the captain and purser of the ships.

Nov. 22. Portsmouth. 56. Dr. Wm. Quatremaine to Williamson. Hopes soon to return to town, but has written to Dr. Clarke about him, though thinking him beyond danger of a relapse.

Nov. 22. Hull. 57. Luke Whittington to Geo. [Jas.] Hickes. Three Bourdeaux ships have arrived, and three from London. The impressed men have sailed for London. An embargo has come down for all Holland ships, which will matter little there, where there are so few.

Nov. 23. Norwich. 58. Willm. Nowell to Henry Muddiman. On search into the report of the plague being in Yarmouth, it was found that, though three died in one house, only one had the plague, and it has not spread. One or two houses are shut up, because persons ventured ashore from a Holland ship, notwithstanding the limitation to the contrary.

Nov. 23. 59. Sir Phil. Musgrave to Sec. Bennet. Gives, as ordered, an account of the affront done to the King in his person. At a meeting of deputy lieutenants and justices of peace at the sessions for Cumberland, the sheriff said he must arrest him at the suit of Wm. Christian, customer of Carlisle, unless he would refer the matter to four gentlemen, or waive his privilege of Parliament, and have it settled by law; refusing this, was taken prisoner a little, till his attorney promised to answer for him. This was done in affront of him, the matter being so small. Christian also spoke slightingly of him. Thinks no governor of a garrison has been so dealt with. [*One and a half pages.*] *Annexing*,

> 59. i. *Statement [by Sir P. Musgrave] that the suit in question is about Christian's claim, as customer, of a halfpenny a beast, which was paid in the late King's time; but now, since the imposition laid on Irish cattle in 1660, the customers receive 6s. for every entry of cattle. The affront to himself is the thing that should be insisted on.*

Nov. 23. 60. Willm. Hall to Sec. Bennet. Sir Wm. Penn, with part of the fleet, set sail to-day. The herring fleet from Yarmouth, of 20 sail, appeared on the back of the sands, stood into the Downs, and is in company with Sir Wm. Penn. Wind N.W.

Nov. 23. Dover. 61. J[ohn] C[arlisle] to Williamson. The fleet, which was in the Downs, 12 ships, with 25 herring vessels from Yarmouth, has

VOL. CV.

1664.

sailed by, and gave rise to an alarm of the Dutch fleet. Two Dutch vessels have been brought in. Asks who are to be head Commissioners for the Prize Office, and whether he must address them or not on his business. There are six prizes now in the harbour.

Nov. 23. Whitehall. 62. Proclamation ordering all seamen who have received press money for entering the service of the navy to repair to their respective ships, at the time appointed, on pain of death and other penalties against offenders, for whose speedy punishment commissions of oyer and terminer are to be appointed; also ordering magistrates to search for and apprehend them. [*Printed, two pages.*]

Nov. 23. Copy of the above. [*Printed. Proc. Coll., pp.* 175–6.]

Nov. 23. Warrant to the Ordnance Commissioners to deliver 70 muskets and bandoleers, 30 pikes, 100 swords, 1 drum, and 2 halberts to Wm. Sheldon, for the use of this company in the island of Guernsey. [*Ent. Book*, 20, p. 37.]

Nov. 23. Commission to Rowland Selby to be Quartermaster to the King's own regiment of Guards, under command of Lord Hawley. Minute. [*Ent. Book* 20, p. 38.]

Nov. 23. Warrant to the Ordnance Commissioners to deliver to Sir John Robinson, Lieutenant of the Tower, such proportions of powder, bullet, &c., as he shall from time to time find requisite. [*Ent. Book* 20, p. 38.]

Nov. ? 63. Petition of Ambrose Atfield, chaplain in the Tower, to the King, for a letter to Cambridge University to admit him Doctor, his service not allowing him to be absent as long as required to perform the duties for his degree.

Nov. 23. Whitehall. The King to the Vice-Chancellor of Cambridge. Recommends Ambrose Atfield for the degree of D.D., and John Chris. Macaker, physician to the late King's armies in Ireland, for that of M.D.; dispensing with the exercises of the former, on account of his constant attendance as chaplain in the Tower. [*Ent. Book* 19, p. 26.]

Nov. 23. Whitehall. Warrant for a grant to Col. John Russell, of the Guards, of a moiety of certain moneys detained by the treasurers, receivers, or collectors of customs, sequestrations, &c., for cos. Norfolk and Cambridge, and Isle of Ely, during the late usurpation; with power to recover the same, paying the other moiety into the Exchequer. [*Ent. Book* 16, p. 270.]

Nov. [23.] 64. Draft of the above. [*Two pages.*]

Nov.? 65. Estimate of the expense of repaving and repairs of the stables; total, 960*l.* 5*s.*; signed by the Duke of Albemarle, [master of the horse], B. Grenvile, and four others.

Vol. CV.

1664.

Nov. 23. Whitehall. Order for a warrant to pay to Ambrose Norton, surveyor of the stables, 960*l.* 5*s.*, for their repair and new paving. [*Ent. Book* 16, p. 280.]

Nov. 23. Privy seal for 500*l.* to Thomas Ross, for secret service, without account. Minute. [*Ent. Book* 16, p. 281.]

Nov. Docquet of the above. [*Docquet, Nov.* 1664.]

Nov. 23. Warrant for a grant to John Madden and Thomas Agar of the office of Surveyor of Woods and Forests on this side Trent, as lately held by Dan. Treswell; fee, 50*l.* a year. [*Ent. Book* 16, p. 281.]

Nov. [23.] 66. Draft of the above.

Nov. 23. Whitehall. Warrant for a grant to Katherine Countess of Chesterfield of an annuity of 3,000*l.* a year, for 17 years, being the term of a lease granted to her late husband, Dan. O'Neale, of the sole making and repairing of gunpowder for the King's stores, which lease has been surrendered by her. [*Ent. Book* 16, p. 282.]

Nov. [23.] 67. Draft of the above.

Nov. 23. Whitehall. 68. Warrant for a grant to James Duke of York of all manors, lands, &c., in co. Warwick, whereof Richard Danford, of London, died possessed, and which are escheated to the Crown for want of heirs.

Nov. 23. Entry of the above. [*Ent. Book* 16, p. 283.]

Nov. 23. 69. Certificate by Jonas Shish of the fitness of George Hipton, shipwright, for the place of Carpenter on board the Dolphin. [*Adm. Paper.*]

Nov. 23. The Hound, Rolling Grounds, Harwich. 70. Capt. John Fortescue to Sam. Pepys. Has brought his ship to anchor, with intent to put all impressed men on board the Drake, but neither that nor any other of the King's ships being at Harwich, requests further orders how to dispose of them. [*Adm. Paper.*]

Nov. 24. Barber Surgeons' Hall. 71. Ralph Thickness and Thos. Hollier, wardens of Surgeons' Hall, to the Navy Comrs. Mr. Solby may well be trusted with the sole fitting of all surgeons' chests for the navy, reserving to other surgeons the privilege granted them by charter, either to make their own medicines, or to have their chests furnished by what apothecary they please, providing the value amount to no more than the freight money allowed by the King; the society to be judges of the price and quality of the goods. [*Adm. Paper.*]

Nov. 24. Harwich. 72. John Browne to the Navy Comrs. A vessel has arrived from Yarmouth, laden with cordage; begs an order to receive it. Men wanted. [*Adm. Paper.*]

Nov. 24. Portsmouth. 73. John Tippetts to the Navy Comrs. Account of contracts entered into for timber, plank, &c. [*Adm. Paper.*]

Nov. 24. 74. Certificate by Capt. Wm. Badiley, and six others, of the fitness of Abel Woollard for the service of boatswain in the Francis. [*Adm. Paper.*]

VOL. CV.

1664.

Nov. 24. Reference to Lord Treasurer Southampton on the petition of Col. Robt. Phillips for a lease for 31 years of certain waste and derelict lands in the hundreds of Colridge Heytor. [*Ent. Book* 18, p. 100.]

Nov. 24. Portsmouth. 75. Wm. Coventry to Sec. Bennet. Mr. King has been to solicit the Duke. Referred him to the Committee [of Council for Navy affairs], not knowing that Taylor was so likely to succeed. Wishes the Eagle were coming, as another fifth-rate is wanted. Thinks Lord Lauderdale right that the Scotchmen cannot be punished amongst the rest of the runaways; but if they run after they are entered on board the King's ships, thinks they might. If the reason given of seizing Holland vessels be the detention by them of that ship of masts, it may blind the Dutch a little longer, and pretty good reprisals are taken. Notice should be sent northward to prepare against the Zealanders, who will be pirating that way. The Committee was also to attend to the protection of trade. Convoys might be spared, if the Dutch have not sent for their fleet, so that a battle is not likely. Prizes are sent to Dover or a near port, because the fleet must not be unmanned by sparing men to carry them up the river. By Opdam's instructions, and De Ruyter's having gone out, it is shown that it is a fallacious assurance that, because they are a commonwealth, their designs will be shown before they can attempt anything. De Ruyter's going out is the cause of the King's ordering ships taking, and therefore of the war; and its being done by De Witt's orders, not those of the States General, might be used by the Prince of Orange's friends to injure De Witt. Sir William Berkeley is sent with six frigates into the Channel, but not to go beyond the Isle of Wight, and to return if the Dutch fleet appear. Hopes orders are given for disposal of Dutchmen taken; they should not be sent home, as that only helps to man their ships for them. The Duke of York is preparing to go on board the Swiftsure. Some landsmen having no arms are sent to Southampton to quarter, and the Duke has sent 200*l.* of his own money to Sir Chas. Littleton for them; none but able, strong-bodied men should be taken; the rest are refused, when the King has been at the charge of raising and marching them. [*Four pages. Begun on the 23rd.*]

Nov. 24. Portsmouth. 76. Wm. Coventry to Sec. Bennet. Cannot see why the Dutch ambassador should be told that the King has resolved to set upon them; his ignorance might have been very fortunate, and perhaps given means to the ship with masts and others to withdraw from Holland. Now he will send up an express, and the traders to the northward, and even in the Downs, when the great ships have sailed, must look to themselves. Does not think the sum demanded by the Committee greater than the war will require, but objects to the grounds on which it is stated; the preparations have not cost nearly 800,000*l.*; the men, at the highest calculation, have not cost more than 504,000*l.* If the replenishing of the stores be included, that makes part of the 1,700,000*l.* mentioned for next year's expense; the

1664. VOL. CV.

House of Commons is so jealous of anything that looks like fallacy, that this may do rather harm than good, and they will see that if 800,000*l.* has been already spent, more than 1,700,000*l.* will be needed to conclude the matter. [*Two and a quarter pages.*]

Nov. 24. Portsmouth. 77. Duke of York to Sec. Bennet. Has consulted with the flag officers on the proposals of the Navy Commissioners, and they agree that it would be better for the victuals for 1,000 men to be prepared at Newcastle, as formerly, than at Hull, because Newcastle, on account of the coal trade, is always supplied with good ships which could carry victuals to the fleet, and this is needed rather than for the ships to come to port for victuals; also, Newcastle is not so far inland as Hull. They think the small reward of 6*d.* per head to commanders for pressed men would do little good. They will do their utmost, from desire to show their diligence by manning their ships. The officers desire that he (the Duke) should have the nomination of one of the Commissioners for prizes. It was suspected in the last Dutch war, that the prize officers, for some bye-ends, prosecuted very slightly; and thus the seamen and public were defrauded of their shares in the prizes; would take care to appoint some one approved by the whole fleet, the appointment to be for six months only, renewable on approbation. [*Two pages.*]

Nov. 24. Order for a warrant to pay to Col. William Legg 20,000*l.*, for the present supply of stores for the Tower. [*Ent. Book* 10, *p.* 280.]

Nov. 24. 78. The King's speech on the meeting of Parliament. Details the circumstances which have brought on the Dutch war; requests aid therein, and rebuts the "vile jealousy," that he intends to gain large supplies for the war, and then make a sudden peace. [*Five pages, printed. Also printed in Lords' Journals*, xi., 614-5.]

Nov. 24. 79. Draft of the above. [*In the King's own hand. Three pages.*]

Nov. 24. Commission for Willm. Montgomery to be Quartermaster to the Earl of Oxford's regiment of Horse Guards. Minute. [*Ent. Book* 20, *p.* 38.]

[Nov. 24.] 80. Note of the preceding commission, and of that of Rowland Selby as quartermaster.

Nov. 25. Egleston. 81. Christopher Sanderson to Sir Philip Musgrave. The party are exalted with hopes of a war with the Dutch, and of troubles from the Presbyterian Scotch. Dares not write without cypher the name of a person who advised another not to take any office under this government, or he would be turned out at the time of deliverance. Asks money for his informer, and a preferment for his own son, who has studied at Leyden and Gray's Inn, is courageous and civil, and speaks Dutch, Polish, Sclavonic, Bohemian, and French. [*One and a half pages.*]

Nov. 25. Warrant to Mr. L'Estrange to apprehend John Westcombe and his wife, Eliz. Ward, and Sarah Kent [Keat]. Minute. [*Ent. Book* 10, *p.* 285.]

VOL. CV.

1664.

Nov. 23. Swiftsure, Spithead. 82. Wm. Coventry to [Sec. Bennet]. The ships from the Downs are near, but cannot come up for the wind, which keeps them in, but will carry the Dutch through the channel. Thinks directions should be sent to Yarmouth, for preventing the spread of the plague. The Parliament men have all left the fleet, except Sir Wm. Penn, Mr. Vaughan, and himself. Will not mind foul weather there, if it be fair at Westminster. Hopes good news thence. [*One and a half pages.*]

Nov. 25. Whitehall. 83. Order in Council for notice to be given in all foreign despatches, especially to the plantations and factories in Africa and America, of the seizure made of all Dutch ships, and for letters to be sent to Lord Willoughby of Parham, Sir Wm. Berkeley, Sir Thos. Modyford, and the Commissioners of New England, to the same effect.

[Nov. 25. Whitehall.] 84. Petition of Frances Lambert formerly Sanders of Bristol, now of Dublin, to the King, for present relief and future support, as referred to the Lord Treasurer to report something for her. Has been often imprisoned for loyalty, and was tried for life, and condemned to death at Abingdon, by Sir Rich. Browne, but escaped. Has lost many hundred pounds, besides sums due to her from his late and present Majesty.

Nov. 25. Reference of the above petition to the Lord Treasurer. [*Ent. Book* 2, p. 101.]

Nov. 26. 85. Account of payments made for the garrison of Carlisle, from 25th June to 26th November, 1664, since which date the monthly pay is to be issued according to the present establishment, and nothing on the former privy seal of 25th June, 1661.

Nov. 26. 86. Trinity House certificate of the fitness of James Kember, of Wapping, to take charge of a fourth or fifth rate ship. [*Adm. Paper, damaged.*]

Nov. 26. Portsmouth. 87. Ben. Johnson to Sam. Pepys. Sends a bill for the last parcel of Holland cordage received from Yarmouth. Arrival of various stores. [*Adm. Paper.*]

Nov. 26. 88. Jonas Shish to the Navy Comrs. Progress of works on the John and Margaret. [*Adm. Paper, damaged.*]

Nov. 26. Royal Charles, near Portsmouth. 89. W. Brouncker to Sec. Bennet. Thanks for a present. The wind being west, all lie still, except Sir Wm. Berkeley, who with five ships has gone to hunt for Dutchmen.

Nov. 28. Isle of Wight. 90. Col. Walter Slingsby to [Williamson]. The watches and guard poles being repaired, few ships can pass the Channel without discovery; 14 or 15 sail of great ships were discovered, pilots sent, and they are now anchored, so that there is a jolly fleet at Spithead. The common people are in good heart, and think the Dutch dare not fight. A galley has brought in three Dutch merchantmen.

Vol. CV.

1664.
Nov. 26.
Edinburgh.

91. R. M[eni] to Henry Muddiman. The boys having broken open Sir Walter Seaton's lodgings and seized his papers, did not regard the Lord Provost and bailies with their halberdiers, on which, not having time to gather the companies, they called the Lord Lyon; he sent 60 musketeers from the castle, who, being opposed, shot one of the boys, and wounded others, whereon the rest fled, but two were secured. The Lord Commissioner held a council, and the Provost was ordered to secure the boys. The Exchequer has met; the merchants petitioned that the Act of Parliament now proceeded on was 60 years old, made for emergency, and never put in execution; that the sealing their cloth and giving oath for goods imported injure their trade, and another Act was pleaded whereby they are not liable to oath: It was therefore ordered that all the goods should be sealed, but the oath delayed till further consideration. The merchants are willing to pay dues, but the new imposition of 80 per cent. troubles them. There were never more English commodities in Scotland than at present, but the 80 per cent. frightening the merchants, they shut their shops, till Council ordered them to open, because the boys were idle, and took to drink, and to revenge themselves on those who disturbed trade. The masters have delivered up 16 or 18 of them. The boys' watchword was "For our posterity!" One of them was proved to have been trying to repress disorders, but the judge being strictly ordered to hang them on conviction, did not liberate him, but remitted him to the Council. The people are willing to serve the King with life and fortune; the disturbance was only with some 20 boys in drink. Sir And. Ramsay, the provost, did all that could be done. The laird of Lundie, brother's son and intended heir of the Earl of Lauderdale, a sweet stately creature, has died of a flux, from drinking small beer when hot with dancing. [*Two pages.*]

Nov. 26.
Royal Charles, Spithead.

92. W. Coventry to Williamson. Knows no objection to the Duke's granting letters of marque. Lord Fitzharding brings news of the excellent votes of the House of Commons. Hopes the King may always be thus happy in the obedience and affection of his people. The whole business has been supernaturally successful; there needs only the key of the arch to make the King glorious and happy. Wants 50 or 100 of the proclamations against runaways, to distribute wherever they can be of the smallest use. The Duke of York is sailing with a fleet of 40 ships, and smaller vessels, able to send back anything the Dutch can set forth as yet. [*Two pages.*]

Nov. 27.
Spithead.

93. Wm. Coventry to [Sec. Bennet]. They are going into the Channel to see whether the letters from Holland which say the Dutch will not come out, or the brags at the Dutch ambassador's are truest. The news sent to the fleet by Lord Fitzharding lays a groundwork of honour and greatness for King and kingdom. Now that His Majesty is assured of money, hopes the building of ships and providing of stores will be set about heartily. Estimates should be made very particularly of all things required, even to the least thing, or else in time of action, either the prices are raised infinitely, or what is

Vol. CV.

1664.

worse, ships delayed till supplies can be sent for. Is glad the report of the plague in Yarmouth is false. Sends a list of pressed men from Hull to be inquired after. A vessel should always remain in the Hope to receive such men. [*One and a quarter pages.*]

Nov. 27. 94. Wm. Coventry to [Sec. Bennet]. As to Holmes, the Duke is not much inclined to condemn a man of mettle at this time; he says Holmes should be heard first. It was as great a breach of orders, and in as high a point as could be, yet the Duke seems inclined to pardon it, on account of the courage and success of the attempt.

Nov. 27. Dover. 95. Thos. Wale to the Navy Comrs. Account of three Dutch vessels captured; one by a boat of lads, another by a shallop of five tons, sent by the governor of the castle, and the third by the Hampshire. [*Adm. Paper.*]

Nov. 28. Forest of Dean. 96. Dan. Furzer and John Jones to the Navy Comrs. Squire Wintour would not allow the removal of the house and pales sold in the yard, claiming rent for the ground used for the yard, satisfaction for damage done by the ship's launching, &c. The house, &c., were offered to him on sale, but he refused to buy them. It was agreed to refer the matter to two arbitrators, who decide that he shall have 10*l.* for damages, and have nothing more to do with house, timber, or anything about the yard. Proposed to him for the King to give up the yard altogether. The storehouse is sold for 40*l.* [*Adm. Paper, two and a quarter pages.*]

Nov. 28. Chatham. 97. Commissioner Peter Pett to Sam. Pepys. Asks what to do with the 62 men pressed at York, Whitby, Scarborough, Lynn, Yarmouth, Dover, Deal, &c., and lately sent in by Capt. Stoakes; they are in no way fit for the service, being made up of all sorts of country trades, and such a ragged crew as never was seen. Progress of ships. Arrival of stores. [*Adm. Paper.*]

Nov. 28. Deptford. 98. Chris. Pett and Jonas Shish to the Navy Comrs. Thinks the Fame may be fitted out as a fire-ship. The charge for carpenter's work will amount to 180*l.* [*Adm. Paper, damaged.*]

Nov. 28. Birkland. 99. Capt. Rich. Green to [the Navy Comrs.] The reason Squire Corbin's servant being employed in procuring the land carriage of timber to Bawtry, and in lading the Love hoy for London, is that the expense was so great, and his [Green's] pay so small that he could not possibly subsist upon it; is now able to perform his duties in the wood, and earns 9*s.* a week by it, but is still unpaid many charges. Begs an extra allowance of 4*d.* a load and a man to help him, out of which undertakes to provide all requisites for two waggons. [*Adm. Paper.*]

Nov. 28. Grant to John Goodgroome of the office of Musician in ordinary for the lute and voice, in place of Henry Purcell, deceased; fee, 40*l.* a year. [*Docquet.*]

Vol. CV.

1664.

Nov. 28. Warrants to the Keeper of the White Lion Prison to deliver [John] Clayton to the Gatehouse, and warrant to the Keeper of the Gatehouse to receive him. Minutes. [*Ent. Book* 10, *p.* 285.]

Nov. 28. Isle of Wight. 100. Col. Walter Slingsby to [Williamson]. The fleet, 45 or 46 sail, has got to sea, and there is a fair wind to bring Opdam out; it is now four or five leagues off; five other ships wait at Portsmouth for men and victuals.

Nov. 28. Royal Charles, near Cape La Hogue. 101. Wm. Coventry to Sec. Bennet. The weather has been very bad, but is better. A small Dutch vessel bound for the East Indies reports that their fleet is dispersed—10 to the Vlie, 14 to the Texel, 12 to Zealand, the rest at Helvoetsluys,—and that the Guinea ships have sailed, and will go about Scotland. Asks the certainty of this as soon as possible. The English fleet is too big to be hazarded in winter time for anything less than a fleet of men-of-war; if this news be confirmed, there will be time to think what should be done for Guinea, and to prepare a lusty fleet for the spring.

Nov. 28. Whitehall. 102. Warrant to the Board of Greencloth to allow to the lords and others of the King's servants board wages, in lieu of the diets suspended from September 20, 1663, to October 1, 1664, excepting those to whom they were granted by special warrant out of the 60,000*l.* allotted for the household; the same to be paid from moneys to be assigned for that purpose.

Nov. 29. Whitehall. 103–105. Warrants of protection, by the Committee of Privy Council for the affairs of the Admiralty and Navy, for Thos. Fotherby, master of the Richard, George Moggeson, of the Adventure, and John Rodman, of the Mary, all employed in carrying alum, coals, and other provisions for the King's alum works. Three Papers.

Nov. 29. Whitehall. Reference on the petition of Dame Wingham to Lord Chancellor Clarendon, who is to compose the differences according to justice and equity. [*Ent. Book* 18, *p.* 101.]

Nov. 29. London. 106. Willm. Gomeldon to Sec. Bennet. Finds that the bearer knows nothing about the receiving of certain books; it was his wife's act only; he is a man of fair dealing, but Calvinistical, and will discover the truth.

Nov. 29. Edinburgh. 107. R. Mein to Hen. Muddiman. The cause of the boys' taking this desperate course in their caps was that the captain of the castle set four sentinels to watch the shop doors; several of the boys are imprisoned and some of their masters also; two of those who were wounded are dead. All is quiet now, and no appearance of further tumult. Mr. Annan preached before the Lord Commissioner a sermon on composing all differences.

Nov. 29. Portsmouth. 108. John Tippetts to Sam. Pepys. Particulars of stores received. Sends dimensions for the new ship's furnaces. Links wanted for use on long winter nights. [*Adm. Paper.*]

Vol. CV.

1664.

Nov. 29. 109. Jonas Shish to the Navy Comrs. Demand for rosin. [*Adm. Paper.*]

Nov. 29. Chatham. 110. Commissioner Peter Pett to Sir John Mennes. Progress of ships. [*Adm. Paper.*]

Nov. 29. Dover. 111. Thos. Wale to the Navy Comrs. Has not been on board any of the Dutch prize ships, nor in the storehouse where the goods are landed, nor has received the value of a ropeyarn; so that no blemish can be brought upon the reputation of the board on his account. Offers to make boats, if Tatnell cannot complete the 20 undertaken in the fixed time. [*Adm. Paper.*]

Nov. 30. Deptford. 112. Thos. Cowley to Sam. Pepys. Mr. Shish daily presses him to enter all shipwrights and calkers that offer themselves. Requests directions, having entered as many as warrant was issued for. [*Adm. Paper, damaged.*]

Nov. 30. Deptford. 113. Thos. Cowley to Sir John Mennes. Forwardness of the Nightingale and Forester. Forty soldiers have been sent to be put on board the said vessels. [*Adm. Paper, damaged.*] *Encloses*,

113. i. *Account of the number of men entered on board six ships named.* *Nov.* 30, 1664.

Nov. 30. Westminster. 114. Passport for Hieronymus Nipho from Flanders, who has served the King for many years, to return to his country. [*Latin.*]

Nov. 30. Whitehall. 115. Warrant from Council to the Keeper of the Gatehouse, Westminster, to take into custody John Furley, of Colchester, found to be a favourer and encourager of Quakers in those parts, and to keep him till further orders. With request that Furley may be removed to Newgate, where he can have better accommodation, and attend better to his business, having two ships laden with wine lately arrived. [*Copy.*]

Nov. 30. Whitehall. 116. Warrant to the Governor of Scarborough Castle to receive John Joplin prisoner, for treasonable and dangerous practices. [*Copy.*]

Nov. 30. Minute of the above. [*Ent. Book* 16, *p.* 285.]

Nov. 30. 117. Report by Lord Chancellor Clarendon and the Earl of Anglesey,—on the petition of Jas. Hamilton, groom of the bedchamber,—that he should have a lease for 31 years of Hyde Park, with all buildings therein, the profit of a former grant being much diminished by the commission granted for relief of purchasers, on which many of them had their leases at half the improved rent. *Annexing*,

117. i. *Description of the messuages and tenements in Hyde Park, included in the proposed grant.* [*Three pages.*]

Nov.? 118. Petition of Thos. Throckmorton to the King, for letters mandatory to the University of Cambridge, to grant him his B.C.L.

VOL. CV.

1664.

degree. Was removed many years ago from Westminster school to St. John's College, Cambridge, but his father, Dr. Throckmorton, being undone by loyalty, he was unable to take his degree.

Nov. 30. The King to the Vice-Chancellor of Cambridge. Recommends Thos. Throckmorton, who for loyalty was ejected from the University, for the degree of B.C.L., dispensing with any subsequent services. [*Ent. Book* 19, *p.* 27.]

Nov. 30. Warrant for creating William Cookes, of Norgrave, co. Worcester, a Baronet. Minute. [*Ent. Book* 16, *p.* 285.]

Nov. [30.] 119. Warrant for a commission to James Duke of York, Lord Admiral, to grant letters of marque and reprisal against the subjects of the States General. [*One and a half pages.*]

Nov. 30. Entry of the above. [*Ent. Book* 16, *p.* 286.]

Nov. [30.] 120, 121. Two drafts of the above.

Nov. 30. Licence to John Browne for four Scottish ships to have free trade with the plantations in Asia, Africa, or America, notwithstanding the Act forbidding such trade to any but English vessels, he having been at great expense in setting up works for refining sugar in Scotland. [*Ent. Book* 16, *p.* 286.]

Nov. 30. Licence for Vavasor and Thweng to travel. Minute. [*Ent. Book* 16, *p.* 287.]

Nov. 30. Warrant for a grant to George Viscount Grandison of a moiety of all fines, issues, amerciaments, &c., for three years, except post fines, issues of jurors, and any others which have been formerly granted to the Earl of Berkshire or any other person. [*Ent. Book* 16, *p.* 287.]

Nov. 30. Poole. 122. Will. Skutt to Williamson. A Bremen ship just come in announces that 17 sail of Holland men-of-war came from Goree to winter in the river off Amsterdam; she also met a Dutch man-of-war, who inquired if she had seen none of their men-of-war; she said not, and was glad to get off, telling the Dutchman she was bound for Rouen.

Nov. 30. Yarmouth. 123. R. B[ower] to Henry Muddiman. A vessel from Rotterdam says 40 men-of-war came to sea, and lay to again, waiting the rest of the fleet; they exercise the men in firing. Sickness spreads, if the reports by the searchers of the number of deaths by plague are true, but they are drunken persons and very poor, and may make false returns, because of the large allowance they have for this work.

Nov. 30. Dover. 124. Jo. Carlisle to Henry Muddiman. Asks who will be Commissioners of the Prize Office. There must be one, for though the Hollanders will not fight, their ships are taken daily; there are seven now in harbour, worth 20,000*l.*, and the goods will be embezzled, if care be not taken. If letters of reprisal were granted

VOL. CV.

1664.

to those who have suffered from the Dutch, a rich ship might be taken without a gun shooting. Will fit out a man-of-war if he may be allowed his proportion of what he takes. If the Hollanders wish to come out, the wind is fair for them; but it is reported they will not engage this winter. [*One and a half pages.*]

Nov. 30. St. Helen's Road. 125. Wm. Coventry to [Sec. Bennet]. The Duke was determined to put to sea, as it seemed the critical time when the Dutch must pass, though less resolution than that of the Duke would scarce have carried anybody to sea in such weather. The fleet could not be kept together,—of 40 sail, there are only 11 or 12 with them. The Duke is returning now, supposing the Dutch harbours will be frozen by this time, and also having tidings from several quarters that their fleet is dispersed. All the flag officers that could be gathered on board think that the fleet should return, leaving eight or nine ships out to cruise; but Lord Sandwich and many more are too far leeward to recover port as yet. Rear-Admiral Sansum has just taken a prize laden with brandy and wine. [*Two pages.*]

Nov. 30. Whitehall. Grant to Simon Van Stingalant, a Dutch merchant, of protection, with licence to continue in his residence at College Hill, London, notwithstanding hostilities commenced between the King and the United Provinces, provided he and his family conduct themselves without offence to government. [*Ent. Book* 14, p. 49.]

Nov. 30. Letter to the Lord Treasurer to pay 10,000*l.* out of the Dunkirk money, for the use of the navy. Minute. [*Ent. Book* 17, p. 74.]

Nov. 30. Grant to Edward Progers, groom of the bedchamber, of the lead piping not used, conveying water from the conduit in Bushy Park to the King's stables at Hampton Court, towards the building of his lodge in the North Park. [*Ent. Book* 17, p. 74.]

Nov. 30. 126. Licence to Sir Edward Musgrave, Bart., high sheriff of [Cumberland], to live out of the county during the year of his shrievalty, when his private concerns require his attendance in London. [*One and a quarter pages.*]

Nov. 30. Entry of the above. [*Ent. Book* 17, p. 75.]

[Nov. 30.] 127. Draft of the above.

Nov. ? 128. Petition of Sir John Hanmer, high sheriff of Gloucestershire, to the King, for leave to reside out of the county, except at the assizes and when his attendance is required, as his house there was burned down during the late war, and has not since been made habitable.

Nov. 30. Licences for Sir John Hanmer, sheriff of Gloucestershire, and for the sheriff of Shropshire [Fras. Charleton], to live out of their counties during their shrievalty. Minutes. [*Ent. Book* 17, pp. 75, 76.]

VOL. CV.

1664.

Nov.? 129. Petition of John Strother, of the county palatine of Durham, to the King, for pardon for manslaughter of Ralph Eden at West Auckland, on 9th September last; was attacked by him, though a stranger, and obliged to fight in self-defence.

Nov.? 130. Petition of the Churchwardens and Overseers of St. Margaret's parish, Westminster, to Sec. Bennet, to remind the King to favour the poor of Westminster as well as of St. Martin's, who have 100*l.* a year, whereas they have had nothing since 1661, three years past. Most of Whitehall Court is in St. Margaret's parish, and the numerous poor are increased by soldiers' widows and children, and others who settle there in attendance on Court or Parliament.

Nov. Remittance to those lately promoted to any spiritual benefice, who compounded for first fruits between 6th October, 1663, and 26th March, 1664, of any part of the four clergy subsidies lately granted, during the first year after their compounding. [*Docquet.*]

Nov. Warrant to pay to the Treasurer of the Navy 304,166*l.* 13*s.* 4*d.*, for sea victuals for 25,000 men for one year. [*Docquet.*]

Nov. Warrant to pay to the Treasurer of the Navy 5,000*l.* on account, for sick and wounded men in the present service. [*Docquet.*]

Nov. Warrant to pay to Stephen Fox, paymaster of the forces, 1,300*l.* 0*s.* 2*d.*, for raising a regiment of foot of 1,200 men, besides officers, of which Sir Wm. Killigrew is colonel. [*Docquet.*]

Nov. Warrant to pay to Stephen Fox 1,000*l.* without account, for the King's secret service. [*Docquet.*]

Nov. Warrant to pay to Col. Wm. Legg 37,198*l.* 10*s.*, for 619 tons 19 cwt. 2 qrs. of refined saltpetre brought by the East India Company, the Lord Treasurer to authorize the delivery thereof to the powder maker, by the King's directions. [*Docquet.*]

[Nov.] Note for —— Gardner to be seized. [*Ent. Book* 16, p. 270.]

Nov. Whitehall. 131. The King to [the Highways' Comrs., &c., about London and Westminster]. Recommends John Lawrence as clerk to the Commissioners, instead of Capt. Read, who has lately quitted the place.

Nov. 132. Draft of the above.

Nov. 133. Memoranda [by Williamson] from the Signet books, of warrants, grants, &c., passed during the month, the uncalendared portions of which are as follow:—

> Note that the Greek professorship at Oxford is granted by the King under the great seal for life, the fee of 40*l.* a year being payable by the treasurer of Christ Church.
>
> Grant to Thos. Cooke, on surrender of Sir John Prettyman, of the receivership of first fruits and tenths, fee 20*l.*, on his giving satisfactory security to the Lord Treasurer.

VOL. CV.

1664.

Note that in selling wood, the woodward values the coppice at so much per acre; the timber trees and saplings are usually preserved for the King's use; the underwood and pollards given away.

Appointment of Thos. Middleton as Navy Commissioner, to take charge of and promote the King's service at Portsmouth, and to sign contracts, bills, orders, &c.; fee, 350*l.* a year.

Grant to the Earl of Castlehaven of two thirds of accountants' [arrears] in cos. Oxon, Berks, Wilts, Hants, and Somerset.

Grant to Rich. Pamplin, King's chaplain, of 100*l.* a year for lodgings, from the treasury chamber.

Grant to Wm. Clayton, musician on the treble hautboy, of 66*l.* a year, wages and livery.

Grant to Viscount Dunbar of the manor and bailiwick of Holderness, with other privileges.

Grant to Amice Andros of the office of Bailiff of Guernsey.

Commission to Thos. Elliott and Wm. Smith, for 31 years, to levy and bring in the fines, issues, and forfeited recognizances not yet granted.

Note that Wm. Rosewell, the Queen's apothecary, is paid out of the treasury chamber for all perfumes for her chapel, the bills being approved by one of the physicians, the Lord Chamberlain, or Vice-Chamberlain.

Grant to the executors of Dr. Ferne, bishop of Chester, of discharge from the gift of a horse, bridle and saddle, cloak with a cape, cup with a cover, bason and ewer, gold ring, and kennel of hounds, usually given to the King by the executors of a bishop of Chester.

Grant to Viscount Brouncker of the office of Navy Commissioner; fee, 500*l.* a year.

Note that the messengers of the Queen's chamber have 50*l.* yearly, and her footman 40*l.*, out of the treasury of the chamber.

Nov. ? 134. The King to [the high sheriff of Nottinghamshire]. Orders were issued in Jan. 1663, for the Court of Record for Peverel honour to be held in the Shire Hall of Nottingham, the castle being demolished in the late war, which order was opposed by Thos. Parkins, sheriff of the county, and others employed by him. Orders him, the future sheriffs, and others concerned, to permit the steward to hold his court in the said places, on pain of high displeasure. [*Draft.*]

Nov. ? Sunday. 135. Lord Chancellor Clarendon to Sec. Bennet. The Lord Mayor of London desired to be heard before the Canary merchants' patent was sealed, and came himself. The King had made an order that on renewing all charters of incorporation, the persons should be obliged to be freemen of London, and though it was thought that

1664. VOL. CV.

the order did not reach this case, the merchants consented to it, to avoid delay. Hopes His Majesty will have the patience to let a clause to that effect be inserted in his presence in the signed bill; it will not take half a quarter of an hour, and it infinitely concerns the merchants to have the patent soon sealed. Cannot stir out of his chamber this cruel weather.

[Nov.] 136. H. P—— to John Knowles. Death of learned and pious Mr. Biddle, [the Socinian], from imprisonment in a stinking place at Newgate. Advises him to go to Holland with other friends, as a proper instrument to manage affairs in foreign parts.

[Nov.] 137. Sir John Bennet to [Sec. Bennet]. Chris. Eyres of Northall, Middlesex, is the person to be put into the commission of peace. Sends a request from Lady Petre; also a pattern of velvet fit for lining his coach, price 24s. a yard. [*With the pattern of velvet attached.*] *Encloses*,

137. I. *Lady Petre to Sir John Bennet. Requests him to obtain from his brother a letter of honour for her sister, Jane Chandos, to answer on oath to the interrogatories that may be put to her.* *November* 12, 1664.

Nov. 138. Proposal by John Tatnell for building long boats and pinnaces at Dover, varying from 21s. to 10s. per foot, according to the length of the boats, from 36 ft. to 16 ft. [*Adm. Paper.*]

Nov. Dover. 139. Thos. Wale to the Navy Comrs. Six Holland bottoms are in Dover pier; one laden with salt had to be lightened for want of water to bring her in safely. Has not a spar that will make a cross-jack, which Sir Wm. Penn sent for. The Downs fleet has set sail, and has sent for pilots for the coast of Flanders. [*Adm. Paper.*]

Nov. The Hulk, Plymouth. 140. John Garratt, boatswain, to the Navy Comrs. Complains of men refusing to assist in conveying ballast, &c., to the different ships, because one lighter was lost. Asks leave to require their services. Is ordered to receive on board 150 pressed men from the south of Cornwall, but the constables leave the best at home, and take such as are unfit for service; offers to procure better ones. Condition of the Hulk. Wants money to pay the men for landing ballast. [*Adm. Paper.*]

Nov. 141. Capt. John Fortescue to the Navy Comrs. Note of the delivery of two tuns of train oil at Harwich, at 25*l.* per tun. [*Adm. Paper.*]

Nov. 142. Capt. Pak. Brooke to [Sam. Pepys]. Begs leave to remove the master of the Eagle with himself into the Foresight. [*Adm. Paper.*]

Nov. 143. Estimate by Chris. Pett for building a second-rate ship, 120 ft. by 39½; total, 9,170*l.* 1s. [*Adm. Paper.*]

[Nov.] 144. Estimate by the Navy Commissioners of the expense of building a second-rate ship, 118 ft. by 37½ ft.; total, 9,176*l.* 1s.

VOL. CV.

1664.
Nov. 115. Estimate by Chris. Pett for a third-rate ship, 116 ft. by 34½; total, 6,884l. [*Adm. Paper, two pages.*]

Nov. 116. Note of guns required for the John and Margaret. [*Adm. Paper.*]

Nov. 117. Note of guns wanting for the William, now taken into the King's service. [*Adm. Paper.*]

VOL. CVI. DECEMBER, 1–18, 1664.

1664.
Dec. 1. Saxlwell, near Newmarket. 1. Isaac Thornton to Sec. Bennet. Has secured a young man called Gillet, unknown in those parts, and very like the description in the News-book of Lewis Gardiner, the great cheat. Wishes some one connected with the Post Office to be sent down to view the party.

Dec. 1. 2. Particulars and valuation of Sayes House, Chertsey, and the lands thereto belonging, with note of demands for the sale thereof. [*One and a quarter pages.*]

Dec. 1. Licence for Mrs. Clayton to see her husband. Minute. [*Ent. Book 16, p. 287.*]

Dec. 1. Chatham. 3. Commissioner Peter Pett to Sam. Pepys. Wonders at receiving no answers to his letters concerning "those pitiful pressed creatures "who are fit for nothing but to fill the ships full of vermin." There is a mutiny amongst the shipwrights from London, on account of the tide-money for extra work being stopped during the short days, when they can only work a quarter of an hour extra. Gottenburg masts wanted. [*Adm. Paper.*]

Dec. 1. The Mary, St. Helen's Road. 4. Capt. Jer. Smyth to the Duke [of Albemarle?]. The Duke of York, Prince Rupert, and Sir John Lawson, with 12 sail, came last night into St. Helen's Road; the Earl of Sandwich and the rest are without, hindered by the wind. Has been cruising between the coast of France and the Isle of Wight.

Dec. 2. St. Helen's Road. 5. Wm. Coventry to [Sec. Bennet]. It is evident that the Dutch laid up their vessels to avoid a war, observing that the King bore all they did very patiently, till they talked of going up the Channel in a bravado, on which he began to arm. They, thinking De Ruyter had done their business in Guinea, thought it best not to pass the Channel, expecting that the King would not meddle with their merchantmen, nor their Straits and East India fleet; but finding their merchant ships are taken, De Witt will be unable, with security to his person, to avoid sending out the fleet. The Duke intends to keep the large ships there in a body, and to send the smaller frigates into several stations, to do service upon the Dutch merchantmen. As to Capt. Allin's letters, cannot tell how best to publish that business; thinks what the Committee have resolved to do by the Farmers of Customs is well and sufficient, unless

VOL. CVI.

1664.

for reputation's sake, a few lines were put in the Diurnal, to make it appear that somewhat is done by way of punishment for the last breach of peace. The Duke thinks of coming to London. Finds that the Committee have ordered 8d. a day to be paid to the landlords of the Admiral's regiment; if so, the King will have to provide shoes and clothes. Thinks less than 8d. ought to do for the landlords, and the rest to be paid to the soldiers; for if they touch no money, few but the very scum of England will enter that regiment. The prizes taken as yet are not numerous nor rich. [*Two pages.*]

Dec. 2. Royal Charles, St. Helen's Road. 6. Wm. Coventry and Sir Wm. Penn to the Navy Comrs. Find the seamen on board the Royal Charles wanting clothes, even to the hazard of their health; other ships have fewer still, some none at all. Request the immediate dispatch of the coarser and useful sort of clothing, according to the regulation of Dec. 12, 1663, which has been much abused by the slopsellers. Standards wanted; they are forced to use the silk one upon every occasion, by which it is much impaired already. The Duke orders the Success and Pembroke to be fitted for sea. [*Adm. Paper.*]

Dec. 2. 7. Declaration by Edw. Viscount Conway and Kilultagh, Baron Ragley, of his appointment of James Duke of Ormond and Earl of Brecknock as his proxy in the ensuing Parliament. [*Latin.*]

Dec. 3. Poole. 8. Wm. Skutt to Williamson. Thanks for his weekly intelligence. The Colchester frigate has brought in a Hollander of small value, laden with pan-tiles, which the collector of customs has taken in charge, as ordered by Council, and the captain sent the prize for Portsmouth.

Dec. 3. 9. Statement by Thos. Clarke, that Rob. Nicholas, of Seend, co. Wilts, one of the barons [of Exchequer] to the late usurper, boasted that he drew up the charge against the late King, and would do it again, if needful, for His Majesty is of the Norman race and unfit to reign; desires a warrant against him. With deposition by John Stokes that the words were spoken in May last, behind St. Clement's in the Strand. Sworn before John Coell, master in Chancery. Endorsed with a note that Stokes lives at Seend, Wiltshire, near Devizes.

10. Copy of the former part of the above; dated Nov. 20.

Dec. 3. Norwich. 11. W. N—— to [Hen. Muddiman]. Sends a letter to the wife of Pooly, the only zealot in those parts for several years, and relating also to Tilham, of Colchester. These two have lately been the most notorious Anabaptists in those parts, and the publication of the letter may tend to undeceive many misled people. Much talk of a blazing star seen this morning about 4 or 5 o'clock, streaming towards the west.

11. I. *John Pigeon to [Mrs. Pooly]. Tilham and his confederates' abominable practices have brought reproach on the English there. He is now afraid to show himself,*

VOL. CVI.

1664.

and has employed Chris. Pooly, her husband, to return with reports of plenty and comfort in Germany, and to sell his estate to remove thither. As her husband has taken another wife, advises her not to go. Details of his ill conduct. Advises her to secure what she can of her own property and his to herself and the children. [*Copy.*]
Rotterdam, Nov. 11, 1664.

Dec. 3. Warrant from Sec. Bennet to Sir George Trevelyan, high sheriff of Somersetshire, to convey —— Hill, now in custody of the Mayor of Bridgewater, to the common goal of the county, to be kept close prisoner for treasonable and seditious practices. [*Ent. Book* 16, *p.* 283.]

Dec. 3. Whitehall. 12. The King to [Sir George Crooke, Bt.], high sheriff of Oxfordshire. Understanding that some accidents have befallen him, which will make it inconvenient for him to live in the county, grants him a dispensation to reside elsewhere, so that it be without prejudice to the service. Endorsed "Mr. Titus."

Dec. 3. Copenhagen. 13. Earl of Carlisle to the Navy Comrs. Requests them to repay to the bearer 203*l.* 12*s.* 11*d.*, and lesser sums, laid out in provisions for five weeks for the Centurion, being the ship ordered to transport him to England. [*Adm. Paper.*]

Dec. 3. Ipswich. 14. Certificate by Capt. Pak. Brook of an agreement with Wm. Kerby, master of the George hoy of London, to transport his pressed men to Portsmouth for 20*l.*, of which 5*l.* is paid him. [*Adm. Paper.*]

Dec. 3. The Francis, Hale Haven. 15. Capt. Robt. Turner to the Navy Comrs. Wants victuals. Twelve vessels have arrived from Hamburg. [*Adm. Paper.*]

Dec. 3. Portsmouth. 16. St. J. Steventon to Sam. Pepys. The muster book of the Elias has been mislaid. Begs that no ill censure may be put upon an accident which might befall the most careful. [*Adm. Paper.*]

Dec. 3. Portsmouth. 17. John Tippetts to Sam. Pepys. Will mark out the 100 trees in Col. Norton's woods. Wants an order for felling trees in the New Forest. Ironwork, blocks, and other provisions wanted. [*Adm. Paper.*]

Dec. 3. Royal Charles, Stokes Bay. 18. W. Coventry to [Sec. Bennet]. The master of a prize laden with masts pretends that they are a present sent from the King of Denmark to the King of France. Asks him to find out the truth of this, as the masts would be most useful, and are indeed necessary for the service; the ship has balks, deals, and other very useful goods. The Duke has ordered the fitting out of what fifth-rate frigates there are, to ply in the Channel this winter; some should ply between Beachy and the French coast, others off Cape la Hogue, and others off the Lizard, so that it would be hard for any Dutch vessel to escape.

Dec. 5. Inner Temple. 19. Ri. Powell to Williamson. Sends an account of the King's fourth part of Wildmore Fen, which shows that the new proposition

VOL. CVI.

1664.

is more advantageous than the tripartite articles. If insisted on, the commoners would part with 2,200 acres to the King, and the incloser, which is requisite, as 200 acres are to be given away to some who have been very instrumental in the affair; therefore only mentions the King as likely to have a fourth of the rent of 2000 acres.

Dec. 5. Westminster. 20. W. Symons to Sir Thos. Clifford. Begs the release of poor Mr. Voysey, prisoner in Windsor Castle, who is likely to perish. As to the question of security, will provide such as will satisfy the governor of the castle and the next justice of peace.

Dec. 5? 21. Petition of Thos. Voysey, prisoner in Windsor Castle, to the King and Council, for speedy trial or discharge. Has groaned almost 12 months in prison, with nothing charged, much less proved against him, being never guilty of sedition or disloyalty. Was suspended from his benefice in Oliver's time, for refusing to take the engagement.

Dec. 5. 22. Earl of Sandwich to [Sec. Bennet]. Whilst the Duke was there, had the benefit of his correspondence, and so did not then trouble his honour with accounts. The Colchester has seized three Dutch vessels, but the weather has kept them out of port. Asks whether to proceed in an affair about a relation of Lord Hawley; stayed before from consideration to Lord Fitzharding, but hears that his lordship is now married.

Dec. 5. Chatham. 23. Commissioner Peter Pett to Sam. Pepys. The St. Andrew is brought up; will employ the 60 men appointed as her guard to carry on the service. Asks leave to discharge the pressed men, they being altogether unfit for service, clothed with rags, full of vermin, and one of them even now ill with the small-pox. Would be willingly rid of the unruly London shipwrights. The Guernsey is ready to sail. [*Adm. Paper.*]

Dec. 5. The Ruby. 24. List sent by Wm. Jennens to the Navy Commissioners of 80 men transferred by order of Vice-Admiral Lawson from the Ruby to the Bristol. [*Adm. Paper, three pages.*]

Dec. 5. Deptford. 25. Jonas Shish to the Navy Comrs. Account of the number of shipwrights in Deptford yard, 119; and the several works on which they are employed. Three inch plank wanted. [*Adm. Paper.*]

Dec. 5. Dover. 26. John Tatnell to the Navy Comrs. Promises a speedy supply of the boats contracted for. Requests a letter to the Governor of Dover Castle, to hasten the country people in furnishing waggons. [*Adm. Paper.*]

Dec. 5. Leghorn. 27. Thos. Clutterbuck to the Navy Comrs. Begs speedy relief from his sufferings and loss in victualling Admiral Smith's squadron. The peace with Algiers is laughed at, no satisfaction being given for any damage sustained, but if the Dutch war continue, it may prove advantageous, as the Kings' ships will have the Dutch only to look after. Arrangements with Mr. Gauden concerning the victualling of the fleet. Convenience of the port of Leghorn, for the supply of

VOL. CVI.

1664.

all sorts of provisions. Offers to provide for the garrison, at Tangiers. Requests the discharge of bills due to him. [*Adm. Paper two and a half pages.*]

Dec. 6. 28. Memorandum by Wm. Bodham of the embezzlement of hemp by two workmen in Woolwich ropeyard; several of the inhabitants of Lambeth have passed their word for their appearance before the Board. [*Adm Paper.*]

Dec. 6. Deptford. 29. Thos. Chikle to Robt. Wayte. Discovery of an embezzlement of junk. [*Adm. Paper.*]

Dec. 6. Portsmouth. 30. Ben. Johnson to Sam. Pepys. Sends two bills of lading of ships. Is busy about surveys, estimates, &c., in order to a complete demand for 12 months' supply. [*Adm. Paper.*]

Dec. 6. The Drake, Downs. 31. Capt. Tobias Sackler to the Navy Comrs. Loss of his boat in chasing and capturing a Dutch prize from St. Martin's Island, laden with wine and brandy. [*Adm. Paper.*]

Dec. 6. Whitehall. 32. Promise by the King to Edw. Backwell, that, if —— Muncaster, a goldsmith on trial for gold-clipping, be convicted, and his goods thus forfeited to the Crown, 250*l*. due from him to Backwell shall be granted out of the forfeited estate.

Dec. 6. Plymouth Fort. 33. J. S. [Sir John Skelton] to Williamson. Major Holmes has arrived with one of his prizes, and the other is expected. Capt. Samson, of the Dunkirk, has brought in four prizes, and sent another to Portsmouth. Three Dutch ships came in through contrary winds.

Dec. 6. Newcastle. 34. Rich. Forster to Jas. Hickes. Some small Dutch vessels are reported to be on the northern coasts, and two small ships to have run ashore near Whitby.

Dec. 6. 35. Comparison of two propositions relative to the partition of the profits of the 4,000 acres of Wildmore Fen, Lincolnshire, to be enclosed, between the King and the commoners, showing that, in either case, the King's fourth part will amount to 383*l*. 6*s*. 8*d*. [*Two pages.*]

Dec. 6. Whitehall. 36. The King to [the Lord Treasurer]. On passing the contract with Dan O'Neale for gunpowder, saltpetre was furnished him at 3*l*. 8*s*. the cwt.; wishes that allowance to be made in stating the accounts of powder in the office, till the Ordnance Commissioners entered on their new contract.

Dec. 6. Entry of the above. [*Ent. Book* 17, *p.* 76.]

Dec. 6. Whitehall. 37. Petition of Bevill Skelton, George Amot, and George Coldham, to the King, for a portion, agreeable to their trouble and expense, of the arrears of rent due by the farmers of excise in the late times, and concealed from His Majesty, some of which they have discovered by diligent prosecution and great expense, and will recover for His Majesty at their own expense, or it would be wholly lost. With reference thereon to the Lord Treasurer and Lord Ashley, and report of the latter, November 24, 1660, that one-third should be

VOL. CVI.

1664.

allowed to the petitioners on the said arrears, and that he delayed his report till he had consulted the Commissioners for the Duke of York's revenue, and Prince Rupert, the Duke, and late Queen of Bohemia having moneys charged on those arrears.

Dec. 7. 38. Petition of Sir James Langham to the King, for licence to reside out of the county of Northampton, for which he is chosen sheriff for the ensuing year. Has no habitation there, and resides with his aged father in London.

Dec. 7. Whitehall. 39. Licence to Sir Jas. Langham, sheriff of Northamptonshire, to live out of the county during the year of his shrievalty, he having no convenient dwelling-house there, and his affairs requiring personal attendance.

Dec. 7. Minute of the above. [*Ent. Book* 17, *p.* 75.]

Dec. 7. Whitehall. 40. Warrant for a grant to Maurice Dalndale of 60*l.*, being the moiety of a fine passed against George Brown, linendraper of London, on the statute of usury.

Dec. 7. Entry of the above. [*Ent. Book* 16, *p.* 288.]

Dec. 7. Hull. 41. Luke Whittington to Jas. Hickes. There are, in the harbour, a Swedish ship and five others bound for London. The embargo being removed, several ships laden for Rotterdam and Amsterdam will be ordered to some part of Flanders.

Dec. 7. Plymouth. 42. J. C[larke] to [Williamson]. Five Dutch ships are brought into the harbour, one of which professes to be from Hamburg. Five ships have arrived from westward, three of which are the King's ships from Guinea, under command of Major Holmes, who brings with him his brother and Col. Belasyse from Portugal.

Dec. 7. Warrant to the Navy Commissioners to order Sir George Carteret to pay to Lord Admiral the Duke of York 2,000*l.*, without account, for secret services, towards his preparation for sea. [*Ent. Book* 16, *p.* 289.]

[Dec. 7.] 43. Minute and draft of the above.

Dec. 7. Warrant to John Lord Belasyse to preserve the game within 12 miles of Worley [Worlaby], co. Lincoln. Minute. [*Ent. Book* 10, *p.* 289.]

Dec. 7. Warrant to Lord General Albemarle to restore the King's own troop in the Earl of Oxford's regiment of Horse Guards, [under Lord Hawley], lately reduced, from 70 to 80 effective men, and to continue it at that number. [*Ent. Book* 20, *p.* 39.]

Dec. 7. Whitehall. Commission to Rich. Phillips to be Ensign to the company, late Capt. Newport's, at Portsmouth. [*Ent. Book* 20, *p.* 39.]

Dec. 7. Commission to Paul Bucknam to be Captain of a company in Portsmouth garrison. [*Ent. Book* 20, *p.* 40.]

Dec. 7. Chatham. 44. Commissioner Peter Pett to Sam. Pepys. Sends a certificate, showing the necessity of disposing of the pressed men on board

VOL. CVI.

1664.

the St. Andrew. Asks what is to be done with Fr. Hurdidge, master of the vessel, there being no employment for him now that the ship is in harbour. [*Adm. Paper.*] *Encloses,*

44. I. *Certificate from Fran. Hurdidge, and three others, of the filthy and destitute condition of the 60 pressed men on board the St. Andrew. The St. Andrew, Dec. 6, 1664.*

Dec. 7. Portsmouth. 45. Certificate by John Tippetts, that the second payment of 100*l.* is due to Edw. Silvester, of Gosport, for making and laying a chain at Portsmouth, according to contract. [*Adm. Paper.*]

Dec. 7. Deptford. 46. Thos. Harper and Jonas Shish to the Navy Comrs. Want 20 labourers to be entered for the dockyard. [*Adm. Paper, damaged.*]

Dec. 7. Portsmouth. 47. Commissioner Thos. Middleton to Sam. Pepys. Has sent up a demand for gun wads by Sir Wm. Penn. Sir Wm. Bartlett has brought in 23 or 24 Dutch ships, laden with French commodities. [*Adm. Paper.*]

Dec. 8. Portsmouth. 48. John Barnard to Thos. Hayter. Two hundred and thirty tickets wanted. Hopes to be able to discharge some of the pressed men for better seamen. Part of the Hollanders' Bordeaux fleet is brought in. [*Adm. Paper.*]

Dec. 8. Harwich. 49. John Browne to the Navy Comrs. Sends contracts for blocks and sacking. Mr. Clarke refuses to deliver tallow without an order from Mr. Gauden. [*Adm. Paper.*]

Dec. 8. The Assurance, Portsmouth. 50. G. Buckeridge to Thos. Hayter. His boatswain and gunner refuse to give copies of their indentures. Asks what to do, that he be not prejudiced by their omission. [*Adm. Paper.*] *Encloses,*

50. I. *G. Buckeridge to Thos. Hayter. To the same purport. Downs, November 22, 1664.*

Dec. 8. 51. Wm. Hall to [Sec. Bennet]. "List from the Downs," being note of the King's ships Drake and Paradox, now cruising there.

Dec. 8. 52. Certificate by Paul and Fras. Holmes, that on 19th November last, Wm. Moyes and Thomas [Alleson?] on pretence of a commission from the Earl of Berkshire, took away two trusses of small calves' skins, which were seized at Kutom, in Kent, to the prejudice of Ant. De Premont, the owner.

Dec. 8. York. 53. Sir Fr. Cobb to Sec. Bennet. Sends a letter from Sir Thos. Davidson referring to an order about John Joplin, which he never received, yet will send Joplin to Yarum, whence he can be conveyed to York Castle and kept close prisoner.

Dec. 8. 54. Sir Will Blakeston to Sec. Bennet. John Brackenbury, who was removed from Lincoln to York, for better discovery of the accomplices in the late plot, has been a prisoner ever since, and his creditors take advantage of his poverty to lay arrests on him, which

VOL. CVI.

1664. is not just, he being already the King's prisoner. Begs that he may be removed to Scarborough Castle, where he will be out of the sheriff's custody, and can be disposed of by order of the deputy lieutenants of Yorkshire.

Dec. 9. 55. W. Coventry to Williamson. If Capt. Taylor's commission for Harwich proceed, some press warrants under the great seal will be needed, for the King's service cannot be carried on without power to command workmen, in cases of urgency.

Dec. 9. Whitehall. 56. Order in Council,—referring to the Farmers of Customs the petition of Chris. Moeyer of London, showing that being a young merchant, he imported from France six bags of red wool, which is much used by beaver and felt makers, not knowing that it cannot be imported from France as well as from Spain, and praying pardon and discharge of his goods. With their report, Dec. 14, that the offence being evidently committed in ignorance, the petitioner a fair trader, and the commodities useful in this country, they should be discharged, on a fair compensation to the officers for their care and trouble.

Dec. 9. Warrant to apprehend Alleson, Moyse, &c. Minute. [*Ent. Book* 16, *p.* 288.]

Dec. 9. Warrant to [John] Blundell to discharge John Wilcox and his wife, they having entered in bond. Minute. [*Ent. Book* 16, *p.* 289.]

Dec. 9. 57. Bond of John and Sarah Wilcox, of St. Peter Cornwall's parish, and two others, in 200*l.*, for the good conduct, &c., of the said John and Sarah Wilcox.

Dec. 9. Warrant to [John] Blundell to discharge Elizabeth Ward, widow, upon bond. Minute. [*Ent. Book* 16, *p.* 289.]

Dec. 9. 58. Bond of Elizabeth Ward, of St. Mary Hill's parish, London, and two others, in 200*l.*, that she shall not contrive nor conceal any design against government, and appear before a secretary on three days' summons.

Dec. 9. Oxford. Warrant for a grant to Rich. Acton, in reversion after Rob. Gregy [Gregory ?], of the office of Examiner in the Court of Exchequer for the county palatine of Chester. [*Ent. Book* 16, *p.* 290.]

Dec. 9. Warrant to pay to Ambrose Norton, surveyor of the stables, 960*l.* 8*s.*, for repairs and new paving the stables in the mews. [*Docquet.*]

[Dec.] 9. Lydney. 59. Daniel Furzer to the Navy Comrs. Urges the expediency of selling the offal timber and storehouse in the forest, rather than of being at the great charge of transporting, taking it down, and setting it up again elsewhere. [*Adm. Paper, two pages.*]

Vol. CVI.

1664.

Dec. 9. Edwinstow, Sherwood. 60. John Russell to the Navy Commrs. Particulars of timber. Unreasonableness of Green's demand of 4d. per load extra, beyond his weekly pay. [*See Nov. 28. Adm. Paper, one and a half pages.*]

Dec. 9. 61. W. Coventry to Sam. Pepys. Masters wanted for the Rainbow and Old James, which are ready rigged, and will shortly be ordered into the Hope. [*Adm. Paper.*]

Dec. 9. Plymouth. 62. John Garratt, boatswain of the hulk, to the Navy Commrs. Supplies sent to ships. [*Adm. Paper.*]

Dec. 9. Chatham. 63. Commissioner Peter Pett to Sam. Pepys. Gives the trades to which the pressed men from Whitby, Scarborough, and Yarmouth belong. Scarce one of the number can be made fit for the service. They complain much of the corruption of the press masters, especially Capt. King, who took 3*l.* for the release of one man. Progress of ships. [*Adm. Paper.*]

Dec. 10. Copenhagen. 64. Earl of Carlisle to the Navy Commrs. The Centurion lies ice bound at Copenhagen; unless a day or two alter the weather, will journey by land, making the best provision possible for the ship. Begs reimbursement for the sums already laid out upon it. [*Adm. Paper.*]

Dec. 10. Portsmouth. 65. John Tippetts to Wm. Coventry. Repairs needed on the Henrietta. Proposes felling a few trees in the New Forest on trial. Good ash and holly to be had in the forest of East Bere. Progress of ships. A new broom-house wanted. [*Adm. Paper.*]

Dec. 10. 66. Wm. Coventry to Sam. Pepys. The purser of the Blackamoor refuses to go the voyage; the best expedient is for the captain to indent for victuals. [*Adm. Paper.*]

Dec. 10. Wapping. 67. Sir Wm. Warren to the Navy Commrs. Will accept the offer of 13*l.* 10*s.* His 60 lasts of pitch is most of it in lighters ready to be sent away; asks where to send it. Endorsed "Sir William Warren accepts of 13*l.* 10*s.* per last for 60 lasts of pitch." [*Adm. Paper.*]

Dec. 10. 68. Warrant from the Navy Commissioners to Mr. Harper and Mr. Cowley of Deptford, to cause the pulley-maker of Deptford to make certain blocks undermentioned, and to hasten them on board the Royal Oak. [*Adm. Paper.*]

Dec. 10. Portsmouth. 69. Ben Johnson to Sir Wm. Penn. Demand for iron and brass work. The new storehouse is much wanted; also lighters to unlade the merchant ships. [*Adm. Paper.*] *Encloses*,

69. I. *Account of anchors in store, with their respective weights. Portsmouth, December 10, 1664.*

Dec. 10. Isle of Wight. 70. Col. Walter Slingsby to [Williamson]. Nothing is talked of but the King's wisdom and greatness, the gallantry and conduct of the Duke of York, and the meanness of the Dutch. All are willing

1664. Vol. CVI.

to part with their money, and most to fight; 30 large ships are lying where they can put to sea at any time. A great Dutch fleet, which pursued some English frigates, is gone, but the wind is against them; they will be driven into English harbours, or have to stand and fight. There are 150 sail brought into the several ports between Dover and Plymouth. Informed Lord Colepeper of a great meeting of Quakers to be held; he sent a party, seized two strangers, desperate and profane ranters who came to seduce, and sent them to the castle; such as were inhabitants, he sent to justices of the peace. Some refusing to pay fines, were sent to Bridewell; and one of them, Priscilla Moseley, being ill, died there, rather than pay half-a-crown fine. Has sent the strangers the Koran in English, to read; if it should make them turn Turks it would be a great blow to the whole sect. [*One and a half pages.*]

Dec. 11. *Lydney.* 71. Daniel Furzer to the Navy Comrs. Thomas Skin, seaman of Bream, near Lydney, was pressed into the service by Francis Fletcher, carpenter of the Montague; but after receiving his conduct money, and ticket to appear at Portsmouth in 10 days' time, he has absented himself. [*Adm. Paper.*]

Dec. 12. Chatham. 72. Commissioner Peter Pett to Sam. Pepys. Urges an increase of wages to the storekeeper and his assistants, at the present juncture of time, when so much business is afoot. Mr. Barrow has fixed on another assistant who is unwilling to act under 3s. a day. [*Adm. Paper.*]

Dec. 12. Deptford. 73. Thos. Cowley to the Navy Comrs. Progress of ships. [*Adm. Paper, damaged.*] *Encloses,*

73. i. *List of* 15 *ships now lying at Deptford. December* 12, 1664.

Dec. 12. Deptford. 74. Capt. Wm. Badiley to Thomas Hayter. Account of ships in readiness to take in men and provisions. [*Adm. Paper, damaged.*]

Dec. 12. Chatham. 75. Edw. Gregory to the Navy Comrs. List of 10 ships remaining in that harbour. [*Adm. Paper.*]

[Dec. 12.] 76. Petition of Humphrey Weld, of Lulworth Castle, co. Dorset, to the King, for protection in his rights as lieut.-governor of Portland Isle, and captain of Portland and Sandsfoot Castles, against Lord-Lieut. the Duke of Richmond, who has entered and inventoried the arms in Portland Castle, and taken possession of that of Sandsfoot. Details other grievances and his own services and losses, in burning down of his mansion house, plunder, sequestration, &c., in the late war.

Dec. 12. Reference of the above petition to the Duke of Albemarle and three others, with commendation of the petitioner, as deserving well for his loyalty in the late rebellion. [*Ent. Book* 18, p. 102.] *Annexing,*

76. i. *Report on the above petition by the Duke of Albemarle and three others, Jan.* 13, 1665, *that it would be better for Sandsfoot Castle to be demolished; but that the jurisdic-*

VOL. CVI.

1664.

tion of Portland Isle should remain independent of the county, and free from taxes as before, and the Duke of Richmond should admit Mr. Weld to his former place as deputy lieutenant, on his submission, in consideration of his services and loyalty.

Dec. 12. Whitehall. 77. Pass for Dr. Francisco Guidaloti into France.

Dec. 12. Minute of the above. [*Ent. Book* 16, *p.* 290.]

Dec. 13. Warrant to Sir John Robinson to receive Dr. Johnson prisoner, for treasonable practices. Minute. [*Ent. Book* 16, *p.* 291.]

Dec. 13. Warrant to Blundell to convey Sarah Keat to the Gatehouse. [*Ent. Book* 16, *p.* 291.]

Dec. 13. Warrant to the Keeper of the Gatehouse to receive her. Minute. [*Ent. Book* 16, *p.* 291.]

Dec. 13. Reference to Lord Steward the Duke of Ormond of the petition of Luke Wicks and the Officers of the standing wardrobe, for payment of their board wages and allowance of diet, much in arrears, through retrenchment and delays. [*Ent. Book* 15, *p.* 104.]

Dec. 13. Commission for Fras. Wall to be Ensign to the Duke of York's company in Portsmouth. Minute. [*Ent. Book* 20, *p.* 40.]

Dec. 13. Dover. 78. John Tatnell to the Navy Commrs. A boat wanted for the Drake. Asks a warrant to the Governor [of the Castle] to provide assistance in carrying board for finishing the boats. [*Adm. Paper.*]

Dec. 14. 79. Capt. Wm. Baliley to the Navy Commrs. Gives account of six merchant ships in the river. [*Adm. Paper.*]

Dec. [14?] 80. Short notes by Pepys of five merchant ships in the river, under consideration to be hired for the King's service. [*Adm. Paper, one and a quarter pages.*]

Dec. 14. 81. W. Coventry to Sam. Pepys. Will send a press warrant for shipwrights and calkers. Harwich should be well supplied with materials for cleaning ships, and the hulk cut down on her arrival, as it will not be long before there will be employment enough for them. [*Adm. Paper.*] *Encloses,*

81. I. *John Tippetts to Coventry. Lord Sandwich says 40 ships are to be graved; 20 calkers and 30 shipwrights will be wanted. Proposes building a new broom-house, and a large lighter of 80 tons, to clear the ships of guns, ballast, &c., and to carry timber. Portsmouth, December 13, 1664.*

[Dec. 14.] 82. Proposed Bill in Parliament for relief of the creditors of the Hamburg Company, whose debts amount to 75,113*l.* 13*s.*, besides interest; viz., that all who wish it may hereafter enter the company on payment of a fine, but that no others shall export woollen goods to places within the limits of the charter, on pain of forfeiture, half of which is to go to the discoverers, and the other half towards payment of the company's debts; also imposing an additional duty on all imports from those places made by any but the company, to be applied to the discharge of their debts. [*Eight sheets.*]

Vol. CVI.

1664.

Dec. 14. The King to [the Dean and Chapter of Christ's Church College, Oxford]. Understands that the 20 senior students ought to be in full orders, unless allowed to study physic or the laws; requests indulgence for Fleetwood Shepherd, M.A., who has studied civil law, and is therefore not prepared to take orders, he being a person of much ability. [*Ent. Book* 19, *p.* 27.]

Dec. 14. The King to the [Dean and Chapter of Windsor]. Requests them to admit [Fras.] Ranger to the next vacant place of a Poor Knight of Windsor, on account of his loyalty and faithful services, that some provision may be made for his old age and decayed fortunes. [*Ent. Book* 17, *p.* 78.]

Dec. 14? Whitehall. 83. Warrant to [Brune] Ryves, dean of Windsor and registrar of the Order of the Garter, and to the Canons and Prebendaries of Windsor, to admit Major Fras. Ranger on the first vacancy, to the place of a Poor Knight of Windsor.

Dec. 14. Letter to Winchester College, recommending Edward Ford to be chosen a scholar upon the first vacancy. Minute. [*Ent. Book* 17, *p.* 79.]

Dec. 14. The King to the Dean and Chapter of Westminster. Informs them of his grant to Edward Kenet of the place of an Almsman in the Collegiate Church of St. Peter's, Westminster, and requires their admission of him accordingly. [*Ent. Book* 17, *p.* 79.]

Dec. 14. Warrant to pay to Capt. Fras. Berkeley 100*l.* out of every 1,000*l.* paid into the privy purse for fines on uncustomed goods. [*Ent. Book* 16, *p.* 290.]

Dec. 14. Warrant for a grant to Sir John Robinson of the goods and estate of Wm. Muncaster, convicted of petty treason at the Old Bailey for clipping coin. [*Ent. Book* 16, *p.* 290.]

Dec. 14. Commissions to Commissioner John Taylor and Commissioner Thos Middleton to take up carpenters, shipwrights, calkers, ropemakers, smiths, &c., for the King's service. Minutes. [*Ent. Book* 16, *p.* 291.]

Dec. 14. Whitehall. 84. Warrant to Sir Jordan Crosland, governor of Scarborough Castle, to take into custody John Brackenbury, for treasonable practices, and to keep him safe prisoner.

Dec. 14. Entry of the above. [*Ent Book* 16, *p.* 291.]

Dec. 14. Warrant to Sir John Robinson to receive —— Green for dangerous practices. Minute. [*Ent. Book* 16, *p* 293.]

Dec. 14. 85. Petition of the Merchants trading to the Canaries to the King. On publication of the proclamation for Canary wines not to be sold beyond 26*l.* the pipe, tried to procure incorporation, to prevent the coming in of a multitude of new traders, and to enable them to keep down the price of wines, but the delays of the farmers of customs in their reports, &c., have prevented the preparation of the charter, and this year more ships have been sent from new

VOL. CVI.

1664.

traders than ever before. Entreat exemption this year from the severity of the wine prizers, and competent profits, hoping next year, by virtue of a Royal charter, to bring down the prices. Signed by Sir Art. Ingram, Sir Wm. Throckmorton, John Turner, and Nich. Warren. Marked "Nothing done."

Dec. 14. Madrid. 86. Capt. Sam. Carrington to the King. Offers to come over to England or Flanders, bringing with him some fireworks which would in half an hour destroy any vessel belonging to His Majesty's enemies, either under or above water, or their custom houses, according to plans never yet put in execution by any man. Will want one assistant, his disbursements paid, money for his journey, and a safe conduct, on account of his debts of 3,000*l.* in England, owing to losses in His Majesty's service in Barbadoes, &c., in 1649 and 1650. Served at Whitehall in the trained bands in 1660, but was forced to fly for debt; has since had a share in a vessel acting under the King of Spain's commissioner, but his partners tried to defraud him of his share, and at length the ship was lost. [*Four pages.*]

Dec. 15. 87. Renaldo Knapton to Sec. Bennet. Asks favour in his behalf as gaoler of Dorset; fears the gaol may be delivered to the new sheriff, and he lose the favour of continuance in office. Will give information about Dorchester, tending to the peace of government.

Dec. 15. 88. Estimate [by the Navy Commissioners] of the charge of providing sea victuals for 5,000 men, for a year; total, 60,833*l.* 6*s.* 8*d.*

Dec. 15. 89. Proposed Act for granting a Royal aid of 2,477,500*l.* to be raised in three years. Endorsed with many later memoranda [by Williamson] relative to the proportions of the monthly payments of the 600,000*l.* to be appropriated to building of ships, &c. [*One and a half pages.*] *Annexing,*

89. I., II. *List of the several counties of England and Wales, and proportion of the aid to be paid by each; with similar memoranda relative to the tax of* 600,000*l.* [*Two papers, three and a half pages.*]

Dec. 15. Deptford. 90. Jonas Shish to the Navy Comrs. The launch is being fitted up according to order. Requests the King's hoy to be sent for six freights of chalk, which may be had for the fetching, and which will serve for making good the ground; 60 tar barrels are wanted for the four fire ships. [*Adm. Paper, damaged.*]

Dec. 15. Dover. 91. Thos. Wale, shipwright, to the Navy Comrs. No one will undertake to tow the two long boats in his custody to Chatham, without hawsers and grapnells. Requests an order to press a hoy and receive hawsers and anchors from some of the prizes. [*Adm. Paper.*]

Dec. 15. Painters' Hall. 92. Sir Wm. Doyley, Sir Thos. Clifford, and Col. Bullen Reymes, Commissioners for the sick and wounded, &c., to the Navy Comrs. Request assistance in distributing their printed instructions

1664. VOL. CVI.

amongst the commanders of the fleet, that proper certificates may be given to all sick or wounded persons sent on shore for cure. [*Adm. Paper.*]

Dec. 16. Harwich. 93. Anthony Deane to the Navy Comrs. Purchase of timber. Arrival of the Rosebush. A small boat wanted for her. [*Adm. Paper.*]

Dec. 16. Harwich. 94. Wm. Baker, boatswain, to Sir Wm. Batten. Arrival of the Rosebush. Wants provisions for fitting her for a bulk, and a house for himself to live in. [*Adm. Paper.*]

Dec. 16. Chatham. 95. Commissioner Peter Pett to Sam. Pepys. There is more fear of a sudden want of timber than of shipwrights, when the third-rate frigate and Victory begin to be built and repaired. The Unicorn is iron-sick under water. Cannot part with any of the Yarmouth small cordage. [*Adm. Paper.*]

Dec. 16. 96. Statement that Ralph Emerson, of Gateshead, exchanged two barrels of sturgeon for plated half crowns, at the rate of 27s. 6d. for 20s. on the price of sturgeon; also account of 20 other persons, in or about Gateshead, Ovington, Newcastle, Raby, and North Shields, engaged in coining, clipping, or selling false coin. [*Three pages.*]

Dec. 16. Whitehall. 97. Warrant to Lord Mordaunt, constable of Windsor Castle, to discharge [Thos.] Voysey, prisoner there, on security for his appearance before two justices of peace. *Annexing,*

97. I. *Blank bond of [Thos.] Voysey in 500l. not to abet any design to the disturbance of the kingdom, and particularly not to frequent nor encourage any unlawful meetings or assemblies.* *December* 1664.

Dec. 16. Entry of the above warrant. [*Ent. Book* 16, p. 294.]

[Dec. 16.] 98. Draft of the above.

Dec. 16. 99. Minutes of documents relating to naval affairs, containing, in addition to those calendared above, the following:—

Letter to the Duke of York to lay an embargo on all ships in His Majesty's ports, except such as carry fish abroad, trade from port to port, the East India ships, and such as may have special passes. October 28.

Commission appointed for the sick and wounded. October 28.

Order for 1,200 land soldiers to be raised for the fleet. October 28.

Note of the latitude of powers allowed for Admiralty and Navy affairs. November 11.

Letters to the chief magistrates of several ports and maritime towns, to assist the Commissioners of the sick and wounded in providing quarters for prisoners at war. November 11.

Vol. CVI.

1664.

Letter to the Governors of St. Bartholomew's and St. Thomas's Hospitals, Southwark, for the reception of the sick and wounded. November 11.

Instructions for the Commissioners of sick and wounded. November 11.

Orders to the Justices of Peace to make out lists of seamen in their respective precincts, with their names and ages. November 18.

Order for all pitch and tar from Virginia and Maryland to be custom free for five years, in order to encourage the planters to apply themselves to commodities more beneficial than tobacco. November 25.

Order for all perishable goods taken from the Dutch to be valued in presence of the master or chief officers of the ship, and of the mayor or chief officer of the place where they are brought in, and then sold by the candle. November 30.

Order for all goods entered as Dutch goods to be seized. November 30.

Order for the farmers of Customs to pay Dutch prisoners the allowance of 20s. to a master, 15s. to an officer, and 10s to a common seaman, out of the product of perishable goods. December 2.

Order for all Dutch prize goods useful for the navy to be sent to the stores, after being surveyed, appraised, and inventoried, and in case they are not prize and are consumed in the service, for satisfaction to be made. December 7.

Order for the Savoy Hospital to be fitted up for the sick and wounded. December 14.

Letter to the Justices of Peace about carriage of ship timber in the Forest of Dean. December 16.

Order for the embargo of ships to be renewed *sine die*, leaving out the clause in favour of transporting fish. December 16.

Order of Council about general reprisals. December 16.

Letter to the Lord Deputy and Council of Ireland about imparting 1,000 men for the King's present service. December 16.

Order for method to be observed in impressing seamen. December 16.

Order for provisions for Landguard Fort. December 16.

Commission to the Lord Admiral, touching granting letters of marque.

Articles and Instructions for such as take out letters of marque and reprisal. December 16. [*Two and a half pages.*]

VOL. CVI.

1664.

Dec. 16. 100. Copy of the last six entries; endorsed with a note that Col. Hen. Norwood bought a vessel at Dunkirk while the town was in the King's possession; that after the town was parted with, it was questioned whether the vessel was free or not, but ordered in Council that it should be inserted into the list in the Exchequer as free, February 3, 1664.

Dec. 16. 101. Request by Sir Willm. Godolphin for 200*l*., for repair of St. Mary's Castle, Scilly Isles; also for six months' pay for supply of provisions in advance, in case of surprise from the enemy or bad weather; also for 1,000*l*. for raising another fort to defend the place, and for ordnance supplies as specified in a report to the Master of Ordnance in 1663. [*One and a quarter pages.*]

Dec. 16. Whitehall. 102. Declaration that on account of the wrongs offered by the Dutch East and West India Companies to British subjects, the King has resolved that letters of reprisal be granted, by commission to Lord Admiral the Duke of York, against the subjects of the States General, all vessels to be brought to judgment in the Admiralty Court, and the crews seized and taken into custody. [*Copy.*]

Dec. 16. Reference to Lord Treas. Southampton on the petition of John Gerlington, late high sheriff for Lancashire, for remission of 1,545*l*. 11*s*. due by him to His Majesty, as collector of the stoves (hearth-money),—he being forced to make use of the money, on account of heavy debts contracted upon him by his late father. [*Ent. Book* 18, *p.* 105.]

Dec. 16. Grant to Wm. Cookes, of Norgrave, co. Worcester, of the dignity of a Baronet, with discharge in the usual form of 1,095*l*. due in respect of that dignity. [*Docquet.*]

Dec. 16. Commission for John Knight to be Surgeon-General of all the forces in England and Wales. Minute. [*Ent. Book* 20, *p.* 40.]

Dec. 16. Whitehall. 103. Warrant for a grant to Hen. Earl of St. Alban's and other trustees of the Queen-Mother, of several lands, tenements, &c., which they now hold in hand for her, for two years after her decease, the profits thereof to be bestowed as she may appoint by her will or other writing. [*Two pages.*]

Dec. 16. Entry of the above. [*Ent. Book* 16, *p.* 294.]

Dec. 16. The King to Robt. Swain, high sheriff of Dorsetshire. Had recommended to his predecessor, by letters of 13 June last, Reynald Knapton to be keeper of the county gaol, in place of [John] Wilson, who is disaffected and unfit therefor, but understands that he has resolved to restore Wilson and displace Knapton. Points out the ill consequence to public affairs of changing an officer approved for loyalty, and requests his continuance. [*Ent. Book* 17, *p.* 80.]

[Dec. 16.] 104. Draft of the above.

VOL. CVI.

1664.

[Dec. 16.] 105. Case of the Tobacco-pipe Makers, addressed to Parliament; showing the great improvement in their trade, since their incorporation, 17 James I., and their threatened ruin because cooks, bakers, alehouse keepers, and others make pipes, but so unskilfully that they are brought into dis-esteem: they request to be comprehended in the statute of labourers, of 5 Eliz., so that none may follow the trade, who have not been apprentices seven years. [*Printed.*]

Dec. 17. Warrant [from Sec. Bennet] for cordage brought from Holland to Yarmouth to be landed. [*Ent. Book* 16, *p.* 205.]

Dec. 17. Portsmouth. 106. Comr. Thos. Middleton to Sam. Pepys. The pursers of several ships complain, and claim allowance for the loss of beer drunk by the workmen on board whilst in harbour. Tender of oars. Account of oak and beech timber in the New Forest. The Henrietta is in port; accommodation wanted to unlade her. The two lighters ordered to be built will be very convenient for the dispatch of business. [*Adm. Paper, one and a quarter pages.*] *Encloses,*

106. I. *Certificate by Thos. Eastwood of the fitness of 500 or 600 oaks, and 50 or 60 beeches in the New Forest, for the King's service.*

Dec. 17. 107. List of 31 shipwrights and 20 calkers impressed for Portsmouth. [*Adm. Paper.*]

Dec. 17. 108. Account of 14 ships at Blackwall docks fit for the King's present service. [*Adm. Paper.*]

Dec. 17. Portsmouth. 109. John Tippetts to the Navy Comrs. Commissioner Middleton approves the building of lighters for clearing the ships, to be commenced as soon as may be. The oak and beech trees in the New Forest should be felled before spring, as they will be much the worse if felled when the sap rises. Two anchors wanted. [*Adm. Paper.*]

Dec. 17. 110. Note that Sir John Packington was afraid of a reported intended rising of Papists in Worcestershire, but denied the truth of the report to Sir Hen. Puckering.

Dec. 17. The Plymouth, Bay of Bulls. 111. Capt. Thos. Allin to [Sir Rich. Fanshaw]. Is hindered taking a dozen great Dutch ships by twos and threes, because only allowed to attack their men-of-war or their Smyrna fleet, and that not in Spanish ports. Details a chase of the Dutch fleet, during which, owing to the darkness, several of his company of nine vessels ran ashore, two were lost, and others damaged. The Governor of Gibraltar refused them assistance. [*Copy, two and a half pages.*]

Dec. 18. 112. Earl of Sandwich to [Sec. Bennet]. Thanks for his return to inquiries about the lady; thought Lord Fitzharding, who is now married, was the only person concerned, but hearing that others also are candidates with the King's recommendation, will suppress any thought that may deviate from His Majesty's pleasure.

VOL. CVII. DECEMBER 19–31, 1664.

1664.

Dec. 19. Harwich. 1. Anthony Deane to the Navy Comrs. Particulars of timber stores wanted for the Rosebush. Arrival of the Golden Star from Sherwood. [*Adm. Paper.*]

Dec. 19. 2. Thos. Wale to the Navy Comrs. A boat was found by two fishermen from Folkstone, supposed to be the long boat of the Drake. The men desire an allowance for salvage, and will deliver her at Dover. Wishes the boats of prizes were on their decks; they form bridges to sally on at low water, and lead to stealing of ropes, brandy, &c. Requests that an Emden ship, now in harbour, may be fitted as a man-of-war, and put under his command. [*Adm. Paper.*]

Dec. 19. Dover. 3. John Tatnell to the Navy Comrs. Richard Hall of Folkstone, the fisherman who found the drift boat supposed to belong to the Drake, refuses 2*l.* 15*s.* for salvage. [*Adm. Paper.*]

Dec. 19. Chatham Dock. 4. Phin. Pett and Jos. Lawrence to [the Navy Comrs]. Commissioner Pett's creek is convenient for laying in masts and boats, and well worth 5*l.* per annum. [*Adm. Paper.*] *Encloses,*

4. I. *Blank form for receipt of rent due to Commissioner Peter Pett, for a creek in the dock at Chatham.*

Dec. 19. Deptford. 5. Capt. Wm. Badiley and two others to the Navy Comrs. A hundred shipwrights and calkers additional, and the materials before ordered will suffice for the speedy fitting up of the ships which are to sail. The Charity and Speedwell, being out of repair, will require a longer time. [*Adm. Paper, damaged.*] *Encloses,*

5. I. *Abstract of Thos. Harper's demand for provisions required for fitting up ships; with note by Peter White of receipt of two copper furnaces.* *19th Dec.*, 1664.

Dec. 20. Portsmouth. 6. Capt. James Alleson to Sam. Pepys. Has sent ashore, by order of the Earl of Sandwich, the bread from the Assurance, damaged by being kept in the damp. [*Adm. Paper.*]

Dec. 20. Hamburg. 7. F. B. to Mr. Slather, merchant in Fenchurch Street. Information of a fire in the tar house at Stockholm, whereby that commodity will rise much in price; also of the departure of the Earl of Carlisle in the Centurion. [*Adm. Paper.*]

Dec. 20. 8. Articles of agreement between the Navy Commissioners and Capt. Hen. Risby and the other Owners of the Coast frigate, whereby the said ship is entered upon the King's service for six months certain, from Jan. 16, 1665, at 150*l.* per calendar month. [*Adm. Paper.*] *Annexing,*

8. I. *Certificate by Capt. John Fortescue, that the Coast frigate, hired for the King's service, is completely equipped as a man-of-war, according to contract.* *January* 16, 1665.

8. II. *John Kirke, boatswain, to Capt. Hen. Risby. Arrival of*

VOL. CVII.

1664.

the Coast frigate in Sole Bay. An anchor wanted; begs him to send one, as he (the captain) is much threatened if they do any damage.
Sole Bay, July 4, 1665.

8. III. *Note of acknowledgment by Henry Bingham, of 12 cwt. of junk received from John Kirke, boatswain of the Coast frigate.* *August 16, 1665.*

8. IV. *Certificate by Wm. Trahearne, that the Coast frigate was cleared out of the King's service, and delivered to the owners December 13, 1665.*

1664? Dec. 21. 9. Statement that certain receivers have not fulfilled their engagement to show up their weekly accounts. Endorsed "Mr. G. Porter's proposition."

1664. [Dec.] 21. Letter to Lord Herbert of Ragland for raising the proportions for cos. Hereford and Gloucester of the 70,000*l*., for the present year. Minute. [*Ent. Book* 20, *p.* 41.]

[Dec. 21.] 10. Warrant to pay to Stephen Fox 10,000*l*. out of the moneys in the Tower remaining from the sale of Dunkirk, for a particular service which cannot without prejudice wait a supply from the ordinary revenue.

Dec. 21. Minute of the above. [*Ent. Book* 17, *p.* 81.]

Dec. 21. 11. Warrant for a grant to Eleanor, daughter of the late Sir Edw. Villiers, of the rent of 300*l*. a year, arising out of the New River waterworks, for 41 years, in reversion after a previous patent for a grant of the same, for 31 years, to John Robinson. [*Two pages.*]

[Dec. 21.] 12. Clause stating that the said patent was granted to John Duckworth on surrender of John Robinson.

Dec. 21. Similar warrant, corrected according to the additional clause, and adding that the grant is to be passed as a future interest, not a reversion. [*Ent. Book* 16, *p.* 290.]

Dec. 21. 13. Draft of the above. [*One and a half pages.*]

Dec. 21. Pass for Mr. Oudart. Minute. [*Ent. Book* 16, *p.* 296.]

Dec. 21. Privy seal for 60,833*l*. 6*s*. 8*d*., for 5,000 men's victuals for a year. Minute. [*Ent. Book* 16, *p.* 297.]

Dec. 21. Order for a warrant to pay to Sir George Cateret 1,306 0*s*. 8*d*. a month, for the service of the Admiral's regiment under the command of Sir William Killigrew, from 26 Nov. last. [*Ent. Book* 16, *p.* 297.]

Dec. [21.] 14. Draft of the above. [*One and a half pages.*]

Dec. 21? 15. Warrant dormant for payment, from time to time, of the sums due to the Admiral's regiment under Sir Wm. Killigrew, according to the establishment lately signed, and the muster-rolls.

VOL. CVII.

1664.

Dec. 21. Warrant to Viscount Fitzharding to order yearly payment of 40*l.* salary to Alex. Man, whom the King has appointed his coffee-maker, to provide and prepare coffee for the Royal person. [*Ent. Book* 16, *p.* 297.]

[Dec. 21.] 16. Draft of the above.

Dec. 21. The King to Col. Edw. Villiers, steward of Richmond Manor. He is to order Edw. Wilkins to forbear the erection of a brew-house in Richmond, which would greatly annoy the neighbourhood, and to give an account of Wilkin's compliance therein. [*Ent. Book* 16, *p.* 298.]

[Dec. 21.] 17. Draft of the above.

Dec. 21. Warrant for creating Sir Jo. Jacob, of Bromley, a Baronet. Minute. Marked Sir Thos. Ingram. [*Ent. Book* 16, *p.* 298.]

Dec. 21. Warrant for creating Thomas Taylor, of Park House, parish of Maidstone, a Baronet. Minute. [*Ent. Book* 16, *p.* 299.]

Dec. 21. Warrant from Sec. Bennet, prohibiting all stationers and printers from printing certain Greek and Latin school-books, until the differences touching a grant to John Seymour of the same be finally determined; caveats having been entered against the passing of the said grant, needless delays are made in coming to a hearing, in order to frustrate the benefit designed to Mr. Seymour. [*Ent. Book*, 16, *p.* 298.]

Dec. 21. Portsmouth. 18. Commissioner Thos. Middleton to Sam. Pepys. The Dutch vessels are to be unladen, and fitted for taking in provisions, ordnance, &c., according to the Earl of Sandwich's order. Requests directions for the disposal of cordage and tar found in some of them. Tender of pitch. Money wanted. Particulars of stores wanted. Complains of the London boats and blocks. The purser of the Henrietta asks what to do with the brandy, cider, &c., on board, and with the boatswain and carpenter's stores. The distance of the writer's house in Portsmouth from the dock hinders the performance of duty, and is prejudicial to health. [*Adm. Paper, three and a half pages.*]

Dec. 21. Harwich. 19. John Browne to the Navy Comrs. Demand for stores. Three vessels from Sherwood have arrived. [*Adm. Paper.*]

Dec. 21. 20. Certificate by Jonas Shish and three others, of the fitness of John Young, master carpenter of the Hound, to serve in any of the King's ships; with note by James Colman, 3rd Aug., 1665, that John Young is an able seaman, and a stout man in the face of the enemy. [*Adm. Paper.*]

Dec. 21. Spithead. 21. Capt. John Tyrwhitt, of the Providence, to Sir Wm. Batten. Sends his boatswain's accounts. Must put into Plymouth for want of a mainsail. [*Adm. Paper.*]

Dec. 22. Chatham. 22. John Brooke to the Navy Comrs. The Rainbow has sailed from Gillingham. Progress of ships. [*Adm. Paper.*]

VOL. CVII.

1664.

Dec. 22. Navy Office. 23. Navy Comrs. to the Officers of the Yard at Chatham. The hemp on board the John and Margaret is to be received into the stores, preserved from damage, made serviceable for the navy, and a report returned of the quantity, and of the loss by the damage. [*Adm. Paper.*]

Dec. 22. Warrant to pay to Fras. Bowman 416*l.* 18*s.*, and 849*l.* 10*s.* 10*d.*, for stationery furnished for Secs. Nicholas and Bennet, from December 20, 1660, to September 14, 1663. Minute. [*Ent. Book* 10, p. 295.]

Dec. 22. Whitehall. 24. Sec. Bennet to Lord Treas. Southampton. The enclosed petition was brought by some of the King's household servants, who might have accompanied it by indecent clamour, if the lord steward had not appeased them with good words. Before moving His Majesty to a reference on the petition, wishes to know whether his lordship is in a condition to pay the board wages. *Encloses,*

24. I. *Petition of His Majesty's Servants above stairs to the King, for board-wages from Michaelmas 1663 to Michaelmas 1664, as allowed to the Board of Greencloth and other below stairs' servants.*

Dec. 22. Warrant to the Ordnance Commissioners to deliver to Lord Chancellor Clarendon six iron sakers and six iron minions, for himself and partners, for the use of Carolina in the West Indies. [*Ent. Book* 20, p. 41.]

Dec. 22. Lowther. 25. Sir Jo. Lowther to Sec. Bennet. Fearing the obstinacy of the party not to discover truth, had recourse to a letter of Mrs. Fell, widow of Judge Fell, a great patroness of those opinions, and found that E. B. is E. Beedell [Biddle], which agrees with the confession of Howgill, who was attainted last assizes in a præmunire, though the latter speaks of E. B. as a woman, whereas Mrs. Fell mentions E. Beedell as a man and a writer of books. There was a London merchant, Beedell, very active in behalf of that party. John Pennyman, half brother to Sir Jas. Pennyman, knows much of their affairs. They are dangerous people, very active, vigilant and obstinate, and numerous in those parts, where the seeds were first sown by Fox and Nayler. Has proceeded against 20 or 30 on the Conventicle Act, and if encouraged, will sentence them to banishment. Asks to what plantation they should go. The gentry are unanimous in a wish to serve His Majesty. *Encloses,*

25. I. *Thos. Gabetis to Sir John Lowther, Bart. The party concerned confessed that a certain letter came from Esther, wife of Thos. Biddle, in the Old Change, he being in the Fleet and she in Bridewell. Could get nothing further from him but impertinent replies. December 21, 1664.*

Dec. 23. 26. Report by Attorney General Palmer, on the competition between Sir James Smith and Sir Edw. Heath concerning Mendip,—that they are suitors for the same thing, though one calls it waste or common, the other manor and demesnes, and detailing his previous reports on the petitions of both parties, in favour of the grants solicited.

VOL. CVII.

1664.

Dec. 23. 27. Minute of a patent to be drawn for Wm. Lord Crofts and Eliz. his wife, of a pension of 1,500*l.* a year, with survivorship.

Dec. 23. 28. Gilbert Thomas, provost marshal, to Wm. Lord Craven. Fears that Mr. Ward, by whose orders he is to act, does not intend to carry on his design faithfully, nor act as he should do. *Encloses,*

28. I. *Reasons for doubting lest Ward fail in performance of his trust; viz.,—that on numerous occasions detailed between 28th November and 20th December, Ward pretended to lead or instruct him in the apprehension of several of the traitors, but the plan always failed, from the parties escaping, the force being insufficient, Ward urging that it would lead to discovery, or some other pretext. Believes that he is intending to get them on shipboard, and let them transport themselves abroad. [Three pages.]* *Dec. 23, 1664.*

Dec.? 29. Account by John Ward of the most eminent Quakers, Anabaptists, and Nonconformists concerned in the plot of 1663, who are now in the county palatine of Durham. Also statement that Mr. Scurr, of Leeds, worth 700*l.* a year, relieved and maintained the plot prisoners in York gaol so well that they said they never lived better, and by his subtilty and means, got them all, including himself, released. Wm. Hotchin, now in the same gaol with himself for not paying tithes, had four horses in readiness. [*Two pages.*]

Dec. 23. Commission to John Taylor to press carpenters, shipwrights, ropemakers, smiths, mariners, soldiers, &c., for service of the navy; and to take up ships and boats at reasonable prices. [*Docquet.*]

Dec. 23. Warrant to pay to Stephen Fox 3,470*l.* 4*s.* a year, for the garrisons of the Scilly Isles, Trescoe and St. Mary's Castle, to begin from Midsummer last. [*Docquet.*]

Dec. 23. Genoa. 30. Notice by William Ellam, resident at Genoa, of his having shipped a cask of wine for Jos. Williamson, to be delivered on his paying 20*s.* freight. [*Printed form with MS. insertions.*]

Dec. 23. Reference to Lord Treas. Southampton on the petition of John Peebles, of Dewsbury, for a grant of the forfeitures and penalties which shall accrue from constables and others in the city of York, for concealing hearths, he having done good service in the discovery of the late plots in the north. [*Ent. Book 18, p. 109.*]

Dec. 23. [Chatham.] 31. Commissioner Peter Pett to Sam. Pepys. Wants six anchors. [*Adm. Paper.*]

Dec. 23. Harwich. 32. John Browne to the Navy Comrs. Watch bells wanted. The Love hoy is arrived from Sherwood, but there is no warrant to unlade her. Complains of the delay caused by not sending letters direct from Colchester, but round by Ipswich, where they wait tide and weather, and only come once or twice a week. [*Adm. Paper.*]

VOL. CVII.

1664.
Dec. 24. Portsmouth. 33. Commissioner Thos. Middleton to Sir Wm. Batten and Sir John Mennes. Begs that able seamen, boatswains, carpenters, &c., may be sent down from London, as it is impossible to procure them at Portsmouth. Detection of fraud in a boatswain and captain. Will endeavour to make the house now building for him convenient, at as little charge as if it were upon his own account. [*Adm. Paper, one and a half pages.*]

Dec. 24. Portsmouth. 34. Commissioner Thos. Middleton to Sam. Pepys. Requests directions concerning the disposal of the Guinea provisions. Is much troubled at the news from Guinea, though not concerned in the company. His rule for contentment is "not to be troubled at two things—one, what a man can help, the other what he cannot help." [*Adm. Paper, one and a half pages.*]

Dec. 24. Portsmouth. 35. Hugh Salisbury to Sir Wm. Batten. The launch of the new ship is put off. Tender of 1,000 double barrels of blacking, at 15*d.* the barrel. Three Dutch prizes sent in by the fleet. Arrival of the Augustine at St. Helen's. [*Adm. Paper.*]

Dec. 24. 36. Jonas Shish to the Navy Comrs. Repairs of ships. Timber wanted; 111 anchors are started, and 30 more ready. [*Adm. Paper, damaged.*]

Dec. 24. Warrant to John Wilson, messenger, to apprehend Leonard Seurr. Minute. [*Ent. Book* 16, *p.* 209.]

Dec. 24. Warrant for a commission to Sir Henry Bennet to be Comptroller of all manner of prize ships and goods, adjudged in the Admiralty Court to belong to the King; he is to assist the Commissioners, have what officers he requires under him, keep counterparts of all indentures, inventories, &c., and accounts of all expenses. [*Ent. Book* 16, *pp.* 299–300.]

Dec. 24. Warrant for a commission to Anthony Lord Ashley to be Treasurer of the prize goods, paying all salaries and expenses; the balance to be paid to the Exchequer, or to the Navy Treasurer or Lieutenant of Ordnance on warrants. [*Ent. Book* 16, *pp.* 300–1.]

[Dec. 24.] Memorandum that the warrant to the Navy Committee to be Commissioners for prize goods is endorsed in the book of commissions, instructions, &c. [*Ent. Book* 16, *p.* 301.]

Dec. 24. Westminster. 37. Grant of denization to Lawrence Du Puy, an alien. [*Latin.*]

Dec. 25. The Plymouth, Cadiz Bay. 38. Capt. Thos. Allin to [Sir Rich. Fanshaw]. On the 19th, attacked with his 7 ships left, a Dutch fleet of 14, three of which were men-of-war; sunk two vessels, and took two others, one a rich prize from Smyrna; the others retired much battered. Has also taken a Dutch prize laden with iron and plank, coming from Lisbon. Is waiting the repair of the Bonaventure, damaged off Gibraltar. The Dover, sailing for Tangiers, has taken three prizes. [*Copy, one and a half pages.*]

VOL. CVII.

1664.

Dec. 26. Covent Garden. 39. De Leyenbergh, Swedish agent, to Sir John Robinson, Lieutenant of the Tower. Begs the release of Arthur Rose, carpenter, pressed out of the Charles of Gottenburg; though an Englishman, he has been a citizen of Gottenburg for 14 years, has his wife and children there now, and is consequently a subject of Sweden. Begs also that the bond given in security for him may be discharged; with note of an order [by the Navy Commissioners] for his release. [*Adm. Paper, two pages.*] *Encloses,*

39. i. *Attested certificate by Geo. Simmion, pressmaster of Languard Fort, of his having impressed Arthur Rose, carpenter and free burgher of Gottenburg, and taken a bond of 40l. for his clearing.* *November 31 (sic), 1664.*

Dec. 26. Harwich. 40. Anthony Deane to the Navy Comrs. Purchase of timber. Stores wanted. Repairs of the Rosebush. It is eight or ten days before they can have an answer to letters sent by way of Ipswich. [*Adm. Paper.*]

Dec. 26. Chatham. 41. Commissioner Peter Pett to Sam. Pepys. Opinions concerning the dimensions of the third-rate frigate. Has examined the pressed men again, but can find no positive proof of the bribery of Capt. King. Is informed that at Yarmouth, the owners of ships hid their own men in hay mows, and pressed these poor creatures. Progress of ships. [*Adm. Paper.*]

Dec. 27. 42. Information of Wm. Mastin, trumpeter to Sir Jordan Crosland. Saw between Scarborough and Bridlington, two Holland men-of-war pursue four English ships, fire, board them, and steer with them towards Holland. With note by F. C. [Sir Fras. Cobb] that the original information was sent to Lord Belasye, Lord Lieutenant.

Dec. 27. 43. W. Coventry to Sam. Pepys. Reminds him to make timely demand from the Officers of Ordnance of guns for the hired ships. Stores required for Harwich, &c. [*Adm. Paper.*]

Dec. 27. Portsmouth. 44. Commissioner Thos. Middleton to Sam. Pepys. The Royal Oak is ready to launch. Thinks her one of the best ships. Asks directions concerning pitch and oars offered. The imprest of 200l. is paid to the clerk of the cheque. Advises the making of blocks and boats in the yard. Is satisfied with his lodgings in the King's yard. Four Dutch prizes are taken, and more expected. [*Adm. Paper, two pages.*]

Dec. 28. The Office. 45. John Shorter to [the Navy Comrs.] Requests the full lading of hemp for the Olive Branch, and protection for the master and men. [*Adm. Paper, two pages.*]

Dec. 28. Chatham. 46. Commissioner Peter Pett to Sam. Pepys. Progress of ships. Thos. Williams asks too much for carrying a raft of masts and yards into the Downs for the Assurance. [*Adm. Paper.*]

Dec. 28. Harwich. 47. Anthony Deane to the Navy Comrs. Particulars of stores wanted for the bulk. Purchase of timber. [*Adm. Paper.*]

Vol. CVII.

1664.

Dec. 28. Dover. 48. Thos. Wale to the Navy Comrs. Can find no man to undertake the long-boats without contract. Leakage discovered in the Swallow. Advice concerning the tallowing of ships. [*Adm. Paper.*]

Dec. 28. Augustine, Portsmouth. 49. Capt. Rich. Teale to the Navy Comrs. Has arrived at Spithead. [*Adm. Paper.*]

Dec. 28. Pass for the Countess of Comminges to return to France, and another for two horses free of custom, for the service of the Count, her husband. Minute. [*Ent. Book* 16, *p.* 303.]

Dec. 28. Leghorn. 50. Thos. Clutterbuck to Sir Wm. Batten. Requests assistance in recovering the money due to him for victualling Capt. Smith's squadron. Forwards the pursers' accounts for the Amity and Bonaventure. Wishes the commanders of the fleet had orders to fall on the Dutch; many considerable ships might be taken without much resistance; should war follow, the prizes are made, and no port will offer a better or more ready sale for them. Sends presents of red and white Florence oil and wine. Desires a list of all ships abroad, their respective force, and commanders' names. The Dutch give out that their differences with His Majesty are now referred to the French King, so that there is no fear of a rupture, but this is looked upon as a design of theirs. [*Adm. Paper, two and a half pages.*] *Encloses,*

50. i. *Account of Thos. Clutterbuck's disbursements for goods provided by order of Capt. James Smith in June 1663, viz., velvets, earthenware, paper, bottles, &c.; total,* 89*l.* 2*s.* 6*d.* *Leghorn, December* 28, 1664.

Dec. 28. 51. Petition of Sir. And. Riccard, Governor, and the Company of the Levant to the King and Council, for protection for a third ship, the Hannibal, and 20 men more, to Smyrna and Constantinople, the other two ships for which they obtained it not sufficing for the lading which they wish to put on board, being 15,000 broad cloths, lead, tin, &c., exported to the great advantage of the kingdom.

Dec. 28. York. 52. Examination of John Clutterbuck, before Sir Edw. Brett, governor of York. Sailed for London on the 26th, with four Scotch gentlemen; discovered near Burlington four Holland men-of-war chasing an English ketch, whereon the examinate's vessel made for land, and he and the four Scotch gentlemen, whose names are subscribed, were put on shore in the long boat.

Dec. 29. Articles between Sec. Bennet, on the King's behalf, and Sir Martin Noel and Matt. Andrews, appointed agents for managing the trade to Mocha, in the Red sea, whereby the latter engage to give His Majesty a fourth part of the profits to be gained by the ship Love, which the former have fitted up at their own cost. [*Case B. Charles II., No.* 2.] *Annexing,*

i. *Declaration by the said Noel and Andrews of their acceptance of the terms of the above indenture.*

VOL. CVII.

1664.

Dec. 29. Whitehall. 53. Warrant for a pension of 1,500*l.* a year to Wm. Lord Crofts, gentleman of the bedchamber, and Elizabeth, his wife, with survivorship. [*One and a half pages.*]

Dec. 29. Whitehall. The King to [the Provost and Fellows of Eton College]. Requests them to elect Hen. Bold, B.D. of Christ Church, Oxford, to their next vacant fellowship. [*Ent. Book* 19, *p.* 29.]

Dec. 29. Chatham. 54. Commissioner Peter Pett to Sam. Pepys. Unserviceableness of the hemp lately delivered. Gottenburg masts wanted. [*Adm. Paper.*]

Dec. 20. Portsmouth. 55. Commissioner Thos. Middleton to Sam. Pepys. Proposes that boats and blocks be made in the yard, those from town are not half so good. Unlading of the Augustine. Tenders of blacking, oars, and handspikes. The new storehouse is finished. [*Adm. Paper.*]

Dec. 29. Portsmouth. 56. Rich. Suffolk, master of the Dreadnought, to Sam. Pepys. Desires to be appointed master of the Royal Oak. [*Adm. Paper.*]

Dec. 29. Victualling Office. 57. Denis Gauden to the Navy Comrs. A month's biscuit, beyond the eight months' victuals, has been put on board the Guinea ships, and will be a loss to the King unless otherwise disposed of. [*Adm. Paper.*] *Encloses,*

> 57. I. *Account of extra provisions put on board the ships designed for Guinea, September,* 1664; *first cost* 3,840*l.* 6*s.*, *present price* 3,250*l.* 9*s.* 2*d.*; *the value of ordinary victualling being* 3,207*l.* 17*s.* 10*d.*
>
> *December* 29, 1664.

Dec. 30. Woolwich. 58. Wm. Bodham to the Navy Comrs. The fence wall of the yard, about 80 yards, declines so much that it cannot stand out the winter, unless supported by eight or ten buttresses. [*Adm. Paper.*]

Dec. 30. Woolwich. 59. Chris. Pett to the Navy Comrs. Repairs of ships. Timber wanted. [*Adm. Paper.*]

Dec. 30. The King to [the Lord Lieutenants of Counties]. They are to require from the sheriffs, collectors, and receivers of the militia tax of 70,000*l.*, raised for the last two years, an exact account of the disposal of the said moneys; to receive from them the surplus, and keep it safely in a castle or garrison, if there be one within 10 miles, if not in some convenient town, to certify the disbursements, and inquire into any defect. The militia are to do duty 14 days this year, as they did last, the officers to be paid at rates specified, and if the pay fall short, the non-commissioned officers are to be paid from the fines of defaulters. In some counties the forces have not been put upon duty, but this is to be attended to at once. With list of eight Lord Lieutenants to whom these letters were sent by Sec. Bennet's secretaries. [*Ent. Book* 20, *pp.* 42–5.]

Vol. CVII.

1664.
[Dec. 30.] 60–62. Three drafts of clauses in the preceding letter.

[Dec. 30.] 63–65. Three lists of letters to be sent to the Lord Lieutenants of Counties, for the raising of the 70,000*l.*; the clerks of the Council, Sec. Morice, and [Sec. Bennet], each undertaking one third; with notes of the towns or castles where the money is to be deposited.

[Dec. 30.] List of the 17 letters dispatched by Council. [*Ent. Book* 20, *p.* 47.]

[Dec. 30.] 66. List of all the counties for which letters are to be written to the Lord Lieutenants about the monthly assessment and 14 days' duty, with the names of some castles for depositing the money.

[Dec. 30.] 67. List of castles for depositing the money of the 70,000*l.* assessments in 16 counties named.

Dec. 30. Whitehall. Petition of Peter La Harque, of Bourdeaux, to the King and Council. Laded a Holland vessel, the Sephears, with wines to sell in Amsterdam, intending with the proceeds to rescue his brother, a captive in Algiers, but his ship was seized by His Majesty's ship the Drake, brought into Dover, and he pillaged both of his clothes and wines. Begs restitution and leave to sell his wines in England, on paying customs. With reference thereon to the judge of the Admiralty Court. [*Ent. Book* 18, *pp.* 110–1.]

Dec. 30. Reference to the Earl of Oxford, Lord Chief Justice in Eyre south of Trent, on the petition of Jo. Leven, to be restored to his office as Under-keeper in Lynwood walk, New Forest, of which he is wrongfully dispossessed. [*Ent. Book* 18, *p.* 112.]

Dec. 31. 68. Sir Will. Blakeston to Sec. Bennet. His trumpeter brought him acquainted with the woman by whose means the traitor Clayton was taken; she is privy to their meetings, and can give good intelligence, as all parties are at work; hopes she may have encouragement.

Dec. 31. Inner Temple. 69. Ri. Powell to Williamson. The allotments of Wildmore Fen made to the commoners amount to 2,200 acres, and 200 more are to be disposed of to commoners not satisfied, so 1,600 will remain, 400 for the King and the residue for Sir John Prettyman, at whose charge the work has been carried on. Wishes Mr. Secretary's consent to some additional acres allowed. Will attend him with Mr. Attorney's award. *Annexing,*

69. I. *Award by Attorney General Palmer to the several persons named concerned in the improvement of Wildmore Fen, of certain portions out of the King's allotment of 4,000 acres, in satisfaction of their damages by the improvement, to which they have subscribed their submission; with the conditions upon which they consent to His Majesty's enclosing the land.* [*Copy, four pages.*]
Dec. 24, 1664.

VOL. CVII.

1664.

Dec. 31. Warrant to pay to Sir Philip Musgrave 3,367*l.* 6*s.* a year, for the garrison of Carlisle Castle, to begin from 26th June last. [*Docquet.*]

Dec. 31. Grant to Sir John Wolstenholme of the dignity of a Baronet, with the usual discharge. [*Docquet.*]

Dec. 31. Warrant confirming to Dr. William Langham the full possession of the Manor of Walgrave, co. Northampton, a remainder thereof vested in the Crown during the time of Queen Elizabeth, by his father, Sir John Langham, not being good in law. [*Ent. Book* 16, *pp.* 306–7.]

Dec. [31.] Whitehall. 70. Licence to Percy Church to transfer his lease of the Manor of Laverton, co. Somerset, belonging to the duchy of Cornwall, to Hopton Shuter, of the Inner Temple.

Dec. [31.] Entry of the above. [*Ent. Book* 16, *p.* 307.]

Dec. 31. Pass for 23 horses for Madame [the Duchess of Orleans]. [*Ent. Book* 16, *p.* 308.]

Dec. 31. Whitehall. 71. Warrant to Colonel Legg, lieutenant of Alice Holt and Woolmer Forests, to have the lop and top of a number of timber trees, felled in the forest for the use of the navy, for repair of the lodges.

Dec. 31. Entry of the above. [*Ent. Books* 16, *p.* 309; *and* 17, *p.* 81.]

Dec. 31. Pass for Mr. St. Johns to France. Minute. [*Ent. Book* 16, *p.* 310.]

Dec. 31. Warrant for a grant to Thomas Lord Colepeper, in trust for James Hamilton, groom of the bedchamber, of a lease for 31 years of certain messuages in Hyde Park, rent, 10*s.*; with the covenant that he shall make leases thereof to purchasers to be appointed, at half the improved rents. [*Ent. Book* 16, *p.* 332.]

Dec. 31. Chatham. 72. Commissioner Peter Pett to Sam. Pepys. Has ordered a bill for the Yarmouth cordage. Progress of ships. [*Adm. Paper.*] *Encloses,*

72. I. *List of New England masts and bowsprits in store; signed by Phil. Barrow.* *December* 31, 1664.

Dec. 31. 73. Capt. John Fortescue to the Navy Comrs. The rate of pay, 10*s.* a day, received with the new trust conferred upon him, is less than his late command; requests 16*s.* a day, bearing his own charge of boat hire, or 12*s.* and that charge to be paid. With note that the latter proposal was accepted. [*Adm. Paper.*]

Dec. 74. Petition of Rich. Watkins of Harwich, anchorsmith, to the Navy Comrs, to be allowed to supply stores of ironwork as formerly, having built, during the last Dutch war, a convenient work-house in Harwich therefor. With note of assent by the Commissioners.

VOL. CVII.

1664.

Dec.? 75. Petition of Rich. Watkins of Harwich, anchorsmith, to the Navy Comrs., for leave to contract at a certain price, and on such terms as not to be liable for damage after the goods are made. [*Adm. Paper.*]

Dec.? 76. Petition of John Clayton, prisoner in the Gatehouse, to Sec. Bennet, for release, or at least for free access of his friends, that he may procure whereof to work at his trade, for support of himself and family; was put to prison 27th Nov. last, and suffers great rigour, though innocent of offence.

Dec.? 77. Petition of Richard Earl of Dorset, William Lord Paget, and Dame Eliz. Harby to the King, for renewal for 21 years, on expiration of the present lease, of their lease of the customs of 4s. a chaldron on coals, detailing the particulars of their former grant.

Dec.? 78. Petition of several Officers of Col. Farrell's regiment, lately discharged at Tangiers, to the King, for provision for them as the rest of the officers; served faithfully in France, Flanders, and Tangiers, seven or eight years; were dismissed 4th May last, but served two months after, and in the fight against the Moors, 4th June, without pay. *Annexing,*

78. i. *Names of 16 Officers in Col. Farrell's regiment, lately dismissed at Tangiers, and of 4 in Col. Fitzgerald's regiment.*

Dec.? 79. Similar petition to the same effect, marked "To be disposed of in garrison, as others have been."

Dec.? 80. Petition of William Gardiner, private soldier in Colonel Legg's company, to Sec. Bennet, for a speedy trial or for release; was sent to the Tower three weeks ago by his order, and is extremely ill, without either fire or friends.

Dec.? 81. Petition of John Kay, merchant of London, to the King, for a Commissioner's place in the prize office now to be erected; lost much by his loyalty, and hazarded his life by preserving in his house, and lending money to Dan. O'Neale, Sir Nich. Armorer, Col. Rich. Talbot, and others.

Dec.? 82. Petition of Wm. Pettifer, prisoner in Oxford Castle, to the King, for release; has been three years and a half in prison, incurring the penalty of a præmunire, for being a quaker and refusing the Oath of Allegiance.

Dec.? 83. Petition of Ann the mother and Mary the wife of Wm. Pettifer, prisoner in Oxford Gaol, to the King, to free him from his long imprisonment of more than three years, because, seduced by evil pretenders to believe that swearing was unlawful, he refused the Oath of Allegiance, and had sentence of præmunire; he will promise to be faithful to His Majesty, and to forbear all conventicles.

Dec.? 84. Petition of Christopher Raleigh to the King, for the passing under the great seal of his pardon, stayed at the privy seal, for being an accessory with Art. Johnson in the murder of John Smith. Served his late and present Majesty during the rebellion.

Vol. CVII.

1664.
Dec.? 85. Petition of several Owners and freighters of small ships, laden in London for Yarmouth, Hull, Lynn, and Boston, to the King, for leave to retain two able English seamen for each vessel, and for a convoy. Since the late proclamation, all their seamen are taken into His Majesty's service, and they do not think it safe to sail with all foreigners. With a schedule of the said vessels, 14 in number.

Dec.? 86. Memoranda [by Williamson] of warrants, grants, &c., passed in the signet office during the month, the uncalendared portions of which are as follow:—

Licence to Sir Wm. Batten for 61 years to erect two light-houses on a piece of ground given him by the town of Harwich, receiving for its maintenance 12*l.* on every 20 chaldrons of Newcastle coal, a halfpenny per ton on English, and a penny on foreign shipping, paying 5*l.* rent to the King.

Grant to Hen. Fane of the governorship of Landguard Fort.

Note that Sir Gilb. Talbot, envoyé to Denmark, had 5*l.* a day, besides allowance for intelligence, and that M. Du Moulin, coming on a message from Copenhagen, had a present of 60*l.*

Appointment of John Taylor as Navy Commissioner at Harwich, to act on instructions from three of the Navy Commissioners in London; fee, 350*l.* a year.

Note that the Queen's horses are provided by the King, and paid for by the master of the horse.

Note that the felling of timber is on a warrant from the Lord Treasurer or Under Treasurer of the Exchequer, to fell so many oaks, &c., within certain forests for the building of ships, to be chosen by the navy purveyors, with assistance of the officers of the forest.

Dec. Whitehall. 87. Warrant for a grant to Jas. Marriott of the place of Keeper of the standing wardrobe and privy lodgings at Hampton Court, void by death of Rich. Marriott.

Dec.? 88. Warrant to the Board of Greencloth to increase the allowance to Dr. Clarke, appointed physician of the household in place of Dr. Whitaker, deceased, to 12s. a day, the sum allowed to other physicians in ordinary. [*Draft.*]

Dec.? 89. [Edw. Riggs to Sec. Bennet]. Will be unfitted for service if Tyler be examined as to anything about him. It should be about Capt. Elton, a great ringleader in prison; the messages he had from several places about the rising; his journeys to several places in England; his knowledge of arms, and sending them to England; his proceedings in the Tower, &c. Tyler will rather suffer anything than accuse Elton, and boasts how easily he deceived the Council by equivocations and reservations. [*Two pages.*]

Dec.? 90. John Hannis to Williamson. Hears nothing of any such grant, and will attend to his caveat. Endorsed "Lord Peterborough's caveat at the Solicitor's."

Vol. CVII.

1664.

[Dec.] 91. Articles of indenture between Sir Hen. Bennet, Secretary of State, on the King's behalf, and Sir Martin Noel and Mat. Andrews, covenanting that, in return for the commission granted to the latter of the sole management of the trade to the Red Sea undertaken in His Majesty's name, they will pay him one fourth of the profits of the present voyage of the ship Love, and of any future voyage they may make. [*Two and a half pages.*]

[Dec.] 92. Draft [by Williamson] of the above. [*One and a half pages.*]

[Dec.] 93. Declaration by Sir Martin Noel and Mat. Andrews, that being appointed agents for the management of a trade to Mocha and other parts near the Red Sea, in consideration of the assistance granted them by Sec. Bennet therein, they agree to give him an eighth part of the clear profits of their voyage. [*One and a half pages.*]

[Dec.] 94. Draft [by Williamson] of the above. [*One and a half pages.*]

Dec. 95. Pass for the ship Love, John Hunt master, to certain ports in or near the Red Sea and back. [*Draft by Williamson.*]

Dec.? 96. Instructions to Parish Clerks to give in accounts weekly of burials, specifying the diseases; monthly of births, baptisms, marriages, and burials; quarterly of the ages of the deaths and their causes; and yearly a census, specifying those who are married or single, Protestants or Papists, &c.

[Dec.] 97, 98. Statement by Renald Knapton, gaoler of Dorchester, that the sheriff neglected both the King's letters of 13th June, 1664, and of 16th of this month, being guided by a son of Denis Bond, one of the late King's judges, and the fanatics having entered into a bond to save him harmless. He sent word to Knapton that he should not be the gaoler, but Wilson, who was in arms against the late King, should have the place. The gentry of the county are afflicted to have its affairs governed by Bond. The Duke of Richmond has twice written to the sheriff, on Knapton's behalf, in vain. Two Papers.

[Dec.] 99. Account by —— Clapton, that out of nine nonconforming ministers at Dorchester, whose names are given, five were lately imprisoned on suspicion of being privy to the plot. Six ministers and 70 others are now in prison for nonconformity. The town is most factious and has daily conventicles, and none of the town ever suffered for loyalty except Renald Knapton, the present gaoler, who has been hated, and an endeavour made to have Wilson, who bore arms against the King, made gaoler. The present sheriff pretends the letter does not concern him, because not directed to him by name.

[Dec.] 100, 101. Two similar documents, not duplicate.

1664. VOL. CVIII. 1664.

Volume of Admiralty Papers, relating to the supply of stores for the Navy, containing—

I. Tenders of Goods, addressed to the Navy Commissioners, by Merchants and Manufacturers, as follow :—

Date.	No.	Name.	Article.	Terms.
1664 Feb. 11 -	1	Wm. Wood and Ed. Gray -	Masts, 6 to 22 hands - -	From 7s. 6d. to 22l.
" 11 -	2	Sir Wm. Warren - -	Planks, timber, deals, &c. -	From 32s. to 3l. 15s. per load, and 5l. per 100.
" 19 -	3	Ed. Gray - - -	Dram timber - -	60s. per load.
" 27 -	4	John Shorter - -	Tar and deals.	
March 14 -	5	Peter Blackborow - -	Plank, 3 to 4 in. deals - -	4l. 5s. per load, and 4l. 14s. per 100.
" 24 -	6	Edw. Silvester - -	Anchors and ironwork -	9 to 12 per cent. abatement from old contract.
" 31 -	7-8	Thos. Chester - -	Timber and deals - -	30s. to 40s. per load, and 3l. 5s. 6d. to 4l. 15s. per 100.
April 4 -	9	Robt. Fowler - -	Tiles - - - -	From 20s. per 100 to 1l. 1s. per 1,000.
May 7 -	10	Chr. Coles - -	Timber, plank, and treenails -	34s. to 76s. per load.
" 14 -	11	Sir Wm. Warren - -	Mast, plank, and treenails -	7s. to 30l. per mast.
June 3 -	12	John Clothre - -	Milan hemp cordage - -	40s. per cwt.
" 4 -	13	Peter Blackborow - -	Timber, boards, masts, &c. -	3l. to 4l. 15s. per load; masts, 7s. to 2l.
" 11 -	14	Capt. Pett - - - -	Elm timber.	
" 20 -	15	Eliz. King - -	Elm timber, 16 in. to 2 ft.	
" 23 -	16	Sir Wm. Warren - -	Masts, deals, timber - -	55s. to 3l. 5s. per load.
" 30 -	17	Sir Wm. Warren - -	Masts, 6 to 22 hands - -	7s. to 33l. each.
" -	18	Mr. Heather - -	Ironwork, 11 tons.	
" -	19	Wm. Wood and Ed. Gray -	Masts, 6 to 22 hands - -	7s. 6d. to 27l. each.
July 14 -	20	Peter Blackborow - -	Timber, planks, spars, &c. -	1l. 15s. to 4l. 15s per load.
" 22 -	21	Sir Wm. Warren - -	New England masts, 22 to 35 in. diameter	95l. to 116l. per mast.
Aug. 16 -	22	John Hayward - -	Oak timber.	
Sept. 1 -	23	John Masterock	Elm timber - - -	30s. per load.
" 3 -	24	Sir Wm. Warren - -	Timber, deals, &c. - -	38s. to 43s. per load.
" 15 -	25	Mr. Harrington - -	Spruce deals, 24 by 16½ in. -	30s. per deal.
" -	26	Thos. Chester - -	Dram timber, 30 ft. per piece Sheathing boards - -	38s. per load. 10s. 6d. per 100 feet.
Oct. 6 -	27	John Downing - -	Anchors, 4 to 30 cwt.	
" 21 -	28	John Hill - - -	Pitch - - - -	10s. 6d. per cwt.(?)
" 22 -	29-30	Robt. Masterock - -	Elm timber - - -	35s. to 40s. per load.
Nov. 3 -	31	Wm. Wood - -	Masts, timber, spars, &c. -	1l. 5s. to 4l. 10s. per 100 spars.
" 9 -	32-4	Ed. Moody - - -	Timber - - - -	40s. to 4l. per load.
" 16 -	35	Phil. Hatton and Chas. Tow-red.	Old masts, bowsprits, and yards	1l. to 22l. 14s. per lot.
" 17 -	36	John Shorter - -	Dram timber, masts, spars, &c.	2l. 9s. to 22l. per mast; 2l. 15s. 6d. to 5l. per 100.
Dec. 9 -	37-39	John Rodbard - -	Anchors and ironwork -	22s. to 27s. 6d. per cwt., &c.
" 10 -	40	John Shorter - -	Timber and deals - -	34s. to 55s. per load; 4l. to 8l. 10s. per 100.
" 20 -	41 †	John Tyson - - -	Deals, fir timber, &c. -	2l. 10s. to 7l. per 100 deals.
" 20 -	42	Wm. Wood and Ed. Gray -	Masts and bowsprits -	5l. 10s. to 28l., and 10l. to 22l.
" 15 -	43	Robt. Walker, Caleb Vaven-	Dram timber, spars - -	46s. per load; 71s. 6d. per 100.
" 16 -	44	Peter Blackborow - -	Deals, timber, &c. - -	31s. to 9l. 10s. per 100; 47s. to 57s. per load.
" 15 -	45-6	John Miller - -	Fire ships.	
" -	47	John Watts - - -	Oars, 15 to 19 ft. - -	3½d. per foot.
	48	Nich. Bradley - -	Anchors and ironwork -	From 33s. to 3l. 10s. per cwt.
	49	James Crane - -	Masts.	
	50	John Harbin - -	French hemp, yarn, and canvas	From 37s. to 48s. per [cwt.]
	51	Thos. Eccleston and Peter Rich.	Oak timber - - -	57s. per load.
	52	Capt. Geo. Cock - -	Plank - - - -	4l. 15s. per load.
	53-6	Peter Blackborow - -	Timber, treenails, &c. - Timber, knees, spars, &c. -	From 31s. to 45s. per load, and 4l. 15s. per load. From 1l. 15s. to 6l. 15s. per load.

† Noted as declined, because of his relation to the Navy.

1664.

Vol. CVIII.

II. Drafts or minutes of contracts with the Navy Commissioners, for work or purchase of goods, or hire of ships; many of them notes in the handwriting of Sam. Pepys. The prices are omitted from this list, as they appear for the most part in those preceding and following:—

Date.		No.	Name.	Goods.
1664.				
March	3	55	Sir Wm. Warren	Deals, planks, and timber.
,,	15	56-7	Alderman Rich. Chiverton	Riga and Quinsborough hemp.
,,	21	58-9	Thos. Harvey	Plasterers' work.
,,		60	Mr. Bradley	Ironwork.
April	7	61	Thos. Harvey	Lanterns, plates, and glass.
,,	15	62	Sir John Hebdon and Mr. Hill	Hemp, and tar.
,,	22	63	Sir Wm. Rider and Wm. Cutler	Tar.
May	24	64	Chris. Coles	Compass and knee timber.
,,	31	65	John Carter	Blocks.
,,		66	John Shorter	Bergen tar.
,,		67	Mr. Rushford	Grapnels.
,,		68	Sir Wm. Warren	Deals.
,,		69	Chris. Coles	Plank, treenails, and elm knees.
June	1	70	Peter Godwin	Oak timber.
,,	2	71	Col. Reymes	Canvas.
,,	7	72	Mr. Bowyer	Train oil and brimstone.
,,	8	73	Mr. Wood	Timber.
,,	9	74	Edw. Benson	Ash oars.
,,	9	75	Edw. Smith	Blocks.
,,	11	76	Mr. Harris	Holland duck.
,,	11	77	Capt. Lowe	Oars.
,,	20	78	John Story	Stockholm tar.
,,		79	Mr. Knight	Quinsborough hemp.
July	13	80	Peter Blackborow	Dram timber.
,,	14	81	Ed. Hubbert	Planks.
,,	22	82	Peter Hazelter	Oak timber.
,,	27	83, 84	Sir Wm. Warren	Gottenburg masts.
,,	28	85	Peter Blackborow	Knees and elm timber.
,,		86	Sir Wm. Warren	Norway masts and knees.
Aug.	2	87	- - - - -	Anchors.
,,	4	88	Owen Lloyd and Hen. Moody	Quinsborough hemp.
,,	4	89	Math. Clements	Blocks.
,,	10	90-1	Sir Wm. Warren	New England masts.
,,	12	92	John Bagley and others	Royal Exchange, hired for Guinea.
,,	25	93	Mr. Harris and Mr. Pruby	Holland duck.
,,		94	Mr. Hewell	Box and Surinam wood.
Sept.	1	95	Capt. Chester and Sir Wm. Warren	Dram timber and knees.
,,	17	96	Wm. Bushell	Spinning of Riga and Quinsborough hemp.
,,	22	97-8	Francis Willard	Best Colleys sacking.
,,		99	Robt. Waithe	Ipswich canvas.
,,		100	John Graves	A barge.
,,		101	Mr. Harrington	Spruce deals.
Oct.	4	102-3	Sir Wm. Warren	Elm boards.
			Mr. Harbing	Small Noyals canvas.
			Mr. Harble	French yarn.
			Capt. Chester and Mr. Halbert	Dram timber.
			Mr. Hewell	Surinam wood.
,,	6	104	John Mason	Straight and compass timber.
,,	12	105	Hen. Lowe	Oars.
,,	20	106	Edw. Silvester	Chain of Spanish iron for Portsmouth.
,,		107	Mr. Swan	Brazen bevins.
,,		108	Mrs. Fley	Noyals and Vitry canvas.
,,		109	Mr. Carter	Brimstone.
			James Wordell and Wm. Bery	Sea Venture smack hired.
,,		110	Robt. Wood	St. George ketch hired.
,,		111	Mr. Downing	Anchors.
			Mr. Harris	Canvas.
,,		112	- - - - -	Oars.
,,		113	Alderman Barker and Wm. Rivett	Hemp.
Nov.	12	114	Alderman Barker	Tarred yarn of Milan hemp.
,,	19	115	Mr. Young and Whistler	Colours.
,,	19	116-18	Mr. Bradley	Anchors, chains, grapnels, &c.

1664. Vol. CVIII.

Date.	No.	Names.	Goods.
1664. Nov. 24	139	Mr. Harrington	Oars.
" 25	140-2	Mr. Rufford	Ironwork.
" 29	143	Mr. Cole	Plank.
"	144	Mr. Bodycoat	Cables.
"	145	Mr. Upton	Quinborough hemp.
"	146	Mr. Margetts	Cordage.
"	147	William Taylor	Dantzic oars.
"	148	-	Ketches—The John, Lea, Bachelor, Desire, and Adam, hired.
Dec. 1	149	Francis Willard	Sacking.
" 3	150	Sir Wm. Warren	Deals.
"	151	Mr. Stanly	Beech oars.
"	152	Peter Blackborow	Drum timber.
		Rob. Wheeler	Brooms.
"	153	Mr. Swan	Reed.
"	154	Edw. Brown	Chalk rubbish.
"	155	Mr. Stanly	Reeds.
"	156	Mr. Hulbert	Plank.
		John Yates	Brooms.
"	157	-	Swedish, Hamburgh Merchant, and Coast frigate, hired.
"	158-9	Sir Wm. Rider, Alderman Edw. Backwell, and Wm. Cutler	Hemp.

III. Warrants from the Navy Commissioners, jointly or severally, to the Storekeeper and Clerk of the Cheque, for receipt of goods into the stores, most of the goods being delivered according to a Contract endorsed on the Warrant, or annexed to it. The papers with contracts are distinguished by an asterisk; C signifies that the stores are to be delivered at Chatham, D at Deptford and W at Woolwich;—

Date.	No.	Contractors or Consignees.		Goods.	Quantity.	Terms.	Directions.
1664 Feb. 9	140	Rich. Hoyle	D	Fishing lines, hooks, &c.	Several casks.	-	For the Westergate and Swallow.
" 11	141	Wm. Wood	D	Bowsprits and spritsail yards.	-	-	For the Expedition.
" 25	142	Thos. Meadows	D	Handerapers, cottons, and kerseys.	6 pairs, 500 yards, and 300 yards.	-	For Portsmouth.
Mar. 10	143	*Edw. Dering	D	Noyals canvas	10 bales.	10l. 16s. 8d. per bale.	
" 31	144	*Sir Wm. Warren	D	Drum timber	54 loads	50s. per load	Part for Chatham.
Apr. 7	145	Mr. Meadows	D	Kerseys and cottons	1,000 yards	-	For waste cloths for the Monmouth.
" 9	146	*Edw. Dering	D	Noyals canvas	100 bales	10l. 5s. per bale.	
" 9	147	*John Harbin	D	" "	"	" "	
" 9	148	*Sir Wm. Warren	D	2, 3, and 4 in. plank	80 loads	5l. 5s. per load.	
" 15	149	Edw. Hayward	D	4 long boats, 2 skiffs, and 2 pinnaces.			
" 20	150	*Sir Wm. Warren	D	Deals, 10 ft. by 10 in.	1,000 deals	4l. per 120	500 for Woolwich.
" 22	151	*John Hill	D	Stockholm tar	50 lasts	11l. per last	Part for Portsmouth.
May 2	152	" "		" "	12 lasts	-	Half to Woolwich.
" 5	153	Arnold Smith	D	Iron hoops and tools	-	-	For the Eagle, bound for Guinea.
" 7	154	*John Stafford	D	6 anchors	43 to 45 cwt. each.	50s. per cwt.	

Vol. CVIII.

1664.

Date.	No.	Contractors or Consignees.		Goods.	Quantity.	Terms.	Direction, &c.
1664. May 16 -	155	Edw. Reyner -	D	Long boat and pinnace.	- - -	- - -	For the Dover.
" 17 -	156	*Peter Blackborow	D	Berwick timber, 30 ft. long.	50 loads -	65s. per load -	25 loads for Chatham.
" 18 -	157	Hen. Russell -	D	Barge oars - -	19 oars -	- - -	For the King's barge.
" 19 -	158	*Edw. Dering -	D	Prussian deals, 24 to 30 ft. long.	1,000 -	6s. 6d. each.	
" 19 -	159	*John Harbin -	D	Noyals and Vitry canvas.	100 bales of 450 yards each.	16l. 18s. 6d. per bale.	
" 21 -	160	*Peter Proby -	D	Holland duck -	30 bolts -	22d. per yard.	
" [illegible] -	161	" " " -	D	" " -	18 " -		
" [illegible] -	162	*John Watts -	D	Oars 16 or 17 ft. long.	40 dozen -	3½d. per foot.	
" [illegible] -	163	*Sir Wm. Rider -	D	Noyals canvas - -	50 bales -	16l. 7s. 6d. per bale.	
" [illegible] -	164	*Rob. Waith -	D	Ipswich canvas -	150 bolts -	27s. per bolt.	
" [illegible] -	165	*Wm. Harrington -	D	Dantzic mainmasts -	[illegible] " -	65s. each.	
" 31 -	166	*Rich. Howell -	D	Holly wood - -	440 ends -	20l. the whole -	Half for Chatham and half for Portsmouth.
" 31 -	167	" " -	D	" " " -	" "	"	Howell to have a hoy to fetch it from Greenwich.
June 2 -	168	Mr. Edgill -	D	Blocks - -	100 dozen	- - -	Half for Portsmouth.
" 2 -	169	*John Radford -	D	Anchors - -	9 -	32s. per cwt.	
" 2 -	170	*Jeffry Wiseheard -	D	" " -	12 -	" "	
" 3 -	171	*Peter Blackborow -	D	Deals 11 ft. by 10 in. -	1,000 -	6l. 5s. per 100.	
" 4 -	172	" " " -	D	Norway masts -	40 -	7s. to 24s. each.	
" 4 -	173	*John Owen -	D	Noyals canvas -	14 bales, 450 yards each.	16l. 5s. per bale.	
" 7 -	174	*Wm. Sawyer -	D	{ Train oil - - Brimstone - -	4 tons - 8 tons -	19l. per ton } 22s. per cwt. }	The oil for Chatham.
" 7 -	175	Mr. Kingston -	D	Boat-hooks - -	8 dozen -	- - -	Same for Chatham, Woolwich, and Portsmouth.
" 9 -	176	*Wm. Wood -	D	Timber 22 to 40 ft. -	45 loads -	50s. a load -	For Chatham.
" 11 -	177	*John Harris -	D	Holland duck -	30 bolts -	22d. per yard.	
" 11 -	178	*Hen. Low -	D	Dantzic oars -	60 dozen -	3½d. and 3d. per foot.	
" 11 -	179	Thos. Edmundson -	D	Forewall - -	- - -	- - -	For the Henrietta.
" 13 -	180	" " "	D	6 anchors and 13 hand-screws.	- - -	- - -	To be repaired.
" 16 -	181	*Jarvis Marplesden -	D	Goats' hair - -	5 tons -	21s. per cwt.	
" 21 -	182	John Harris -	D	Old canvas -	- - -	- - -	To be put on board the Augustine, reserving so much for the Matthias.
" 23 -	183	*Sir Wm. Warren -	D	{ [illegible] deals - Dram timber - Oak plank -	[illegible] - [illegible] loads - [illegible] loads -	3l. 16s. per 120 [illegible] per load. 3l. 16s. per load.	} Same for Woolwich.
" 28 -	184	*Rob. Waith -	D	Ipswich canvas -	300 bolts -	27s. per bolt.	
" [illegible] -	185	Sir Wm. Rider and Mr. Cutler	D	Pitch - -	[illegible] lasts.		
July 5 -	186	Mr. Young and Mr. Whistler.	D	Ensigns and jacks -	20 of each.		
" 5 -	187	Mr. Mitchell -	D	Colours.			
" 9 -	188	Wm. Cooper -	D	Timber from Alleyholt.			
" 13 -	189	Sir Wm. Warren -	D	Gottenburg masts, spars, and deals.			
" 14 -	190	*John Harris -	D	Holland duck -	100 bolts -	22d. a yard.	
" 14 -	191	*Edw. Hulbert -	D	English oak plank -	100 loads -	3l. 13s. per load.	
" 14 -	192	*Sir Wm. Warren -	D	Norway masts -	50 -	As before -	Half for Woolwich
" 21 -	193	*Capt. John [illegible] -	D	Holland cordage -	4 tons -	66s. per cwt. -	For Portsmouth.

1664. VOL. CVIII.

Date.		Contractors or Consignors.		Goods.	Quantity.	Terms.	Directions.
1664.							
July 21	194	*Peter Blackborow	D	Dram timber	25 loads	57s. per load	For Chatham.
" 25	195	* " "	D	Oak and elm timber	120 loads	51s. and 30s. per load.	Half for Woolwich.
" 26	196	Sir Wm. Warren	D	Norway masts, deals.			
" 28	197	" "	D	Norway masts	300.		
" 28	198	Mr. Hayles	D	A sayce and tassel	- - -	- - -	To be sent to the Downs.
Aug. 4	199	*Mat. Clements	D	Blocks	40 dozen	8s. per doz.	
" 7	200	Mrs. Ann Ingram	D	Spades shod with iron	30		
" 8	201	*Col. Rulleyn Bryson.	D	Noyals canvas	150 bales	16l. 5s. and 10l. 16s. 6d. per bale.	
" 11	202	Arnold Smith	D	Rivets, punches, hammers, chisels, &c.	Various	- - -	For Capt. Allin's squadron.
" 13	203	- -	D	Spanish table	- - -	- - -	For Plymouth.
" 19	204	Edm. Rayner	D	Elm board	200 feet	- - -	For Plymouth.
" 22	205	*Daniel Bradley and John Ruffhead.	D	Anchors	10	25s. to 26s. per cwt.	Deliver three two old anchors to barrel.
" 25	206	Jas. Clark	D	Rubbing stones	84.		
" 27	207	Mr. Pomfield	D	German hemp cordage	2 tons	33s. per cwt.	For Portsmouth.
Sept. 3	208	*Thos. Chester	D	Dram timber, 70 ft.	500 loads	1l. 1s. per load	Half to Woolwich.
" 6	209	*Sir Wm. Warren	C	Deals, 8, 10, 11 ft.	15,000	3l. 16s. per 100.	
" 13	210	*John Watts	D	Danzic oars	50 dozen	8½d. per foot.	
" 13	211	*Capt. Hen. Lowe	D	Oars	"	"	
" 14	212	Edw. Smith	C	Blocks	140 dozen		
" 15	213	John Young and Hen. Whistler.	D	Jacks and ensigns	20 of each.		
" 15	214	*John Graves	D	A barge	32 ft. long	30l. - -	For the Admiral bound for Guinea.
" 16	215	- -	D	Bass ropes	- - -	- - -	Now in a lighter before the dock.
" 17	216	John Brett	C	Sherwood timber	All that is brought in.		
" 19	217	Mrs. Davey	C	Compasses, watch, minute and hour glasses.	2 to 20 dozen.		
" 20	218	Mr. Morris	D	Pitch and tar	- - -	- - -	For the Guinea fleet.
" 21	219	Peter Blackborow	C	Deals	2,400	- - -	Above those in his contract.
" 23	220	*John Hill	D	Oil	3 tuns	21l. 10s. per tun.	
" 24	221	*Sir Wm. Warren	D	Whale oil	12 tuns	22l. per tun.	
" 24	222	* " "	D	Gottenburg masts, spars, and deals.	977 masts	From 6l. to 12l. per mast.	Some for Chatham and some for Portsmouth.
" 29	223	—— Parker	C	Sand	90 tons.		
" 30	224	*Rob. Apps	C	Oak timber	60 loads	43s. 6d. per load.	
Oct. 1	225	Mr. Coles	C	Timber, treenails, knees, &c.	7 to 100 loads.		
" 3	226	Mr. Downes	W	Tables	6	- - -	For the Henrietta, bound for Guinea.
" 4	227	*Peter Pauley	D	Holland duck	200 bolts	1s. 10d. per yard	To be sent to Chatham.
" 4	228	*Wm. Bowyer	C	Black rosin	15 tons	9l. 10s. per ton.	
" 4	229	* " "	D	"	5 tons	6l. per ton.	
" 4	230	*Robt. Waith	D	Linen cloth	3,000 ells	9d. per ell.	
" 4	231	*John Harbin	D	Noyals canvas; Vitry canvas	50 bales; 8,000 ells	11l. 10s. per bale; 15d. per ell.	
" 4	232	*Sir Wm. Warren	W	Elm timber, 30 ft.; Elm board, 15 ft.	600 loads; 100,000 ft.	30s. per load; 11s. per 100 ft.	Half for Deptford.
" 4	233	*Rich. Howell	D	Hornbeam wood	8 tons	6l. per ton.	
" 4	234	* " "	C	"	4 tons.	"	
" 4	235	Capt. John Taylor	D	Sloops	2 -	- - -	For the Guinea fleet.
" 4	236	John Mason	C	Beech and oak timber	6 loads		
" 4	237	*John Morris	D	Holland duck	250 bolts	1s. 10d. per yard.	

1664. Vol. CVIII.

Date.	No.	Contractors or Consignees.		Goods.	Quantity.	Terms.	Directions.
1664. Oct. 5	238	*John Mason	C	Timber	250 loads	44s. per load.	
„ 6	239	*Capt. Hen. Lowe	D	Oars, from 16 ft. to 22 ft.	20 dozen	8½d. and 9d. per foot.	To be sent to Chatham.
„ 6	240	*John Downing	D	Anchors	13	44s. to 47s. per cwt.	
„ 8	241	Thos. Staines	C	Poop lanterns	4.		
„ 8	242	*James Askew	D	Whale oil	20 tons	22l. per ton.	
„ 8	243	Capt. Fras. Steward	D	Cable, 8½ in.	1	-	Lent him by the Captain of the Hampshire.
„ 11	244	Thos. Alrabull	D	Tallow	2 tons	-	Half for Chatham.
„ 11	245	*Sir Wm. Warren	D	Elm timber Elm board	500 loads 200,000 ft.	38s. per load 11s. per 100 ft.	Half for Woolwich.
„ 11	246	*Fras. Willard, jun.	D	Colliers marking	100 pieces	21s. a piece	For Portsmouth.
„ 13	247	-	D	Hammocks	1,000	-	For Chatham.
„ 13	248	*Rich. Hale	D	White oakum	3 tons	27s. per cwt.	
„ 14	249	*Thos. Carter	D	Brimstone	10 tons	22l. per ton	Part for Portsmouth.
„ 18	250	*Wm. Sawyer	W	Stockholm pitch	10 lasts	9l. 15s. per last	For Portsmouth.
„ 20	251	Young and Whistler	D	Bewpers	8,000 yards	6d. per yard	To be wrought into colours.
„ 26	252	*Sir Wm. Warren	D	Spars, 10 to 18 ft.	1,500	1l. 5s. per 120.	
„ 27	253	Jarvis Maplesden	W	Ox hair, liquored, Leather Leather scraps, &c.	1 ton. 10 backs. 20 dozen.		
„ 29	254	Sam. Moore	W	Wooden screws	2 pairs	-	To be sent to Harwich.
Nov. 1	255	*Sir Wm. Warren	D	Compass timber Knees ¾ in. sheathing board	600 loads 100 100,000 ft.	2l. per load. 3l. per load. 10s. per 100 ft.	
„ 4	256	Wm. Attaway	C	Pictures, 10 ft. by 6 ft. 3 in.			
„ 4	257	*Humph. Swan	D	Broom bavins, 30 in.	40,000	47s. per 1,000	Half for Woolwich.
„ 4	258	*Capt. Hen. Lowe	C	Oars, 15 to 24 ft.	100 dozen	8½d. to 9½d. per ft.	
„ 7	259	*John Hayward	C	Oak and elm timber, knees, &c.	115 loads	40s. to 42s. per load.	
„ 7	260	*Edw. Smith	C	Elm timber	60 loads	30s. per load.	
„ 7	261	*Chris. Cockrell	C	Copper kettles, brass skillets, ladles, &c.	1 dozen of each.		
„ 7	262	John Curtis	C	Reed, 14 in.	60,000.		
„ 7	263	Sir Wm. Warren	D	Cables.			
„ 17	264	*Wm. Castell	D	Knees	40 loads	4l. 15s. per load.	
„ 17	265	*Capt. Rich. Haddock	D	Hemp rope, 3½ in.	300 coils	5s. per coil.	
„ 17	266	*Hugh Upton	C	Riga Rhine hemp	20 tons	43l. per ton.	
„ 17	267	*John Shorter	C	Masts Drum deals Drum timber	37 35 cwt. 84 pieces	1l. 6s. to 17l. 15s. 3l. 10s. per 120. 30s. to 47s. per load.	
„ 17	268	*Robt. Apps and John Avery.	C	Timber	80 loads	1l. 15s. per load.	
„ 17	269	*Wm. Attaway	C	Yards, 13 ft. and 14 ft. long.	2.		
„ 21	270-1	*Chris. Cole	C	Plank Timber, &c. Treenails	1 to 5 in. 467 loads 64,000	4l. per load. 1l. 16s. to 3l. per load. 2l. 11s. to 7l. 12s. per 1,000.	
„ 24	272	*Robt. Walsh	D	Ipswich canvas	50 bolts	30s. per bolt	
„ 24	273	*Nich. Bradley	D	Anchors, grapnels, &c.	-	From 30s. to 32s. per cwt.	
„ 28	274	*Robt. Walsh	D	Suffolk canvas	500 bolts	18½d. per yard.	
„ 29	275	Rich. Greenstead	C	Birch brooms	365 dozen.		
„ 29	276	*John Young and Hen. Whistler.	D	Ensigns, flags, &c.	-	8½d. per yard.	
„ 29	277	*John Shorter	D	Masts 5 to 6 hands	84	7s. to 17s. 6d. each.	
„ 29	278	*Alderman Wm. Hooker.	D	English tallow	11 tons	46s. per cwt.	

1664. Vol. CVIII.

Date.	No.	Contractors or Consignees.		Goods.	Quantity.	Terms.	Directions.
1664, Nov. 30	279	John Young	D	Bags	400	- - -	For Portsmouth.
„ 30	280	*John Harris	D	Holland duck	200 bolts	1s. 10d. per yd.	
„ 30	281	John Shorter	C	Dram deals, 18 ft.	650		
				Birchen handspikes	300		
Dec. 1	282	*Wm. Taylor	D	Ash oars, 15 to 21 ft.	40 dozen	8½d. and 9½d. per foot.	
2	283	Mr. Whitton	C	Handspikes and knees	52 dozen.		
„ 2	284	*Edw. Hill	C	Elm and oak timber	80 loads	21s. to 24s. per load.	
„ 2	285	*Mrs. Constance Pley	C	Noyals canvas	500 bales	11l. 10s. per bale.	Part for Portsmouth.
				Vitry canvas	6,000 ells	13d. per ell.	
„ 2	286	*Jarvis Maplesden	C	[illegible]	- - -	11d. per lb.	To be cut down the trunk of a well-grown ox hide.
„ 3	287	Edw. Dering	C	Tar and hemp.			
„ 3	288	*Sir Wm. Warren	D	Gottenburg masts	- - -	32l. 17s. 6d. to 43l. each.	Imperfect.
„ 4	289	Thos. Wood	C	Double blocks	1s.		
„ 5	290	Mr. [illegible]	C	Globe lanterns	3	- - -	For the Charles.
„ 5	291	*Robert Moorcock and John Mason.	C	Elm timber	210 loads	2l. 8s. per load.	
„ 6	292	*Sir Wm. Warren	D	Deals, 22½ to 24 ft.	1,200	6s. 6d. to 11s. each.	
„ 6	293	*Rich. Sparrman	D	Cables, 12 and 11 in.	4 tons	40s. per cwt.	
„ 6	294	*Wm. Bowyer	D	Black rosin	10 tons	10l. per ton.	
„ 6	295	*Rich. Goodlaughter	D	Anchors	20	32s. per cwt.	
„ 7	296	Mr. Pepys	D	Harwich hempen	22 pieces	- - -	Two pieces to be kept as patterns for future contracts.
„ 10	297	*Sir Wm. Warren	D	Gottenburg pitch	60 lasts	13l. 10s. per last.	
„ 13	298	Mr. Burkland and Mr. Burrows.	D	Copper furnace	2	- - -	For Portsmouth.
				Fire engine	1	- - -	
„ 14	299	*John Clarke	C	Linen hoops for tops of ships.	2,000 feet	3½d. per foot.	
„ 15	300	*John Watts	D	Oars, 16 to 19 ft.	30 dozen	9½d. per foot.	
„ 17	301	*Wm. Harrington	D	Oars, 15 to 25 ft.	1,700	3½d. to 4d. per ft.	
„ 20	302	Sir Wm. Warren	D	Pitch	See plan from late contract.		
„ 20	303	*Edw. Hulbert	D	Plank	200 loads	2l. 17s. per load	
„ 24	304	*Nich. Bradley and John Bulford.	D	Grapnels, bolts, hooks, anchors, &c.	Various	Various.	
„ 30	305	Stephen Elph	C	Burning [illegible], 1½ lb.	20,000		
„ 30	306	Thos. Ray	C	„	25,000.		
„ 31	307	John Mason	C	Elm timber	100 loads	42s. 6d. per load.	

Vol. CIX. 1664? Undated.

1664?

Warrant to the Master of the Great Wardrobe to allow 23*l*. 8*s*. 2*d*. each, for immediate liveries, to Willm. Chiffinch and three other pages of the bedchamber to the Queen, and to John Forbes and John Bork, pages supernumerary, and to continue the same half yearly. [*Docquet.*]

VOL. CIX.

1664?

Warrant to the Master of the Great Wardrobe to allow 16*l.* 2*s.* 6*d.*, for an immediate livery to John Goodgroom, musician in ordinary for lute and voice, in place of Angelo Notario, deceased, and the same half yearly. [*Docquet.*]

Warrant to the Master of the Great Wardrobe to allow 40*l.* 0*s.* 6*d.*, as an immediate livery to George Stepney, groom of the privy chamber supernumerary, and to continue the same yearly. [*Docquet.*]

1. Note of a grant to John Pinecombe of all logwood or blockwood forfeited for nonpayment of custom, and of all forfeitures arising on importations thereof contrary to the Act of Navigation, &c. [*Imperfect.*]

Whitehall. 2. Warrant for a licence to Thos. Killigrew to set up a lottery for three years, after the expiration of the three years' lottery granted to the Royal Fishing Company, called the Pricking Book Lottery, on rental of 50*l.*, to be paid to the said company. *Annexing,*

2. I. *Account of payments in the Exchequer made to Thos. Killigrew, on his pension of* 100*l. a year, since* 1638, *and of balance due thereon, up to* 1664; *total,* 9,200*l.*; *signed by himself.*

Whitehall. 3. Passport for Hen. Howard, of Norfolk, with his two sons, and Sir Samuel Tuke, Bt., and Lady Tuke, to travel for three years, with servants, horses, plate, &c.

4. Warrant to Sam. Pepys and Rob. Long to search for treasure said to be concealed in the Tower or Hamlet precincts, in presence of the Lieutenant of the Tower, or some one appointed by him, and to deliver the same to Sec. Bennet. [*Draft.*]

5. The King to [Sec. Bennet]. Sam. Pepys and Rob. Long, with assistance of the Lieutenant of the Tower, are permitted to search the Tower, the hamlets, precincts, &c., thereof, for gold, silver, and jewels concealed, which they are to bring to him. Of these 2,000*l.* is to be given to the Earl of Sandwich, as a free gift; 2,000*l.* to the discoverers, and the rest retained in his hands for His Majesty's use. [*Draft by Bennet.*]

6. The King to Col. Wm. Legg, lieutenant of Ordnance. The new-raised officers and soldiers are to allow for the arms they receive from his stores. An account is therefore to be sent in to Stephen Fox, paymaster, that he may deduct the money from the payments at the 7 yearly musters.

7. The King to the [Attorney General]. Understands that many ill-affected people in Hertfordshire refuse to conform to the church, and attend conventicles, notwithstanding the Act against them, whereby a third of the forfeitures thereon becomes due to the Exchequer; but the mayor and burgesses having been careful and active in putting them down, he is to prepare a grant to them of the said third of the forfeitures, on conviction of the offenders. [*Copy.*]

Vol. CIX.

1664?

8. C. O. [Lord Chancellor Clarendon] to Sec. Bennet. Requests for the author [Sam. Butler] a licence for the sole printing of the first, second, and third parts of Hudibras.

9. Francesco Corbott to the King. Was ill on his journey to Paris, and too ill on his arrival to see Madame. His Majesty promised him favour, if owing to the impediments that Sir Hen. Bennet makes to his game, he cannot profit by his promised letter of change. Has received no profit, and failed to obtain the money which he hoped for in Paris; begs that he may return to throw himself at His Majesty's feet. [*Italian.*]

10. [Sec. Bennet?] to the Mayor of Norwich. The King gave authority in 1662 to the magistrates of that town to allow or disallow the keeping of shows, games, and lotteries, in order to avoid abuses happening by their licentious exercise; but now signifies his pleasure that no lotteries are to be allowed, except as appointed by Sir Ant. Desmarces, to whom the management of the same is granted, for benefit of the Royal Fishing Company. [*Draft.*]

11. Edw. Arundel to Sec. Bennet. Requests favour, as the son of Paul Arundel who was in Ireland in Queen Elizabeth's time. Has served in the Imperial armies till 1661; came over to find employment in England, but failing in this, begs a passport to return to Germany. [*French.*]

12. —— to [Sec. Bennet]. Requests him to obtain the King's toleration for his seeming a friend to his enemies; and freedom from harm for a person to be sent from them, to offer compliance with the writer's proposals. Asks also a grant of money to persons necessary to effect the business.

13. Wm. Reid to Sec. Bennet. Has lost 500*l.* from the seizure of the St. Francis, and is now under restraint. Begs him to sign a paper, by which he may be freed from debt and restraint. [*Damaged.*]

14. Peter Cullum to Sec. Bennet. Has brought his adversary to consent to take 8*l.* 10*s.* and a bond for the rest of the debt, which with charges comes to 16*l.*, but he threatens an execution, unless it be paid at once. Begs help, fearing to be ruined by being kept where he is.

15. Elizabeth Countess of Guildford to Sec. Bennet. Hopes that Lord Crofts has satisfied him as to her behaviour. Wishes to vindicate Col. Gilbert Carr to the King and Duke of Ormond, and to obtain a pass for him to live abroad. [*Two pages.*]

16. Sir Rob. Howard to Sec. Bennet. Wishes he could have been heard, before the King or Mr. Killigrew had been in the way, the informations given being utterly false. Mrs. Weavers brought in all her parts three weeks before, told the company that she would act no more, and refused to stay though pressed; she afterwards proved

Vol. CIX.

1664?

to be with child, and therefore they were glad of her absence, wishing the stage to be a place of credit, and not one that persons of honour would avoid. [*One and a quarter pages.*]

17. Phil. Frowde to Sec. Bennet. Begs to be informed of the difference between the true and false packet, if two are sent to Sir George Downing, lest he commit an error.

Friday. 18. H. Slingsby to Sec. Bennet. Has 40,000*l.* to pay to Mr Backwell, on receipt of the King's warrant justifying the paying it.

Monday. 19. H. S[lingsby to Williamson]. The King and Council are considering the rates of gold, and therefore want a speedy account of the price of our 20*s.* piece of gold in the Paris mint, and whether any work is doing there. Endorsed "Write to Lord Holles about gold, &c."

20. G. P. to [Williamson ?] There are four regiments of discontent Scotch and English forming in Holland, and they intend in that way to trouble the King's affairs; the management of the business is left to De Witt. There is a great desire for Lambert's liberty; he is thought necessary for any occasion that may arise, but is probably ignorant of or averse to such things himself. A messenger has been sent to tell him that there is a commission for his execution, on the least stir; he writes back that he hesitates to escape, because he is under several bonds not to do so. The messenger has returned with a letter to say that the thing, being necessary, is just by all laws both divine and human. [*Two pages.*]

21. John Steward [a madman ?] to Williamson. Begs help to establish King James's son, the founder of many cities, in the house where Mr. Cornish dwells. His cows have been killed; wishes all cow killers blinded till the wronged are satisfied. Wants an appointment in the King's chapel or bedchamber for his son, Mark Coleman, who can sing, play on the viols and preach extempore. [*Two pages.*]

22. Sir Phil. Meadowes to Williamson. Hopes by a search amongst his papers to recover the declaration he formerly had of Cromwell's; knows not where else to direct him for it.

23. H. Lady Yarborough to Williamson. A boy whom she had in charge has been stolen away by spirits, as they call them, who convey such boys to ships for New England or Barbadoes. Begs a warrant for the bearer, whose apprentice he was, to search the ships going out, in order to reclaim him.

24. Sir Wm. Fleetwood to Williamson, at Lady Anderson's, Strand. Rejoices at his recovery. Sends him a buck as requested, though they decrease both in number and goodness.

Friday. 25. Lord St. John to Williamson. Requests notice before any new warrant is given for Mr. Brooke, of Cheshire, who petitions for one concerning a trial depending between him and Earl Rivers.

Vol. CIX.

1661?

26. Thos. Killigrew to Williamson. His friends offer Williamson 600*l*. at once, or 650*l*. in two payments, for the pricking lottery, which Sir Ant. [Desmarces] and his associates have power to dispose of. Argues that it is improbable he will dispose of it to better advantage.

27. —— —— to [Thos. Killigrew(?), reversioner of the mastership of the revels]. Requests him to prevail with Sir Hen. Bennet that some friends may have liberty from Sir Ant. Desmarces and Co. to use the pricking lottery, paying 200*l*. a year, as long as Sir Anthony has the management of it, which, excepting 100*l*. fine, is as much as the Fishing Commissioners ever offered. Reasons why they offer no more:—there were never more than eight lotteries in England, and they were licensed by the Master of the Revels, and let at such rent as from 25*l*. to 30*l*. a year; the person addressed having the reversion of the lotteries promised after the Royal Fishing Company, there will be no difficulty in securing the reversion by giving it up into Desmarces' hands, and suffering his friends to continue the farm. The Fishing Company's interest lasts two years from Easter next. [*One and a half pages.*]

28. Proposal to give 1,000*l*. to Sir Ant. Desmarces and Co. for the reversion of the pricking lottery, which expires in two years, provided the propounders may hold it those two years, likewise to pay expenses and the 100*l*. a year which Mr. Killigrew paid to the Fishing Commissioners; this offer is a great adventure, and Sir Anthony cannot hope for a better.

29. Barth. Hesketh to [Williamson]. The person about whom Capt. Dale speaks is a tall man called Smith, much disguised, who only goes out at night, he is said to be a rumper, and in fear of his life. With note that he lodges at the Key, St. John's Street, opposite Hickes Hall.

30. E. Montague to Williamson. Requests a copy of his brother [Ralph Montague]'s warrant for tenancy of a third part of Gillingham Forest.

31. Chevalier de Gramont to [Williamson ?]. Requests a passport for the Marquis de Raie, for some dogs which are already bought. [*French.*]

32. —— Joly to Williamson. Reminds him of the Savoy gentleman to whom he promised a letter to the Prince of Orange. [*French.*]

33. Thos. Harper to Williamson. Sends a packet directed for Sir Hen. Morice, but which must be a mistake, for Sir Hen. Bennet, as Mr. Coke, Sir Wm. Morice's secretary, has a packet of the same hand and seal.

34. ——— to [Williamson]. Professions of grateful respect to [Sir Hen.] Bennet. [*French, damaged.*]

VOL. CIX.

1664?

35. Thos. Agar to Williamson. Has failed to find the record he asks for, though he has searched the book, from the passing of the Earl of Strafford's patent as lieutenant of Ireland to his death; thinks it must have passed the signet only, and not the great seal. [*Damaged.*]

36. John Hatcher to Williamson. Has been prevented visiting him by the stay of his Hertfordshire relations. [*Damaged.*]

37. Marquis of Montbrun to the King. Driven by his expenses to restore his fortune by His Majesty's justice, came over three years ago, and having obtained it, sounded his praises through the court of France. Hopes this justice will continue; must be a beggar for it, contrary to the tenor of his past life, the history of which is now being written and waits his revision. His Majesty is mentioned in it as he ought to be, such an opportunity of succouring a distressed prince rarely happening; considers this action the finest of his life. [*French.*]

38. —— Dacres to Lord General [Albemarle]. Dares not presume to address the King for himself, but begs his Grace to intercede with His Majesty to forget what has been represented to his disadvantage, and free him from imprisonment; the King shall never have reason to repent his clemency; will endeavour to show cordial affection to his person and welfare.

39–43. Letters in short-hand in 1663 and 1664, addressed to Edw. Martindale, of Taunton, Somersetshire. With a key to a few of the symbols. Five papers.

44. List of 43 persons in England, and one in Ireland, who are dispersers of Quakers' books. Endorsed "Q. how proved."

45. Declaration of belief that the King has an undoubted right to the throne, and that none has any right to depose him therefrom, or to excommunicate him, or absolve his subjects from their allegiance; also of willingness to defend him, and disclose any plots made against him; of detestation of the doctrine that the Pope can depose, deprive, or murder princes, &c. Endorsed "Quakers' oath." [*Two pages, damaged.*]

46. The same declaration as made by Hen. Foster, of Sutton, Isle of Ely.

47. Order that a person described be secured, if found near Whitehall or St. James's, and notice given to Sec. Bennet. Endorsed "The Ironmonger espion, Sir T. Gower."

48. Note of the correspondence of Chris. Eyon, of Barnard Castle, a great fanatic, with merchants in Holland, and George and Reynold Faucett, in London; also of John Cock, Lady Vane's steward, at Raby Castle, a dangerous person, who writes to Caleb Perior in London. Endorsed "Sir P. Musgrave."

VOL. CIX.

1664?

49. Request by Sir J. Coughter (?) for the Secretary to hear George Withams' replies to what may be objected against him.

50. Names and addresses of numerous persons in the bishopric of Durham, some in gaol, who have frequent communion with a certain party, and of others suspected to be dangerous persons.

51. Note that Theop. Hart, of Wappenham near Towcester, and Tim. Hart, of Mixbury, co. Oxford, ministers, are most pernicious persons, and probably connected with any plot in those parts.

52. Particulars of the proceedings of George Cooke, of Essex, of Wm. Miller, formerly belonging to Blackwell Hall, and of their mutual acquaintance.

53. Order [in Council] that Sec. Bennet write to —— Streter to hinder meetings of Quakers, &c.; also that Carr be taken, and Knight proceeded against.

54. Note that young Desborough of Norwich rides about with pistols visiting the Quakers, and is intimate with Col. Scrope, who revolted from General Monk in Scotland.

55. Charge of Sir Fras. Wortley, Bart., at the sessions. Lauds the cause of order; praises monarchy as the best form of government; shows the provisions made by the English constitution for the liberty of the subject, and recalls the miseries of the late disorder. Describes the duties of the justices and juries at sessions, viz.: to enquire into, though not to punish treason, stating what actions are treasonable; to enquire into and present felonies to the next assizes, describing their different kinds, and also misdemeanors. Exhorts all constables and other civil officers to do their best for prevention and prosecution of crime; and the juries to act without fear or favour, not lessening crimes, as the country would else be filled with desperate rogues and sturdy thieves. Endorsed "For Mr. Garrett." [*Six pages.*]

56. Account [by Edm. Potter], of conventicles, fasts, and meetings held by the Presbyterians at the houses of Col. Hunt, of Shropshire, Mr. Benbow, near Laurence Lane, London, &c. Details of numerous persons of that party and their proceedings. They boast that they have intelligence of all that passes at Court, and laugh at the three regiments more of horse which the King will raise, boasting that they are assured of 50,000 men in London. Col. Hunt's eldest son keeps 30 horses at Shrewsbury ready for service. Hampden, Baxter, and Dr. Manton often meet to confer at a lord's house 17 miles from London, towards Oxford. Col. Hunt has a dinner, called the parsons' ordinary, at his lodging every Tuesday. Before discovery of the Yorkshire conspiracy, they boasted that it was carried on so closely that all the wisdom of Council should never disappoint it, and said that Oliver had a quicker scent for discovering a plot than any now have; they are more reserved now, admit none to their meetings but by ticket, and sometimes exclude their daughters

VOL. CIX.

1664?

and wives. Great persons are requested to leave their coaches and come privately; they make collections often, and stave off with gifts those who for poverty are likely to conform, as Dr. Bryan, of Coventry. Mr. Calamy has lately had 500*l.* to distribute. Mr. Baxter often preaches at Hampden's house near St. John's, fitted up on purpose, Mr. Jacom, Mr. Whittaker, and Mr. Poole at the Countess of Exeter's. They advise that all the ejected ministers take their own pulpits again, and see if the people will not stand by them. Mr. Calamy preached every Sunday at his own house, till he was taken ill. Names of other preachers and places of worship. Sam. Gellibrand, of St. Paul's Churchyard, and Fras. Titon, of St. Dunstan's, are their booksellers; Dr. Wild is their poet. [*Two pages.*]

57. Note [by Edw. Potter] that And. Pyke, a loyal and discreet young man, is servant to Col. Hunt, and account of the best way of sending for him by a servant of Mr. Blunden, of Paternoster Row.

58. Note that Ralph Alexander, tailor of Moorfields, sent 400 tons of goods by a Coventry carrier, and query as to what is become of them. Endorsed "Arms dispersed."

59. Memorial of Col. Evils and Mr. Bronyen, late chaplain to Bradshaw, seditious subjects now residing in France, the latter of whom runs from place to place, exclaiming against King and government, seducing young gentlemen, and too much encouraged by English faction. Noted "East Greenwich, Mr. Thomas's patent."

60. Information sent to Council of John Bull, a silk throwster, Brick Lane, Whitechapel, a very dangerous person, who has a meeting house in his yard, has great acquaintance of soldiers and seamen, and influences them against their loyalty, and that it will be great damage to the kingdom and to the affairs now on foot, if he is allowed to remain free.

61. Notes [by Williamson], that Widow Harrison of Scarborough is to watch Joplin, that he have no concern there; that Eleanor Simcox, who carried the letters to and from Durham, and was with Joplin, is in London; and query as to the proceedings on Waller's examination at Durham.

62. Note that Eleanor Simcox lives in Bishopsgate Street, and would best be heard of from the letter carrier; he knows all people by their names who correspond with their accomplices by letter.

63. Note that counsellors, procurers, aiders, &c., of certain treasons are all within the compass of high treason.

64. Account, addressed to Lord Crofts, of 13 fanatics at East Sheen, where conventicles are innumerable; Col. Shepherd and his son Matthew; John Ireton, formerly lord mayor; Nich. Juxon, justice in Oliver's time, &c.

65. Proposal to let a piece of land, the draining of which cost the late King 8,000*l.*, at the rent of 1,000*l.* for two thirds, the other

Vol. CIX.

1664?

third to be granted for charges of repairing and finishing the draining. Endorsed "Proportion of fen—Earl of Shrewsbury's petition."

66. Report by Mr. Garret that Carey, late verger of St. Paul's, says that Alderman Pack, of Blackwell Hall, or Mr. Jermyn, the city carpenter in Little Moorfields, can discover the will of Henry VII., with seals affixed in silver boxes; also a chalice, crozier, staff, and other things formerly belonging to St. Paul's, in which Warner, a verger, may assist.

67. Statement of the scope of the bill to compel Lady Leveson, widow of Sir Rich. Leveson, to sell three fourths of the manor of Balsall, in order to pay the debts of her sister, Lady Anne Holbourn, who died in August 1663, and to whom she was residuary legatee. A fragment, endorsed with notes on the subject, showing that both ladies and Douglas Lady Kniveton were daughters of Sir Rob. Dudley, son of Rob. Earl of Leicester, and that he died in 1630.

68. Charge by John Williams against several persons, most of them men of good estate still living, for embezzling and carrying goods from the King's mint and storehouse in Cardiganshire, value 3,000*l*., in 1647; coining money without warrant, stealing coining irons and stamps, sending over silver, lead, &c., to Holland, and relieving Shrewsbury with money against His Majesty.

69. Answers to objections for building a bridge over the Thames, between Westminster and Lambeth, with a plan of the arches of the proposed bridge; the objections being danger of its breaking, interruptions to the course of the river, and injury to the employment of watermen. The reasons in favour of a bridge are the convenience of passage to the King and two Queens to their residences at Greenwich, Nonsuch, and Hampton Court; increase of trade to Westminster; better and more speedy access for soldiers to Southwark, the nest of fanatics, where in two or three days, they assembled 4,000 or 5,000, and whither the troops cannot now go in less than three hours; and the formation of a strong quarter to lodge troops on the bridge. The expense to be borne by a voluntary contribution of neighbouring gentry, and such a toll as London Bridge now receives for repairs. [*Three pages.*]

70. Abstract of the case of James Pickering, Gilbert Havers, and other owners of the Unity of London. In 1638 their ship, bound for a port in Biscay, then besieged by the French, was taken by the Duke d'Epernon, then Lord Admiral of France, for the French navy, and the men were turned ashore and satisfaction promised. The loss was estimated by the French at 14,500*l*., but now they falsely pretend that satisfaction was given in 1640.

71. Statement by Mr. Gelson that he is engaged by the owner of some money and cloth taken by a Dutch caper, to recover it. He proposes sending the master and a judicious seaman to the ports of Holland, who in seeking the caper, would take account of the ships,

Vol. CIX.

1664?

garrisons, disposition of the people, &c., in Holland. The sum taken away from the master is 165*l.*, and there is a design to let 50*l.* go to the King, and divide the rest with the owner, but the poor man who has been abused by delays, &c., for six or seven months, should be considered. [*One and a half pages.*]

72. Proposition of Erasmus Purling, engineer, and subject of His Majesty, to construct an engine to row with 100, or 120 and carry 1,000 or 1,500 men, safe from musket or cannon shot, wherewith he can enter a fleet of ships of war, and fire or sink the whole; and can take blockhouses or forts at the entrance of a harbour, and all at inconsiderable expense.

73. Account of the town of Hartlepool, its harbour, situation, inhabitants—chiefly fishermen, Norway merchants, and tradespeople,—and size, showing that it may be easily fortified and rendered very strong. *Annexing,*

73. I. *Plan of the town, and of the sea coast thence to Stockton.*

74. Report by Lord Chamberlain Manchester, the Earl of Lauderdale, and Sir. Jo. Denham, that Thos. Killigrew has not exceeded the powers granted him by his patent; it gave him entire authority over the actors, which he has hitherto used but little, and the complaints against him for giving powers of attorney to Moon, Hart, and Lacy to superintend the rest are not well founded, as the letter of attorney is recalled, &c. [*Two pages.*]

75. Reference by Lord Treas. Southampton,—on a petition of —— Spencer and five others for commissions to recover marsh land in Essex—to the Surveyor General and Attorney General, to consider how it can be done without injury to particular persons, yet reserving the King's rights; and report of Surveyor General Harbord, advising that inquisitions of the lands petitioned for be fairly taken, on public notice that all persons concerned may be heard and their leases granted; and of Attorney General Palmer, recommending the issue of a commission thereon, and nominating nine Commissioners. [*Copies.*]

76. Account of the reception and treatment of the King at Fontarabia, at the Treaty of the Pyrenees. With note that the first misunderstanding between Sir Hen. Bennet and the Earl of Clarendon arose from the free advertisement he gave as to those whom "the Spaniards would or would not look well upon."

77. Memoranda by Sir Wm. Tyringham of the rents at which the excise of six counties is farmed, with the farmers' names; viz., Oxford, Sir Thos. Pennystone and Robt. Knowles, 4,700*l.*; Somerset, George Skipp, 5,400*l.*; Hants and Isle of Wight, Benj. Thistlethwaite and Wm. Warner, 3,900*l.*; Lancashire, Pierce Lee and Hen. Houghton, 4,950*l.*; Bedfordshire, Fras. Crawley, 1,870*l.*; Bristol and Gloucestershire, Edm. Chamberlain, 8,800*l.*

78. Account of the expenses of "Charles's journey" from London to Newcastle, and back; total, 12*l.* 3*s.* 6*d.* [*Two pages.*]

VOL. CIX.

1664?

79. List [by Sec. Bennet] of 12 garrisons which have sent in their accounts, and of nine which have not.

80. List [by Wm. Coventry] of the Navy Commissioners, with the number of commissions, from two to six each, issued to them, for pressing men, &c., for the navy, leaving out purveyance of goods, as taken away by the last Act of Parliament, but specially mentioning ropemakers.

81. Statement of the large sums already discovered by Rich. Pight, the Earls of Dorset and Carlisle, and others, to whom commissions have been issued for discovery of prize goods, besides above 300,000*l.* which will be lost without a commission, proceedings by that mode being so much speedier and less costly than by the Exchequer or Admiralty Courts; Dr. Walker is willing to be both a commissioner and counsellor in the business. Endorsed "Hatchett, &c., Duke of Monmouth."

82. "Catalogue of books brought in [to the State Paper Office] from Haberdashers' Hall," being 17 books of Indemnity, from 1647 to 1603.

Project by Sir S. Crow, thrown into a tabular form, for a great addition to the wealth and common stock of our nation, by thrift in making more use of our own commodities and abstaining from foreign commodities, and by improvement in tillage, draining, planting, shipping, fishing, navigation, trade, &c. [*Case B., Charles II., No 3.*]

83. Proposals addressed to the King and Council to erect an office for transporting to the plantations all rogues, beggars, and felons convicted of petty larcenies, sending them to the next seaport, where provision shall be made for their transportation; all persons to be sent thither who cannot give a good account of themselves; such persons to serve 4 years when abroad if above 20 years of age, and 7 years if under; all such persons to be first registered, on penalty of 20*l.* Half the fines paid by merchants, mariners, or planters, for persons to be transported to be given to the King, the other half to the officers for transport.

84. Proposal to meet the extraordinary public necessities by putting the public seal on papers or parchments relating to business, as bonds, bills, licences, petitions, custom house entries, &c., on payment of from 1*d.* to 4*s.* a sheet, acording to the importance of the document. [*One and a quarter pages.*]

85. Remarks by John Bowring, on the importance of re-establishing the Courts of Survey and Augmentation, as the best mode of improving the revenue. He has other most material things to communicate, but wishes to do so to the King in person, rather than to commit them to paper, and also to explain to him the project of the late King for settling his revenue, so as to assist himself, in case of domestic broils.

VOL. CIX.

1664?

86. Proposal, signed Eady, for taking off chimney-money and all other taxes, except customs, impost and excise, and increasing the excise in lieu thereof, on a scale proposed.

87. Note [by Williamson] that the Society for the Plantation of Ulster had lands granted them, some of which they gave to the 12 London companies, for being at the expense of the plantation; that the society's patent was repealed, but is now re-granted, with a licence of mortmain to the 12 companies. Also, list of the officers of the Mint.

88. Account of the present state of the Mint; that no foreign coin or bullion is brought there to be sold, because of the efforts now making to obtain permission for export of gold and silver, whereby higher rates are expected, so that 100*l.* in silver has not been brought for coining since the Restoration. With an account of the Mint officers and their salaries, and of the nature of incidental charges there. [*Two and a quarter pages.*]

89. Extracts from Acts of Parliament, &c., 4 Edw. III. to 16 Charles II., relative to the intervals at which Parliaments are to be held. [*Two and a half pages.*]

90. Order of precedency of noblemen and their families.

91. [John Evelyn's] "Kalendarium Hortense, or Instructions for each Month of what is required to be done in the Orchard and Olitory Garden, and in the Parterre and Flower Garden." With title and a table of the contents of the chapters of his "Sylva," printed 1664. Particulars of large oak trees found in different localities, and of the prices for which they were sold. Discourses on cider by Dr. Smith and Capt. Taylor, and extracts from [Evelyn's] "Sylva, or a Discourse on Forest Trees." Extracts from sermons (?) on the causes of heresy and schism, of error in Christian life, of the evils of sects in the Church, and the sin of transgressing against the powers that be. [*Book in parchment cover, of 57 written and several blank pages. At the end of the book are accounts of money transactions, in Spanish,* 1642, 1643, *and* 1651.]

92. Information as to the printers of the following books:—"The Juryman's Charge," by Rich. Creaven, a Fifth-Monarchy man; "Pure Encouragement," by Wm. Baillie; "England's Warning;" "A book to the judges and jury," by Wm. Smith; "Election of Reprobation," by George Bishop; "Christian Religious Meetings allowed," and "The Soul's Duty and Safety in a Trying Time," by Rich. Fernswith; also note of Rebecca Trewish, of Watling Street, as a writer. The printers named are Widow Dover, of Bartholomew Close; Sam. Simmons, of Aldersgate Street; Widow Jennens, of Addlehill; and Redman, in Paul's Alley. Endorsed "Concerning printers of seditious books."

93. Expedients proposed to prevent the disturbance of the government; viz.,—care to be taken in the North to allow no great meetings

VOL. CIX.

1664?

till Spring is past, and to watch over six officers of the old army, who go and come thence; also over Portsmouth, and such part of the navy as served the Parliament and refused to serve the King; and over persons seemingly neuter, who keep Presbyterian ministers, or soldiers or officers of the late army, in their houses; 200 horsemen rose in Suffolk on the late plot, but not finding the plotters of their own party, retired quietly. Enquiries should be made in Holland after such as have retired to the Spaw, &c., amongst whom are Sidney and Ludlow, and after money and letters sent to them. Their chiefest reliance is on the old army in Ireland, which they think has been preserved to finish the work begun, and 32 officers have invited Ludlow over; they intend to seize Kinsale and Limerick. They are not discouraged by the failure of their plot at Dublin. [*Three pages.*]

94. List of the ships in the Royal navy; total, 132 ships, 18,671 men, and 4,519 guns, besides 14 smaller vessels, not men-of-war, and several yachts, &c., belonging to His Majesty.

95. List of 47 ships in the King's pay, giving the names of the captains, some of the lieutenants, and of the ships' destinations; with note that some are to be paid off and larger ones sent out in their places; others to be paid off, in order to lessen the expense of setting out the 13 first named. [*Two pages.*]

96. Preface to an account of the English navy, completing up to the present time the list of 125 ships published a few years before, because many imperfect lists are published, with design to represent the navy as inconsiderable.

97. Certificate by Sir Wm. Berkeley, that 21 men named out of the Dreadnought, were victualled for two days, whilst assisting to bring the Resolution to Spithead. [*Adm. Paper.*]

98. Plasterer's rates for making, poop and hand lanterns. [*Adm. Paper, two pages.*]

99. Report by Mr. Harris of Vittry canvas fit for service, at Mr. Berry's, Mr. Lordell's, and Mr. Ovlatt's. [*Adm. Paper.*]

100. Estimate for making provision for preserving 200 great masts at Portsmouth; total, 816*l.* 13*s.* 4*d.* [*Adm. Paper.*]

101. Abstract of victuallers' declarations from May to December. [*Adm. Paper.*]

102. Certificate by Moses Butler of his survey of timber, &c., tendered by Mr. Newburne, for Woolwich. [*Adm. Paper.*]

103. Tender by Chris. Cole of plank and treenails. [*Adm. Paper.*]

104. Memoranda relative to Mr. Lowe's rafters and John Watts' oars. [*Adm. Paper.*]

105. Minutes of several contracts for purchase of deals, dram timber, and oaken plank for the navy. [*Adm. Paper.*]

Vol. CIX.

1664?

106. Order for reference of a petition, not specified, to Sir Orlando Bridgman, Lord Chief Justice of Common Pleas, and Sir Matthew Hale, Lord Chief Baron.

Petitions, all addressed to the King, unless otherwise specified.

107. John Alcock, prisoner in the Gatehouse, to Sec. Bennet, for release on bail, in order to expose the odious malice of his enemies, who suborned false witnesses to swear treason against him; he was acquitted, and recovered 100*l.* damages against them, in revenge for which they renew their charge, and have thrown him into prison.

108. Anonymous. For the erection of an office for Survey of all Vessels coming in or going out of ports, so that none be permitted to enter without a certificate of health, in order to avoid the introduction of the pestilence. [*Much damaged.*]

109. Sir John Armitage, of Kirklees, co. York. Marching to the assistance of Lord [Sir George] Booth, in Lancashire, before the Restoration, was attacked and taken prisoner by George Denham, and his horses, value 100*l.*, taken from him, for which he recovered 72*l.* damages at law; but before he could obtain the money, Denham was hanged at York for high treason, and his lands, by attainder, devolved on His Majesty. Begs permission to retain such land as he has extended for his debt, until it be satisfied.

110. Thomas, son of Sir Humphrey Bennet, Lieut. in Sir Wm. Killigrew's company in the Duke of York's regiment. For the command of the said company, in case of the death of Sir William, who is now dangerously ill.

111. Rebecca Brown, of Middlesex, widow. That her son Matthew, who as a porter haberdasher, is constantly passing and repassing in the City, may have a protection from being pressed for His Majesty's service, as his family are dependent upon him.

112. Nathaniel Cale, late mayor of Bristol. For reversion of a tellership in the Exchequer. Was sequestered and decimated in the late troubles, and spent much money in the office of mayor, undertaken to remove disaffected persons from the government, even before the late Act of Regulation [of Corporations], by which he has contracted much envy and malice.

113. Nic. Carter. For a mandamus to the University of Cambridge for his Doctor's degree; is a Fellow of Clare Hall, M.A. of 12 years' standing, but long deprived of his fellowship, and of the advantage of taking his M.D. degree at the usual time. [*Degree granted* 1665.] *Annexing,*

113. i. *Certificate by Fras. Glisson, professor of medicine, and Drs. Chr. Terne and Gasp. Nedham, in favour of the petitioner.*

Vol. CIX.

1664 ?

Petitions—continued.

114. Peter, son of the late Elizabeth Carey. For relief, the pension of 40*l.* a year, paid to his mother for her hazardous services to his late and present Majesty, having ceased on her death.

115. Capt. John Cary. Details his services to the late King as captain of horse, in which service he lost some of his limbs, raised troops at his own expense, and afterwards left employment, and a pension in the [Spanish] Low Countries, to serve as adjutant to the Duke of Gloucester, but has waited two years in vain for employment. Begs a pension, employment in a garrison, or money for a horse and equipage to serve in the Royal Guards.

116. Capt. John Cary. For employment, or a letter to the Governor of the Low Countries, to restore him a pension which he formerly had there, but left in order to serve in the late Duke of Gloucester's regiment; served as captain, and raised a company at his own charge in the late war.

117. Thomas Chiffinch. Begs that for avoidance of the pestilence, which in 1603, 1625, and 1636, were brought into this kingdom from the Mediterranean, precautions may be used here as in all those ports, except by the Turks who believe in predestination; that an office be erected to visit goods or passengers, none to land without certificate, and that all diseased persons remain first on shipboard, and afterwards apart on shore.

118. Thos. Davies, His Majesty's servant. For substitution of Rob. Vyner, of London, goldsmith, and Thos. Vyner, instead of George Digby and Thos. Lisle, as the two lives during which he has a grant of the place of Water Bailiff of Dover; has contracted debts by building a place on the bank side for the King's game of bears and bulls.

119. Sir Fras. Dodington. For the place of a Commissioner for reprisals in the port of London.

120. Charles Viscount Fitzharding, Wm. Lord Crofts, and John Lord Berkeley. For a commission of inquiry into the right of common possessed by divers towns, &c. in Whitwood Forest, co. Northampton, and satisfaction to the claimants thereof; the rest to be improved to the King's use, the soil being dirty and unfit for hunting; also for a lease for sixty years to the petitioners of a moiety thereof, in recompense for the pains and penalties they are willing to undergo in effecting the said improvement.

121. Abraham Forester. For a patent for his new invention to mend highways and pave streets in the kingdom, enforcing the former laws for highways, and having a moiety of the forfeitures; the Commissioners of Highways have approved the trial he has made near St. James's Palace. Has waited a year without receiving any encouragement from Parliament, to which His Majesty recommended him. Asks also a commission to discover gifts made for the benefit of highways, and to recover the arrears.

VOL. CIX.

1664?

PETITIONS—*continued.*

122. Sir Faithful Fortescue. For a grant of the King's moiety of the forfeitures of such as have resolutely disobeyed the third proclamation for moderating the unconscionable prices of wines, on account of His Majesty's bounty in forgiving the penalties of disobeying the first; some of them are very rich men, exact unreasonable prices, and give mingled wines and false measure.

123. Similar petition to the same effect. *Annexing,*

123. I. *Sir Faithful Fortescue to Mr. Godolphin. Asks what is done in his petition, and if granted, wants a chapman for it. The gentleman keeps him prisoner in his chamber.*

124. Jane Gerrard, widow. For a lease of a small piece of ground in the tilt yard, to finish building a house in which to entertain His Majesty's Guards, to which she is continued sutler, in place of her late husband.

125. Matthias Grayson, of Knaresborough, co. York. For such rewards as are set forth by proclamation; being a gunsmith, not only refused to make arms for the rebels in the late horrid plot, but was the first to discover it to Rich. Hatton, Justice of peace, 31 July, 1663, and is the first who was examined thereon. Has been in [London] ever since May last, to the neglect of his calling, and received no reward. With certificate by Sir Thos. Gower and Sir John Goodrick to the truth of his petition. *Annexing,*

125. I. *Certificate by Lord Fauconberg, that Matthias Grayson is a well-affected servant, and in the most dangerous times furnished him and others with arms, powder, &c.*

126. The Partridge Keeper at Hampton Court. For order for such conveniences as shall enable him better to rear birds for His Majesty's pleasure. With note that the King wished the petition commended to Lord Fitzharding.

127. Wm. Harewood, quartermaster, Tim. Boughey, chaplain, and John Hounsborne, surgeon of the King's regiment of Guards, under Lord Wentworth. For re-establishment and continuance of their pay, which has been stopped since 3 Oct., 1663, at which time they were dispersed into garrisons, although His Majesty had declared his intention for the field and staff officers to remain entire. With note that the Lord General has seen and approved their petition.

128. Wm. Harrington. For permission to freight four or five ships from Lubec, or any other Baltic port, to convey the 700 loads of spruce planks with which he has contracted to supply the navy, English ships being so unfit for that service that they can be but half laden; will not else be enabled to fulfil his contract, while the French King engrosses the planks, and raises them to extravagant prices.

1664 ? Vol. CIX.

Petitions—*continued.*

129. James Haswell and Ant. Loraine, majors of horse; Hen. Horsdenel, lieutenant-colonel of foot; Thos. Selby, Wm. Carr, John Erington, and Thos. Carleton, captains of horse. To be enlisted, as disbanded officers, into some of the garrisons, so as to be in continual readiness for service. Are almost ruined by serving the late late King, from the beginning of the wars. *Annexing,*

129. i. *Certificate by Thos. [Lord] Wentworth and Sir Arthur Slingsby of the loyalty and good service in the army of Major Jas. Haswell. London, June 2, 1662.*

130. Col. Ralph Hebourne. For a company on a vacancy in a garrison. Served the late King through imprisonments and miseries; after the Restoration, had a foot company in Berwick, but was disbanded when the garrison was reduced.

131. Rebecca Herne. For release of her husband; he being at York on important business, although he is an officer of great trust in the City, and attorney at Westminster, was sent for and put in charge of Copley, a messenger, who keeps him close in a dismal garret; he had, by verbal order of the Lord Chamberlain, arrested Lawrence Seyrs, who owing him 900*l.*, procured himself to be sworn of the privy chamber, and then sold his estate, and was going to France.

132. Robert Hope, John Trethewy, and Alexander Croston, clerks of the spicery. For a similar warrant to that given to the first three clerks of the kitchen, for board wages from Michaelmas 1663 to 1664, notwithstanding the suspension of pensions.

133. James Houseman, Stephen Rogers, Thos. Perkins, and John Tyler, officers of the Customs of Dover. In pursuance of the proclamation of September 15, 1660, they have prosecuted more offences in export of wool than the whole nation besides, the forfeitures being above 1,800*l.*, one moiety of which has been paid into the Exchequer, but their moiety has not covered the expenses of serjeants-at-arms, messengers, intelligencers, suits-at-law, &c., and they meet with much discouragement and misrepresentation; pray that they may have the benefit of the said proclamation; that the messengers may be ordered privately to apprehend certain persons named by them for His Majesty's examination, and that he will hear their obstacles and proposals for removal thereof. [*Two pages.*]

134. Sir R. Langley. For the same grace as bestowed on other loyal persons; viz., a confirmation of his fee-farm rents of 80*l.* purchased during the usurpation, which have been taken from him and restored to the Crown; pleads his loyal services, especially in promoting the Restoration. Endorsed with abstract of the same. [*Draft by Williamson.*]

135. Bevis, brother of the late Sir Evan Lloyd, governor of Chester. For fulfilment of the King's promises to his brother, made when he was called upon, on a petition of the gentlemen of

VOL. CIX.

1664?

PETITIONS—*continued.*

Cheshire, to resign Chester Castle and fort to Sir Geoffry Shakerley, of reimbursement of sums expended about the garrison; his brother spent his estate and life in service of the late King. *Annexing,*

135. I, II. *Accounts by Sir Evan Lloyd of his disbursements concerning Chester Castle; total,* 408*l.* 4*s.* 2*d.* *Two papers.* *August* 1663.

Inhabitants of the suburbs of London. For establishment by Act of Parliament of the rate of prices for coal, established in 1638, on complaints of bad coal sold at excessive rates, and which was very useful whilst it lasted, but being interrupted by the late wars, the former abuses returned, and in 1657, many poor people were starved to death, from the unreasonable price of fuel. [*East India Papers, Vol.* xv., *f.* 78.]

136. Edm. Madocks. For pardon; but if guilty of bloodshed, he submits to the law; served at Dunkirk till the disbanding of Major Bridges' troop, and on his return, being out of employment, was induced to ill company.

137. Thos. Marsh. For a recommendation to be Chief Clerk to the Commissioners for the port of London, for prize goods. Is clerk assistant to the House of Commons, and was industrious to show, in the Committee for Trade, how His Majesty's honour was intrenched on by the Dutch. Had waited on him at Bruges with the original MS. of the proceedings of his father's murderers. His own father, Col. John Marsh, lost his inheritance by his loyalty.

138. Andrew Mollett, workman in the new royal garden in St. James's Park. For special order to pay the workmen, now one and a half years in arrears, or the garden must run to ruin, and cannot supply the privy kitchen of the King or Queen.

139. James Duke of Monmouth. For a lease, in reversion after the Farmers of Customs, of the impositions on coals exported, and in the meantime, for the defalcation of 2,000*l.* a year allowed to the farmers, till the termination of a lease thereof nearly expiring, granted by the late King to Henry Lucas and others.

140. Isaac Montague, gunsmith, born in France. For a warrant to continue his trade in Westminster, and for restitution of things seized from him by those of his own trade, who threaten his ruin. With note, that it is done by his being sworn King's servant extraordinary.

141. The Field Officers and Captains of the English Regiment of Horse which served in Portugal. For admission for the soldiers to the Royal Guards, as the foot soldiers who came from Portugal have been, many of them being in perishing condition.

Vol. CIX.

1664?

Petitions—*continued.*

142. Col. Henry Pearson and Col. Francis Moore. For employment or pensions, being recalled from their commands in Portugal, and having no means of subsistence.

143. Col. Henry Peirson and Col. Fras. Moore. To be put in some condition to serve, being called home from their commands in Portugal.

144. Matthew Penlall, of the Chapel Royal, to Sec. Bennet, to give him the fees incident to his service, or to remit them till he receives his salary, now much in arrears. Suffered much for his loyalty; and the want of a letter which is directed to Lord Holles, ambassador for France, will be his ruin.

145. Eliz. Countess Dowager of Peterborough and others. To pass their lease of derelict lands in several counties, which they have discovered at charge of 2,000*l.*, but are obstructed in the passing thereof, although they agreed with the Earl of Cleveland, Earl of Suffolk and Lord Fitzharding, who pretended to part thereof.

146. Elizabeth Countess Dowager of Peterborough, Eliz. Countess of Anglesey, and George Howard. To add six weeks to the time of two years prescribed by their warrant, during which to have concealed and derelict lands discovered by them, the inquisitions on the same not being perfected. *Annexing,*

146. i. *Warrant for a grant to the petitioners of concealed encroached, or derelict lands in Kent, Sussex, Hants, Norfolk, and Middlesex, discovered by them.*

147. Porters of the Gate. To order payment of the arrears of their board wages for 1664, as they alone of the officers below stairs were suspended from the allowance of board wages, notwithstanding their constant attendance day and night.

148. Teige Power, footman to the Duke of York. For a grant of a ruined house in King Street, Westminster, with leave to rebuild it; it is contested in law, and meanwhile is in a very dangerous condition, falling into the highways, and has already pulled down part of his house.

149. Sir George Reeve. Served the late and present Kings in the wars. As executor to the late Sir Hen. Reeve, advanced to his creditors 1,000*l.* due to him for wages as gentleman pensioner; had a warrant for 500*l.* of it from the arrears of excise, which cost him 26*l.*, but has done him no good; begs to receive the sum from the growing excise, or some other way.

150. Sir George Reeve. For some other way of paying the said 500*l.*

151. Willm. Saffery, of Deal, mariner. For relief; lost an arm and both hands eight years ago, in a fight against the Turks, for the honour of the English nation, and preservation of merchant's goods, and has received no reward.

Vol. CLX.

1661 ?

Petitions—*continued*.

152. Francis and John Simpson, His Majesty's jewellers in ordinary. For help to restore their lost credit, injured by reports both here and abroad, of their being so disabled by His Majesty's nonpayments that they want moneys to buy bread, all which is very true. Ask reparation from those who have so often disobeyed His Majesty's commands, on purpose to ruin them.

153. John Southcote. For appointment as a Commissioner for Prizes in Devonshire. Spent most of his fortune in His Majesty's service, seven years before the Restoration. *Annexing*,

153. i. *The King to* [*John Southcote*]. *Hears that he is ready to assist him, and has done so. Begs him to continue in the same good affection, and hopes he will soon have an opportunity to express it; will repay, if God bless him, any money expended on his account.* [*Copy.*]

154. Clara, wife of Capt. Edw. Spragg. For payment of 50s. a month, decreed for her by the Duke of York from the pay of her husband, who has deserted her, or if he will return her the money he had with her, she will go to Dunkirk where she was born, and leave him with his new mistress.

155. John Staybanck, oarmaker. For payment of 34*l.* 8*s.* due for several sets of oars for His Majesty's barges; has waited several days on the Treasurer of the Chamber, but cannot obtain a penny, and is very poor.

156. Henry Stubbe, physician. To be appointed to the charge of such seamen as may contract any sickness during their service, at Yarmouth, Dunwich, Aldborough, and Southwold.

157. Robt. Swan. Had an order for the Town Clerk's place of Newcastle, but Sir John Marley slighting it, bought the place for his own son Robert, and refused him admission; having contracted debts in obtaining the place, has now been five months in prison; begs that as Sir John Marley's mayoralty is over, he may have an order for admission to the place, and for dismissal of Rob. Marley.

158. The Serjeant and Officers of the 16 Trumpeters and Kettledrummers. For a year's salary, from the 15,000*l.* now assigned to the Treasurer of the Chamber; they are three years in arrears, and some of them reduced to great want.

159. Justina, daughter of Sir Ant. Vandyck. For continuance of her pension of 200*l.*, stopped a year ago, or some other relief, having nothing else to subsist upon.

160. Ralph Wallis to Sec. Bennet. Begs him not to crush a worm unworthy of his hand, but restore him to liberty, being in a messenger's custody, and not to starve a poor family for scribbling a little drollery, stories picked up, for bread; only touched the priests

1664?

VOL. CIX.

PETITIONS—*continued.*

that they may learn better manners, and will scribble as much against fanatics, when the worm gets into his cracked pate, as it did when he wrote those books.

161. Ralph Wallis, the scribbling cobler, still in Newgate, to Sec. Bennet, for an intimation to Sir Rich. Browne, that he leaves the petitioner to the court of justice, and will not withstand his release, which was ordered by sessions, on bail of Sir Rich. Browne, but Sir Richard declines to give the bail till he knows his honour's pleasure.

162. Captn. John Walsh and David Lacy, late of Col. Fitzgerald's regiment. To be placed in the same condition as their fellow officers dismissed at Tangiers, none of whom are left unprovided for but themselves.

163. Edw. Warren. For relief; discovered and caused the apprehension of George Elton, a person dangerous and malicious to His Majesty, and the fanatics who abound there so threaten his abode and practice that he has been obliged to remove to Westminster, where he must perish without aid.

164. Col. Stephen White. For relief; served in the Foot Guards till their first reducement, but has now been a year without pay.

165. The Widows and Orphans of those who were slain in the Royal service. For some provision for their present and future relief, to save them from perishing, as neither Act of Parliament has provided for them. With a list of 162 names of females. *Annexing,*

165. i. *Proposals on behalf of the widows and orphans in the petition annexed; that the benefit shall be confined to those whose husbands had real commands, whose accounts will bear an audit, and who have received nothing from the 60,000l. or the Act for widows and orphans; that they shall have divided amongst them, according to rank, the profits resulting from their discoveries of arrears of rent, benefit of renewing leases, and moneys charged on accountants in the Savoy and Whitefriars; that they shall be excused the fees on passing grants, &c., and have persons appointed to carry on the business.*

166. Luke Wilkes, yeoman, and the Officers of the removing wardrobe. For payment of the arrears of their salary and other allowances, and for due provision therefor in time to come: their allowances for attendance, &c., were fixed to a stated sum, 620l. a year and 40l. for washing; they are two years in arrears of their salary and seven months of their board wages of 14s. a day, granted in lieu of five dishes a meal.

167, 168. Two drafts of the above [*written or corrected by Williamson*].

VOL. CIX.

1664?

PETITIONS—*continued.*

169. Sir Edw. Wingfield. For a place as Commissioner for prize goods.

170. Henry Wynn, solicitor general to the Queen-Mother. For a grant to Roger Mostyn and John Wynn, both of the Inner Temple, of the reversion of the office of Prothonotary and Clerk of the Crown for cos. Carnarvon, Merioneth, and Anglesey for life; Wm. Wynn and Wm. Jones, to whom it was granted by the late King, being dead.

171. Robt. Wyvill. For pardon of 1,248*l.* 17*s.* 6*d.*, which he is in arrears in bringing up the monthly assessments, owing to loss by bills of exchange, &c. His late brother, Wm. Wyvill, sold his estate, value 4,000*l.* and engaged him as security in debts for promoting the Restoration, for some of which he is now involved in vexatious suits. *Annexing,*

171. I. *Request for a privy seal for the said remission, to save him from utter ruin.*

VOL. CX. JANUARY 1–10, 1664–5.

1664–5.

Jan. 1. Coldmoor, Herefordshire. 1. Herb. Aubrey, jun., to Williamson. Rejoices in his employment under so good a prince. Enquired after him through Mr. Westfaling, burgess of Hereford. Would be glad to hear from him and their eternally honoured friend, Mr. Ball. [*One and a half pages.*]

Jan. 1. Warrant for a commission to James Duke of Ormond of the office of Lieutenant for Somersetshire and the city of Bristol. [*Ent. Book* 16, *p.* 323.]

Jan. Entry of the above, dated Jan. 2. [*Ent. Book* 16, *p.* 238.]

Jan. 1. The Augustine, Portsmouth. 2. Capt. Rich. Teale to the Navy Comrs. Has arrived at Portsmouth; part of the goods are delivered. Wants victuals. [*Adm. Paper.*]

Jan. 1. The Drake, Downs. 3. Capt. Tobias Sackler to the Navy Comrs. Wants a boat to replace his own, lost in chasing a Dutch prize; also some provisions, and repair of the brickwork of two furnaces. [*Adm. Paper.*]

Jan. 1. The John and Margaret, Downs. 4. Capt. Geo. Chappell to the Navy Comrs. Has arrived in the Downs with the Greyhound; but the other two men-of-war and the ships bound for East India are not yet come up. The sea provisions want recruiting; is constrained to buy wood for the present spending, not having heard of nor seen his purser lately; begs another appointed if he is ill. [*Adm. Paper.*]

Jan. 2. Chatham. 5. Commissioner Peter Pett to Sam. Pepys. Finds the cordage in the yard stronger than the Yarmouth cordage. Sends a certifi-

VOL. CX.

1664–5

cate of two parcels of hemp, lately delivered into the stores; hopes by dear bought experience to convince the Board of the necessity of buying provisions from merchants, to be served in immediately. There is a demand from Deptford for black oakum. [*Adm. Paper.*] *Encloses*,

5. I. *Edw. Gregory, Phil. Barrow, and John Owen to [the Navy Comrs.] Account of the hemp lately delivered at Chatham; 11 tons are dry, five tons wet, but dried again, at an expense of 40l.; eight tons wet and rotten. The Quinsborough hemp was five cwt. short of weight, and a ton had to be dried.* *Chatham, January* 2, 1665.

Jan. 2. Lydney. 6. Dan. Furzer to the Navy Comrs. Has met no great encouragement from the justices of the peace for Gloucestershire about carriage of timber; those on the other side the Severn plead that they are free, the river lying between them, and those on this side refuse to do any more till those on the further side come forward. Has applied to Judge Hale, but he refuses to give an opinion. Is unable to send the two drafts required, for want of vellum, which cannot be had at Gloucester or Bristol. [*Adm. Paper, one and a half pages.*]

Jan. 2. Rotterdam. 7. John Harcourt to Nic. Constable, Woodstock. Private business. War is expected there, for they hear of flat-bottomed boats provided for coming over, and great preparation of ships. Asks whether there be any hopes of peace.

Jan. 2. Dover. 8. J[ohn] C[arlisle] to Williamson. Hears that the lords of the Admiralty are chosen, and supposes the prize office will follow; wishes to be a sub-commissioner; could show that the King is much wronged in reference to prizes brought into that harbour. The Blackamoor has brought in a Dutch vessel, but as all are French on board, and it is bound for Dunkirk, fears it will not prove a prize.

Jan. 2. 9. Leonard Williams to Sec. Bennet. Details notices which he gave, and which, had they not miscarried, would have sufficed for apprehending Carew, Atkinson, and 16 others. Is in condition to give timely notice of fanatics' designs; but will unavoidably be discovered, if set to find out single persons. Capt Thomas is willing, but his men oversway him to act beyond instructions. These men are fittest to use, for being exiled, their friends trust them, and they are inquisitive after news, and eager for contrivances to redeem themselves. Begs to be dismissed unless his information is thought worth a comfortable maintenance, as he would not be beholden to those he must betray. Will wait on Sir Thos. Osborne for instructions.

Jan. 2. 10. Petition of the Royal African Company to the King. Being established two years before, they raised a joint stock of 120,000l., and sent abroad 158,000l. worth of manufactures in English ships; they have increased the stock and taken up money on credit; their

VOL. CX.

1664–5.

effects are now worth 273,807*l.* 6*s.* 2*d.*; but owing to their present and apprehended future losses by De Ruyter's expedition, their credit is failing, and they request some plan to be contrived to support a trade which brings in 200,000*l.* or 300,000*l.* yearly of gold to the Mint, and supplies the American plantations with negroes; they request also that the Dutch prizes taken by Major Holmes may be ceded to them, as De Ruyter declares that the mischief he has done them is in retaliation for that loss.

[Jan. 2.] 11. Brief narrative of the trade and present condition of the African Company, showing their successful establishment on the North coast and Gold coast, on each of which they have nine factories in places named; their great prosperity, by which they were induced to take up a large stock on credit; and their present danger from want of credit, owing to their heavy losses through the capture of Gold Island by De Ruyter. [*Two and a half pages.*]

Jan. 3. 12. Earl of Sandwich to [Sec. Bennet]. Hears that the lady expresses a disposition to choose for herself; would not be out of hope, yet must banish her from his thoughts, unless assured that the King would not be displeased; begs to know His Majesty's pleasure in a matter of much importance to his family.

Jan. 3. 13. J. Uthwayt to the Navy Comrs. Requests an assistant in the survey at Deptford and Woolwich, as granted to his predecessor and to himself formerly, in time of action; also his former allowance for travelling charges to Woolwich. [*Adm. Paper, damaged.*]

Jan. 3. Portsmouth. 14. Commissioner Thos. Middleton to Sam. Pepys. Particulars of stores. Can employ ten boatmakers and six blockmakers. Great want of seamen. The new ship is to be launched next month, and he has not one man belonging to her "except the officers, whose work is to look about them." It is hard to make bricks without straw; is content, the small time he has to live, to serve his King and country, but would rather be buried alive than put upon impossibilities. Has received orders to discharge the ship of masts lately taken. Complains of not being able to afford a clerk. [*Adm. Paper, two pages.*]

Jan. 3. Woolwich. 15. Wm. Bodham to Sam. Pepys. The Lord Mayor has released one of the two thieves concerned in the late embezzlement of hemp, upon security for appearance. The other is at work in the rope-yard, also on security. [*Adm. Paper.*]

Jan. 3. Plymouth. 16. John Garratt, boatswain of the Hulk, to the Navy Comrs. Stores wanted. Requests money to pay the boatmen, and directions concerning Capt. Sansum's demand for nails, plank, pitch, oakum, &c. [*Adm. Paper.*]

Jan. 3. The Mary. Rolling Grounds. 17. Capt. Jer. Smyth to Wm. Coventry. Account of damage sustained in a storm off Aldborough Bay. One of his anchors which broke proved to be made of broken iron, beaten over to cover it, and several captains in the fleet have been so served. Wants two

1664-5. VOL. CX.

anchors, cables, masts, &c. Particulars of other ships damaged. Many sailors are sick, from the terrible storms of wind and much snow. [*Adm. Paper.*]

Jan. 3. London. 18. Robt. Waith to Sam. Pepys. Has purchased 15 tons of tallow at 44*l.* per ton, ready money upon delivery at Porter's quay; will be a loser unless 46*l.* be allowed on delivery thereof at Deptford, but will take 45*l.* rather than keep it. [*Adm. Paper.*]

Jan. 4. Dublin. 19. Capt. Jas. Sharland to the Navy Comrs. Has not received the stores sent for the Harp, though two other ships have arrived which left the Downs at the same time. Hears that the vessel was forced into Galway. [*Adm. Paper.*]

Jan. 4. Woolwich. 20. Chris. Pett to the Navy Comrs. Arrival of the Francis. Repairs of ships. Timber wanted. [*Adm. Paper.*] *Encloses*,

20. I. *Account by Jos. Horn, carpenter, of repairs needed for the Francis.* *Jan.* 4, 1665.

Jan. 4. Harwich. 21. Anthony Deane to the Navy Comrs. A boat is wanted for the Adventure, and a mainmast for the Eagle. [*Adm. Paper.*]

Jan. 4. Bristol. 22. Dan. Adams to the Navy Comrs. No blacksmiths will contract for anchors of the weight required, having no shops fit for such great work, and fearing to lose their other employments of small anchors, bolts, &c. Advises that an able workman be sent down, and a place appointed for the purpose. Good forest iron is to be had at 16*l.* the ton. All the smiths asked what advance money they should have, and how they should be paid, if they undertook the work, &c. [*Adm. Paper.*]

Jan. 4. Chatham. 23. Commissioner Peter Pett to Sam. Pepys. Thos. Jenkins, master of the Margaret ketch of Margate, was the person who brought the damaged hemp. Wants the long boats bringing up speedily, and more reeds, which are now at 30*s.* a thousand. [*Adm. Paper.*]

Jan. ? 24. Petition of George Fell, of Swarthmore, co. Lancaster, to the King, for the estate of his mother, forfeited for life, because she has run herself into a præmunire for embracing the fanatic opinions of the Quakers, during the late usurpation, and obstinately adhering thereto. *Annexing,*

24. I. *Certificate by Sir Roger Bradshaigh and Rich. Kirkby in favour of the petitioner, as favouring the Restoration, and doing his utmost to persuade his mother to conformity with the church.* *Dec.* 1, 1664.

Jan. 4. Warrant for a grant to George Fell of the estate of [Marg.] Fell of Swarthmore, county palatine of Lancaster, forfeited on her conviction of præmunire at the last Lancaster assizes. [*Ent. Book* 10, *p.* 311.]

Jan. 4. Warrant for a declaration that Henry Earl of St. Alban's and the other trustees for the Queen-Mother may retain all the profits

VOL. CX.

1664-5.

of her lands for two years after her death, except Nonsuch, Nonsuch Little Park, co. Surrey, Denmark House, *alias* Somerset House, and the Royal Palace and Park at Greenwich, to be employed to such purposes as the said Queen shall direct by her will. [*Ent. Book* 16, *pp.* 311-3.]

[Jan. 4.] 25. Copy of the above. [*Two pages.*]

Jan. 5. Warrant for a grant to Abraham Cowley and Baptist May, on nomination of Henry Earl of St. Alban's, of certain parcels of ground in the bailiwick of St. James's, as described in a map sent therewith. [*Ent. Book* 16, *p.* 313.]

Jan. 4. Whitehall. 26. Warrant for a lease to the Earl of St. Alban's, at request of the Queen-Mother, of a parcel of ground, 24 ft. by 510 ft., between Somerset House and the Savoy, whereon a gallery is built, formerly used by the Chancellor of the duchy of Lancaster, on rental of 10s., excepting the ground for building stables for the Queen-Mother. [*One and a half pages.*]

Jan. 4. Entry of the above. [*Ent. Book* 17, *p.* 82.]

Jan. Another entry of the above, dated Jan. 21. [*Ent. Book* 16, *p.* 335.]

[Jan. 4.] 27. Petition of Arthur Barclay, gentleman of the privy chamber, to the King, for present relief, and compensation for a pension of 400*l.* a year, given him by the late King, in exchange for his surrender of the profits on wine and aqua vitæ licences in Ireland.

Jan. 4. Reference of the above petition to the Lord Treasurer. [*Ent. Book* 18, *p.* 113.]

Jan. 5. Cockpit. 28. Duke of Albemarle to Sec. Bennet. The pay of the officers of the Duke of York's regiment, under command of Sir Wm. Killigrew, is to begin from Nov. 16 last, the date of their first muster.

Jan. 5. Chatham. 29. Commissioner Peter Pett to Sam. Pepys. Advises for better improvement of the spinners' time, that the new ropeway be perfected, and a slight house erected of deals, to be removed when necessary, whereby half as much again would be spun and laid as now. [*Adm. Paper.*] *Encloses*,

29. I. *Account of cordage now in store at Chatham.* *January* 3, 1665.

29. II. *Philip Barrow and four other Officers of the Yard to Commissioner Peter Pett. In answer to the Navy Commissioners' queries, give a detailed account of the cordage that could be made before Lady Day, by the* 100 *men now at work, and of the quantity required for use; also of the anchors that are wanted; none can be made at Chatham, the fires not being able to overcome the other work. The forge at the old dock should be repaired and set to work.* [*Three pages.*] *January* 5, 1665.

VOL. CX.

1664–5.

Jan. 5. 30. Capt. James Cadman to the Navy Comrs. Recommends Wm. Burstow for a lieutenant's employment. [*Adm. Paper.*]

Jan. 5. 31. Jonas Shish to the Navy Comrs. There is no mast in store large enough for the Mary. Timber wanted. [*Adm. Paper, damaged.*]

Jan. 5. 32. Capt. Wm. Badiley to the Navy Comrs. Has been with Mr. Cadbury to Woolwich, and chosen a large mast for the Mary. [*Adm. Paper, damaged.*]

Jan. 5. Woolwich Ropeyard. 33. Wm. Bodham to the Navy Comrs. Gives Edw. Rundells' estimate for erecting a slight house of deals in the ropeyard. Complains of the workmen's delay in the building [of the new ropehouse], under the false pretext of wanting timber, and the master carpenter's non-attendance since Christmas; 12 tons of cordage can be made in the yard weekly. [*Adm. Paper.*]

Jan. 5. Portsmouth. 34. Commissioner Thos. Middleton to Sam. Pepys. The Earl of Sandwich has ordered several ships to come into port, to be cleaned and provisioned for three months. Complains of his want of power to act, and wishes either not to have the name, or to have the power; desires further instructions. Half the provision offered him by the pursers of ships will be lost, because he knows not how to dispose of it. Fears he has been too free with his pen. Seeks not his own interest, but the King's. [*Adm. Paper, two and a half pages.*]

Jan. 5. Woolwich. 35. Edw. Rundalls to Sam. Pepys. Reports progress of the new spinning house. Six house carpenters wanted. [*Adm. Paper, damaged.*]

Jan. 5. 36. Capt. Wm. Badiley to the Navy Comrs. Repairs of ships. [*Adm. Paper, damaged.*]

Jan. 6. Deptford. 37. J. Uthwayt to Thos. Wilson. There is no vessel now going into the Downs, and the things will not be half a freight. Proposes sending them by the first vessel. [*Adm. Paper, damaged.*]

Jan. 6. Dover. 38. Thos. White to the Navy Comrs. Repairs needed for the Drake and Paradox. Will undertake to procure supplies for the ships, husbanding as though they were his own, as he did under the former Commissioners, consulting them on any considerable business, and leaving it to them to make him some small allowance. If the new cordage were taken out of every prize at her first coming into port, and put into the storehouse, it would not damage the prize a quarter as much as it would profit the stores. [*Adm. Paper.*] *Encloses,*

38. I. *Thos. White to the [Navy Comrs.] At request of the boatswain of the Drake, has ordered the sailmaker to alter his sails, which are dangerous in a gale of wind.*

Jan. 6. 39. Capt. Wm. Badiley to the Navy Comrs. Mr. Catiel, the pilot appointed to carry over the Kitchen to Rouen, was detained by the parishioners for other duties till the afternoon; the vessel waited for him at Gravesend. [*Adm. Paper, damaged.*]

1664–5. Vol. CX.

Jan. 6. Harwich. 40. Anthony Deane to the Navy Comrs. Account of boats, masts, &c., required for several ships now fitting out. [*Adm. Paper.*]

Jan. 6. Whitehall. 41. Petition of Col. Robt. Broughton to the King, for authority to search for treasure concealed in cos. Middlesex, Hants, and Somerset, and for His Majesty's interest in the said treasure, a reward being promised him for his services and sufferings in the cause of the late King. With reference thereon to the Solicitor General, and his report, Jan. 9, in favour of the petitioner, limiting the grant to a year; also suggesting that he should not have leave to dig other men's lands, but reap the benefit of voluntary compositions. *Annexing,*

41. I. *Form of an order for a warrant as requested, for Col. Broughton to dig for treasure trove.*

Jan. 6. Entry of the above reference. [*Ent. Book* 18, *p.* 113.]

Jan. 7. 42. Certificate by eight of the crew of the Mary Fortune of Bristol,—that on 6th Dec. last, Callender Britton, Barth. Crooke, and Lewis Rogers, Quakers, were brought on board their ship for transportation; that the said Quakers were put on shore again on the 23rd, because of a stay for all ships, but brought back on the 31st; but that they the crew, being smitten by the Lord with a terrible fear, durst not carry away innocent persons who walk in the fear of the Lord; they are persuaded the King does not wish to destroy his subjects, nor make void the Act that Englishmen shall not be carried abroad without their consents; moreover, these men are bound by no indenture nor agreement for their passage, and there is a law in Barbadoes that whoever brings persons into the island against their will, is liable to heavy penalties, and to be forced to take the said persons back to their habitations: on these accounts they have put the men on shore again.

Jan. 7. Hull. 43. Capt. Luke Whittington to James Hickes. Has nothing to record since his letters of the 4th and 6th instant.

Jan. 7. Warrant to Captain Robert Holmes, commander of the Jersey frigate, to deliver up the ships and goods taken from the Dutch on the coast of Guinea, to a person appointed by the Duke of York, to be employed for the benefit of the Royal African Company. [*Ent. Book* 10, *p.* 320.]

Jan. 7. Portsmouth. 44. Commissioner Thos. Middleton to Sam. Pepys. Sends particulars of damage sustained by the Yarmouth, and of a dispute between Capt. Jennings of the Ruby and the master of that ship. As they could not work together, has discharged the master, and appointed Mr. Bowell in his stead. Begs his approval. Recommends Anthony Smith as master of the Tiger or Lizard. One side of the Royal Charles is completed. [*Adm. Paper, two pages.*]

Jan. 7. Portsmouth. 45. John Tippetts to the Navy Comrs. The furnace ordered for the Barbadoes Merchant has been made long since, but not called

VOL. CX.

1664-5.

for. Advises that the felling of trees in the New Forest and Bere Forest be hastened. The 100 trees are marked in Col. Norton's grounds. [*Adm. Paper.*]

Jan. 7. 46. John Paule to the Navy Comrs. Begs consideration for having a long and tedious journey to Stockwith, and then a journey thither for money. Wishes his vessel for carriage of timber from Sherwood to be hired by the month, as it cannot go without convoy, now the Holland men-of-war are abroad. [*Adm. Paper.*]

Jan. 7. 47. Report by Capt. Fortescue of the state of two vessels in the river, and of the stores at Woolwich and Deptford, as regards cables and anchors. [*Adm. Paper.*]

Jan. 7. Harwich. 48. Sir Wm. Batten to Wm. Coventry. Condition of the ships at Harwich. [*Adm. Paper.*]

Jan. 8. Dover. 49. John Tatnell to the Navy Comrs. The Blackamoor pink was forced to let slip in a gale of wind; had her anchor and cable taken up, and has restored them to her. Begs payment of his disbursements therein. [*Adm. Paper.*]

Jan. 8. Dover. 50. Thos. Wale to the Navy Comrs. Repairs of ships. The hoy men ask 3*l.* 10*s.* each for carriage of the long boats to Chatham. The Folkstone men demand 40*s.* salvage for the Drake's long boat; understands that she was too big, being built for the Hector. Mr. Tatnell promises to supply another. [*Adm. Paper.*]

Jan. 8. The John and Margaret, Downs. 51. Capt. Geo. Chappell to the Navy Comrs. Hearing nothing of his purser, was constrained to purchase wood and candles at Gravesend, for which a bill is passed, payable to John Paige, merchant of London, as the Deal men would not sell wood on bills upon the Navy Commissioners. Is sorry the credit of the Board is not better in Deal. The William and two other ships are ready to sail. [*Adm. Paper.*] *Encloses,*

51. I. *Account of money spent for wood and candles for the John and Margaret; total, 28l. 12s. January 6, 1665.*

Jan. 8. Deptford. 52. Jonas Shish to Mr. Coventry. Repairs of ships. Proposes to launch the Garland. [*Adm. Paper, damaged.*]

Jan. 8. Warrant to Matthew Butler to apprehend Richard Harland. Minute. [*Ent. Book 16, p. 314.*]

Jan. 9. 53. Certificate that Charles Anderson was admitted to Magdalen College, Cambridge, 10th June 1653, and stayed there till Christmas 1657, applying himself to physic, in which he gave promise of excellency. Endorsed "Lord Belasyse." [*Lower half torn off.*]

Jan. 9. 54. Wm. Castell to Sam. Pepys. Has altered the measurement of a third-rate ship about to be built, the King so much desiring breadth; 1,800*l.* should be paid in advance for it. [*Adm. Paper.*]

VOL. CX.

1664–5.
Jan. 9.
The William, Downs.

55. Capt. Wm. Basse to the Navy Commrs. Account of stores required. Begs that the purser may be sent for, and examined whether he intends to go in the ship, as she only waits the first opportunity of wind to set sail. [*Adm. Paper.*] *Encloses,*

55. I. *Account of provisions received on board the William, for six months' indent for sea store.*

Jan. 9.

56. Wm. Coventry to Sam. Pepys. The Earl of Sandwich sends word that the purser of the Royal Exchange delivers but three quarters of a pint instead of a pint of oil for 1lb of butter, on the plea that it is so charged in his indent. Mr. Gauden must attend the Board on this matter, and touching the short allowance of victuals in the Channel fleet. The cutting down wood in the King's forests must be hastened. [*Adm. Paper.*]

Jan. 9.
Harwich.

57. Sir Wm. Batten to the Navy Commrs. Particulars of ships fitting out. Captain Smyth much wants Langley's ketch, which was the packet boat, fitted up with four small guns. *Encloses,*

57. I. *List by John Wright, bailiff of Ipswich, of thirty-two ships belonging to Ipswich, fit for the King's service, with the masters' names; twenty-seven of them are between 250 and 300 tons; there are other good ships, but too short, being built only for the coal trade.* Jan. 8, 1665.

57. II. *Similar list, endorsed as sent to Mr. Coventry.* January 14, 1665.

Jan. 9.
Woolwich Ropeyard.

58. Wm. Bodham to the Navy Commrs. The three cables of 17 inches will be ready to-morrow, and no time shall be lost upon other works. [*Adm. Paper.*]

Jan. 9.
Portsmouth.

59. Commissioner Thos. Middleton to [the Navy Commrs.] Requests boat-makers and block-makers to be sent down. All the ships are now fitted but the Royal Oak. Purchase of stores. Has suggested to the Earl of Sandwich that 50 of the Dutchmen now in prison be employed as labourers in the yard, victualled by petty warrant, and lodged on board the two hulks. In order to keep the idle mariners to their duty, has desired the mayor to send orders to all the houses of entertainment, not to entertain any seaman without a note under his captain's hand, on forfeiture of 10s. Has persuaded the governor to send soldiers to search all the houses for them, and those taken are kept upon the guard, and suffer so with hunger and cold before released, that he thinks it will be a warning to the others. Wants more authority; would rather be buried alive than accept employment to the ruin of his reputation. The King is likely to be at a great loss in the Guinea provisions. [*Adm. Paper, three pages.*]

Jan. 9.
Portsmouth.

60. Commissioner Thos. Middleton to [the Navy Commrs.] Sends account of cordage in store, and of what is demanded and can be

VOL. CX.

1664-5.

made by Lady Day; all the ships in port want some, but is sparing in supplying them. Yarn wanted. [*Adm. Paper, one and a quarter pages.*] *Encloses,*

60. I. *List of cables and other cordage required for ships abroad; with note that those in port are already fitted out.*

60. II. *Report by Gr. Prachy of the weekly manufacture of cordage, 10 tons; 130 tons could be furnished by Lady Day; 60 spinners are employed, and 159 tons were delivered into the stores since October last.*
Portsmouth Ropeyard, January 6, 1665.

60. III. *Account by Ben. Johnson of cordage remaining in store, and of that already ordered to be issued, but not in store.* *Portsmouth, Jan. 6, 1665.*

Jan. 10. Portsmouth. 61. Commissioner Thos. Middleton to Sam. Pepys. Thanks for his intention to procure him instructions from the Duke of York. The many obstructions he meets with in the performance of his duty have given him oft times cause to repent of his sudden coming to Portsmouth, before his instructions were finished. Backwardness of the new ship for want of men and materials. Stores wanted. The use of ready money would save the King at least 2s. 6d. in the pound. Some will not sell for London pay, they say they shall have so much time and expense in going up to beg it. Has written to the Earl of Sandwich to send two or three ketches for bringing provisions from the Augustine. Working without tools is like setting him to make bricks without straw. [*Adm. Paper, three pages.*]

Jan. 10. Harwich. 62. Sir Wm. Batten to the Navy Comrs. Repairs of ships. [*Adm. Paper.*]

Jan. 10. Reference to the Lords of the Council for Admiralty Affairs, on the petition of Fras. Godolphin, vice-admiral for the south coast of Cornwall, that having taken three Dutch ships, two of which are to be delivered to the Customers of Falmouth, he may be allowed to keep the third, in consideration of his expenses in seizing her. [*Ent. Book* 18, p. 114.]

Jan. 10. Whitehall. 63. Petition of Rich. Erwin, gentleman sewer, to the King, for payment of six years' arrears of a pension of 300*l.* a year, granted by the late King to his father, Sir Wm. Erwin, for 21 years which are now expired, the interest in which is vested in himself. With reference thereon to the Lord Treasurer, and his report, Feb. 10, that if pensions granted from the time when the late King ceased to be master of his revenue to the Restoration be made grounds for suits, His Majesty would be too much pressed, but that a moderate sum may be allowed to the petitioner.

Jan. 10. Entry of the above reference. [*Ent. Book* 18, p. 114.]

Jan. 10. Reference to the Lord Treasurer,—on the petition of Sir Bernard de Gomme, for continuance of his pension, stopped by the general

VOL. CX.

1664–5.

stay of pensions,—recommending the clearing of arrears, and its regular payment in future, as the King has immediate occasion for him at Tangiers. [*Ent. Book* 18, *p.* 115.]

Jan. 11. Whitehall. 64. Petition of Christopher Pett, master shipwright of Deptford and Woolwich, to the King, to allow him, as increase of salary, the offals of trees soon to be felled in Waltham and Aliceholt, for building ships. Has held his office 12 years, but the meanness of his salary, 103*l.* 8*s.* 4*d.*, his growing family, and the loss of 500*l.* by navy debts, have brought him into debt. With reference thereon to the Lord Treasurer, to decide how far it can be granted without prejudice to Col. Legg's grant of the offals of Alicholt Forest, for repairing the lodges and mounds there.

[Jan. 11.] 65. Draft of the above reference.

Jan. 11. Entry of the above reference. [*Ent. Book* 18, *p.* 115.]

Jan. 11. 66. Capt. Wm. Badiley to the Navy Comrs. Certifies the fitness of Giles Bond to take charge of the Harwich hoy. [*Adm. Paper.*]

Jan. 12. 67. Capt. John Taylor to the Navy Comrs. Tenders a sample of New England tar, offered for contract. [*Adm. Paper.*]

Jan. 12. The Harkaway, Downs. 68. Capt. John Barton to the Navy Comrs. Having sprung a leak, requests an order for repairs, and for the entering of 15 more men, having only 50. Has brought in another vessel laden with French wines and brandies, which pretends to be from Dunkirk. [*Adm. Paper.*]

Jan. 12. Dover. 69. Thos. Wale to the Navy Comrs. The long boats are ready. Repairs and stores for ships. As some complained of the powder being kept in his storehouse for safety, has removed it to the West Fort; the carriage will be 3*d.* a barrel. [*Adm. Paper.*]

Jan. 12. Portsmouth. 70. Commissioner Thos. Middleton to Sam. Pepys. Progress of works in the yard. Eight ships being ordered to be cleaned each spring tide, has to employ men from the fleet at 18*d.* a day and 2*s.* a night, or they will not dispatch the work. Particulars of stores wanted or purchased. The French yarn lately delivered is not good. Money wanted. A ship is brought in laden with cordage, sails, &c. The Hollanders now all go under the name of Hamburghers, French, Lubeckers, &c. [*Adm. Paper, two and a half pages.*]

Jan. 12. Portsmouth. 71. Commissioner Thos. Middleton to Sam. Pepys. Boat and block makers wanted. One boat made in the King's yard is worth two elsewhere. [*Adm. Paper.*]

Jan. 12. 72. Wm. Blackburn to the Navy Comrs. Has brought John Bresford to contract for three tons of well-spun cordage. [*Adm. Paper.*]

Jan. 12. Navy Office. 73. Navy Comrs. to the Clerks of the Store and Cheque at Chatham. Desire a ship's lading of Gottenburg masts, deals, &c., to be received

1664-5. VOL. CX.

from Sir Wm. Warren, for the securing and bringing on shore of which, ropes, staples, and lighters are to be delivered to the master of the ship. [*Adm. Paper.*]

Jan.? 74. Enquiry [by Sec. Bennet] from Lord Carbery, whether he consents that the [militia] moneys [for Wales] be lodged in Ludlow Castle, in case there be no strong place within his lieutenancy. With his reply, that if the King pleases, the moneys for North and South Wales might be safely kept in each respectively, or if not, in Ludlow Castle, which is within 10 miles of both.

Jan. 12. Whitehall. 75. The King to the Earl of Carbery [lord lieutenant of Wales]. Duplicate of the letter to the lords lieutenants of counties, of Dec. 30, 1664, ordering the money raised to be deposited in Ludlow Castle. [*Four pages.*]

[Jan. 12.] 76. Alteration in the above letter, as addressed to the Earl of Carbery, that the money be put into a trunk or chest, to be conveyed to the nearest castle or town.

Jan. 12. 77. Information concerning the fanatics, that they intend to surprise Bristol, where they have a sufficient party to master the honest party. They hear that Lambert is escaped, and Ludlow removing from Switzerland to Holland, where he has enlisted the discontented English. Some propose to land at Burlington, some in Scotland, but most in Kent, where the castles are commanded by negligent persons.

Jan. 12. 78. Solicitor General Finch to Sec. Bennet. Has not received orders about Col. Broughton's grant of treasure trove; he is willing to be limited to a short time and one county, and to digging in the King's soil, so that the only objection to his modest desire is the little profit he will make of it.

Jan. 12. Warrant to Sir Robert Henley, prothonotary of the Court of King's Bench, to pay 60*l.* to Maurice Deladale, being the King's moiety of a fine levied on George Browne, linen draper of London, for usury. [*Ent. Book* 16, *p.* 321.]

Jan. 12. 79. Draft of the above.

Jan. 12. Warrant to Lord Herbert to deliver up Paul Hobson, prisoner in Chepstow Castle, to be conveyed to the Tower. [*Ent. Book* 16, *p.* 321.]

Jan. 12. Two similar warrants (*mutatis mutandis*) for receiving and conveying the above Paul Hobson. Minute. [*Ent. Book* 16, *p.* 321.]

Jan. 12. Warrant to pay to Sir John Shaw 521*l.* without account, for secret services. Minute. [*Ent. Book* 16, *p.* 322.]

Jan.? 80. Petition of the Churchwardens and Overseers of St. Martin's-in-the-Fields to the King, for the continuance of His Majesty's former charity of 100*l.* towards the relief of their poor, and for no delay in the payment.

VOL. CX.

1664-5.
Jan. 12. Warrant for 100*l.* to the poor of the parish of St. Martin's, as a gift from His Majesty. Minute. [*Ent. Book* 16, p. 322.]

Jan. 13. Southampton House. 81. Declaration by Lord Treas. Southampton of his suspension of Mr. Christian, customer of Carlisle, from his office, for violently arresting Sir Phil. Musgrave, deputy lieutenant and justice of the peace, on a suit between them for toll of cattle, until Christian has attended His Majesty to know his pleasure, and appointment of Wm. Kirkby to execute the office meanwhile.

Jan. 13. Lisbon. 82. Thos. Clutterbuck to the Navy Comrs. Has passed a bill for 294*l.* 12*s.* 3*d.*, payable to Charles Longland, and begs punctual satisfaction. [*Adm. Paper.*]

Jan. 14. Portsmouth. 83. John Tippetts to Sam. Pepys. Mr. Eastwood states that there may be 500 oaks and 60 beeches in the New Forest, fit for felling, but the beech must be felled speedily. Holly and ash may be had from East Bere Forest. [*Adm. Paper.*]

Jan. 14. Dover. 84. Thos. Wale to the Navy Comrs. The Drake and Paradox have set sail. Has often spoken to Nich. Eaton, the mayor, and the other Commissioners of the harbour, for removing 60 lighters of ballast to restore the former depth of water in the harbour, but they are cold about it. A fourth-rate frigate could only come in on a spring tide. [*Adm. Paper.*]

Jan. 14. Dover. 85. E. Wivell to the Navy Comrs. Notifies the sailing of certain ships. [*Adm. Paper.*]

Jan. 14. Southampton House. 86. Capt. Wm. Badiley to the Navy Comrs. Recommends the employment of a ship lying at the ballast quay, to assist the Harwich hoy in towing down the mast, bowsprit, and other provisions belonging to the Mary. [*Adm. Paper, damaged.*]

Jan. 14. Warrant to apprehend Andrew White with all his papers. Minute. [*Ent. Book* 16, p. 322.]

Jan. 14. 87. Examination of Major Robt. Holmes, before Secs. Morice and Bennet. Being ordered to protect trade on the coast of Africa, to discover the strength of the Dutch there, and particularly to find out the Golden Lion which had chiefly injured the Royal company, he sailed from Cape Verd; the Dutch first attacked him, but afterwards offered to surrender the place; he accepted the offer, treated the officers, &c. courteously for a month, and then sent them back to Holland. Having settled a governor and garrison, and stored the place with provisions and water, went to Cestus the place of rendezvous, laid the foundation of a fort there and went along the Gold Coast, the Dutch constantly affronting him. Seized the Golden Lion, left a garrison in Cape Corso, and on complaints by the English of Dutch oppression, seized several other of their vessels. Brought home 2,000*l.* or 3,000*l.* in gold, some hides, wax, teeth, &c., but will be accountable for all. Can satisfy the world

VOL. CX.

1664–5.

from Dutch papers of the wrongs they have done, and greater would have been committed, had he not arrived in season to protect the English trade. [*Three and a quarter pages.*]

Jan. 14. 88, 89. Two drafts of the preceding.

Jan. 15? 90. Petition of Thos. Rogers, of Distington, co. Cumberland, labourer, to the King, for a letter to Sir Patricius Curwen, Bart., Sir Wm. Huddleston, and Rich. Tolson, justices of the peace of Cumberland, to order Hen. Jenkinson to show cause why he detains a tenement in Emerdale Forest, belonging to the petitioner, as heir to his brother William, on a false pretext of purchase. Has come 300 miles to obtain His Majesty's favour, being too poor to go to law.

Jan. 15. The Paradox, Margate Road. 91. Capt. Leo. Guy to Sir Wm. Penn. In coming out of Dover pier, got aground, but received no damage. With a little labour, three feet more water may be made there. [*Adm. Paper.*]

Jan. 15. Dover. 92. John Tatnell to the Navy Comrs. A Dutch pink just taken will make a good man of war, and can be fitted in four days; would willingly take the command of her. Has several boats ready. [*Adm. Paper.*]

Jan. 15. Portsmouth. 93. Commissioner Thos. Middleton to Sam. Pepys. Is glad the boat and block makers may be expected so speedily. Has made progress in taking account of the Guinea provisions, but much must be left to the examination of the Board. Cannot procure any men for the dockyard. Broom wanted. Finds he was mistaken in supposing that ready money could be had, though it would save the King 3s. 6d. in the pound. Complains of the large demands for cable by the 15 ships lately come into port. All the cordage in store will signify nothing for such a supply. Is at a loss how to satisfy the humours of such unreasonable men, but will let them know that although a young Commissioner, he is an old sailor. [*Adm. Paper, four pages.*]

Jan. 16. Victualling Office. 94. Denis Gauden to the Navy Comrs. Asks directions about victualling 1,500 men for a year, at Leghorn. [*Adm. Paper.*]

Jan. 16. Bristol. 95. Dan. Furzer to the Navy Comrs. Sends a draft of a ship about to be built. Would have presented it in a better form, but there are no workmen about there who understand the manner of doing it. [*Adm. Paper.*]

Jan. 16. Harwich. 96. Anthony Deane to the Navy Comrs. Repairs of the Elizabeth. Contracts for timber. None will be delivered but for ready money, without a charge of 20 per cent. more. There is much work yet to be done on the Hulk. [*Adm. Paper.*]

Jan. 16. Portsmouth. 97. John Tippetts to the Navy Comrs. Has marked out in Col. Norton's woods 80 oaks and 2 large elms. Desires a bill of imprest for 120*l.* [*Adm. Paper.*]

VOL. CX.

1664–5.

Jan. 16. Chatham. 98. John Steward, lieutenant of the Prince, to Sam. Pepys. Is ready to sail. Hopes the London will not come up, or they would lose all the men whom they pressed in her. Wishes the Commissioners to examine one Lovimar, who owns all the deals, plank, pitch, &c., embezzled from the King's stores. [*Adm. Paper.*]

Jan. 16. Leghorn. 99. Thos. Clutterbuck to the Navy Comrs. Requests punctual discharge of his bill for 294*l.* 12*s.* 3*d.*, due for six weeks' provisions made ready for the Bonaventure. There is no news of Admiral Allin, therefore it is to be feared he has left those seas, which will prove ominous to the poor merchants, for on removal of the King's frigates, the Algerines would forget their late articles of peace. The Dutch begin to talk of arming their merchant ships. Capt. Allin might easily have taken many rich vessels, but now they are more wary in their movements, and being assured of relief from home, determine to maintain their interest in those seas; they much eye the port of Leghorn, as being the chief seat of trade. [*Adm. Paper, two pages.*]

Jan. 16. Portsmouth. 100. Commissioner Thos. Middleton to Sam. Pepys. Particulars of stores. Mr. Gauden's agent refuses to weigh the Guinea provisions, saying he understands nothing of the business. [*Adm. Paper.*]

Jan. 16. Grant to James Marriott of the office of Keeper of the Standing Wardrobe and Privy Lodgings at Hampton Court, in place of Rich. Marriott, deceased. [*Docquet.*]

Jan. 16. Warrant to pay to Sir George Carteret, treasurer of the navy, 1,396*l.* 8*s.* monthly, from Nov. 16 last, for pay of the Admiral's regiment, under Sir Wm. Killigrew, Bart. [*Docquet.*]

Jan. 17. Warrant to a messenger to repair to Lyme in Dorsetshire, and apprehend Amos Short, with all seditious books, papers, or writings found on him. Minute. [*Ent. Book* 16, *p.* 329.]

Jan. 17. Warrant to [Thos.] Widowes to repair to the Three Cups, Bread Street, the usual inn of Robert Hawsey, carrier between London and Bristol, and to search all warehouses, boxes, packs, &c., belonging to him. [*Ent. Book* 16, *p.* 329.]

Jan. 17. Whitehall. 101. Order to the Clerk of the Signet, to enter a caveat that no grant pass for making a market in East Smithfield, without notice to [Sec. Bennet].

Jan. 17. Harwich. 102. Wm. Baker, boatswain, to the Navy Comrs. Six frigates having sailed, only the Mary and Elizabeth are left in port. [*Adm. Paper.*]

Jan. 17. Woolwich. 103. Chris. Pett to the Navy Comrs. The Fountain cannot be launched, by reason of the frost and ice. The Royal Katherine is not unfit for service, as reported. Wishes people would learn to know more and speak less. She will vindicate herself when tried,

VOL. CX.

1664–5.

and "cast all her dirt in the faces of the others." [*Adm. Paper.*] *Encloses,*

103. I. *List of eight pressed men who have not yet appeared.*

Jan. 17. 104. Answers by Wm. Castell to Lord Brouncker's proposals calculating the tonnage of the new ship he is to build, to carry 300 men. [*Adm. Paper, two pages.*]

Jan. 17. Deptford. 105. John Shish to the Navy Comrs. Repairs of ships. Timber wanted. [*Adm. Paper, damaged.*]

Jan. 18. Chatham Dockyard. 106. John Owen and Robt. Sliter to [Sam. Pepys]. Certify the danger of placing the wet hemp received from the Thomas and Margaret, in any storehouse, for fear of its firing. Advise that it be speedily disposed of. [*Adm. Paper.*]

Jan. 18. 107. Capt. Wm. Badiley to the Navy Comrs. Asks their reply about employing the Sirack of Ipswich to carry down the Mary's foremast, &c. [*Adm. Paper, damaged.*]

Jan. 18. Commission to John Earl of Lauderdale, Charles Viscount Fitzharding, Wm. Lord Crofts, John Lord Berkeley, John and Wm. Ashburnham, Hen. Coventry, Sir Thos. Clifford, and Edw. Thurland, to manage the affairs and estates of James Duke of Monmouth, in Scotland and elsewhere in the King's dominions, during his minority, see that his household is well ordered, and settle his debts. [*Ent. Book* 10, *pp.* 324–8.]

Jan. 19. 108. Information of sixty-two conventicles held in London between Nov. 27, 1664, and Jan. 8, 1665, with the names of the ministers. With note of the purchase of arms and horses by the master of the Golden Lion, Bread Street, and two others. [*One and a half pages.*]

Jan. ? 109. Petition of Thos. Voysey, prisoner in Windsor Castle, to Sec. Bennet, for a speedy trial or release, being unable to bear his great charges as a prisoner, or provide for his family. Has been almost twelve months in prison, and nothing proved against him, and is innocent of any sedition or disloyalty.

Jan. 19. 110. Bond of Thos. Voysey, of Newbury, Berkshire, and two others, in 500*l.*, that he shall not disturb government, nor encourage unlawful meetings, and shall appear before a Secretary of State when required.

Jan. 19. Harwich. 111. John Browne to the Navy Comrs. The money disbursed exceeds the 100*l.* imprest by 37*l.* 8*s.* 10*d.* Wants another 100*l.* for paying poor labourers for oakum picking, and hiring vessels. [*Adm. Paper.*]

Jan. 19. Norwich. 112. Wm. Baker to the Navy Comrs. Certifies the arrival of the Mary's mainmast, cables, and anchors; one anchor is unserviceable. [*Adm. Paper.*]

Jan. 19. Portsmouth. 113. Commissioner Thos. Middleton to Sam. Pepys. Fears to be blamed if any misfortune should happen the ships. Allows no

VOL. CX.

1664-5.

cables to be delivered except on his order, but complains that those of 110 fathoms delivered to the ships are seldom returned above 80 or 85 fathoms, under the plea that they must be cut to make scrubs, spun yarn, &c. Thinks this should be prevented. Particulars of stores. Ready money wanted. [*Adm. Paper, two pages.*] *Encloses,*

113. I. *Blank contract for 20 tons of cordage to be served into the stores at Portsmouth.* *Portsmouth, Jan. 16, 1665.*

VOL. CXI. JANUARY 20–31, 1664–5.

1664–5.
Jan. 20. 1. Wm. Coventry to Sam. Pepys. Asks a list of the names of Jones' and Langley's ketches, and of the ships lately hired, which must be sent to the Ordnance Office, with the number and quality of guns required for them. Wishes the Victualler to be hastened in his dispatches every where, especially in supplying the ketches which are to fetch pressed men. Capt. Fortescue must hasten the work at Deptford, which has been stayed by the frost. [*Adm. Paper.*]

Jan. 20. Deptford. 2. J. Uthwayt to Sir Wm. Batten. Sends the measurement and valuation of cables lately delivered at Woolwich. Farley Stevenson, the gunner of the Hope prize, is the person who embezzled the cable and anchors from Deptford stores; the boatswain, his confederate, has run away. Other cables are missing. Shows the conveniency of a hulk at Deptford. [*Adm. Paper.*]

Jan. 20. 3. Certificate by Capt. James Locke that the second payment is due to Mr. Page, for the ketch now building at Wivenhoe. [*Adm. Paper.*]

Jan. 20. Plymouth. 4. John Garratt, boatswain of the Hulk, to the Navy Comrs. Damage sustained by the Bristol. Repairs needed. [*Adm. Paper.*]

Jan. 20. Warrant for removing John Le Flored from Dorchester gaol to London. Minute. [*Ent. Book 16, p. 330.*]

Jan. [20?] 5. Release to Bold Boughey, warden of the Fleet, from the custody of Jas. Seaborne, currier of London, in prison for a debt due to the late John Sparkes, which debt he has now discharged to Rich. Deacon, and Eliz. Deacon, *alias* Sparkes, the rightful claimants.

Jan. 20. 6. "Mr. Phillip's information," on the enlisting of men in cos. Bucks and Herts, the lists being in the hands of Capt. Harris and Tanner of Amersham. It is not general, but the work of the forwardest; most have arms, and the rest are promised them. Mr. Rogers, *alias* Capt. Jones, is among them, in a carter's habit. They are glad that the horse are to be removed from Watford, though they say they fear them not.

VOL. CXI.

1664-5.

Jan. 20. Westminster. 7. Patent to Sec. Bennet of the office of Comptroller of all prize ships and goods, with their furniture, ammunition, &c., whether adjudged prizes by the Admiralty court or otherwise, and of those inventoried, appraised, or sold by order of the Navy Commissioners; requiring him to assist the Commissioners for Prizes, and certify to them what officers he requires under him, who shall thereupon be appointed; ordering him also to keep account of all proceedings of the Admiralty Court and Navy Commissioners relating to prize ships, of the moneys arising from their sale, &c. [*Copy, two pages.*]

Jan. 20. 8. Appointment by the Commissioners for Prizes during the Dutch war of Hen. Brabant as storekeeper and warehouse-keeper for prizes and prize goods in Newcastle-on-Tyne and the adjoining districts.

Jan. 21. Whitehall. 9. Order by the Commissioners for Prizes to Jos. Williamson, that he request some intelligent merchant at Bilbao to give information relative to four Dutch ships, laden with wool and iron at Bilbao, and bound for Holland, but which, on report of the war with England, dismissed their Dutch crews, manned their ships with Biscainers, and passed them and their goods over to merchants of Bilbao, on whose account they are to come into Holland.

Jan. 21. Whitehall. Warrant to the Commissioners for Prizes to appoint certain Sub-Commissioners in the ports of London, Dover, Portsmouth, Plymouth, Bristol, Hull, Newcastle, and other places where it may be thought necessary. With a list of Sub-Commissioners nominated. [*Ent. Book* 16, *pp.* 330-1.]

[Jan. 21.] 10. Draft of the above warrant.

[Jan. 21.] 11. Drafts of the above list of Sub-Commissioners.

[Jan. 21.] 12. Clause in the instructions to the Commissioners for Prizes, that in order that the Sub-Commissioners may be tied to exact performance of their duties, they are to be suspended if found faulty, and the King is to nominate others instead of those displaced for misdemeanor.

[Jan. 21.] 13. Twentieth clause in the instructions to the Sub-Commissioners for Prizes, that if any prize come in within their bounds, it is to be brought into the prescribed port, unless the goods will be injured, in which case they are to be sold to the best advantage, and speedy notice given to the Commissioners.

Jan. 21. Whitehall. 14. Instructions [by the Commissioners for Prizes] to the Sub-Commissioners for Kingston-upon-Hull, upon their taking possession of prize ships and goods in the ports, hitherto taken in charge by the officers of customs, as to their disposition, the prevention of embezzlement, the keeping of accounts relative to them, payment of customs, &c. [*Copy,* 31 *pages.*]

Jan. 21. Warrant for a grant to Col. Rob. Broughton, of all such hidden treasure in Middlesex as shall be discovered within a year, with

VOL. CXI.

1664-5.

power to sue for, recover, or compound for the same. [*Ent. Book* 16, p. 331.]

[Jan. 21.] 15. Draft of the preceding.

Jan. [21.] 16. List of 26 ships now lying at Blackwall, not taken up for the King's service, with account of their dimensions, age, &c.; also, notes of others at Deptford, &c. Endorsed "Capt. Fortescue's note of merchants in the river." [*Adm. Paper, one and a half pages.*]

[Jan. 21.] 17. Note of one of the above ships, the John and Abigail. [*Adm. Paper.*]

Jan. 21. 18. List of 11 of the above ships, in treaty to be hired for men-of-war, with their age and number of guns. [*Adm. Paper.*]

Jan. 21. Chatham Dock. 19. Phin. Pett to [Sam. Pepys]. The three globe lanterns made by Mr. Staines for the Royal Charles are well worth 36*l.* [*Adm. Paper.*]

Jan. 21. Portsmouth. 20. John Tippetts to the Navy Comrs. Requests an order for felling 20 of Col. Norton's trees. Fears it will be too late to fell the beech, ash, and holly, in the King's Forest. Shipwrights and calkers are wanted to careen the great ships ordered in. [*Adm. Paper.*]

Jan. 21. Chatham. 21. Lieutenant John Stewart to Sam. Pepys. Account of the forwardness of the Prince, which will soon be ready to sail. [*Adm. Paper.*]

Jan. 21. Harwich. 22. Anthony Deane to the Navy Comrs. Repairs of ships. [*Adm. Paper.*]

Jan. 21. Chatham. 23. Edw. Gregory and four other Officers of the Yard to the Navy Comrs. Mr. Bilton's hemp is foul, and not worth the charge of working. [*Adm. Paper.*]

Jan. 21. Dover. 24. Pass from Nicholas Eaton, mayor of Dover, for Robert Magdogell and Robt. Moore, who have lately discharged themselves from the service of the States of Holland, in order to serve His Majesty, permitting them to go to London without molestation, and requesting relief for them in their necessities. With notes of their relief at Canterbury, 24 Jan., by Jo. Whitfield, treasurer, and 26 Jan., by S. Horne, treasurer. [*Adm. Paper.*]

Jan. 22. Portsmouth. 25. Commissioner Thos. Middleton to Sam. Pepys. The French cordage lately delivered is very unserviceable. The Duke of York orders the Royal Charles and James to be careened, &c.; 30 calkers and 20 carpenters are wanted, or orders cannot be executed: account of the Guinea provisions. Urges the want of ready money; it is a commodity that cannot be done without. Particulars of stores. [*Adm. Paper, three pages.*] *Encloses,*

25. I. *Commissioner Thos. Middleton to Sam. Pepys. Capt. Suffolk is entertained by Capt. Mynge, as master of the Royal Oak. The Earl of Sandwich is sailing for the Downs.* *January* 22, 1665.

1664–5. **Vol. CXI.**

Jan. 22. The Augustine, Portsmouth. 26. Capt. Rich. Teale to the Navy Comrs. Wants a supply of victuals for the Augustine, and a convoy. [*Adm. Paper.*]

Jan. 22. Order for a warrant to pay 30,000*l.* by quarterly instalments to Sir Henry Wood, Bart., for the use of the Queen-Mother, to be accounted for to her revenue commissioners. [*Ent. Book* 16, *p.* 329.]

[Jan. 22.] 27. Warrant for payment to Sir Hen. Wood as ordered above.

[Jan. 22.] 28. Minute of the above warrant.

Jan. 23. Warrant from Sec. Bennet to John Fowell, deputy lieutenant of Devonshire, to release Nicholas Battersley, minister of Dartmouth, on bail for his good behaviour and appearance, he having cleared himself, and given proof of his loyalty. [*Ent. Book* 16, *p.* 330.]

Jan. 23. Warrant to Sir John Robinson to deliver Major Robert Holmes to Percival Stanney; with a like warrant for Stanney to receive and keep him prisoner. Minute. [*Ent. Book* 16, *p.* 330.]

[Jan. 23.] 29. "Reasons most humbly presented to His Majesty and his Parliament, why men's persons should not be imprisoned for debt or damages, or anything thereto relating."

Jan. 23. Reference to the Solicitor General on the petition of the Earl of Cleveland and Lord Wentworth, that as they are damaged in the sale of part of their estate by the claims of Blackwall's granters, he shall ascertain truly what remains due on Stepney and Hackney, they declaring that nothing is due. [*Ent. Book* 18, *p.* 116.]

Jan. 23. Woolwich. 30. Chris. Pett to the Navy Comrs. Progress of ships in the yard. Timber wanted. Is troubled that what he said about the clamour raised against the Royal Katherine should give offence; only said that the report was false. [*Adm. Paper.*]

Jan. 23. Portsmouth. 31. Commissioner Thos. Middleton to Sam. Pepys. The 200*l.* is spent; wants money. [*Adm. Paper.*] *Encloses*,

31. i. *Account by St. J. Steventon of his disbursements since the receipt of the last 400l.; total, 454l. 0s., besides outstanding debts. Portsmouth, January 24, 1665.*

Jan. 23. Portsmouth. 32. Commissioner Thos. Middleton to Sir Wm. Penn. Thinks the careening of the Royal Charles and James a most unnecessary and chargeable work, and therefore will have no hand in it without a positive order. Damage sustained by ships. [*Adm. Paper, two pages.*]

Jan. 23. Portsmouth. 33. Commissioner Thos. Middleton to [Sam. Pepys]. Desires a warrant for felling beeches. The officers of the yard take great care to forward the service, but the seamen are rude, and it cannot be

Vol. CXI.

1664–5.

remedied. A parcel of good French hemp has arrived. Damage sustained by ships. [*Adm. Paper.*] *Encloses,*

33. i. *Blank contract for 50 dozen oars at 25s. per foot, and 100 dozen handspikes at 6s. the dozen.* *July 23, 1664.*

Jan. 24. Dover. 34. Thos. Wale to the Navy Coms. Has delivered the two long boats; five or six men-of-war are lying off Deal; has fetched the Drake's boat from Folkstone, and will satisfy the men who saved her. [*Adm. Paper.*]

Jan. 24. Chatham. 35. Edw. Gregory to the Navy Coms. Arrival of the Guinea frigate; sends her muster book. [*Adm. Paper.*]

Jan. 24. Chatham. 36. Rich. Burton, locksmith, to the Navy Coms. His rates of work have been so often lessened, that now they are the lowest allowed in any yard; no man can make a livelihood and do his work well at a less rate, without making proposals which he never intends to perform. Desires the continuance of his usual allowance. [*Adm. Paper.*]

Jan 24. 37. Jonas Shish to the Navy Coms. Sends measurement of the St. George, lying in Mr. Janson's dry dock. [*Adm. Paper.*]

Jan. 24. Order to the Lord Treasurer for a warrant for felling 60 beech trees in New Forest, co. Hants, for flank and keel pieces for the navy. [*Ent. Book* 22, *p.* 3.]

Jan. 24. Warrant for a grant to Thos. Laney, B.D., of the prebend of Ailesbury, Lincoln Cathedral. [*Ent. Book* 19, *p.* 29.]

Jan. 24. Warrant to pay to Sir Oliver Boteler, Bart., 1,600*l.* lent by his father, Sir Wm. Boteler, to the late King. [*Ent. Book* 22, *p.* 2.]

Jan. 24. Warrant to pay to Col. Wm. Legg, lieutenant of the ordnance, 67,520*l.* on account for iron ordnance, &c., and for 200 tons of copper to be provided in Sweden. [*Docquet.*]

Jan. 24. Warrant to pay to Col. Wm. Legg 73,162*l.* 8s., for saltpetre, &c. to be converted into gunpowder for furnishing the King's stores. [*Docquet.*]

Jan. 24. Warrant to pay to the Churchwardens and Overseers of the Poor of St. Martin's-in-the-Fields 100*l.*, as the King's free bounty. [*Docquet.*]

Jan. 24. Reference to Lord Treas. Southampton on the petition of Sir John Denham and Sir Willm. Morley, who desire the King's title for making a sea-wall across the creek from the sea. [*Ent. Book* 18, *p.* 121.]

[Jan. 24.] Reference to Dr. Exton, judge of the Admiralty Court, on the petition of Rich. Batson, merchant, requiring him to take such order as is consistent with the rules of the court, or report his opinion to the King. [*Ent. Book* 18, *p.* 121.]

Vol. CXI.

1664–5.

Jan. 23. 38. Receipt by Thos. Dixon from Mr. Williamson of seven letters to be delivered to the Lord Lieutenants. Endorsed "70,000*l.* letters."

Jan. 25. 39. Account by Jas. Harman of the Jersey's provisions brought by Thos. Streaton, in the Samuel hoy of Chatham, from the Gore, and her long boat from Deal. [*Adm. Paper.*]

Jan. 25. Woolwich. 40. Certificate by Chris. Pett and Capt. Wm. Badiley, that John Moore, boatswain of the Royal Katherine, having performed all the cutting out of ropes and rigging of the said ship, gets only the allowance of a common man. [*Adm. Paper.*]

Jan. 23. Chatham Dock. 41. Phin. Pett to the Navy Comrs. Begs that Mr. Lewsley may not be sent far away; his employment in keeping cheques upon all timber and plank, and as purveyor in viewing all timber contracted for, make his services indispensable. [*Adm. Paper.*]

Jan. 26. Harwich. 42. Anthony Deane and Wm. Baker to the Navy Comrs. Repairs of the Mary. Want money. [*Adm. Paper.*]

Jan. 20. Portsmouth. 43. John Tippetts to the Navy Comrs. Col. Norton's timber is not dear in proportion to its goodness; 30 calkers will be enough for careening the Charles, Royal James, and Henry. [*Adm. Paper.*]

Jan. 16. Woolwich. 44. Chris. Pett to the Navy Comrs. Repairs of ships. Asks leave of absence to attend the funeral of Commissioner Pett's late wife. [*Adm. Paper, damaged.*]

Jan. 20. Portsmouth. 45. Commissioner Thos. Middleton to Sam. Pepys. Repairs needed for the York and Bristol. There are now 70 mast-makers and boat-makers employed; 20 axemen and 30 calkers are required. Eight tons more of French cordage have arrived, equally unfit for service. [*Adm. Paper.*] *Encloses,*

45. I. *Certificate by Thos. Eastwood of the charge for felling, converting, and carrying* 700 *trees, amounting to* 800*l.*

Jan. 26. Reference to Lord Treasurer Southampton on the petition of Sir Geo. Carre, keeper of the New Park, New Forest, Hampshire, and John Gwin, for a grant for the sale of what alder and yew trees are in that forest. [*Ent. Book* 18, p 117.]

Jan. 20. Whitehall. 46. Petition of the Gentlemen of Cornwall now serving in Parliament to the King, for transfer of the assize courts from Launceston to Bodmin, where is a public hall and all necessaries; the former place is in one end of a county 80 miles long, is inconvenient to witnesses, jurors, and suitors, and improper in taking the deputy lieutenants and other officers so far away from some parts of a county exposed on two sides to the sea. With reference thereon to the Attorney General.

Jan. 20. Entry of the above reference. [*Ent. Book* 18, p. 117.]

Jan. 26. Whitehall. 47. Petition of the Mayor, &c., of Launceston, co. Cornwall, to the King, that the assizes and gaol delivery of the county, held there by

VOL. CXI.

1664–5.

ancient charter, and the chief support of the town, may not be removed, as proposed by some gentlemen of the county, to Bodmin, a mean town, lying 20 miles further within the county, and inconvenient for the judges by the badness of the ways. With reference thereon to the Attorney General.

Jan. 26. Entry of the above reference. [*Ent. Book* 18, p. 118.]

Jan. 26. Reference to the Officers of Greencloth, at request of Lord Steward the Duke of Ormond, on the petition of Jon. Batailhé for aid; he ordered 110 tuns of French wines for the King's household, which remain on hand because of the suspension of diets, and he is much damaged by the sale of Dutch prize wines. [*Ent. Book* 18, p. 18.]

Jan. 26. Reference to the Lord-Steward of the Household and Board of Greencloth on the petition of Christopher Musgrave, clerk of the robes to the Queen, for payment of his wages and board-wages. [*Ent. Book* 18, p. 119.]

Jan. 26. Whitehall. 48. Robt. Southwell to [Sec. Bennet]. The Commissioners for Prizes wish him to inform the King that on perusal of the letters, &c., of Solicofre, merchant of Marseilles, they think fit that his ship, Le Pigeon-Blanc, driven into Falmouth by weather, and seized as a prize, should be released.

Jan. 27. Whitehall. 49. Robt. Southwell to Sec. Bennet. The Commissioners for Prizes want commissions for Mr. Read and Capt. Taylor, for prize goods in the Caribbee Islands; and blank commissions to be sent to Sir Thos. Modyford, Sir Wm. Berkeley, the Commissioners of New England, and Sir Thos. Temple, each to appoint a fit man in their respective places.

Jan. 27. Recommendation to Lord Treas. Southampton and the Attorney General, of the petition of George Bishop of Winchester for discharge of a fee-farm rent of 10*l*. per annum on a house and grounds at Chelsea, purchased by him, the house, &c., being a small part of the whole manor; the whole rent is to be charged on the remaining part. [*Ent. Book* 18, p. 120.]

Jan. 27. Order to the Duke of York, on the petition of the Owners of the ship African, for her discharge; they contracted with the East India Company, but the ship is stopped in her passage, and the King wishes to gratify the company, and also to make use of the ship, to bring home the forces remaining under Sir Abraham Shipman. [*Ent. Book* 18, p. 120.]

Jan. 27. Reference to Lord Treas. Southampton on the petition of Edw. Progers, for the felling and selling of a coppice called Great Wotton, towards payment for building the lodge in Hampton Court Park, His Majesty having promised that he should be reimbursed. [*Ent. Book* 18, p. 121.]

Vol. CXI.

1664–5.
Jan. 27.
Feb. 6.
Chelsea.

Amb. Van Gogh to the [States General]. The Guinea fleet is to stay and await further tidings of what is done by De Ruyter, and Capt. Allin to remain in the Straits with his fleet; 30 merchants' ships more are fitting out for war, and the press greater than ever. They have got 200 men about Yarmouth, and expect 500 from Scotland. The Earl of Sandwich is ready for the Downs with 15 ships. A new duty of 40s. a tun on Spanish, and 20s. on French wines was projected in Parliament, to be given to the Duke of York, but was laid aside. Prince Rupert had an accidental hurt in the head, but is past danger. The news of Major-General Lambert's escape is not confirmed. [*Holl. Corresp., Jan.* 27, 1665.]

Jan. 27.
Woolwich.

50. Chris. Pett to Sam. Pepys. Thinks Mr. Cooper could undertake the service in Waltham Forest as well as Alicsholt. The Fountain is launched. [*Adm. Paper.*]

Jan. 28.
Portsmouth.

51. Commissioner Thos. Middleton to Sam. Pepys. Particulars of ships; 500 men will be wanted for the ships now in port when they go out, for few bring in more than 150 or 200 men. Vessels are wanted to carry provisions on to the ships; there are two laden with chesnuts, which if emptied could be so employed. Fears the King will become debtor to the account of many vessels in port. For want of money, is obliged to issue press warrants for carts to fetch broom. Desires an order to land all goods useful to the navy out of the prize ships. Mutiny amongst the block-makers. Account of stores wanted. [*Adm. Paper, three pages.*]

Jan. 28.
Deptford.

52. Jonas Shish to the Navy Comrs. Asks whether the men are to work on the 30th of the month. Cannot launch vessels on account of the thick ice in the wet dock. [*Adm. Paper, damaged.*]

Jan. 28.
Deptford.

53. Capt. Wm. Badiley to the Navy Comrs. Has employed a hoy to carry ballast out of the Royal Katherine. [*Adm. Paper, damaged.*]

Jan.?

54. Petition of John Dale, rector of Standlake, co. Oxford, to the King, for a dispensation to hold with the said rectory that of Rombald-kirk, diocese of Chester, though above 30 miles distant; has been at great charge in repairing the chancel, parsonage house, &c.

Jan. 29.

The King to the Archbishop of Canterbury. Requests him to grant a dispensation to John Dale, for holding the rectory of Standlake, diocese of Oxford, with that of Rombald-kirk. [*Ent. Book* 19, p. 31.]

Jan.?

55. Petition of Francis Coventry, the younger, to the King, for free pardon; has already obtained respite of burning in the hand, being convicted of manslaughter, because engaged in the unfortunate quarrel in which Rupert Dillon and Hen. Proby were killed, though neither died by his hand.

Jan. 28.

Warrant for a pardon to Fras. Coventry, for the death of Rupert Dillon and Hen. Proby, he being found guilty of manslaughter only; with restitution of goods and chattels. [*Ent. Book* 23, p. 1.]

[Jan. 28.]

56. Draft of the above.

VOL. CXI.

1664-5.
Jan. 28. Whitehall.
57. Warrant for a commission to the Duke of York to grant letters of marque and reprisal against ships, vessels, &c., belonging to the States of the United Provinces, for the injuries done by their East and West Indian Companies to British subjects. [*Two and a half pages.*]

Jan. 28. Entry of the above. [*Ent. Book 22, pp. 5, 6.*]

[Jan. 28.] 58. Blank form of obligation in 1,000*l.*, entered into by private men-of-war furnished with letters of reprisal against the Dutch, to pay to the King a fifteenth part of the value of all prizes taken by them, or the customs on the goods. Also

Similar form of obligation in 1,000*l.*, to pay a tenth of the value of such prizes into the Admiralty Court, for the Lord Admiral. Also

Similar obligation in 2,000*l.* not to attack the ships of any subject, especially those of Jersey and Guernsey; to bring their prizes into a British port or into Tangiers; and not to meddle with such ships or goods till adjudged lawful prizes by the Admiralty Court. [*Three pages, copies.*]

[Jan. 28.] 59. Statement of the mischief done to the clothworkers, dyers, &c., by the unlimited export of unwrought cloths, kersies, &c., which are bought up by the Dutch, dressed and dyed abroad, and so stretched that they can be sold at the same price when re-imported here, as was paid for them unwrought; with proposal for a remedy by Act of Parliament, by laying impositions on cloths, &c., exported white, and on those imported dyed. [*Printed.*]

Jan. 28. / Feb. 7. Dieppe.
60. Jean Belliard to Sir [Sam.] Moreland. Thanks for recommendations of his two sons to the Governor of Jamaica. Begs favour for the bearer, Capt. Jesfin Contentin, whose ship, going from Barnstaple, has been taken into Plymouth, it being a vessel in which many of his friends are interested. [*French.*]

Jan. 28. Grant to Col. Robt. Broughton of all treasure trove discovered since June 24, 1660, not claimed by any proprietor, and of all that shall be found in Middlesex within a year; with power to compound and sue for the same, but not to enter on any subject's land to dig for treasure, on penalty of 100*l.* and the loss incurred. [*Docquet.*]

Jan. 28. Warrant to pay to Sir George Carteret, treasurer of the navy, a further sum of 5,000*l.*, for the relief of the sick and wounded at sea, maintenance of Dutch prisoners, repairing and fitting Chelsea College for such as shall be sent thither, &c. [*Docquet.*]

Jan. 28. Warrant to pay to Sir George Carteret 60,833*l.* 6*s.* 8*d.*, for providing sea victuals for 5,000 men for one year. [*Docquet.*]

Jan. 28. Warrant to the Lord Treasurer and Lord Ashley to assign upon the rent of 1,838*l.* 12*s.*, reserved on a lease to Lord Mordaunt and others, of the 12*d.* per chaldron on Newcastle coal, 1,100*l.* yearly, to be paid to William Lord Crofts and Elizabeth his wife, as part of a

1664–5. VOL. CXI.

pension for their joint lives of 1,500*l.* a year, granted them on surrender by Lord Crofts of his pension of 1,000*l.* a year as gentleman of the bedchamber. [*Ent. Book* 17, *pp.* 85–6.]

[Jan. 28.] 61. Draft of the preceding. [*Three pages.*]

Jan. 28. Warrant for a grant to Sir John Griffin of the office of Captain and Keeper of the Blockhouses at West Tilbury and Gravesend; fee, 4*d.* a day and 20*l.* a year. [*Ent. Book* 22, *p.* 2.]

Jan. 28. Warrant to the Commissioners for Prizes to release and restore the goods of the St. Francis of Brest, lately brought into Portsmouth by the Diamond frigate, it appearing on petition of Peter Crolnoy and others, her owners, that she ought to be discharged from present service and restraint. [*Ent. Book* 22, *p.* 3.]

[Jan. 28.] 62. Draft of the above.

Jan. 28. Warrant by the Commissioners for Prizes, appointing Sir Thos. Strickland, Bart., sub-commissioner for prizes in the port of London. [*Ent. Book* 22, *p.* 7.]

Jan. [28.] 63. Draft of the above.

Jan. 28. Warrant by the Commissioners for Prizes, appointing Henry Dethick solicitor to the Prize Office, for prosecution of the King's title in the High Court of Admiralty. [*Ent. Book* 22, *p.* 8.]

Jan. 28. Chester. 64. Dr. Allan Pennington to Williamson. Recommends Sam. Burges, a person of great parts and merit, for some employment, such as ambassador's secretary, he having already travelled.

Jan. 28. Deal. 65. Ric. Watts to Williamson. The post office makes him pay for his letters, although they are marked with Mr. Hickes' name, and free; many letters of consequence are never delivered, and some are kept five or ten days in the office. The Earl of Sandwich, with Rear-Admiral Teddeman, arrived in the Downs on the 27th, with 13 ships, and two of the King's ships have arrived from Margate Road.

Jan. 28. London. 66. Fras. Godolphin to Col. Lewis Tremayne, deputy vice-admiral at St. Mawes Castle, Cornwall. Orders him to deliver to Capt. Erasmus De Brewer the ship lately seized in Fowey harbour, in obedience to an order of the Duke of York, he paying necessary expenses. *Encloses,*

66. I. *Warrant from the Duke of York to Fras. Godolphin, vice-admiral of the south of Cornwall, to deliver up the said ship taken by Capt. Brewer in the late wars between France and Spain, and adjudged in the Admiralty Courts to be lawful prize.* [*Copy.*] *Jan.* 10, 1665.

Jan. 20. 67. Information of 17 conventicles held in London, from January 10 to 20, 1665, with note that many of Cromwell's officers have withdrawn from the City, on hearing that there will be an order from

VOL. CXI.

1664–5.

Council to search for them. Major Jordan, formerly Nonconformist preacher at York, is lodged in Alderman Webb's house. On 20 doors in Paternoster Row and Ludgate Hill, papers were posted, inscribed "Murder will out."

Jan. 29. Warrant to the Commissioners for Prizes to permit the departure of the Pigeon-Blanc, belonging to —— Sollcofre, of Marseilles, driven by weather into Falmouth, and there detained by virtue of the present seizure; as the vessel belongs to Frenchmen, it should be discharged from further restraint. [*Ent. Book* 22, *p.* 4.]

[Jan. 29.] 68. Draft of the above.

Jan. 29. Warrant to Sir Thos. Ingram, chancellor of the duchy of Lancaster, to pay from the revenues of the duchy 400*l.* a year, being the remainder unassigned of a pension of 1,500*l.* granted to Lord Crofts and Elizabeth his wife, on surrender by the former of a pension of 1,000*l.* a year as gentleman of the bedchamber. [*Ent. Book* 17, *pp.* 83–4.]

Jan. 29. 69. W. Coventry to Sam. Pepys. To-morrow being a day of such great solemnity, it will be improper to receive friends. If the York must be girded, it is better to do it now. [*Adm. Paper.*]

Jan. 29. 70. W. Coventry to Sam. Pepys. Desires the names of the seven ships which refuse the King's price, and some order about cleaning the merchant ships. A messenger must be sent to Deptford, to inquire whether the Richmond or Coventry be gone down. The captain of the Garland complains of delay in sending victuals. Commissioner Middleton's advice about the inconvenience of new shrouds is very important, and should be laid before the Board. [*Adm. Paper, one and a half pages.*]

Jan. 30.
The Hind,
Harwich. 71. Capt. John Withers to the Navy Comrs. Sends the muster-book of the Hind. Has brought several volunteers and pressed men from Aldborough, and is ready to fetch others from Scarborough. [*Adm. Paper.*]

Jan. 30.
Dover. 72. E. Wivell to the Navy Comrs. The two pilots employed by him have performed their duty well, and been punctually paid. Refuses to satisfy the large demand of the young man who brought in the Hind, for his unskilful services. Offers to inspect the dispatch and good husbanding of the different vessels, as they come into port. [*Adm. Paper.*]

Jan. 30.
Portsmouth. 73. Commissioner Thos. Middleton to Sam. Pepys. The Royal Charles, James, and Henry being ordered to be careened, vessels will be wanted to receive their ballast, ammunition, &c. Proposes that the Guinea provisions be taken out of the Augustine, that she may be used. The 200*l.* and 100*l.* sent are right welcome; people take such advantage of the present necessity. Particulars of stores. [*Adm. Paper, two pages.*]

VOL. CXI.

1664–5.

Jan. 31. 74. Jonas Shish to the Navy Comrs. Wants some black oakum. [*Adm. Paper, damaged.*]

Jan. 31. Woolwich. 75. Chris. Pett to Sam. Pepys. Recommends Henry Sturton, lately pressed from Capt. Taylor's yard at Wapping, an able workman, to be employed in converting the timber intended to be felled in Waltham Forest, or to be appointed sideman on one of the new ships. [*Adm. Paper.*]

Jan. 31. 76. Account of the number and nature of guns required for five hired merchant ships. [*Adm. Paper.*]

Jan. 31. Harwich. 77. John Browne, storekeeper, to Sir Wm. Batten. Has made out bills for the smith who worked before Mr. Watkins came, but will not fill them in without the approbation of the Board. Thinks as the work was small, he should have 32*s.* 8*d.* per cwt. [*Adm. Paper.*]

Jan. 31. 78. Certificate by Capt. Henry Fenn of the discharge of Francis Fletcher, carpenter of the Montague, and the appointment of John Sear in his stead. [*Adm. Paper.*]

Jan. 31. Victualling Office. 79. Certificate by Thos. Lewis that Edw. Bond, master of the Harwich hoy, has passed his account. [*Adm. Paper.*]

Jan. 31. Harwich. 80. Anthony Deane to the Navy Comrs. The most convenient place for building the new third-rate ship will be the King's yard. Particulars of timber wanted or offered. [*Adm. Paper.*]

Jan. 31. Dover. 81. Nicholas Eaton, mayor of Dover, to the Navy Comrs. Promises to have the bank near the boom removed as soon as possible, in order to give free passage to the ships as formerly. The sixth-rate ship named in their letter was not in danger, but she went out in a neap tide and with an east wind. [*Adm. Paper.*]

Jan. 31. The Dartmouth, King's Road. 82. Capt. Rich. Rooth to the Navy Comrs. Has arrived with the Duke of York's command to press as many able seamen as can possibly be procured, and to receive others from the Vice-Admirals of Gloucestershire and Somersetshire. Has got a small supply of cordage, &c., from Capt. Dan. Adams, of Bristol. [*Adm. Paper.*] *Encloses,*

82. I. *Account by Capt. Dan. Adams of provisions furnished for the Dartmouth.* *Bristol, January* 28, 1665.

Jan. 31. Whitehall. 83. Pass for —— Leicester to embark from any port with two horses for Ireland.

Jan. 31. Warrant for a grant to Sir Edw. Heath, K.B., and Edm. Vernon, of the forest of Mendip, co. Somerset, and lands thereto belonging, with all casualties, liberties, and lead mines, on their discovering and making good at their own charge the right of the Crown to the same. [*Ent. Book* 22, *pp.* 11–2.]

[Jan. 31.] 84. Draft of the above. [*Two and a half pages.*]

Vol. CXI.

1664–5.

Jan. 31. 85. John Lord Belasyse to Williamson. Requests the King's signature to commissions for Hen. Darcy to be lieutenant to Capt. Chas. Daniell at Tangiers; George Leslay, ensign to Sir Rob. Hildyard at Hull; and Rob. Hildyard, lieutenant to his father, Sir Rob. Hildyard.

Jan. 31. 86. Lord Ashley to Wm. Wardour. Requests to know what has been paid in on the 18 months' assessment, and also on the assessment for October 1664, up to January 28, 1665.

Jan. ? 87. Petition of the Prisoners for Debt throughout the kingdom to the King, to remind the Parliament to pass before rising the Act for their release, the bill for which has been twice read; they fear that through press of time, and the petitions of gaolers against it, it may be laid aside. Many of them served the late King, and are willing to pay their just debts according to their abilities.

Jan. ? 88. Petition of Daniel Ferrand, of Bourdeaux, to the King and Council, for restoration of the goods of his brother-in-law, Jean de Ridder, of Bourdeaux, laden at Middleburg and Amsterdam for Bourdeaux, before any letters of reprisal against the Dutch were issued or heard of, on proof that they really belong to Ridder, who is a French merchant of good account.

Jan. ? 89. Petition of Abraham Gregory, master of the Free School, Gloucester, to the King, for a letter to Cambridge University, to grant him his M.A. degree, which he was unable to take during the late rebellion, on account of his loyalty. *Annexing,*

89. i. *Certificate by Wm. Bishop of Gloucester to the orthodoxy, conformity, and good conduct of the petitioner.* *Jan. 23, 1665.*

Jan. ? 90. Petition of Paul Hobson to the King, for fulfilment of the desire to which His Majesty formerly expressed favour, viz., to grant him an order to go beyond seas; his long imprisonment having brought him to great weakness, and ruined his estate. [*See* 1664, *Aug.* 18.]

Jan. ? 91. Petition of Edw. Kennet, of Westminster, to the King, for the reversion of the first vacancy in the almshouses near the Gatehouse. Kept an inn at Ross, Herefordshire, during the late wars, and was miserably vexed and plundered by the Parliament party for his loyalty.

Jan. ? 92. Petition of Col. Walter Slingsby to the King, for continuance for a second year of the captain's pay allowed him on giving up Sandham Fort to Capt. Holmes, that he may subsist and repair to his charge in the Isle of Wight.

Jan. ? 93. Petition of Capt. John Strode, lieutenant governor of Dover Castle, to the King, for His Majesty's share of the benefit of three Dutch prize ships, the Raven, Jacob, and Golden Sun, which with great

VOL. CXI.

1664–5.

trouble, and at an expense of 1,000*l*., he has brought into Dover harbour, and according to an order of Council of 18 November last, secured them by taking away their sails, &c. [*See May* 26, 1665.]

Jan. Memoranda [by Williamson from the Signet books] of warrants, grants, &c., passed during the month, the uncalendared portions of which are as follow:—

Commission to Prince Rupert and other Lords of the Council to be the principal Commissioners for Prizes, with power to appoint such sub-commissioners as the King shall nominate.

Note that the grooms and pages of the Queen's chamber have 100 marks yearly at Christmas, as the King's free gift for the preceding year.

Appointment of Thos. Duppa as assistant gentleman-usher daily waiter, with 100 marks yearly out of the treasury of the chamber, for his attendance on progresses.

Note that the Treasurer of the Chamber sometimes passes a privy seal to empower him to make payments.

Grant to Dan. Deine of the keepership of the King's garden, his beds and other harness, and his wardrobe at the Tower.

Grant of incorporation to the Canary Company, to consist of all English subjects who have traded to the Canary Islands to the amount of 1,000*l*. yearly for the past seven years, and who are not retailers. [*Domestic Corresp., December* 1664.]

Jan.? 94. Warrant to pay to John Lord Berkley of Stratton, Sir John Duncombe, and Thos. Chicheley, appointed Commissioners of Ordnance, 21 Oct. 1664, 200 marks each per annum, as paid to the late Master of Ordnance, out of the 12,000*l*. a year allowed for that office; and also allowances for a clerk and three servants.

Jan. Whitehall. 95. Licence to [Sir George Crooke, Bart.], high sheriff of Oxfordshire, to reside out of the county during his year of office, on account of some accidents lately befallen him, so that the public service be not neglected.

Jan. Deptford. 96. Thos. Childe to the Navy Comrs. Wants either a warrant to seize goods purloined from the King's stores, as discovered by him, or that his affidavit and papers may be returned. [*Adm. Paper.*]

Jan. 97. Thos. Eastwood to the Navy Comrs. Asks an imprest of 100*l*., to go on with the felling of trees in the New Forest and Bere Forest. [*Adm. Paper.*]

Jan.? 98. Capt. Wm. Badiley to the Navy Comrs. Cannot remove the Francis from Woolwich to Deptford, the river being full of ice. [*Adm. Paper, damaged.*]

Jan. 99. Certificate from Watermen's Hall to the Navy Comrs., that in order to provide as many watermen as possible for the King's service, they have searched every place on the river, from Gravesend to Windsor, and find 4,883 watermen, and that now there are 1,700 at sea in the service. [*Adm. Paper.*]

VOL. CXI.

1664–5. [Jan.] 100. Certificate of the amount of fines and issues of jurors, given in by the sheriffs of the several counties of England, for the year 16 Charles II.; total, 1,158*l*.

Jan.? 101. Comparison, drawn up in parallel columns, between the numbers of horses kept for the King and Queen, and allowed to the household officers, 7 Charles I. and 16 Charles II., with the allowances for wages, board wages, &c., showing that in the former year the stable establishment cost 15,203*l*. 19*s*. 5*d*., which, without the composition for hay, oats, and straw, would have been 18,465*l*. 13*s*.; in the present year, it will amount to 16,640*l*. 12*s*. 3*d*. [*Twenty-five pages.*]

Jan.? 102. Note of a request by Sir Gilbert Talbot, [envoy in Denmark], for a release from the clause in the commission requiring all prizes to be brought into England or Ireland to be adjudged there; and for a commission to John Paul and John Perkins to judge prizes taken on those coasts; supposed to mean those on the Baltic Sea.

Jan.? 103. Account by George Markham, that on 30th Jan., the day of fasting and prayer in memory of the late King, many persons at Weymouth, although warned by the mayor, kept open their shops and would not go to church. Sent a letter to the mayor and a party of horse, on which the fanatics shut up their shops and ran out of town. Edw. Tucker, Bart. Beare, John Owner, and Rob. Roberts had their shops shut by the mayor, but opened them again in despite of him.

VOL. CXII. FEBRUARY 1–18, 1664–5.

1664–5. Feb. 1. Warrant for creating Sir Nicholas Crisp, of Middlesex, a Baronet. Minute. [*Ent. Book 22, p. 64.*]

Feb. 1. 1. Sir Jo. Lawson to Williamson. Encloses the original warrant, which must be new drawn with certain additions, and signed. Hopes then to get the money in time.

Feb. 1. The Jersey. 2. Daniel Sindrey, purser of the Jersey, to Mr. Hayter. Sends muster books of the Expedition and Jersey. Desires 10 tickets. [*Adm. Paper.*]

Feb. 1. Portsmouth. 3. Commissioner Thos. Middleton to Sam. Pepys. The York must be girded with fir timber for want of oak. Particulars of ships. Recommends the practice of stoving hawsers for shrouds; it is a business of great importance. Wonders that the masts of great ships stand, considering how they are supported. Requests an order for employing, in the King's service, the great galleys lately come into port laden with rotten chesnuts. With postscript, dated Feb. 2nd: Has just received the Commissioners' orders concerning the careening of ships in port. Will send up samples of French cordage to be viewed by the Board. [*Adm. Paper, two pages.*]

VOL. CXII.

1664–5.

Feb. 1. Portsmouth. 4. John Tippetts, John Cox, and John Tinker, officers of the yard, to the Navy Comrs. Value the set of lanterns on board the Royal Charles at 28*l.* [*Adm. Paper.*]

Feb. 2. The Assistance, Plymouth. 5. Capt. Za. Browne to the Navy Comrs. Certifies the wilful damage done to his vessel off Scilly by Mr. Cratey, of the Bristol, from Malaga. Capt. John Price of the Blackamoor can give information where the fault lies. A new mainsail is wanted. [*Adm. Paper.*] *Encloses,*

5. I. *Certificate by Thos. Loader, carpenter of the Monk, and two others, of damage sustained by the Assistance, and estimate of her repairs, amounting to 20l.*

January 28, 1665.

Feb. 2. The Mary, Harwich. 6. Capt. Jer. Smyth to Sir Wm. Batten. Arrival of his stores. Will soon be ready to sail. The Elizabeth is ready; her purser has taken short provisions; hopes he may be made an example of, as an idle and debauched fellow. [*Adm. Paper.*] *Encloses,*

6. I. *Account by Capt. Edw. Nixon of provisions received on board the Elizabeth, and of what they are short of the proper proportion.*

Feb. 2. Woolwich. 7. Chris. Pett to the Navy Comrs. Recommends Andrew Rogers, a shipwright of Chatham, for converting timber in Waltham Forest, and hewing the frame of the second-rate ship in Alkeholt, at the rate of 12*s.* per load. Timber wanted. Progress of ships. [*Adm. Paper.*]

Feb. 2. Deptford. 8. Thos. Cowley and Jonas Shish to Sam. Pepys. Account of a mutiny among the workmen, because they are kept in the yard during the half hour allowed for breakfast. Requests orders and some speedy remedy: it would never do to comply with them. [*Adm. Paper, damaged.*]

Feb. 2. Prison, Westminster. 9. M. De la Fabvollière, engineer, to Sec. Bennet. Being in the apartment of Prince Rupert at court, presented a humble supplication to one of his gentlemen, to be given to the Prince, when the gentleman abused him, and on his replying, struck him several times with his own sword on the head; then aided by several scoundrels of the Prince's stable, hustled him out of the door, and gave him up to the guard, whence he was sent to prison. Begs favour and release. [*French.*]

Feb. 2. Privy seal for 15,000*l.* to Bishop Rassel, in discharge of payments made by him, and in recompense for service. [*Ent. Book 22, p. 9.*]

Feb. 2. Privy seal for 2,000*l.* to Lady Elizabeth Fielding, of the King's free gift. Minute. [*Ent. Book 22, p. 14.*]

Feb. 3. Reference to Lord Ashley on the petition of Mr. Elliot, for a commission to prosecute all persons formally issuing counterfeit bills and debentures. [*Ent. Book 18, p. 122.*]

VOL. CXII.

1664–5.
Feb. 3. Warrant for a discharge to Peter Pett, navy commissioner, of an imprest of 250*l.*, advanced to him in 1660 and 1661 for navy expenses. [*Ent. Book* 22, *p.* 8.]

Feb. 3. Warrant for a grant to Richard Earl of Dorset, Sir John Rivers, Bart., and Sir George Courthope, and their heirs, in trust for the inhabitants of East Grinstead, Sussex, of a change of market day and of two yearly fairs there. [*Ent. Book* 22, *p.* 9.]

Feb. 3. 10. Reasons read in Council why at this juncture the trade of the Straits should be preserved: it employs a million of people, being half the trade of the kingdom; 100 sail of ships, worth 600,000*l.*, are returning, and without convoy will fall into the enemy's hands; the goods ready for Turkey and Leghorn will be spoiled by delay, and clothiers, &c., reduced to great distress; the ships should go off at once with 12 or 13 men-of-war as convoy, before the Holland fleet assembles, as the Hollanders will have difficulty to find men in the general call for sailors. [*Two pages.*]

Feb. 3. Lydney. 11. Dan. Furzer to the Navy Comrs. Sends particulars of ironwork required for the new ship. The smith and ironmonger will both expect ready money. Difficulty of finding a convenient place for making the great anchors; the storehouse lately hired at Coppill may be enlarged for the purpose for 12*l.* Will forbear making moulds for the new ship, until he hears whether the draft is to be altered. Robert Foley, ironmonger, intends to treat for the supply of anchors and ironwork. [*Adm. Paper, two pages.*] *Encloses,*

11. I. *List of the prices for ironwork, as offered by Mr. Furzer, compared with those paid in London, the latter being the larger.*

Feb. 3. The Plymouth, Gibraltar Bay. 12. Capt. Thos. Allin to Sir Geo. Carteret. Has been necessitated to order a bill of 229*l.* 3*s.* 4*d.* to be taken up of Capt. Rich. Beach, for the emergent occasions of the fleet, their treasury being exhausted in buying provisions, &c. [*Adm. Paper.*]

Feb. 3. 13. W. Coventry to Sam. Pepys. Sends Steventon's application for an assistant; and thinks that for the present it should be allowed. Asks the names of the merchant ships agreed for, and the number of guns they will carry. [*Adm. Paper.*] *Encloses,*

13. I. *St. J. Steventon to Wm. Coventry. Complains of his press of business, from only having one clerk. At Chatham the clerk of the cheque has three. Begs for one or two more assistants. Portsmouth, January* 28, 1665.

Feb. 3. Deptford. 14. Giles Bond to the Navy Comrs. Gives an account of stores taken on board the Harwich hoy. Is ready to sail for Harwich. [*Adm. Paper, damaged.*]

Feb. 3. 15. Thos. Hobson to Thos. Hayter. Isaac Morrice, a shipwright pressed for Portsmouth, desires leave to send another able man in his stead. Asks directions thereon. [*Adm. Paper.*]

VOL. CXII.

1664–5.

Feb. 3. Milford. 16. Lieutenant John Steward to Sam. Pepys. Forwardness of the Prince; she can carry six more guns than allowed. Men wanted. Mr. Norman has taken a prize of pitch, tar, and plank, which will be useful to the fleet. [*Adm. Paper.*]

Feb. 4. The Mary, Harwich. 17. Capt. Jer. Smyth to the Navy Comrs. Forwardness of his ship. The men pressed by the constables are of all trades; out of 11 sent from Colchester, there were only two seamen. Sent the mayor a list of the able seamen in the town, but he would not cause them to be impressed. [*Adm. Paper.*]

Feb. 4. Deptford. 18. Capt. Wm. Badiley to the Navy Comrs. Survey of provisions on board the Golden Lion. Wants powder and gunners' stores from the Tower. [*Adm. Paper, damaged.*]

Feb. 4. Warrant for taking Elizabeth Calvert to the Gatehouse. Minute. [*Ent. Book 22, p. 9.*]

Feb. 4. Prison, Westminster. 19. M. De la Fabrollière to [Sec. Bennet]. Hopes his petition has done good. Prince Rupert sent him word to obtain a discharge of some things received by him from the Tower, and which are now on the Royal James, in the hands of the master gunner. This is just, but impossible, the account of them being with other papers, in his trunk at Portsmouth, of which he (the writer) has the key. Begs release, and a little money to take him to Portsmouth, to attend to these matters. [*French.*]

Feb. 4. Hull. 20. Luke Whittington to Sir Edw. Walker. Cannot agree with the Doctor, who threatens to petition the Lord Treasurer to sequester his office. Thinks this cannot be done, as he holds it under the great seal, but asks whether a protection for his person and goods could be had. The fishermen have seen 30 Holland ships, most of them men-of-war, off Flamborough, coming from northwards.

Feb. 4. London. 21. Jo. Corrance to Edw. Viscount Conway. Rejoices at his safe arrival in England, and hopes for his lady's recovery in the spring. Private business. [*One and a half page, damaged.*]

Feb. 5. Queen's College, Oxford. 22. Jo. Wakefield to Williamson. The vicarage of St. John, Isle of Thanet, worth 100*l.* a year, is void by removal of Mr. Overing to Old Fish Street, London; it is in the gift of the Archbishop of Canterbury. Begs assistance to obtain it, if he thinks it worth the having.

Feb. 5. Spalding. 23. Anthony Oldfield to Edw. Christian, Westminster. Mr. Lane, a Lynn merchant, who came from Dordrecht, dined there with Opdam and with Walton, former governor of Lynn, one of the scarlet die, who is received into the Dutch councils. He was disguised in a periwig down to his waist. A Dutchman threatened Lane to knock his brains out if he did anything concerning Walton, finding that he knew him.

VOL. CXII.

1664–5.
Feb. 5. Portsmouth. 24. Commissioner Thos. Middleton to Sam. Pepys. Wants small vessels for carrying provisions to and from the great ships. The prize officers refuse to deliver any of the prize ships for the King's use. There will be oak plank sufficient for the girding of the York. [*Adm. Paper.*]

Feb. 6. Portsmouth. 25. Commissioner Thos. Middleton to Sam. Pepys. Believes 1,000 of the best men will be lost out of the various ships coming into that port to be cleaned; the only remedy for it is to set up a gallows in every town between Portsmouth and London, and out of every ten men taken, going away without leave, to hang one by lot. Captain Salmon misses 120 men, and every ship 20, 30, 50, and some 100. Particulars of ships and stores. The Yarmouth is come to anchor, having lost all her masts through the defect of her shrouds. Complains of the rigging of the King's ships in general. [*Adm. Paper, one and a quarter pages.*]

Feb. 6. 26. Commissioner Peter Pett to Sam. Pepys. Returns the contract for a third-rate ship to be built by Mr. Castell, sent him by the Board to view and correct. [*Adm. Paper.*]

Feb. 6. Dover. 27. Thos. White to the Navy Comrs. Solicits the appointment of Clerk of the Cheque and Storekeeper at Dover, if vessels should be sent in to man, and stores kept there, as in the former Holland wars. The tradesmen of the town wish to furnish commodities for the service, at reasonable rates. [*Adm. Paper.*]

Feb. 6. Dover. 28. Thos. White to Sir Geo. Carteret. Beseeches his interest with the Board to procure him the employment of Agent or Clerk of the Cheque there. Will not buy nor sell anything, but only keep accounts. [*Adm. Paper.*]

Feb. 6. Victualling Office. 29. Denis Gauden to the Navy Comrs. Sends an account of victuals as nearly as it can be computed. [*Adm. Paper.*] *Encloses,*

29. I. *Account of victuals in store and under contract for ten seaports named.* *February* 6, 1665.

Feb. 6. Pass for two geldings into France. Minute. [*Ent. Book* 22, *p.* 10.]

Feb. 6. Pass for two horses into France for Mr. Leicester. Minute. [*Ent. Book* 22, *p.* 10.]

Feb. ? 30. Petition of Fras. White to the King for denization; was born at Sedan in France, but brought up in England, chiefly in service of Lord North.

Feb. 6. Grant of denization to [Fras.] White. Minute. [*Ent. Book* 22, *p.* 10.]

Feb. 6. Whitehall. 31. Warrant to Sir Fras. Cobb, high sheriff of Yorkshire, to deliver John Brackenbury, prisoner at York, to Sir Edw. Brett, commander of the forces, to be conveyed to Scarborough Castle.

Feb. 6. Minute of the above. [*Ent. Book* 22, *p.* 10.]

VOL. CXII.

1664–5.

Feb. 6. Whitehall. 32. James Povey to Sec. Bennet. The Duke of Albemarle wishes him to remember the caveat formerly entered, that nothing pass to the prejudice of the grant to his Grace's nephew, Sir Jas. Smith, of Mendip Manor, Somersetshire.

Feb. 6. The King to [the Vice-Chancellor of Cambridge]. Requests a D.D. degree for Thos. Holt, B.D., Chancellor of Wells Cathedral, in consideration of his loyal services to the late King, &c. [*Ent. Book* 19, p. 31.]

Feb. 6. Letter recommending Abraham Gregory to take his degree as M.A., at Cambridge. Minute. [*Ent. Book* 19, p. 32.]

Feb. 6. Warrant to the Board of Greencloth for a yearly salary of 50*l.* to Simon Menselli, keeper of the King's snow and frost houses. [*Ent. Book* 22, p. 12.]

[Feb. 6.] 33, 34. Warrant to Wm. Ashburnham, cofferer, to pay to Simon Menselli, keeper of the snow and frost houses, 50*l.* a year for his service and charges, beginning from Dec. 1662. [*Two drafts.*]

Feb. 6. Privy seal for 10,000*l.* to the privy purse. Minute. [*Ent. Book* 22, p. 13.]

Feb. 6. Commissions for Robt. Hildyard to be Lieutenant, and Geo. Lasley, Ensign, to Sir Robt. Hildyard's company at Hull. Minute. [*Ent. Book* 20, p. 46.]

Feb. 6. Commission for Lord Hawley to march to York. Minute. [*Ent. Book* 20, p. 46.]

Feb. 6. Letter to the Lord Treasurer to pay to Stephen Fox 15,000*l.*, out of money received from the sale of Dunkirk. Minute. [*Ent. Book* 17, p. 64.]

Feb. 6. Corroboration of a grant to Thos. Laney, B.D., of the Prebend of Ailesbury, in Lincoln Cathedral. [*Docquet.*]

Feb. 6. Warrant for discharging Thos. Chiffinch from all writs of *distringas* and other processes, for not accounting for several sums received and disbursed by him according to the King's commands, notwithstanding any grant thereof to others. [*Docquet.*]

Feb. 6. Warrant to pay 250*l.* to John Fisher, to be paid to Edw. Jolley for his interest in the houses without the park wall, near the Cockpit, on his surrender thereof to the King's use; also to pay 50*l.* to Adrian May, for repair of the said houses, and making for a bridge in the park, &c. [*Docquet.*]

Feb. 6. 35. Petition of Allan Smallwood, D.D., to the King, to corroborate his title to the Rectory of Graystock, Cumberland, to which he was presented, since the Restoration, by Eliz. Countess Dowager of Arundel and Surrey. With note in his favour by Gilbert Archbishop of Canterbury.

VOL. CXII.

1664–5.
Feb. 6.
Whitehall.

36. The King to [the Dean and Chapter of Salisbury]. Requested leave, on Feb 3, 1664, for Dr. Thos. Hyde, chanter of the cathedral, to remove to the house void by death of Dr. Hollis, notwithstanding the statute to the contrary, so that Dr. Rich. Clayton, B.D., a residentiary, who should have had the said house, was left destitute. Begs the next vacant residentiary's house for him. [*Copy.*]

Feb. 7.
Newcastle.

37. Rich. Forster to James Hickes. There is a greater storm of snow than any one can remember. Begs intelligence. An action with the Dutch is expected.

Feb. 7.

Warrant for Sir John Shaw, of London, to be a Baronet. Minute. [*Ent. Book* 22, *p.* 64.]

Feb. 7.

Grant to Sir John Griffith of the office of Keeper of the Blockhouse at West Tilbury, fee, 2*d.* a day; and of that at Gravesend, fee, 4*d.* a day, with six acres of land, &c. [*Docquet.*]

Feb. 7.

Warrant to pay to Sir Allan Apsley, master and surveyor of the hawks, 800*l.* per annum, with arrears, for providing hawks, and paying falconers; to be paid by the Receiver of Lincolnshire, or if that revenue will not bear the charge, from some other branch of revenue. [*Docquet.*]

Feb. 7.

Warrant to pay to Sir Henry Wood, Bart., treasurer and receiver general to the Queen-Mother, for her use, 30,000*l.*, to be paid quarterly. [*Docquet.*]

Feb. 7.

Grant to Baptist May and Abraham Cowley, on nomination of the Earl of St. Alban's, of ground in Pall Mall, whereon 13 or 14 houses are intended to be built, on rent of 160*l.* a year, to begin from Michaelmas, 1666; and also lease to them of part of the ground sometimes used as a highway from Charing Cross to St. James's, with the usual provisoes and exceptions. [*Ent. Book* 72, *pp.* 490–501.]

Feb. 7.

38. Wm. Wardour to Lord Ashley. States the sums paid in from the several counties of England and Wales, on the assessment for October, 1660; total, 65,853*l.* 11*s.* 2½*d.* [*Two and a half pages.*]

Feb. 7.

39. Wm. Wardour to Lord Ashley. States the sums paid in for the 18 months' assessment, up to Jan. 28 last; total, 941,711*l.* 17*s.* 4*d.* [*One and a half pages.*]

[Feb. 7.]

40. Petition of Katharine Countess Dowager of Chesterfield, executrix of Daniel O'Neale, to the King, for extra allowance for continual dispatches, which she is required daily to send during the raising of the great power at sea, to the sea-side counties where the ships lie, and sometimes to the vessels themselves, for which she has no allowance, nor means of reimbursement. [*Draft, corrected, one and a half pages.*]

VOL. CXII.

1664–5.

Feb. 7. Reference of the above petition to Secs. Morice and Bennet, and their report, June 22, in favour of the petition. [*Ent. Book* 16, *pp.* 122, 174.]

Feb. 7. Reference to the Lord Chancellor, Lord Treasurer, and two others, on the petition of the poor tenants in Cumberland, praying not to pay more than the ancient rent of 49*s.* for certain tenements. [*Ent. Book* 18, p. 123.]

Feb. 7. 41. [Wm.] Cooper, purveyor of timber, to the Navy Comrs. Begs to be excused waiting on the justices, as it takes up so much time, and will obstruct the moulding of the frame of the new ship building in Aliceholt woods. Requests allowances, materials, and a letter of credit for continuing the work. [*Adm. Paper.*]

Feb. 7. Woolwich. 42. Chris. Pett to Sam. Pepys. Mr. Morehouse and Mr. Denis were employed years since in felling and converting timber for the navy. Can say nothing of their ability. Recommends Mr. Cooper as knowing the forest better than any other man. Timber wanted. Repairs of ships. [*Adm. Paper.*]

Feb. 7. 43. W. Coventry to Sir Wm. Penn. Desires that the fire ships and other small ships be hastened down from Deptford, to serve against privateers and gather in men. The Success has spent her mainmast and gone into Plymouth. Col. Middleton's notion of new cordage loosing the masts, and of storing it to preserve them, is new, and worth consideration. Suggests making the carpenter of the Breda purveyor of one of the forests, so as to make the purveyors more reasonable and industrious, and encourage the builders, as "there is nothing but a Cooper or a Rogers to be found on English ground." Timber wanted. [*Adm. Paper.*] *Encloses,*

43. I. *Note by Wm. Coventry of a bill of imprest for* 1,000*l. required by James Johnson.*

Feb. 7. Harwich. 44. Anthony Deane to the Navy Comrs. Repairs of ships. Want of labourers. Proposes a bargain of good timber. It will make 3*s.* a load difference in price, if it be brought in by the King. [*Adm. Paper.*]

[Feb. 7.] 45. Note by Sir Wm. Batten of the number of guns, &c., on 13 merchant ships agreed for. [*Adm. Paper.*]

[Feb. 7.] 46. Note of guns for five merchant ships taken up, part of which are the King's, and part their own. [*Adm. Paper.*]

Feb. 7. 47. Account of guns decided on for four of the merchant ships. [*Adm. Paper.*]

[Feb. 7.] 48–51. Further particulars of the size and quality of the guns for the said ships. Four papers. [*Adm. Paper.*]

Feb. 7. 52. Account of the number of men and guns on ten merchant ships hired into the service. [*Adm. Paper.*]

N 2

Vol. CXII.

1664–5.

Feb. 7. Harwich. 53. Giles Bond, of the Harwich hoy, to the Navy Comrs. Has arrived at Harwich from Deptford, and hopes soon to come to London. [*Adm. Paper.*]

Feb. 7. Dover. 54. John Tatnell to Sir John Lawson. Begs his interest in procuring him the place of a Shipwright at Dover; has experience and ability. [*Adm. Paper.*]

Feb. 7. Lizard frigate, Portsmouth. 55. Capt. John Andrews to the Navy Comrs. Is appointed to the command of the Lizard; her condition is good, but she has neither master nor gunner. An able man has been presented for the former place. [*Adm. Paper.*] *Encloses,*

55. I. *Certificate by Robt. Salmon and Laurence Browning of the fitness of Rich. Bone to take the employment of master on the Lizard.* *Feb. 4, 1665.*

Feb. 7. Burnham Market. 56. Capt. Thos. Lardge to Sam. Pepys. Hears the rumour of a sudden war with the Dutch; was in all former engagements, and had command of the Lark, but that ship being laid up, retired to Norfolk, his country. Offers his services. [*Adm. Paper.*]

Feb. 8. Chatham. 57. Lieut. John Steward to Sam. Pepys. The bearer, Mr. Adams, is an able master, owner of a good hoy, and would willingly attend the Earl of [Sandwich] in the Prince. Asks directions about getting men, and will then soon be ready to sail. [*Adm. Paper.*]

Feb. 8. Whitehall. Proclamation of the prices of wines for the ensuing year, as fixed by the Lord Chancellor and others; Canary, Alicant and Muscadel, 26*l.* the pipe, or 9*d.* a pint; French wines, 8*d.* a quart; Rhenish wines, 12*d.* a quart, &c. [*Printed, Proc. Coll., p. 177.*]

[Feb. 8.] 58. Reasons against the bill for settling the estate of Sir Rob Carr, Bart.: viz, that it is preferred by the son, Sir Rob. Carr, without consent of his parents; that it is dangerous to admit a son to dispose of his father's estate, and unjust for the father to be compelled to sell his estate in his lifetime, to pay his son's debts, &c. With answers to these objections, showing that Sir Rob. Carr, sen., has been locked up by Lady Carr in the country, and by ill usage rendered incapable of management; that all the children wish a settlement of the property, and that Lady Carr, being nobly provided for, has no ground of complaint, &c. [*Printed.*]

Feb. 8. Yarmouth. 59. Rich. Bower to Williamson. A small ketch, bound to Hull and Scarborough for men, and the Hind ketch, which went in chase of a Flemish buss, are out in a great storm. The ketch sent for men is so small that they do not like to go in it, saying they shall be prize for any that attack them; 200 or 300 are waiting conveyance, and had better be gone, as one person has died and another sickened of the plague in the town. A sloop from Nieuport in Flanders has been cast ashore.

VOL. CXII.

1664–5.

Feb. 6. 60. Sec. Bennet to the King. The money hitherto spent on Castle Cornet, Guernsey, has been of little use for defence of the island, as the castle does not command the landing place near: nothing should be done more for it, except to fit it as a garrison for 60 soldiers and to repair the granaries, &c.; but a line should be thrown up for retreat in danger, the islanders ordered to secure their moveables from incursion, and each parish to build a storehouse, to which they can retire; breastworks should be thrown up, and the castle stored at the King's expense; the cost will be 700*l.*; 25 men should constantly be kept in the Castle Du Val, which commands a landing place. [*Three pages.*]

Feb. 9. 61. Leonard Williams to Sec. Bennet. Has delivered his letters; only keeps company with his honour's professed enemies, and omits no charge nor trouble to hear of anything against government. In spite of rumours, nothing serious is intended at present. Atkinson wants to go to Holland, but there is hazard in getting over, and when the war with the Dutch begins, they hope to manage their business.

Feb. 9. London. 62. Speech of Sir Edw. Turner, speaker of the House of Commons, to the King, on his passing the Act for granting a Royal aid of 2,477,500*l.* to be paid in three years, for the Dutch war. [*Printed, four pages; also printed in Lords' Journals, Vol.* XI., *p.* 654.]

Feb. 9. Deal. 63. Ri. Watts to Williamson. The Earl of Sandwich has gone for Holland; five of the King's ships from Portsmouth and 17 merchant ships have arrived.

Feb. 9. Woolwich. 64. Wm. Bodham to Sam. Pepys. Will make trial of the New England tar. Progress of the new ropehouse. Timber wanted. [*Adm. Paper.*]

Feb. 9. The Plymouth, Gibraltar Bay. 65. Capt. Thos. Allin to Sir Geo. Carteret. Has taken up a bill of 183*l.* 6*s.* 8*d.* of Capt. Robt. Clerk, in 800 pieces of 8, to supply the emergencies of the fleet. [*Adm. Paper.*]

Feb. 9. Chatham. 66. Rich. Burton, locksmith, to the Navy Comrs. Will serve the King for one year with all ironwork, at 20*s.* in 100*l.* cheaper than any other person; performs his works himself, while those who make tenders employ men under them, and fall short in goodness and workmanship. [*Adm. Paper.*]

Feb. 9. River's Mouth. 67. Capt. John Barton, of the Blackamoor, to the Navy Comrs. His ship is ordered to Harwich, to ply between Alford [Orford] Ness and the Hope. Had a leak stopped at Harwich. [*Adm. Paper.*]

Feb. 9. Harwich bay, Harwich. 68. Giles Bond to the Navy Comrs. Has arrived at Harwich, and is detained there by weather and by repairs of other ships. [*Adm. Paper.*]

Feb. 9. Harwich. 69. Anthony Deane and Wm. Baker to the Navy Comrs. Have careened the Mary safely. The success of the new engine is com-

VOL. CXII.

1664–5.

plete; its cost is only 35*l.*, and the guns of a fourth-rate ship can be taken on deck without capstan. Seven tons more of yarn offered. [*Adm. Paper.*]

Feb. 9. 70. Wm. Coventry to Sam. Pepys. Hopes some ketches have been hired. There has been much talk about cleaning the merchant ships, but nothing has yet been resolved on; proposes it to be done at Portsmouth, distinct from the King's yard. Asks the determination of the Board about a purveyor, and the stowing of cordage. More merchant ships must be hired, if possible. [*Adm. Paper, one and a half pages.*]

Feb. 9. Warrant to Lord Ashley to pay to Francis Godolphin 600*l.* out of the proceeds of prize ships and goods. [*Ent. Book 22, p. 14.*]

Feb. 10/20. Charing. Ambassador Van Gogh to [the States General]. The equipping of ships and pressing of seamen goes on as much as ever. The Royal Oak, an English East India ship, was cast away about Sally. Capt. Holmes is still under guard, but it is not known whether his business is taken in hand before the King or Royal Company. The Duchess of York was delivered of a princess on the night between Monday and Tuesday, and both are doing well. [*Holland Corresp., Feb. 20, 1665.*]

Feb. 10. 71. Susanna Arnott to Williamson. Begs dispatch of her business; when she gets her money, will give him 50*l.* and Mr. Secretary a fitting gratuity. Hopes it will not have to pass the great seal, as she can hardly get money to pass it through.

Feb. 10. St. James's. 72. Pass from the Duke of York for the St. John Baptist, a ship belonging to the French East India Company, but built in the United Provinces, to go thence to France, provided she carry no goods belonging to persons in hostility with His Majesty, nor do wrong to any of his subjects.

Feb. 10. St. James's. 73. Like pass for the St. Mary belonging to the said company.

Feb. 10. Warrant to Sir John Robinson to receive —— Marchant prisoner, for dangerous practices. Minute. [*Ent. Book 22, p. 15.*]

Feb. 10. Warrant to the Commander of a frigate to receive —— Marchant from Guernsey, to be conveyed to the Lieutenant of the Tower. Minute. [*Ent. Book 22, p. 15.*]

Feb. 11. Bristol. 74. Willm. Colston to Williamson. Begs a licence for his small vessel, the Angel Gabriel, bound for Portugal with corn, his son having given bond for its delivery. Will give 10*l.* to have the licence quickly.

Feb. 11. Warrant for confirmation of Allan Smallwood in the Rectory of Graystock, diocese of Carlisle. Minute. [*Ent. Book 22, p. 14.*]

VOL. CXII.

1664–5.

Feb. 11. Commission for Willm. Sheldon to be Lieut.-Colonel to Col. Pearson's regiment employed in the service of the King of Portugal, and Captain of a company of foot in the regiment lately commanded by Lieut.-Col. Belayse. Minute. [*Ent. Book* 20, *p.* 47.]

Feb. 11. Whitehall. 75. Articles or Instructions set down by the King in Council, for merchants and others who have letters of marque from the Duke of York against the States of the United Provinces. They are to seize their ships wherever they find them; to enter into bond to bring them before the Admiralty Officers, when they are to answer queries about the proprietorship of the ships; also to take care of them and the goods, or of the proceeds of sale of any perishable articles, and to attempt nothing against the King's subjects or allies; they may dispose of what is adjudged to them for their own benefit free from all molestation, and buyers are to be authorized to purchase the goods. They shall, before taking out commissions, give in the name and tonnage of their ship, and an account of her crew, stores, &c., and enter security for the Lord Admiral's tenths, and for the usual customs. [*Copy, five pages.*]

[Feb. 11.] 76. Copy of the above, with slight differences. [*Six and a half pages.*]

Feb. 11. Whitehall. Order granting the petition of Sir Chas. Stanley for leave to offer a bill to Parliament for his pardon and restoration in blood. [*Ent. Book* 18, *p.* 123.]

Feb. 11. Reference to the Lord Treasurer and Lord Ashley on the petition of Sir John Lowther, Bart., for corroboration of his title to the Manor of St. Bees, co. Cumberland. [*Ent. Book* 18, *p.* 124.]

[Feb. 11.] 77. Petition of Charles Earl of Norwich and Lady Elizabeth his sister, widow of Wm. Lord Brereton, to the King, for a patent to buy and export yearly 3,000 barrels of Welsh butter, as formerly granted to Sir Hen. Compton and Thos. Nevett; the late Earl of Norwich and Lord Brereton suffered much for loyalty.

Feb. 11. Reference of the above petition to the Lord Treasurer and Attorney General. [*Ent. Book* 18, *p.* 125.]

Feb. 11. Reference to the Duke of Buckingham on the petition of Major Willm. Gower, for the office of Serjeant-at-arms at York, if one be needed. [*Ent. Book* 18, *p.* 125.]

Feb. 11. Reference to the Lord Chancellor, Lord Treasurer, and Lord Ashley of the petition of Sir Hugh Cartwright for payment of 3,000*l.* on account of his great expenses for arms in the service of the late King. [*Ent. Book* 18, *p.* 126.]

[Feb. 11.] 78. Draft of the above reference.

Vol. CXII.

1664–5.

Feb. 11. Whitehall. 79. Petition of Charles Lord Gerard to the King, that if he takes the two acres of land called the Military Ground, parish of St. Martin's-in-the-Fields, co. Middlesex, belonging to the petitioner, he will pay for it as another would, or will grant him in fee farm two other acres there, which he now holds on lease, rental 4s. a year. With reference thereon to the Lord Treasurer.

[Feb. 11.] Entry of the above reference. [*Ent. Book* 18, *p.* 126.]

Feb. 11. Credach. 80. James Scudamore to Williamson. Cannot trouble Sec. Bennet with private affairs, therefore begs Williamson to let him know some ten or twelve days before the Duke puts to sea, that he may be in readiness.

Feb. 11. Portsmouth. 81. Commissioner Thos. Middleton to Sam. Pepys. Progress of ships. The ropemaker there understands stoving cordage, and proposes building a stovehouse, with a copper to contain 30 barrels of tar. Capt. Stoakes lies speechless. [*Adm. Paper, one and a quarter pages.*]

Feb. 11. Woolwich. 82. Wm. Rodham to the Navy Comrs. The New England tar is well conditioned, and reasonably free from water. Fears that the trial barrel is refined, and that the parcel will not hold out as good as the sample. Timber wanted. [*Adm. Paper.*]

Feb. 11. Harwich. 83. E. Lynde, purser of the Elizabeth, to Sam. Pepys. Capt. Nixon is displeased with his complaining of the officers refusing to give up copies of their indents, and tries to prejudice him. Desires leave to come up and vindicate himself. [*Adm. Paper.*]

Feb. 11. Portsmouth. 84. Commissioner Peter Pett to Sam. Pepys. Progress of ships. Begs Sir John Mennes may be told that something is ordered to be done to his darling Henry, which will make her go better. Intends going with the purveyor to the New Forest. [*Adm. Paper.*]

Feb. 12. Dover. 85. John Tatnell to the Navy Comrs. Requests an order for furnishing the Providence with a long boat; has six more boats by him; wants money. [*Adm. Paper.*]

Feb. 12. Deptford. 86. Jonas Shish to the Navy Comrs. There is one decayed mast at Deptford, and three at Woolwich, fit for the floating stage at Harwich. Requests a warrant for their delivery. [*Adm. Paper, damaged.*]

Feb. 12. Abbey Holme. 87. Mungo Dalton to Williamson. Begs his interest to obtain for him the place of Bailiff of Abbey Holme, which, though of little profit, is convenient on account of his residence in Holme Cultram.

Feb. 13. 88. Orders to be observed for the future government of the Ordnance Office; forbidding the further sale of places in the office, but increasing the fee of the master of ordnance from 200 marks to 1,000*l.* a year; regulating the payment of fees in the office, the passing and payment of bills and debentures for goods, &c. On the death

VOL. CXII.

1664–5.

of Col. Wm. Legg, the present master of armory and lieutenant of ordinance, the place of master of the armory is to cease, and the lieutenant of ordinance is to have his salary raised from 384*l.* to 800*l.*, but no longer to hold the office of treasurer or paymaster, and that officer is forbidden, on pain of loss of place, to receive any gratuities from merchants or others, but is to have a salary of 400*l.* a year, &c. [*Copy, five pages.*]

Feb. 13. 89. J[ohn] I[ronmonger] to Sir Thos. Gower. Has been at two very private meetings. A letter from Holland says that Washington and Whalley have returned through France. Ludlow is at Cumfeer, much made of; he has been twice with De Witt, and is promised ammunition and men, if they make a head in any port near the sea. The parties are confident, and say there will be a rising in the west of England, backed by France. Col. Fulthorp and Captains Lascelles, Hutton, and others engaged in the last conspiracy met privately, with several from Scotland, at Northallerton, and dispatched letters thence. Capts. Carter, Best, and others, met at Cowton; they have a design, and are mad enough to venture on anything, but they will begin in London or the west.

Feb. 13. Dover. 90. Thos. White to the Navy Comrs. Stores wanted for ships. Desires to be clerk of the cheque and storekeeper at Dover. [*Adm. Paper.*]

Feb. 13. Dover. 91. E. Wivell to Sam. Pepys. David Grant offers his ship of 100 tons for the King's service. Wishes to serve as the Commissioners' agent at Dover, to inspect the refitting and dispatch of ships. [*Adm. Paper.*]

Feb. 13. 92–95. Notes of the weight and dimensions of guns on several hired ships. Four papers. [*Adm. Paper.*]

Feb. 13. 96. Certificate by Thos. Padnall, and three other ship officers, of the death, on Feb. 11, of Capt. John Stoakes, commander of the Triumph. [*Adm. Paper.*]

Feb. 13. The Montagu. 97. Capt. Hen. Fenn to the Navy Comrs. Is ordered into Chatham for repairs. [*Adm. Paper.*]

Feb. 13. Chatham. 98. Stephen Lee to the Navy Comrs. No notice has been taken of his paper of the price of ironwork, [and his tender to do it cheaper than Burton, the locksmith at Chatham]. Asks if he shall attend again at the office. [*Adm. Paper.*]

Feb. 13. Portsmouth. 99. Commissioner Thos. Middleton to Sam. Pepys. Repairs of ships. Recommends Smith to be master of the Tiger. As to merchant ships, their companies cannot clean them; carpenters must be had from shore; desires positive orders about it. If all the navy were in distress, an empty galliot with a few rotten chesnuts could not be obtained without an order, and that order could not be got till the loss to the King amounted to more than the vessel

Vol. CXII.

1664–5.

was worth. Particulars of stores. Complains of the smallness and badness of scuppers sent from London. Asks what is to be done with the Swiftsure. [*Adm. Paper, three pages.*]

Feb. 14. 100. Capt. Wm. Badiley to the Navy Comrs. The owners of the merchant ships promise to get them fitted with all speed, according to contract; they complain of not being able to keep men, as they are all pressed away. [*Adm. Paper, damaged.*]

Feb. 14. Woolwich. 101. Chris. Pett to Sam. Pepys. Is glad Mr. Morehouse gives satisfaction as purveyor of Waltham Forest. Mr. Cooper will undertake the converting of timber in Aliceholt, although much disheartened by his former extraordinary trouble in waiting upon the justices to get the timber carried. The hewing the frame of the new ship is worth more than 12s. per load; will be a loser unless he be allowed the waste wood. Forty shipwrights and calkers may be discharged. Proposes sending them to Blackwall until required again. Timber wanted. [*Adm. Paper.*]

Feb. 14. 102. Sir Robt. Brooke to Wm. Coventry. Recommends John Browne, master of the William, as a victualler for the navy. [*Adm. Paper.*]

Feb. 14. Chatham Ropeyard. 103. John Owen, clerk of the ropeyard, to Sam. Pepys. The best of the damaged hemp will do for twice-laid stuff, the rest is unfit for anything but paper stuff. Requests further orders concerning Mr. Bilton's hemp. [*Adm. Paper.*]

Feb. 14. Warrant to Stanney for recommitting Major R. Holmes to the Tower, and warrant to Sir John Robinson to receive him. Minute. [*Ent. Book 22, p. 10.*]

Feb. 14. 104. *List* of letters written by the Clerks of the Council to 10 Lieutenants of counties, about the arrears of the 70,000*l.*, and sent by Widowes, the messenger.

Feb. 14. Prize Office, Portsmouth. 105. Christopher Barker to Williamson. Requests assistance if anything happens concerning him, and begs a line from him.

Feb. 15. Whitehall. 106. [Sec. Bennet] to the English Consuls abroad. The King, fearing danger to merchant ships during the disputes with the Dutch, wishes the ships in foreign ports to be warned not to sail alone, but to wait the passing of other merchant vessels or of the King's ships. Any vessels that wish for it may have letters of reprisal, on giving proper security. [*Draft.*]

Feb. 15. Deal. 107. Will. Skutt to Williamson. The coast is clear of enemies, in spite of the talk of so many privateers coming out of Zealand.

Feb. 15. Yarmouth. 108. Rich. Bower to Williamson. An Ostender says he saw 20 sail of Dutch ships about Scarborough; they had taken three ketches; they use small fishing cobbles civilly, paying for the fish, but take away the masts from the larger ones; there are 10 sail abroad. Has 250 stout, able seamen, ready to go on board the Nightingale and a small ketch.

Vol. CXII.

1664–5.

Feb. 15. 109. Lord Chief Justice Bridgeman to Sec. Bennet. On the King's orders about Hall's discoveries of the coiners in the north, has removed Sharper from Durham to London, transmitted him and his discoveries, and Hall also to Judge Twysden, who has removed Ovingdon from Durham to be tried at York, thus breaking that northern combination. Begs that none of the coiners who may be convicted be pardoned without certificate from the judges, as some who had good estates have obtained pardons, and the prosecutors had not even their charges; requests that out of the estates of convicted coiners, the charges of prosecution, &c, may be borne, and fit persons rewarded, which has been hitherto done out of the King's purse. Has given Hall 5*l.* Begs a protection for him from arrest, as being on the King's service.

Feb. 15. Warrant to John Prescot to seize ——. Minute. [*Ent. Book* 22, p. 16.]

Feb. 15. Letter of protection from Sec. Bennet to —— Hall, sent on the King's service to York, Newcastle, Durham, and other places, on an occasion much importing the public good. [*Ent. Book* 22, p. 16.]

Feb. 15. London. Levant Company to Capt. Hudson and Capt. Hill, at Scanderoon. The King being engaged in a downright war with the Dutch, who are arming all they can in the Straits, the passage home will be extremely dangerous. They must keep their ships clear and fit for defence. A good convoy will be sent with ships now at Gravesend, but it may not perhaps go so far as Smyrna. With note of the dispatch of seven copies of this letter by different routes, and of the like letter sent to Capt. Cole. [*Levant Papers, Vol.* v., *p.* 90.]

Feb. 15. 110. [Order in Council], referring to the Committee for the Admiralty and Navy a petition of the gentlemen and merchants of Devonshire trading to Newfoundland, for licence to proceed in the fishing there, as the chief means of support for many poor.

[Feb.] 15. 111. Abstract of the above.

Feb. 15. 112. Petition of the Merchant Adventurers to the King and Council, that John Browne, officer to Mr. Thomas, in custody for not delivering up, according to order, 40 white cloths seized by him, may be required to perform the said order; that all others may be ordered to abstain from attempts to seize white cloths shipped, until the whole cause is decided on; also, that if Browne continue contumacious, the 40 cloths may be delivered to the warehouse-keeper of the Commissioners and Farmers of Customs.

Feb. 15. Chatham Dock. 113. Phin. Pett to the Navy Comrs. Repairs of ships. Tallow wanted. [*Adm. Paper.*]

Feb. 15. East India Merchant, Spithead. 114. Capt. John Willgresse to Sam. Pepys. Will try to procure the 180 men allowed him. Great want of a cable and boats. Cannot get supplied, his being a hired ship. [*Adm. Paper.*]

VOL. CXII.

1664–5.

Feb. 16. Harwich. 115. Anthony Deane to the Navy Comrs. The Mary's works are completed, and the carpenters paid by him. Proposes employing soldiers, in the present time of need, to fill the wharf and level the ground, there being no labourers nor shipwrights to be had. [*Adm. Paper.*]

Feb. 16. 116. W. Coventry to Sam. Pepys. Sends a survey of the Guinea provisions on board the Maryland, and a paper from the bailiff of Ipswich about pressed men; also the waterman's list, which should be sent soon to Gravesend and Chatham, lest the ships should sail before defaulters are apprehended. [*Adm. Paper.*]

Feb. 16. 117. W. Coventry to Sam. Pepys. Urges dispatch in hiring the merchant ships. Wishes orders sent to Harwich for marking the broad arrow on some of the Ipswich ships, and for their owners to come up to treat about them. If an hour were appointed every morning for all commanders and owners to meet one of the Board at Blackwall, it would be very convenient. Dispatch of small vessels at Deptford. [*Adm. Paper.*]

Feb. 16. Deptford. 118. Capt. Wm. Badiley and J. Uthwayt to the Navy Comrs. The main course of the Henrietta is so thin and beaten as to be unfit for repairs. [*Adm. Paper, damaged.*]

Feb. 16. Portsmouth. 119. Commissioner Thos. Middleton to [Sam. Pepys]. The Swiftsure shall be brought into port to grave. Detailed advice concerning the better making of cordage for standing rigging, &c. The yarn should stand long and be pickled before it is put to use. The boatswains use any rope they find of a fit size, however unfit it be for service; the more masts lost, the more profit for them. Total loss of the rigging of the Yarmouth. Meets with very different husbandry in the King's service from what he was accustomed to in his youthful time. Men and materials are wanted for cleaning the merchant ships. Complains of the delay in ordering needful vessels to carry on the work. Progress of ships. [*Adm. Paper, four pages.*]

Feb. 16. Warrant to Ralph Rutter and John Wilson to repair to Hounslow Heath, and apprehend Benjamin Olding and Roger Williams, of Brentford, for contempts and misdemeanors. Minute. [*Ent. Book 22, p. 17.*]

Feb. 16. Privy seal for 300*l.* to Lieut.-Col. Carr, of the King's free gift. Minute. [*Ent. Book 22, p. 17.*]

Feb. 16. Grant, at the nomination of the Earl of St. Alban's, to Baptist May and Abraham Cowley of a piece of ground, part of Pall Mall field, whereon 13 or 14 great houses are intended to be built, rent 80*l.* a year; and also grant of the highway from Charing Cross to St. James's. [*Docquet.*]

Feb. 16. Demise, at the nomination of the Earl of St. Alban's, to Sir Thos. Bond, Bart., for 31 years, of a parcel of land, buildings, &c., adjoining the Duchy House near the Savoy, co. Middlesex, 24 feet by 310, on rent of 10s. [*Docquet.*]

VOL. CXII.

1664–5.
Feb. 16. Reference to Lord Admiral the Duke of York of the petition of Sir John Coryton, Bart., for leave to erect lighthouses at the Isle of Wight, Portland Road, Rame Head, and the Lizard Point, for which the merchants and shipmasters have several times petitioned; he receiving 6d. per ton on all strangers' vessels anchoring between the Isle of Wight and Mount's Bay. [*Ent. Book* 18, p. 127.]

Feb. 16. Whitehall. 120. [Sec. Bennet] to the Lord Treasurer. The King being satisfied in the particulars about which he had taken just offence against Mr. Christian, customer of Carlisle, wishes on his petition, and at the request of Sir Phil. Musgrave, that he should be restored to his place, from which he was suspended. [*Draft.*]

Feb. 16. Letter Office, London. 121. James Hickes to Williamson. Wrote to Mr. Hall about the complaint of Mr. Watts, of Deal, against the postmaster at Deal, for detention of letters, &c. The latter denies the charges, and is spleenful against Mr. Hall, calling him a fanatic and an intelligencer to Kelsie, governor of Dover Castle during the rebellion, though he was a faithful asserter of the King's interests, and deserves encouragement, for he gives 40s. a year for the constant lists of shipping in the Downs. Begs repayment for him, his salary being unable to bear this payment.

Feb. 17. 122. Leo. Williams to Sec. Bennet. Atkinson still intends to go for Holland, but is willing to stay till March, if nothing unexpected occur. He is to stay a little while there to see what the English are doing; as to maintenance, he can gather 20*l.* or 30*l.* amongst his acquaintance there. May perhaps find a pretence before then to go himself to Holland, as it were out of fear.

Feb. 17. 123. Sir John Colleton to Sec. Bennet. Entreats the speedy signing of a warrant for the 12 guns for Barbadoes, as the owners are at great loss waiting for them.

Feb. 17. Whitehall. 124. The Council to Secs. Morice and Bennet. The proposed method of impressing seamen is for the Duke of York to issue warrants to the vice-admirals to impress the numbers in their respective limits, corresponding with the Lord of the Council to whose care the county is committed, and with persons appointed by him to elect fit men. A speedy supply being needful, request them to do their utmost to complete the number of 200 for Essex; to direct justices of peace to order the constables of each parish to leave tickets at the houses of seamen, ordering them to appear and enlist; those who fail to be apprehended and sent to common gaol, to remain till they engage in the service by taking imprest money. The constables are to give monthly accounts of their proceedings therein. [*Two pages.*]

Feb. 17. Wrexham. 125. Ellis Sutton to Rich. Earl of Carbery. Being appointed lieutenant to Col. John Robinson's militia company, in Bromfield, co. Denbigh, was ordered by three deputy lieutenants to summon the trained bands, and dispose of them for preservation of peace, and

VOL. CXII.

1664–5.

apprehension of suspicious persons frequenting unlawful assemblies, &c. On 12 Feb., Ensign David Edwards heard of a conventicle of 80 or 100 persons, meeting at the house of John Manley of Wrexham, a nonconformist once in arms against the King. Soldiers were got together, who knocked at the door; for some time they were not answered, the people hiding and getting away by back doors; Manley then appeared at a window, and entered into a dilatory dispute about their authority in coming in arms without a justice of peace; at length they entered, and found some persons who, not being of the family, were convicted by the Conventicle Act. Some of them had been formerly indited for seditious meetings, were in arms against the late King, and are notoriously obstinate in their principles. *Encloses*,

125. I. *List of 21 persons taken in the aforesaid house.*

Feb. 17. 126. Petition of the Merchant Adventurers to the King and Council, recapitulating the seizure of 40 cloths by John Browne, and complaining that, although according to their order of the 15th instant, the cloths have been restored to the owner, Browne had meanwhile caused them to be opened and appraised, whereby they were damaged and dirtied, and the proprietor sees that he is still liable to suit for the value of the cloths. Request that Browne may not, by such pretence of compliance, elude punishment.

Feb. 17. 127. Thos. Agar, surveyor-general of woods, to Sam. Pepys. Begs speedy return of a warrant for the auditor of Essex, sent up for further cognizance. Is waiting for warrants for felling the 2,000 trees in the New Forest, and those in the Holt and East Bere. [*Adm. Paper.*]

Feb. 18. 128. Certificate by Hen. Rogers, mayor, and John Imber, minister of Christ Church, co. Hants, that Mellor Bullock is the lawful wife of Robt. Bullock, who went volunteer in the Elias, and perished with the ship; leaving his widow and children in destitute condition. [*Adm. Paper.*]

Feb. 18. 129. W. Coventry to Sam. Pepys. Sends an extract of a paper from the Earl of Sandwich, concerning the wants of several ships in the Downs, for which supplies must be hastened. The Portland is ordered to Chatham for repairs. [*Adm. Paper.*]

Feb. 18. Edwinstow. 130. John Russell to the Navy Comrs. Particulars of felling and carriage of timber. Mr. Corbin refuses to meddle with the payment of land carriage any more. [*Adm. Paper.*]

Feb. 18. Cockpit. 131. Sir Wm. Clarke to Sam. Pepys. Recommends Henry Curvett, master of the Foresight, as Lieutenant of the Welcome. [*Adm. Paper.*]

Feb. 18. 132. Jo. North, a quaker, to the King. Complains of the barbarous murder of one of his sons, 27 March last, shot at his own door, by Curtis, an apothecary of Doncaster, without even a constable; the murderer, being a member of the corporation, got off

VOL. CXII.

1664–5.

by a packed jury, who decided that be acted in self defence. Asks if His Majesty would not have challenged a jury sitting on his father's death, if all composed of Cromwell's creatures, with Ireton, Fleetwood, or Lambert as foreman. Applies to him, as father of his country, to order an impartial trial, and to charge the judges on the circuit to examine the right, lest innocent blood cry against him. Details a vision of his murdered son. If his petition be not replied to, must exclaim, with Job, "I cry, but there is no judgment." [*Three pages.*]

Feb. 18. Bristol. 133. Willm. Colston to Williamson. Is still in hopes that he will not be denied the small favour of sending a ship of eight men, when others have been allowed to send ships of 30. Cannot otherwise dispose of his corn. The letters of marque should be sent by the first post to his son Richard. Requests Williamson to give the security and will indemnify him.

Feb. 18. 134. Ro. Benson to Williamson. Sends a certificate about the nine Quakers whom the judges would have set at liberty. They have lost their estates, and are so infinitely impudent and provoking that all are tired out with them. *Annexing,*

134. I. *List by Judges Thos. Twysden and Chris. Turner of nine Quakers, convicted of præmunire for refusing the Oath of Obedience, who have been imprisoned for two and a half years.* *Feb. 15, 1665.*

Feb. 18. Beaudesert. 135. Sir Brian Broughton to Williamson. Hears that Lambert intends an escape; gave 50s. to the intelligencer, a captain who is engaged to raise a troop of horse for them; he went 100 miles into the west for the information, and may be of use if not disobliged by so small rewards. Mr. Secretary need pay nothing, the week's pay for the militia would discharge all and more.

Feb. 18. Pay Office, Portsmouth. 136. Christopher Barker to Williamson. Hears that Sec. Bennet intends to employ a deputy comptroller, to give a constant account of all that passes at Portsmouth; begs the office for himself, because being clerk, everything passes through his hands.

Feb. 18. Whitehall. The King to the Lord Treasurer. Allows his former proceedings in forbearing to receive from the arrears of excise, granted to His Majesty by the Act of Convention after his return, 6,248*l.* 7*s.* 1*d.*, in regard of the like sum allowed by him to Alderman Backwell out of the growing excise; the said sum being now all paid except 2,907*l.* 0*s.* 4½*d.*, wishes further receipts to be suspended, until such moneys as were assigned from the said arrears to the Duke of York, Capt. Titus, and Mr. Peck are provided for. [*Ent. Book* 17, *pp.* 91–2.]

[Feb. 18.] 137. Draft of the above.

Feb. 18. Presentation of Dr. Lloyd to the Rectory of Hambledon, co. Bucks. Minute. [*Ent. Book* 19, *p.* 32.]

Feb. 18. Commission for Morgan Jenkins to be Quartermaster of a troop of horse in the Earl of Oxford's regiment of Horse Guards. Minute. [*Ent. Book* 20, *p.* 48.]

VOL. CXII.

1664–5.
Feb. 18. Warrant to the Ordnance Commissioners to deliver 200 muskets with bandoleers, 100 barrels of powder, 50 pikes, and 30 halberts, with shovels, spades, and pickaxes, to —— Sindane, governor of the island of Shetland. [*Ent. Book* 20, *p.* 48.]

Feb. 18. Whitehall. Warrant to Col. William Legg, lieutenant of the forests of Alice-holt and Woolmer, co. Hants, to preserve the game in the said forests, now much destroyed. [*Ent. Book* 22, *p.* 17.]

Feb. 18. Warrant to the Ordnance Commissioners to deliver certain pieces of ordnance, for the service of Barbadoes. [*Ent. Book* 22, *p.* 18.]

Feb. 18. Whitehall. 138. Pass for Cornelius Geesdorp Van Laen to go to Holland and return.

Feb. 18. Minute of the above. [*Ent. Book* 22, *p.* 18.]

Feb. 18. Order for a warrant to pay to Rob. Lye 1,230*l.*, for jewels given to the Portuguese Ambassador and his secretary. [*Ent. Book* 22, *p.* 18.]

Feb. 18. Warrant for a grant to Thos. Ravenscroft of the place of Keeper of the Council chamber, on surrender of the same by his father, George Ravenscroft, who held it by patent from King James. [*Ent. Book* 22, *p.* 19.]

[Feb. 18.] 139. Draft of the above.

Feb. 18. Warrant to the Rangers and other officers of Rockingham Forest to allow Viscount Cullen, verderer there, his yearly warrants for deer, and also a buck out of each of the other six walks of which he is not verderer, he having lost many deer by gifts to the King, and by unusual mortality among them. [*Ent. Book* 22, *p.* 20.]

Feb. 18. Warrant for a lease to Sir Jordan Crosland, Bart., of Harum-baugh, co York, of the manors and sundry tenements in Braffer-ton and Helperby, and all other forfeited estates and goods of Ralph Rymer, sen., and Ralph Rymer, jun., his son, attainted for misprision of treason, on his redeeming the same from Sir Thos. Osborne by payment of 2,000*l.* [*Ent. Book* 22, *pp.* 25–27.]

Feb. 18. Gatehouse, Westminster. 140. M. De la Fabvollière, engineer, to the King. Has languished four weeks in that miserable prison, friendless and perishing. Has never intentionally offended Prince Rupert, but done his utmost to show him affection. Entreats for liberty. [*French.*]

Feb.? 141. Petition of Dan. Fabureau De la Fabvollière to Lord Arling-ton, for pardon and liberation. Would never have offended had he known his offence would appear so great; did not think it would prejudice his lordship or any man, but merely preserve himself from unjust persecution.

Feb.? 142. Petition of D. De la Fabvollière to the King. Would not have committed the offence had he known that by the laws of the kingdom it would seem so odious as it does.

VOL. CXII.

1664–5. Feb. 18. Deal.

143. Ri. Watts to Williamson. The Earl of Sandwich, with his fleet and six other ships, has come into the Downs. A foot company of soldiers has arrived.

VOL. CXIII. FEB. 19–28, 1664–5.

1664–5. Feb. 19. Portsmouth.

1. Andrew Newport to Williamson. At Sec. Bennet's request, nominated a deputy comptroller for prizes in the port, Arth. Bradshaw; begs that he or some other deputy may be appointed, since by instructions from the Commissioners of Prizes, the officers are often to have recourse to the deputy comptroller.

Feb. 19. Rye.

2. Jo. Dallatt to Williamson. The Hope of London has come in from the Canaries, laden with Canary [wine], and the Speedwell of London from Seville, laden with oranges and olives.

Feb. 19. Blackstakes, The Hope.

3. Capt. John Barton to the Navy Commrs. Wants provisions; has brought up 50 pressed men from Harwich for the St. George. [*Adm. Paper.*]

Feb. 19. Southwark.

4. Lieut. Martin Gardiner to Sam. Pepys. Requests redress of the abuse committed by seamen pressing soldiers out of the Duke of York's regiment. [*Adm. Paper.*]

Feb. 19. Dover.

5. Thos. Wales to the Navy Commrs. Account of work performed according to general warrant. [*Adm. Paper.*]

Feb. 20.

Warrant for a pardon to William Ring, of Netherhaven, co. Wilts, for all offences committed before 24 June last. [*Ent. Book* 22, *p.* 20.]

Feb. 20.

Corroboration of presentation of Allan Smallwood, D.D., to the Rectory of Graystock, co. Cumberland. [*Docquet.*]

Feb. 20.

Warrant to pay to Lady Elizabeth Gage 2,000*l.*, as the King's free gift. [*Docquet.*]

Feb. 20.

Warrant to pay to Col. John Frescheville 2,000*l.*, as the King's free gift. [*Docquet.*]

Feb. 20.

Warrant to pay to Chas. Viscount Fitzharding, keeper of the privy purse, 10,000*l.*, for the use of the said purse. [*Docquet.*]

Feb. 20.

6. Wm. Coventry to Sam. Pepys. Ballast for the London must be hastened down; her men are to be turned into the Prince, either by ticket or book. The merchant ships are to be got out of the docks, to take their stores on board. The Montague and London are almost ready for victualling. [*Adm. Paper.*]

Feb. 20.

7. Capt. Wm. Badiley to the Navy Commrs. The work of carrying ballast to the London cannot be done by lighters; six hoys must be employed. The Briar is ready to take in her provisions. [*Adm. Paper, damaged.*]

VOL. CXIII.

1664–5.
Feb. 20. Ipswich. 8. Anthony Deane to the Navy Comrs. Particulars of the dimensions, &c., of the six Ipswich ships pressed for the King's service. [*Adm. Paper.*]

Feb. 20. 9. List of 25 prize ships brought into Dover since November last; stating the masters' names, destination, lading, number of guns, by whom taken, and when brought in. [*Adm. Paper, two pages.*]

Feb. 20. Portsmouth. 10. Commissioner Thos. Middleton to Sam. Pepys. It is impossible to take the measure of any ship, unless she be dry upon the ground, and even then it must be done by a skilful man. No orders have been received, nor men sent down, to clean and grave the merchant ships. Particulars of timber. Purchase of cordage from Weymouth, and other stores. Great want of money; 200 men are employed who beg money to diet themselves, which would be 50*l.* a week. Account of the Royal Charles having narrowly escaped a disaster, only breaking a hawser. Never knew a worse ship to careen than the Henry. [*Adm. Paper, three pages.*] *Encloses,*

10. I. *Invoice by Jacob Bryan of canvas to be sold on board the Violet from St. Malo.* *Portsmouth, Feb. 16, 1665.*

10. II. *Contract with Giles Hounsel, of Weymouth, for cordage, at 39s. per cwt.* *Portsmouth, February 17, 1665.*

Feb. 20. Gravesend. 11. James Pugh to the Navy Comrs. List of nine ships at Gravesend with the number of men on board, and of those absent and sick on shore. They are now well supplied with clothes. [*Adm. Paper.*]

Feb. 20. Portsmouth. 12. Commissioner Peter Pett to Sam. Pepys. Danger incurred by the Royal Charles, through the indiscretion of her officers, who in clearing an anchor supposed to be foul, cast her ashore; no damage was sustained; proposes to sail her to-morrow. [*Adm. Paper.*]

Feb. 20. Yarmouth. 13. Rich. Bower to Williamson. Complains of wrong three years ago, in being detained 12 months in London to give information of some Custom House abuses, and then dismissed without reward and rendered ridiculous, because three of the accused Commissioners were members of the Committee to which the business was referred. Delay of sailing of the pressed men, because one was sent whom Bailiff Cubitt would not spare; he allowed him to go on board, lest the others should refuse to go, but had him put ashore again, and Sir Thos. Meadows sent a warrant to take him. The town has at length agreed to incorporation with Little Yarmouth.

Feb. 20. Whitehall. 14. Warrant to Ralph Rutter and John Wilson, messengers, to set at liberty Benj. Olding and Roger Williams. With draft of an order for the names of the Duke of Buckingham and others to be inserted as Commissioners of Appeals in the business of prizes.

Feb. 20. St. James's. 15. Pass by Lord Admiral the Duke of York for the Crown, a ship built in the United Provinces for the French East India Company, to go to France, provided she carry no goods belonging to persons in hostility with the King.

VOL. CXIII.

1664–5.

Feb. 20. 16. Edw. Adams to Williamson. Asks his commands to Consul Maynard in Portugal. Presents him with part of a box of China oranges.

Feb. 20. Rydal. 17. Dan. Fleming to Williamson. Requests him to share with himself and his cousin Kirkby, in the next lease of the Lancashire excise, for which they are willing to give within 100*l.* of the present rent.

Feb. 20. Reference to the Lord Chancellor and three others on the petition of Lord Paget. [*Ent. Book* 18, *p.* 127.]

Feb. 21. 18. Aug. Fen to Edw. Raynes. Expects soon to be employed elsewhere. Wants Erastus, if he can spare him. Has been skirmishing with the Nigri, who are ignorant and knavish beyond imagination, for the sake of Mr. Sharples, an honest man and former justice of peace, who is staggering. Wishes that Rayner, being near to Blackburn, would see Mr. Sharples and do the deed with him.

Feb. 21. 19. J[ohn] I[ronmonger] to Sir Thos. Gower. The consultation at Northallerton was to arrange how they may meet with least suspicion, to agree on ways of writing, places where their agents may be furnished with fresh horses, money, &c.; their pretence of meeting will be a suit-at-law, bargain, or arbitration, and their letters will always have some real business. Letters from Holland say that the English settled there are 3,000 good men; believes them to be only 800, but good soldiers and ready to hazard anything. If the Dutch would land them, they would venture themselves. The Dutch vary in counsels; sometimes they talk of landing in March or April, sometimes of spinning out the war till the King's money is spent, and they think he could hardly get more; much depends on the issue of the French Ambassador's journey to England. There may be an attempt in the bishopric, but not till the Dutch are at sea. The chief agitators are now in London. Col. Gilby Carr in Holland manages the affairs of the Scottish remonstrators. Leving may be taken in London.

Feb. 21. Woolwich. 20. Chris. Pett to the [Navy Comrs.] The sample of broom sent in by Isaac Sanderson, minister of Plumstead, is large and fit for service. [*Adm. Paper.*]

Feb. 21. 21. Ro. Richbell to Sam. Pepys. Being ill, sends his kinsman, John Shattock, to sign his contract for 20 tons of rosin, at 10*l.* per ton, and allowance for carriage from Southampton to Portsmouth.

Feb. 21. Chatham. 22. Edw. Gregory to the Navy Comrs. Sends muster-books of several ships; the last 300*l.* imprest is all paid away. [*Adm. Paper.*]

Feb. 21. 23. W. Coventry to Sam. Pepys. Desires men to be set to work immediately, to refit the bread-room, powder-room, &c., of the John and Thomas, as the owners make difficulty about it. [*Adm. Paper.*]

Vol. CXIII.

1664–5.
Feb. 21. London. 24. Certificate by Stephen Pyund that the Sea-flower ketch sailed from Chatham on the 15th, with pressed men from Rochester and elsewhere on board, and is at anchor over against Horseydown, in readiness to sail. [*Adm. Paper.*]

Feb. 21. 25. W. Coventry to Sam. Pepys. John Langrack is the carpenter of the Breda proposed as purveyor for Aliceholt; he is to have his dispatch as soon as possible. [*Adm. Paper.*] *Encloses,*

25. I. *Earl of Sandwich to Coventry. Recommends John Langrack for the employment of purveyor. Downs, Feb. 18, 1665.*

Feb. 21. 26. Wm. Coventry to Sam. Pepys. Concurs in the opinion that Mr. Pett must not think himself so wholly master of the office as to impose both men and rates; thinks the man had better be employed the old way, till Pett proposes the other way. Asks in what readiness the fire-ships are for sailing. Endorsed "About the fitness of choosing Langrack as purveyor, with regard to Mr. Pett at Woolwich. [*Adm. Paper.*]

Feb. 22. Woolwich. 27. Wm. Bodham to Sam. Pepys. A chimney has fired in the George alehouse, near the ropeyard, at 3 a.m.; it was caused by the keeper's entertaining some ropemakers, and suffering them to be drunk; has turned him out of the work. Recommends an honest fellow in his stead, but being one whose private opinions suffer him not to go to church, is doubtful whether he may be entered. Proposes that a good middle-sized water engine be kept in the yard; one could be provided for 20*l.* [*Adm. Paper, two pages.*]

Feb. 22. The Downs. 28. Capt. Thos. Teddeman to Sam. Pepys. Particulars of ships. The Earl of Sandwich intends setting out for London. [*Adm. Paper.*]

Feb. 22. Harwich. 29. Anthony Deane to the Navy Comrs. Contracts for timber. Requests a press warrant for providing shipwrights. [*Adm. Paper.*]

Feb. 22. 30. W. Coventry to Sam. Pepys. A warrant must be sent to Woolwich for receiving some yarn; does not presume it to be very bad, and they cannot be very curious at this time. Is of Mr. Bodham's opinion that the King's own spinning would be best. [*Adm. Paper.*] *Encloses,*

30. I. *Wm. Bodham to Wm. Coventry. Entreats an order for the receipt of nine tons of Hamburg cable yarn, delivered by James Johnson of Yarmouth without any warrant or copy of contract. If time permitted, it would be more to the King's profit to have yarn spun by his own workmen. Woolwich, Feb. 21, 1665.*

Feb. 22. Woolwich. 31. Wm. Bodham to Sir Wm. Batten. There are 24 tons of yarn received from Mr. Harris. Asks what cordage shall be made of it. Some Hamburg cable yarn is taken in. [*Adm. Paper.*]

Vol. CXIII.

1664–5.

Feb. 22. Portsmouth. 32. Commissioner Thos. Middleton to Sam. Pepys. The *Royal Charles* is unable to get out of harbour for want of wind. [*Adm. Paper.*] *Encloses*,

32. i. *Certificate by John Kempthorne of the fitness of the Mayflower ketch, under command of Thomas Norwood, to wait on the Royal James.* *Feb.* 18, 1665.

Feb. 22. Ollerton. 33. Thos. Corbyn to W. Coventry. Particulars of felling and carriage of timber in Sherwood Forest. Thinks carriages may be had from Yorkshire and Derbyshire, being within 12 miles. The watermen pretend they dare not stir without some security, for fear of pressing. Begs to be discharged from the service, and reimbursed for money spent out of his own pocket. Mr. Russell will cheerfully serve in his stead, and Capt. Green will manage the loading in the wood. [*Adm. Paper, two pages.*] *Encloses*,

33. i. *List of three justices in Derbyshire, four in Yorkshire, and three in Nottinghamshire, and names of the 21 watermen employed in the two great ketches.*

Feb. 22. Pass for Philip De Marinis, returning to China and other Eastern parts, for the conversion of infidels. [*Ent. Book* 22, *p.* 22.]

Feb. 22. Privy seal for 1,000*l.* to George Lord Berkeley, of Berkeley Castle, for repairs of the fences, &c., at Nonsuch Park. Minute. [*Ent. Book* 22, *p.* 22.]

Feb. [22.] Whitehall. Pass for Anthony Carew, of Ostend, sent for by the King to England for two months, and protection from trouble in reference to any prizes taken during the usurpation. [*Ent. Book* 22, *p.* 23.]

Feb.? 34. Petition of Major Rob. Walters, prisoner in the Tower, to the King, for release; confesses his heinous offence in concealing the late horrid treason in the Northern parts, yet has now not only confessed to His Majesty and Lord Lieutenant the Duke of Buckingham all he knows, but has witnessed against the conspirators who are brought to trial, omitting not the least thing against any of them.

Feb. 22. Warrant to Sir John Robinson to release Robert Walters. Minute. [*Ent. Book* 22, *p.* 23.]

Feb. 22. Reprieve for Jean Mesandière from being burnt in the hand. Minute. [*Ent. Book* 22, *p.* 24.]

Feb. 22. Whitehall. Order in Council, on full debate about the Newfoundland fishery, that the Lord Admiral shall give licence to one ship of Dartmouth only to go for Newfoundland. [*Domestic Corresp., Feb.* 15, 1665.]

Feb. 22. London. 35. "John Keymer's observations made upon the Dutch fishing about the year 1601, demonstrating that there is more wealth raised

Vol. CXIII.

1664–5.

out of herrings and other fish in His Majesty's seas, by the neighbouring nations in one year, than the King of Spain hath from the Indies in four, and that there were 20,000 ships and other vessels and about 400,000 people there set on work by both sea and land, and maintained only by fishing on the coasts of England, Scotland, and Ireland." Printed for Sir Edw. Ford, and licensed by Roger L'Estrange, Feb. 22, 1665. [*Twelve pages.*]

Feb. 22. Deal. 36. Ri. Watts to Williamson. The Earl of Sandwich landed last night, expecting orders to go up by land. A fleet of Hollanders is near the Spurn.

Feb. 22. Warwick. 37. Sir Hen. Puckering and John Rous to Sec. Bennet. Wish through him to inform the Council that they have committed to gaol several persons suspected of clipping money. Three ounces of clippings, chiefly from shillings and sixpences were found; yet the people concerned are beloved among their neighbours, and in a few hours, got a good certificate of their past deportment from many of the better sort.

Feb. 22. Gainsborough. 38. Note that 30 sail of Hollanders have been for ten days about Flamborough, have taken the ketch with the pressed men from Hull, and by their long boats, fetched many sheep from the coast.

Feb. 22. Whitehall. 39. Order in Council for the printing and publishing of the King's declaration on his proceedings for reparation of affront and injuries done by the States of the United Provinces. [*Printed.*] *Annexing,*

39. i. *The King's declaration that many spoils have been committed by the Dutch East and West India Companies, and instead of reparation as demanded, De Ruyter is sent to act hostilely against the English in Africa, and they have granted letters of marque against the English; therefore the Dutch being clearly the aggressors, letters of marque shall be issued to seize their ships as prizes, and also any other vessels that carry soldiers, arms, &c., to their territories, and all merchandise belonging to them in any vessel whatsoever, unless it have a safe conduct from the Duke of York.* [*Printed, four pages.*]

Feb. 22. 40. Examination of Edward James, before Sir Hen. Wroth. Being at Ely, in the house of Cornet Graves, a late officer under Col. Hacker, Graves taking him for one of their party, told him that 60 of old Oliver's boys met and mustered in the town, and they should have a day soon.

Feb. 22. Hull. 41. Luke Whittington to James Hickes. The fleet of 13 sail, bound for London, are to go under convoy of the Convertine, which has arrived for the pressed men.

Feb. 22. Dover. 42. Jo. Carlisle to Williamson. A prize is taken; 24 sail of ours are in the Downs, and four sent to cruise in Margate Road. The

Vol. CXIII.

1664–5.

Earl of Sandwich is ashore, and intends for London. No prize goods are landed yet, for want of an order from the Admiralty.

Feb. 22. Poole. 43. Wm. Skutt to Williamson. A vessel arrived from Kinsale has seen nothing of the enemy. Begs influence with the Commissioners of the wine licences, in the renewal of a licence for a house at the end of the town which he holds in behalf of his mother-in-law, Melior Allen of Sarum, at 10*l.* a year, to which sum it has been raised from 4*l.*; some whose houses are in the heart of the town [Sarum] can give 40*l.*

Feb. 23. Whitehall. 44. The King to Aubrey Earl of Oxford, chief justice in Eyre south of the Trent, the Earl of Southampton, warden of the New Forest, and the Officers of the court of Lyndhurst. Orders John Lewin to be continued gamekeeper of Lynwood walk, New Forest, from which office he was likely to be dispossessed by one Tarvor, as he appears on examination to be an able and fit person. [*Copy.*]

Feb. 23. Entry of the above. [*Ent. Book* 16, *p.* 337.]

Feb. 23. Note of the above letter. [*Ent. Book* 22, *p.* 27.]

Feb. 23. Dover. 45. Jo. Carlisle to Hen. Muddiman. Sends a letter on a quarrel between Mr. Watts and Mr. Lodge of Deal. Watts is honest, willing to serve, and loyal; but Lodge was always a factious impertinent fellow. Wishes Williamson would silence him. *Encloses,*

45. I. *Ri. Watts to Mr. Carlisle. Complains that Lodge of the post office abused him for an old fanatic, turned him out of the office, and refused to send to Williamson his letter, in which he reported a large Holland fleet to be in sight off the Spurn, because he had not put the date outside; asks if Lodge can command this to be done.* *Deal, Feb.* 22, 1665.

Feb. 23. Yarum, Yorkshire. 46. News from the North. There are 20 or 30 Dutch men-of-war and 60 Flushing capers coasting between Flamborough and Berwick. A Dutch 40-gun vessel came into Burlington, hoisting English colours, and sent a counterfeit letter, pretending to be sent as a convoy to any ships in that or the parts near land. A Scarborough ketch went on this false summons, and has not been heard of since. A vessel manned with half Dutch is in the Tees, and may easily send spies ashore to spy out the naked places of the coast, such as Redcar, Whitby, Hartlepool, Stockton, &c.; see where men may be landed, do mischief enough, and go away scot free.

Feb. 23. 47. Leonard Williams to Sec. Bennet. Fawcett, having brought himself incautiously into suspicion with his party, to ingratiate himself with them, informed against Leving, as a trapanner, on which some of them enticed Leving to an obscure place, threatened to murder him, and charged him with his treason; he denied it, saying that had he betrayed their lodgings, as he could have done, they would have been taken; they produced testimony, but at last spared his life, on condition that he would retire and have nothing to do with Sec. Bennet. With note by Wm Leving, that Sir Roger Langley can give an account of the unworthiness of "this man."

VOL. CXIII.

1664–5.
Feb. 22. Whitehall. 48. Warrant to Sir Thos. Ingram to order payment by the Receiver General of the duchy of Lancaster of 1,000*l.* to Sir John Denham, surveyor of works, towards the buildings and works now in hand at Greenwich.

Feb. 23. Entry of the above. [*Ent. Book* 17, p. 92.]

Feb. 23. Reprieve for Jean De la Court, condemned for murder at the Old Bailey sessions. Minute. [*Ent. Book* 22, p. 24.]

Feb. 23. Warrant to the Navy Commissioners to order payment to Sir Allan Apsley of 2,000*l.*, by appointment of the Duke of York, to be employed for secret services, by the Duke's directions. [*Ent. Book* 22, p. 24.]

Feb. 23. 49. Capt. Wm. Badiley to the Navy Comrs. The Paul and Fame are ready to take in provisions. [*Adm. Paper, damaged.*]

Feb. 23. Barking. 50. Thos. Cartwright, minister, to Sir Wm. Batten. Has been much injured by John Barnard, a drunken innkeeper in Barking, in confidence of not being arrested or called to account for it, because he is purser to the Henrietta. Begs counsel and assistance to take remedy at common law. [*Adm. Paper.*]

Feb. 23. Woolwich. 51. Chris. Pett to the Navy Comrs. Repairs of ships. Plank wanted. [*Adm. Paper.*]

Feb. 24. 52. Certificate by John Fortescue of the measurement of the Loyal George, 91½ ft. by 8 ft. 11 in. [*Adm. Paper.*] *Annexing,*

52. I. *Calculations of the said measurement.*

Feb. 24. 53. Capt. Wm. Badiley to Sam. Pepys. The vessel employed to carry down ballast to the London was stopped at Deptford, and all her men pressed away, in spite of a warrant of protection signed by the Board. [*Adm. Paper, damaged.*]

Feb. 24. Whitehall. 54. Order in Council,—on petition of the Merchant Adventurers' Company and of John Browne, clothworker and officer employed under Rob. Thomas, farmer of the duty on white cloth, now in custody of a messenger,—that he be so continued till the Lord Treasurer and Lord Ashley report their opinions on the whole business, and meanwhile Mr. Browne be desired to surcease all proceedings in the Exchequer; also that the report be dispatched, the Board having often been troubled on this business.

Feb. 24. Gersdall, Yorkshire. 55. Abraham Nelson to Sec. Bennet. The fanatics there hope that the Dutch wars will open a gap. They hear that General Lambert has escaped to Holland, and that there are two full regiments of English fugitives there. The trained band was called up to receive six days' pay; wishes an oath were imposed on them to be true to the King, not only in foreign wars, but in insurrections on what pretence soever. A competent number of horse would do the work.

VOL. CXIII.

1664–5.
Feb. 24.
Egglestone.

56. Christopher Sanderson to Sir Phil. Musgrave. A grand Quaker reports that the Dutch intend to plague the English by keeping from engagements till their provisions are exhausted. He says their party have several persons of quality in the country for their friends, so that, however the tide turns, they will be well used. John Joplin, when leaving Durham, said, "Farewell to subjects' liberty, or having the benefit of the known laws of the nation." He said many of their banished friends were in London, being safer there than elsewhere, and cannot be discovered, having periwigs and other disguises. Has given 3*l.* to an intelligencer, with a letter of recommendation from this Quaker to Grisell Pate, who knows where all the parties are in London, and what is transacted there or elsewhere.

Feb. 24.
Dover Castle.

57. Capt. John Strode to Williamson. Sir Wm. Berkeley has passed for Portsmouth. A Denmark ship in port was examined by a Dutch galley, which, after a little plundering, let her go, as she was bound for France. Hen. Howard and his brother and Fras. Digby have gone for Calais. Fears the Dunkirk packet will fall into the hands of a Zealand privateer in the road.

Feb. 24.
Dover Castle.

58. Capt. John Strode to Sec. Bennet. No such ship as that he mentions has come into the road, only a Denmark vessel which might give rise to the report.

Feb. 24.
Deal.

59. Ri. Watts to Sec. Bennet. The soldiers and money for Tangiers have gone on board. Account of vessels in the Downs.

Feb. 24.
Yarmouth.

60. Rich. Bower to Williamson. A ketch has come down for 100 men, but they will hardly be got in the town, unless Capt. Saunders were sent; every man in the town would have gone with him voluntarily, he is so winning on all seamen, and as stout as ever salt water bore. The works about the town are in such a condition, and so wanting in powder, gun-carriages, &c., that there is not wherewithal to defend the ships in harbour.

Feb. 25.
Newcastle.

61. John Dobson to Sir Phil. Musgrave. Asseverates the truth of his report about a design being in hand against the government; Sir Philip will hear of it from other hands.

Feb. 25.

Commission to Sir Henry Belasyse to be Captain of a company of foot lately commanded by Lord Belasyse. Minute. [*Ent. Book* 20, p. 50.]

Feb. 25.

Warrant to Sir Ralph Freeman and Hen. Slingsby, masters and workers of the Mint, to pay to Hen. Brouncker 2,974*l.* 5*s.*, for 63 pounds weight of gold brought by the Royal African Company; also warrant for coining the same into medals or healing pieces, after a form described, with a hole to pass a ribband through; the said medals to be delivered to Viscount Fitzharding, keeper of the privy purse. [*Ent. Book* 22, pp. 28–30.]

VOL. CXIII.

1664–5.
Feb. 25. Warrant prohibiting any person whatsoever from entering the attiring house of the Duke of York's theatre, under the management of Sir William Davenant, except such as belong to the company, complaints having been made of great disorders, through resort of persons thither. [*Ent. Book* 22, *p.* 32.]

Feb. 25. Order for a warrant to pay to Sir Philip Musgrave, Bart., governor of Carlisle, 3,607*l.* 6*s.* monthly, for the service of the garrison, according to an establishment made Nov. 26, 1664; and also 71*l.* 17*s.* 4*d.*, for arrears of the said forces. [*Ent. Book* 22, *pp.* 32–3.]

Feb. 25. Whitehall. Warrant to Sir Francis Cobb, high sheriff of Yorkshire, to discharge Samuel Poole, John Levens, and eight other Quakers convicted of præmunire for refusing to take the Oath of Obedience, who have been imprisoned two years and a half, and should have so continued for life, but His Majesty takes compassion on them, in hopes of their proving more obedient in future. [*Ent. Book* 22, *p.* 33.]

[Feb. 25.] 62. Draft of the above.

Feb. 25. Pass for six horses for the Earl of Lincoln. Minute. [*Ent. Book* 22, *p.* 34.]

Feb. 25. Privy seal for 1,560*l.* to Robert Lye, for jewels to the Portuguese Ambassador, Envoy, and Secretary. Minute. [*Ent. Book* 22, *p.* 35.]

Feb. 25. The King to [the Dean and Chapter of Salisbury]. Requests Richard Clayton, B.D., to have the next residentiary's house vacant. [*Ent. Book* 17, *p.* 95, *similar to the entry of Feb.* 6.]

Feb. 25. York. 63. Sir. Fr. Cobb to Sec. Bennet. Would neither appear too officious nor too negligent. Sends depositions, a paper taken from a Quaker, and a letter from Acklom, chief of the sectaries in the East Riding, written on his being sent to York. *Encloses*,

63. I. *Information of Henry Lathley of Hollam, East Riding of Yorkshire, taken before Sir Fras. Cobb. Heard John Nicholson of Risam say, that if God put the sword into his hand, he must strike, and that the Quakers had ships of their own, which they employed for intelligence beyond seas. Has had several Quakers' books sent him, and a book has been written of the sufferings and deliverance of seven sent to be banished, but after three months, the ship was beaten back by weather. Peter Johnson has not been lawfully married, and he and other Quakers named were not at church on 30 January. Also,*

Information of Tim. Rhoades, of Hornsea, and John Tompson and Edw. Gall, of Hollam. Peter Acklom of Hornsea has often held meetings at his house, since his release from prison, at Hull. He said tithes would soon be put

VOL. CXIII.

1664–5.

down, and they would fight the Lord's battles; he reproached Hen. Lathley, minister of Hollam, as preaching lies. Also,

Information of John Giles, of Hollam, that John Isaac of Tunstall carried two guns from John Wetson's house. [Three pages.] Beverley, Feb. 21, 1665.

63. II. *Peter Acklom, [a Quaker,] to [Sir] Fras. Cobb, high sheriff of Yorkshire. Requests him not to do so unjust an act as to send him to prison, only because some men and women were seen coming towards his house; remonstrates that an unjust act is against his oath as justice of the peace. Feb. 25, 1665.*

Feb. 25. Whitehall. 64. Warrant for a grant to the Earl of Middleton of 1,000*l.* as the King's free gift.

[Feb. 25.] Minute of the above. [*Ent. Book* 22, *p.* 24.]

Feb. 25. Dorchester. 65. John Cole to [Williamson]. M. Dumas, an envoy from the King of France, landed at Weymouth and has gone for Portsmouth to clear away French goods on board of Dutch vessels. He says the French troops preparing are meant for Portugal, and that M. De Verneuil and another ambassador extraordinary are coming to mediate a peace between the English and the Dutch. A courier has been sent from France to Spain for explanation of the forces sent from Germany to Flanders; also to demand Namur and other provinces, belonging to the Queen of France, after the King of Spain's death.

Feb. 25. Lichfield. 66. Sir B. Broughton to Williamson. Sends him a scout's information. Is marching to a fellow justice, with a company of conventiclers. *Encloses,*

66. I. —— *to [Sir B. Broughton]. The party will not rise till the Dutch are fighting our ships, which will be in May. Dispute between the Presbyterians and the Council in London. The North is pretty firm, and Leicestershire, but no other place to be counted on, except London. The Quakers will not fight, but wish them well. Some of the Scots are drawn off; only the Independents and Baptists stand firm. They want not arms, having those that Hewson commanded. [One and a half pages.] Feb. 20, 1665.*

Feb. 25. London. Levant Company to [the Earl of Winchelsea]. Send Hen. Denton, Fellow of Queen's College, Oxford, as minister to Constantinople, and John Luke to Smyrna, to succeed Mr. Bradgate, for whose irregular and hasty dismissal they blame the consul. Are sorry that Mr. Bendish should suffer by dismissal from the consulate at Cairo, but it is much to the advantage of the Company, in preventing avanias, &c. Still wish Mr. Pickering's removal, on account of his ill-example to the young men at Smyrna. Think it needless to have a dragoman

1664–5. Vol. CXIII.

always residing at the Grand Seignior's court, which they hope will soon return to Constantinople. Instructions as to consulage, &c. in particular cases. Beg him to obtain the settlement of the customs at Aleppo, without their being paid in kind; also the repairs of Moral Bs. bridge. Hope the four general ships sent with great quantities of cloth, &c., will arrive safely, having a good convoy. Send him a gratuity of 2,000 dollars. [*Levant Papers, Vol.* v., pp. 91–94.]

Feb. 25. London. Levant Company to Willm. Hedges. Exceptions to his accounts as to charges of feasting, over-payment to the minister, personal avanias, &c. The tents provided for the ambassador's intended journey to Adrianople will not be needed, and had better be sold. [*Levant Papers, Vol.* v., pp. 94–5.]

Feb. 25. London. Levant Company to Consul Cave. His proceeding in dismissing Mr. Bradgate, contrary to their positive order, is adjudged irregular and prejudicial, therefore the payment of any gratuity to him is stopped during pleasure; one of 700 dollars is ordered to Bradgate, and his books, &c., are to be allowed to be sent over. Each should give the other a general release, and avoid lawsuits. Send another minister, John Luke, B.D., very well recommended, and hope he will not meet with neglect and indignity. To avoid the ill custom of leading women about the streets, those who have no husbands are to quit the country. Particulars of duties to be levied in individual cases. Roger Rayner, a poor man, asks aid in gathering in the goods of his brother, Thos. Rayner, a cooper, who died three years ago at Smyrna. Shipmasters are now ordered to land goods at his or the Treasurer's scale, unless by licence, which is only to be given to conformable factors, that the others may not escape the fines. Particulars of ships and their ladings. Refuse to allow the gratuities granted to dragomen and the cancelier, &c. Damages are to be allowed to merchants, according to the bills of lading. The enforcing duties and fines should not be wholly left to the Treasurer. [*Levant Papers, Vol.* v., pp. 95–100.]

Feb. 25. London. Levant Company to Rich. Mowse. Similar to the last as to the landing of goods, &c.; exceptions to his accounts, and to those of former treasurers. Refuse to allow his own consulage to Capt. Woodgreen, who went to Constantinople on his own occasions. [*Levant Papers, Vol.* v., pp. 100–103.]

Feb. 25. London. Levant Company to Consul Lannoy. Four ships are now departing for Smyrna, but as they cannot all have a lading back, Capt. Hill's ship Hannibal is to be considered a general ship, and allowed to seek a freight at Scanderoon, and he to have a gratuity of 100 dollars. [*Levant Papers, Vol.* v., p. 103.]

Feb. 25. London. Levant Company to Capt. Hill. Permit him to go to Scanderoon if he wish it, and grant him 100 dollars for port charges. [*Levant Papers, Vol.* v., p. 104.]

VOL. CXIII.

1664–5.

Feb. 25. The Garland. 67. Capt. Charles Talbot to Sam. Pepys. Sends the names of four seamen to be discharged from the Golden Lion, being entered on the Garland. [*Adm. Paper.*]

Feb. 25. 68. Jonas Shish to the Navy Comrs. Progress of ships. [*Adm. Paper, damaged.*]

Feb. 25. John and Katherine, Spithead. 69. Capt. John Whalley to the Navy Comrs. Desires a new master, his late one being dead. [*Adm Paper.*]

Feb. 25. Harwich. 70. Giles Bond, master of the Harwich hoy, to the Navy Comrs. Has arrived at Harwich, and hopes to sail for London shortly. Account of stores transported by him. [*Adm. Paper.*]

Feb. 25. 71. Certificate by Nicholas Hill, and two others, that three and a half tuns of beer leaked out in the hold of the Resolution. [*Adm. Paper.*]

Feb. 25. 72. Certificate by Capt. John Fortescue that the Return is completely equipped and fitted by the owners, according to contract. [*Adm. Paper.*]

Feb. 25. Portsmouth. 73. Commissioner Thos. Middleton to Sam. Pepys. The Royal Charles and James are still in port for want of wind. The Henry cannot be careened with an engine. Fifteen tuns of whale oil, taken in a Dutch vessel, are brought into the stores. Particulars of stores. Thinks the Royal Oak will prove the best man-of-war in England. Details of a new house to be built for himself, with accommodation for any of the Commissioners when they come down. [*Adm. Paper, three pages.*]

Feb. 25. 74. Report by Wm. Acworth that Mr. Morison refuses to deliver the remainder of the 200 lasts of tar contracted for by Mr. Cutler, until he has made sure of his money. [*Adm. Paper.*]

Feb. 26. The Augustine, Portsmouth. 75. Capt. Rich. Teate to the Navy Comrs. Has arrived, but is delayed in unlading, owing to the want of lighters and the lowness of the tide. Was prevented sailing by contrary winds. [*Adm. Paper.*]

Feb. 26. The Blackamoor, Harwich. 76. Capt. John Barton to the Navy Comrs. Asks whether his ship is to be tallowed this victualling. [*Adm. Paper.*]

Feb. 26. 77. W. Coventry to Sam. Pepys. Desires money, and a warrant to Mr. Hill for pressing watermen to carry down the merchant ships. [*Adm. Paper.*]

Feb. 26. Warrant to the Keeper of the Gatehouse to discharge De la Brillere. Minute. [*Ent. Book 22, p. 24.*]

[Feb. 26.] Warrant for Sir Robt. Smyth, of Upton, Essex, to be a Baronet. Minute. [*Ent. Book 22, p. 24.*]

Feb. 26. Hull. 78. Willm. Gower to Williamson. The Convertine frigate is waiting with 130 pressed men, and the ketch with 50. The

Vol. CXIII.

1664-5.

London first of 17 sail comes with this convoy, and among them John Williamson, commander of the Endeavour of York, by whom he sends him a cask of ale.

Feb. 27. Cradock. 79. James Scudamore to Williamson. Thanks for his letter. The ripening of the counsels for sea must follow such barbarism as none but the Dutch could have acted. Hopes to repay their inhumanity with interest, and is glad that, being water rats, they will not drown so soon, and then their punishment will last the longer.

Feb. 27. Isle of Wight. 80. —— —— to Williamson. Four of the Royal Company's ships have set sail for Guinea. The prodigious news of throwing the English overboard will make the seamen more desperate against the Dutch. Capt. Douce, in the Pembroke, has sailed to Morlaix, to convoy some vessels laden with linens. No appearance of enemies.

Feb. 27. Margate. 81. Joh. Smith to Williamson. Will give notice as requested of ships, &c., at North Foreland. The Paradox is ordered about Margate Roads, to convoy vessels in and out of the Thames. Several of the King's ships are going to Chatham to repair.

Feb. 27. Dover Castle. 82. Capt. John Strode to Williamson. An order having come to stop Hamburghers, has brought in one off the coast, which pretends to be bound for Newcastle for coals.

Feb. 27. 83. James Hickes to Williamson. Regrets the misunderstanding between Watts and Lodge of Deal. Will write to call the latter to account for miscarriage of letters, and order him to more civil behaviour. Mr. Hall wants favour in something that may contribute to the King and Williamson's service. There has been neglect in delivery of letters.

Feb. 27. "Ad vada Boum." [Oxford.] 84. Anthony Trevor to Williamson. Is out of temper with the news. Has a surfeit of Holland cheese. Exhorts him to take care of his health. Dr. Owen, sometime dean of Christ Church, has a bill found against him for unlawful assemblies for religious worship.

[Feb. 27.] 85. Petition of Col. Edward Grey, Sir Chas. Cotterell, Edw. Progers, Col. Thos. Culpeper, and Col. Bullen Reymes, to the King, for a lease on moderate rent of lands left by the sea in Lancashire, now withheld from His Majesty, the embanking and improving thereof to be done at their expense, they will advantage His Majesty, and render those lands of great benefit to the country.

Feb. 27. Reference of the above petition to the Lord Treasurer. [*Ent. Book* 18, p. 128.]

Feb. 27. Whitehall. 86. Warrant to the High Sheriff of Surrey to reprieve William Ashenhurst, condemned to death for felony at the Surrey assizes, on consideration of his former services and sufferings. [*Copy.*]

Feb. 27. Entry of the above. [*Ent. Book* 22, p. 29.]

Vol. CXIII.

1664–5.

Feb. 27. Order that all persons attending the Royal theatre pay at the first door, their money to be returned if they leave before the end of the act, complaint having been made that they refuse to pay, whereon the doorkeepers have to send after and solicit them for their entrance money; the names of offenders are to be reported to the Lord Chamberlain of the Household. With memorandum that a duplicate of the above warrant was signed, the same date. [*Ent. Book* 22, *p.* 31.]

Feb. 27. Order to the Constable of Windsor Castle, the Comptroller and Surveyor of works, and the inferior officers, to obey certain instructions. [*Ent. Book* 22, *p.* 35.] *Annexing,*

i. Instructions to the said officers, relative to confining themselves to their respective charges; the drawing up of warrants for repairs, felling and sale of timber and old materials, payment of labourers, &c.

Feb. 27. Grant to Wm. Lord Crofts and Eliz. his wife of an annuity of 400*l.* from the revenues of the duchy of Lancaster. [*Docquet.*]

Feb. 27. London. Sir And. Riccard, governor of the Levant Company, to Morgan Read, consul at Leghorn. Thanks for his interposing to detain a Turk who escaped from Spain in Capt. Rand's vessel, and was left at Leghorn with Arena Milenet, as the matter might have proved of ill consequence to their trade. Capt. Rand must be blamed for meddling in such a business, and the captive returned in safety to his own country. [*Levant Papers, Vol.* v., *p.* 105.]

Feb. 27. London. Sir And. Riccard, governor of the Levant Company, to Capt. Chamblet. The King having promised a good convoy to accompany them out, they may wait for it, without breach of articles. With note of like letters to Captains Hill, Bradenham, and Bates. [*Levant Papers, Vol.* v., *p.* 105.]

Feb. 27. 87. Certificate by Sir Wm. Berkeley that 121 Dutch prisoners, as per list prefixed, were victualled on board the Resolution for a day; with note by Jer. Smyth, Sept. 1, 1666, that they had the whole allowance of 81 men for a day. [*Adm. Paper.*]

Feb. 27. Portsmouth. 88. Commissioner Thos. Middleton to Sam. Pepys. The Eagle wants nothing but ammunition. Ketches demanded for the Royal Oak and James. Has no hemp fit for standing riggings. Discovery of a hawser and some hemp suspected to be embezzled. Will vex his heart out to see the ruin made by such a pack of rogues. Particulars of ships. Account of stores found in one of the prizes. [*Adm. Paper, two and a half pages.*]

Feb. 27. Woolwich. 89. Estimate by Chris. Pett and Francis Fletcher of repairs for the Golden Lion; total, 446*l.* [*Adm. Paper, two pages.*]

Feb. 27. Lee. 90. Dan. Furzer to the Navy Comrs. Requests orders concerning the shipwrights, squarers, carpenters, &c., waiting to be employed upon the new ship. [*Adm. Paper.*]

VOL. CXIII.

1664–5.
Feb. 27.
Harwich.

91. Anthony Deane to the Navy Comrs. The masters of the Ipswich ships will shortly be in London. Purchase of timber; there is not an elm within 12 miles. [*Adm. Paper.*]

Feb. 27.

92. J. Sotherne to Thos. Hayter. Mr. Coventry desires that some laws of war be hastened down to the ships at the Hope. With order to Mr. Pugh for one book and two sheets to be distributed to each commander in or near the Hope. [*Adm. Paper.*]

Feb. 28.
Chatham.

93. Jas. Norman to Sir Wm. Batten. Wants 5,000 hammocks, as the men have to lie on deck. Other stores are not sent, though often asked for. Is obliged to be importunate, the service being so exceedingly urgent. [*Adm. Paper.*]

Feb. 28.

94. Certificate by Capt. John Fortescue of the St. George being ready to sail. [*Adm. Paper.*] *Annexing,*

94. I. *Account of her length, 90 ft., and burthen, 260 tons.*

Feb. 28.
Chatham Dock.

95. Phin. Pett to the Navy Comrs. Repairs of ships. Timber wanted. Provisions necessary to make the place more serviceable for carrying on the works. [*Adm. Paper.*]

Feb. 28.
Portsmouth.

96. John Tippetts to the Navy Comrs. Has received no advice from Sir John Lawson about the ketch to be built, nor from the Board whether to proceed upon the second-rate ship. [*Adm. Paper.*]

Feb. 28.
Leghorn.

97. Captain Thos. Clutterbuck to the [Navy Comrs.] Has received no reply to his repeated demands for repayment of the 1,300*l.* expended two years past, in victualling Capt. Smith's squadron. Begs that it may be paid without further loss of time. The Mantua ordinary has been robbed of all his letters. English letters coming by the same mail as those from Holland are opened by the ministers of health, and often so burnt in the smoking that one cannot read their contents. Requests that his letters may be forwarded by the French ordinary. Twelve of the King's ships are at Gibraltar, where lie 23 Dutchmen laden with corn. Wishes that ships might have orders often to visit Legborn; at no port could they be more speedily and cheaply supplied with stores, or receive more certain intelligence of all that passes in the Mediterranean. The Dutch are in fear for their Smyrna convoy, which in 10 or 14 days will be at Messina; ten sail of frigates might easily surprise them; they will be worth near a million of pieces of eight. [*Adm. Paper, three pages.*]

Feb. 28.
Deptford.

98. W. Coventry to Sam. Pepys. Finds a want of good hammocks, though plenty of bad; a supply must be sent down immediately; if the persons usually serving will not send good ones, they must be had of some others. [*Adm. Paper.*]

Feb. 28.
The Triumph, Spithead.

99. Wm. Blundeston, surgeon to the Triumph, to Sir. Wm. Penn. Begs satisfaction for three months' service, and great expense of medicine, on board the Royal Charles, before being appointed to the Triumph. [*Adm. Paper.*]

Vol. CXIII.

1664–5.

Feb. 28. Dover. 100. Thos. Wale, shipwright, to the Navy Commrs. Has commenced deepening the water at the pier head. Has had in his custody, ever since the last Dutch war, some oars and a boat. Daily demands of the carpenters for canvas, nails, and pump chains. [*Adm. Paper.*]

Feb. 28. Newcastle. 101. Rich. Forster to James Hickes. There are some Holland men-of-war and freebooters off the coast. The news of the Dutch cruelty is much lamented, and has inflamed the people to revenge the blood of their innocent fellow subjects, shed by those barbarous people.

Feb. 28. 102. Grant to Wm. Longueville, in reversion after Thos. Sparkes, of the office of Chirographer in the Court of Common Pleas; with note of the grant of the said office, June 15, 1660, to Thos. Sparkes and John Perrott. Minute.

Feb. 28. Warrant to pay to Dr. Hardy, vicar of St. Martin's-in-the-Fields, 18*l.*, for four years' allowance in lieu of tithes for Lower Crowfield close, taken into the King's physic garden, and for the same to be continued yearly. [*Docquet.*]

Feb. 28. Reference to the Attorney General on the petition of James Duke of Monmouth and Wm. Lord Crofts, for examination by him of Sir Thos. Hyde's title to the Manor of Albury. [*Ent. Book* 18, p. 130.]

Feb. 28. Hull. 103. Luke Whittington to Williamson. The pressed men are on board the Convertine and ketch, except 60 taken to man the fleet of 18 sail going under their convoy, laden with lead, brass, oats, iron, hemp, butter, &c., worth 40,000*l.*,—a large adventure for one convoy in these times. Two Hull ketches have been taken by Holland freebooters; 40 Holland and Zealand men-of-war are on on the coast; and coals have risen very high, no ships venturing to Newcastle. The fleet from London is daily expected. Some of the Convertine's men were ill, but are recovered.

Feb. 28. Whitehall. 104. Petition of Lieut.-Col. Thos. Duncan to the King, for a letter to Lord Belasyse, governor of Hull, that he may be mustered in his company as a reformado, free of duty, as granted by the Duke of Albemarle; also for some other office for relief of his wife and children, whom he has not seen for five years. With order thereon that the King will remember him if he can find any fit gift not already disposed of. [*Copy.*]

Feb.? 105. Petition of Lieut.-Col. Thos. Duncan to Sec. Bennet, to expedite his dispatch according to the annexed petition and report, and deliver it to Mr. Williamson; he promised him a letter seven months ago, according to the Duke of Albemarle's reference on his petition, but it has been omitted to his great damage.

Feb.? 106. Petition of Lieut.-Col. Thos. Duncan to the King, for dispatch of a letter to Lord Belasyse, governor of Hull, to grant him a Reformado's place in the garrison there, duty free; it was promised on 17 September last, on an order by the Duke of Albe-

Vol. CXIII.

1664–5.

marie on his former petition, but through great poverty, he has not been able to obtain the letter.

Feb. 28. Chester. 107. Alexander Rigby to Sir Geoffrey Shakerley. Lord Derby, Lord Cholmondeley, and Mr. Cholmondeley, of Vale Royal, keep the keys of the chest. There was a meeting of Quakers in Castle Lane; 20 of them are sent to the Northgate. Mr. Dutton, of Hatton, apprehended some Anabaptists who met in the country; those fanatic sort of people are of late very peremptory.

[Feb. 28.] 108. Notes from the Parliamentary journals of addresses made by the Houses of Parliament to the King, from 1662. [*Four pages.*]

Feb. 28. Warrant for the Dukes of Buckingham, Albemarle, and Ormond, and 11 others to be appointed Commissioners for Appeals in the business of prizes and prize goods. [*Ent. Book* 22, *p.* 37.]

Feb. 28? 109. List of eight Commissioners of Appeal for prizes, to be presented to the King.

Feb. 28. Warrant to the Lord General to order the levying of 1,200 men to be added to Colonel John Russel's regiment of Guards, in order to raise it to 2,400 men, and 1,000 to Lieut.-Col. Morgan's, to raise it to 2,000. [*Ent. Book* 22, *p.* 38.]

[Feb. 28.] 110. Draft of the above.

Feb. 28. Warrant to the Farmers of Customs to permit 300 barrels of gunpowder to be shipped for the use of the King of Portugal. [*Ent. Book* 22, *p.* 38.]

Feb.? 111. Petition of Henry Bruncard to the King, for a grant to him, as promised to the late Hugh Boteler, of licence to erect one or more lighthouses at Milford Haven, co. Pembroke, and to receive 2*d.* a ton on English ships, and 4*d.* on foreign, towards the expenses.

Feb. 28. Warrant for a licence to Henry Bruncard to erect and maintain for 31 years, on rent of 20 nobles, one or more lighthouses at Milford Haven, co. Pembroke, receiving therefor 2*d.* a ton on English ships, and 4*d.* from strangers,—the said grant to be confirmed by Act of Parliament,—the Navy Officers and Masters of Trinity House certifying that shipwrecks often happen for want of such lights. [*Ent. Book* 22, *pp.* 39–40.]

Feb. [28.] Whitehall. 112. Order for a warrant to pay to the Earl of Lindsey, as keeper of the Manor of Woodstock, 40*l.* a year for wages of the keepers, 40*l.* for purchase of hay for the deer, and other necessary sums.

Feb. 28. Whitehall. 113. Similar warrant, premising that the allowances are the same as granted by the late King to Philip Earl of Montgomery, on finding that the expenses of the manor and park amounted to more than the rent of 114*l.* 1*s.* 10*d.*, which he was to pay for it. [*Two pages.*]

[Feb. 28.] 114. Draft of the above. [*One and a half pages.*]

Feb. 28. Entry of the above, assigning the payment on the Receiver-General of Oxfordshire. [*Ent. Book* 22, *p.* 43.]

Vol. CXIII.

1664–5.
Feb. 28. Petition of Sir Chas. Stanley, K.B., to the King, for leave to present a bill in Parliament for restoration in blood and absolute pardon of all offences; His Majesty's pardon touching the death of George Symonds, slain when in his company, not sufficing for his restoration. With order thereon, granting the petition. [*Ent. Book* 18, *p.* 133.]

Feb.? 115. Petition of Alexander Eakins, of Weston-Favell, co. Northampton, to the King, for a letter to the mayor and aldermen of the town to elect him to the stewardship of the corporation, void by death of Wm. Rushton. Was loyal and lost most of his estate during the late war.

Feb.? 116. Petition of the Gate Porters to Sec. Bennet, for payment of the arrears of their board wages, they being five in number with their five servants; have attended day and night, and received nothing for 18 months. Endorsed with a list of numerous petitions, including the 16 immediately following.

Feb.? 117. Petition of Monsieur Ferdinand to the King. Requests on his dismissal, which he hears is intended, a recompense proportionate to his expense, incurred in leaving France and settling in England, on understanding that His Majesty wished to have his services, and also to the pension and allowances that he had, as one of the first musicians of the King of France, to which place he cannot hope to return. [*French.*]

Feb.? 118. Petition of the Churchwardens of St. Margaret's parish, Westminster, to the King, for continuance of his bounty of 100*l.* a year to the poor, 50*l.* of which is for relief of the poor children in the hospital in Tuttle Fields, founded by the late King.

Feb.? 119. Petition of James Lord Lundoris, prisoner in the Fleet, to the King, not to suffer his grey hairs to go with dishonour to the grave, but to be his good angel and lead him through these iron gates of misery into freedom. Has divested himself of his small fortune in behalf of his late and present Majesty, and has no hope but in his favour.

Feb.? 120. Petition of the Canary Company to the King, that Edw. Prescot and John Smith, jun., of Teneriffe, may be called home and punished, as the ringleaders who incited the islanders to a tumultuous rising against the Company's factors, thereby endangering their lives; and that Sam. Wilson, merchant of London, who by his letters has encouraged them therein, may be called to account.

Feb.? 121. Petition of John Gregory, prisoner in Sandown Castle, to the King, for release on security, or for a hearing, or for some maintenance to preserve his life. Has been there and in the Tower two years, and never heard the cause of his commitment; must starve to death if he remain longer, having no maintenance there as he had in the Tower.

Vol. CXIII.

1664–5.

Feb. ? 122. Petition of John Sherman to the King, for the colours in Capt. Gray's company in His Majesty's now regiment of Guards, commanded by Col. Russell. Details his services.

Feb. ? 123. Petition of Katherine Haswell to the King, for the next small office that falls void for her husband, who though formerly an officer serves under Sir Wm. Berkeley, as a foremast man in this Dutch war. Her father was kept in chains during the late rebellion; her brother slain at Edgehill, and she, after many services in carrying letters, was dangerously wounded at Basing House, and disabled from a livelihood. Marked "for Sir Wm. Berkeley."

Feb. ? 124. Petition of Elinor, wife of Daniel Bailey, who is imprisoned in Maidstone gaol for horsestealing, to the King, for suspension of the execution of her husband, who is to die the next day; and for his reprieve, this being his first offence.

Feb. ? 125. Petition of Col. Hen. Starkey to the King, for a free pardon for Dan. Baily, late an expert soldier under his command in service of the late King, but now prisoner in Kent gaol for stealing a mare, which he says he intended to return, after riding her to Deptford to enlist in His Majesty's service at sea.

Feb. ? 126. Petition of Hugh Jones ap Price, of Newbury, Anglesea, to the King, for a commission to himself and others to discover lands, &c., in the north of Wales, concealed from the Crown by their inhabitants for many years past, and converted to their own uses; and for the benefit thereof for himself, according to Act of Parliament. Endorsed with a blank certificate, that in the late King's time many Crown lands in cos. Pembroke and Cardigan were taken for private purposes.

Feb. ? 127. Petition of the Pages of the Bedchamber to the King, for payment of their board wages in future, with arrears since Michaelmas, 1663.

Feb. ? 128. Petition of Elizabeth Calvert, widow, to the King, for pardon and release from the King's Bench, where she is close prisoner, for having helped John Wilson of Chester, author of a book called Nehuston, to print it, she being wholly ignorant of the sedition contained therein; faithfully promises never to be concerned in such books for the future.

Feb. ? 129. Petition of John, son of the late murdered Dr. John Hewitt, to the King, for payment of a pension of 100*l.*, promised four years ago, with arrears; has hitherto been at great charge in soliciting, but received nothing.

Feb. ? 130. Similar petition to the same effect. Has paid the fees of the several officers to procure his patent, and was obliged to borrow from his friends, who are now urgent for payment.

Feb. ? 131. Petition of Lady Diana, relict of Sir Joseph Colster, Bart., to the King, for a grant of a debt of 500*l.*, which though desperate, she hopes to compound for; it was left by Isaac Gould to his son Isaac,

VOL. CXIII.

1664–5.

who being convicted of felony, this money became due to the Crown, though he afterwards released it to his brother John, who is lately dead.

Feb.? 132. Petition of Col. John Russell of His Majesty's regiment of Guards to the King, for restoration to liberty and to his attendance on His Majesty, being still continued in his displeasure. Marked "Col. Russell's 2nd petition."

Feb.? 133. Petition of two Clerks of the Cheque and 40 Messengers of the Chamber in ordinary to the King, for an assignment of their arrears of wages, and future settlement of the same. Notwithstanding their several petitions and references, they are still two years and a quarter in arrear at Lady Day next.

Feb.? 134. Petition of John Matthew Magra, banker at Turin, to the King, to depute some of the Council to do him and his partners justice, their ship, bound for Amsterdam, being taken in the Channel, before the declaration of the present war with Holland, and their goods belonging to themselves.

[Feb.] 135. Petition of Abraham Meza and David Baruh and their families to the King, for permission to come on shore, being all in perfect health. Came from Rotterdam, and are on their way to Surinam, but were stopped at Tollhaven in the Thames, by his order.

Feb.? 136. Petition of Sir Rich. Mauleverer and 14 other gentlemen, sufferers for the late King, to His Majesty, for a commission to take such Dutch vessels as they may encounter in the Straits, and for a small frigate to execute it therewith, a war against the Dutch being resolved on.

Feb.? 137. The King to the Lord Lieutenants of Counties. Recapitulates the directions given in his letter of 30 Dec. last, relative to the gathering in of the month's assessment for the last two years, the drawing out the militia, and paying the officers, as he understands the orders have been neglected in some counties. [*Three and a half pages, see 1664, Dec. 30.*]

Feb.? 138. Memoranda of letters to the Lord Lieutenants for the arrears of the 70,000*l.*, delivered out to sundry persons.

Feb.? 139. List of the Lord Lieutenants of Counties to whom letters were addressed for arrears.

Feb.? 140. Commission to Capt. Gilbert Thomas and three others to execute the office of Provost Marshal of Middlesex, Westminster, Southwark, Surrey, and other places adjoining the King's palace; to prevent murders, robberies, and misdemeanors by rogues and vagabonds disguised as persons of quality, or as Quakers or sectaries met for divine worship, but who plot against government, through neglect of the constables in keeping watch. They are to suppress

VOL. CXIII.

1664–5. seditious books, apprehend offenders and sectaries assembling more than five in number, suppress tumults, quarrels, and unlawful games in the streets, keep watch and ward, try weights and measures, test provisions, &c., receiving a third of all fines allowed to prosecutors. [*One and a half sheets.*]

Feb. Memoranda from the Signet books [by Williamson] of warrants, &c., passed during the month, the uncalendared portions of which are as follow:—

Commission to the Duke of York to empower the Governors of Colonies to grant commissions to whom they shall think fit, against the Dutch.

Grant of 400*l.* to Sir Charles Cotterel, going as envoy to Brussels, to congratulate Castelrodrigo, the governor. [*Domestic Corresp., Dec.* 1664.]

Feb. 141. Similar memoranda, the uncalendared portions of which are as follow:—

Grant to Hen. Robinson of the sole use of his inventions for quenching fire, for preserving ships in war, and for raising water.

Notes that the Queen's five gentlemen ushers daily waiters have 100 marks each yearly; the 11 gentlemen ushers, quarter waiters, 12*l.*; the seven yeomen ushers, 7*l.* 2*s.* 6*d.*; the two yeomen harbingers, 30*l.*; the two yeomen attending her robes, 20*l.*; the two yeomen attending her beds, 20*l.*; all paid out of the treasury of the chamber.

Grant to the Earl of Carlisle of 1,000*l.* on his return from his embassy to Russia.

Grant to the Duke of Monmouth of a pension of 6,000*l.* a year.

Lease to Lord Mordaunt, Sir Thos. Peyton, and Sir Jeremy Whichcott, for 31 years from Jan. 1661, of the duty of 12*d.* a chaldron on coals; rent, 1,838*l.* 12*s.* 6*d.*

Grant to George Johnson of 12*d.* a day for life, as yeoman o the bows.

Note that all payments assigned on the duchy of Lancaster are to be made payable by the Receiver-General of the duchy.

Note that M. De Persigny, envoy from France, had a jewel of 470*l.*

Note that the pages of honour have 120*l.* annuity, on the King's pleasure signified by the master of the horse.

Grant to —— Brimsmead of pardon for having two wives.

Licence to Sir Edw. Ford and [Thos.] Togood to erect water houses at Wapping and Marybone, and one between Temple Bar and Charing Cross, not above 15 feet high.

Vol. CXIII.

1664–5.

Feb. ? 142. Form of letters of reprisal granted by the Duke of York to private men-of-war, against the ships and goods of the United States. [*Four and a half pages.*]

Feb. ? 143. Commission of especial reprisals to Sir Edmund Turner and George Carew against the ships and Merchandise of the States General, until they have recovered 151,612*l*., the value of the Bona Esperanza and Hen. Bonaventure, ships of the late Sir Wm. Courteen, spoiled by the Dutch East India Company, in 1613. [*Fifteen pages.*]

Feb. ? 144. Earl of Peterborough to [Williamson]. Is still on shore, his stores not being ready; shows kindness to the Duke's servants and officers of the fleet, especially Mr. Coventry; is sorry to hear of more coming this way. The Lord Constable [of Windsor Castle?] had better have stayed and gathered laurels more easily in his own garden, but his wife's envy expenses all they have; the Duke's forces will soon be completed, but some captains secretly complain of want of men, and say that the order for their not being harboured in the country where they lie is ineffectual. [*Two pages.*]

Feb. ? 145. Request that, in spite of the King's prohibition against correspondence with Holland in the declaration of war, a warrant may be granted for the Postmaster-General to dispatch the Holland mails to and fro, as necessary for corresponding with ambassadors in the Northern courts, and for enabling merchants to withdraw their estates and effects.

Feb. ? 146. Statement that the King, wishing to encourage the fishing trade, lately incorporated the Royal Fishing Company under the Duke of York, but at Lynn in Norfolk, their bank of money was seized and squandered by Capt. John Rookewood, their agents beaten, and their implements broken. The King refers the case to the person addressed, to see that the rights of the Royal Fishing Company may be preserved.

Feb. ? 147. Brief notes of commissions issued since the King's restoration. [*Thirteen pages.*]

Feb. ? 148. Regulations proposed by Mr. Millington for carrying on trade in the present time of war. The plantations and Turkey trade to be managed by English shipping only; in other trades the shipping of any friendly nation to be allowed on payment of strangers' duties; and convoys to be provided at certain months for vessels trading to certain places. [*Two pages.*]

Feb. ? 149. List of the King's fleet, with the names of the commanders, and an account of the present disposal of the fleet under the Duke of York, Prince Rupert, and the Earl of Sandwich, or in harbour; also a list of ships not appointed to any squadron. [*Three pages.*]

Vol. CXIII.

1664–5.
Feb.

Lists sent by Margin Lodge to Williamson of ships in the Downs during the month, the state of the wind, &c. :—

No.	Date.	King's.	Merchants'.	Wind.	Remarks.
150	Feb. 18	29	0	W.	Will send two lists daily.
151	„ 19	26	1	N.W.	
152	„ 20	25	1	N. by E.	
153	„ 21	20	1	N.N.W.	Earl of Sandwich goes to London to-morrow.
154	„ 27	14	1	E.S.E.	
155	„ 28	11	1	S.W.	

Vol. CXIV. March 1–15, 1664–5.

1664–5.
March 1.
Whitehall.

Proclamation forbidding all sailing of vessels from any English port for foreign trade or commerce without licence, on pain of confiscation, on account of the great perils and inconveniences of these times of danger. [*Printed. Proc. Coll., Charles II.*, p. 178.]

March 1.

Warrant to pay to Lord George Berkeley of Berkeley Castle 1,000*l*., for the repairs of the pales and fences in Nonsuch Park. [*Docquet.*]

March 1.
Hull.

1. Luke Whittington to James Hickes. Two Ostend vessels are stayed, lest meeting with the Holland fleet, they should inform them of the fleet of 18 vessels, under convoy of a man-of-war, which are to go to London with the first fair wind. Two Holland privateers seized a Humber keel, the men escaping in their boat. Holland vessels are seen every day from Bridlington.

March 1.
Edinburgh.

2. R. M[ein] to Hen. Muddiman. Lord Lauderdale writes to the Lord Commissioner that the reported barbarities of De Ruyter at Guinea are lies, and the liars are to be hanged or sent into Holland. Three Scotch ships trading to Bourdeaux are taken. The advertisement for Glasgow is to be put in the London diurnal.

March 1.
Portsmouth.

3. Commissioner Thos. Middleton to Sam. Pepys. Particulars of ships. The masters of the merchants come to him for stores for graving, and he has no orders to supply them. Tenders of rosin and cordage. Requests an order for the delivery of various goods out of the prize ships to the stores. Expects the news from Holland will be confirmed, but it may be worse, for drowning is an easy death, and the Dutch know how to torment men before death; has been a spectator of their actions, and a very great sufferer by them. [*Adm. Paper, three pages.*]

VOL. CXIV.

1664-5.

March 1. 4. Wm. Coventry to Sam. Pepys. The paying by the prize office formerly of those who brought in prizes ought not to alter the resolution to pay Capt. Talbot, as the goods of his prize were given to the Royal Company, and the men were part of the Jersey and Expedition's crew; 2,000 trees are to be felled in Alicesholt, 700 in Waltham, and 700 in New Forest. [*Adm. Paper.*]

March 1. 5. Wm. Coventry to Sam. Pepys. Desires the Articles of War to be sent to Capt. Jordan, for distribution among the ships in the Hope. The practice of moulding timber in the woods wastes a great deal. Particulars of stores wanted. When Capt. Allin returns, most of that fleet will come to Harwich, which ought to be well provided with stores for cleaning and refitting. [*Adm. Paper, two pages.*]

March 1. 6. Certificate by Capt. John Fortescue of the John and Thomas being completely equipped and fitted, according to contract. [*Adm. Paper.*]

March 2. Dover. 7. John Tatnell to the Navy Comrs. Repairs of the Mermaid and several boats at Deal. John Cooley offers to furnish leather scuppers. [*Adm. Paper.*]

March 2. Dover. 8. Thos. Wale to the Navy Comrs. Wants stores. Repairs of the Paradox. [*Adm. Paper.*] *Annexing,*

8. I. *Account by Capt. John Johnson of boatswains and carpenters' stores required for the Little Gift.*
Dover Road, March 2.

March 2. Dover. 9. E. Wivell to the Navy Comrs. The Paradox and Little Gift are at anchor before the harbour, waiting a tide to get in. [*Adm. Paper.*]

March 2. Whitehall. 10. Petition of Thos. and Hen. Killigrew to the King, for the felling of several coppices, containing 100 acres, in Whittlewood and Sanlcey forests. With reference thereon to the Lord Treasurer and Chancellor of the Exchequer, and report of the latter, March 20, in favour of the petition.

March 2. The King to the Gentlemen of Surrey. There have always been deer and heath-poults preserved in Windsor Forest for the Royal hunting, but in the late times they have been much destroyed. Asks them to consider of some way to preserve a competent number of deer there; if they serve him therein, he may be induced to part with some part of what he accounts his right there. [*Ent. Book* 17, *p.* 96.]

March 2. Pass for two horses to France. Minute. [*Ent. Book* 22, *p.* 38.]

March 2. Warrant from Sec. Bennet to apprehend Thomas Glass, Major Vernon, and others, with their papers, and bring them before him. [*Ent. Book* 22, *p.* 44.]

Vol. CXIV.

1664-5.
March 2. Warrant from Sec. Bennet for apprehending —— Strange, *alias* Captain L'Estrange, and another. Minute. [*Ent. Book* 22, *p.* 44.]

March 1 11. Information of A. W——. Capt. Lieut. Strange tried to persuade the Fifth Monarchy men to take this juncture to attempt Whitehall, but the soberer fanatics argued that it was more rational to stay and see what advantage they might have by the war with Holland. Strange would only wait one month; his first attempt was to be on the King and Monk. Capt. Cox, who served in Sweden, was urged to take the command of a frigate building against the Dutch, that he might bring back any of the banished party, or Lambert, now in prison, who is of good repute with the sober fanatics, but not with the Fifth Monarchy men. Roberts, an ejected Scotch minister, beneficed in Martindale, assures them that Westmoreland and the Borders only wait an apportunity to appear. John Goodwin, who wrote "Mene, Tekel," has another similar book almost ready for press. [*Two pages.*]

March 2. 12. W. Coventry to [Williamson]. Sends two blank commissions for Lord Holles, and a copy of the bonds that Lord Holles must use, as the required security cannot be given in the Admiralty court. His Lordship should encourage persons wanting commissions to send for them regularly, but more of these will be sent, rather than lose friends. Endorsed "Commissions to Frenchmen."

[March 2.] 13. Book of notes [by Williamson] from the Journals of Parliament, 12–17 Charles II., arranged according to subjects. [*Eighteen pages.*]

March 3. 14. Bill of lading of the Lucas frigate, from Mallamocca, bound for the Downs, containing 8 cases of spirits, birding pieces, &c., for the King's use, consigned to Sir John Shaw. Endorsed "Willm. Burrows, master of the Mayflower, from Locke," &c. [*Printed form, filled up.*]

March 3. 15. Ger. Lady Anderson to Williamson. Requests him to have a pardon signed for a nephew of hers, a canon of Hereford, who with some of his brethren, had committed an error which cannot be solved but by the King's dispensation. The Dean is willing that it should be passed by. [*See March 6, 1665.*]

March 3. Dover Castle. 16. Capt. John Strode to Williamson. A fleet of 13 sail has passed; Zealand freebooters ply on the Flemish and French coasts, and a privateer of theirs with 30 guns has gone northward. Lord Castlemaine has returned from France and gone to London, and Thos. Howard from Zealand.

March 3. Dover Castle. 17. J[ohn] C[arlisle] to Williamson. There have passed into the Downs 17 sail of our men-of-war and four Smyrna merchants; also a Hamburgher, which reports that 60 Holland vessels, laden with Bourdeaux wines, set sail northwards, three weeks ago. The Earl of Castlemaine and Thos. Howard, of Suffolk, have this day landed.

VOL. CXIV.

1664–5.

March 3. Deal. 18. Ri. Watts to [Williamson]. About 16 of the King's ships have sailed southward; three more, with one prize and one merchantman, are in the Downs.

March 3. Whitehall. 19. Examination of Major Robt. Holmes. Shown his instructions, ordering him to protect the goods, ships, forts, &c., of the Royal Company, and to preserve their freedom of trade with the natives, by force if needful, and if he were able to do it; shows narratives of the wrongs committed on the English in Gambia, by the King of Barra, at instigation of the Dutch, and alleges the universal complaints of the English factors on the coast against the Dutch. Gives a full account of his taking of Cape de Verde, and his respect to the private property of the Dutch. Details the fraudulent practices of the Dutch at Sestos. Account of his taking the Golden Lion; of the Dutch taking Anta; of their setting a price on his head on the Gold Coast; of his amicable overtures to their general Valkenburg, to compose differences; of the taking of Cape Corso; of the treachery of the Dutch in blowing up the English at Aga; and of the taking of Anamaboa. [*Five and a half pages.*] *Annexing,*

19. I. *Extract from the Instructions given to Captain Holmes concerning the protection of the agents, goods, ships, factories, &c., of the Royal [African] Company, by force if needful, and if he be strong enough, especially from the molestation of the Golden Lion of Flushing.* [*Copy.*]

March 3. 20. Draft of the above examination. [*Three and a half pages.*]

March? 21. [Chris. Sanderson to Sir Phil. Musgrave.] His intelligencer reports that an old Presbyterian inveighed much against this devilish Parliament, and said the King would never part with it. Col. Ludlow, Capt. Mason, and several others are now privately in London. Wants 20*l.* to pay the intelligencer; the wheels must be oiled to make them go. A colonel under restraint [Lilburn] has asked his father to send him money, as there will soon be a change. Wants a cypher to correspond in. Care should be taken of the King's person, of his Court, and of that factious city, the receptacle of all this rebellious brood. Will do his best to find out the hiding place of the rebels. [*One and a quarter pages. Imperfect.*]

March 3. Egglestone. 22. Christopher Sanderson to Sir Philip Musgrave. Cannot find out from Grisley Pate, *alias* George Bateman, of Durham, where these good fellows lie in London. Bateman doubts not but there will be a good appearance for the old cause, and April showers may bring something; he would be able to ride a horse, though old, but would not get one too soon, as cavaliers are jealous of Quakers and others who have good horses. He says the Dutch intend to land some regiments in Scotland, whither their friends from the northern parts will repair. Chris. Eyon, a quaker merchant of Barnard Castle, says there are eight or nine regiments of English and Scots in Holland, who are for landing in Scotland; wants money for his friend to get a good horse, that

VOL. CXIV.

1664–5.

he may obtain better intelligence. It is reported amongst them that Lambert, with the governor of the Isle [Guernsey], and two more are gone to the Dutch, and Dr. Richardson, with six ships, came to receive them. Also that the Earl of Argyle has retired to his house in the north, determined to oppose the King on account of some affronts. Col. Lilburn says his father, Rich. Lilburn, has got up 80*l.*, and will send it him, for he expects a speedy alteration. Is using every effort to have timely notice of what is doing. Expects to have to bind his intelligencer over to good behaviour, so as to avoid suspicion, in order that when he comes to him, it may be on pretext to procure his enlargement. [*Two pages.*]

[March 3.] 23. Sec. Bennet to the Lord Mayor of London. The King being resolved to make public his late declaration of Feb. 22, relating to the injuries done by the Dutch, has ordered two heralds, with serjeants-at-arms and trumpeters, to proclaim it at Whitehall Court gate, and in the accustomed places in London. His lordship, with the aldermen and sheriffs, is to be ready to receive and assist them therein. [*Draft.*]

March 3. Warrant to the King's Heralds and Pursuivants-at-arms to choose two heralds to attend at Whitehall Gate at 10 a.m. on the 4th instant, to meet the serjeants-at-arms and trumpeters, and proclaim war with the United Provinces, on account of the injuries of the Dutch East and West India Companies. [*Ent. Book 22, p. 45.*]

March 3. The Dartmouth, Liverpool. 24. Capt. Rich. Rooth to Sir Wm. Penn. Complains of the unserviceableness of the 71 pressed men sent on board by Sir John Owen. Has disbursed them, since it is the Duke of York's pleasure that none but seamen be received. Enough might have been had if done timely, but 19 vessels were allowed to sail from Liverpool without one man impressed, and then the 58 seamen ordered from that town were taken chiefly from the plough. Can get no assistance either from the mayor of Liverpool or the Earl of Derby who is vice-admiral. Has only received 20 seamen above his own number as yet. The provisions are exhausted and little service done. [*Adm. Paper.*] *Encloses,*

> 24. i. *Names and trades of 20 pressed men sent by Sir John Owen, but discharged for inability.* *March* 3, 1665.

March 3. Portsmouth. 25. Commissioner Thos. Middleton to Sam. Pepys. Recommends John Merritt as blockmaker at Portsmouth. [*Adm. Paper.*]

March 3. Revenge, between Queenborough and Sheerness. 26. Capt. Thos. Teddeman to the Navy Comrs. Has acquainted Commissioner Peter Pett with his arrival from the Downs, in reference to refitting his vessel. [*Adm. Paper.*]

March 3. Portsmouth. 27. John Tippetts to Sir Wm. Batten. Will prepare a draft of the second-rate ship to be built. The Royal Oak has sailed to Spithead. [*Adm. Paper.*]

Vol. CXIV.

1664–5.

March 4. 28. Certificate by Capt. John Fortescue of the John and Abigail being completely equipped and ready to sail. [*Adm. Paper.*]

March 4. 29. Similar certificate in behalf of the Satisfaction. [*Adm. Paper.*]

March 4. Harwich. 30. Anthony Deane to the Navy Comrs. Sends an account of provisions necessary against the arrival of the Straits' fleet. Repairs of ships. [*Adm. Paper.*]

March 4. Portsmouth. 31. Commissioner Thos. Middleton to Sam. Pepys. If the form and manner of use of the careening wheel be sent, it may be put in practice as occasion requires. Never does and never will contract for provisions without an order from the Board. Begs that the new second-rate ship may be built after the model of the Royal Oak. Promises dispatch and cheapness in erecting a dwelling house for himself in the yard. Has discovered the stolen hawser; the man must be hanged, being a very knave. Thinks all the mischief done in this matter arises from allowing perquisites in the navy. Particulars of ships and stores. [*Adm Paper, three pages.*]

March 4. Lydney. 32. Dan Furzer to the Navy Comrs. The iron there is good, but the stock small; although it is risen in price, there are a dozen poor men who will willingly do the work required, at the price mentioned by the Board. Particulars of timber in the Lea Baly. Wishes an opinion of his draft for the ship. [*Adm. Paper, one and a half pages.*]

March 4. Chatham Ropeyard. 33. John Owen, clerk of the ropeyard, to the Navy Comrs. John Brown, officer of ordnance, refuses to receive the damaged hemp without an order. [*Adm. Paper.*]

March 4. Warrant to Lord Chamberlain Manchester to admit James Earl of Suffolk, as gentleman of the bedchamber, in place of the late Lord Wentworth. [*Ent. Book 22, p. 40.*]

March 4. Order for a warrant to Sir Thos. Trevor to join with the Queen-Mother in an assignment to the Earl of St. Alban's and others, her trustees, for her life and for two years after her decease, of certain lands and tenements granted by the late King to Sir John Walter, Sir Jas. Fullerton, and Sir Thos. Trevor, the last named being the only survivor, and Sir John Trevor, his son, being his executor; these lands were transferred by the said persons to the Queen-Mother for life, but are now granted to her trustees for two years after her death. [*Ent. Book 17, pp. 96–7.*]

March 4. Grant to Sir Robt. Smith, of Upton, co. Essex, of the dignity of a Baronet. [*Docquet.*]

March 4. Grant to the same of the usual discharge. [*Docquet.*]

March 4. Warrant to pay to Col. Wm. Legg, lieutenant of ordnance, 586*l.* 13*s.* 11¼*d.*, for the repair of Portland Castle, and furnishing it with provisions of war. [*Docquet.*]

VOL. CXIV.

1664–5.
March 4. Warrant to pay to Col. Wm. Legg 205*l.* 19*s.* 11*d.* for ordnance, &c., to be delivered to Sir John Colleton, Bart., for the use of the island of Barbadoes. [*Docquet.*]

March 4. Warrant to pay to Col. Wm. Legg 158*l.* 8*s.* 4*d.*, for carriages, arms, &c., to be delivered to Sir George Carteret, for service in the island of Alderney. [*Docquet.*]

March 4. Plymouth. 34. J. C[larke] to [Williamson]. Lord Belasyse came there yesterday, and is waiting the Smyrna fleet, which is to go with the same convoy that takes him to Tangiers. Seven of the King's ships are in port, and ten vessels laden with Bourdeaux wines.

March 4. Deal. 35. Ri. Watts to Williamson. There are 70 of the crews of ships who were sent on shore for water left behind, the winds being high. They are sent with tickets to Portsmouth. A gentleman has come to survey quarters for the Duke of York.

March 4. 36. George Williamson to Jos. Williamson. Finds difficulty in executing his commission for collecting the hearth-money. Has made a perfect survey, but many disputes arise. Has written to the Lord Treasurer, and hopes a reply before rent-day, to satisfy objections which are very great. Will take in his bonds for the excise. Hears he is to be put out of the lease, though he has paid his rent as punctually as any in England. Asks his brother to speak a word in season for him. [*Damaged.*]

March 4. Whitehall. 37. Petition of Rich. March, keeper of the ordnance stores, to the King, for a grant of the place of Keeper of small guns in the Tower, which formerly belonged to the store keepers; it was granted by the late Sir Wm. Compton to Mat. Bayley, his clerk, but from some misconduct he is suspended from office. With reference thereon to the Attorney General.

March 4. Whitehall. 38. Petition of George Arnott to the King, for a grant of several small fines payable in the duchy of Cornwall, discovered by him. Was formerly a page of honour, but having an employment in the French army before the Restoration, which he has now lost by the death of the Earl of Tiveot, never received the annuity of 120*l.* granted to other pages. With reference thereon to the Lord Treasurer, and his report, March 18, in favour of the petition. *Annexing,*

38. I. *Account of fines in arrears in the duchy of Cornwall; total, 545l. Endorsed "Mr. Arnott."*

March 4. Entry of the above reference. [*Ent. Book* 18, p. 129.]

March 4. Reference to the Bishop of Winchester and four other Commissioners for repair of St. Paul's, on the petition of Edw. Dallowe for relief by the dean and chapter, in reference to a small piece of waste land lying on the north side of St. Paul's, purchased by him, and on which he has expended great sums. [*Ent. Book* 18, p. 130.]

VOL. CXIV.

1664–5.

March 4. Margate. 39. John Smith to Williamson. Thos. Frizley, an Englishman who has long lived in Rotterdam, and is suspected as a spy, has arrived, with a letter from Sir George Downing. Has stayed him according to the King's declaration of February 22, till further directions.

March 5. [Deal.] 40. Mor. Lodge to [Williamson]. A Dutch caper threatened the Eaglet ketch in the Downs, but neither could get to the other, and the thick weather prevented the townsmen from manning boats and going to her.

March 5. 4 p.m., Deal. 41. Ri. Watts to Williamson. A Dutch man-of-war is in the Downs. Orders are sent to Sandown Castle to shoot off two pieces of ordinance.

March 5. Plymouth. 42. —— to Williamson. There are eight King's ships in the Downs, four bound for Tangiers, and three merchant ships waiting for Lord Belasyse; also other vessels from Bourdeaux, &c., five of which are secured by the sub-commissioners of prizes, as they are found to be Hollanders. Four Dutch prisoners escaped from the castle, but were taken again, on board an Ostender. Two ships discharged by the Commissioners have sailed away.

March 5. Hull. 43. Luke Whittington to James Hickes. The fleet intended for London has gone down to the convoy, to sail the first fair wind. Holland men-of-war are still seen off the coasts.

March 5. 44. Sir Wm. Coventry* to Sec. Bennet. Gives the names of the ships at or near Gravesend, bound to the plantations, and a list of those that had passes, but are not yet gone.

March 5. Assistance, Plymouth. 45. Capt. Zach. Browne to the Navy Comrs. Did not discharge the men who have complained to the Board, but sent them ashore sick, to go to the hospital, and return when recovered. Wants a new master in the room of one deceased. [*Adm. Paper.*]

March 5. The Harp, Holyhead. 46. Capt. James Sharland to the Navy Comrs. Was ordered by the Lord Deputy and Council [of Ireland] to wait, at Holyhead, the arrival of Richard Earl of Arran, who has not yet come. Great part of the carpenters and boatswains' stores are lost, owing to the oversetting of the ship in which they were sent. Asks a fresh supply and an increase of men. [*Adm. Paper.*] *Encloses,*

> 46. I., II. *Account of what was lost of the carpenters and boatswains' stores, sent by Mr. Carier to Dublin.* [*Two papers.*]

March 6. 47. Robert Southwell to Sam Pepys. Has entered the order for the Friesland prize, when condemned, to be appraised by the Commissioners of Prizes of London, and delivered over for the use of the navy. Advises that the Court of Admiralty put her speedily on the list to be tried. [*Adm. Paper.*]

* Coventry was knighted on March 2, 1665, and is therefore so named, although the endorsements of his letters frequently speak of him as Mr. Coventry, for several months later.

VOL. CXIV.

1664–5.

March 6. Victualling Office. 48. Denis Gauden to the Navy Comrs. Sends account of victuals in store and under contract, in ten ports named. [*Adm. Paper.*]

March 6. 49. Sir Wm. Coventry to Sam. Pepys. The Duke of York recommends Sir John Knight's proposal to hire a ship at Bristol for pressing and receiving pressed men thereabouts, and transporting them where they are required. If a ship of reasonable size be selected, she might serve as a convoyer in those seas, or perhaps catch a privateer; she should be hastened, for the Virginia ships are expected, and will bring 300 men, who would be a great prize. The Earl of Sandwich advises that two long boats be always stationed at Deal, to supply the fleet with ballast, water, &c., as needful. The officers at Deptford desire a wall instead of a pale to be built in the timber-yard, which would quit cost, by keeping the men in the yard. Mr. Gauden's pork is found too light. Account of guns on board the Eagle and Ferdinand. [*Adm. Paper, two pages.*]

March 6. The Centurion, Downs. 50. Captain of the Centurion to the Navy Comrs. Has arrived in the Downs. None but Capt. Jennings in the Ruby is there, the rest are gone westward. [*Adm. Paper.*]

March 6. Portsmouth. 51. Commissioner Thos. Middleton to Sam. Pepys. Sends inventories of the Eagle, Ferdinand, and Madras's stores, and will have them appraised. Particulars of stores. Complains of the abuse in pressing men utterly unfit for service, some 50, 60, and even 70 years of age. No man will admit them into his ship; they cannot return without pay, and no one has power to send them home again, so they wander up and down the streets, starving and spreading infection in the town; if they go home they will be put into gaol. Some of the pressmasters should be made an example of. [*Adm. Paper, two pages.*]

March 6. The King to the [Vice-Chancellor] of Cambridge. Recommends John Beale, B.D., and Thos. Fuller, B.D., late of Christ's College, for their D.D. degrees, with seniority according to their standing in the University. [*Ent. Book* 19, *p.* 32.]

March 6. The King to the Dean and Chapter of Hereford Cathedral. Discharges from all penalties certain members of their chapter, who have lately presented Lawrence Williams to the church of Norton Cannon, co. Hereford, contrary to the local statutes of the church, which forbid presentations except at general meetings of the chapter. [*Ent. Book* 19, *p.* 33.]

[March 6.] 52. Draft of the above.

March 6. Warrant to Sir John Robinson to release Capt. Robert Holmes. [*Ent. Book* 22, *p.* 45.]

March 6. Warrant for a grant to James Earl of Suffolk of a pension of 1,000*l.* a year, as gentleman of the bedchamber. [*Ent. Book* 22, *p.* 47.]

VOL. CXIV.

1664–5.

March 6. Whitehall. Warrant to the Keeper of Newgate to deliver up [Jean] Le Court to James Bridgman, to be transported in 14 days, and not to return, on pain of the execution of the sentence of death against him. [*Ent. Book* 22, *p.* 47.]

[March 6.] 53. [Rob. Southwell] to Williamson. He is to draw up a letter from the King to the Commissioners of Prizes, stating that whatever may be the decision of the Court of Admiralty, they are to discharge without trouble or delay some French wines, which John Quesnall of Legborn laded for Holland, as steward to M. De Turenne.

March 6. Whitehall. 54. Warrant to the Commissioners of Prizes to restore to John Quesnall, of Lisbon, certain French wines, laden by him as steward to the Marshal De Turenne; he has a suit pending about them in the Admiralty Court, from which he is to be discharged, as a mark of the King's esteem for the said Marshal.

March 6. Entry of the above. [*Ent. Book* 22, *p.* 49.]

March ? 55. Petition of Anthony Choqueux to the King, for his board wages from the Greencloth, or for reference to Council of the case between him and Mr. Pierce. Was employed in 1634, on advice of Sir Theodore Mayerne, to attend the King's servants and others in London, wherein he had great success; served the late King by sea and land; in 1642, was commanded to attend Prince Rupert as surgeon, and in 1643, sworn surgeon in ordinary, but has not yet succeeded to pay and board wages; a report has been spread to his prejudice that he has turned merchant, and Mr. Pierce has applied for reception of board wages.

March 6. Whitehall. Warrant to pay to Ant. De Choqueux, surgeon in ordinary, 883*l.* 12*s.*, in discharge of so much due to him from the late King for services. Minute. [*Ent. Book* 22, *p.* 51.]

[March 6.] 56. Draft of the above.

March 6. Warrant for a grant to Ant. De Choqueux of the place of King's Surgeon in ordinary, salary 60*l.* a year, to begin from 1661. Minute. [*Ent. Book* 22, *p.* 52.]

March ? 57. Sir Allan Apsley to Williamson. Requests him to remind Mr. Secretary of warrants for Rich. Swift to be falconer in place of Hugh Wright; Lord Herbert to preserve the game within 12 miles of Ramsbury, Wiltshire, and Lord St. John within 12 miles of Bolton Castle, Yorkshire.

March 6. Warrant for a grant to Richard Swift of the office of Falconer in ordinary, in place of Hugh Wright, deceased; fee, 13*l.* 13*s.* 9½*d.* a year, and 2*s.* a day. Minute. [*Ent. Book* 22, *p.* 52.]

March 6. Whitehall. 58. Warrant to Lord St. John to preserve the game within 12 miles of Bolton Castle, Yorkshire.

March 6. Minute of the above. [*Ent. Book* 22, *p.* 53.]

Vol. CXIV.

1664–5.

March 6. Whitehall. 59. Warrant to Henry Lord Herbert to preserve the game within 12 miles of Ramsbury, Wiltshire.

March 6. Minute of the above. [*Ent. Book* 22, *p.* 53.]

March 6. 60. Minutes of the above three warrants and of one to Sir George Stowell to preserve game.

[March 6.] Pass for Monsieur Girault to France. Minute. [*Ent. Book* 22, *p.* 53.]

March 6. Warrant for a grant to Charles Viscount Fitzharding of the title of Earl of Falmouth, co. Devon, and Baron Botetort of Langport; with the usual fee of 20*l.* a year for better support of his dignity. [*Ent. Book* 22, *p.* 55.]

March 6. Whitehall. 61. Warrant for a grant to Sir Henry Bennet of the title of Lord Bennet of Arlington, co. Middlesex.

March 8. Entry of the above, giving the title as Lord Cheney. [*Ent. Book* 22, *p.* 55.]

March 6/16. Chelsea. Amb. Van Goch to [the States General]. On Saturday last, the King's declaration [of war] was solemnly proclaimed. Two heralds in their coats of arms, with four mace-bearers, nine trumpeters, and two troops of horse, assembled at Westminster, where the trumpet sounded, and the declaration was read with great shouting and rejoicing of the people; thence they went to Temple Bar, where the Lord Mayor and aldermen, in scarlet gowns on horseback, conducted them to Temple Gate, over against Chancery Lane, where it was read with more acclamation than before, the Horse Guards drawing their swords and clattering them; then again in Cheapside and before the Royal Exchange, with great demonstration of joy and sounding of trumpets; after which many nobles of the Court came into the City, to dine with the Lord Mayor. Nine prizes have been sold, but after all deductions, out of three ships and their ladings, only 27*l.* came into the Exchequer. [*Holl. Corresp., March* 6, 1665.]

March 6. Reference to Sir Henry De Vic, chancellor of the order of the Garter, on the petition of Capt. Edm. Barber, for a Poor Knight's place in Windsor. [*Ent. Book* 18, *p.* 131.]

March 6. Whitehall. Proclamation enforcing the late Act for regulating the measures and prices of coals, whereby, to prevent deceits, all sea coals are to be sold by the chaldron of 36 bushels, according to a bushel kept at Guildhall, and those sold by weight at 112 lbs. the cwt.; the prices to be set by the Lord Mayor and justices of peace for London; offenders to pay double the value, half to the informer, and half for repair of highways; and a report of proceedings therein to be made to Council. [*Printed. Proc. Coll., p.* 180.]

[March 6.] 62. Draft of the above. [*Two sheets.*]

March 6. Whitehall. Proclamation ordering a general fast on April 5, to pray for the success of the naval forces set out to vindicate the rights of the

VOL. CXIV.

1664–5.

kingdom from the injuries of the Dutch, for which a public form of prayer is to be prepared. [*Printed. Proc. Coll., p.* 180.]

March 6. 63. James Hickes to Williamson. Hopes Col. Frowde has given him satisfaction about the differences between Mr. Watts and Mr. Lodge. A man's actions should have credit as his truth and honesty deserve. *Encloses,*

63. I. *Mor. Lodge to James Hickes. Hears that Mr. Watts has complained of him to Mr. Williamson. Watts falsely accused him of neglect and of detaining his letters, &c., and spoke so abusively that he turned him out of the office. Suffered much for loyalty, and had his estate sequestered, whilst Watts, who now tries to brand him, was a sequestrator's clerk.* *Deal, March* 1, 1665.

March 6. Deal. 64. Ri. Watts to Williamson. The supposed Dutch ship was forced into the Downs in a storm; arrival of several vessels. The Katherine, a richly-laden merchant ship, bound for the Straits, has run aground near the North Foreland.

March 6. Portsmouth. 65. Deposition of Denis Bossinet, before Sir Hum. Bennet, justice of peace for Hampshire. The Lieutenant of the Ruby frigate took from the Thomas and the George, both of St. Malo, indigo, logwood, and soap, value, 5,000 or 6,000 livres.

[March 6.] 66. Complaint by Denis Bossinet to the King, against the Lieutenant of the Ruby, detailing particulars of the taking of the aforesaid goods. [*French.*]

March 6. 67. Attorney General Palmer to the King. Sends a Commission for Appeals in cases of prizes, as ordered by Council. [*Copy.*] *Prefixing.*

67. I. *Commission to John Lord Robartes, the Dukes of Buckingham and Ormond, and ten others, to act as Judges or Commissioners of Appeal, in cases of prizes taken by letters of marque, on which the party against whom sentence is given in the Admiralty Court may desire to appeal.* [*Three pages.*]

[March 6.] 68. Detailed narrative, by Major Rob. Holmes, of his proceedings against the Dutch in his late expedition to Guinea; to the same effect as that given in his examination of March 3, but much fuller. [*Copy. Twelve and a half pages. Read in Council, March* 6, 1665.]

March 6. Essex House. 69. Memoranda relating to sums agreed to be paid to the Earl of Sandwich, for his journey to Portugal, &c., a privy seal to be drawn out for the whole sum, but not specifying that any part is to be for interest.

March 7. Newcastle. 70. Rich. Forster to James Hickes. In the impress of seamen, the mayor, Sir Ralph Delavale, and others agreed to make volunteers of Capt. John Wetwyng's pressmasters, who knowing the haunts of most of the seamen of the town, managed so well that almost as great a number of volunteers and pressed men will be

Q 2

Vol. CXIV.

1664–5.

returned as will be had out of Scotland; as none can escape the pressmasters, many come in as volunteers because they will not be pressed; there are hundreds of stout young keel and barge men who could do good service, and hundreds would go volunteers, if they may be employed.

[March 7.] 71. Memorandum to obtain and send to Mat. Anderton, of Chester, a warrant for the Earl of Arran to export 30 horses to Ireland, for the officers of the King's regiment of Guards.

March 7. Pass for 30 horses to Ireland for Lord Arran. Minute. [*Ent. Book* 22, *p.* 47.]

March 7. Sec. Bennet to the Lord Chief Justice. There being now several ships in the Thames bound for the plantations, the King, wishing to repress the more than ordinary insolence of Quakers and other sectaries, orders that those condemned to transportation be sent off in those ships. Is attending His Majesty to Portsmouth, and therefore his lordship must communicate with his fellow secretary, if there should be occasion. [*Ent. Book* 22, *p.* 48.]

March 7. Royal Charles. 72. Sir Wm. Coventry to Sec. Bennet. Expects that Capt. Smith, with his ships, is now in the Downs, where the Duke has ordered him to remain; other ships are also sailing, so that a good body of the fleet will soon be together, sufficient to make good that station against any fleet the Dutch now have together. One of the Smyrna ships has run aground entering the Downs, and is in great danger. A vessel, supposed to be one for the Barbadoes, has blown up below the Hope. Dutch letters give good hopes that we shall be earlier than they; God send it.

March 7. Grant to Fras. White, born in France, of denization, with all usual liberties, &c. [*Docquet.*]

March 7. Westminster. Passport for Hen. Boyle, second son of Roger Earl of Orrery, returning abroad to prosecute his studies. [*Latin. Foreign Ent. Book*, *No.* 11, *p.* 63.]

March 7. Dover. 73. Thos. Wale to the Navy Commrs. The storehouses which were used as the magazine in the late war are to be let; Mr. Gauden's agent is in hand to take them for laying provisions in; they ought to be secured by the Commissioners. Particulars of ships. [*Adm. Paper.*]

March 7. 74. Robert Magors, purveyor, to the Navy Commrs. Particulars of timber marked out by him in the wharfs westward, fit for shipbuilding. [*Adm. Paper.*]

March 7. Harwich. 75. Anthony Deane to the Navy Commrs. Cannot spare any small masts. Repairs of ships. The convoys for the northern fleet came into harbour last night. [*Adm. Paper.*]

March 8. Woolwich Ropeyard. 76. Memorandum by the Clerk of the Ropeyard of the want of laying places for cordage in the yard; with proposition to use Mr. Clothier's ground in the warren. [*Adm. Paper.*]

VOL. CXIV.

1664–5.

March 8. Garland, Harwich. 77. Capt. Charles Talbot to Sam. Pepys. Desires tickets for his three servants, discharged from the Golden Lion. [*Adm. Paper.*]

March 8. Dover. 78. Thos. Wale to the Navy Comrs. The Paradox and Little Gift will set sail to-morrow. The gunner at Capt. Daniel's fort demands 3*d*. a barrel for handling the powder to be stowed there in and out of the waggon, and 3*d*. a barrel for carriage. [*Adm. Paper.*]

March 8. The Mary, Downs. 79. Capt. Jer. Smith to Sam. Pepys. Desires 300 printed tickets for men discharged from the Mary into other ships. [*Adm. Paper.*]

March 8. Woolwich. 80. Chris. Pett to the Navy Comrs. Estimate of ironwork on board the Royal Katherine; total, 38*l*. 0*s*. 6*d*. [*Adm. Paper.*]

March 8. 81. Sir Wm. Coventry to Sam. Pepys. Orders must be sent to Harwich for supplies and victuals to be dispatched to the ships in the Hope. [*Adm. Paper.*] *Encloses*,

81. I. *Capt. Henry Hyde to [Sir] Wm. Coventry. Stores wanted for repairs of his ship, the Sapphire. Harwich, March 7.*

March 8. Chatham Dock. 82. Phin. Pett to the Navy Comrs. Particulars of ships. Compass timber wanted; if not speedily supplied, the shipwrights and calkers may be discharged. [*Adm. Paper.*]

March 8. Grant to Willm. Langham of the Manor of Walgrave, co. Northampton, and other lands lately conveyed by John Browne to Sir John Langham his father. [*Docquet.*]

March 8. Grant to Edw. Gregory, jun., on surrender of Edw. Gregory, sen., of the office of Clerk of the Prick and Cheque of the navy provisions and stores at Chatham; fee, 40*l*. a year. [*Docquet.*]

March 8. Warrant for Jean De la Court to be transported beyond seas, within 14 days. Minute. [*Ent. Book 22, p. 47.*]

March 8. 83. Decree of the High Court of Admiralty, that the Dutch ship Abraham's Sacrifice, Garret Hendrick Rapier master,—seized by the King's ship Oxford, and brought into Dartmouth by virtue of His Majesty's letters of reprisal,—is lawful prize. [*Latin, copy, three pages.*]

March 8. Dover. 84. Jo. Carlisle to Williamson. The brave ship London has blown up near the Hope, only the hull and stern left. Was sent by Sir Edward Massey, a Commissioner, to take the sails and ropes off a small vessel from Bayonne, pretended to be of Nieuport, but there were five Dutchmen on board, who are sent prisoners to the castle. Refused to allow the Customs' officers to fasten the warehouse doors where the sails and ropes are kept, as these things pay no custom; else would give nothing for the office of warehouse keeper.

March 8. Hereford. 85. Ar. Trevor to Williamson. There is foul weather and foul work among the younger sons of the law, who are come to a hog-

VOL. CXIV.

1664-5.

shearing, and help to make up the cry with the pigs. The fifth form have a weary occupation, and if St. Francis of Assisi were there, he would need all his patience and that of his capuchins.

March 8. London. 86. Geo. Evans to Williamson. Thanks for his kindness to Mr. Gregory about Cambridge. Asks assistance for a lady in her business at Court.

March 8. Portsmouth. 87. Robt. Lye to Williamson. Sec. [Bennet] has arrived, and wishes Williamson with his own hands to deliver to foreign ambassadors the King's declaration about the Dutch war, that they may have no pretence for not taking notice of it. The place is cold and unwholesome. The King has that day gone on board four ships, and found all in good condition and well manned, but wanting in numbers. His Majesty sails to-morrow if the bad weather permit. Mr. Secretary wishes to take precedence of Col. Frescheville, but hesitates whether to choose for his title Colbrooke, Lymington, or Paddington; he prefers the first, and unless Sir Edw. Walker says it is taken up, wishes it to be inserted. [*Two pages.*]

March 9. 88. Statement by Sir Edw. Walker, [Garter king-at-arms,] that Sec. Bennet being most nobly descended, on the mother's side, from several Earls' families, might take the name of one of them, as Bradston, or Ingoldsthorp; the titles of St. Amand and Dunsmore are void; or he might take one from some place in his possession, as Dawley, his father's house, or be baron of the place near Andover where he received his honourable star, if it have a good termination. [*One and a half pages.*]

March 8. 89. John Ironmonger to Sir Thos. Gower. Those abroad promise great things, and are glad to have their designs attempted at other people's hazard, yet promise to come also. They say 600 or 700 could take Newcastle. The chief agitators, Atkinson, Marsden, and others are in London, about Shoreditch and Wapping, and are written to under feigned names, altered every month. Women are employed about letters, which are sent for Lady Danvers, to be communicated to Lady Vane. All the monied men there are to send their moneys beyond seas, as is done in London; if any alarm is given, they will never be caught. There are practices at Dublin also. The governors of Holland fear lest the Prince of Orange should withdraw himself from their power: they have spies on him, but dare not do more for fear of the people. Many old officers in the North have better horses than the cavaliers.

March 9. Coffee House. 90. ——— ——— to Sec. Bennet. The selling of places makes men steal to raise their money. The blowing up of the London was caused by chapmen selling powder 20s. a barrel cheaper than in London. The Hollanders call the King's proclamation damnable, devilish, and such like, and are raising an army of 30,000 men. A Dutch man-of-war has taken two small Scotch ships. On reading the Order in Council for suspending the Act of Navigation, a Commonwealth man said it should have been done by privately warning the

VOL. CXIV.

1664–5.

merchants, for it looked as though we feared the Dutch, since the last war was wholly on the Act of Navigation and might discourage the seamen, that Act being for their benefit; but it was replied that the cases were different, and the seamen would now have better pay than the merchants gave before the expedition. The Dutch lord who made the match between the Prince of Orange and the late King's daughter said he wondered they would print so dirty a reply to the King of England's ambassador, for in abusing his person, they abused His Majesty; they say the King is their enemy, and defend their News-book. There is a rumour in the City that the aldermen and several companies will build the King a ship, to be called the London, and that another regiment of foot is to be raised and sent into Ireland.

March 9. Cambridge. 91. Rich. Bower to Williamson. Is coming to town to see Mr. Muddiman. One has died at Cambridge of the plague. The pressed men ordered on board by Sir Thos. Meadowes complained that their meat was black and stunk.

March 9. Deal. 92. Ri. Watts to Williamson. The fleet and merchant ships are still in the Downs. The Forester has sent in a prize to Margate, laden with butter, hides, &c.

March 9. Portsmouth. 93. Wm. Godolphin to Williamson. He is to give the King's declaration to the hands of foreign ambassadors, and send it to all the consuls abroad, to publish in their respective ports. Sec. Bennet will not have his own name in his title, to avoid any appearance of evil in his future lady, Lady Bennet being of too famous reputation in the world. He has considered almost all places, Falmouth, Paddington, and Colebrooke; he prefers the latter, if not already bestowed. The King has but a small train, to the shame of the nobility who will not be at the expense of following him. He is much pleased with the new frigate built at Portsmouth, the Royal Oak, and has ordered Tippetts, the shipwright who built her, to build just such another, and not to mend her in any part, being assured that anything which is not just so, cannot be so good; these were his very words. He is delighted with his entertainment among the ships. [*Four pages.*]

March 9. Henrietta. Portsmouth Harbour. Warrant to Sir George Ayscue to sail with all the King's ships now ready in Portsmouth harbour and in Spithead to the Downs, and there to remain till further orders. [*Ent. Book* 22, p. 33.]

March 9. Portsmouth. Order to the Captain and Lieutenant of the Ruby frigate to restore some chests of indigo, logwood, and other merchandise, belonging to Denis Bossinet, merchant of St. Malo, and taken by him from two St. Malo vessels, though knowing them to be French. [*Ent. Book* 22, p. 31.]

March 9. London. Levant Company to Capt. Bradenham. Are glad that his ship is got off and fit to proceed on her voyage, and receive the goods which were unladen. He is to go with Capt. Chamblet to Plymouth, where they will find the convoy ready. [*Levant Papers, Vol.* v., p. 106.]

Vol. CXIV.

1664–5.

March 9. Warrant to pay to Sir Phil. Musgrave, Bart., 282*l.* 2*s.* a month, for the forces of the garrison at Carlisle, and 71*l.* 17*s.* 4*d.*, due for their arrears from 23 June to 20 Nov., when the new establishment began. [*Docquet.*]

March 9. Portsmouth. Commission to Capt. Willm. Barker to be Captain of a company of foot in Col. Russell's regiment of Guards. [*Ent. Book* 20, *p.* 21.]

March 9. 94. Account by Capt. John Fortescue of the condition of 10 merchant ships in the Thames. [*Adm. Paper, two and a half pages.*]

March 9. 95. Thos. Lewis to Sam. Pepys. Cannot give the Dartmouth a supply a victuals at Dawpool, Mr. Gauden being at Portsmouth. [*Adm. Paper.*]

March 9. 96. Lambert Wood to Sam. Pepys. Requests an order for one month's provision for the Sarah pink, his being consumed by pressed men received on board and discharged. [*Adm. Paper.*]

March. 9. Harwich. 97. Anthony Deane to Sam. Pepys. Complains of the disorder occasioned by men going on shore, notwithstanding a warrant to the contrary; some course must be taken that the taverns do not entertain them, or a severe check put upon them. Danger to the Sapphire during her repairs, from neglect of the men. [*Adm. Paper.*]

March 9. Whitehall. 98. Rob. Southwell to [Sec. Bennet]. Sends him an account of what passed before the Lords Commissioners yesterday. Has received the Duke's answer to them, about regulating the disorders of seamen, and the draft of an order proposed to be printed and set up in the ships to caution the men; wishes it may not breed discontent among them. Laments the great loss of the London.

March 10. 99. Capt. John Taylor to [the Navy Comrs.] Arrival of the Blackcock from New England, laden with great masts. Offers to convey them direct to Chatham, where they are most wanted, if extra costs be allowed him. [*Adm. Paper.*]

March 10. Chatham Dock. 100. Phin. Pett to the Navy Comrs. Repairs of ships. Has sent to enquire what quantity of compass timber can be had in those parts. [*Adm. Paper.*]

March 10. Margate. 101. Joh. Smith to Williamson. The master of the Rotterdam vessel has gone to London, to get clear if he can. There is a vessel in Sandwich not yet stayed, which some will swear to be a Zealander. No Dutch frigates come near, the King's ships being always on the look out. A New England ship has arrived with masts for the service. A Smyrna merchant ship was aground, but has got off again.

March 10. Plymouth. 102. Da. Grosse to Williamson. Account of ships at anchor; Lord Belasyse has arrived, and is preparing his equipage, awaiting the Straits' fleet. Sir John Skelton, deputy governor of Plymouth, has arrived, being met six miles off by the most eminent persons of

1664–5. Vol. CXIV.

the town. A ship of St. Malo, pretending to be French, has been brought in, and the master and others imprisoned, because counterfeit seals of the King and Duke of York were found on board.

March 10. Lower Dillam. 103. James Hickes to Williamson. It is resolved to make an example of Mr. Watts, because five sea captains complained that neither the Mayor of Deal nor any of the 12 chief magistrates, of whom Watts was one, would help them in pressing several men who had absented themselves, and Watts denied their power to press them.

March 10. Rotterdam. 104. ——— to Henry Smith [Sec. Bennet?]. Will do all the service in his power. Finds eight men-of-war at Helvoetsluys and seven in the Maes, whose names he sends; they are building two others, and making fly boats into fire-ships. The prizes have been sent in, one from Bourdeaux bound for Aberdeen; one from Leith for Rouen, laden with salmon, herrings, tallow, and butter; one for Newcastle for coals. The prisoners are brought to prison, chained two together, none suffered to go near them, kept on bread and cheese, and allowed neither fire nor candle. Amsterdam furnishes 60 ships and the East India Company 20, all manned with young resolute men, of whom they have such abundance that they pick out the best, and pay them only 12 guilders a month. The Provinces are well united and earnest in the war, and think they can fight much better than the English. The prohibition of commerce and of the Greenland fleet and herring fishery gives them 30,000 men. The commonalty are enraged with the King for stealing their ships and goods, as they say, without declaring war first; but they blame most the Lord Chancellor, the Duke of York, Sir George Downing, and Sir Wm. Davidson; they say the Lord Chancellor wants to set the Duke of York on the throne. The English in Holland are very cruel and disaffected towards the King. Sir John Webster of Amsterdam reports having heard from a privy councillor that His Majesty is willing for some accommodation for a treaty of peace; he was answered that the fit persons to be entrusted were the envoy Van Goch in England, and Sir George Downing at the Hague. The States General have issued proclamations forbidding the import of English goods, on pain of confiscation and fine, warning foreign nations to receive no English commissions against the Dutch, on pain of being judged pirates and punished with death, if taken, and forbidding the Greenland fleet to go forth. Account of Dutch ships at Helvoetsluys and the Maes. [*Three pages.*]

March 18. Chelsea. Amb. Van Goch to [the States General]. The King went on Tuesday to Portsmouth, to view the fortifications and hasten the ships, and has not returned. The Duke of York is recovered and will soon go to Deal; it is believed he will go out with the fleet; the Duchess goes with him and has taken a country house near, so as to be at hand to receive news of him during the expedition. The London, prepared for Vice-Admiral Lawson, was blown up whilst sailing up the river, and only 19 out of the crew of 3?1 saved. Capt. Allin is returning with 12 ships of war, 5 prizes and 50 mer-

VOL. CXIV.

1664–5.

chantmen, and sends word that he has men enough to man 12 other ships of war. Capt. Holmes is released, having satisfied the Council about his expedition to Guinea. [*Copy, Holl. Corresp., March* 10, 1665.]

March 10. Bristol. 105. Sir George Norton and five other Deputy Lieutenants of Bristol to the Duke of Ormond, Lord Lieutenant [of Somersetshire]. Have consulted with the militia officers, and find the provision made in the Militia Act, of one fourth of the monthly contribution for the charge of drummers and serjeants, is not a sixth part of the necessary charges. Beg his influence to obtain for the officers the whole contribution for last year, now in the hands of the late sheriffs.

March 10. 106. Sir W. Coventry to [Williamson]. Sends for Sir Gilb. Talbot two blank commissions for private men-of-war, with copies of the security usually given.

March 11. Edinburgh. 107. Rob. Mein to Hen. Muddiman. Lord Ballantyne, deputy treasurer of Scotland, has left for London. The other 500 seamen are appointed to be in readiness against the convoys come down with the Scots' fleet now in England, that they may return in those vessels. A Dundee ship has been taken and carried into Flushing. The country will be undone for want of trade. There have been great storms of snow, so that it is impossible to travel.

March 11. 108. Capt. Robt. Turner to Thos. Hayter. Wants tickets, and an order to enter men on board the Francis. [*Adm. Paper.*]

March 11. Ollerton. 109. Thos. Corbin to the Navy Comrs. Wants a warrant to the Justices for the speedy conveyance of timber; a good deal will be fit for carriage before what is already at Hawtry is taken away. Begs an order for Mr. Russell to pay him the 50*l.*, disbursed for carriage of timber, beyond the money received. [*Adm. Paper.*]

March 11. The Prince. 110. Capt. Roger Cuttance to the Navy Comrs. Requests stores for the Prince, which are not to be had at Chatham. The Eagle is arrived with 89 pressed men, to be disposed of among the ships in the Hope. [*Adm. Paper.*]

March 11. 111. Sir Wm. Coventry to Sam. Pepys. Complains that the delay at Harwich, by having to wait for orders before any stores can be delivered, causes the running away of seamen. Some other method must be adopted, even though loss attend it; "dispatch is now above all." Particulars of stores. Asks whether Mr. Creed will retain the muster-master's place. There are sufficient ships for Tangiers, without Col. Atkin's demand, 11 being licensed since 23 December. He wanted to engross the 1,500 chaldrons of coal, on pretext of Tangiers; fears some private interest. [*Adm. Paper, two pages.*]

March 11. 112. Capt. John Taylor to the Navy Comrs. Has with vast charge and hazard brought in his ship, laden with 32 New England masts. Requests a warrant that they may be received at Chatham. [*Adm. Paper.*]

VOL. CXIV.

1664–5.

March 11. 113. Giles Bond to the Navy Comrs. The Harwich hoy is ready to sail, and awaits orders. There are sails at Deptford to be transported to Harwich. [*Adm. Paper.*]

March 12. Portsmouth. 114. Commissioner Thos. Middleton to Sir Wm. Penn. Requests payment of 87*l.* 10*s.*, his salary for four months at 350*l.* a year, and of 15*l.* incidental expenses; total, 102*l.* 10*s.* Also his clerk's salary at 30*l.* a year. [*Adm. Paper, two pages.*]

March 12. Deal. 115. Thos. Wale to the Navy Comrs. Particulars of boats. Repairs of the Dreadnought. [*Adm. Paper.*]

March 12. 116. Sir Wm. Coventry to Sam. Pepys. Asks whether there be flags, pendants, and ensigns sufficient, and what is done for lodging stores at Dover and Hull. Requests an immediate order to Capt. Fortescue to get the arms returned to Sir Chichester Wray. Some one must be sent down to take account of all ships below Woolwich, as far as the Hope, as to what men, victuals, and stores are on board. [*Adm. Paper.*]

March 12. Portsmouth. 117. Commissioner Thos. Middleton to [Sam. Pepys]. Will be glad to see the description of the careening wheel. Promises to send a copy of the oath taken before the mayor and magistrates, concerning the embezzled cordage. Begs that some one else may be appointed to prosecute it; cannot prosecute a man to death for theft, even against himself. Has cautioned the ropemakers against buying anything that has been the King's. The merchant ships shall be graved next spring tide. Particulars of stores and timber. Has acquainted the King with abuses in pressing, and by His Majesty's orders, discharged some men, and written to the press-masters to send more and better, on penalty of being sent to London, and thence to Tyburn themselves. Begs that the boatsman of the yard may not be dismissed; he is better than ten other men, and well acquainted with his business. Has bought a parcel of English hemp at 3*l*s. per cwt. Recommends Jacob Bryan for some employment, and two men as masters of the galliot prizes to be fitted out for carrying stone from Portland. [*Adm. Paper, four pages.*]

March 12. Hull. 118. Luke Whittington to James Hickes. The London fleet is still detained by the easterly winds. Hopes the Hollanders have been forced from the coast, that it may sail safely.

March 12. Plymouth. 119. Lord Belasyse to Williamson. Will obey the Duke's commands in waiting for the Smyrna merchant ships, but waits with impatience away from [Tangiers] a place where his service is so much required.

March 13. Dorchester. 120. John Cole to [Williamson]. Capt. Seymour, of the Pearl, has brought into Portland Road three prizes, laden with wine and brandy, part of the Holland fleet of 30 sail from Bourdeaux, now come into the Channel. They are manned with half French, and all have French colours. Many French privateers are setting out with Dutch commissions. Some Anabaptists were surprised, at their meeting at Fordington, a parish near, and carried before a justice.

VOL. CXIV.

1664-5.

March 13. Deal. 121. Ri. Watts to Williamson. Three more prizes have been sent into the Downs; three French vessels and an Ostender came in.

March 13. 122. Duke of Albemarle to Sir George Carteret, navy treasurer. Orders him to pay 600*l.* to Lieut. Godfrey Dennis, appointed to conduct 600 soldiers from Ireland to Bristol, for their maintainance for a month, allowing each soldier 8*d.* a day, and the serjeants and corporals accordingly.

March 13. Portsmouth. 123. Commissioner Thos. Middleton to Sam. Pepys. Great embezzlements are carried on under the name of perquisites. Is much troubled at the loss of the London; 40 calkers and 20 axemen may be discharged. [*Adm. Paper.*]

March 13. Dover. 124. Thos. Walo to the Navy Comrs. Wants a mizen-yard for the Dreadnought, and a main-yard for the Assurance. [*Adm. Paper.*]

March 13. Forest of Dean. 125. Dan. Furzer to the Navy Comrs. Sends an estimate for fitting the forge with a blast, &c.; total, 45*l.* 3*s.* The smith will undertake the biggest anchors at the lowest rates he can; a workman fit to be his assistant will deserve 15*s.* per week. Asks orders about iron offered to be served in by several poor men. [*Adm. Paper, two pages.*]

March 13. 126. Sir Wm. Coventry to Sam. Pepys. The captain of the Fox has received no order to fit out. Sir John Knight has taken up the George of Bristol, to carry 20 pieces of ordnance; she must be well victualled, and have a good complement of men; it will be a way to get volunteers entered for service in that sea, and being thus trapanned, they may be used other ways. Wishes clerks to be sent to take an exact muster of the fleet in the Downs, before the arrival of the Duke of York. [*Adm. Paper.*]

March 13. 127. Report of the state of 17 ships now in the river, as to their number of men, stores, victuals, &c. [*Adm. Paper, three and a half pages.*]

March 14. The Lily, Harwich. 128. Capt. Amos Beare to the Navy Comrs. Begs a new boat in lieu of one lost in a storm. [*Adm. Paper.*]

March 14. Harwich. 129. Anthony Deane to the Navy Comrs. Progress of the new ship. Purchase of timber. Wants money, for nobody will come up to London to be paid. [*Adm. Paper.*]

March 14. 130. J. Sotherne to Thos. Hayter. A copy of the bond usually given to pursers, and some blank warrants for officers are to be sent to Sir John Knight, at Bristol. [*Adm. Paper.*]

March 14. Warrant for creating Richard Earl of Cork an Earl of England, by the name of Earl of Burlington, *alias* Bridlington, co. York. Minute. [*Ent. Book* 22, *p.* 59.]

VOL. CXIV.

1664–5.

March 14. The Dartmouth, Liverpool, Chester Water. 131. Capt. Rich. Rooth to the Navy Comrs. As Mr. Gauden could not procure provisions, has set brewers and bakers of the place to work, to supply two months' victuals for 120 men. They will be at as easy, if not cheaper, rate than the victuallers would have done it. Has only received 90 instead of the 330 pressed men ordered in Cheshire, Lancashire, and North Wales; 100 more men were sent, but being taken from the plough or from trades, he sent them back. The number cannot be completed till the shipping, which is expected with the first westerly wind, arrives. [*Adm. Paper.*]

March 14. Newcastle. 132. Rich. Forster to James Hickes. There are 300 and more young lusty fellows from Newcastle or Gateshead, volunteers or pressed men, longing for the convoy to come, that they may get to the fleet and to service; never saw men promise more courage. No news of the Dutch on the coasts.

March 15. Dover. 133. J[ohn] C[arlisle] to Williamson. Taking of three more prizes; 5,000 soldiers have come to Calais, to guard their coasts, and it is said that the French will soon have 50 sail of ships on the Narrow Seas. The States of Holland have set out a book showing how the King has broken his promise with them, and are high in their threats. Between the Prize Commissioners and the Customs' officers, none of the goods landed are given up, which is a great loss to the King.

March 15. 134. Rich. Bower to [Williamson]. Two Yarmouth vessels going for London, with two ketches, were taken near Aldborough by a Dutch man-of-war. [*Imperfect.*]

March 15. Whitehall. 135. Order in Council, that the late proclamation about foreign trade and commerce shall not be understood to hinder trade between England and Ireland and the King's islands in Europe, and that notice be sent to the officers of the several ports accordingly.

March 15. Whitehall. 136. Order in Council,—on complaint of the Levant Company, that Thos. Stanton and Hawly Bishop, two of their factors at Aleppo, have fled away with great sums of money belonging to the Turks, to the scandal of the English and danger of their trade,—that letters be sent to the Great Duke of Tuscany and Republic of Venice, requesting them to secure the said persons, should they come into their territories.

March 15. Yarmouth. 137. News letter. Two frigates are in chase of a Dutch caper. Several Holland private men-of-war are abroad. The proclamation touching the Holland war was proclaimed at Yarmouth in the ordinary manner, not with the solemnity used in other places.

March 15. Pass for six horses for Sir Nich. Armorer to Ireland. Minute. [*Ent. Book* 22, *p.* 58.]

March 15. Whitehall. Proclamation prohibiting the import or retailing of any commodities of the growth or manufacture of the United Provinces, they having prohibited all English goods. Printed. [*Proc. Coll., Charles II.*, p. 181.]

Vol. CXIV.

1664–5.

March 15. 138. Certificate by Abraham Ansley, that the Mereland merchant ship is now riding in Plymouth Sound. [*Adm. Paper.*]

March 15. Chatham Roperyard. 139. John Owen to Sir Wm. Batten. Has but 100 tons of hemp in store, which will be spent in six weeks' time. Requests a supply. [*Adm. Paper.*]

March 15. Woolwich. 140. Wm. Bodham to the Navy Comrs. Complains of the insolence of John Clark, shipwright in the dock, who, having endangered the ropeyard wall by digging in his garden close under its foundation, refuses to allow the repairing of it, threatening to arrest all workmen who come upon his ground. Advises that he be suspended from his employment till he is more compliant, and his wages stopped towards repair of the damage. [*Adm. Paper.*]

March 15. The Pearl, The Hope. 141. Capt. Peter Foote to [Sir] Wm. Coventry. Cannot sail before to-morrow night, on account of want of men and stores; 12 of his best men are gone to press seamen. [*Adm. Paper.*]

March 15. 142. Sir Wm. Coventry to Sam. Pepys. A mizen mast and yard must be sent to the Dreadnought in the Downs, and stores hastened to Dover. [*Adm. Paper.*]

March 15. 143. John Uthwayt to the Navy Comrs. Survey of cordage, junk, &c., at the Tower. [*Adm. Paper.*]

Vol. CXV. March 16–23, 1664–5.

1664–5.

March 16. 1. Jonas Shish to the Navy Comrs. Wants canvas and timber for the new ship. [*Adm. Paper.*]

March 16. Dover. 2. Thos. White to Sam. Pepys. Begs for some employment in the navy. [*Adm. Paper.*] *Encloses,*

2. I. *Certificate by Nich. Eaton, mayor, and Wm. Eaton, George West, and Rich. Barley, jurats of Dover, recommending Thos. White, for many years master of attendance at that port, as still fit for that employment.*
Dover, March 10 1665.

March 16. 3. Sir Wm. Coventry to Sam. Pepys. The Royal Katherine is to be unstowed and iron ballast put in her, and vessels and all other helps imaginable dispatched for it forthwith. [*Adm. Paper.*]

March 16. 4. Sir Wm. Coventry to Sam. Pepys. Offers free use of the lodgings fallen to him upon Lord Berkeley's leaving the office, to any of the commissioners or persons employed by them in this time of haste, until his return. Will change lodgings with Sir John Mennes, if he prefer it. [*Adm. Paper.*]

Vol. CXV.

1664–5.

March 16. 5. Sir Wm. Coventry to Sam. Pepys. The increase of men demanded for the Harp is reasonable, and the supply of stores necessary. Wants the names of the vessels lying on the river to receive men, that they may not be disturbed. [*Adm. Paper.*]

March 16. 6. Sir Wm. Warren to the Navy Comrs. Finds it difficult to hire ships to fetch the masts from Gottenburg which he bought for the King's service. Will pay the freight of a ship sent for them at the usual rate in times of peace, if they will hire the ship and run the risk at sea. [*Adm. Paper.*]

March 16. Harwich. 7. Anthony Deane to the Navy Comrs. Sends a draft of the careening engine. Has pressed 33 shipwrights at or near Ipswich. Purchase of timber. Desires two men to look after the lighters. [*Adm. Paper.*]

March 16. Harwich. 8. John Browne to the Navy Comrs. Sends Mr. Johnson's bill for cordage, and a certificate of the defects in Sir Wm. Warren's Gottenburg masts. [*Adm. Paper.*]

March 16. Victualling Office. 9. Denis Gauden to the Navy Comrs. Is ordered to supply every ship of the fleet with four months' provisions, computed from the last of March, and another two months' by the end of May. Begs directions about delivering oatmeal in lieu of one day's fish in a week. [*Adm. Paper.*]

March 16. Cockpit. 10. Petition of Abraham Robotham to the Duke of Albemarle, for the command of a frigate or victualler. Served in the Henry last summer, and was owner of a merchantman for many years. With note by the Duke, recommending the petitioner to the Navy Commissioners. [*Adm. Paper.*]

March 16. 11. Chris. Pett to [the Navy Comrs.] Proposes the cheapest and most expeditious way of converting timber in Aliceholt for the frame of the new second-rate ship; viz., to send his foreman with 20 able shipwrights, to have the timber hewed to the moulds in the wood. Elm timber is wanted for the fourth-rate ship now building. [*Adm. Paper, damaged.*]

[March 16.] 12. Warrant to Sir George Carteret, treasurer of the navy, to pay the salaries of the Admiral's regiment, according to the muster rolls delivered, and also 20s. per man for such as shall be raised in lieu of men sent to sea, and to certify the same to the Duke of Albemarle, who will issue warrants for its repayment. [*Draft.*]

March 16. Entry of the above. With note of a similar warrant for Mr. Vice-Chamberlain [Sir G. Carteret], to pay the Admiral's regiment, to remain with the Lord General. [*Ent. Book 22, pp. 62–3.*]

March 16. Warrant to the Keeper of the Gatehouse to take John Atkinson into custody for high treason, and keep him close in the dungeon till further order. Minute. [*Ent. Book 22, p. 63.*]

Vol. CXV.

1664–5.
March 16. Order to Sir Thomas Ingram, chancellor of the duchy of Lancaster, for a warrant to Sir John Curzon, Bart., receiver general of the duchy, to pay 1,000*l.* to Hugh May, paymaster of the works, for the King's buildings at Greenwich. [*Ent. Book* 22, p. 70.]

March [16.] 13. Copy of the above.

March 16. Warrant assigning the pension of 6,000*l.* granted to the Duke of Monmouth to be paid from the receipts of excise for Yorkshire. [*Ent. Book* 17, p. 98.]

March 16. 14. Draft of the above. [*Two pages.*]

March? 15. Petition of Edw. Traffles, of Winchester, to the King, for his letter to the electors of Winchester College, that his son Richard may be sped to New College, Oxford, at the next election.

March 16. The King to the Wardens of New College and other electors of Winchester College. Recommends Rich. Traffles, child of Winchester College, for transplantation to the University, on account of the loyal sufferings of his parents in the late rebellion. [*Ent. Book* 19, p. 34.]

March 16. Edinburgh. 16. R. M[ein] to Hen. Muddiman. A fleet of 32 ships now in the Frith is hoped to be the Scots' fleet, with four of the King's ships in convoy, the granting of which convoy is thought a great favour. The very being of Scottish trading depends on the 500 brave seamen ready to go when the convoy returns. They are picked men, far beyond the others who went up, most of whom perished in the London. Mr. Mall, laird of Melgem, has a device by which he can stay six or eight hours under water, coming up to recover breath, and is most willing and able to serve His Majesty in recovering the guns, &c. of the London. The Dutch are a false, subtle people, and lurk for advantages.

March 16. 17. Estimate by Rob. Child and Wm. Bowles, masters of tents and toils, of the charge of the waggons, toils for the deer, tents, &c., for the Queen's use, ordered in 1664, and request for payment of the same; total, 1,322*l.*

March 16. Whitehall. 18. Order for a warrant to the Exchequer and to the Receiver General for Oxfordshire, to pay to the Earl of Lindsey, Lieutenant of Woodstock Manor, 40*l.* a year, for wages for the park keepers, and 40*l.* for provision of hay for the deer, as granted by the late King to Phil. late Earl of Montgomery, when he had the custody of the park. [*One and a half pages.*]

March 17. Newcastle. 19. Rich. Forster to James Hickes. Arrival of the long looked-for ships. Dined with Sir Ralph Delavale and the three captains, and saw many volunteers sent aboard the men-of-war. The people are much encouraged with the fleet, and hope a constant trade. Two men-of-war passed lately, convoying 23 Scottish ships.

VOL. CXV.

1664–5.
March 17.
Plymouth.

20. Da. Grosse to Williamson. The Straits' vessels have arrived and wait Lord Belasyse's departure. A prize is taken by the Dover. Arrival of vessels of the town from Marseilles, Leghorn, Genoa, Majorca, and St. Lucas, all bound for London. Capt. Allin's fleet, with 30 merchant ships, is eastward of Lyme, beating up the Channel. The Bear is to carry the pressed men thence to the fleet.

March 17.
Plymouth.

21. Sir John Coryton to Williamson. Has tried the temper of the people of Kellington, and finds them much altered in their esteem of him (the writer), because their last members neglected to get them two fairs, and suffered their opposers to get fairs for the very days which they desired; also they never had a token of respect from their members, but were sued by the agents of Mr. Rowley, who is lord of the manor, and forced to compositions. Paid the poorer sort their money again, and would have paid the charge of the fairs. Had they been obtained, Lord Bennet would have secured an interest in the place for ever.

March 17.
Serjeants' Inn, Chancery Lane.

22. Warrant from Lord Chief Justice Hyde to the Sheriff of Surrey, to command the execution of Wm. Ashenhurst and Rob. Kilvert, condemned to death for felony last assizes, but the former reprieved and the latter stayed from execution, without warrant.

March 17.
Letter Office.

23. James Hickes to Williamson. Sends letters from Newcastle and Plymouth. The prisoners being taken from Ilchester gaol to go to Taunton, to their trial, the under-keeper desired the old witch to show the people one of her pranks before she went, which she did.

March 17.

Warrant for creating George Rawdon a Baronet of Ireland. Minute. [*Ent. Book* 22, *p.* 63.]

March $\frac{17}{27}$.
Chelsea.

Ambassador Van Goch to the States General. The King has accepted the offer of the Lord Mayor and Aldermen to build him a ship instead of the London, adding that it is to be called the Loyal London. They meanwhile undertake to support three ships in the fleet at their own charge; 300 land soldiers, lately drawn out of the Guards to be sent on board the Duke's ship, were mustered, when his Highness made a speech, assuring them they should go no further than he would in his own person, whereon with a shout and great acclamations of joy, they were sent to the Downs. The sailors from an Emden vessel, formerly unmolested, are now made prisoners at Plymouth, on pretence that Emden is garrisoned by the States; all Dutch mariners are imprisoned. The people belonging to a Swedish ship are discharged from Chelsea College, perhaps to be put on board colliers' vessels. [*Copy, Holland Corresp., March* 17.]

March 17.
Chatham.

24. Commissioner Peter Pett to Sam. Pepys. Wants an order for deals intended for making a small house to keep provisions in at Sheerness. Particulars of ships. Timber wanted. [*Adm. Paper.*]

VOL. CXV.

1661–5.

March 17. The Expedition, The Hope. 25. Capt. Tobias Sackler to the Navy Comrs. Requests a new master, as his present one does not look after the ship. Is ordered to the Downs. [*Adm. Paper.*]

March 17. The Prince, The Hope. 26. Capt. Rog. Cuttance to Sam. Pepys. Wants kerseys and waste cloth. [*Adm. Paper.*]

March 17. 27. Certificate by Capt. Rog. Cuttance, that Henry Adams, master of the John boy, has waited on the ship Prince since Feb. 16. [*Adm. Paper.*]

March 17. Deptford. 28. Certificate by Thos. Cowley that Rob. Hutison was entered on the Expedition at Deptford, on Dec. 10, 1663. [*Adm. Paper, damaged.*]

March 18. 29. Certificate by G. Bowerman, that 76 persons, a list of whom is prefixed, have been constantly employed in the ballast office for three years, and are not to be impressed, nor compelled upon any other service. *Enclosing,*

> 29. I. *Reasons offered for preserving a certain number of men for ballasting in the river, who are poor men, pressed from country labour, most of them never having been inside a ship; showing that the rent of 2,000l. could not else be paid for the ballast office; that they have always been exempt, and that the supply of ballast is very important, &c. Of 240, the total number, 75 have entered as volunteers; request that at least 70 may be secured.* [*Two pages.*]

March 18. 30. Wm. Philpott, master of the Mayflower of Margate, to Sam. Pepys. Sends dimensions of the Mayflower boy, offering her services as formerly. [*Adm. Paper.*]

March 18. 31. Peter Rossell to the Navy Comrs. Has surveyed yarn and old rope at Mr. Spireman's, at Rodrith; the price of the latter is 16s. per cwt. [*Adm. Paper.*]

March 18. Portsmouth. 32. Comr. Thos. Middleton to [Sam. Pepys]. Will give all possible dispatch to Sir Wm. Warren's ship of deals, but all are busy about a prize from which 10,000 or 12,000 deals may be had. Particulars of stores bought and offered. Account of ships lying at Spithead. Col. Reymes has recommended two able seamen as masters of the galliot prizes. Progress of ships. Will not yet discharge calkers or axemen, lest Capt. Allin's fleet should come in suddenly, and want all hands at work. Reproved the captain of one of the merchant ships for not making quicker dispatch, but he threw the blame on the master of the ship. The embezzlement of cordage is not proved against the man suspected, or he would have been hanged. Particulars of timber felling. Money wanted by the purveyors. Requests press warrants to be sent down to each captain. [*Adm. Paper, four pages.*]

Vol. CXV.

1664–5.

March 18. Portsmouth. 33. Comr. Thos. Middleton to [Sam. Pepys]. Cannot fix the date of his commission, nor send it up as desired before payment of his allowance, as Morris Eady who was employed in the business, has it at Dover. [*Adm. Paper.*]

March 18. Dorchester. 34. John Cole to [Williamson]. Several captains have landed and gone up to London. The rest of Capt. Allin's fleet, with 30 merchantmen, are near Portland. The Dutch have taken an Englishman off Gibraltar, laden with herrings, and sold her at Malaga. They, as well as the English, have leave to sell their prizes in any port of Spain. A shallop built at Cadiz by the Dutch is not allowed by the governor to go to sea, till further orders from the King of Spain.

March 18 ? 35. Leonard Williams to Sec. Bennet. Thanks for receipt of 20*l.* for himself and 20*l.* for Mr. Betson. The money is insufficient. Has run great hazards and spent much money in the cause; a good reward would encourage Mr. Betson, and tend much to the King's service. Hears from Capt. Thomas of the taking of Capt. Newbury, an old officer, and of Terrill the waterman, who has carried persons up and down about the new design. Knows not either of them.

March 18. 36. Leo. Williams to Sec. Bennet. Has been early and late with Capt. Thomas, to show him the places where they meet. Atkinson can confirm what he says. Has sent a paper of their new design to Sir Roger Langley, a man faithful to the King and well beloved in the country. Thinks Mene Tekel would confess if fairly treated, being poor and having a large family. Pleads for a reward, having caused the taking of 16 at once, some more considerable than Atkinson. *Annexing,*

36. I. [*Leo. Williams and —— Betson*] *to Sir Roger Langley. In March 1663, Atkinson was active in the design, and got a council together, viz., Blood, Lockyer, Capt. Wise, Jones alias Mene Tekel, Carew, and Major Lee. They meant to take houses near the Tower and Whitehall, gather arms, and destroy the King, Dukes of York and Albemarle, and Lord Chancellor. Atkinson knows where most of these persons lodge; will tell anything else wanted to pinch Atkinson to a confession.* *March 17, 1665.*

March 18. Westminster. 37. Warrant to the Lord Treasurer and Chancellor of the Exchequer, authorizing certain payments made by them to excise officers, and to Rowland Laugharne and Sarah Gardiner, out of the arrears of excise of 6,248*l.* 7*s.* 1*d.*, due to His Majesty for so much paid to Ald. Backwell out of the growing duty of excise, and ordering that payments be first made from the remainder to the Duke of York, Capt. Titus, and Mr. Peck, before the rest be reimbursed to the King. [*Two sheets.*]

March 18. Whitehall. 38. Examination of John Atkinson, stockinger of Askrigg. Has been in London ever since the intended rising in the North. Knows

R 2

Vol. CXV.

1664–5.

the chief men, Lockyer, Jones, Blood, &c. When any are taken, the rest dislodge and cannot well be found. Was engaged by Baptists of desperate fortune, but grew wearied of their selfish designs, and looked for an opportunity to discover them. Particulars of many of the plotters and their residences. [*Three and a half pages.*]

March 18. Warrant to Sir John Robinson to receive [John] Atkinson, commonly called the Stockinger, prisoner for treasonable practices. Minute. [*Ent. Book* 22, *p.* 63.]

March 18. Whitehall. Note of the King's approval of Sir Richard Egerton, Sir Richard Brooke, and Sir Geoffrey Shakerly, as deputy lieutenants of the county palatine of Chester. [*Ent. Book* 22, *p.* 64.]

March 18. Whitehall. Warrant to the High Sheriff of Surrey for the execution of William Ashenhurst, the late reprieve notwithstanding. [*Ent. Book* 22, *p.* 64.]

March 18. London. 39. "The Rosie Crucian Heavenly Court and their Throne of Light discovered and communicated to the world by John Heydon, gent., φιλονόμος, a servant of God and secretary of nature." With a second title page "Hampaaneah Nvelamiu, or the Fuman of Rosie Crucian philosophy, teaching the wonderful power of the Pantarva, and the perfect, full discovery of the true Cœlum Terræ, or first matter of mettales and their preparation into incredible extraordinary medicines or elixirs, to cure all diseases in young or old, being fitted for the poor afflicted people of the world, admirable for all." Licensed by Roger L'Estrange. [*One hundred and nine pages, imperfect.*]

March 19. Hull. 40. Luke Whittington to Jas. Hickes. The rich fleet of 24 vessels of the town, with the convoy, has sailed from the Humber, and was joined by the frigate from Scarborough, with the pressed men. Col. Morley, the present governor of Hull, sent out several files of musketeers to Serjeant Bullock's house, two miles off, where a conventicle of 100 to 300 fanatics was held; only 20 were seized, as their scouts were out, and they fled. Report that the Hollanders have landed in Scotland or Shetland.

March 19. Hull. 41. Willm. Gower to Williamson. Sent him a cask of ale by the fleet that has just sailed; a fleet of 60 ships, with six convoys, has passed northward. Mr. Comings and Mr. Fairfax will give intelligence from Whitby. Asks Sir Henry Bennet's new title.

March 19. Plymouth. 42. Da. Grosse to [Williamson]. Arrival and departure of ships. Another prize taken. The rest of the Smyrna fleet has arrived, to go under convoy of Lord Belasyse, when the wind allows; 100 soldiers put aboard for Tangiers, 50 from Plymouth garrison, and 50 from Pendennis shouted their joy to serve the King, which much satisfied the spectators.

March 19. 43. J[ohn] I[ronmonger] to Sir Thos. Gower. The last letters from Holland gave assurance that the French would support the States. They consent to the stay of all the ships lately built for

VOL. CXV.

1664–5.

them in Holland. The Admiral of France will bring 42 ships from the Italian seas to Brest in April. Marsden is in London like a great gallant, and often at Court. Col. Carr promises much to the States of what will be done in the west of Scotland.

March 19. 44. Examination of [Wm.] Ashenhurst, prisoner in the White Lion. There are frequent meetings in the prison of 40 or 50 Anabaptists, some of whom were his judges, and condemned him when he was in Sir George Booth's business. They rent a chamber there, sometimes stay all night, and some bring arms; looking through the key-hole, heard them earnest in discourse of something to be done in April next.

March 19. The King to Col. Russell. He is to follow the 300 soldiers late of the Guards, who are ordered on board the fleet to repress the mutiny which has arisen from some unknown cause, and the Judge Advocate is to proceed to a speedy trial and execution of the chief offenders, by a council of war near the place where the offenders live, according to the Articles of War published at Oxford in the time of the late King, so as to discourage others from such presumptuous attempts in future. [*Ent. Book* 17, *pp.* 99–100.]

[March 19.] 45. Draft of the above [*by Sec. Bennet and Williamson.*]

March 19. Sunday. 46. Sir Geo. Carteret to the Navy Comrs. The King wonders that the Dutch galliot lying at Deptford, bound for the north of Scotland, is not yet dispatched. Asks if the captain's complaint of not having all his stores be true, or where the fault lies. [*Adm. Paper.*]

March 20. Deptford. 47. Thos. Harper to Thos. Turner. Particulars of stores. Timber wanted; also the standards for the Royal Charles. [*Adm. Paper, damaged.*]

March 20. Coxpill. 48. Dan. Furzer to the Navy Comrs. Requests a warrant for felling keel-pieces, plank, &c., in the Lea Baly, for the new ship. [*Adm. Paper.*]

March 20. 49. Certificate by Capt. Zach. Browne, that a fresh supply of medicine is needed by John Powell, surgeon of the Assistance. [*Adm. Paper.*]

March 20. 50. Capt. John Taylor to Pepys. Desires a bill for the large deals at Chatham. The allowance demanded for the Blackcock's coming into Chatham till a time of leisure is 98*l.* 8*s.* [*Adm. Paper.*]

March 20. Dover. 51. Thos. White to the Navy Comrs. Account of naval stores which may be bought at that port; viz., sheet lead, cordage, tar, ironwork, and canvas. [*Adm. Paper.*]

March 20. Bridgewater. 52. Sir Hugh Smyth, Sir John Sydenham, and five other Deputy Lieutenants of Somersetshire to the Duke of Ormond, [lord lieutenant]. Could not deposit the month's assessment now in the

VOL. CXV.

1664–5.

late sheriff's hands, as ordered, as the sea affairs and assizes prevented many gentlemen from meeting, but will soon do it; find that of 4,784*l.* 5*s.* 6*d.*, 403*l.* 7*s.* 6*d.* has been disbursed as ordered, 4,348*l.* 18*s.* is in Sir George Norton, the late sheriff's hands, and 441*l.* 9*s.* 2*d.* not yet collected. Hope fuller instructions when his Grace visits the country. *Annexing,*

52. I. *Account [by Williamson] of the arrears of 70,000l. collected in Somersetshire, as certified by the Lord Lieutenant, corresponding with the above statement.*

March 20. Guildhall. 53. Order at a meeting of the Lord Mayor and Justices of the Peace for London, Middlesex, Kent, and Surrey, that the Earl of Newport and Lord Craven be desired to move the King to order no ships laden with coal to be stayed at Harwich or other ports at the river's mouth, except for supply of the said ports, in order that the City and neighbourhood may be supplied.

March 20. Guildhall. 54. Order in the said meeting, that from March 22, the price of coals shall not be more than 30*s.* a chaldron; none are to refuse to sell at that rate, and the justices of peace to see the order put in execution. With marginal list of 14 persons present. [*One and a half pages.*]

March 20. 55. John Madden and Thos. Agar to Lord [Treas. Southampton]. Report the state of the several coppices in Whittlewood and Sauleey forests; their total value is 534*l.*, after deducting 82*l.* for fencing; but if the value of the acres or half-acres claimed by the lord warden, lieutenant, ranger, and verderers be deducted, it will be 495*l.* 10*s.* [*Two and a half pages.*]

March 20. Derby. 56. Sir Chas. Dallison, Wm. Ellis, and Nich. Wilmot to Attorney General Palmer. Calton was the only evidence against Wright and Howe, and the other prisoners at Derby, therefore they were not proceeded against. It was proved against Wild that he knew of the plot for which several were executed, and knew that Lockyer would raise 500 men at Nottingham; that he often spoke of the plot, offered press money to enlist persons, and said there would soon be an alteration. The prisoner's defence was that he remembers nothing of this, but that his head was once hurt and a piece of his skull taken out, that his brain was sometimes distempered, and that he had been drinking. He proved that he did not act at all in the late troubles, and that he frequented church. The judge has ordered the execution for Easter week. [*One and a quarter pages.*]

March 20. Leicester. 57. Edw. Darwell to Matthew Johnson, at the Attorney General's chambers, Brick Court, Middle Temple, London. Phil. Wild was the only one tried, the others were released on bail, there being only one witness against them. The gentry think the verdict against Wild is hard, his defence being that he was sometimes distracted, and was in drink at the time.

VOL. CXV.

1664-5.
March 20. Derby. 58. Anchitell Gray and H. Every, justices of peace of Derby, to Mr. Boulteale, the Lord Chancellor's secretary, Worcester House, London. Ask whether Phil. Wild, condemned for treason, may be capable of pardon. The jury were satisfied that he was drunk when he tried to enlist soldiers, and that he is distracted on the changes of the moon. He has confessed who employed him therein. Thos. Calton, now prisoner in the gaol, was witness against him. *Encloses,*

58. I. *Confession of Phil. Wild. Was employed by his master, Col. Hutherson, and his son Thomas, to enlist soldiers against the Yorkshire rising, Oct. 12, and had a horse given him; went to Thos. Greensmith of Coventry, and George Hollis, of Newbold, near Chesterfield, to know if they were ready. Being at Milton, in drink, tried to enlist his brother, Timothy Wild, Lieut. Wild, Allin, and Roper. Before this, Hutherson had threatened to fall on a troop of the King's horses, and to take Warwick Castle.*

March 20. Grant to Anthony De Choqueux of the office of Surgeon in ordinary, fee 80*l.* a year, to begin from Midsummer, 1661. [*Docquet.*]

March 20. Warrant to pay to Anthony De Choqueux 383*l.* 12*s.*, due to him from the late King. [*Docquet.*]

March 20. Grant to James Earl of Suffolk of an annuity of 1,000*l.* as gentleman of the bedchamber. [*Docquet.*]

March 20. Warrant to pay to the Earl of Sandwich, master of the great wardrobe, 5,000*l.* on account, for extraordinary charges in his office since Michaelmas, 1664. [*Docquet.*]

March 20. 59. Arthur Trevor to [Williamson]. The only business on hand is about the length of the hoods of Capuchins and Recollets, the black and grey monks at Coventry, and the bishop whose head was broken with his own crosier in trying to settle the question of precedency with his pastoral staff; also about a pig, said not to be one because he was whole-hoofed. A miller, when indicted, justified taking excessive tolls, because the rector on Palm Sunday said "Tolle, tolle, &c."

March 20. 60. Information by Thos. Gray, an Englishman who sailed with the Dutch two years, and has now escaped by way of Ostend, with loss of 18 months' pay. There are 50 men-of-war at Texel preparing under young Trump, 50 at Flushing under Evertsen, 5 at Camphire under young Banckart, and 30 at Helvoetsluys under Opdam. There are few English amongst them, and those cannot get away. They have 12 fire-ships. Many of De Ruyter's men are ill or dead at Guinea, and they want provisions.

VOL. CXV.

1661–5.

March 21. Deal. 61. Rl. Watts to Williamson. Arrival and departure of vessels. Great guns and broadsides have been heard all day, and it is thought that the fleet under Sir George Ayscue is engaged. Our ships are 18 sail, the rest being on the scout.

March 21. Sandwich. 62. Capt. John Strode to Williamson. The fleet has sailed from the Downs eastward, and a great many guns have been fired from seaward. Can send him white wine, but there was not a drop of claret in all the prize ships.

March 21. 63. Deposition of Robt. Westcomb. Being sent with Gilbert Thomas, provost marshal, to apprehend —— Terry, Terry said "you have missed your prize; you came to take Doctor Johnson, and he is far enough out of your reach." When in Flanders, Johnson told him that he was the best artist in the world for making rich metals, and could live well in England, if he could find some one that could adulterate mercury. Johnson showed him an ingredient which would change brass to the colour of perfect silver.

March 21. Licence to Alice De l'Ecluse to pass into Holland on her particular occasions. Minute. [*Ent. Book* 22, p. 65.]

March 21. Warrant to Sir Edward Griffin, treasurer of the chamber, to deliver to Humphrey Lord Bishop of London, chief almoner, or the sub-almoner, 133*l*. 6*s*. 8*d*., to be distributed in alms on Maunday Thursday, Good Friday, and Easter week. [*Ent. Book* 22, p. 68.]

March 21. Grant to Rich. Swift of the office of Falconer in ordinary, in the place of Hugh Wright; fee, 2*s*. a day, and 13*l*. 13*s*. 0½*d*. for yearly livery. [*Docquet*.]

March 21. Harwich. 64. Anthony Deane to the Navy Commrs. Sends particulars of the dimensions and use of the careening wheel. Justice Scrivener refuses to meddle with the carriage of his timber; it must be bought on the place. Sir Philip Parker makes the same agreement. These bargains will come to 700*l*. [*Adm. Paper*.]

March 21. Deal. 65. John Culmer to Sir John Mennes. Offers to convert two long boats in his possession into water boats, for the use of the fleet. [*Adm. Paper*.]

March 21. 66. Sir Wm. Coventry to Sam. Pepys. Complains that Capt. Fortescue does nothing towards restoring the arms to Sir Chichester Wray. Desires orders for it to be done whatever it costs. Suggests iron stone ballasting for the ships building at Bristol, as cheaper in the end. Timber wanted at Deptford. [*Adm. Paper*.]

March 21. 67. Sir Wm. Coventry to Sam. Pepys. The stores demanded by Sir Wm. Penn for the Charles must be hastened into the King's Channel, and not into the Downs. [*Adm. Paper*.]

VOL. CXV.

1664–5.
March 22. 68. Sir Wm. Coventry to Sam. Pepys. Desires stores for the Lily, against her coming up to Woolwich. [*Adm. Paper.*] *Encloses*,

68. I. *Capt. Amos. Beare to Sir Geo. Askew, commander of the fleet in the Downs. Is ordered to ply between the buoy of the Nore and North Foreland, calling sometimes at Margate for orders. Wants a cable and other provisions. The Lily, Margate Road, March 19.*

March 22. Woolwich. 69. Wm. Bodham to the Navy Comrs. Three men, strangers by their language, have been observed to walk and pry suspiciously round the ropeyard. In these times of hostility with the Dutch, some worse mischief than thieving is feared. Advises a third watchman for the yard during the war, and arms to be ready; 200 deals wanted. [*Adm. Paper.*]

March 22. Woolwich. 70. Richard Dowson to the [Navy Comrs.] The joiners' work for the new ship will cost 190*l*., or 216*l*. deducting for work already done. [*Adm. Paper.*]

March 22. 71. Sir Wm. Coventry to the Rulers of Watermen's Hall. Complains of pressed watermen hiring others in their places, whereby the service is encumbered with useless men, while able seamen are left at home. The same persons are to be impressed again, notwithstanding their having hired others, in order to make people more cautious. [*Adm. Paper.*] *Encloses*,

71. I. *List of 70 men given in by order of the Rulers of the Watermen's Company.*

March 22. Chester. 72. Capt. Rich. Rooth to the Navy Comrs. Has drawn a bill of exchange on them for 221*l*., for provisions. Has 130 pressed men on board, besides his company, and hopes that the number imposed on Cheshire and Lancashire will soon be complete. [*Adm. Paper.*]

March 22. Dover. 73. Thos. White to the Navy Comrs. Wishes navy stores brought in by prizes to be delivered into his charge, appraised by four men when landed, housed in the stores, and delivered out by the Prize Commissioners when required by the King's ships. [*Adm. Paper.*]

March 22. Chatham. 74. Peter Pett, jun., to Sam. Pepys. Writes during his father's absence to transmit certain packets. Asks if the contracts received are to be kept till his father's return, or sent to London. [*Adm. Paper.*] *Encloses*,

74. I., II. *Account of provisions required for Dover, noting such as are ready to be sent. Two papers.*

March 22. Whitehall. Warrant for a grant to Horatio Lord Townshend of two thirds of certain marsh lands in or near Walton and other places, cos. Cambridge, Lincoln, and Norfolk, as settled upon the late King when he undertook to drain the same, and spent 6,000*l*. therein, on condition of his lordship's prosecuting His Majesty's right and title thereto at his own expense, and paying such fee-farm rents as may be agreed upon. [*Ent. Book 14, f. 53.*]

Vol. CXV.

1664–5.

March 22. Whitehall. Warrant to Lord Townshend to examine the King's claims to the land mentioned in the preceding warrant; to agree with persons interested therein for restoring and perfecting the embankment, two thirds to be for the King, and the other third for pretension of soil and common; and to require all evidences or writings relating thereto to be produced. [*Ent. Book* 14, *f.* 54.]

March 22. The King to the [Dean and Chapter of Christ Church, Oxford]. The legacy of 900*l.* a year, bequeathed by —— Thurstan to that college, having come to their hands after long suit, and the present dean and chapter having greatly improved the revenue of the college, the money is to be employed in increasing the salaries of the singing men 5*s.* a quarter, and in adding one to the 100 students founded there. [*Ent. Book* 19, *f.* 35.]

March 22. Warrant to the Commissioners of Prizes, to restore certain brandies and wines, seized on board the Crowned Pen, to Sire Tavart and Dr. Lopes of Bourdeaux, their owners. [*Ent. Book* 22, *p.* 71.]

March 22. Warrant to Sir Ralph Freeman and Henry Slingsby, masters and workers of the Mint, to allow three pennyweights Troy in the pound as a remedy in weight on 3*d.* and 4*d.* pieces, and four pennyweights on 2*d.* and 1*d.* pieces, since great exactness cannot be observed in the small coins, of which a great quantity is to be made. [*Ent. Book* 22, *p.* 72.]

[March 22.] 75. Draft of the above. [*Imperfect.*]

March 22. Whitehall. 76. The King to the Duke of York. Has prepared a great and powerful fleet to assert his right to the dominion of the Narrow Seas, and has, at his request, given him the command of it, confiding in his wisdom, valour, and conduct, by God's blessing, for happy success. He is to act by advice of the Council of War, either sailing to the North, into the Channel, or to the coast of Holland; to endeavour directly to secure the mastery of the seas and safety of navigation, and for this object to fight or not fight, as he thinks best. [*Two pages.*]

March [22.] 77. Draft of the above. [*Two pages.*]

March 22. Entry of the above. [*Ent. Book* 21, *p.* 162.]

March 22. Deal. 78. Ri. Watts to [Williamson]. The shooting that was heard was only salutes. A Straits prize has come in, and other ships.

March 22. Hull. 79. J. C—— to James Hickes. Three strong Holland men-of-war have been seen off Bridlington.

March 22. Plymouth. 80. J. C[larke] to James Hickes. Lord Belasyse, his officers and 200 soldiers, have sailed in the Foresight, Elizabeth, and Eagle, along with the Smyrna fleet and some ships bound for Leghorn, Cadiz, Barbadoes, &c. Vessels have arrived from Portugal, Seville, and the Canaries, all bound for London.

Vol. CXV.

1664–5.
March 22. Whitehall. 81. Order in Council, revoking the word Ireland from the dispensation lately granted in reference to certain clauses in the Act of Navigation, suspending the said Act as to commodities from Norway or the Baltic; also from Germany, Flanders, or France, if the owners be the King's born subjects; empowering not only subjects, but merchants of any nation in amity, to import hemp, pitch, tar, masts, saltpetre, and copper; and authorizing English merchants to employ foreign ships, or seamen of any nation at amity, provided no goods be imported into the plantations except direct from England and Wales, nor from thence except to ports in England and Wales, for which the custom house officers are to take bonds and other securities.

March 22. Whitehall. 82. Sir Wm. Coventry to Lord Arlington. Sends a paper given him by the Duke, but thinks it cannot be dispatched during his Royal Highness's short stay, as he will be cautious in granting passes to foreign ships without positive directions from the King or Council, or at least the opinion of the Prize Commissioners that the service will not be prejudiced thereby.

March 22. 83. Sir Rob. Wiseman, advocate general, to the Commissioners for Prizes. As to the account required of French claims on prizes, nine tenths of the claims made in the Admiralty Court are on the plea of the goods being French. Although the Dutch were known to be the great traders at sea, and these goods are in Dutch vessels, going between Dutch ports, and the crew Dutch, yet they are sworn to belong only to Frenchmen. Those French who went on with their claims were soon dispatched, but some would not proceed in them, saying they could right themselves elsewhere; this failing, they resumed them, and on their own proofs, without any proof on the other side, have been discharged. This has been done because the court was ordered to respect the alliance of the two crowns, and to prefer French claims before those of any other nation. If the charges complained of are those incident to seizure and detention, and the court proceedings, they are justified by law, as the French gave ground for seizure by using Dutch vessels and equipage, and sailing between Dutch ports. The notion that the King's declaration of February 22 was made to condemn all French goods taken in Dutch vessels before that time is disproved, because it runs altogether in the future; and because, since its publication, the Admiralty Court has discharged many French goods taken in Dutch ships. [*Two and a half pages.*]

March 22. 84. Copy of the above. [*Four and a half pages.*] *Annexing,*

84. I. *List of 11 French ships and their goods discharged without trial in the Admiralty Court, from January 28 to March 22, 1665.*

March 23. Dover. 85. Jo. Carlisle to Williamson. Vice-Admiral Allin has sailed with 11 ships, and Sir Wm. Berkeley with 13, bound for Sole Bay, which will be the rendezvous. Sir And. Browne has arrived from Lord Fanshaw. Report that six Holland ships are taken. Sends him a box of oranges and lemons, the first fruits of his labour as storehouse keeper.

Vol. CXV.

1664–5.

March 23. Deal. 86. Rl. Watts to Williamson. Sir Willm. Berkeley's fleet and prizes have arrived. Twenty King's ships are in the Downs.

March 23. Warrant for leave to Henry Killigrew to fell, cut down, and carry away the coppices and coppice wood in the forests of Whittlewood and Saukey, co. Northampton, as the King's free gift. [*Ent. Book* 22, *p.* 66.]

March ? 87. Petition of Capt. Rob. Holmes to the King, for pardon under the great seal for whatever passed in the Guinea expedition, His Majesty having declared himself well satisfied with his explanations thereon. [*Draft by Williamson, damaged.*]

March 23. Warrant for a pardon and release to Capt. Rob. Holmes of all debts and demands concerning shipping or ammunition, and all felonies and offences in England or elsewhere, up to the present time. [*Ent. Book* 22, p. 69.]

[March 23.] 88. Draft of the above.

March 23. Warrant to pay to Stephen Fox 3,500*l.*, for secret services, without account. Minute. [*Ent. Book* 22, *p.* 73.]

March 23. Warrant to pay to Stephen Fox 1,000*l.*, for secret services, without account. [*Docquet.*]

March 23. 89. Thos. Kendall to Williamson. The two East India ships being ready to sail, wants the letters to Sir Abraham Shipman. Left with the Navy Commissioners copies of the contract about bringing home and sending to Fort St. George the men he has left.

March 23. 90. Agreement between the Navy Commissioners and the East India Company for the hire of the African and the St. George, for the transport to Surat or Fort St. George, of such of the King's forces as remain at Anjadiva, under command of Sir Abraham Shipman, at 15*l.* per head. [*Adm. Paper, damaged.*]

March 23. 91. Capt. John Taylor to the Navy Comrs. There are 28 New England masts and 160 large deals delivered at Chatham. [*Adm. Paper.*]

March 23. Chatham Dock. 92. Phin. Pett to the Navy Comrs. Particulars of timber. The Monk is ready to launch. [*Adm. Paper.*]

March 23. Victualling Office. 93. Certificate by Thos. Lewis that Devereux Wyatt, purser of the Adventure, has cleared his accounts. [*Adm. Paper.*]

March 23. Portsmouth Dockyard. 94. Commissioner Thos. Middleton to Sam. Pepys. Account of St. John Steventon's wife, a drunken and debauched woman, being burnt to death; had the house taken fire, it would have burnt ships in dock, storehouse, &c. and happening at low water, could not well have been put out. Asks how to dispose of ships when ready. A press warrant wanted. [*Adm. Paper.*]

VOL. CXV.

1664–5.

March 23. Portsmouth. 95. Commissioner Thos. Middleton to Sam. Pepys. Particulars of stores. Repairs of ships. The Greyhound is come in with about 100 poor pitiful men on board, and no order how to dispose of them. Will put them on board the Ferdinand, Eagle, and Fox. [*Adm. Paper, one and a half pages.*]

March 23. Victualling Office. 96. Denis Gauden to Sam. Pepys. Recommends the Hopewell, pink, and Cane Merchant, as victualling ships. [*Adm. Paper.*]

March 23. 97. Sir Wm. Coventry to Sam. Pepys. Has come to Queensborough and got under sail. White and blue colours are wanted for the fleet. The ketches, smacks, and hoys hired must be allotted to the great ships, and the rest sent down to the Gunfleet, that they may not hide themselves in holes whilst they eat the King's bread. The merchantmen must be hastened. The rulers of Watermen's Hall are to give an account of the number of men pressed by them, and the men to be viewed when sent, for they have lusty fellows, if they will send them. Stores wanted. Forwards the Duke of York's warrant to the Marshal of the Admiralty, to send away some prisoners in his hands. [*Adm. Paper, two pages.*]

March 23. Royal Exchange, Downs Road. 98. Capt. Giles Shelley to Capt. John Bagby. Notifies his arrival. Account of his charges for graving, repairs, &c. Is troubled at the order to go into harbour, being so perplexed with the men taking liberty to themselves to go and see their friends; "it is an epidemical disease among the sailors when they come into harbour," and then they are pressed into other men-of-war. [*Adm. Paper.*]

March 23. Deptford. 99. Thos. Harper to Sam. Pepys. Is ordered to hasten stores to the Prince; asks what sort of hammocks are to be sent. Proposes some abatement to be made in kerseys and cottons, for want of breadth, as well as in canvas. [*Adm. Paper, damaged.*]

VOL. CXVI. MARCH 24–31, 1665.

1665.

March 24. 1. Certificate by Capt. John Fortescue of the Golden Phœnix being completely equipped as a man-of-war. [*Adm. Paper.*]

March 24. The Harp, Holyhead. 2. Capt. James Sharland to the Navy Comrs. Wants stores and ammunition. [*Adm. Paper.*]

March 24. Holyhead. 3. Capt. James Sharland to Mr. Sansfield. Is ordered to enter 18 men on board the Harp. Begs his efforts to get his supply of stores speedily sent down. [*Adm. Paper.*]

March 24. Milford. 4. Capt. John Whateley to Capt. John Miller. Has received orders to go to Portsmouth, but is not yet ready. Has heard nothing of the master spoken of. Would have got a master at the Navy Office, but for the great charge. [*Adm. Paper.*]

Vol. CXVI.

1665.

March 24. The Unicorn. 5. Capt. Henry Teddeman to the Navy Comrs. Wants a ketch to attend upon the Unicorn, to supply her with water and other necessaries. [*Adm. Paper.*]

March 24. Surgeons' Hall. 6. Rich. Reynell to Thos. Hayter. James South, lately appointed surgeon of the Guinea, has disappeared. Will send to inquire after him. [*Adm. Paper.*]

March 24. April 3. Ambassador Van Goch to the States General. Yesterday the Duke of York, with the chief sea officers, Prince Rupert, Duke of Monmouth, Earl of Sandwich, and others, went down to Hawsans, between the Downs and Harwich, the place appointed for the rendezvous of the fleet. The Queen and Duchess accompanied them to the Hope. Capt. Allin and his ships have joined the fleet. [*Holland Corresp., March* 24, 1665.]

March 24. The King to the [Dean and Chapter of Christ's Church, Oxford]. Requests re-admission of Thos. Ireland, B.L., who resigned his student's place there in order to be capable of election to the readership of moral philosophy, which is otherwise disposed of; wishes him to retain his former seniority, without advancement to any higher table. [*Ent. Book* 19, p. 30.]

March 24. The King to the Mayor and Aldermen of Coventry. Recommends William, son of Sam. Bird of Claybrooke, co. Leicester, now scholar in their free school, to the Scholar's place in St. John's College, Oxford, to be supplied by their choice. [*Ent. Book* 10, p. 37.]

March 24. Commission to Fras. Fortescue to be Lieutenant in Capt. Paul Bucknam's company of foot in Portsmouth. Minute. [*Ent. Book* 20, p. 51.]

March 24. Warrant for a pardon to Charles Cornell and Mary his wife, accused of seducing Miles Ward, apprentice to William Warren, to expend 225*l.* of his master's money in taverns, &c., as it appears that they were unjustly prosecuted by Ward and Warren, with intent to deprive them of goods, value 2,000*l.* [*Ent. Book* 22, *pp.* 65–6.]

March 24. Warrant to James Earl of Northampton, chief ranger, and the other officers of Whittlewood and Sauleey forests, co. Northampton, to permit persons appointed by Dame Philippa Mohun to cut down and carry away 1,500 old dottrell and decayed trees out of the said forests. [*Ent. Book* 22, p. 67.]

[March 24.] 7. Draft of the above.

[March 24.] 8. Another draft of the above, with proviso that the wood be carried away within three years.

March 24. Deal. 9. Ri. Watts to Williamson. The fleets of Sir Wm. Berkeley and Adm. Allin have sailed, and Sir George Ayscue's is nine leagues to the south-west of North Foreland. There are three Dutch privateers about Newport.

VOL. CXVI.

1665.

March 24. 10. List of 72 ships cleared at Newcastle during the past week, the greater number bound for London.

March 24. 11. Leonard Williams to Sec. Lord Bennet. Thinks that his friends believe he can serve them, as they apply to him, and want him to come in for a protection; will be wary to trust himself among them. Wants to go privately to the bishopric of Durham; will tell them that he only confessed to save his own life, but that he will not witness against any of them, and as nothing has been done against them, they will believe him. If Sir Roger Langley were to write him a letter to bring him in, which he could show, and say how honest Sir Roger has been to him, it would lead men to confess and find the same benefit; when any are taken, will give particulars against them which will make them confess. Wants a protection, under the King's hand and seal.

March 24. Egglestone Hall. 12. Christopher Sanderson to Sec. Bennet. The informer hopes soon to tell where the parties meet, because Col. Lilburne's father, Rich. Lilburne, has asked him to go and see his son, and he hopes letters will be sent by him. Mrs. Gower writes to her husband, Capt. Gower, or her son, at Mr. Washburne's, near Bishopsgate. Col. Lilburne's letters are addressed to Ralph Stapleton, near Charing Cross; if the letters are intercepted, care should be taken not to discover the informer; when any search is made for the party, they hide in Southwark. They are much exalted, saying they shall have an army to resort to, for the Dutch will land in the north of Scotland, with 10 regiments and plenty of arms. "Mene, Tekel, or the Downfall of Tyranny" is much cried up amongst them; also another seditious book called "George Withers' New Year's Gift." Has framed a writing to which the informer might try to get subscriptions, and thus discover their whole party. Wants a commission against the rebels, without which he dares not act; nothing but death or exile will supersede their bloody contrivances. Thinks of coming up to London in April, to meet his informer about the discovery of these good fellows. [*Two pages.*] *Annexing,*

12. I. *Form of a commission to Christopher Sanderson, of Egglestone, to give directions to an intelligencer employed for the King in the county of Durham, and especially to put him on an endeavour to procure the subscriptions of the disaffected to such engagements as may bring them under the compass of the law.*

12. II. *Form of a proposal to assist Christian brethren in distress, by contributions, and promises to go or send to visit them, or persuade others to go; to be signed—*

1st, by Peter Presbyterian who will go in person with horse and arms;

2nd, by Hugh Independent who will send a man with horse and arms;

3rd, by Praisegod Fanatic who will give assistance in money, naming the sums, but shilling is to stand for pound, in the amount stated.

12. III. *Duplicate of the above, but giving the names in each class as John Rebel.*

Vol. CXVI.

1665.

March 24. Royal Charles. 13. Sir Wm. Coventry to Lord Arlington. Has been in the fleet so short a time as not to gain any information except what was sent to the Duke of Albemarle. Forwards a letter to Lord Craven from Prince Rupert.

[March 25.] 14. Account of the charge of keeping and planting Greenwich Park, with the 16 coppices and dwarf orchard, from Lady Day, 1662 to 1665, and building the garden house; total, 580*l.* 17*s.* With a request for 118*l.* yearly allowance, in lieu of all bills and demands. Noted "payable to Sir Wm. Boreman, keeper of the new-planted dwarf-orchard."

March 25? 15. Six forms of cyphers for Sir Hen. Bennet, now Lord Arlington, of his name or initials, surmounted by a baron's coronet.

March 25? 16. Three forms of cyphers of the name or initials of Lord Arlington, by Mr. Harris.

March 25. Whitehall. 17. Henry Bennet Lord Arlington to the Lord Chancellor. The seal is to be put without delay to Lord St. Alban's grant of St. James's fields, even though it should not have the Lord Treasurer's recommendation; also to his other grant of the Duchy House. [*Damaged.*]

March 25. 18. Isabella Lady Curwen to Williamson. Asks assistance as to the enclosed. Mr. Dugdale is now in Cumberland, and will stay till the sad solemnity, and perhaps create disturbance, which would much afflict her. The heralds threatened her man when in London; the King-at-arms promised that no disturbance should be offered, but the engagement was only verbal. Begs an order for the escutcheons and ensigns to remain in the church without defacing. *Annexing,*

18. i. *Wm. Dugdale, Norroy, king at arms, to Sir Philip Musgrave, Bart. As to the funeral intended for Sir Patricius Curwen, if, in spite of civil warning, they are persuaded by the painter to carry those hatchments, hopes they will not pay him for them till they see whether they will stand; will assuredly pull them down in Easter week, when he comes, or if falser, deface them, as empowered to do; and if they are not set up till after his return, will do it in the face of the country, at the next assizes at Carlisle. Heralds' Office, Feb. 20, 1665.*

March 25. Poole. 19. Wm. Skutt to Williamson. All is quiet on the coast, the fishermen see no appearance of the enemy. Admiral Allin's fleet has passed eastward.

March 25. 20. Account of customs received in the port of London, from Michaelmas 1662 to Lady Day 1665, showing what is received on the King's account and the farmers' account; sum total, 995,731*l.* 13*s.*

VOL. CXVI.

1665.

March 25. London. 21. James Hickes to Williamson. Has been very ill. Mr. Muddiman complains that some of his letters are taxed, though Sec. Morice ordered them to go free. Muddiman has been to the Custom House to get the names of correspondents in the ports. Is anxious about his petition; wants vindication, or punishment if guilty.

March 25. Westminster. 22. Pass for Vincentio and Bart. Albrici, the King's composers in music, to go abroad, and return. [*Latin.*]

March 25. 23. Particulars of alterations made since 3 October, 1663, in the garrisons of Guernsey, Lord Wentworth's company in Portsmouth, and those in Landguard Point Fort, and Ludlow Castle.

March 25. 24. Certificate by Capt. John Fortescue that the Constant Katharine is completely equipped as a man-of-war. [*Adm. Paper.*]

March 25. Chatham Dock. 25. Edw. Gregory to the Navy Comrs. The delay in sending up the quarter books is caused by the greatness of the extras, the infinite trouble occasioned by the late call books, and the multiplicity of business. [*Adm. Paper.*]

March 25. The Prince. 26. Earl of Sandwich to Sam. Pepys. The fire booms sent are too large to be used. Begs a supply of others, not above 22 inches at the butt-end, and 40 feet long. [*Adm. Paper.*]

March 25. 27. List of 62 seamen impressed, granted to 16 London ships named. [*Adm. Paper, one and a half pages.*]

March 25. 28. Sir Wm. Coventry to Sam. Pepys. All kinds of colours are wanted. Victuallers and ketches must be hastened down from the Hope. No more calico colours are to be made; they do not last. [*Adm. Paper.*]

March 25. London. 29. Sir Anthony Bateman to Sir Wm. Batten. Offers for sale a small parcel of reed near Woolwich, at the usual price. [*Adm. Paper.*]

March 25. Portsmouth. 30. Commissioner Thos. Middleton to Sam. Pepys. St. John Steventon has not forwarded his accounts, owing to the disaster to his wife. The Greyhound is arrived with 200 pressed men from Wales; has disposed of them amongst the ships; most of them are pitiful souls, not understanding a word of English, and fit for nothing. Particulars of ships. Desires a press warrant for securing men suspected of embezzling prize goods. Wants coal; proposes sending one of the galliots, now lying idle in port, to Sunderland, to fetch some. [*Adm. Paper, three pages.*]

March 25. The Assistance, The Hope. 31. Capt. Zach. Browne to the Navy Comrs. Notifies his arrival. Asks what quantity of provisions he is to take in. Has only 120 men left; 50 are sick at Plymouth and Chatham, and several went to London and are pressed on board other ships. [*Adm. Paper.*]

Vol. CXVI.

1665.

March 25. The Reserve, Cowly Bay. 32. Capt. John Hubbard to the Navy Comrs. Is ordered to remain three days there for his better manning. [*Adm. Paper.*]

March 23. The Monk, Chatham. 33. Capt. Thos. Penrose to [Sir] Wm. Coventry. Cannot join the fleet at the Gunfleet until his victuals and stores are on board. Death of his master, Rob. Sayers. Recommends Petter Wappall for that employment. [*Adm. Paper.*]

March 25. Bristol. 34. Sir John Knight to the Navy Comrs. Account of ammunition and stores required for the George; money must be had. Sends the purser's bond and security; has given him his instructions and the Duke's commissions. Is made to pay postage for all his letters. [*Adm. Paper.*]

March 20. Chatham. 35. Commissioner Peter Pett to Sam. Pepys. Cannot hear of any red silk flag in store. Sir Edw. Dering's timber is ordinary, and only worth 30s. a load. The Monk sails to morrow. The Dover provisions will be ready for the Augustine when she comes. Will soon give his opinion of the fourth and fifth rate vessels to be built by contract. [*Adm. Paper.*]

March 26. 36. Robt. Magors and John Tooker to the Navy Comrs. Account of several prize vessels in the Thames, suitable for carrying timber from Sherwood Forest. [*Adm. Paper.*]

March 26. Milton, near Gravesend. 37. John Marlow, mayor of Gravesend, to the Navy Comrs. Sends examinations, &c., concerning two barrels of gunpowder now in custody of Sir John Griffith, having the Tower mark upon them, which were sold by Henry Mason to John Watson, shopkeeper in Gravesend, at 55s. per barrel. Has taken recognizances for the appearance of Mason at the next assizes, and bound over persons to give evidence against him. [*Adm. Paper.*] *Encloses,*

37. i. *Information of Thos. Webb of Gravesend, labourer. Was desired, by Henry Mason, to carry a burden for him to John Watson's; delivered it to a servant girl of Watson, and returned for another burden, which was a tub covered with a cloth; while delivering that, was taken into custody, and has been ever since kept in the fort. Did not know that the burdens were gunpowder, or had the Tower mark upon them; and is ignorant whose they were, or whence and how they came to Henry Mason. March 24, 1665.*

37. ii. *Examination of Henry Mason. Sold two barrels of gunpowder to John Watson for 55s. each; bought them for 50s. each, of a person unknown, met with accidentally, who brought them on horseback to his house in Milton. Does not know the Tower mark, nor the King's mark on gunpowder barrels; never bought gunpowder before; did not think he had offended in buying this. March 24, 1665.*

VOL. CXVI.

1665.

37. III. *Examination of John Watson. Bought of Henry Mason, collar-maker, two barrels of gunpowder, which were to be brought to him; the barrels were seized by Serjeant Smyth and other soldiers under command of Sir John Griffith, for the King's use.* *March 24, 1665.*

37. IV. *Information of Serjeant John Smyth and company of soldiers. Going down the streets of Gravesend, observed a man with a burden, which they conceived to be gunpowder from the King's stores; followed him, viewed the barrel, and found the Tower mark upon it. The porter deposed to having received it from Henry Mason. Seized the barrels by order of Arthur Ingram, ensign of Sir John Griffith's company, and kept the porter in guard for some time.* *March 24, 1665.*

March 26. Commissions to Col. Edw. Grey to be Lieut.-Col., and Wm. Rolston, Major, in Col. John Russell's regiment of Guards. Minute. [*Ent. Book* 20, *p.* 32.]

March 26. Deal. 38. Ri. Watts to Williamson. Note of ships in the Downs. The Providence has brought in three prizes.

March 26. Royal Charles. 39. Sir Wm. Coventry to Lord Arlington. Was troubled to see the Duke with so small a fleet as he found, but now Sir Wm. Berkeley has brought up the ships from Portsmouth, and Capt. Allin those from the Straits; these, with a few others which have come in, make 23 sail, and they would think themselves invincible, but the want of men reminds them that they are mortal. The Duke ordered a ketch to go out yesterday and meet the Dutch packet boat, and to take and give a receipt for the letters, before the boat came in sight of his fleet, the latter being so small. Hopes Lord Sandwich will soon bring ships from the river. If all in the river could be manned and sent, they might defy the Dutch. [*Two pages.*]

March 27. Royal Charles, Harwich Road. 40. T. Ross to Williamson. There are 48 good, well manned ships in the road, and Lord Sandwich is expected. The Straits men and Sir Wm. Berkeley have arrived. Capt. Utbird goes to London, laden with 60,000*l.* in bullion and goods. When they come to an engagement, will send him the first Dutchman's ears for an umbrello to the south window of his lodgings; if their thickness will not secure him from the sun, knows not what will. A blazing star has been seen at 2 a.m., 20 degrees to the eastward. Hopes he knows the Exchequer is *excellent* pay, though some think the public faith was as good. Thinks his present abode a pleasant monastery retirement, for most of the society say their prayers backward. Lets him know that he is alive, lest the solicitous Jesuit get the survivorship of his lands in Kent.

March 27./April 6. Chelsea. Ambassador Van Goch to the States General. Many merchant ships, colliers from Hull and Newcastle, have arrived in the river. The Duke of Buckingham and Earl of Peterborough offered to

Vol. CXVI.

1665.

attend the Duke of York in his ship as volunteers, but that offer was, for several good reasons, declined. The King has given a ship to each of them, and also to Major Holmes the ship Revenge, which he accepted with much thankfulness, and declared he would maintain the name of his ship against the enemy. [*Holland Corresp., March* 27.]

March 27. 41. Certificate by Capt. John Fortescue of the Loyal Merchant being completely equipped as a man-of-war. [*Adm. Paper.*]

March 27. Harwich. 42. Anthony Deane to the Navy Comrs. Account of masts there and of money disbursed. Repairs of the Adventure. [*Adm. Paper.*]

March 27. Fareham. 43. John Langrack to the Navy Comrs. Particulars of timber in the Holt. Requests warrants to the justices of Surrey and Hampshire for carriage of timber. The money levied by them upon their several hundreds or parishes should be gathered by the constable and two others, on bond to pay any money needed for carrying on the work. [*Adm. Paper.*]

March 27. The Expedition, Margate Road. 44. Capt. Tobias Sackler to Sam. Pepys. Is to remain in Margate Road till further notice, to press men; wants a surgeon. [*Adm. Paper.*]

March 27. Portsmouth. 45. Commissioner Thos. Middleton to [Sam. Pepys]. Repairs of the Eagle and Ferdinand. Has received no orders about the Madras. Sends the names of the masters chosen for the galliot prizes. Has discharged the London calkers, Capt. Allin's fleet having passed the port. Has bound Jones and his security in 40*l*. bonds to appear at the next assizes. Has been obliged to act on his own authority, for want of a press warrant; hopes for the King's pardon, in the form of a press warrant under the broad seal. Fears none but Lord Colepeper, who will find it a hard matter to get him out of Portsmouth. Particulars of stores. The Commissioners of Prizes refuse to deliver goods without ready money. Progress of ships in dock. [*Adm. Paper, three and a half pages.*]

March 27. Royal Charles. The Gunfleet. 46. Sir Wm. Coventry to the Navy Comrs. Has written to the Duke of Albemarle to order convoy for the New England masts from the Downs. The Lizard is sent to St. Malo. Thinks the Augustine, being gunned, and a few men and soldiers on board, may convoy a vessel thence; the fleet should not be distracted with various convoys. [*Adm. Paper.*]

March 27. 47. Sir Wm. Coventry to Sam. Pepys. Recommends the hire of Thos. Snidall's hoy for sending to the fleet; she holds 80 or 90 tons, and her master is used to the King's Channel and the North. [*Adm. Paper.*]

March 27. 48. Robt. Southwell to Sam. Pepys. Desires for the Commissioners of Prizes, a copy of the instructions printed and given to captains of ships. The Freeland of Amsterdam is condemned, and may be had for the use of the navy. [*Adm. Paper.*]

Vol. CXVI.

1665.

March 27? 49. Capt. Jos. Saunders to the Navy Comrs. The Breda is prevented going to sea for want of men, and hindered by weather from getting her provisions, &c., on board. [*Adm. Paper.*]

March 27. Royal Charles. 50. Sir Wm. Coventry to Sam. Pepys. Advises the slopsellers' account to be taken of the clothes on board each ship, and money to be sent to them for a further supply. Flags, stores, and ammunition wanted; also ketches and small vessels for watering the fleet. The men left sick at Portsmouth may now be fit to man the merchant ships. The surgeons of the ships returned from the Straits demand medicaments; the Plymouth and Portsmouth are ordered into dock at Chatham, the rest of the ships to be kept out at present. When the Earl of Sandwich returns, there will be no fear of the Hollander, in whatever condition he may be; though not a numerous fleet, yet the quality of the ships considered, ours will be able to give them odds, but in the present condition of victuals and stores, we can do nothing against them. Everybody must be quickened to the utmost, this being a pinch of time when all diligence is required. Many of the Fame's men are without clothes, because the slopsellers failed to send them as promised. The service suffers by such neglect. Most of the Straits' ships are well supplied with cable, but want shrouds, &c. [*Adm. Paper, four pages, imperfect.*]

March 27. Dover. 51. Thos. White to the Navy Comrs. Has received the Duke of York's warrant to act as agent for the navy in that port; promises a worthy discharge of his trust. Begs an order to buy navy stores when persons will not wait an answer from London; has storehouse room for 200 tons of provisions, and a private yard for timber adjoining his dwelling house. [*Adm. Paper.*]

March 27. 52. John Tooker to Sam. Pepys. Particulars of his agreement with Mr. Warren to carry 50 tons of goods to Tangiers for 20*l*. Difficulty in settling the accounts; only claimed what he was properly entitled to. [*Adm. Paper.*]

March 27. Bristol. 53. Sir John Knight to the Navy Comrs. Urges the speedy furnishing of the George with stores and ammunition. Has already 150 pressed men on board; 110 men is too great a number for the ship's company. Requests payment of 100*l*. to the owners for two months' hire. [*Adm. Paper.*]

March 27. 54. Jonas Shish to the Navy Comrs. The men refuse to work; suspects the calkers as being the ringleaders. [*Adm. Paper.*]

March 28. Castle frigate, Harwich. 55. Capt. Ph. Evatt to the Navy Comrs. Was ordered to take on board men from the Vice-Admirals of Essex and Suffolk, but not one is provided. Must lie in harbour at great expense, while probably the whole fleet engages; has 100 men on board, but very few are seamen. Particulars of stores wanted, especially clothes, without which they cannot perform their duty, being eaten up with vermin; four are discharged sick, from want of necessaries in the extremity of the weather. [*Adm. Paper.*]

VOL. CXVI.

1665.

March 28. Harwich hoy. Harwich. 56. Giles Bond to the Navy Comrs. Is unlading and awaits orders. [*Adm. Paper.*]

March 28. Chatham Ropeyard. 57. John Owen to Sir Wm. Batten. Wants a speedy supply of hemp. [*Adm. Paper.*]

March 28? 58. Edw. Gregory to Sam. Pepys. Account of money disbursed; great expense in wages, &c. The 150*l*. lent by Mr. Perry, and long since paid away in the King's service, is not yet repaid to Perry's wife, notwithstanding the absolute orders of the Board. [*Adm. Paper.*]

March 28. The Monk, The Hope. 59. Capt. Thos. Penrose to the Navy Comrs. Notifies his arrival after repairs. Is ready to take in provisions. Begs an addition of 20 men to his 260. [*Adm. Paper.*]

March 28. King Ferdinando, Portsmouth Harbour. 60. Capt Fras. Johnson to the Navy Coms. Account of stores required for his ship. Has 120 men on board, about 40 seamen amongst them. Desires a press warrant for boatmen and carpenters' stores. [*Adm. Paper.*]

March 28. 61. Agreement between the Navy Comrs. and Capt. Simon Nichols and Ben. Henshaw, for hire and freight of the King Ferdinando, 400 tons burden, at 8*s*. per month per ton, for six months certain, and twelve months uncertain. [*Adm. Paper, one and a half pages.*] *Enclosing,*

> 61. i. *Note of the Ferdinand's entry into the King's service, April 5th, continuing until Oct.* 5, 1665.

March 28. Plymouth. 62. John Lanyon to the Navy Comrs. The Hulk is ready. Proposes converting the Dutch prize, St. Mary Conception, into a man-of-war. [*Adm. Paper.*]

March 28. Cockpit. 63. Duke of Albemarle to the Navy Comrs. Recommends Rich. Smyth as master of a ship. [*Adm. Paper.*]

March 28. Cockpit. 64. Duke of Albemarle to the Navy Comrs. Has ordered the Pembroke into Dover to clean. Desires that she may be revictualled there. [*Adm. Paper.*]

March 28. 65. Warrant from the Duke of Albemarle to Gilbert Thomas, provost marshal of Westminster and Middlesex, to deliver to Capt. Rich. Newbury the papers concerning the ship Hopewell, and any other private papers which he lately took from him.

March 28. Whitehall. 66. Warrant from Lord Arlington to the Farmers of Customs in the port of London, to permit the landing, duty free, of certain wines for the use of M. Courtin, French ambassador. [*Draft.*]

March 28. The Charles, Harwich. 67. H. Brouncker to Williamson. Requests him to deliver the enclosed.

March 28. Royal Charles, off the Gunfleet. 68. Sir Wm. Coventry to Lord [Arlington]. Keeps a paper of marine intelligence to make extracts from. Has been too busy to do it, having been writing incessantly, or attending the Duke at the

VOL. CXVI.

1665.

Council of war; the fleet has been divided into three squadrons, leaving out ships that are very backward, or are upon the Irish coast, or Tangiers, but taking in all that may be expected in three weeks' time, if want of men hinder not. Are putting the fleet into good condition for active service. Capt. Gilpin, a good commander, was drowned in his boat. The Duke is unwilling to give a reference on Mrs. Lisle's petition, thinking nothing could be got thereby, but if she has a right, she may try it. Lord Sandwich has arrived with the Prince and the Unicorn. [*Two pages.*]

March 28. Reference to Lord Treas. Southampton and Lord Ashley on the petition of John Harvey, receiver for Lincolnshire, for repayment of 300*l*., paid in gold by his late father for the use of the late King, His Majesty wishing to gratify the petitioner, but without prejudicing his own service by the example in future. [*Ent. Book* 18, *p.* 134.]

March 29. Reference to the Lord Treasurer and Chancellor of the Exchequer on the petition of Rice Powell, for relief from debts contracted in the King's service. [*Ent. Book* 18, *p.* 130.]

March 29. London. 69. Robt. Sainthill to Williamson. Begs the return of some papers which he gave three years ago to the King, who delivered them to Sec. Bennet. The Lord Treasurer being unable to pay him, tried to obtain payment from the customs, excise, or chimney money, but in vain. Was ordered to think of something that could be done for him, and has now a proposal to make about a beneficial trade to Tangiers.

March 29. The King to Sir John Clayton, professor of physic in Oxford University, and master of the Almshouse of Ewelme, co. Oxford. Orders admission of John Taylor to the next Almsman's place vacant, he having received many wounds in fighting against the rebels, and being now very impotent. [*Ent. Book* 17, *p.* 101.]

March 29. 70. Trinity House certificate that Edw. Watts, of Limehouse, is an experienced mariner, and able to take charge of a fourth or fifth rate frigate.

March 29. The Plymouth, Blackstakes, over Queenborough. 71. Capt. Thos. Allin to the Navy Comrs. Is on his way to Chatham for repairs. Wants provisions of all sorts. [*Adm. Paper.*]

March 29. Dover. 72. Thos. White to the Navy Comrs. Intreats dispatch in sending down stores. Can get nothing at a tolerable rate. Asks an order for the use of goods in prize ships, and directions about ironwork, employment of ropemakers, &c. [*Adm. Paper.*]

March 29. Royal Charles. 73. Judge Advocate Fowler to the Navy Comrs. Is returned from the Straits, and wants stores after his long voyage of 16 months, and full payment of money due to him. [*Adm. Paper.*]

Vol. CXVI.

1665.

March 29. Royal Charles. 74. Judge Advocate Fowler to Sam. Pepys. Is safely returned from the tedious Mediterranean expedition, and incorporated with the fleet off Harwich. Solicits his influence with the Board for the payment of all moneys due to him; wishes Mr. Ewers to state what moneys his wife has received during his absence. Is on board the Unicorn. [*Adm. Paper.*]

March 29. Chatham Dock. 75. Phin Pett to the Navy Comrs. Great want of timber for the Victory and new ship. Mr. Cole of Sussex has contracted for 300 loads, but has not above 60 ready. [*Adm. Paper.*]

[March 29.] 76. Account of the division of the English fleet into squadrons:—37 ships under the Duke of York, 35 under Prince Rupert, and 35 under the Earl of Sandwich; also list of 4 fire-ships and 20 ketches, and account of the subdivision of the Duke of York's squadron under the admiral, vice-admiral, and rear-admiral. [*Two and a half pages.*]

March 29. 77. Similar list of the fleets as subdivided into squadrons, containing also the numbers of men and guns on each, and the names of the commanders, with the distribution of the smaller vessels. [*Three pages.*]

March 29. Royal Charles. 78. J. Pearse to Sam. Pepys. Begs that Rider, surgeon of the Nonsuch cast away in December last, may be paid for his former services, and appointed to the Portsmouth. The hospital ship must be sent down speedily, with all provisions necessary. Recommends Robinson as surgeon for it. [*Adm. Paper.*]

March 30. Harwich. 79. Anthony Deane to the Navy Comrs. Repairs of ships. Merchant vessels are ordered into the Rolling Ground for supply of stores. Boats wanted. Sends bills of timber and plank, paid for out of the imprest money. [*Adm. Paper.*]

March 30. Royal Charles, near the Gunfleet. 80. Sir Wm. Coventry to the Navy Comrs. The Duke of York consents to the making out monthly bills for slopsellers, to ensure a better supply of clothes, which are greatly wanted, even to endangering the health of the men. If there be not sufficient persons to supply the fleet, others must be procured. Capt. Kempthorne will yield to anything reasonable concerning his ship at Wivenhoe, required for the King's service, but refers the business to the owners, Sir Andrew Riccard, Mr. Kendall, and others. Rigging must be hastened down for the new ketch, intended to wait on Prince Rupert. Boats and hammocks wanted. Persons should be appointed to overlook the shipping of stores. [*Adm. Paper, two pages.*]

March 30. Pass for the Earl of Ailesbury, his lady and suite, to France, and to transport 25 horses. Minute. [*Ent. Book 22, p. 74.*]

March 30. Warrant to [Roger] Harsnett, serjeant-at-arms, to apprehend the Duke of Richmond, and convey him to the Tower. Minute. [*Ent. Book 22, p. 74.*]

Vol. CXVI.

1665.

March 30. Warrant to [Roger] Harsnett, serjeant-at-arms, to apprehend Lord O'Brien. Minute. [*Ent. Book* 22, *p.* 74.]

March 30. Warrant to Sir John Bishop to apprehend William Russell. Minute. [*Ent. Book* 22, *p.* 74.]

March 30. Warrant to Mr. Barkust (?) to apprehend Col. Russell. Minute. [*Ent. Book* 22, *p.* 74.]

March 30. Four warrants to Sir John Robinson to receive them all into his custody. Minute. [*Ent. Book* 22, *p.* 74.]

March ? 81. Petition of Charles Duke of Richmond and Lenox to the King, to withdraw his displeasure, and discharge him from restraint incurred by his being concerned in a late difference.

March ? 82. Petition of Lord William O'Brien to the King, for release from restraint. Was engaged in a business which justly incurred His Majesty's displeasure, he having strictly prohibited such differences.

March ? 83. Petition of Col. John Russell, of His Majesty's regiment of Guards, and of Wm. Russell, his nephew, son of the Earl of Bedford, to the King, for discharge from confinement; acknowledge the justice of His Majesty's displeasure, but were always obedient before, especially in accidents of this kind.

March ? 84. Draft of the above [*by Williamson*].

March 30. Westminster. 85. Warrant to the Exchequer and to the Auditor and Receiver for Oxfordshire to pay to Montague Earl of Lindsey, lieutenant of Woodstock Manor, 40*l.* a year for the park keepers, and 40*l.* for hay for the deer. [*Copy, two sheets.*]

March 30. Ipswich. 86. Capt. Robt. Wilkinson to the Navy Comrs. Was sent to press able seamen for the Charity, now in dock at Deptford. Has procured about 25, but they are very scarce. Will send them to London by land, there being no passage by water. [*Adm. Paper.*]

March 30. Royal Charles. 87. Sir W. Coventry to [Lord Arlington]. All the courtesy he has paid the French Ambassador has been quick dispatch of passes for French ships out of Holland, or release of mariners seized. Will send a list of those ships if required. Refers him to Sir Thos. Clifford for tidings of the fleet.

March 31. Royal Charles. 88. Sir Wm. Coventry and Sir Wm. Penn to the Navy Comrs. The London Stone ketch is to be hired, and dispatched forthwith. [*Adm. Paper.*]

March 31. Gravesend. 89. Capt. Hugh Hyde to the Navy Comrs. The Jersey is ready to sail, having 150 men on board; it is impossible to procure more seamen, for the merchant ships are altogether stripped of men before coming into port, by the vessels they meet abroad. Requests an order to join the fleet at once. [*Adm. Paper.*]

Vol. CXVI.

1665.

March 31. 90. Contract between [Sir] Wm. Coventry, Sir Wm. Penn, and Wm. Hotchin, for the hire of the Pelham ketch of Wivenhoe, upon the same terms as the Isabella, she being warranted to carry equal freight. With memoranda thereon relating to the contract. [*Adm. Paper.*] *Annexing*,

90. i. *Certificate by Thos. Lewis, of Wm. Hotchin having cleared his victualling accounts from March 30, 1665, to December following. Victualling Office, May 30, 1666.*

90. ii. *Certificate by John King, and four others, of the Pelham being equal in burthen to the Isabella, viz., 85 tons. March 9, 1667.*

90. iii. *Certificate by Rich. Dickenson, of the care and diligence of Wm. Hotchin, master of the Pelham, in attending the Swiftsure, under command of Sir Wm. Berkeley, deceased, from April 1, 1664, to Nov. 15, 1665. April 12, 1667.*

March 31. Forest of Dean. 91. Dan. Furzer to the Navy Comrs. Requests an assistant for the smith. Sends rates and prices of lesser anchors, and an agreement for ships' work and supply of stores. Is much hindered for want of an order to fell keel-pieces, plank, stocks, &c. [*Adm. Paper.*] *Encloses*,

91. i. *Indenture whereby Dan. Furzer of Lydney agrees to pay to Rob. Tampler and Wm. Eddy, both of Lydney, blacksmiths, 25s. 8d. per cwt. for larger descriptions of ironwork, and 28s. for smaller, to be delivered into the storehouse at Conpill; any found not good to be returned to the makers. [Damaged.] March 16, 1665.*

March 31. Kinsale. 92. Capt. John Johnson to the Navy Comrs. Capture off the Land's End, of a Hamburg pink, the St. Peter, 80 tons burthen, laden with wine. Has delivered her to Rob. Southwell, vice-admiral of the place. [*Adm. Paper.*]

March 31. Yarmouth. 93. James Johnson to Sam. Pepys. Recommends Ben. Stedman to build a fifth-rate ship; will send his demands and a draft speedily. The Edgars are willing to contract for a fourth and fifth rate frigate. [*Adm. Paper.*]

March 31. Woolwich. 94. Chris. Pett to the Navy Comrs. Particulars of timber needed; labourers are wanted, many of the men being gone to sea in the service, &c. [*Adm. Paper.*]

March 31. Warrant to Ralph Hutter to take John Blackwell into custody, till further order. Minute. [*Ent. Book* 22, *p.* 75.]

March 31. Warrant to the Commissioners of Prizes to release the Gustavus Horne of Riga, the King having, at request of the resident of Sweden, pardoned the master of the said vessel for attempting to transport away 40 Dutchmen. [*Ent. Book* 22, *p.* 77.]

Vol. CXVI.

1665.

March 31. Warrant to the Officers of Exchequer, Farmers of Customs, &c., to remit the fine of 64*l.* 17*s.* 8*d.* imposed upon Jacob Mariette, for importing three bags of red wool not brought direct from the place of growth, it appearing that the wool ought to come free, and that there was no design of fraud in the importer. [*Ent. Book* 22, *p.* 78.]

[March 31.] 95. Draft of the above. [*Damaged.*]

March 31 Warrant for a grant to Edward Villiers and his heirs for ever of the lighthouse at Tynemouth Castle, with power to receive 12*d.* toll of every ship trading to Newcastle or Sunderland, instead of 4*d.* received before, on condition of his rebuilding the lighthouse which is now in decay, and paying a rent of 20 marks to the Crown. [*Ent. Book* 22, *pp.* 79, 80.]

March 31. Egglestone Hall. 96. Christopher Sanderson to Lord Arlington. John Atkinson, the fugitive of Askrigg, is in London. Chris. Eyon approves the book mentioned in his last as the best book that ever fell into his hands; the name put to it is "Laophilus Misotyrannus." The King should take more than ordinary care of his person till this rumour of a Dutch war is blown over; the first design of the traitors now lurking in London will be against him. Description of Atkinson's person; he was a volunteer against the King in the late times; hopes the party may be discovered by the addresses of their letters which he gave. There should be great care taken that Lambert does not escape. As nothing will satisfy them but dominion, hopes nothing will satisfy the King but hanging and banishing them. [*Some names in cypher, decyphered.*]

March? 97. Account of letters, &c., sent to or delivered from the Government authorities in Ireland and Scotland, the Duke of Albemarle General of the forces, the Members of Parliament, and Ministers of State, from 31 December 1664 to 31 March 1665, for which allowance is demanded by Katherine Countess of Chesterfield, widow of Dan. O'Neale, late postmaster general.

March? 98. Petition of Capt. Walter Braems to the King, for a warrant to dig for plate and jewels said to be concealed in cos. Hants, Somerset, or Leicester, not digging within walls or under ground sown with corn, nor prejudicing the proprietors, and reserving a third on his discoveries to the King, and another third to the discoverers.

March? 99. Petition of Thos. Holland to the King, for the place of one of the Commissioners for Appeals. Has failed in many similar attempts, though His Majesty has often expressed an intention of serving him, on account of the loyalty of himself and his relations. [*Draft by Williamson.*]

March? 100. Petition of Capt. Rich. Minors to the King, for some gratuity to enable him to serve on the present expedition; in 1662, conveyed the Viceroy Antonio Melho de Castro and 80 Portuguese to Portugal,

1665. Vol. CXVI.

in his ship bound for the East Indies, without any return made him, and the President of the East India Company there sent him home with 60 tons of pepper, when he could have made 7,000*l.* freight.

March ? 101. Petition of Dame P. Mohun to the King, for an order to the keepers, &c. of Whittlewood and Saulcey forests, to permit her to cut down and carry away 1,500 dottrell and decayed trees there, fit only for firewood, according to her order of 24 March last, pursuant to which she employed agents to view and mark the trees, but they were stayed in their work by the under officers.

March ? 102. Similar petition, stating that the grant was made her on consideration of her voluntary delivery of her patent for the coinage duty, long before it was expired.

March ? 103. Petition of J. Neril to Lord Arlington. Complains that though a servant of M. De Cominges, the French ambassador, he was arrested by officers of the liberty of the duchy, who refused his liberation, though he showed the ambassador's protection; that a special writ was issued against him for 500*l.* on a mere verbal allegation, and 30*s.* offered to a person whom he never saw to swear against him; has given bail for 1,000*l.* to show that he intends no fraud, but begs that the parties may ask his pardon, and be ordered not to do the like again.

March ? 104. Petition of John Williams, porter to the mint and mines in Wales, to Sec. Lord Bennet, for a warrant to summon John Port, now a merchant in London, before him, because he and his agents, about 1647, broke open the mint and storehouse, and took bullion or coin worth 30,000*l.*, and other materials, from the petitioner's custody, conveying them into Holland or elsewhere.

March ? 105. Petition of James Robinson, merchant, to the King and Council, for admission as surveyor of the Royal fishing, or for the place in the post office, held by the late Dan. O'Neale, on condition of his employing his profits in building busses, and promoting the fishing trade. Was ordered relief for his former great losses by the Dutch, yet in the treaty, the public concernment required him to be left out; was ordered other compensation, and proposed the propagation of the Royal fishing; but in spite of references on his petitions, nothing has been done.

March ? 106. Petition of William Sanders, draper of London, to Lord Arlington, for payment of 323*l.* 13*s.* 5*d.*, for cloth delivered at ready money prices, which was ordered by his lordship for the funeral of the late Lord Wentworth. *Annexing,*

106. i. *Bill for the aforesaid cloth, with certificate of its delivery, by Wm. Harwood.* 2 *March*, 1665.

March 107. Petition of Herbert Throckmorton, disbanded ensign, to the King, for the place of Ensign in the late Lord Wentworth's regi-

Vol. CXVI.

1665.

ment at Portsmouth; served three years at Berwick, was dismissed on the reduction of the garrison, and then trailed a pike under Lord Wentworth.

March. Whitehall. 108. Warrant to Sir George Carteret to pay to the Admiral's regiment under Sir Wm. Killigrew such allowances as shall be directed on debentures, according to the muster rolls of the several companies.

March. Whitehall. 109. Warrant for Major Wm. Gower to be serjeant-at-arms to the Duke of Buckingham, appointed President at York. [*One and a half pages.*]

March. Whitehall. 110. Order for a warrant to the Attorney of the duchy of Lancaster to prepare a grant to Charles Lord Gerard, of Brandon, of 1,000*l.* a year for life, to be received from the revenues of the duchy, he having resigned the office of Captain of the Guard. [*One and a half pages.*]

[March.] 111. Draft of the preceding, with a clause that the payment is to begin from 25 Dec., 1661, the arrears for the last three years and the payment for the present to be made 24 June next. [*Two and a half pages.*]

March. Memoranda [by Williamson] of warrants, &c., passed in the signet office during the month, the uncalendared portions of which are as follow:—

Grant to Jer. Gobory, dancing master to the Queen, of 140*l.* for life.

Note that on the Earl of Carlisle's return from Russia, the plate for his house and chapel, which had been furnished him as usual on an indenture with the master of the Jewel House, was all given to him.

Grant to Wm. Rumbold and Thos. Townsend of the office of Clerk of the great wardrobe, on their surrender of a former patent.

Grant to William, son and heir of the late Sir William Craven and his brother Sir Anthony, of the title of Baron Craven, of Hampsted Marshall, in default of heirs male of the Earl of Craven.

Commission to Sir Denny Ashburnham, Sir George Benyon, Fr. Smith, and Edw. Wingate, to manage the revenue of excise, with allowance of 2*d.* out of every 20*s.* received.

Creation of Lord Arundel of Trerice, Cornwall.

Note that when an inclosure is allowed in a forest, there must be a clause commanding its allowance at the next justice seat in Eyre.

Vol. CXVI.

1665.

Licence to Sir Barth. Pell, Thos. Killigrew, and others, for 31 years, to appoint places for shooting with the long bow, wrestling, running, &c., and to set prizes.

Note that the under-housekeeper at Whitehall is paid yearly for cleaning the house, on a bill signed by the *Lord Chamberlain*.

Licence to Nich. Pitts to use his new invention of making salt out of sea brine, without fire or sun.

Note that Sir John Finch, resident at Florence, had 500*l.* for his equipage, and 1,000*l.* quarterly entertainment, besides intelligence money. [*Domestic Corresp., Feb.* 1665.]

March ? 112. ——— to [Sir Edw. Bagot]. He is to tell Sir Nicholas [Armorer] that he conversed with an Anabaptist who feared lest the Dutch have already corrupted the navy, for no man would be firm to the King who had fought against him; he thinks the Dutch war is wholly on account of the old English rebels. Treachery must be prevented. Great matters are expected by the rebels from Scotland, when the Dutch and we engage. Marked [by Williamson] "Sir Edw. Bagot to Sir Nich. Armorer." [*Fragment.*]

March ? 113. John Buckworth to Chas. Porter. Has traced the report of letters of marque being granted in Holland against the English to Capt. Gospritt, a sober discreet person, and sends his letter thereon.

March ? 114. Request that Thomas Ball and four other mariners of Bristol, sent to Newgate in November, 1664, for running away after they had been impressed for the navy, who have been long in prison ready to starve, and are very ready to serve, may be discharged and sent on board the fleet.

March. 115. Account by Rich. Royston, stationer, of goods delivered to Mr. Williamson for Lord Arlington, Feb. and March, 1665; total, 73*l.* 7*s.* *Annexing,*

115. I. *Bill of former goods delivered for Lord Arlington from* 1662 *to February* 1665; *total,* 58*l.* 8*s.* [*One and a half pages.*]

March. 116. Statement of the mode of publishing, by the heralds and pursuivants, &c., the King's declaration of his resolution to exact satisfaction for the injuries done by the Dutch to the East and West India Company. [*Imperfect.*]

[March.] 117. Note of Mr. Draynar's embalming the body of Lord Wentworth.

[March.] 118. Bill of [Sir Alex.] Fraser of 80*l.*, for embalming the body of Thos. Lord Wentworth.

[March.] 119. Apothecary and surgeon's bill of 80*l.*, for embalming the body of Lord Wentworth.

[March.] 120. Bill of expenses at the funeral of Thos. Lord Wentworth; total, 537*l.* 8*s.* 7*d.*, beside the herald-at-arms.

VOL. CXVI.

1665.

March ? 121. Bill by Thos. Simons, King's seal engraver, for 23 seals made for Lord Arlington as Sec. Bennet, with the three alterations in his coat of arms; total, 49*l.*

March ? 122. Statement of the advantages of a quarantine, beside that of keeping off the sickness as mentioned in the petition; viz., securing the customs, regulating imports, making freer and cheaper markets by its being known what merchandise is in port, discovery of persons coming in, which are merchants and which travellers, &c.

March. 123. Account of 45 ships mustered by Mr. Gelsthorp and another, with the numbers of men on each, varying from 607 to 72. [*Adm. Paper.*]

March ? 124. Account by Capt. John Fortescue of the dimensions of 14 ships hired for the King's service. [*Adm. Paper, three pages.*]

March ? 125. List of goods on board the ship Mary of Dieppe, pretending to be for the Earl of St. Alban's.

March ? 126. Directions from the Duke of Albemarle that Atkinson, now in the Tower, is to be sent to the assizes at Carlisle; Oldroyd, in the Gatehouse, to the York assizes; and Bovet, in Somersetshire, now only in the Marshal's hands, to be sent up prisoner. With marginal notes of warrants required for these transfers.

March ? 127. Note that no action of the Fifth-Monarchy men ever need be feared till they see the issue of the war; one of them confessed, at a meeting of 30, that his conscience troubled him for giving intelligence of their actings, and discovered that three others, Ward, North, and Fryer, were also intelligencers. They disputed whether to murder them, but decided in the negative. It is reported that Ludlow, Whalley, and Goffe are in Holland.

March. Lists sent by Mor. Lodge to Williamson of the King's and merchants' ships in the Downs during the month, and the state of the wind, viz.:—

No.	Date.	King's.	Merchants'.	Wind.
128.	March 3	4	0	N.E.
129.	„ 4	3	0	N.E.
130.	„ 9	22	10	S.
131.	„ 10	23	7	S.W.
132.	„ 11	24	10	E.S.E.
133.	„ 12	26	8	W.S.W.
134.	„ 13	28	8	S.E.
135.	„ 23	21	11	N.N.W.
136.	„ 25	3	4	S.W.

VOL. CXVII. APRIL 1–11, 1665.

1665.
April 1. 1. Sir W. Coventry to Williamson. Thanks for his news, which much consoles them when separated from the world, especially the volunteers, who have succeeded in losing all their money, and have nothing to do but to read. Some ships join them daily poorly manned, but with a supply of old soldiers which helps them much.

April 1. York. 2. Sir Fras. Cobb to Williamson. Will deliver the secretary's letters to the justices of the East and West Ridings of Yorkshire. Fears a tumult in York, as a person has written to order home his daughter, who is a servant there, for fear of troublesome times. A blazing star has been seen, which lasted a good while after daylight; the tail turned upwards and towards the west. Asks Mr. Secretary's title.

April ? 3. Petition of John Miller to the King, for release, on taking the Oath of Allegiance, and giving bail for his good demeanour and appearance. Was taken prisoner, 12 January 1664, from his house in Bedfordshire, and sent to Bedford gaol for a month, then brought up to London, examined by Sec. Bennet on his acquaintance with the treasonable practices of Capt. Nich. Cordey, then prisoner in the Gatehouse, but since released; was sent to the Gatehouse, and thence to Windsor Castle, where he has been above a year, not knowing any charge against him.

April 1. Warrant from Lord Arlington to Lord Mordaunt to discharge John Miller, on bond for his loyalty and appearance. [*Ent. Book* 22, p. 80.]

April 1. Royal Charles. 4. Duke of York to Lord Arlington. Hopes soon to have the fleet in such order as to execute the King's commands, and therefore begs written directions whether to annoy the enemy or protect subjects, when both cannot be done. Cannot make a good choice, being far from intelligence and from His Majesty's consultations. With note of reply.

April 1. Royal Charles. 5. Sir Wm. Coventry to Lord Arlington. The business is taking in victuals and stores. Three merchant ships have come in, poorly manned, but the old soldiers partly supply the defect of men; from the new-raised ones, the commanders pray to be delivered.

April 1. Plymouth. 6. Henry Pike [deputy vice-admiral] to the Navy Commrs. Sends Browning's bond. Is glad to hear of so many good men out of one ship. [*Adm. Paper.*] *Encloses,*

6. I. *Bond of Robert Browning, commander of the Robert and George of London, in 200l., to the Duke of York, lord admiral, for the delivery, upon his arrival in the Thames, of 17 impressed seamen now on board his ship at Plymouth, for whom he has received impress money.*
November 17, 1664.

Vol. CXVII.

1665.

April 1. Bristol. 7. Sir John Knight to the Navy Comrs. Acknowledges the order for payment of 100*l.* His ship is ready to sail. Asks what is to be allowed for the surgeon's chest. A pinnace is wanted. Has written to Mr. Coventry and is writing to the Duke of Albemarle, who acts for the Duke of York in his absence, to know where the ship shall carry the seamen; if no orders are received, will complete his number of 300 seamen, and start for Portsmouth to join the fleet. Persons must be appointed to appraise the ship upon oath, according to the articles. [*Adm. Paper.*]

April 1. The Portsmouth, Black Stakes, in the Medway. 8. Capt. Robt. Mohun to the Navy Comrs. Is on his way to Chatham for repairs. Requests directions to the officers of the dock for speedy dispatch to rejoin the fleet. [*Adm. Paper.*]

April 1. Portsmouth. 9. John Tippetts to the Navy Comrs. Six hundred oaks and 100 beeches may be had in the New Forest, and holly to supply the stores for many years. [*Adm. Paper.*]

April 1. Royal Charles. 10. Sir Wm. Coventry to Sam. Pepys. Sends a draft of an order about the slopsellers' business, to be amended by the Board before rather than after publication. A ship's lading of timber, taken by Capt. Allin near Cadiz, goes to Chatham, unless the King lay aside the thought of Commissioner Pett's building a ship by contract. Advises as many ships as possible to be built out of the River Thames, at Newcastle, Yarmouth, Winchelsea, Bristol, &c., owing to the scarcity of timber. Particulars of stores. The Council of War desire three water ships and two hospital ships, well fitted with cradles and surgeons, to attend the fleet. Recommends Robinson as surgeon; 2,000 hammocks are wanted. Clothes should be sent to Harwich before the Straits' men are paid; it would prove a good market, employ the men's money out of the alehouse, and take away a pretence of going to London for clothes. Demands cables for the Maryland and Hopewell. The Leopard and Adventure were aground between the Rolling Ground and Harwich, but sustained no damage. [*Adm. Paper, two and a half pages.*] *Encloses*

10. i. *Note by Abraham Ausley of what cables are on board the Maryland.* *April* 1, 1665.

April 1. 11. Contract for a fourth-rate ship, 100 feet long, to be built by Commissioner Pett at Chatham, for 2,000*l.* [*Draft, four leaves. Adm. Paper.*]

April 2. Portsmouth. 12. St. J. Steventon to the Navy Comrs. Sends quarter books from July 1 to December 31, 1664. [*Adm. Paper.*]

April 2. Harwich. 13. Sir Wm. Penn to the Navy Comrs. Is there by the Duke of York's orders, to give all possible dispatch to ships in harbour. The Straits' fleet cannot go to sea until their demand for provisions be supplied. The delay of the Augustine in bringing down cables is prejudicial to the service; the nimblest vessel that can be obtained should be employed. [*Adm. Paper.*]

VOL. CXVII.

1665.

April 2. Deptford. 14. Capt. Wm. Badiley to Sir Wm. Batten. Details his proceedings on board the Sarah pink towards taking up the wreck of the London. The master desires four more men. [*Adm. Paper.*] *Annexing*,

14. I. *Note of provisions required on the Sarah for carrying on the work.* *April 2, 1665.*

April 2. The Vanguard. The Hope. 15. Capt. Jonas Poole to the Navy Comrs. Arrived and sent the gunner up to procure stores. Is in readiness to receive victualling. Great want of men; despairs of getting his full number, unless he may have a convenient vessel to secure them better when pressed. [*Adm. Paper.*]

April 2. 16. Certificate by John Lloyd and John Turner to the Watermen's Company that Nath. Evans came on board the Dragon for a certain consideration, in room of Wm. Salmon, waterman.

April 2. Warrant to the Ordnance to deliver to the Master of the Mecklin and Black posthouse, Greenwich, 500 wheelbarrows, with 80 spare wheels, &c., and 300 pickaxes, for the use of the garrison at Portsmouth. Minute. [*Ent. Book* 16, *p.* 381.]

April 3. 17. Earl of Cleveland to Lord Arlington. Thanks for favours. A reference was obtained by his lordship to the Solicitor General, to take account of the sum pretended to be due from Stepney and Hackney to [Rich.] Blackwell, which is granted to Lady Belhaven; she would not then answer the writer's bill in the Exchequer, but having since done so, he is advised to proceed in court rather than on the reference. Requests a privy seal to the Barons of the Exchequer, to take the accounts in the King's name as mortgagee. Is sure His Majesty would be sorry for the obstructions he suffers from Lady Belhaven in settling his affairs. [*One and a half pages.*] *Annexing*,

17. I. *Account of the case between the Earl of Cleveland and Lady Belhaven, relative to the estate of Rich. Blackwell in the manors of Stepney and Hackney. Endorsed, "Returned."* *April 4, 1665.*

April 3. Royal Charles. 18. Sir Wm. Coventry to Lord Arlington. The fleet begins to be very strong, and if the river ships came up, would fear nothing but fire and sands. The fleet of colliers having come out, hopes the ships will soon be manned. The old soldiers have done good service towards the manning, but all are afraid of the new, ragged men. Sir Walter Vane, who came over with this packet, says the Dutch will come out; hopes it will be a short business and a good one.

April 3. Harwich. 19. Earl of Peterborough to Williamson. Has been with the Duke, and finds the Unicorn appointed for him. The fleet rides five or six leagues off; they provide for a business of some months. Thanks for aid towards getting his privy seal, and his business concluded with Mr. Povey.

VOL. CXVII.

1665.

April 3. Whitehall. 20. Robt. Southwell to Lord Arlington. The Prize Commissioners want the King's directions about the Prophet Daniel, a vessel laden with brandy and wines at Dunkirk and bound for Rochelle, driven by weather into the Isle of Wight, and there detained as a prize. M. Vandeper, the owner, confesses that the vessel belongs to an Englishman, to whom he is willing to restore it, but the goods are his own; yet some depositions in the Admiralty Court prove that the mariners speak nothing but Dutch.

April 3. Warrant to pay to Sir Roger Langley, Bart., 805*l.* 14*s.* 6*d.*, for disbursements on the trial of several persons in Yorkshire, where he was high sheriff. [*Docquet.*]

April 3. The George, Farnham, Surrey. 21. John Langrack to the Navy Comrs. Has marked 2,000 trees in Aliceholt, which will contain 2,800 loads; has been obliged to mark young trees, not finding serviceable timber sufficient for the required number. Requests warrants to the justices of Surrey and Hampshire for carriage of 2,700 loads, and for proper parish officers to be appointed to see the work performed. [*Adm. Paper.*]

April 3. Cockpit. 22. Duke of Albemarle to the Navy Comrs. The Royal Sovereign is to be graved; two sixth-rate frigates or one fifth-rate should be in readiness to sail to Barbary; 20 more good merchant ships must be hired and hastened to the fleet, amongst them a ship at Wivenhoe, whereof Sir Andrew Ricart, Capt. Kempthorne, and Mr. Kendall are owners; waterships carrying 800 tons of water are to be provided, and two hospital ships. Desires them to order a supply of masts for Commissioner Middleton at Portsmouth. [*Adm. Paper.*]

April 3. 23. Account of stores borrowed out of the prize ship, Young Hovelin. With note of an order, April 19, for these goods to be taken into the King's stores by Commissioner Pett. [*Adm. Paper.*]

April 3. Woolwich. 24. Capt. John Best, of the Marmaduke, to the Navy Comrs. Is prevented by illness from impressing seamen; begs that the imprest money may be paid to his lieutenant for a time. [*Adm. Paper.*]

April 3. The Lea, Bristol. 25. Dan. Furzer to the Navy Comrs. Business in the forest is delayed for want of the warrant lately demanded. Asks a warrant to press shipwrights, &c., for the ship at Bristol. Mr. Bayley, who is coming up to contract for a ship to be built, has the advantage that the Bristol men prefer being employed near home. [*Adm. Paper.*]

April 3. 26. Sir Wm. Coventry to Sam. Pepys. Must repeat the want of clothes and colours until they are provided; without the first the men must fall sick, and the others are so wanted that scarcely a ship in the squadron wears an ensign; is told that all the blue colours were lost in the London. The surgeon alluded to in the Duke of York's letter is Michael Behols. Sir Wm. Penn is ashore at Harwich, to dispatch the fleet there. The victualler at Dover does not play his part well; ships are much delayed there. Clothes, &c., must be hastened down to Harwich, not waiting for the Augustine. [*Adm. Paper, two pages.*]

Vol. CXVII.

1665.

April 3. The Castle frigate, Harwich. 27. Capt. P. Evatt to the Navy Comrs. Has received but two men from the Vice-Admirals of Essex and Suffolk. Is ready to sail; demands a speedy supply of stores and clothes. [*Adm. Paper.*]

April 3. Edwinstow. 28. John Russell to the Navy Comrs. Hoys wanted for carrying away the timber lying at Stockwith. Particulars of timber. Wants money and warrants for land carriage. [*Adm. Paper.*]

April 3. Royal Oak. 29. Sir John Lawson to Sir Wm. Batten. Wants a suit of pennants and some red ensigns, for the Royal Oak. [*Adm. Paper.*]

April 4. Harwich. 30. Wm. Coventry to Sam. Pepys. Has come on shore to see he place, not out of curiosity, but in order to understand it better when spoken of. Stores wanted, especially hammocks and clothes, also lighters, for want of which the service suffers much. The business of scrapers must be resumed for cleaning the sides and decks of ships; commanders complain of their ships not being so healthy since it was left off; health and cleanliness should be considered, men being so hard to get. A ketch of 90 tons is to be had at Colchester for 400*l*. The delay in victualling is intolerable, as from want of casks, the empty casks have to be got out and refilled at Ipswich, and there are no vessels to take them out; it would be well to employ some of the prize ships for that service. Proposes a hulk or two at Harwich, to ensure more safety in clearing out vessels; hulks much wanted there. Shows the bad effect produced by letting tradesmen's bills remain so long unpaid; some of the shipwrights have six months' pay due. Stores must be hastened down without waiting for the Augustine; hopes to be supplied and gone to sea before she arrives. Ships must be dispatched speedily to join the fleet; all depends upon the first appearance in the seas. [*Adm. Paper, five pages.*]

April 4. 31. John Greene to Sam. Pepys. Requests an order for the discharge of three pressed men, now on the Loyal Merchant at Gravesend, belonging to Mr. Turner, who fears his ship will be gone before he can get others. [*Adm. Paper.*]

April 4. 32. Sir Wm. Warren to the Navy Comrs. Can no longer supply Gottenburg masts upon the terms of his former contract, owing to many losses sustained, and both masts and freight have risen in value. Since the public notice by the King and Council of Sweden forbidding any more masts to be felled for seven years, has received commands from the Duke of York to buy up all that remained unsold, that such a necessary provision may not be wanting in time of war. Has now at Gottenburg seven or eight ships loading; requests vessels to convoy them to England, and a reasonable advance for the increased price. [*Adm. Paper, three pages.*]

April 4. Dover. 33. Thos. White to the Navy Comrs. Has made two contracts for cordage. Wants a supply of all sorts of stores, being cheaper in London than there; also a warrant to take up such men as shall be

VOL. CXVII.

1665.

needful. Asks the rate of carpenters and labourers' wages. Arrival of Lord Castlehaven from Ostend, and an ambassador from Flanders. An East Indiaman outward bound set sail. The King's pleasure boats have arrived from Calais, with the French ambassador. [*Adm. Paper.*]

April 4. 34. Jonas Shish to the Navy Comrs. Progress of the new ship. Timber wanted. [*Adm. Paper.*]

April 4. Plymouth. 35. John Lanyon to the Navy Comrs. Begs satisfaction for disbursements on the Hulk, now ready for service. Asks directions touching the St. Mary of Amsterdam prize ship; she will carry 46 pieces of ordnance. Mr. Barker's cable yarn is good. [*Adm. Paper.*]

April 4. Cockpit. 36. Duke of Albemarle to the Navy Comrs. Desires that two good fire-ships be provided with all possible speed, and dispatched to the fleet. [*Adm. Paper.*]

April 4. 37. Discourse on the reasons which England has to reject the Stuarts; viz., the taxes, exactions, and episcopal tyranny of the late King; the heavier yoke of this King, who permits none to speak publicly in the name of Jesus, but he must worship the Liturgy, or be thrown into a dungeon; men are hauled up and down, by 50 or 100, to prisons, wounded and slashed for praying, &c.; corporations enslaved, taxes multiplied, and public spirited men hunted down by the blood-hounds of the Court, and murdered. Exhortation to the people to say "To thy tents, O Israel!" and call the Stuarts to account for their stewardship! Those who received the King may as lawfully reject and put him to death, for falsity and perjury. Appeal to God to inspire the people to discern their duty, and to put a two-edged sword into their hands, to execute his judgments, &c. Endorsed, "Sectaries' papers"; also with the names of John Atkinson, of Askrigg, Chrs. Eyon, John Atkinson, —— Atkinson, and Mrs. Gower. [*Two pages.*]

April 4. 38. Leonard Williams to Sir Roger Langley. Lord Arlington promises him a few lines under the King's hand, for his security. The party are all in confusion about Atkinson's being taken, and are jealous of one another, not knowing whom to accuse about it; another besides himself is suspected. Southwark should be searched, as most of those about London lodge there; they would think Podsell or Atkinson was the cause of it, and would then come to this side the river, where they could not stir but they would be lighted upon. Can find the house in Thames Street where he was with Atkinson, if Atkinson confess that the arms are there now. Podsell would confess much if promised release on bail. [*Two pages.*]

38. i. *Note by W. L., that Podsell is looked upon as one of the fanatic party, a stout, faithful fellow, and was at the great meeting, of which the writer gave an account to Capt. Thomas, at the Rose and Crown tavern, near the Tower.*

VOL. CXVII.

1665.
April 5. 39. Warrant from the Duke of Albemarle to Sir George Carteret to pay to Sir Chas. Littleton 218*l.* 5*s.*, on account of ten days' pay for a company of 606 private soldiers at 8*d.* a day, 21 corporals and a drummer 12*d.*, and 7 serjeants 18*d.*, being a party lately come from Ireland.

April 5. Royal Charles. 40. Duke of York to the King. Read His Majesty's letter of the 3rd to the flag officers; the debates on it were tedious to relate, and they have not yet come to a fixed resolution, hoping further news of the present posture of the enemy, which may give more light. Meanwhile all think they should remain where they are till fully victualled, and till the ships at Harwich and the Rolling Grounds, and the second and third rate ships ready in or near the Hope join them. They think this for the same reason that made His Majesty resolve on that place for a rendezvous; viz., that the Downs would be hazardous for other ships to join them, and that where they are, the Dutch can gain less information of their strength. Meets the officers daily to discourse on this great affair, and is losing no time in getting victuals and water on board. Fears the Dutch may be before them, for Sir Walter Vane says that Opdam was to go on board this week, and that the wind favours their coming out. All, except Prince Rupert, think they will immediately come out and fight. Sends a list of the ships, but begs that no copies may be given of it, as it would be very serviceable to the enemy. Gives this caution, because he has seen a list in Dutch of the ships, so exact that it must have been copied from some of His Majesty's books, which are in the hands of persons of quality. Lord Muskerry sends a proviso which he wishes inserting in the Act for Ireland, and none have a better title to it by services and sufferings than the late Marquis of Clanricard. Begs that the new ketch may not wait for the Duke of Buckingham, as he is staying some time longer. [*Five pages, holograph.*] *Encloses*,

40. I. *Proviso for payment to Charles Viscount Muskerry, out of the security for commissioned officers serving before June 5, 1649, of the arrears due to the late Marquis of Clanricard, to Dec. 10, 1650, for his services in Ireland.*

April 5. Royal Charles. 41. Sir W. Coventry to the King. Was no further concerned in the wish for punctual orders to be sent to his Royal Highness than from due respect to His Majesty's resolutions. Shall himself always act as ordered.

April 5. Hague. 42. Charles Henry Lord Wotton to Lord Arlington. Was ready to cross the sea and tender his duty to the King, when the Princess Dowager [of Orange] threatened, if he did so, to deprive him of all he has under the Prince, which is very considerable. Does not wish to be a burden to his friends, but will still come if he may be serviceable to His Majesty.

1665. Vol. CXVII.

April 5. Yarmouth. 43. James Johnson to the Navy Comrs. If the Edgars' contract for fourth and fifth rate ships be taken, Yarmouth is as convenient a place as any in England for the building. [*Adm. Paper.*]

April 5. 44. Bills of the weight of tobacco stalks received from George Hudson. [*Adm. Paper.*]

April 5. Swiftsure. 45. Sir Wm. Berkeley to the Navy Comrs. Being ordered to carry the red flag, as Rear-Admiral, has caused his ship to be provided with extra lights for the poop and top. [*Adm. Paper.*]

April 5. Royal Charles. 46. Sir Wm. Coventry to Sam. Pepys. Asks the number of guns and men allotted to each merchant ship; if clothes be not speedily sent to the several ships, they will be full of incurable sickness. Victuals and tickets must be hastened for Harwich. Complains of the abuse of sending down boys instead of soldiers and watermen; has ordered them to be discharged and set on shore, unless the commanders in the river will have them. [*Adm. Paper, one and a half pages.*]

April 5. Lyme. 47. Capt. Wm. Hall to Sam. Pepys. Request repayment of 10*l.* taken up for Mr. Gauden's victualling agent; is appointed as convoy to several vessels, and has need of the money for impressing men on the coast of Norfolk. [*Adm. Paper.*]

April 5. Chatham. 48. Commissioner Peter Pett to Sam. Pepys. The plan of having only one deck for ships was found so bad that most of those built after the last Dutch war had an extra deck, but by this they lost their quality of bearing sail and carrying ordnance; asks whether the fifth-rate frigate now building is to have one or two decks. Urges the Board to converse with parties intending to build, to prevent the gross mistakes which have formerly arisen. [*Adm. Paper.*]

April 5. Dartmouth frigate, Dawpool. 49. Capt. Rich. Rooth to the Navy Comrs. Has drawn a bill for 224*l.*; is under sail for Milford, to dispose of 86 seamen impressed from Lancashire, 29 from Cheshire, 47 sent by Sir John Owen from North Wales, and 57 impressed by himself whilst there. [*Adm. Paper.*]

April 5. Gravesend. 50. Fr. Hosier to Thos. Hayter. The Satisfaction is still in the Hope with 120 men. Arrival of the Colchester and Hamburgh Merchant. [*Adm. Paper.*]

April 5. Yarmouth. 51. James Johnson to the Navy Comrs. Henry and Edmund Edgar, builders of the three last frigates, are willing to contract again, having the most commodious place in Yarmouth, for that purpose. [*Adm. Paper.*]

April 6. Yarmouth. 52. James Johnson to the Navy Comrs. Benjamin Stedman is willing to contract for the building of a fifth-rate frigate. [*Adm. Paper.*]

VOL. CXVII.

1665.

April 6. Woolwich. 53. Account by Capt. John Fortescue of 14 merchant ships taken up by him for the King's service, at Woolwich and Blackwall. [*Adm. Paper, two pages.*]

April. The Prince. 54. Capt. Roger Cuttance to Sam. Pepys. Colours wanted for the Earl of Sandwich's squadron, consisting of 37 ships and 6 ketches. A worn flag received from Sir George Askew has been used till now; when the Rear-Admiral comes, there will not be one for him to wear. Most of the blue colours in the fleet before were blown up in the London. [*Adm. Paper.*]

April 6. Barber Surgeons' Hall. 55. Rich. Reynell or Reynolds to Thos. Hayter. A surgeon wanted for the Portsmouth; if Mr. Pepys will send bills for the freight and imprest money, one shall be supplied forthwith. [*Adm. Paper.*] *Encloses*,

55. I. *Hugh Rider to Rich. Reynolds, clerk of the Surgeons' Company. Details his misfortune and loss as surgeon to the Nonsuch, lately wrecked; is appointed by the Duke of York to the Portsmouth, but being incapacitated by sickness from undertaking the service, begs that another may be provided in his stead.*

Harwich, April 1, 1665.

April 6. 56. Sir Wm. Coventry to Sam. Pepys. Has small vessels enough. Sends the order for slops, signed, that 400 copies of it may be printed for distribution amongst the fleet. The contract ships must be speedily dispatched; the Dutch have divers of their own ships built before the keels of ours are laid. Sends duplicates of the ticket made out for men discharged from the Loyal George, in case they apply for money. The pursers do not attend, pretending accounts at the victualling office. [*Adm. Paper.*]

April 6. Bristol. 57. Dan. Furzer to the Navy Comrs. Francis Bayley is willing to contract for the building of a ship at or near Bristol. [*Adm. Paper.*]

April 6. The Fox, Portsmouth Harbour. 58. Capt. Wm. Dale to the Navy Comrs. Will be ready to sail for Spithead in three days. [*Adm. Paper.*]

April 6. London. 59. Capt. Valentine Tatnell to Sam. Pepys. Begs the command of the Constant Warwick; would willingly wait, upon any promise of her, otherwise must hasten to the fleet; cannot remain on shore when so many of his old acquaintances are engaged at sea. Requests the speedy payment of his disbursements for pressing men. [*Adm. Paper.*]

April 6. Deptford. 60. Capt. Jonas Poole to Sam. Pepys. Has received 52 able seamen from Yarmouth and Lowestoft, who are now on board the Vanguard. The master of the vessel which brought them up demands payment for his freight; suggests hiring the said vessel to attend the Vanguard, and facilitate her dispatch to the Earl of Sandwich's fleet. [*Adm. Paper.*]

Vol. CXVII.

1665.

April 6. Harwich. 61. Sir Wm. Batten and Sir Wm. Penn to the Navy Comrs. Want a supply of various stores, colours, and tickets. [*Adm. Paper.*]

April 6. Portsmouth. 62. Account of the nature and value of loans and stores delivered to various merchant ships at Portsmouth, from Jan. 12, 1665. [*Adm. Paper, four pages.*]

April 6. 63. Copy of the above, with many more of the prices of goods filled in. [*Adm. Paper, two pages.*]

April 6. Harwich. 64. Sir Wm. Batten to the Navy Comrs. Will not begin to pay the Straits fleet till the ships now in harbour are repaired and victualled. [*Adm. Paper.*]

April 6. Chatham. 65. Sir John Mennes to [Sam. Pepys]. Survey of the new ship building by Mr. Pett. Counted six ketches over against St. Katherine's; questioned them what they did there, and was told that their commanders had orders, but none of them were on board. [*Adm. Paper.*]

[April 6.] Reference to the Attorney General on the petition of John Hargrill, to be quieted until his trial can be had at the Exchequer bar. [*Ent. Book* 18, *p.* 138.]

April 6. The King to [the Corporation of Leicester]. Approves their election of John Huckle to the office of Town Clerk, void by decease of Edward Palmer. [*Ent. Book* 14, *f.* 55.]

April 6. Pass for —— Sherwood to go and come. Minute. [*Ent. Book* 22, *p.* 80.]

April 6. Tower. 66. Examination of John Atkinson. Denies seeing John Hill, of York, and other persons named, at any meeting, or having more than ordinary discourse with Capt. Hodgson, Lieut.-Col. Beckwith, or Capts. Carter and Best. Lieut.-Col. Mason brought news from London and the west of England, that the north need not take the business upon them, as there would be assistance from other places. Knows not what was said at Capt. Lockyer's house, when the examinat was there with Marsden.

April 6. Tower. 67. Examination of John Atkinson by [Lord Arlington] alone. Cannot direct to the lodgings or meetings he formerly confessed of, nor tell where their magazines of arms are, but might if he had his liberty, and would faithfully return. Capt. Lockyer and Mene Tekel have moneys in their hands; the latter, if taken, would confess all he knows, and has long thought of putting himself into the King's mercy; they only talk at random as to help from the Dutch. [*One and a half pages.*]

April 7. Durham. 68. E. Matthews to Sir Herbert Price. Is kept in prison on false, feigned actions, to prevent his discovering something. Wishes to be removed to London by a *habeas corpus*, and brought before the King without delay, for fear of danger. Will pledge his life for the truth of what he has to tell

VOL. CXVII.

1665.

April 7. Plymouth. 69. John Lanyon to the Navy Comrs. Has sent Mr. Andrews an account of the hulk's repairs, and other disbursements for ships. The Sorlings is the only vessel now in port. [*Adm. Paper.*] Encloses,

69. I. *Account by John Lanyon, of money spent upon various ships in port; total, 527l. 18s. 3d. With note requesting payment of the sums to Thos. Andrews.*

April 7. 70. Pass and protection from impress, by Sir Wm. Penn, for the Michael of London, now at Ipswich, which has been hired for the King's service. [*Adm. Paper, damaged.*]

April 7. 71. Jonas Shish to the Navy Comrs. The only ships left at Deptford are the Charity and Hound, which are not fitted for fireships, the one not sailing well, the other being out of repair. [*Adm. Paper.*]

April 7. Barber Surgeons' Hall. 72. Rich. Reynell to Thos. Hayter. The wardens are desired to send a surgeon to Portsmouth for the Fox. Desires bills for her, as likewise for the Truelove and Maryland Merchant. [*Adm. Paper.*]

April 7. Chatham. 73. Commissioner Peter Pett to Sam. Pepys. Sir Edw. Dering's timber is much better than was reported; he demands 1,000l. for the 400 trees standing, or 31s. per ton of 40 feet. Particulars of ships. Desires money, for the poor men clamour much, some of them having eaten no flesh for weeks. [*Adm. Paper.*]

April 7. Chatham. 74. Commissioner Peter Pett to Sam. Pepys. Requests directions concerning 10 or 12 tuns of rosin come into the river, pronounced by the storekeeper to be very good, and offered at 18l. per tun. [*Adm. Paper.*]

April 7. Yarmouth. 75. James Johnson to Sam. Pepys. The two Edgars and Mr. Stedman are on their way to London, to contract for the fourth and fifth rate frigates required; it will be well to close with them at their first coming, to prevent a combination with the city builders. [*Adm. Paper.*]

April 8. Ordnance Office. 76. Edw. Sherburne and Fr. Nicholls, officers of ordnance, to the Navy Comrs. Request that the Harwich hoy may be assigned to assist in weighing the London's guns, and convoys appointed for two vessels now ready to convey stores to the fleet.

April 8. 77. List of 10 ships riding in the Hope, with numbers and particulars of men on board. [*Adm. Paper.*]

April 8. Bristol. 78. Sir John Knight to the Navy Comrs. The George is ready to sail as soon as her victuals and stores can be put on board; will not have above 200 seamen to send away, unless the easterly wind changes, and enables the many ships daily expected to come in, when there would be a considerable number in a few days; asks the proper charge for fitting up a surgeon's chest; desires an order on Mr. Morgan, collector of customs, for the payment of 100l. [*Adm. Paper.*]

VOL. CXVII.

1665.

April 8. Reference to the Ordnance Commissioners, on the petition of Robt. Holmes, for licence for powder and other ammunition, which he has put into Capt. March's hand, to be sold. [*Ent. Book* 18, *p.* 138.]

April 9. Weymouth. 79. George Pley to Sam. Pepys. The cloth from St. Malo shall be shipped for Portsmouth as soon as any convoy can be procured. Is wearied with waiting so long for a necessary supply of money to carry on the manufacture of English sailcloth, and will desist this week unless paid. It is a pity that so hopeful and necessary a manufacture should be let fall, for want of timely assistance, when it had need be increased, seeing the French have forbidden, under great penalties, the exportation of any sailcloth. Begs the consideration of the Board upon the matter, for once let fall those looms, and farewell the commodity. [*Adm. Paper.*]

April 9. Portsmouth. 80. St. J. Steventon to Sam. Pepys. Sends a blank for another imprest, the former of 400*l.* being more than expended. Gives account of weekly payments. Commissioner Middleton is dissatisfied, and will leave for London. [*Adm. Paper.*]

April 9. 81. Sir Wm. Coventry to the Navy Comrs. Hear that his proposal for more hulks at Harwich is approved, if they may be procured. Suggests that condemned prize ships, at Dover or Portsmouth, be set aside for that service, or a great ship whose upper works are decayed be fitted up. The Plymouth and Portsmouth must be hastened to the fleet, that Capt. Allin may attend a court of war on some who have misbehaved in the South. The Hound and Greyhound are proposed for fire-ships. Sir Wm. Batten thinks the Augustine may be fitted up to lie at Harwich to receive stores, &c. Great want of colours; could not fight if they would, for want of a flag to make signals with, the only remedy being the red coats of the volunteers. Particulars of small ketches hired. The merchant ships, though not fully manned, may do much good service if sent speedily. Clothes wanted. Sir Wm. Batten's agreement with the town of Harwich for some ground, being made by one of themselves, should be confirmed. [*Adm. Paper, three pages.*]

April 10. 82. Report [by Capt. John Fortescue] of the state of 12 ships in the river near Gravesend, Long Reach, Woolwich, Deptford, and Ratcliffe. [*Adm. Paper, three pages.*]

April 10. Chatham. 83. Edw. Gregory to Sam. Pepys. The Governors of the Chest have resolved, with Sir John Mennes' consent, to commence the general payment of the pensioners on the 8th of next month; begs the insertion of this into the News-book, to continue there 14 days; and for bills to be set up on the Navy and Treasury Office doors. [*Adm. Paper.*]

April 10. Custom. 84. Sir Wm. Clarke to Sam. Pepys. Recommends Wm. Earle for a Lieutenant's or Purser's place in one of the ships now to be hired. [*Adm. Paper.*]

Vol. CXVII.

1665.

April 10. Dover. 85. Thos. White to the Navy Comrs. Urges the expediency of all naval stores out of the prize ships being delivered at once into the stores, rather than bought second-hand; much money would thus be saved. [*Adm. Paper.*]

April 10. Farnham. 86. John Langrack to Sam. Pepys. Has received warrants for the Justices of Hampshire and Surrey; desires another for the Justices of Sussex, and a copy of the Act of Parliament. Wants money. [*Adm. Paper.*]

April 10. The Lee. 87. Dan. Furzer to the Navy Comrs. Requests that Peter Blackborow's offer of plank may in no wise be neglected in the present exigency. Asks directions concerning the trees blown down in the forest, whether they may be made use of without a warrant. A press warrant for men is wanted. Asks what sorts of ironwork are most needed, and how far the contract is accepted. [*One and a quarter pages.*]

April 10. Warrant to the Commissioners of Prizes to release the Charity, belonging to the French farmers of salt, and carrying salt for the King of France's storehouses, but driven by weather into Falmouth, and there detained 10 weeks. [*Ent. Book* 22, *p.* 81.]

April [10]. 88. Warrant for payment of a salary of 500*l.* each to the Commissioners of Ordnance, John Lord Berkeley of Stratton, Sir John Duncombe, and Thomas Chicheley.

April 10. Entry of the above. [*Ent. Book* 22, *p.* 83.]

89. Draft of the above, dated March.

April 10. Pass for 12 horses to Ireland for Col. Thomas Howard. Minute. [*Ent. Book* 22, *p.* 83.]

April 10. Warrant to [John] Bradley to apprehend a person calling herself Tarleton. [*Ent. Book* 22, *p.* 85.]

April 10. Warrant for making Lawrence Dibusty, native of Bayonne, a free denizen. Minute. [*Ent. Book* 22, *p.* 87.]

April 10. Warrant to the Commissioners of Prizes for release of a vessel called the Prophet Daniel, belonging to Dan. Van de Pere and Capt. Jacob Johnson, laden with wine and brandy at Rochelle, and bound for Dunkirk, but driven by weather into the Isle of Wight. [*Ent. Book* 22, *p.* 87.]

[April 10.] 90. Warrant appointing Dr. Macdowell, of Scotland, now residing in Holland, to transact certain affairs of importance there, and correspond with the Secretaries of State.

April 10. Entry of the above. [*Ent. Book* 22, *p.* 88.]

April 10. Whitehall. 91. Order for a warrant to the Woodwards and other Officers of the New Forest, to cause 600 oaks and 100 beeches to be felled in the forest for the use of the navy, and as much holly as the master shipwright of the yard at Portsmouth finds necessary.

April 10. Entry of the above. [*Ent. Book* 17, *p.* 104.]

VOL. CXVII.

1665.

April 10. Warrant to pay to Sir John Jacob and other farmers of customs 110,000*l.*, balance due of 190,000*l.*, at the rate of 20,000*l.* half yearly, from Michaelmas 1664 to 1667. [*Docquet.*]

April 10. Warrant to Sir Edw. Griffin, treasurer of the chamber, to pay to Constantine Magennis, footman to the Queen, 40*l.* a year. [*Docquet.*]

April 10. Westminster. 92. Grant to Thos. Bacon, on surrender in his behalf by Cuthbert Bacon, of the office of Ranger or Riding Forester in the New Forest, Hampshire. [*Latin, six sheets.*]

April 10. Royal Charles. 93. Sir Wm. Coventry to Lord Arlington. The Duke of York recommends to the Duke of Albemarle Col. Reymes' desire for a better convoy, and for better performance of such services, will assign his grace a competent number of ships for convoy, and for securing the channel against pickaroons; therefore the Duke of Albemarle must be referred to on such occasions in future. Sir John Monson's proposal, for the Newcastle convoys to join in point of time and tide with the Whitby men, will be difficult, and it will be still more so to make a fleet of colliers stay for three or four small boats to join them. If it be the King's pleasure, the Whitby vessels must have a convoy, but none of the King's ships can enter that harbour. They will have to ride out till the alum men come to them. [*Two pages.*]

April 10. The King to the Dean and Chapter of the Chapel Royal, Windsor. Requests them to dispense with the days of residence of John Durel, one of their canons, on account of his appointment as one of the constant preachers of the French congregation in the Savoy, for which he receives no allowance. [*Ent. Book* 19, *p.* 38.]

[April 10.] 94. Note of the above letter.

April 10. 95. Lord Ashley to Wm. Wardour, clerk of the Pells. Wishes to know the sums paid on the 18 months' assessment, from January 28 to March 25.

April 11. The Falcon. 96. Earl of Peterborough to [Williamson]. Has just saluted the Duke, and visited Prince Rupert and the Earl of Sandwich on their ships. The two latter think he (the writer) ought to have a better ship; is determined to be pleased with what the Duke of York thinks fit. The Duke of Buckingham has arrived when past expectation, but is not in the esteem a great man should be. [*One and a half pages.*]

April 11. Whitehall. 97. Petition of several Scotch Artificers in London and Westminster to the King, for letters patent to erect a charitable corporation for relief of their indigent and sickly persons and orphans, by providing them with a convenient workhouse. With reference thereon to the Attorney General, and his report, April 19, in favour of the petition. Signed by Rob. Caldwell, And. Paterson, and 17 others. *Annexing,*

97. I. *Queries in reference to the legality of the said corporation, and reply by Wm. Prynne, in its favour, quoting as*

Vol. CXVII.

1665.

presidents the Dutch corporations in Canterbury, Norwich, and Colchester; Jesus College in Oxford for Welsh scholars, and Queen's College for Northern scholars.

April 11. Entry of the preceding reference. [*Ent. Book* 18, p. 140.]

April 11. 98. List of seven Lieutenants and eight Ensigns who have quitted the service of the States of Holland, and are now in London. With note of three other Scottish Lieutenants come from Holland.

April 11. Reference recommending to the Lord Treasurer, the petition of Lady Frances Tyldesley, for payment of an annuity, on account of the eminent worth and loyalty of her late husband. [*Ent. Book* 18, *p.* 139.]

April 11. Reference to the Solicitor General on the petition of the Earl of Cleveland for a privy seal; and further reference, April 16, on Mr. Solicitor's report upon the case to the Lord Treasurer. [*Ent. Book* 18, *p.* 139.]

April 11. Reference to Lord Steward the Duke of Ormond on the petition of Luke Wilkes and five other yeomen of the removing wardrobe, for their allowance of six dishes, the King preferring to allow diet rather than board wages. [*Ent. Book* 18, *p.* 140.]

April 11. The Prince. 99. Earl of Sandwich to Lord [Arlington]. Thanks for his favour by Mr. Montague and Lord Falmouth.

April 11. 100. Phil. Tandy to Viscount Conway. Private affairs. Sends his accounts from December 4, 1664. [*One and a half pages.*]

April 11. Warrant for a grant to Thomas Killigrew, groom of the bedchamber, and Henry his son, of the coppices in Whittlewood and Saulcey forests, co. Northampton, and warrant for the same to be cut and felled, and the money to be paid to them, defalcating the allowances to the officers of the forest, &c. [*Ent. Book* 22, *pp.* 81–3.]

April 11. Warrant from Lord Arlington to [Wm.] Goldsburough, clerk of the House of Commons, to deliver to John Bradley, messenger, certain papers and books concerning affairs hitherto agitated by the committee of Darby House, which are of much importance for the service of Ireland. [*Ent Book* 22, p. 85.]

April? 101. Petition of George Moretto, His Majesty's surgeon, to the King, for leave to erect a stage in both the Universities, and in any other place in the Kingdom, free from all impositions, and notwithstanding any other person's having one erected at the time of his coming. *Annexing,*

101. i. *Certificate by Rob. Fox, and eight other residents in London, to the wonderful cures of wens, hare-lips, cancers, blindness, &c., performed by George Moretto on his stage at Tower Hill, those for the poor being done for charity. March* 13, 1665.

Vol. CXVII.

1665.

April 11. Whitehall. Licence to George Moretto, in consideration of his skill in medicine and surgery, to practise in any part of the King's dominions, and to expose his medicines for sale publicly, by erecting a stage in the market place, or any other mode which he deems convenient, without molestation to himself or servant. [*Ent. Book* 22, *pp.* 86-7.]

[April 11.] 102. Draft of the above. Endorsed "Mountebank." [*Two pages.*]

April 11. Whitehall. The King to the Lord Mayor, Recorder, and Aldermen of London. Many disorders daily arise for want of due execution of the late Act for repair of highways and sewers. Wishing to preserve that great and populous city from fire and other accidents, recommends more diligent execution thereof, and a strict review of all sewers. As irregularities in building are punished with less damage in the beginning, whereas the law only appoints punishment when they are done,—authorizes them, after due warning, to imprison such owners and workmen as continue to erect buildings made unlawful by the Act, and to pull down the said buildings. Desires them forthwith to open Temple Bar, and the passage and gatehouse of Cheapside, in St. Paul's Churchyard, as mentioned in the said Act, and will take care to inspect their progress therein. Has made the City his royal residence, and received from it such marks of loyalty and affection as will ever make him concerned for its wealth, trade, reputation, beauty, and convenience. [*Ent. Book* 17, *pp.* 102–3.]

April 11. Whitehall. 103. The King to [the New River Company]. Recommends Simon Middleton, son of Sir Hugh Middleton, who conferred a great benefit on London by bringing the New River from Chadwell, as clerk of the company. He holds the moiety thereof from the Crown in fee farm, and therefore his interest will be a pledge of his integrity. Wishes them also to admit Edw. Somes, merchant, as the agent whom by charter the King is to have, to be present and vote at all their meetings.

April 11. 104. Warrant from the Navy Comrs. to the Clerks of the Stores and Cheque at Deptford, to visit Mr. Boddicot's ropeyard in Goodman's Fields, and see the weight of some strands for five cables made by order of the Board. [*Adm. Paper.*]

April 11. Deptford. 105. Jonas Shish to the Navy Comrs. The Charity cannot be launched until the high tides. Repairs needed for the Hound. [*Adm. Paper.*]

April 11. 106. Capt. John Taylor to Thos. Hayter. Wants two bills for the New England masts lately delivered at Chatham, and a bill of imprest for 500*l.* on account, as promised. [*Adm. Paper.*]

April 11. London. 107. John Shorter to Wm. Pypes [Sam. Pepys?], Navy Office. Cannot comply with the terms of his contract for Norway masts, &c., owing to the increased rate of freight demanded; the master of the Olive Branch asks 400*l.* for what he formerly received 210*l.* [*Adm. Paper.*]

Vol. CXVII.

1665.

April 11. Deptford. 108. Capt. Wm. Badiley to the Navy Comrs. Has received two letters from Lambert Wood, concerning the wreck of the London, and things necessary to be sent down to further the work of recovering her. [*Adm. Paper.*] *Encloses,*

> 108. i. *Lambert Wood to Capt. Wm. Badiley. Has sounded round the wreck of the London, at low water, but finds she is all dispersed about, and can do no harm to any ship. There is no need to put up another beacon. His long boat is leaky; wants pitch for repairs.*
>
> *The London, April 6, 1665.*

April 11. Harwich. 109. Sir Wm. Batten to the Navy Comrs. The merchant ships must be hastened down; they will be better manned in Harwich than in London; 400 pressed men have arrived from Cambridgeshire and Lincolnshire. Is much plagued to get the Straits fleet's victuals. Cables and hemp wanted, also water ships. Has sent money to pay off the Straits' seamen, or there would be no keeping the men on board. Provisions wanted in the stores. [*Adm. Paper.*]

April 11. Chatham. 110. Sir John Mennes to Sam. Pepys. The Forester and Pembroke are dispatched. Desires the pursers' books of the Phœnix and Nonsuch. Fearful complaints among the seamen for want of clothes; the slopsellers have none but fine clothes and linen in store; shirts at 5s. each, and stockings at 6s. a pair, of no substance for service; it is their drift to send no more down of the proper quality, until necessity compels the seamen to take the remains of the fine. Asks how to dispose of the great number of men now unemployed in the yard. The new ship in building is at a stand for timber, and no other work in hand but pulling down the old Victory; the men are clamorous for money, and three quarters of a year behind in their pay. A full congregation of Quakers and the like were seized upon by Sir Francis Clark, and all, men and women, sent to Maidstone Gaol. Has ordered the unlading of the prize containing knees, timber, Spanish iron, &c. [*Adm. Paper.*]

April 11. 111. Thos. Lewis to Sam. Pepys. Mr. Brown, purser of the Drake, coming into Queenborough water destitute of victuals, had four days' petty warrant for 85 men granted, without order from the clerk of the cheque; the purser must now pay for it or get the warrant of the Board for his discharge. [*Adm. Paper.*]

April 11. York. 112. Math. Norwood to Sam. Pepys. Has made all possible progress with the business mentioned by Mr. Honeywood; viz., the dangers and the landmarks to shun them; the harbour within and above the dock, &c.; will do more the first opportunity. [*Adm. Paper.*]

VOL. CXVIII. APRIL 12-22, 1665.

1665.

April 12. Yarmouth. 1. James Johnson to Sam. Pepys. Perceives that a conclusion is made with the Edgars for the fourth and fifth rate frigates, the one at 6*l.* per ton, the other at such a proportion as was given during the last Dutch war. Mr. Stedman will accept the same terms. Three such ships are as many as can be well performed in the town. Offers 20 cwt. of great shot for sale. [*Adm. Paper.*]

April 12. Royal Charles. 2. Sir Wm. Penn to Sam. Pepys. Wants pilots. Wm. Sanders of Yarmouth, and Anthony Lowes of Tower Wharf must be pressed to serve in the Royal Charles, and hastened down with all speed. [*Adm. Paper.*]

April 12. [Deptford.] 3. Jonas Shish to Sam. Pepys. The King was yesterday in the yard, and well pleased with the proceedings. Begs that Mr. Edmonds may make the sails for the new ketch. [*Adm. Paper.*]

April 12. Royal Charles. 4. J. Pearse to Sam. Pepys. Is sorry Mr. Robinson is not to be surgeon of the hospital ship. Mr. Ringet, chief surgeon-general ashore to the King, would assist in procuring a good one; 50 sail of colliers passing to the river bring news of the Mermaid having chased and taken a Dutch man-of-war. The passengers from Portland say that 30 Dutch men-of-war set sail from the Brill last week for their rendezvous, and one for the East Indies. Mr. Ringet's house is in Durham Yard. [*Adm. Paper.*]

April 12. 5. Account of colours sent from Deptford to the Royal Charles and to Harwich, for the use of the fleet, since March 30. [*Adm. Paper, three pages.*]

April 12. St. Malo. 6. Geo. Pley to Col. Bullen Reymes. Sent a former petition, signed by 13 homeward-bound ship masters, for help. Some naughty fellows have given advice to Brest of the rich fleet homeward bound from St. Malo, and its small convoy; 4 Flushing men-of-war arrived to attend the setting forth; unless good convoy be sent forthwith, escape is impossible. Has entreated the stay of the Lizard for safe-guard until more force arrives. Begs and beseeches "haste, haste, haste." [*Adm. Paper.*]

April 12. 7. Thos. Harper to Sam. Pepys. Has dispatched colours, boats, and hammocks by the Royal Oak to the fleet. As distinction colours come in, they shall be sent. [*Adm. Paper.*]

April 12. Cockpit. 8. Duke of Albemarle to the Navy Comrs. Ships must be provided for carrying beer and dry victuals to the fleet, as soon as the victuallers have them ready. [*Adm. Paper.*]

April 12. Whitehall. 9. Pass at request of Benigne Heliot, merchant of Paris, for the Flying Eagle of Dieppe, to lade at St. Valery and Dunkirk, with wines, brandy, ribbons, &c., to sail to Stockholm for a lading of pitch, tar, copper, &c., and thence to London. [*Copy.*]

April 12. Entry of the above. [*Ent. Book*, 14, *pp.* 55-6.]

Vol. CXVIII.

1663.

April 12. Warrant to pay to Stephen Fox, paymaster of the forces, 3,500*l.*, for secret service, without account. [*Docquet.*]

April 12. Warrant to the Farmers of Customs to permit wine to be landed for the use of Mons. De Verneuil. Minute. [*Ent. Book* 22, p. 89.]

April 12. 10. Examination of Edw. Parrott, before Lord Chief Justice Hyde. Jas. Browne, prisoner in the King's Bench, complained to him of the wickedness of the times, but hoped things would grow better, and asked him if he could ride a horse. Browne wanted a buff coat and arms; thinks he can discover what Browne means to do, if he may have leave to go to him.

April 12. 11. Sir Fr. Cobb to Williamson. Finds the countryman who wrote to his daughter ingenuous in his answers, and of good life. Hopes good effects from the Lord Chancellor's excellent letters read at the quarter sessions. Will be careful to have constant intelligence from all parts of the county. Wants the order for the month's assessment.

April 13. Royal Charles. 12. Sir W. Coventry to Lord [Arlington]. After all this expense and pains, the fleet is likely to remain unserviceable, through defect on the victualler's part; supposed before that the delay proceeded from contrary winds, or sloth in the hoymen, but as other vessels and stores from the Navy Office come in, and only two small vessels of victuals, fears that Mr. Gauden has not the stock pretended. Beer especially is deficient; is afraid there is a lack of casks. The defects from Harwich are worse and more inexcusable, Mr. Gauden having orders, four months ago, to provide victuals in that port, and to prepare for the whole Straits fleet to return there; but though two of that fleet went to Chatham, yet now the rest are cleaned and ready to leave Harwich, their beer is not brewed. They are melancholy about the victuals, for if a store be not provided within a month, to last till November, the weather will be too hot to prepare them so that they can be relied on. It will be said that if the victualler send bad victuals, it is his loss, they must be thrown overboard; but that will not repair the King's loss, if his fleet cannot keep the sea, when he has most need of their service. Has long thought one man insufficient for such a task. Has had Mr. Gauden brought before Council, but although his own agent showed that he had only victuals at Portsmouth for 1,700 men, when he said he had enough for 4,000, he was dismissed without a chiding, affirming that the agent did not know, though upon the place, whilst Gauden was remote from it. When such neglect is not punished, people only make themselves enemies by complaining. Wishes inventories may be taken of masts, cordage, anchors, &c., in store, to supply a fleet which employs 4,000 tons of cordage; supplies should be ready to refit the ships after a fight, even if the King had to pawn the ring off his finger for money. Blind and general discourses that "we have a brave fleet, and we will be

1665. Vol. CXVIII.

at them," will not avail, where there is neither money, victuals, nor materials to carry on the war. Does not wish to be over officious in informing His Majesty of these things, and would not do it now, if all were not at stake. Unless the King stir vigorously in the matter, fair words and friends will destroy the business. Goes somewhat beyond bounds, from an earnest desire that His Majesty should be served, and that nothing under his Royal Highness's name and conduct should be reflected upon. Understands M. Choqueux is going to London, to complain that he has not what is fit; is threatened with Prince Rupert's anger about it. Does cheerfully what he is commanded, but cannot set new precedents without the King's directions as to private men's goods, or the Admiral's as to public, though few have taken less liberty than the Duke. Begs to be heard before he is condemned, on M. Choqueux's business. [*Four pages.*]

April 13. 13. Dr. F. Warner to Lord Arlington. Has no private ends in stopping Sir John from travelling, but thinks him under an influence that will force him out of religion, and out of his estate, entailed on him by his father, but cut off by himself; has therefore summoned him to appear and settle his estate first, without a power of revocation.

April 13. 14. Wm. Wardour to Lord Ashley. States the sums paid on the 18 months' assessment from 12 counties in England and Wales, from January 28 to March 25, 1665; total, 9,773*l.* 9*s.* 6*d.*

April 13. Letter for a lease to Henry Isham of the tithes of Darley, near Derby. Minute. [*Ent. Book* 14, p. 62.]

[April 13.] Letter to the Chancellor of the Duchy, for a lease to Henry Isham of the tithes of Belper, Chevin, and Holland, co. Derby. Minute. [*Ent. Book* 14, *p.* 62.]

April 13. Warrant to Sir Edward Broughton to apprehend John Low. Minute. [*Ent. Book* 22, *p.* 90.]

April 13. Reference to the Ordnance Commissioners on the petition of Henry Clarke, dismissed from his office as storekeeper at Portsmouth by unjust accusations, for examination as to his department. [*Ent. Book* 18, p. 141.]

April 13. Cadiz. 15. Jo. Bland to [Sam. Pepys]. [*First part of this letter dated March* 30 *from Tangiers.*] Has supplied Capt. Sam. Price with a bowsprit. A storehouse should be set up in Tangiers, to supply ships of war passing to the Mediterranean; at present vessels in extremity return home for assistance, thereby losing great advantages. During the war with Holland now begun, such a thing must be provided. Should a ship want powder, masts, cordage, &c., to go home immediately is a consideration and loss. It would also bring the town into request, and be a beginning for greater things. Is passing to Spain, being invited by the Spaniards to enter into

Vol. CXVIII.

1665.

contracts for several English manufactures. Foresees that in a few years, with proper encouragement for men of property to reside there, Tangiers will prosper and be made a beautiful and delightful place.

[*Continued April* 13.] Is now in Cadiz. Three Dutch men-of-war in port escaped from the fight with Admiral Allin, which dare not go to sea; also a brigantine and 13 merchant ships are preparing. They know not the forces in Tangiers, nor with how little strength Lord Belasyse came. Has been in Spain 10 days. The desire for contracts is renewed. Wishes the King would let goods be brought by frigates to Tangiers during the war. [*Adm. Paper, four pages.*]

April 13. 16. Jo. Perriman to Sam. Pepys. Is waiting for dispatch of his business concerning the Swallow. [*Adm. Paper.*]

April 13. Royal Charles. 17. Sir Wm. Coventry and Sir Wm. Penn to the Navy Comrs. Stores should be hastened to Harwich for repairs of various ships in the Duke of York's squadron. The John and Margaret is out of stores, and must be supplied by her owners. [*Adm. Paper.*]

April 13. Woolwich. 18. Wm. Acworth to the Navy Comrs. Twelve labourers are wanted for Woolwich, to lay up and stack timber. [*Adm. Paper.*]

April 13. Portsmouth. 19. John Tippetts to the Navy Comrs. Requests warrants to four Justices named of the New Forest and five of the Portsdown division, for the land carriage of timber. [*Adm. Paper.*]

April 13. Harwich. 20. Anthony Deane to the Navy Comrs. Requests a warrant to Justice Thos. Scrivener for the land carriage of 140 trees. Does not know the name of the other justices, but if a blank be left, will get it filled up. [*Adm. Paper.*]

April 13. Harwich. 21. Sir Wm. Batten to the Navy Comrs. Is commanded to remain at Harwich until the fleet is dispatched. The beer and water casks being found, the only delay now is for cables expected by the Augustine; 50 or 60 sail of colliers passed. [*Adm. Paper.*]

April 13. Dover. 22. Thos. White to the Navy Comrs. Is desired by the Commissioners for Prizes to appraise 14 ships and some goods. Asks what price he may give for some of them; wants letters of credit that what he buys at the candle may be paid for in London. [*Adm. Paper.*]

April 13. Royal Charles. 23. List of 16 men discharged from the Mary into the Unicorn, on March 13, 1665; with note by Sir Wm. Coventry, of the said list being delivered by the captain of the Unicorn, to ensure payment of the wages due to them on board the Mary. [*Adm. Paper.*]

April 13. Royal Charles. 24. List of 16 men discharged from the Pearl into the Unicorn, March 13, 1665; with similar note by Sir Wm. Coventry. [*Adm. Paper.*]

Vol. CXVIII.

1665.

April 14. 25. Certificate by Capt. John Fortescue that the John and Elizabeth, hired for the King's service, is well provided and ready to take in provisions. [*Adm. Paper.*]

April 14. Gravesend. 26. Account by Fr. Hosier of 12 ships in the Hope; the dates of arrival and departure, and the numbers of men giving good attendance on each. [*Adm. Paper.*]

April 14. Ordnance Office. 27. Edw. Sherburne to Sam. Pepys. The stores for the Pembroke were ordered some days since, but no gunner appearing, knows not into whose charge to deliver them. The over-metalling of the new cannon cannot be remedied; it is an error of the founders. The Drake was appointed convoy to a vessel of gunners' stores for Harwich; asks if she has arrived there. [*Adm. Paper.*]

April 14. Venice. 28. Pasino Panini to the King. Money being the food of armies, begs leave to offer a proposition by which His Majesty may raise a revenue of five millions, and yet the subject only feel an almost insensible imposition. Endorsed "Mr. Brunetti." [*Italian, two pages.*]

April 14. York. 29. Rich. Hewet, mayor of York, to Edw. Sheppard, alderman of Doncaster. The messenger secured seems an absolute cheat; his packet was stuffed with blank paper, bills with the names of parties torn out, &c. He should be sent to the common gaol, to be tried for his roguery. *Encloses,*

29. i. *Examination of George Hudson, before Alderman Edw. Sheppard. Is a soldier in the Tower, and on Wednesday last was ordered, with three others, to wait on the King, who had received news of his navy being beaten, two of his best ships lost, the Duke of York escaping with his life, &c. The King stood in his shirt till the Duke of Albemarle directed a packet for the Mayor of York, which he was ordered to carry to him, and the other soldiers were sent in other directions. April 14, 1665.*

April 14. Durham Prison. 30. Edw. Matthews to Sir Herbert Price. Repeats his former request to be removed by *habeas corpus* to London, to discover something to the King, and wishes the same for his wife Grace Matthews, who is with him in prison. Reminds him that they were fellow students in the Temple, and that he gave him a tract on the star that appeared on the King's birth, which tract His Majesty graciously accepted.

April [14?] The Fleet. 31. Earl of Peterborough to Willinmson. Is stowing his goods on the Unicorn. There are not yet 60 men of war assembled. Was sorry to miss Pine, on account of his humour, but does not wish his convenience to give any disturbance.

April 15. Gloucester. 32. Wm. Bishop of Gloucester to Gilbert Archbishop of Canterbury. Informs him, at request of the Bishop of Hereford, that Wallis, a soldier of scurrilous wit, convented at the Council table for a scandalous pamphlet called "Magna Charta, or more News

VOL. CXVIII.

1665.

from Rome," denies the King's supremacy in ecclesiastical causes, and depraves the Liturgy, and that his scoffs are read with much applause by the people. He sells the books publicly in the town and elsewhere, and glories in them; though much favour has been shown him, he boasts of his scurrility.

April 15. Custom House. 33. Sir Jo. Wolstenholme to Lord Arlington. Sends letters received from the collector at Ipswich, which came over in the packet boat. *Encloses*,

33. I. *Robt. Forman to Beatrice, widow of William Cary, of Yarmouth. Wants an answer to his last, and to know how he may receive his moneys.*

Rotterdam, April $\frac{8}{18}$, 1665.

33. II. *Robt. Foreman to Wm. Foreman, mariner of Newcastle. Private affairs. There are sad times in Holland; hopes things are better in England.*

Rotterdam, April $\frac{8}{18}$, 1665.

April 14. 34. Sir W. Coventry to Williamson. Three privateers have been taken by some of the frigates. The fleet is well increased and in good condition. The order to bring the prizes to England is according to the King's directions.

April 15. Royal Charles. 35. Duke of York to Lord [Arlington]. Begs a truce to compliments when his lordship writes to him. Thinks the French will not quarrel with them, as it is not their interest, and what their ambassadors say should not change the counsels. M. D'Humières could tell nothing; the courtiers in France are not well informed. Three small ships have been taken, after some resistance, in which Capt. Golding, of the Diamond, and nine of his men were killed. Thinks the prizes may be repaired and manned again. Sir Thos. Clifford will take care of the prisoners. [*Two pages.*]

April 15. Royal Charles. 36. Sir Wm. Coventry to Lord [Arlington]. The fleet is considerable enough to have a fair game at the Dutch, if they have a fair meeting. Though the victualler has not fully played his part, they hope soon to put to sea. Thanks for his lordship's inclinations of favour and promotion for him, as related by Lord Falmouth. [*One and a quarter pages.*]

April [15?] 37. Earl of Peterborough to [Williamson]. Has little news; a battle is exceedingly desired by all; longs for it with passion himself, on account of his stock in the Guinea company. Will remove into the ship Montague, at request of the Earl of Sandwich. [*Two pages.*]

April 15. Whitehall. Reference to the Lord High Chancellor and the Lord Chief Justice of the Common Pleas on the petition of Sir Wm. Scroggs, for redress; being one of the city of London's council, it is his duty to walk before the Lord Mayor on certain days of solemnity, but he is unable to perform it from wounds sustained in the cause of the late King, and has therefore been suspended from his place. [*Ent. Book 18, p. 142.*]

Vol. CXVIII.

1665.

April 15. 38. Sir Wm. Rider to Sam. Pepys. Recommends John Horne for the survey of ships now building by contract. [*Adm. Paper.*]

April 15. Chatham. 39. Commissioner Peter Pett to Sam. Pepys. Dispatch of the Portsmouth and Plymouth. Sir John Mennes lies at Queensborough; would fain have invited him to Chatham for the night, but such is his zeal that he would rather inconvenience himself by taking a lodging at Queensborough, than run the hazard of the Portsmouth not sailing away on the afternoon of Monday. Fears Mr. Lewsley cannot fell all Sir Ed. Dering's timber this season. [*Adm. Paper.*]

April 15. Cockpit. 40. Duke of Albemarle to the Navy Comrs. The building of the second-rate frigate at Woolwich and the third-rate at Chatham is to be stopped, and no new contracts entered into for ships building or hiring without special orders; three fifth-rate frigates are to be built, and no more of the 20 merchant ships hired. The men lately come from Guernsey are to be turned over to Capt. Wilkinson for the Great Charity. [*Adm. Paper.*]

April 15. Royal Charles. 41. Sir Wm. Coventry to Sam. Pepys. Will patch up the ships lately come out of the river in their manning, so as to make them serviceable in some measure; whilst they lay in the river they were only a scandal. Will send an account as soon as any experiment of the tobacco stalk is made, but wishes even leather shavings might be sent down to supply the great want. Is sorry money is so scarce. Has not heard whether those men made prisoners by the Admiralty for running away were shipped on board any vessel, to be brought back to the fleet. The Augustine has arrived. The Diamond and Yarmouth have been in fight, and Capt. Golding killed; three privateers taken.

April 15. 42. Account of the Dutch man-of-war captured by the Mermaid. and of two others brought in by the Diamond and Yarmouth. [*Adm. Paper.*]

April 15. Royal Charles. 43. Sir Wm. Coventry to the Navy Comrs. Neither tobacco stalks, nor shoemakers' shavings for wadding have arrived. The colours sent are too few, more must be supplied forthwith as the fleet is about to sail; ketches should be hastened down. The victualler is a man of good words, and provides good victuals, but very much short of the quantity; he professes to send 600 tons weekly, and 700 tons are consumed. The water cask allowed is too small in proportion, besides being bad and leaky. Urges the settling Mr Deane's salary, of Harwich; every encouragement should be given him for his good husbandry; his place during the war is likely to be an active one. The Augustine has arrived. [*Adm. Paper, two pages.*] *Encloses,*

43. i. *Note by Wm. Sheldon, that Mr. Deane's warrant for Harwich is dated Oct. 15, 1664, and Mr. Fletcher's for Woolwich, Jan. 7, 1665.*

VOL. CXVIII.

1665.

April 15. Woolwich.
44. Chris. Pett to Sam. Pepys. Begs allowance for his extra services when without assistance. Has received a good account of the proving of the Royal Katherine. Great want of timber. [*Adm. Paper.*]

April 15. Dieppe.
45. Peter Crucefix to Commissioner Peter Pett. Though unknown to him, is acquainted with his brother. Offers yarn and cordage at 38s. per cwt. Refers to Sir John Lawson and other navy officers, to whom he is well known. [*Adm. Paper.*]

April 15. Victualling Office.
46. Thos. Lewis to the Navy Comrs. Cannot get vessels to convey beer to the fleet; the masters object to be hired by the run, because some have lately been taken by the month; others who would go cannot for want of men. Begs some speedy remedy. [*Adm. Paper.*]

April 15. Bristol.
47. Sir John Knight to the Navy Comrs. Renews his request for an order to Mr. Morgan, the collector of customs there, to pay him 100*l.* due; has gone on daily disbursing his own money for stores, ammunition, &c., till it amounts to 150*l.* The ship is ready to sail; has 200 men on board. She is appraised at 1,400*l.* [*Adm. Paper.*]

April 15.
48. Henry Thurston and Peter Tomlin to the Navy Comrs. Certify that the third payment is due to Robt. Page, for the ketch building at Wivenhoe. [*Adm. Paper.*]

April 15.
49. List of seven ships sailed away, five remaining in the river, and four at Sheerness taking in provisions. [*Adm. Paper.*]

April 16. Royal Charles.
50. List of 12 men discharged from the Pearl, March 10, 1665, and entered upon the Prince, March 13; with note by Sir Wm. Coventry of their having no tickets, owing to the captain's absence; but their claim for wages is to be secured to them or their friends. [*Adm. Paper.*]

April 16. Royal Charles.
51. Sir Wm. Coventry and Sir Wm. Penn to the Navy Comrs. Have received some clothes from the slopsellers, but not nearly sufficient. Beg directions for a speedy supply and convenient proportion of shirts, waistcoats, drawers, and stockings. More colours wanted. [*Adm. Paper.*]

April 16. Royal Charles.
52. Sir Wm. Coventry to Sam. Pepys. Desires that Sanders and Anthony Lawes be found out, and hastened down with all speed, being intended as mates for the Royal Charles. The Satisfaction is arrived; other merchant ships are expected daily. The Vanguard, Plymouth, and Portsmouth are to be hastened away. Sails wanted for the Ann yacht; also white and blue colours. [*Adm. Paper.*]

April 16. Chatham.
53. Jas. Norman, clerk of the survey, to Thos. Hayter. Wastecloths and kerseys wanted for the Portsmouth. Sends a messenger to bring the cloth at once on board the ship now at Black Stakes. [*Adm. Paper.*]

Vol. CXVIII.

1665.

April 16. Villeroy. 54. [John Viscount Mordaunt] to the Earl of Peterborough. Standers by see the best of the play. Harry Killigrew got to the King six hours before the Duke of Buckingham, with letters from the Duke of York. The affront was intended, for it happened before His Majesty's letter to the Duke of York on the Duke of Buckingham's reception arrived; the King will most likely refer the case to the Duke of York. Is concerned for his lordship, Buckingham's pretences being not on his peerage, but on his being a privy councellor. Offers service as his brother and friend.

April 16. The Unicorn. 55. Earl of Peterborough to Williamson. The fleet is much satisfied with the noble fight of two of the ships, and the prize they have taken. Had the noble Lord who has left thought that men could outlive such an encounter, he might not have gone. The Lord Constable has set a good example, to be content with being a hero of his own making. Had better have written verses last time, and after reaching at laurels too hard to come by, been contented with rosemary or lavender. [*One and a half pages.*]

April 17. Whitehall. 56. Warrant for a grant to George Arnott of certain fines due from lands in the duchy of Cornwall, in a schedule annexed, with power to recover and compound for the same, or to receive them if already paid into the Exchequer. *Annexing,*

56. i. *Schedule of the fines above alluded to; total value, 525l.*

April 17. Licence for the Anstice and Mary of Dartmouth, laden with fish for Portugal, to depart without embargo, on consideration that Dartmouth sent in more seamen for the fleet than were imposed upon it. [*Ent. Book* 14, p. 56.]

April 17. The King to [the Vice Chancellor of Cambridge]. Recommends Edmond Yarborough, M.A., for the degree of M.D., on account of his experience in physic, any statute to the contrary notwithstanding. [*Ent. Book* 19, p. 38.]

April ? 57. Petition of James Palmer, Fellow of Trinity College, Cambridge, to the King, for a letter, &c., to the Master of the college to obtain him a dispensation to travel for three years. Was visited with a dropsy during his former dispensation, and therefore confined to one place, and unable to visit the famous universities and places of learning in Europe.

April 17. The King to the Master and Fellows of Trinity College, Cambridge. Requests them to renew to Jas. Palmer, Fellow of that college, their licence for him to travel for three years, for improvement in learning, as he was prevented by illness from making the proposed use of their former licence. [*Ent. Book* 19, p. 39.]

April 17. Letter for Fras. Monday to be Almsman in place of David Evans, at Canterbury. Minute. [*Ent. Book* 19, p. 40.]

VOL. CXVIII.

1665.

April 17. Letter for Willm. Tempest to be Almsman at Canterbury, in place of Robt. Hornsby, who is ejected. Minute. [*Ent. Book* 19, *p.* 40.]

April 17. Pass for George Symonds, going on his private business, to India, for four years. [*Ent. Book* 22, *p.* 97.]

April 17. Warrant to the Sheriff of Lancashire to convey George Fox, prisoner there, to the confines of York, to be thence conveyed to Scarborough; noted Col. Kirkby. Minute. [*Ent. Book* 22, *p.* 97.]

April 17. Warrant to Anthony Lord Ashley to pay 5,000*l.* to Sir Arthur Slingsby, out of the proceeds of prize ships. [*Ent. Book* 22, *p.* 98.]

April 17. Pass for Mr. Freer to go beyond sea. Minute. [*Ent. Book* 22, *p.* 98.]

April 17. Whitehall. 58. Pass for Wm. Leving to go abroad on secret matters of importance to the King's service. [*Copy.*]

April 17. Minute of the above. [*Ent. Book* 22, *p.* 98.]

April 17. Whitehall. Warrant to allow to Sir Roger Langley, Bart., 600*l.*, out of hearth and other moneys in his hands as sheriff of Yorkshire, in consideration of sums expended by him in the management and discovery of the late plot. [*Ent. Book* 22, *p.* 98.]

April 17. Warrant for a grant to Walter Brames of all hidden treasure discovered within one year, in the parish of St. Peter's-Cheesehill, co. Hants. [*Ent. Book* 22, *p.* 99.]

April 17. Licence for Sir John Warner to travel. [*Ent. Book* 22, *p.* 102.]

April 17. The King to the Lord Treasurer. He is to signify to the respective officers through whose hands the grant lately made to the Queen-Mother of the benefit of her jointure for two years after her decease shall pass, that His Majesty consents and approves of the same. [*Ent. Book* 17, *p.* 105.]

April 17. London. Levant Company to [the Earl of Winchelsea]. Thanks for his great care in reference to the vile and treacherous design of Thos. Stanton and Hawley Bishop, and their infamous departure from Turkey. The King has sent letters to Tuscany and Venice, to have them secured if they come there. The charges of their crime must be borne by those interested in their estate, not by the Company, and the Turks should be warned that the persons they trust are alone liable for their debts; it is against the Company's will that their factors are trusted by Turks or others. [*Levant Papers, Vol.* v., *p.* 100.]

April 17. London. Levant Company to Martin Loe. At his father's importunity, they abate 100 out of the 154 dollars excepted against in his first account; also the 583 dollars in the latter account, except 183 disbursed on the Pasha's passing Scanderoon, which they refer to the

VOL. CXVIII.

1665.

consul and treasurer at Aleppo, without whom no presents are to be given. He is bound to repair and keep up the warehouses. [*Levant Papers, Vol.* v., *p.* 107.]

April 17. London. Levant Company to Man Brown [treasurer at Aleppo]. Similar to the above. [*Levant Papers, Vol.* v., *p.* 108.]

April 17. London. Levant Company to Consul Lannoy. Are pleased that the factors have taken the oath, and that by his care about charges, he has now cash in hand. Think the consulage of 453 dollars paid by the merchant stranger does not countervail the prejudice of introducing a stranger to the trade; desire him to enforce substantial repair of the warehouses at Scanderoon. Great scandal arises from the conduct of Thos. Stanton and Hawley Bishop, in possessing themselves of a great estate of Turks, and then running away. Will do their utmost to bring them to justice, &c.; fear that the marine factor has been an accessory; his conduct should be enquired into, and he be suspended if needful. Exceptions against Mr. Lee's accounts. Single consulage should not have been accepted from the Eagle, or any other than general ships. [*Levant Papers, Vol.* v., *pp.* 109–112.]

April 17. Reference to the Lord Treasurer of a petition of Charles Roberts to the King, for two thirds of an estate in Yorkshire, worth 700*l.* or 800*l.*, concealed from the Crown, to be discovered by him. [*Ent. Book* 18, *p.* 148.]

[April 17.] 59. Draft of the above-named petition, soliciting only a moiety of the estate.

April 17. Islington. 60. R. Neville to Lord Arlington. States the reasons why Simon Middleton is not thought a fit man to be clerk of the New River; that he was once mad, and spoke traitorous speeches, and would be apt to relapse; that he was treasurer of the corporation, detained the profits of divers shares, and when dismissed, refused to give up the key of the chest; that he put the company to much cost in suits, and has still suits pending, and is therefore unfit to cast up their accounts, seal their leases, keep their books, instruct their counsel, &c.; also that the office is beneath his estate and dignity. [*Two pages.*]

April 17. Royal Charles. 61. Earl of Falmouth to Lord [Arlington]. Found the Duke inclined to sail on Thursday. The news of the fleet on the Irish coast will incline the council of war to make all possible haste to the coast of Holland. The fleet is much augmented since he saw it.

April 17. Commissions to —— Sherrard to be Lieutenant, and —— Adderly Cornet to Sir Fras. Compton's troop. Minute. [*Ent. Book* 20, *p.* 53.]

April 17. Order—on petition of the Earl of Shrewsbury and others interested in the Bona Esperanza and Henry Bonaventure for letters of

VOL. CXVIII.

1665.

reprisal,—that Sir Robt. Wiseman, advocate general, and Sir Wm. Turner, advocate of the Duke of York, prepare a special commission as desired. [*Ent. Book* 18, p. 146.]

April 17. Reference to the Lord Treasurer and the Earl of Oxford, lord chief justice in Eyre south of Trent, on the petition of John Lewyn Groom—keeper of Lynwood walk in the New Forest, Hampshire, complaining of disturbance in the quiet execution of his office. [*Ent. Book* 18, p. 147.]

April 17. Cockpit. 62. Duke of Albemarle to the Navy Comrs. The King wishes no ships laden with coals to go out of the river; the commanders of some ships in the river must take care that none but empty colliers pass out. [*Adm. Paper.*]

April 17. 63. Robt. Magors to the Navy Comrs. Cannot find above 23 loads of compass timber fit for service in all the yards on the river. [*Adm. Paper.*]

April 17. Deptford. 64. Jonas Shish to the Navy Comrs. Recommends Mr. Bull, a carver of good experience, to undertake the cutting of any ship in the country. [*Adm. Paper.*]

April 17. The Lea, near Lea Baily. 65. Dan. Furzer to the Navy Comrs. Will only fell breeches sufficient for the keel of the new ship until further warrant; if instructions had been sent concerning the iron work necessary for the present occasion, could have sent a parcel by the next ship. The smith must soon have an assistant. [*Adm. Paper.*]

April 17. The Coventry, Lyme. 66. Barth. Coke, boatswain, to Sir Wm. Batten. Has taken up a bill of 8*l.* for hammocks and twine, for the use of the frigate. [*Adm. Paper.*]

April 17. The Speedwell, Leith Road. 67. Capt. J. Lightfoot to the Navy Comrs. Has brought the Galliot hoy in safety to Leith, expecting thence to attend her to Shetland and Bracy Sound; Col. St. Clare, who commands the Galliot, and is at Leith to raise soldiers and money to transport, will not be in readiness to depart for a fortnight. The enemy's men-of-war appearing on the coast, is ordered by Lord Commissioner Rothes to convoy several merchant ships to Aberdeen, and then carry directions to Caithness and the Isles of Orkney, for raising 200 men more for Col. St. Clare, to take with him to fortify the Sound. Asks how to be supplied with victuals during this extra service. [*Adm. Paper.*]

April 17. Dover. 68. Thos. White to Sam. Pepys. Hears that the Dutch are at sea with 100 sail of ships; believes it to be the Zealand squadron from the Brill, going to the East land; the Norwich and Little Mary have brought in five Flemish built ships, manned with Frenchmen and laden with French goods; the Bristol sailed into the Downs; other ships in sight. The Little Mary has also sent in a Lubecker. [*Adm. Paper.*]

VOL. CXVIII.

1665.

April 18. 69. Wm. Castell to Thos. Hayter. Desires a warrant of protection from imprest for Ralph Watson, Thos. Cullinder, and Joseph Haynes, shipwrights coming out of Suffolk to work upon the third-rate ship now building. [*Adm. Paper.*]

April 18. The Plymouth, Black Stakes. 70. Capt. Thos. Allin to [Sam. Pepys]. Will not neglect a minute in setting sail; has had much trouble in getting the men together; 248 are now on board. Wants sails and tackling, and his purser to be dispatched forthwith. [*Adm. Paper.*]

April 18. New Forest. 71. Thos. Eastwood to the Navy Comrs. Particulars of the felling of timber; requests an order to the justices to grant warrants for land carriage; also money for carrying on the work. [*Adm. Paper.*]

April 18. Deptford. 72. Jonas Shish to the Navy Comrs. Launch of the Charity; the Hound may be docked in her room; 5,000 treenails wanted and three tons of oakum. [*Adm. Paper.*]

April 18. Chatham. 73. Commissioner Peter Pett to Sam. Pepys. The staves and posts are sent away to Sheerness, to be placed upon the beach; the hulk will speedily follow; 10 seamen must be borne upon her, besides the boatswain and carpenter; proposes to take them from the guard of the Sovereign, till part of the navy return. Desires an imprest of 80*l.* to Mr. Lewsley, for carrying on the business of Sir Edw. Dering's timber. [*Adm. Paper.*]

April 18. Little Gift, Galway. 74. Robt. Swan, purser, to Sam. Pepys. Engagement, pursuit, and escape of a Dutch man-of-war off the west coast of Ireland; eight men were wounded; his captain, who behaved nobly, is come into port for repairs; victualled at Kinsale, but as there is no allowance for the sick and wounded, they are forced to be turned on shore. [*Adm. Paper.*]

April 18. Royal Charles, near the Gunfleet. 75. Sir Wm. Coventry to Lord Arlington. The fleet is now preparing to sail at once; if only the stores were arrived from the Ordnance Office, and from the victualler who is very backward, neither ships, men, nor good-will would be wanting to give the King the desired victory. They are obliged to dismiss some men, though not very able ones, for want of victuals. The proportion of land soldiers is large, yet on the whole, the commanders who had experience in the late Dutch war say that the fleet is better manned now than then. They will probably sail towards the Dutch coasts, to try if the Dutch will come out and venture a battle, which is much desired whilst the men are in good health. Sir George Downing's letters seem to show it probable that they will come out. The King would be pleased could he see the temper of the commanders, —no rhodomontade, but an assurance of beating them. The men are discouraged by great want of surgeons. Begs that the wardens of the hall may be sent for, and empowered to press surgeons if needful. [*Two pages.*]

Vol. CXVIII.

1665.

[April 18.] 76. Petition of John Lowe to Lord Arlington for release or permission to clear himself. Was suddenly seized and put into the Gatehouse dungeon, three days ago, only for answering a prisoner who called to him out of a window to know how his wife and children are. Marked, "Speak to Sir R. Langley."

April 18. Whitehall. 77. Petition of Francis Roper to the King for a grant in remainder of several small tenements, parcel of the duchy of Cornwall, rental 23*l.* 3*s.* 5*d.*, possessed by persons holding two, three, or four lives therein, some of which are expired. With reference thereon to the Lord Treasurer.

April 18. Warrant to Ralph Retter to discharge John Blackwall. Minute. [*Ent. Book* 22, *p.* 88.]

April 18. Grant to Sir Rich. Browne, Bart., of 200*l.* yearly increase upon his former allowance of 50*l.*, as clerk of the Council. [*Docquet.*]

April 18. Like grants to Sir John Nicholas, K.B., Sir Edw. Walker, and Robt. Southwell, clerks of the Council. [*Docquet.*]

April 18. Warrant to pay to John Colville, goldsmith of London, 2,000*l.* for secret service, to be paid by the receiver of the royal aid for Hampshire upon the year 1665. [*Docquet.*]

April 18. Reference to the Lord Treasurer, on the petition of Dame Anne, relict of Sir Fras. Gurdon, for repayment of vast sums expended by her husband in the King's service. [*Ent. Book* 18, p. 143.]

April 18. Reference on the petition of Sir Robt. Long to the Attorney and Solicitor General and Sergeant Glynne, to certify if any money be really lent on the bond, and if not, how it may be discharged; meanwhile no process is to be issued on it. [*Ent. Book* 18, p. 143.]

April 18. 78. Draft of the above reference.

April 18. 79. Writ of attachment from Sir Thos. Pettus, Bart., sheriff of Norfolk, for the appearance of John Lynes and Phillippa Cullyer, of Windham parish, before the Barons of the Exchequer at Westminster, on the day after Ascension Day, to answer for divers transgressions, contempts, &c. [*Latin.*]

April 18. 80. Certificate by Sir W. Maynard that Rob. Jocelin, of Hide Hall, co. Hertford, has always been a loyal subject, is a justice of peace for Essex, has 1,000*l.* a year, and is of an ancient family. Endorsed "Sir Alex. Nesbitt's baronet."

April 18. 81. Petition of Henry Brunsell to the King, for the Vicarage of Wisbeach, Isle of Ely. With note in his favour by Gilbert Archbishop of Canterbury.

April 18. 82. Sir P. Warwick to Williamson. Lord Sandwich's paper is suitable to the King's intention to grant him 4,000*l.* a year, but part of it being in reversion, while the reversion lasts, this way of supply is to be made.

Vol. CXVIII.

1665.

April 19. The Unicorn. 83. Earl of Peterborough to Williamson. Was on the Earl of Sandwich's ship at return of the Duke of Buckingham, who was not expected any more; did not see him, not wishing to hear what might not please him, for a prince cannot be obliged to do what he promises. Waits on the Duke [of York] every few days, when there is no assembly of officers, and hopes he will not break his promise. Thanks for the care of his great business; thinks there is something of Mr. Povey in the obstruction.

April 19. Whitehall. 84. Robt Southwell to Lord [Arlington]. The Commissioners for Prizes request the King's directions about the St. Margaret of Treport. The ship is said to be French; the master says the wines were landed at Ostend, but two of the men say it was Middleburg. Mademoiselle has written to M. de Comminges about it.

April 19. Whitehall. 85. Warrant to Lord Treas. Southampton to grant to Percy Church the first vacant King's Waiter's place in the port of London. [*Copy.*]

April 10. Edwinstowe. 86. John Russell to the Navy Comrs. Wants boys for the carriage of timber from Bawtry; has obtained warrants from the justices of Derbyshire and Yorkshire for 400 loads, and for sending in 10 carts a day. Wants money; has paid 140*l.* since his last accounts, for land carriage and workmen. Capt. Greene broke his leg while lading a waggon; prays continuance of his pay until his recovery. [*Adm. Paper.*]

April 19. Woolwich. 87. Chris. Pett to the Navy Comrs. Little progress is yet made with the new second-rate ship, owing to the want of timber; will forbear, as ordered, any further proceedings upon her. Great want of timber for completing the mould of the fourth-rate ship; begs that Mr. Morehouse may be hastened in sending in what he has converted from Waltham Forest. [*Adm. Paper.*]

April 19. Ordnance Office. 88. Edw. Sherburne and two other Officers of Ordnance to Sir John Mennes. Request a warrant to Capt. Ferne for impressing 25 men to assist in the recovery of the London's guns.

April 19. 89. Thos. Lewis to Sam. Pepys. Requests warrants to Stephen Garland, master of the Isabel and Providence, and Jack Taylor, of the Golden Falcon, to press 19 men for their vessels, appointed to carry beer to the fleet. [*Adm. Paper.*]

April 10. Bristol. 90. Sir John Knight to the Navy Comrs. Has received 100*l.* from the collector of customs, and passed his bill of exchange upon Sir Geo. Carteret for the same. The George has set sail, with 226 able seamen on board. [*Adm. Paper.*]

April 20. Ordnance Office. 91. Edw. Sherburne and two other Officers of Ordnance to the Navy Comrs. Have endeavoured to furnish the Madras with guns, according to directions received; if the Royal Company's guns now on board be removed, there are not sufficient in store to make good her proportion. [*Adm. Paper.*]

Vol. CXVIII.

1665.

April 20. Chatham. 92. Commissioner Peter Pett to Sam. Pepys. The Victory goes on apace. If the third-rate frigate be stopped, two fifth-rates should be built by the assistants at Chatham and Portsmouth. Has appointed three or four suits of masts to be in readiness upon all occasions, which is but necessary in these times of danger. [*Adm. Paper.*]

April 20. The Marmaduke, the Hope. 93. Capt. John Best to the Navy Comrs. Wants 60 tons more ballast; has already, by the bills, 210 tons. Thinks they give base tonnage. Requests 30 or 40 more men, that he may get into the fleet. [*Adm. Paper.*]

April 20. 94. Sir Phil. Musgrave to Williamson. Has no news. Thanks for favours.

April 20. The Unicorn. 95. Earl of Peterborough to [Williamson]. Thanks for his timely notice of the attacks of malice; hopes to hinder the harm. The assertion has no ground, as he never meant to leave an occasion of so much glory; receives only civility, but no contrary treatment would drive him from the fleet. The Duke of Buckingham's fickleness gives great scandal; he has left his ship, sent back his goods, and thrust himself as volunteer on the Earl of Sandwich's ship, to the dislike of everyone. Is courted to better ships, and even to the Duke's, but stays where he is, to show that he came not to seek safety. Hopes the King will be assured that if he do little service, he is incapable of any example which could be to the prejudice of affairs. [*Two pages.*]

April 20. 96. Sir W. Coventry to Williamson. The fleet sails to-morrow for the Texel, to see if the Dutch will come out; hopes, in spite of their brag, to bring his Royal Highness safe back. Sends a letter for M. Dumas, the gentleman sent by the King of France to solicit the French merchants' business.

April 20. Royal Charles. 97. Duke of York to the King. According to his orders, has sent up Emerson with the prizes, and ordered Capt. Trafford of the Unity to accompany him. Several vessels are coming up, so that the fleet is about ready. Hopes to sail to-morrow for the Texel, and plying at a safe distance from the coast, in case it should blow hard, to send out scouts to give notice of the Dutch coming out, and to interrupt their trade. Is sorry that the failure of the victualler about beer will make the ships able to stay so little a time on the coast; refers for information on this and other things to his letter to the Lord General; sends an account of the order of battle, and will write as often as possible. Begs His Majesty's care of D. Talbot, if the proviso that will ruin him stands. Should the indiscretion of the Governor of Landguard Fort be punished by putting him out of his command, recommends Sir Robt. Brookes for the place. [*Four pages.*]

April 20. Royal Charles. 98. Sir Wm. Coventry to Lord Arlington. Sends his reply to the Swedes and Frenchmen's complaints by itself, so as to be shared

1665. Vol. CXVIII.

with them, if needful. Has a glut of business, and few helps, on account of the sickness of his chief clerk; the fleet sails to-morrow. Its setting forth in the state it is would have been avoided if advertisements had been seasonably hearkened to.

April 20. Royal Charles. 99. Earl of Falmouth to [Lord Arlington]. The Duke pressed the council of war very hard to sail this morning, but they would not consent till to-morrow, in hopes of some stores coming that they cannot do without. Want of beer and other provisions will force them back sooner than would be requisite; there never was seen so brave, well-manned, and resolute a fleet as this of 80 good ships, though the enemy brag much of being more numerous. Wonders what the French will say about it; what they do looks as though they proposed by their mediation for Holland to make peace without them. Heard of M. Cominges not standing up when the King's health was drunk, but thinks it a trifle. Begs assistance to Mrs. Ross in her petition. He [her husband?] deserves well, considering his service there to the Duke of Monmouth, and the occasion he is going upon. The business will not be long, for if the Dutch come not out soon, they will not be seen this summer. [*Four pages.*]

April 20. Royal Charles. 100. B. May to [Lord Arlington]. Thanks for his letters; will not give him the trouble of reading professions of service; their trunks were overboard this morning, and there is great confusion to bring all into order.

April 20. Whitehall. 101. Petition of the Lords, Knights, and Gentlemen in and about London who delight in archery, to the King, for commissions, as granted them by the two last Kings, to shoot at marks and set up stakes, which, in these late times, the insolent farmers and field keepers pull down and take to their own use, setting their mastiff dogs at the petitioners. With order thereon to the Attorney and Solicitor General, to prepare a grant to the petitioners of liberty to shoot within their usual bounds.

April 20. Whitehall. 102. Petition of Major-General Rowland Laugharne to the King, for payment from the growing excise of South Wales of 875*l.* arrears, and his pension of 500*l.* a year. Has lost 37,030*l.* in the service, and has only received 1,200*l.* out of 3,000*l.* ordered him by Parliament; has little hopes of the remainder, and his pension of 500*l.* a year is stayed. With reference thereon, strongly recommending his relief, to the Lord Treasurer, and his report, April 24, that the excise and exchequer revenues are taken up by pre-assignments for public occasions, but if a privy seal were issued in some other name, he would try to pay it, stopping it in future from the petitioner's pension.

[April 20.] Entry of the above reference. [*Ent. Book* 18, p. 147.]

April 20. 103. Warrant to the Lord Treasurer, Lord General, and Stephen Fox for payment to eight Lieutenants and eight Ensigns, who have refused the oath imposed by the States of Holland, and were there-

Vol. CXVIII.

1665.

upon discharged the service, of 3s. per day each, to the lieutenants, and 2s. 6d. to the ensigns, till further orders, to be paid by Fox, on warrants from the Duke of Albemarle. With list of names annexed, and note of additions of seven more names, in January and February 1666. [*Two pages.*]

[April 20.] 104. Draft of the preceding.

April 20. Whitehall. Entry of the preceding warrant and list. [*Ent. Book* 22, *pp.* 102–3.]

[April 20.] Warrant for an addition of two Captains, two Lieutenants, and one Ensign to the said establishment, the captains to receive 5s. a day each. [*Ent. Book* 22, *p.* 103.]

April 21. Warrant to Roger Harsnett to apprehend Lord Morley, for fighting contrary to the late proclamation. Minute. [*Ent. Book* 22, *p.* 103.]

April 21. Warrant to the Lieutenant of the Tower to discharge the Duke of Richmond and Lenox. Minute. [*Ent. Book* 22, *p.* 104.]

April 21. Grant to John Browne of Casome, (Caversham,) co. Oxford, of the dignity of a Baronet. [*Docquet.*]

April 21. Grant to the same of the usual discharge. [*Docquet.*]

April 21. 105. Signor Brunetti to [Lord Arlington]. Is sorry to have displeased him by asking a favour, but begs protection and influence with the King for his assistance, having resolved to establish himself in England, whatever his fortune may be. [*French.*]

April 21. 5 a.m. Royal Charles. 106. Duke of York to the King. Col. Farr of Languard Fort has been to give information about the complaint against him; the Colonel's fault seems to have been rather over-exactness than anything else, and he is very sensible of it. Thinks a good reprimand will be enough for him. The fleet is under sail, wind S.E. No endeavours shall be wanting to serve his Majesty. [*One and a half pages.*]

April 21. 107. Account by Jacob Blackleech of water cask delivered on board the Mary and Elizabeth, John and Elizabeth, and Hope pink. [*Adm. Paper.*]

April 21. Chatham. 108. Edw. Gregory to Sam. Pepys. Is glad that the alteration of the day intended for paying the pensioners is approved; will fix notices on the dock gate and Hill House door. Requests that the chests, books, &c, may be sent down. [*Adm. Paper.*]

April 21. Royal Charles. 109. Sir Wm. Coventry to the Navy Comrs. Supplies of stores must still be forwarded to Harwich, although the fleet has sailed; would wish them sent in large vessels, for the more security in bringing them after the fleet, should the Duke of York so order it. Desires an account of the rate of wages paid at Portsmouth, to regulate the payment of Harwich yard. [*Adm. Paper.*]

VOL. CXVIII.

1665.

April 21. Woolwich. 110. Wm. Acworth to Sir Wm. Batten. Account of timber served in by Sir Wm. Warren, since his last contract of Dec. 15, 1664.

April 21. Farnham. 111. John Langrack to Sam. Pepys. Has received no answer from the justices as to whether they will make any better dispatch than formerly. Proposes letting a quarter or a third of the trees in Alicholt stand for this year; has more felled already than can be carried in one summer. Asks what to do with the timber converted by Mr. Cooper. [*Adm. Paper.*] *Encloses*,

112. I. *List of 8 justices of Surrey and 16 of Hampshire.*

April 22. Victualling Office. 112. Thos. Lewis to the Navy Comrs. Sends an account of water cask provided for such ships as were ready to receive it. The principal hindrance in sending beer to the fleet has been for want of men, the watermen sent being generally unfit or unwilling to work. [*Adm. Paper.*] *Encloses*,

112. I. *Account of beer ready to be sent from London to complete the victualling of the fleet for four months; of what is already laden, and what in lighters by the ships' side; 470 tuns are remaining at the brewery; total, 1,524 tuns 1 hogshead 20 gallons.* *April* 22, 1665.

112. II. *List of 65 watermen impressed and put on board the victuallers, &c.* *April* 17 *and* 18, 1665.

112. III. *List of 27 watermen on board the four victualling ships.*

112. IV. *Similar list, with eight names added, and note of their unfitness and refractory conduct; also that many go ashore to sleep, and are discontent that they, as masters of families, are pressed, while single men are excused on giving money to the pressmen.* *April* 22, 1665.

April 22. 113. Sir W. Coventry to Mr. Deane, master shipwright at Harwich. Desires the payment of 6*l.* 10*s.* to Thos. Brown, master of the Michael of Ipswich, on his bringing a receipt from Capt. Earle of the Loyal George. With a power of attorney from Thos. Brown for Thos. Weekes, of Harwich, to receive the same. Nov. 5, 1666. [*Adm. Paper.*]

April 22. 114. Edw. Gray to the Navy Comrs. Requests an order to receive seven masts out of the 12 brought to Chatham by Captain Taylor, for fitting up the frigates now building. [*Adm. Paper.*]

April 22. The Paradox, Downs. 115. Capt. Leo. Guy to the Navy Comrs. Is arrived from Portsmouth; waits for orders. [*Adm. Paper.*]

April 22. Lea. 116. Dan. Furzer to the Navy Comrs. Sends a list and prices of the iron work intended; begs money for carrying on the work and buying materials for the house, which will soon be fit to work in. [*Adm. Paper.*]

Vol. CXVIII.

1665.

April 22. Woolwich. 117. Chris. Pett to Sam. Pepys. Begs to be allowed to build the fifth-rate ship ordered, in place of the second-rate lately stopped; has a considerable quantity of small timber in the yard, and every convenience. Begs allowance for two divers, employed when the estimate for the mast dock at Blackwall was made, and for two barrels of beer drunk when the Royal Katherine was launched. The Golden Lion is ready to launch. A small Dutch frigate is brought in by the Mermaid; the two taken by the Yarmouth and Diamond are coming up to be trimmed. [*Adm. Paper.*]

April 22. York. 118. Geo. Stubley to the Navy Commrs. Offers services in impressing seamen, or any other duty required. [*Adm. Paper.*]

April 22. Gravesend. 119. Account of three ships in the Hope, with the number of men on each giving good attendance. [*Adm. Paper.*]

April 22. 120. Robert Magorn to the Navy Commrs. Gives a list of eight ships impressed for the present service. [*Adm. Paper.*]

April 22. Royal Charles, off Orfordness, 5 a.m. 121. Sir Wm. Coventry to Lord [Arlington]. Mr. Penn will relate their condition, under sail with a brave fleet, wind and weather fair. Are looking for the Dutch, and think they see some of their scouts. If the Dutch find out our condition as to victuals, they will play their game very ill if they come out. Begs that letters from his lordship and the Duke of Albemarle may be sent to Harwich, whence some ketches will be ready to bring them. The Duke commends to his lordship a business of Sir George Ayscue's, a very honest, gallant man, depending upon the Irish bill. He does not serve mercenarily, for he lives handsomely and honourably in the fleet, beyond his pay. [*Two pages.*]

April 22. Royal Charles. 122. Earl of Falmouth to Lord [Arlington]. They are sailing as fast as they can with a small gale; there are 92 sail in the fleet; are hoping for news of the enemy. Begs favour for Sir George Ayscue; his cause is most just, and Lord Ormond is his friend; he cannot solicit for himself, whilst absent on the king's service. Are in battle order; only wishes the King could see them. [*Two pages.*]

April 22. 123. Answer by Simon Middleton to the reasons why he is not thought fit to be clerk of the New River Company; the traitorous words he was reported to have uttered were said in a violent fever, in which his mind was distempered. Particulars of the unjust suits brought against him by Sir Wm. Backhouse and other shareholders; wishes to be clerk chiefly to reduce the extravagant allowances made to Sir William's serving man; if his having an income of 2,000*l.* a year be the objection to his having the place, wishes it were stronger, as if the Company were better managed it might be 2,500*l.*

April [22]. 124. Memorial of passages at the court held for the New River, viz., that the river was brought to London from Chadwell, 17 James; that the King having advanced money therefor, had

Vol. CXVIII.

1665

one half, which he let in fee farm to Sir Hugh Middleton, for 500*l.* a year, the other half being divided into 36 shares, of which Middleton had 13; that, until the troubles, the King always had a member on his behalf at the court; that the salary of the clerk is 100*l.*, increased by profits of leases to above 300*l.* Mr. Middleton offered to be their clerk, and had the King's letter on his behalf, of which Mr. Nevill spoke slightingly, said that such were to be had for 5*s.* each, declared during the reading that it was false, and would hardly let it be read through; he and some others refused good offers of Mr. Middleton and another, and chose Harrison, a serving man, instead; the governor also caused Mr. Gardner, who has no interest in the river, to be admitted as trustee for himself, but refused to admit Mr. Somes for the King.

April 22. Order for a warrant to pay to John Napier 240*l.*, due on his pension as a page of honour. Minute. [*Ent. Book* 22, *p.* 104.]

April 22. Westminster. 125. Inquisition on the death of Hen. Hastings, who was mortally wounded on April 21, in St. Giles' parish, London, and died on the following day, giving a verdict of wilful murder against Thomas Lord Morley and Monteagle, who gave him a wound on the head with a sword, and against Fras. Cromwich, as aiding and abetting the same, but the jury are ignorant what property the said persons are possessed of. [*Latin, two sheets.*]

[April 22.] 126. Presentation of the above-named persons, as guilty of the murder of Hen. Hastings. [*Latin.*]

April 22. Reference on the petition of the Earl of Cleveland to the Lord Treasurer, Chancellor of the Exchequer and Solicitor General, who are to consider what can be done for relief of the honourable petitioner, who has deserved so eminently in the King's service. [*Ent. Book* 18, *p.* 144.]

[April 22.] 127. Draft of the preceding.

April 22. 128. Sir W. Coventry to Lord Arlington. Requests an alteration in the grant to Capt. Allin of 1,000*l.* from the groats allowed for the maintenance of ministers, which will make it available if the past arrears are all paid away, as he hears they are. The King's interest is not concerned, as he would not like to make a profit of what comes through want of chaplains in the fleet. [*Two pages.*]

1665. VOL. CXIX. APRIL 23–30, 1665.

April 23. Drayton. 1. Capt. E. De Belle Tour to Williamson. Thanks for the honour he has done him in accepting his protection; begs him to tell M. Vernatti, who is returning, that he wishes him (the writer) well. [*French, two pages.*]

April 23. 2. Thos. Lewis to Sam. Pepys. Sends an account of beer ready to be shipped; has already shown how much the service is hindered by want of men, and by the unfitness of those sent; one vessel is entirely deserted; begs a speedy supply for the six vessels in the list sent. [*Adm. Paper.*] *Encloses,*

2. I. *List of 32 watermen on board the four victualling ships, and of six ships on which 40 more men are required.* *April* 22, 1665.

April 23. 3. Receipt by Wm. Rayne of six puncheons of water for the Loyal George, from Thos. Browne, master of the Michael. [*Adm. Paper.*]

April 24. The Swallow. 4. Jo. Perriman, master of the Swallow, to the Navy Commrs. Desires warrants for his boatswain, carpenter, and joiner. [*Adm. Paper.*]

April 24. Barber Surgeons' Hall. 5. Rich. Reynell to Thos. Hayter. Has provided more mates and barbers, as ordered by Mr. Pearce, surgeon general, now with the fleet. Asks how to convey them thither. [*Adm. Paper.*] *Annexing,*

5. I. *List of four ships wanting surgeons.*

[April 24.] 6. Petition of John Bagwell, shipwright, to the Navy Commrs., for employment as carpenter in the Young Lion; served in the yards at Deptford and Woolwich for many years. [*Adm. Paper.*] *Encloses,*

6. I. *Certificate by Jonas Shish of the fitness of John Bagwell, of Deptford, for a Master or Carpenter's place in any sixth-rate ship.* *April* 24, 1665.

April 24. Lowestoft. 7. Capt. Jas. Wilde to [Sam. Pepys]. Capt. Wm. Hill of the Coventry has arrived with a convoy of 30 small vessels from Lynn, wanting a supply of wood and candles. He sent to shore for them, but would not allow his men to go near any one, had the goods left on the sea shore, and then sent to fetch them, being ordered so to demean himself, though his men were in good health; he lies wind bound, but will sail for Lee Road when he can; he asks directions for victualling his ship. [*Adm. Paper.*]

April 24. 8. List by Capt. James Blake of three officers belonging to the Constant John, with request for warrants for their continuance. [*Adm. Paper.*]

VOL. CXIX.

1665.

April 24. Woolwich. 9. Chris Pett to Sam. Pepys. Has surveyed the two Dutch prizes, and made an estimate of their repairs. Was invited by the King to go with him in his barge to see them, and His Majesty expressed pleasure at the success of the proof of the Royal Katherine. Hopes this will shame all those who did such ill service as to asperse this ship, not only at home, but abroad in the enemy's country. Was never frowned on by the King, amidst these ill reports, but had they proved true, would have sunk under the burden. Recommends James Fletcher for the Carpenter's place in the Unity prize. [*Adm. Paper.*]

April 24. Yarmouth. 10. James Johnson to Sam. Pepys. Wishes to treat with Mr. Stedman for a fifth-rate frigate, upon the same terms as the Edgars. Offers 20 cwt. of great shot for sale. [*Adm. Paper.*]

April 24. Whitehall. Declaration that if Capt. Thos. Allin, now engaged in the Dutch war, where his experience and courage promise good service, should be killed, his son Thos. Allin shall succeed him as Captain of Sandgate Castle, Kent. [*Ent. Book* 22, *pp.* 105–7.]

April 24. 11. Warrant to the Navy Commissioners to pay 100*l.* to the widow of Capt. John Golding, of the ship Diamond, slain in an engagement with two Dutch ships, as an acknowledgment of his services, and an encouragement of others to a cheerful performance of the like.

April 24. Entry of the above. [*Ent. Book* 22, *p.* 107.]

April 24. 12. Draft of the above.

April 24. Warrant to pay from the Exchequer to Edward Earl of Sandwich 676*l.* a year, to make up the sum of 4,000*l.* a year granted him from lands in the duchy of Lancaster, until the reversions of certain leases in the manor of Brampton, co. Hunts, fall in. [*Ent. Book* 22, *pp.* 108–10.]

April 24. The King to [the Master and Fellows of Christ's College, Cambridge]. Recommends Charles Smithson, B.A., student of that college, to the first vacant fellowship, on account of his father's loyalty during the late distractions. [*Ent. Book* 17, *p.* 106.]

April 24. Warrant for a lease to Theobald Earl of Carlingford and two others, for three years, of marsh lands in Cumberland, to be recovered by them, reserving one fourth of the value to the Crown, except certain houses, saltpans, anchorage and quayage of vessels, &c., at Whitehaven. [*Ent. Book* 17, *pp.* 107–8.]

April [24]. Whitehall. 13. Warrant for a grant to Theobald Earl of Carlingford and two others of the said marsh lands, and also of the tenements, saltpans, anchorage, and quayage at Whitehaven, &c.; with the usual commissions for the discovery of the lands, &c. [*Two pages.*]

April 24. The Charles. 14. Sir Allan Apsley to Lord [Arlington]. Requests favour for Capt. Noakes, a man of courage and parts, who served under him

VOL. CXIX.

1665.

in the West, and who wishes to be employed in Guernsey, where he now resides. Has no greater ambition than to have an interest in his lordship, as one of the best men and best friends. [*Two pages.*]

April 24. Royal Charles, off the Texel. 15. Duke of York to the King. Sent an account by Sir Wm. Penn's son that they got upon the broad forteens; got within them yesterday, off Egmont and Camperdown. The weather being thick, durst not stand near the shore, but sent in Capt. Smyth, with three frigates, for the Texel, and resolved at a Council of War to remain there to interrupt ships going into the Texel or Vlie, and to ride at anchor to keep their station, and avoid the hazard of tacking with so great a fleet at night. Has scouts always every way, to give timely notice of anything that may come. Capt. Smyth has returned, and reports that the Dutch have more than 80 sail in the Texel, three of which are flag-ships; one of them fired at him. A Flushing privateer and some fisher boats are taken; will keep one of them, a new Bessano yacht, which was hard to capture, because she plies well up to windward. Intends proposing to the Council of War to lie nearer the Texel, if the weather prove fine; as the Dutch know of their being there, has a mind that they should see them. [*Four pages.*]

April 24. Royal Charles, off the Texel. 16. Sir Wm. Coventry to Lord [Arlington]. Capt. Chicheley does not think the Dutch fleet so many as Capt. Smyth reported. They heard the Admiral's gun shot off for calling a Council, and think the Dutch fleet has seen theirs. Cannot hear that the Zealand fleet has come to the Texel, or intends it. Some ships have come up, which prove to be Hamburgers or Danes, and there is no cause for their detention. [*Two pages.*]

April 24. Royal Charles. 17. Earl of Falmouth to Lord [Arlington]. Are at anchor 10 or 12 leagues N.N.W. of the Texel. Thinks the Dutch fleet will not come out till the ships in the Weelings have joined them, and Reuter has come in. Expects to be nearer them by six leagues, after to-morrow's council of war. The weather is very fair and no accident, but nothing considerable taken, only fisher boats and a little miserable privateer. [*Three pages.*]

April 24. Licence to Fras. Williamson and Ralph Wayne, for 60 years, to convey springs of water discovered by them near Piccadilly, St. James's Field, Haymarket, and Suffolk Buildings, in pipes through the highways to the houses thereon to be built, they compounding for any damage they may do, and paying 6*s.* 8*d.* rent. [*Docquet.*]

April 24. Warrant to pay to John Watson, messenger of the chamber to the Queen, 50*l.* a year for life. [*Docquet.*]

April 24. Warrant to make allowance to Lord Townshend, on his rent of 2,000*l.* a year for the duty of 4*s.* a chaldron on coals exported, of the moiety of forfeitures paid into the Exchequer or elsewhere for nonpayment of the duty, or for false entries or forfeited bonds. [*Docquet.*]

Vol. CXIX.

1663.

April 24. Warrant to pay to Sir Roger Langley, Bart., late high sheriff of Yorkshire, 600*l.* for his expenses in the management and discovery of the late plot. [*Docquet.*]

April 24. Inner Temple. 18. Arthur Trevor to Williamson. Sends the assignment of the stables which Lady Chesterfield desires from Lord Arlington; she saves his lordship harmless as to rent and repairs, except for his part of Goring House; she is in fear of Davies, who always demanded his rent assisted by an attorney or bailiff.

April 24. Exeter. 19. Seth Bishop of Exeter to the Archbishop of Canterbury. Has waited on Lord Mohun, and promised, on his Grace's commands, to give Landilp Rectory to his lordship's nominee, Mr. Harding. Finds Exeter as well conditioned as may be, with 40 revolted ministers nestling there, and no power to remove them. Begs authority to disable Amos Short, of Lyme, Dorsetshire, from making pestilent excursions into his diocese.

April 24. 20. Report by Lord Treas. Southampton on Sir Jas. Bunce's petition, that vouchers are found for disbursements by Sir James of 3,691*l.*, of which he swears that he only received 500 Holland guilders, but that many of the payments being for services in Scotland, cannot be brought upon the English Exchequer, which is not in a condition to bear them.

April 24. 21. Account by Mr. Watts of schismatics in Deal; viz., Capt. Sam. Taverner, formerly commander of the castle; John Milford, an Anabaptist and post-office clerk, who has the view of the letters hours before they are delivered; James Coston, whose wife is a great hearer and preacher, and 10 others; with particulars of their proceedings. [*One and a half pages.*]

April 24. 22. Queries suggested by Sir Roger Langley to be put to the prisoner [John Lowe].

April 24. 23. Examination of John Lowe before Lord Arlington. Works at a brewhouse; goes sometimes to church. Knows Patshull [Podsell?] and has seen him in prison. Does not know John Atkinson the stockinger; nor anything of the late plot; saw Nath. Strange at a meeting, but did not know him till after. Knows of no concealed arms, and never saw Danvers nor Jones (Mene Tekel), nor Tim. Butler, Green, nor Loving. Was baptised a fortnight before, but will not say by whom. Has received money since he was in prison. [*One and a quarter pages.*]

April 24. Reference to the Lord Treasurer and Lord Ashley, on the petition of Fras. Roper, for several small tenements in Cornwall, rent 23*l.* 5*s.* 4*d.* per annum. [*Ent. Book* 18, *p.* 143.]

April 24. Reference to the Lord Treasurer on the petition of Viscount Ogle of Caterlough, for relief, being detained prisoner for debts contracted in the King's service. [*Ent. Book* 18, *p.* 143.]

Vol. CXIX.

1665.

April 23. Reference to the Lord Treasurer on the petition of Edw. Progers, for 1,500 decayed trees out of Hampton Park, on account towards the expenses of his building. [*Ent. Book* 19, *p.* 144.]

April 23. London. 24. Anonymous to the Archbishop of Canterbury. Knowing the general disquiet likely to be produced by want of sea coals, wishes to have it laid before the King, and presents it through his Grace, having formerly succeeded in presenting an important paper to the late King, by means of Archbishop Laud. *Encloses*,

24. I. *Suggestions as to the settlement of coals at a constant rate, to prevent the frauds of engrossing them, by a pretended company of coal and wood sellers;—viz., by the coal mines being taken by the King as mines royal; no coal exported till the country is supplied, and great consumers enjoined to burn coals, if living within* 10 *miles of a port, or portable river; by constant maintenance of a coal fleet; the King taking to farm both the export and home vent of coals, and by appointing a council for trade, to find out the cause of its decay, &c.*

April 23. Worcester. 25. Lord Windsor to Sec. Bennet. Hearing that John Knowles of Pershore was ill affected, sent Major Wilde to seize his letters; he refuses to explain the obscure expressions in them, saying that he is not legally accused. Will keep him close prisoner, and has sent up the letters and books. The country is quiet. *Encloses*,

25. I. *Memoranda relative to John Knowles, professed minister at Pershore, Worcestershire, taken prisoner by order of Lord Windsor; and of queries to be put to him relative to some letters addressed to him, &c.* [*One and a half pages.*]

25. II. *Mr. Knowles' "articles of faith, to be principally inquired into in reference to these times;" e.g.,—the doctrine of the Trinity, original sin, election, inspiration of the Scriptures, the moral law, oneness of saints with God, repentance, the resurrection, heaven, the sabbath, church ordinances, baptism, perseverance in grace, &c.* [*Two and a half pages.*]

25. III. "*A confutation of certain reasons which were framed against Laymen's preaching of the word.*" [*Twelve pages.*]

25. IV. "*Towards the Vindication of a Minister from a false accusation, and (on that occasion) an examination of Laymen's preaching, by way of answer to a writing some years since published in this city by a nameless author, and now subscribed by one John Knowles.*" *Signed Giles Workman.* [*Twenty-one pages.*]

25. V. "*Catalogue of the most material books found in the study of Mr. Knowles.*" *Signed J. W.* [*Two pages.*]

1665. VOL. CXIX.

25. VI. *Edw. Atkinson to John Knowles. Apologizes for not answering his letter. Has a sickly child, and has lately lost his wife who was an eminent Christian.*

Aldersgate Street, Oct. 14, 1662.

25. VII. *H. P—— to John Knowles. Private affairs. Knows not what freedom they have of meeting. His friends keep up a small meeting, but are very strict in the qualifications of those they admit; wishes Knowles would come among them two or three months. The necessities of the Poles increase, the Emperor having driven them from his territories. With later note that Mr. Knowles is looked on as a master builder, and that the Poles named will prove to mean a pack of English rebels.*

25. VIII. *H. P——, to John Knowles. Was at Oxford with his Transylvanian friend, and sorry not to meet Knowles there. Private affairs; religious advice. Gives Mr. Biddle's reading of the 1st of St. John. With notes by another hand, showing the danger of these expositions.* [*Two pages.*]

April 1, 1665.

25. IX. *R. Y—— to* [*John Knowles*]. *Hopes his heart will be stirred to come over, and that the Lord's work will prosper in his hands. Trusts this land of darkness will become a land of light; there is a great work to do, and he may be instrumental therein. Noted as a strong invitation to sedition, in which Mr. Knowles is expected to be very instrumental.*

April 25. Warrant to the Commissioner of Prizes to discharge the St. Margaret of Treport, which is proved to be a French vessel, at the interposition of Mademoiselle. [*Ent. Book* 22, p. 104.]

April 25. Whitehall. 26. Warrant to the Farmers of Customs to exempt certain coaches, horses, wines, &c., belonging to Monsieur Courtin, French ambassador, from all duties, and the vessels that carry the same from the duty of 5s. a ton, usually levied on French ships. [*Draft.*]

April 25. Entry of the above. [*Ent. Book* 22, p. 111.]

April 25. Warrant for release of a vessel now at Dover, which brought 24 horses for the Duke of Verneuil, the French ambassador, and is detained for not paying the duty of 5s. a ton. [*Ent. Book* 22, p. 112.]

April 25. 27. Jonas Shish to the Navy Comrs. Wants 50 or 60 loads of large elm timber, to saw into four inch planks, for completing the works of the new ship. [*Adm. Paper.*]

April 25. The Dartmouth, Kinsale. 28. Capt. Rich. Rooth to the Navy Comrs. On his return to his station off the Black rock to the north-west of Ireland, after victualling, &c., at Kinsale, encountered and captured a Dutch privateer of 80 tons, six guns, and 48 men, whereof two were killed and six wounded; six of his own men were also wounded; is obliged to put back again into Kinsale for repairs; understands from the cap-

VOL. CXIX.

1665.

tain of the prize that seven Dutch men-of-war are already on the coast, and five others ready to follow; requests that some course may be taken, both in Ireland and England, for the care of sick and wounded men; recommends John Gasbave, an experienced surgeon, who was employed at Portsmouth during the last Dutch war, to be appointed for Kinsale. [*Adm. Paper.*]

April 25. 29. Capt. John Tayler to the Lord Mayor of London. Requests that the King may be moved to signify to the Navy Commissioners the necessity of issuing warrants to the justices for land and water carriage of timber for the works of the new ship; and that the shipwrights and artificers employed may be secured from being impressed, in order that he may complete his contract in the time expected. [*Adm. Paper.*] *Encloses,*

29. I. *Names of justices in Essex,—Petit, Pascall, Wild, and Sir Thos. Abdy.*

29. II. *Particulars to be mentioned in the warrants issued to justices.*

April 25. 30. Account of four ships tendered to the Navy Commissioners, by Mr. Lewes, with their tonnage and masters' names. [*Adm. Paper.*]

April 25. 31. Jacob Blackleech to the Navy Comrs. Particulars of progress of the three water-ships. [*Adm. Paper.*]

April 25. Cockpit. 32. Duke of Albemarle to Sam. Pepys. Victuallers and others concerned in sending away beer and water to the fleet must be hastened. The Unity, a Dutch prize, is to be fitted out as a man-of-war. [*Adm. Paper.*]

April 26. Woolwich. 33. Certificate by Chris. Pett and five others to the Navy Comrs., that the scandalous report of John Clarke, yeoman of Woolwich, such a turbulent spirit that his neighbours could not possibly live with him, is false. [*Adm. Paper.*]

April 26. Cockpit. 34. Sir Wm. Clarke to Sam. Pepys. Capt. Guy, of the Paradox, is ordered to Harwich, to await the arrival of the beer, water, and other provisions, and convey them to the fleet; he is meanwhile to give an account of all ships and provisions that come thither. Has not yet heard of Capt. Stuart, who is to be commander of the Happy Entrance. [*Adm. Paper.*]

April 26. The Fox, Downs. 35. Capt. Wm. Dale to the Navy Comrs. Has taken into convoy the Robert and John, laden with stores for Portsmouth. [*Adm. Paper.*]

April 26. 36. Edw. Holbert to the Navy Comrs. Has served in plank value 700*l*., although as by contract, the first 30 loads were to be paid in ready money, he sold it cheaper than could otherwise have been done; cannot supply more until paid for that already delivered. [*Adm. Paper.*]

Vol. CXIX.

1665.

April 26. 37. Recommendation by E. Osborne of Nic. Day as gunner to the Sarah and Elizabeth, and request of warrant for his entry. [*Adm. Paper.*]

April 26. Harwich. 38. Invoice of timber and plank sent by the Love boy to Harwich. [*Adm. Paper.*]

April 26. Bristol. 39. Sir John Knight to the Navy Comrs. Will send his accounts for disbursements on board the George. Has been obliged to pay the press-master 18*l.* Will keep the 1,200*l.*, imprested to Francis Bayley for building the new ship, till there is occasion for it. Hears nothing of the seamen who ran away from the Hector. Continues pressing seamen, but fears that, being mostly strangers, they will run away also and not be found, he having no ship to put them in. Asks if he shall proceed in it. [*Adm. Paper.*]

April 26. Whitehall. Proclamation recalling the proclamation of March 1, which forbade any ships to go to sea for commerce; also promising letters of marque to any who will set forth private men-of-war against the Dutch, and declaring that on account of the importance of the coal trade, no seamen employed therein shall be pressed, and that convoys shall be provided for the coal vessels. [*Printed, Proc. Col., p.* 182.]

April 26. Doctors' Commons. 40. Will. Turner to Williamson. Sir Rob. Wiseman, King's advocate, returned the treaty between France and Holland to Lord Arlington, along with what was drawn up in conformity to order.

April 26. The Plymouth, Texel. 41. Capt. Thos. Allin to [Williamson]. Asks his favour in the alteration of his grant, but wishes the former date to be preserved, lest Sir John Lawson and Sir Wm. Berkeley should be paid before him. Begs not to be prejudiced if knocked off in this expedition. Has had many promises of favour, but the sea has taken up all his time. Hopes there is no obstruction in the warrant for his son, Thos. Allin, to succeed him in Sandgate Castle.

April 26. 42. Earl of Exeter to Lord Arlington. Requests further commands as to how the money in the sheriffs' hands, is to be disposed of, there being no castle nor garrison in or near the county.

April 27. Royal Charles. 43. Earl of Falmouth to Lord [Arlington]. They are now within four leagues of the Texel, that the enemy may have the pleasure of seeing them, but will not lie so near. Nothing could be so advantageous to His Majesty [as the Dutch coming out], but that is a good argument against their doing it. Will be obliged to return in two or three weeks for beer, water, &c.; is expecting the Dutch fleet from Rochelle and Bourdeaux; is now in sight of their whole fleet, so as to distinguish their flags. Does not think the Dutch like the sight of them. [*Three pages.*]

April 27. Warrant to pay to the Earl of Sandwich 40,000*l.* from the customs, by 20,000*l.* the half year, beginning from Michaelmas 1667, to defray arrears due upon the great wardrobe; to be distributed amongst the tradesmen who have supplied commodities, and in wages and other allowances. [*Docquet.*]

VOL. CXIX.

1665.

[April 27.] [Whitehall.] 44. Petition of Edward Trussell and other tradesmen belonging to the great wardrobe, to the King, for redress. His Majesty, on their petition, ordered the Lord Treasurer to assign the moneys due to them on some certain branch of revenue, whereas he has drawn up a warrant ready to pass for 40,000*l.*, part thereof on half-yearly payments from the Customs, but not to begin till Michaelmas 1667, whereby they will be ruined.

April 27. Reference of the above petition to the Lord Treasurer, who is ordered to allow the petitioners ordinary interest from Lady Day last, till their moneys are fully paid. [*Ent. Book* 18, *p.* 148.]

April 27. Warrant for permitting a ship, freighted with wine, baggage, &c., for the Duke of Vernueil, to unlade in the port of London, free from all duties. [*Ent. Book* 22, *p.* 113.]

April 27. Privy seal for 500*l.* to Charles Viscount Andover. Minute. [*Ent. Book* 22, *p.* 114.]

April 27. Whitehall. 45. Petition of Sir John Lowther, Bart., to the King, for a grant of the soil between high and low water at Whitehaven, Cumberland, on which his ancestors erected a pier and other buildings, but a late grant being made of the derelict lands there, his title has been called in question. With reference thereon to the Lord Treasurer and Lord Ashley, and their report, June 13, 1665, in favour of the petition.

April 27. Entry of the above reference. [*Ent. Book* 18, *p.* 148.]

April 27. London. 46. Jacob Blackleech to the Navy Comrs. Particulars and progress of the three water ships. [*Adm. Paper.*]

April 27. Cockpit. 47. Duke of Albemarle to the Navy Comrs. Desires a month's provisions for the 25 men employed in the Harwich hoy for taking up the ordnance, cables, and anchors belonging to the London, lately wrecked near Chatham. Beer and water should be hastened to the fleet. [*Adm. Paper.*]

April 27. 48. Account of press warrants given to four victualling ships, for 42 men. [*Adm. Paper.*]

April 27. Deptford. 49. J. Uthwayt to Sir Wm. Batten. A brewer's servant, apprehended for embezzling a piece of a stay, supposed to be the forestay of the Unity prize, is an able seaman and has sheltered himself a long time under the disguise of a drayman. [*Adm. Paper.*]

April 27. London. 50. Wm. Bodham to Sir John Mennes. John Clark, of Woolwich, is hovering about the Navy Office, to petition for his wages; he has made an overcharge for buttressing the wall. Cautions the Commissioners against false petitions and certificates, made more by favour than right or knowledge. Few men reckon it a sin to damnify the King, if they can but be indemnified themselves. [*Adm. Paper.*]

VOL. CXIX.

1665
April 27. 51. Thos. Lewis to Sam. Pepys. Account of cask delivered by the three water ships; 171 tons are already gone, and the rest will be ready on half an hour's warning. [*Adm. Paper.*]

April 27. 52. Thos. Lewis to Sam. Pepys. Gives an account of the watermen on board the victualling vessels, not one of whom was pressed by the watermen. Begs for press warrants. [*Adm. Paper.*] *Encloses,*

52. I. *Account of beer sent to the fleet as part of the 2,100 tuns needed for the first four months; total, 1,031 tuns.* *April 27, 1665.*

52. II., III. *Similar account of beer, 1,835 tuns; with notes relating to beer and other provisions.*

April 27. Victualling Office. 53. Thos. Lewis to the Navy Comrs. Only three men have appeared of all those ordered to be pressed by the Marshal of the Admiralty, and many of the watermen have deserted. Three ships laden with beer cannot sail through want of men, and through neglect of the masters, who are seldom on board, and will not come for bills of lading. Mr Blackleech, appointed for filling the water casks, does not mind his business as be ought. [*Adm. Paper.*] *Encloses,*

53. I. *Account of the appearance of watermen on the victualling ships, and neglect of the masters in suffering lighters of beer to remain at the sides of ships, and not unlading them.* *April 24, 1665.*

April 28. 54. Muster of the watermen on board the 12 ships ready to take in provisions. [*Adm. Paper.*]

April 28. 55. Note that only four watermen are found on board the Constant Anne, and one on board the Hopewell. [*Adm. Paper.*]

April 28. 56. Account of press warrants required for 20 men for two victualling ships. [*Adm. Paper.*]

April 28. The Coventry, Hole Haven. 57. Capt. Wm. Hill to Sam Pepys. Went on shore at Lowestoft to buy wood and candles. Ascribes the strange report of the plague being amongst his crew to Sir Thos. Meadowes, of Yarmouth, who "may be an honest man to the King, but no wise man in his actions." His company are, and have been all the voyage, very well. The ship is very foul, being four months off the ground, and all provisions expended. Desires to bring up a small prize captured, supposed to be Dutch, to be submitted to the Admiralty Court. [*Adm. Paper.*]

April 28. The Greyhound, Downs. 58. Capt. Rich. Country to the Navy Comrs. Has arrived with 10 sail of merchant ships from the Levant. The ship has not been upon ground since November, and has but one month's provisions on board; is ambitious for action, and cheerful to be employed; awaits orders. [*Adm. Paper.*]

Vol. CXIX.

1665.

April 28. Royal Charles, six leagues from the Texel.

59. Sir Wm. Coventry to Sam. Pepys. The whole fleet has passed within two leagues of the Texel. Could discern the Dutch flags, but most of their fleet was hid behind the island; ours was quite visible; thinks it the best that ever was upon the sea. Slop-sellers' supplies will be welcome, whenever they come. To hasten all stores and provisions to Harwich must still be the burthen of his song. Arrival of the Eagle and John and Katherine, bringing men. The Vanguard and Success are still wanting. [*Adm. Paper.*]

April 28. The Sorlings, Plymouth.

60. Capt. Jonathan Waltham to the Navy Comrs. Has been waiting at Plymouth for orders. Wrote twice to Coventry and Sir John Skelton, but received no answer. Is heartily willing to do service; begs a more favourable construction of his actions. [*Adm. Paper.*]

April 28. Chatham.

61. Commissioner Peter Pett to Sam. Pepys. Asks directions in regard to a letter received from the Justices of Kent, in answer to a warrant, issued by Sir John Mennes and himself, for the carriage of 350 loads of timber. Also whether the Act for carriage gives the latitude of charging two counties with the carriage of timber growing on one. Mr. Moorcock complains of hard usage from the carters last year, who forced him to pay them before any of the timber was carried to the places assigned, and then left it in their several parishes where they live, and where it yet remains. Sends instructions given to Mr. Lewsley for Sir Edw. Dering's timber, for correction. The new hulk is sent down to Sheerness. Thinks the galley, for about 500*l.*, may be made into a very useful sixth-rate frigate. Has ordered six masts for Mr. Grey. [*One and a half pages.*] *Encloses,*

61. i. *Instructions for Thos. Lewsley, purveyor, as to the sale of bark, measuring, topping and lopping, squaring, and carriage of 400 oak trees, bought of Sir Edw. Dering, of Pluckley, Kent.* [*Two pages.*] *April 25, 1665.*

April 28. Off the Texel.

62. Duke of York to Lord Arlington. Will send Holmes's examination on oath about the Guinea business, that all the world may see how the Dutch abuse them by false reports. Yesterday the whole fleet stood to shore, within sight of land, and again to-day they have approached within a league. The Dutch ride between the Texel and the Helder, but so thick that their numbers could not be counted. Their flag-ships are great ships; they have had a fair wind to come out, but there is no sign of it; will try to meet with their ships homeward bound. [*Two and a half pages.*]

April 28. Royal Charles, near the Texel.

63. Sir Wm. Coventry to Lord Arlington. Rode so near the Dutch fleet as to hear their guns fire. Supposes it was at healths, though not at ours. That they might not want notice of the fleet, the Duke permitted a fisher boat which had been taken to go to them. The Duke will lay Sir George Downing's proposal before the council of war, but cannot conjecture how it will be taken. The fleet will soon return for beer, &c., but unless a greater proportion

VOL. CXIX.

1665.

be supplied than the victualler promised, the fleet cannot do service, unless supplied with wine instead, which would be a great charge. Reminds him that the victualler's defects have already been brought before Council. Asks what should be done if the Dutch will not come out, but send their East India and Smyrna ships to some foreign port, and then do as they please in the Straits and Guinea. "If we divide our fleet, they may come out and do what they please here; if we do not, they carry all before them there." If M. De Beaufort comes into these seas, supposes the King will have an exact account of his errand, and, if His Majesty do not like it, will soon drive him into harbour or out of those seas again. [*Two pages.*]

April 28. Swiftsure, off the Texel. 64. Sir Thos. Clifford to Williamson. They have been all day braving the Dutch, sailing in sight of their fleet, but they seem afraid, and will not come out. Fears they will keep them too long without fighting. Thanks for his tidings about the French ambassadors.

April 28. Royal Charles. 65. Sir W. Coventry to Williamson. Have shown the Dutch the best fleet they ever saw; part of the Dutch fleet was riding at anchor, within the island; they had flags in the maintop of a very high ship, and the foretop of another. The English ships are in good order, well manned, and for the most part in good health.

April 28. Reference to the Lord Treasurer and Lord Ashley on the petition of Theobald Earl of Carlingford and Wm. Dyke, complaining that a grant of certain lands belonging to the Crown, discovered by them at great cost, is obstructed by the claims of others. [*Ent. Book* 18, *p.* 149.]

April 28. Whitehall. 66. Pass for the ship Count Eric of Riga, belonging to the French East India Company, and laden with deals, pitch, lead, and quicksilver, from Hamburg to Havre de Grace, or any other French port, provided she carry no goods nor merchandise belonging to persons in hostility with the King.

April 28. Entry of the above. [*Ent. Book* 22, *p.* 113.]

April 28. Letter Office. 67. James Hickes to Williamson. Sends intelligence, as required, about the principles of Wm. Foreman, who is a fanatic, and his owners no better; thinks his correspondent's letters to Holland should be inspected, as they may transmit the present state of the kingdom, and the designs intended against the King. *Encloses,*

67. I. *Rich. Foster to Jas. Hickes. Could hear nothing of Wm. Foreman, except as master of a small vessel trading for Berwick. Went with Sir Fras. Anderson, member for Newcastle, to the mayor, about it. They sent for* [Thos.] *Swan, the postmaster, who said Foreman had had no letters*

Vol. CXIX.

1665.

from Holland lately, but several from the north. Sends Forman's examinations and bond. There are a few capers off the coast, but they do little hurt. The people say they shall be great losers by the Lord Mayor's proceedings about coal; the coal works have ceased, and many thousands will go begging. The fanatics prick up their ears, but the mayor and gentlemen take good care of them. *Newcastle, April 25, 1665.*

67. II. *Examination of Wm. Forman, master of the Prosperous of Newcastle. Has not been in Holland for more than a year, nor had any letter thence for three months, except one from Robt. Forman, nor sent any but one to him. Signed by Fras. Liddell, mayor, Sir Fras. Anderson, and Ralph Carr.* *Newcastle, April 24, 1665.*

67. III. *Bond of Wm. Forman, and two others, in 500l., that he shall not plot against government, and shall appear before the deputy lieutenants, if summoned within a year; with names of the five owners of the Prosperous.*

April 28. Privy seal for 800l. to Jeremy Snow, for secret service without account. Minute. [*Ent. Book* 22, p. 113.]

April 28. Warrant for a grant to Dame Mary Killigrew, dresser to the Queen Consort, of a pension of 300l. a year. [*Ent. Book* 22, p. 114.]

April 28. Licence extending for two months the time granted by the Duke of York for the ship St. Mary, built in the United Provinces for the French East India Company, to pass to France, provided she carry no goods belonging to the King's enemies. [*Ent. Book* 22, pp. 116–7.]

April 28. Similar licence for the St. John Baptist. Minute. [*Ent. Book* 22, p. 117.]

April 28. Privy seal for 500l. to —— ——, for secret services, without account. Minute. [*Ent. Book* 22, p. 117.]

April 28. Warrant to the Farmers of Customs to take particular care to prevent the exportation of saltpetre, for which there will be more than ordinary need, to make gunpowder during the war with the Dutch. [*Ent. Book* 22, p. 117.]

April [28.] 68. Draft of the above.

April 28. Pass for Madame de Fiennes. [*Ent. Book* 22, p. 118.]

April 29. Warrant for an allowance of 1,000l. a year to George Viscount Grandison, from Lady day, 1661, when the office of Captain of the Yeomen of the Guards was surrendered to him by the late Earl of Norwich. [*Ent. Book* 22, p. 119.]

Vol. CXIX.

1665.

April 28. Warrant to pay to Sir Edward Carr and Edward Heball, equerries to the Queen, who have served ever since her arrival but received no salary, 150*l.* each, for board and standing wages for one year and a half. [*Ent. Book* 22, p. 120.]

April 29. Order for a grant of confirmation of the charter of Totness, co. Devon. [*Ent. Book* 22, *p.* 128.] *Annexing,*

1. *Heads of alterations and additions to be inserted in the above charter.*

April 29. Warrant to Lord Ashley, treasurer for prizes, to pay to the Earl of St. Alban's 1,000*l.* out of moneys for the sale of prizes, for the use of Mons. Blanchford. [*Ent. Book* 22, p. 131.]

April 29. Warrant to pay to John Napier 240*l.*, due to him as page of honour. [*Docquet.*]

April 29. Grant of denization to Lawrence Dibusty, native of Bayonne, he paying strangers' customs and subsidies, and obeying the laws of the kingdom. [*Docquet.*]

April 29. 69. Jacob Blackleach to the Navy Comrs. Particulars and progress of the three water ships. [*Adm. Paper.*]

April 29. 70. Report of the condition of 11 ships now in the river. [*Adm. Paper, three pages.*]

April 29. The Augustine, Harwich. 71. Capt. Rich. Teale to the Navy Comrs. Hopes in three days to be full ballasted, and will then make all speed to Chatham. [*Adm. Paper.*]

April 29. The Fox, Spithead. 72. Capt. Wm. Dale to the Navy Comrs. Is arrived with the Robert and John, laden with stores for Portsmouth; hears that the Fox is ordered for Sally; requests that a half deck may be raised in her to make her more serviceable. [*Adm. Paper.*]

April 29. 73. John Russell to the Navy Comrs. Account of the timber sent by the Love hoy from Stockwith. More hoys are wanted. Requests money. [*Adm. Paper.*]

April 29 May 9. Dieppe. 74. Peter Crucefix to the Navy Comrs. Wishes to send yarn and hemp on trial at 36*s.* and 34*s.* per cwt.; is well known to Sir John Lawson, Capt. Rich. Rooth, and others. Begs leave to freight two English vessels to Newcastle for coals. [*Adm. Paper.*]

April 30. Warrant for a grant to Philip Packer, of Groombridge, Kent, and John Packer, his son, in reversion after Wm. and Robt. Packer, of the office of Usher of the receipt of Exchequer, and Keeper of the Star Chamber. [*Ent. Book* 22, p. 133.]

April 30. 75. Deposition of Andrew Higgins, that Sir Robt. Reynolds said the King was but a single person, and if he did anything contrary to the laws, he might be tried for his life by his subjects.

VOL. CXIX.

1665.

April? 76. Petition of Sir William Boreman, His Majesty's servant, to the King, to confer upon him the estate of Hubert Arnold, his relative, who has committed suicide, in trust for the widow and family.

April. Golden Lion. 77. Rich. Morris, purser, to the Navy Coms. Part of the 60 men brought home in the Golden Lion prize are discharged by tickets; about 20 remain upon sea pay. Mr. Sheldon, clerk of the cheque, refusing to grant them provisions, they have entered themselves in other ships, and advise their friends to come to the writer for tickets. Requests an order to discharge them. [*Adm. Paper.*]

April. 78. Capt. Jonas Poole to Sam. Pepys. Sends tickets for the 24 men belonging to the London, granted him by the Earl of Sandwich; the men are on board the Vanguard, and cannot well be spared to come up; begs an order to Philip Solomon to receive their respective moneys from Sir Geo. Carteret. Has granted passes to London, for five days, to 11 pressed men received from ships coming in, and written to their masters not to pay them any wages till they return to their duty. [*Adm. Paper.*]

April. Plymouth. 79. John Lanyon to Sam. Pepys. Sends account of cable yarn received from Dan. Barker; asks what size to lay it; has given a three months' bond for the money, 481*l.* 14*s.* 8*d.* The Sorlings has been in dock three weeks, the captain pretending he has no order to wash and tallow, though he cannot go to sea before it be done, which is thought strange. The St. Mary prize is still in port, and all her company discharged: she needs repairs, and would serve for a convoy to Tangiers. [*Adm. Paper.*]

April. 80. Complaint of Augustin Punnett and four other pilots, of their usual pay being lessened, till it is impossible to subsist by the employment. Must omit the service unless payment be made as formerly. [*Adm. Paper.*]

April? 81. Measurement of the masts in the 10 Gottenburg ships. [*Adm. Paper.*]

April. 82. Navy Commissioners' warrant of protection to 10 bargemen employed in bringing up timber from Reading to Woolwich. [*Adm. Paper, copy.*]

April. 83. Mr. Harris's account of sails to be provided to remain in store. [*Adm. Paper.*]

April. 84. Account of press warrants granted to eight victualling vessels; pressmen to be provided if the watermen fail. [*Adm. Paper.*]

April. 85. Account of guns belonging to the Sarah and Elizabeth water ship. [*Adm. Paper.*]

April. 86. Account of guns belonging to the Constant John water ship. [*Adm. Paper.*]

April. 87. Account by James Cooke of the Madras's guns. [*Adm. Paper.*]

1663. VOL. CXX. MAY 1–9, 1663.

May 1. 1. Certificate by Ro. Benson, clerk of Assize for Yorkshire, that Phineas and Thos. Hodgson, Oliver Cave, John Holbrooke, and Edw. Greene, were indicted last summer for robbery, and the two first condemned and executed, but that nothing further was objected against the other three.

May 1. 2. List of 15 victualling ships, their respective masters, length, breadth, depth, and burthen; with the number of men on each. [*Adm. Paper.*] *Annexing*,

2. I. *List of eight of the above vessels, noting that they are now at Dover and offered for service.*

May 1. Winchester Street. 3. Jas. Houblon to Sam. Pepys. Requests the discharge of the ship St. Lucar Merchant, lately hired; both ship and master are unfit for northward service, and he and his brother, who are the owners, have a voyage for her. [*Adm. Paper.*]

May 1. Cockpit. 4. Sir Wm. Clarke to Sam. Pepys. Encloses for correction the directions for sending the Coventry to Portsmouth. [*Adm. Paper.*]

May 1. Farnham. 5. John Langrack to Sam. Pepys. Wants money for the carriage of timber; several towns in Hampshire have measured themselves out of the 12 miles appointed for carriage; if timber be sawn into 3 or 4-inch planks in the forest, not one out of four would come safe to London, as they throw them down and take them up so often by the way. [*Adm. Paper.*]

May 1. Victualling Office. 6. D. Gauden to the Navy Commrs. Account of the tonnage of two months' victuals to be sent to the fleet from several ports named; total, 44,000 tons. Requests that shipping may be provided for receiving them. The greater part of the beer must be supplied from London. [*Adm. Paper.*]

May 1. Chatham. 7. Edw. Gregory, jun., to Sam. Pepys. Complains of the encroachments of Mr. Barrow, the storekeeper, upon his privilege as clerk of the cheque, in the pre-eminency of signing; it was attempted, but positively forbidden, in his father's time. Has applied to Commissioner Peter Pett, who promises to lay it before the Board. Begs his favour. [*Adm. Paper.*]

May 1. The Lea. 8. Dan. Furzer to the Navy Commrs. The smith is willing to accept an assistant in making the biggest anchors, in consideration of the trouble and preparation of their honours in almost fitting a house for the purpose, although 23s. a week is more than he believed would have been demanded. Wants money for the carriers. [*Adm. Paper.*]

May 1. Yarmouth. 9. James Johnson to the Navy Commrs. Will acquaint the Edgars that for the imprest of 700*l.* they must give security. Asks in what manner the security must be taken. Mr. Stedman is

Vol. CXX.

1663.

willing to build a ship on the same terms. Offers great shot for sale. [*Adm. Paper.*]

May 1. Cockpit. 10. Duke of Albemarle to the Navy Comrs. Requests the release of John Crussone, engaged to serve in the Vanguard, but detained prisoner in the Marshalsea for a debt of 3*l*., this debt to be satisfied out of the first wages that become due to him. [*Adm. Paper.*] *Encloses,*

10. I. *Petition of John Crussone, prisoner in the Marshalsea, to the Duke of Albemarle, for release and liberty to return to the King's service; John Fox, commander of the Constant Elizabeth, with whom he made a voyage to Virginia, has cast him into prison for a debt of 3l., and detained his wages, which amount to more than that sum, on the plea of his being the cause of his men being pressed into the King's service.*

May 2. Hamburg. 11. Nath. Cambridge to Edward Dering, merchant of London. Account of goods sent by the Royal Catherine to Gluckstadt, and of various bills drawn. [*Adm. Paper.*] *Annexing,*

11. I. *Nath. Cambridge to Edw. Dering. Invoice of goods laden on the Royal Catherine. Asks his determination about insurance; it cannot be done under 8 per cent.; heard from Amsterdam that two private men-of-war were going out for the Elbe, to intercept the Hamburg fleet.*

May 2. Elias hulk, Catwater, Plymouth. 12. John Garratt, boatswain of the hulk, to the Navy Comrs. Begs an increase of salary and more help, in consideration of extra work now that the hulk is employed, having also to attend the ships coming in for ballast, and to overlook the masts in store. *Encloses,*

12. I.–III. *Receipts for money paid to Simon Hatsell, former boatswain of the hulk, at 10s. a week,* 1656–1658.

May 2. 13. Warrant from the Navy Comrs. to the Storekeeper and Clerk of the Cheque at Deptford, to overlook the weighing of strands in the respective yards of those rope merchants lately contracted with for cables, and to cause the same, when laid into cables, to be weighed by the King's beam at Deptford. [*Adm. Paper.*]

May 2. Harwich. 14. Anthony Deane to the Navy Comrs. Particulars of timber to be had from Sir Philip Parker and Mr. Tyler. If remitting money is troublesome, the King's collector, Mr. Keane, of Ipswich, would be glad to advance it. Hears of a good mast at Woolwich for the Ann yacht. The great lighter for the carriage of timber is ready to launch. [*Adm. Paper, three pages.*]

May 2. Plymouth. 15. John Lanyon to the Navy Comrs. Asks directions concerning the size and length of cordage to be laid. The Sorlings will be ready to sail in two days. [*Adm. Paper.*]

Vol. CXX.

1665.

May 2. 16. Ellis Osborne to Thos. Hayter. Requests a warrant for John Sly, carpenter of the Sarah and Elizabeth, to be entered at Deptford. [*Adm. Paper.*]

May 2. 17. Jacob Blackbeech to the Navy Comrs. Account of three water ships in readiness; 3,000 wood billets more are wanted for each. [*Adm. Paper.*]

May 2. 18. Jonas Shish to the Navy Comrs. Advises the building of a house crane, to go with a wheel of 14 feet, by the new launch in the plank yard at Deptford. [*Adm. Paper.*] *Encloses,*

18. i. *Estimate by Jonas Shish and Edw. Randells, for building a house crane 30 feet long by 13 feet wide, and 30 feet high, to stand by the new launch at Deptford yard; total, 217l. 10s. 8d.* *Deptford, May* 1, 1665.

May 2. Carlisle. 19. Certificate by Sir Edw. Musgrave, sheriff, and eight Justices of the Peace for Cumberland of the careful and prudent conduct of George Williamson, chief collector for hearth money for the county, in raising the rent, without forcing it from the people.

May 2. 20. "The exercise at arms to be performed by the Artillery Company in the Artillery Garden, and the passes that lead to it from Moorgate, on Tuesday 2nd May 1665," being a mock battle between the Romans and the Grecians, in which the former are victorious; giving the names of the officers who assume the different characters. [*Thirteen pages.*]

May 2. Garsdale. 21. Abraham Nelson, of Garsdale, Yorkshire, to Lord Arlington. Is one of the indigent officers; has always been watchful over insurrections, and often given notice of them to Parliament men; there is danger for want of a moving army of horse. Has suffered deeply for his zeal in the Royal cause, and is now obliged to keep in private for fear of an arrest. Begs a protection for 10 or 12 months.

[May 2.] [Whitehall.] 22. Petition of Henry Peters, yeoman of the field, to the King, for something from the privy purse; the slack payments of these ill times and the small benefit he makes by his office have left him 100l. in debt, and not able to pay for lodging and diet.

May 2. Reference of the above petition to the Lord Treasurer. [*Ent. Book* 18, p. 148.]

May 2. Reference to the Duke of Ormond on Sir Rob. Parkhurst's petition. [*Ent. Book* 18, *p.* 149.]

May 2. Warrant for a grant to Dr. James Hyde of the office of Public Reader of Physic in the University of Oxford, void by resignation of Sir Thomas Clayton; fee, 40l. a year. [*Ent. Book* 22, *p.* 122.]

May 2. Warrant to Sir Richard Ford and Sir Richard Reeves, late sheriffs of London, to deliver to the Commissioners for lieutenancy of London

Vol. CXX.

1665.

the moneys remaining in their hands, raised on the Act for 70,000*l*. a year for the militia; the said money is to be paid for the arrears of officers and other services for the City. [*Ent. Book* 22, p. 127.]

May 3. Warrant to Lord Ashley to pay to Sir John Denham, surveyor of buildings, 1,030*l*. out of money in his hands from sale of prizes, in satisfaction for the same sum disbursed by him. [*Ent. Book* 22, p. 114.]

May 3. Warrant to the Commissioners for Prizes to deliver to John Young, storekeeper of Portsmouth, all empty casks brought in as prizes in or near that port. [*Ent. Book* 22, p. 122.]

May 3. Whitehall. 23. The King to the Commissioners for execution of the Act for repair of highways. Wishing to provide not only for the prosperity but the safety and beauty of the City, recommends the diligent prosecution of the said Act. Orders a review of all offences against it and a due levying of penalties; as no punishment is appointed to offenders by irregularities of building, authorizes them to commit to prison such as continue obstinate, and to demolish the said buildings; also to open the passage to St. Martin's Lane from the Strand, and other passages mentioned in the Act. [*One and a half pages*.]

May 3. Entry of the above. [*Ent. Book* 17, p. 108.]

May 3. Hinton. 24. P—— to Lord [Arlington]. When in London, engaged leading persons of every persuasion to correspond with him, especially the Fifth Monarchy men and Anabaptists. Their pastor was formerly that frantic prophet, Feake, but is now Helmes; they hold principles near to Venner's, and none are so likely to make a bold, desperate attempt. Told them he was going into the West to serve the Lord's people, as it was high time to look about them. They want a narrative of the strange sights in the skies seen by many at Honiton in Devonshire, for some ministers are now writing a book about such things; the book should be stopped, as it will be stuffed full of disloyal scandalous observations on the government, as well as on persons. Hopes soon to send the names of the authors. Lord Poulett is at Col. Piggot's near Bristol, and is not well enough to attend to business. Is going to Exeter and Taunton, having the Duke of Albemarle's pass. Endorsed "From P. in the West." [*Two and a half pages*.]

May 3. Carlisle. 25. —— to [Williamson]. Thinks the spirit of rebellion as vigorous in the south and west of Scotland as it was when the Scots entered into that wicked covenant, the bane of these three nations. Col. Gibbie Ker [Gilby Carr ?] is said to have taken a commission from the Hollanders to levy men in Scotland, and to have built up some forts in Shetland. The honest stout Archbishop of Glasgow thinks the securing of Col. Rob. Montgomery, Major-Generals Hoburn and Mourne, Davie Lesly, now Lord Newark, and some few others, would do much to keep the country quiet. It is thought that more standing forces are necessary, and the demolishing of the

VOL. CXX.

1665.

citadels is much lamented. A commission was given by the Council to search for arms in Galloway, but it did not signify much. Is glad that Carlisle has so vigilant and careful a governor, as the garrison is environed with discontented persons.

May 3. The Paradox, Downs. 26. Capt. Leo. Guy to the Navy Comrs. Awaits orders for victualling and tallowing. [*Adm. Paper.*]

May 3. Chatham. 27. Sir Wm. Clarke to Sam. Pepys. The Duke of York has ordered, as requested, commissions for the master of the ketch bought at Colchester, and other officers; the naming of the ketch and of the one building at Wivenhoe is referred to the Board. [*Adm. Paper.*]

May 3. Cockpit. 28. Duke of Albemarle to the Navy Comrs. Desires that such of the wives and mothers of divers mariners in the Westergate as have letters of attorney may receive part of their husbands' pay, to relieve their present distress, it being uncertain what is become of the ship. [*Adm. Paper.*] *Encloses*,

28. I. *Petition of several wives and mothers of the mariners in the Westergate to the Duke of Albemarle, for payment of some part of the money due to their respective husbands, through whose long absence they are reduced to great want and misery.*

May 3. 29. Account of five ships freighted by Sir Wm. Rider and Wm. Cutler, merchants of London, for Dantzick, Riga, Stockholm, &c., to fetch home the King's goods. Press warrants and protections for the men are required. [*Adm. Paper.*]

May 4. London. 30. Jacob Blackleech to [the Navy Comrs.]. The three water ships are ready to set sail, and can fill no more water until they come lower down in the river into deeper water. [*Adm. Paper.*]

May 4. 31. Certificate by Matthew Hayden of the readiness of the Sea Venture smack for service as a victualler. [*Adm. Paper.*]

May 4. The Coventry, Holehaven. 32. Capt. Wm. Hill to Sam. Pepys. Begs to come up and give account of the ship, which wants cleaning and stores. [*Adm. Paper.*]

May 4. The Unity. 33, 34. Accounts by Thos. Trafford, captain, and Wm. Foster, purser, of provisions remaining on board the prize ship Unity. Two papers. [*Adm. Paper.*]

May 4. Woolwich Ropeyard. 35. Wm. Bodham to Sam. Pepys. Sends three estimates for carpenters' work by Ellery; suggests that Mr. Rundells be called upon for his prices for the same particulars. Esteems Ellery "an honester man and not so cunning a snapp as the other." [*Adm. Paper.*] *Encloses*,

35. I. *Estimates for carpenters' work; viz., for altering the shed, 75l. 0s. 8d.; repairing the wharf at the crane in the gun-yard, 63l. 6s.; building a gallery, 25 ft. long, to take up bundles in the street without opening the gates, 23l.;*

1665. Vol. CXX.

with statement of the conveniences and profit of such works. [Two pages.] Woolwich Ropeyard, May 2, 1665.

May 4. Cockpit. 36. Duke of Albemarle to the Navy Comrs. The victualler in London gives account of victuals ready for 5,500 men. The King wishes a survey may be taken of the beef, pork, &c. provided, and of what beer can be served in by the 20th of the month, and an account of the several proportions sent with all speed; the victualler is to permit persons appointed to survey the same. Has ordered Capt. Amos Beare into Dover, to victual and repair the Lily. [*Adm. Paper.*] *Annexing,*

36. i. *List of proportions of victuals in store or contracted for, being nearly what is required for 5,500 men for 6 months; with note [by Sir Wm. Coventry] that it was shown to the Duke, in reply to his letter of the 4th, and that some provisions are put out to various contractors, who may be relied on for punctuality. May 6, 1665.*

May 4. 37. Agreement between the Navy Comrs. and Capt. Wm. Porter, for the hire and freight of the Loyal Subject, 561 tons burthen, at 10*s.* per month per ton, for six months certain and twelve months uncertain. [*Adm. Paper, damaged.*]

May 4. Seville. 38. John Blood to Sam. Pepys. Has passed over to Spain, to engage his old acquaintances, upon the present opportunity offered by the Dutch war, to establish Tangiers convoys, and lay the foundation of a sound trade for time to come; requests that good passage and freight may be given to all victuallers and ammunition ships for Spain, by way of Tangiers, thus making it the deposit of all commodities between Spain and England. Nothing can be of greater service to the King than to make Tangiers famous, which can be done by making it cheaper for ships to land and re-ship from thence than go direct to Spain. [*One and a half pages.*]

May 4. Portsmouth. 39. John Tippetts to the Navy Comrs. Requests an imprest of 150*l.* towards squaring and breaking the trees bought of Col. Norton. Is sorry Peter Blackborow's 4-inch plank is gone by, that being a provision much wanted. [*Adm. Paper.*]

May 4. Wapping. 40. Sir Wm. Warren to the Navy Comrs. Has hired two great ships to fetch the masts from New England. Demands sufficient convoy, according to contract, for their safe conduct beyond Land's End. [*Adm. Paper.*]

May? 41. Statement that the late Lord Langdale sold the rectory of Holme in Spalding moor, co. York, 40 years ago, to Dr. Hodgson, for the use of St. John's College, Cambridge; that it was then an impropriation, but is now a donative for one of their fellows, value 160*l.*, but 20*l.* is paid to the King for fee-farm rent. Lord Langdale requests the King to exchange it with the college for one of like value, and to confer Holme upon him.

Vol. CXX.

1665.

May ? 42. Petition of Marmaduke Lord Langdale to the King, to inform the governors of St. John's College, Cambridge, that His Majesty wishes to dispose of the rectory of Holme Cultram, co. York, value 160*l*., but paying only 23*l*. fee-farm rent, which was sold to the college by the late Lord Langdale, and will convey to them one nearer and of better value in compensation. [*See* 1665, *May* 26.]

May ? 43. Request by Lord Langdale, that the King will signify his pleasure to the governors of St. John's College, Cambridge, to have the disposal of the rectory of Holme, Yorkshire, and that he wishes to know its true value, so as to give them full compensation in exchange.

May [4]. Whitehall. 44. The King to the [Master and Fellows of] St. John's College, Cambridge. Requests leave for Marmaduke Lord Langdale to exchange the rectory of Holme in Spalding moor, co. York, yearly value 160*l*., sold by his late father to the college, for some rectory of equal or better value, to be granted to them by His Majesty, in compensation for the late Lord's loyalty and sufferings; offers them Polebrook, Burton Latimer or Stoke Brewen, co. Northampton, which are at a convenient distance. [*Draft, two pages.*] *Annexing*,

44. i. *Account of the value in the First Fruits' Office, of the rectory of Holme in Yorkshire, and of the three others named in Northamptonshire.*

May 4. Entry of the above. [*Ent. Book* 19, *pp.* 40–1.]

[May 4.] 45. Draft of the above.

May 4. The King to [the Fellows of Emmanuel College, Cambridge]. Recommends Dr. John Breton, prebendary of Worcester, and late member of that college, for election to the mastership, void by resignation of Dr. Sancroft, now Dean of St. Paul's, London. Grants him also a dispensation from the unusual severity of their college statutes, which would discourage and render him less useful, at a time when the Church most needs the labours of such persons. [*Ent. Book* 19, *pp.* 41–2.]

[May 4.] 46. Draft of the above, with differences.

May 4. The King to [the Fellows of Emmanuel College, Cambridge]. Grants a dispensation in behalf of Dr. John Breton from the statute whereby absence from college for more than a month is forbidden; from that prohibiting the master to hold any other benefice with cure of souls, or from any other that should interfere with Breton's election as their master. Latin. [*Ent. Book* 19, *pp.* 43–4.]

May 4. Whitehall. The King to the Earl of Carbery and the Deputy Lieutenants and Sheriffs of North and South Wales. Having appointed a small garrison at Ludlow Castle, for security of the militia money and the plate and jewels kept there, authorizes them to pay the said garrison out of the money for the militia tax of 70,000*l*. a year. [*Ent. Book* 20, *p.* 54.]

VOL. CXX.

1663.

[May 4.] Whitehall. 47. The King to the Lord Lieutenants of Counties. The late Act having authorized the raising of 70,000*l.* yearly, if needful, for the militia, it was raised the two last years, on account of the danger by plots and conspiracies; the same seditious spirit remaining, especially now that he is at war abroad, the month's assessment is again to be raised, and paid in before June 23, and safely lodged in a castle prescribed; also the accounts of the receivers and collectors for the last two years are to be examined, and any balance left in their hands to be paid in; all to be disbursed for the ends appointed by the Act. The forces are to do 14 days' duty this year as they did last, and the commissioned officers, from a captain downwards, to receive pay for that time; those not commissioned are to be paid from money raised by the Act for trophies, non-commissioned officers, &c. [*Six pages.*]

[May 4.] 48. Draft of the above. [*Two and a half pages.*]

May 4. Entry of the above, with notes of the dispatch of the above letters. [*Ent. Book 20, pp. 53–60.*]

[May 4.] 49. Draft of the above, as addressed to the Lord Lieutenant of Berkshire. [*Six pages.*]

[May 4.] 50, 51. Drafts of two clauses of the above. Two papers.

[May 4.] 52. Fair copy of two clauses in the above.

May 4? 53. List of Lord Lieutenants' letters to be written by the clerks of the Council, with the style of address to be adopted, according to their respective ranks. [*Two pages.*] *Annexing,*

53. I. *Account of 26 letters received from Lord Arlington, May 3, and sent by different messengers to the Lord Lieutenants of counties, for the 70,000l.*

[May 4.] 54. List of 20 letters to Lord Lieutenants of counties for the 70,000*l.*, delivered to Thos. Dixon.

May 4. 55. List of five letters, for the 70,000*l.*, delivered by Thos. Trulocke.

[May 4.] 56. List of some of the persons to whom the above letters are sent, and note of the castles where the money is to be kept. [*Draft.*]

May 4? 57. Memoranda of Lord Lieutenants of certain counties, &c. [to whom letters were sent].

[May 4.] 58. Note of circular letters dispatched to the Lieutenants and Deputy Lieutenants of counties.

May 4. Pass for the ship Crown. Minute. [*Ent. Book 22, pp. 123 and 130.*]

Vol. CXX.

1665.

May 4. Order for a warrant to the Commissioners of Ordnance to impress such boats and lighters, seamen or bargemen, as shall be needful to convey arms and ammunition on board vessels in the Thames. [*Ent. Book* 22, *p.* 123.]

May [4]. 59. Warrant to pay to Lord Arlington 3,000*l.*, for secret service, without account. Minute.

May 4. Entry of the above. [*Ent. Book* 22, *p.* 124.]

May [4]. 60. Warrant for a grant to the King's nephew, the Duke of Cambridge, of a pension of 3,000*l.* a year, to be managed by others for his benefit, till he is 14 years old, and thenceforward by himself.

May 4. Entry of the above. [*Ent. Book* 22, *p.* 124.]

May 4. Warrant to the Commissioners for sick and wounded soldiers, the Lieut.-Governor of Plymouth, and others, carefully to effect an exchange of five Dutch prisoners named, now in Plymouth, with seven English prisoners, not dismissing the prisoners till the Dutch release theirs. [*Ent. Book* 22, *p.* 125.]

May 4. Warrant [to the Farmers of Customs] to prohibit the export of sulphur, as it is required for an extraordinary provision of gunpowder. [*Ent. Book* 22, *p.* 126.]

May 4. Warrant for creating Robert Jocelyn, of Hyde Hall, co. Herts, a Baronet. Minute. [*Ent. Book* 22, *p.* 130.]

May 4/14. Dunkirk. 61. —— to Lord [Arlington]. Will pay M. de St. Saveur 500*l.* as ordered. Letters are to be addressed to Eliz. Sagelstraten, and sent viâ Helvoetsluys. Finds he is suspected, so will send his intelligence viâ Harwich. Will forward the books for Antwerp and the Hague as ordered. The Holland fleet is not put to sea. [*Two and a half pages.*]

May? 62. Petition of Thos. Macdonnell to the King, for the Lieutenancy of Capt. Atkins' foot company, void by death of Rob. Warner. Has been promised employment.

May 4. Commission for Thos. Macdonnell to be Lieutenant to Jonathan Atkins' company of foot. Minute. [*Ent. Book* 20, *p.* 53.]

May 5. Warrant to pay to Jeremy Snow 800*l.*, for secret service, without account. [*Docquet.*]

May 5. Warrant to pay to Lord Grandison, Captain of the Guard, 1,000*l.* yearly, as salary of his office, from Lady Day 1661. [*Docquet.*]

May 5. Whitehall. 63. Petition of the Farmers of the King's alum and of the Owners of coals at Sunderland to the King, for a ship to ply for two months, on purpose to secure the trade of the Northern parts from the attacks of the Dutch, whilst they lay in a provision of 6,000

Vol. CXX.

1665.

chaldrons of Sunderland coals, without which they cannot make the alum which is now in His Majesty's hands; the loss of that trade would injure the revenue, and thousands who live by dyeing, leather dressing, &c. Sunderland being a barred haven, will only admit vessels bearing 24 or 26 chaldrons. With reference thereon to Lord Admiral the Duke of York, and note that the King orders the petition to be sent to the Lord General.

[May 5.] 64. Petition of Chas. Gifford to the King, for 500 or 600 young beech trees from the New Forest, towards making piles for certain derelict lands in Dorsetshire leased by him, in which he intends to make improvements that will benefit the subject, and bring in rent to His Majesty.

May 5. Reference of the above petition to the Lord Treasurer. [*Ent. Book* 18, *p.* 150.]

May 5. Off the Vlie. 65. Duke of York to Lord Arlington. Has been hindered by cross winds from receiving letters from England, and also from getting at more of the Dutch fleet which came round Scotland. They chased 10 last night, and have taken 8. Hopes Capt. Smith may have lighted on 20 or 30 bound for the Vlie and the Texel. Refers to Sir Thos. Clifford for a list of prizes, and to his letter to the General for particulars. [*Two pages.*]

May 5. 66. [Earl of Falmouth to Lord Arlington]. Had such ill luck, by contrary winds and mist, that 24 or 25 of the Dutch fleet from Ireland got into the Texel; capture of 10 of them. Major Smith is sent with six sail before the Vlie; two ships from each squadron were ordered to join him, but could not for the mist; one of the prizes is worth 20,000*l.*, the others are of Bourdeaux wines, brandy, &c. [*Four pages.*]

May 5. Royal Charles, off the Vlie. 67. Sir Wm. Coventry to Lord Arlington. They had notice on Saturday of 30 ships coming out of the Texel, and stood into shore to meet with them; it proved a mistake, but it lost the opportunity of getting to the station designed to intercept the Dutch merchantmen. The Duke ordered seven ships to intercept such as would enter the Vlie, but four being prevented by mist from joining them, the rest would do little good, though the 30 merchantmen are without any convoy, having parted from the two men-of-war, and eight vessels bound for Zealand and Rotterdam, all of which are taken, except the men-of-war, which forsook the merchantmen on perceiving the fleet to be English. The Council of war thinks it best for the fleet to return to the English coast to take in supplies, and then wait the return of the Dutch East India fleet. [*Three pages.*]

May 5. Royal Charles. 68. Sir Wm. Coventry to Lord Arlington. Private letter. Fears the taking off the embargo and allowing privateers to carry any number of English seamen they please will have bad effects in the recruiting of the fleet, or the detaining those who are on board, as all have great inclination for private men-of-war, in which they flatter themselves they shall get mountains of gold. Is surprized

VOL. CXX.

1665.

that no more ships are to be fitted out, considering the condition of the Straits and Guinea fleet. The main fleet will not bear dividing, considering that Sir George Downing pronounces the enemy's fleet better by 50 ships than in the last Dutch war. The enemy will still build and increase, while by casualties, &c., the English fleet must decrease, and if one battle is lost, ten times the money that would have ensured victory will not bring it to equal terms again. The expense will tire the English before the Dutch, because the latter still carry on their East India, Straits, and Guinea trade, destroying that of the English there, and they would therefore be foolish to risk a battle without great advantage. They should be pressed at all points; their courage is not to be despised. Thinks that leave to trade, without sufficient security for it by superiority at sea, would be the greatest mischief that could happen to the nation. [*Three pages.*]

May 5. Royal Charles. 69. Sir Wm. Coventry and Sir Wm. Penn to the Navy Comrs. Cables wanted for several ships. Provisions of all sorts should be sent to Harwich, in readiness for the ships coming there next spring [tide] to tallow; the fleet is not yet supplied with sufficient clothes; 10 Hollanders were sighted; two were men-of-war, which escaped when the eight merchant ships were taken; two days before they parted with 30 sail bound in at the Texel; this was the fleet discovered near Ireland, come about to the northward. [*Adm. Paper.*]

May 5. Barber Surgeons' Hall. 70. Ralph Thicknes and Thos. Hollier to the Navy Comrs. List of things necessary for the hospital ships to attend the fleet; the master surgeons chosen are Edmund Higgs and Wm. Smart, experienced surgeons employed in the last Dutch war. They must have three mates to each ship. [*Adm. Paper.*]

May 5. The Dartmouth, Kinsale Harbour. 71. Capt. Rich. Rooth to the Navy Comrs. Capture of a Dutch frigate of 12 guns, between Cape Clear and the Mizen Head; four of the enemy slain and 17 desperately wounded. Has had little damage; only 4 men wounded and two slain, Wm. Lundy, the master, being one; has substituted John Painter, mate, in his room; his gunner's stores are much exhausted; can only get supplied at Cork by special order from the Lord Lieutenant; has taken up a few necessaries, for the present want, from Mr. Thos. Chudleigh; proposes the prize to be fitted up as a man-of-war; hears from the prisoners that five frigates are lying towards the west; begs that the four vessels lately sent to ply on the coast may be continued longer than was intended. [*Adm. Paper.*]

May 5. Carlisle. 72. Sir Wm. Clarke to Sam. Pepys. John Page, recommended by him as purser of the Happy Entrance, has received his warrant. [*Adm. Paper.*]

May 5. The Hastings, Plymouth. 73. Capt. Jonathan Waltham to the Navy Comrs. Has received orders to go for Portsmouth; is warping out and will set sail in the morning. [*Adm. Paper.*]

VOL. CXX.

1665.

May 5. Chatham. 74. Edw. Gregory and Jas. Norman to the Navy Comrs. The provisions ordered to be sent in the Augustine to Dover are ready, with exception of a few things not in store. [*Adm. Paper.*]

May 5. The Nightingale, Galway. 75. Capt. Rich. Long to the Navy Comrs. Capture of a Dutch privateer, of 15 guns; nine of the enemy killed, and only one of his own men; the vessel is so damaged that she cannot keep the sea; has endeavoured to secure her so as to reach Plymouth, where he is ordered to victual. Complains of not being able to obtain any stores, nor yet suffered to take anything out of the prize. [*Adm. Paper.*]

May 5. Whitehall. 76. Robt. Southwell to Sam. Pepys. Has taken great concern for Mr. Coleman, since the foundering of the Elias, in which he was master; obtained him a commission as lieutenant of the Warwick; she being under repairs at Portsmouth, and not likely to sail for four months, recommends him now for command of the Hound, intended for a fine ship. [*Adm. Paper.*]

May 5. Chatham Dockyard. 77. Phin. Pett to Commissioner Peter Pett. Sends dimensions of the two fly-boats, Black Cock and St. Jacob. [*Adm. Paper.*]

May 5. Plymouth. 78. Receipt by John Lanyon for 10 tons of cordage, bought by order of the Navy Commissioners of Thos. Tente, ropelayer of Plymouth, for 410*l.* [*Adm. Paper.*]

May 6. Cockpit. 79. Duke of Albemarle to the [Navy Comrs.]. The St. Lawrence and Young King are to be appraised and delivered to Mr. Cole, who is employed to fetch timber from Sussex, for the ships building at Chatham. He is to pay the wages, and allow a third of the freight to the King. [*Adm. Paper.*]

May 6. 80. Certificate by Matthew Hayden of the readiness of the Hopewell to serve as a victualling ship. [*Adm. Paper.*]

May 6. 81. Jacob Blackleech to the Navy Comrs. The three water ships have sailed to Deptford. [*Adm. Paper.*]

May 6. Cockpit. 82. Sir Wm. Clarke to Sam. Pepys. The Coventry is to be cleaned and victualled, and the Greyhound sent in her stead to convey a merchant ship to Ostend. [*Adm. Paper.*]

May 6. Victualling Office. 83. Thos. Lewis to the Navy Comrs. The four ships laden with beer and biscuit for the fleet neglect to sail, though they have had fair wind to carry them to Harwich; 400 tuns of beer and a quantity of dry provisions are ready for a further supply. John Nutt, master of the Sarah ketch, has two lighters with flesh by his side, and cannot take it in for want of men. [*Adm. Paper.*]

May 6. Deptford. 84. Thos. Cowley to Thos. Hayter. The captain of the Swallow requires victuals for five men above his allowed number; a warrant is wanted for entering men on the Young Lion prize. [*Adm. Paper.*]

Vol. CXX.

1665.
May 6. 85. Report of John Burrowes and Thos. Beckford, slopsellers, to the Navy Commissioners, of money due to them for the navy during the last two years; total, 21,800l., of which they have received only 800l.; not only is their stock dishonored, but their credit; unless a speedy supply be ordered, they will be incapable to accommodate the service, and ruined both in their estates and families. [*Adm. Paper.*]

May 6. Bristol. 86. Sir John Knight to the Navy Commrs. Sends account of money paid for the George, and for pressing 34 seamen; total, 64l. 9s. 7d. Desires payment; asks whether he shall proceed in pressing men. Marked "Continue the press." [*Adm. Paper.*]

May 6. Woolwich. 87. Wm. Bodham to [the Navy Commrs.] Gives a comparative view of the three estimates by Robt. Ellery and Edw. Rundell for wharfing, altering the shed, and building a gallery: Ellery, 50l. 10s.; Rundell, 15l. 1s. One of them must be a knave, their estimates are so different. Ellery will not abate 40s. in his, and advises that Rundell be obliged to undertake the work as he has estimated it; if he refuse, it is knavery; will endeavour to find the hare, if the dogs be set on; that is, will discover the roguery, if the Commissioners will correct it. [*Adm. Paper, two pages.*]

May 6. 88. List of 7 letters to Lord Lieutenants of counties, delivered by Jas. Holbrooke, May 4 and May 6.

May 6. Whitehall. 89. Warrant from Lord Arlington to Wm. Benson to deliver to Jos. Williamson, keeper of State Papers, the books and papers belonging to affairs heretofore agitated by the Committee of Gurney House, which are of much importance to His Majesty's service.

Minute of the above, dated March 4. [*Ent. Book 22, p. 133.*]

May 6. Whitehall. 90. Like warrant to John Dorney to deliver up to Williamson the books and papers relating to the Yorkshire engagement, heretofore agitated by the Committee for advance of money.

May 6. Carlisle. 91. Abraham Nelson to Lord Arlington. The country is divided into the old cavaliers, who are either Catholics or old Protestants, and think themselves slighted that their enemies are preferred before them, but yet maintain their loyalty; casuists, who want peace, free trade and no taxes, and care not who rules, nor what is the religion; and libertines, who would tolerate any religion for advantage, gape for preferment, and would carry the bag and betray their master. Hopes a safe return for the navy, till which the party cannot be dealt with; no penalty should be inflicted on Quakers meanwhile, but officers should be on the watch against insurrections. Renews his request for a protection, being in danger for a pretended debt of 89l.

May 6. 92. Ro. Clark to John Sicklemore, Gray's Inn, London. Sam. Jacob, who brought the books taken at Woodbridge from Holland, has been sent to gaol, by Bailiff Wright and Mr. Robinson, for

VOL. CXX.

1665.

saying that the Dutch have 170 sail of well-manned ships, and so many volunteers that they can pick and choose; also that they have a ship with the Covenant on the stern, and underneath is written, "If the King take me, he will not keep me." Jacob does not deny this, but says that he heard it by report; that he came from Holland five weeks ago, landed at Harwich, and went to London. Asks the Earl of Suffolk's advice whether he is to be kept in prison or released on bail.

May 7. Lathom. 93. Dorothea Helena Countess of Derby to Lady Killigrew. Requests her husband's favour in behalf of Mr. Calcott, who killed a Lancashire gentleman in self-defence, and was condemned, being a loyalist, by a jury of sequestrators; the jury refused a reprieve, though all the gentry of Cheshire begged for it, but the Bishop obtained three weeks for him. The King had granted a reprieve, but it was stopped on misinformation. Is sure that when His Majesty knows the truth, he will pity the poor man, who is allied to the Cheshire gentlemen by his marriage with Sir Francis Gambul's daughter. [*Two pages.*] *Annexing*,

93. I. *Statement of the circumstances of a quarrel, at Sir Phil. Egerton's in Cheshire, between Hen. Banaster and Major Rob. Calcott; the former used abusive language to the latter, who did not take offence, and they seemed friends, but the next morning Banaster took Calcott out to walk, and attacked him; Calcott slew him in self defence, and refused to escape, as he could not avoid doing it; but a jury of sequestrators committed him, found him guilty, and he is condemned to die. When young, he showed his fidelity, by being concerned for the late Countess of Derby in the Manx rebellion; he was active in Sir George Booth's business, was long imprisoned, and with much ado escaped hanging. The high sheriff of the county had chosen a jury of gentlemen, but the judge changed them.*

93. II. *Certificate by the Earl of Derby, and 17 other justices of peace for the county palatine of Chester, present at the trial of Rob. Calcott, that he is a fit object of mercy, as his provocations were very great and often renewed.*

93. III. *Copy of the above.*

93. IV. *Certificate by the Earl of Derby, that there was no grudge between Calcott and Banaster; that the dispute was unpremeditated, and the thing a great misfortune, Calcott having loyally served both the late and present King.* *April 23, 1665.*

93. V. *Certificate by Thos. Nedham and Chas. Cotton, that at Sir Phil. Egerton's house, Hen. Banaster used abusive language, unprovoked, to Major Rob. Calcott, who did not reply offensively, and they seemed afterwards friends; yet soon after Mr. Banaster was slain, acknowledging that he died fairly, sword in hand.* *April 23, 1665.*

1665.

VOL. CXX.

93. VI. *Certificate by Rich. Taylor, mayor, and 10 other Aldermen of Chester, to the modest and peaceable demeanour of Major Rich. Calcott, who is well affected, and was in the Cheshire engagement.* *Chester, April 24, 1665.*

May 8. London. 94. Thos. Tyte to Sir Wm. Batten. Desires the second payment of 323*l.* 10*s.* 2*d.* upon his account for powder; hears of Capt. Ant. Archer's arrival at Hamburg, with a Dutch prize of 300 tons, which he intends to lade with stores for England. Asks whether he may bring thence 7 cables ordered which are ready to ship; sends an account of their measurement and value. [*Adm. Paper.*]

May 8. Deptford. 95. Thos. Cowley to Thos. Hayter. Returns Sir Wm. Warren's contract. Asks directions about victualling the five men in the Swallow. [*Adm. Paper.*]

May 8. The Paradise, [illegible]. 96. Capt. Leo Guy to the Navy Comrs. Is ordered by the Duke of Albemarle to go to the westward, off Scilly, and to victual at Plymouth. [*Adm. Paper.*]

May 8. Chatham. 97. Comr. Peter Pett to Sam. Pepys. The cordage, masts, and treenails shall be sent to Harwich. Mr. Lawsley wants letters to the Justices about the carriage of Fluckley timber. [*Adm. Paper.*]

May 8. Plymouth Sound. 98. Capt. John Stanesby, of the Eagle, to the Navy Comrs. Is returned from Tangiers; has only three weeks' provision. On the 7th inst., at night, met with two Dutch men-of-war; the engagement lasted two hours and a half; much damage was done to the ship, himself shot in the head, the master and corporal also wounded. [*Adm. Paper.*]

May 8. Plymouth. 99. Capt. Edw. Nixon, of the Elizabeth, to the Navy Comrs. Has hastened from Tangiers without stop, except to exchange two or three broadsides with two Dutch men-of-war met with off Scilly; not much injury was done on either side, being stopped by night. At break of day, found the Hollanders at a considerable distance, and being bound by his instructions, dared not venture to pursue them. [*Adm. Paper.*]

May 8. Lea Daly. 100. Dan. Furzer to the Navy Comrs. Acknowledges an imprest for 200*l.*; the matter of wages for the smith's assistant should have been more largely stated before such progress was made in the business; promises to overlook all the ironwork, that not a bar be wrought before it be sufficiently proved and tried; fears an obstacle from the smith having gone so low in his charges, upon thoughts of having an assistant at an easy rate; begs that a person may be found at 25*s.* per week, with expenses of coming down allowed. Warrants are wanted for felling plank, and for impress of six trow men for the carriage of timber by water. [*Adm. Paper, two pages.*]

May 8. Dover. 101. E. Wivell to the Navy Comrs. Account of money paid to pilots since September 1664; total, 13*l.* 15*s.* Begs re-payment. [*Adm. Paper.*]

Vol. CXX.

1665.

May 8. 102. Account of beer shipped to the fleet from London, Dover, and Ipswich, in March and April last; total, 3,357 tuns. [*Adm. Paper.*]

May 8? 103. Note by Mr. Tooker that not one waterman appeared since Monday, whereby four lighters of beer have lain, to a considerable damage, by the sides of the ships. The water casks are complained of as musty and leaky. The masters who complain of want of hands wish to employ the Dutch prisoners from Chelsea College to load their ships. [*Adm. Paper.*]

May 8. Warrant to pay to the Earl of Sandwich 676*l.* a year, during the continuance of certain estates on the manor of Brompton. [*Docquet.*]

May 8. Warrant to imprest to William Mordaunt 500*l.*, for secret service. [*Docquet.*]

May 8. Warrant to pay to Charles Viscount Andover 500*l.* as the King's free gift. [*Docquet.*]

May 8. The King to Sir Francis Cobb, high sheriff of Yorkshire. Appointed Humphrey Hareward housekeeper of the Mansion House at York, 24th July 1660, and on 5th February 1661, granted the reversion thereof to Capt. Richard Harland; many controversies arising between them thereon, on 15th March last, ordered Hareward to be removed, and Harland put into possession, but on further representation, commands that this last order be not executed, but that Hen. Parry, of whose loyalty he has had long experience, be put into the place, and Hareward is to depute Parry to receive all the profits and allowances of the office. Hopes thus to put an end to all disputes. [*Ent. Book* 14, *f.* 59.]

May 8. Whitehall. The King to the Commissioners for levying the royal aid in the county palatine of Lancaster. Wishes them to rectify irregularities in the assessments of the hundreds of Derby, Salford, and Lonsdale, that the levies thereof may not be obnoxious to complaint. [*Ent. Book* 14, *p.* 60.]

May 8. Warrant from Lord Arlington to search for the person of Rich. Knowles, at his dwelling house, and to seize and bring him with his papers before himself. [*Ent. Book* 22, *p.* 132.]

May [8]. 104. Draft of the above.

May 8. Whitehall. 105. Draft of the above, ordering the Mayor of Gloucester and all other magistrates concerned to assist in the search.

May 8. York. 106. J. Sotherne to James Hickes. Lord Sandwich has met with several of the Dutch fleet, dispersed by a storm, and taken four men-of-war and ten merchantmen, of which two are East Indiamen. His letters were dated on the 5th, 40 leagues W.N.W. from the Texel. They were in hopes of meeting the main of the Dutch fleet. The Hector was sunk, and the captain and all the men lost.

Vol. CXX.

1665.

May 8. Kirkby Mallory, Leicestershire. 107. Sir Verney Noel to Lord Arlington. Wm. Leving and Wm. Frear were seized as suspected persons. Has stayed them, as they do not agree in their report, though they have passes from the King and his lordship. Leving confesses that he escaped from prison, and is probably the person against whom the proclamation was issued.

May 8. Kirkby Mallory. 108. Wm. Leving and Wm. Frear to Robt. Lye, Whitehall. Beg a letter to Sir Verney Noel to free them, being detained and their passes questioned, on the ground that Leving was lately in a proclamation.

May 8. Badminton. 109. Lord Herbert of Ragland to Williamson. The remissness, not to say worse, of his deputy lieutenants has prevented his giving a good account of His Majesty's commands, but hopes by the end of the month to have the accounts perfected, and the remains of the two months' tax lodged as directed. If there be any failure, will acquaint Lord Arlington where the fault lies.

May 9. York. 110. Walter Strickland to Williamson. The two brothers Wilson are come from Ireland, because what they were about to do got wind, and they were threatened by their own clan, durst not stay, and came to London. Their father and brother are at York, in prison on the same account, and both will certainly die, unless they can do something to move the King to grant them their lives. Will be in London in a fortnight, and thinks he can make them do more than any one else. All is quiet, and the people pay their money to the royal aid cheerfully. *Encloses*,

110. I. *W. Wilson to Rich. Wilson, in York Castle. Asks whether to go to hear Mr. Wharton. Supposes Anthony is with Sir Walter, if none murder him: they both were in great danger. Wishes him to address to Rich. Appleby's lodgings, and not to let their father's heart be cast down.*
London, May 6, 1665.

May 9. Pass for Abbot Montague to France, with four horses. Minute. [*Ent. Book* 22, p. 131.]

May 9. Pass for Mr. Riorden to France, with four horses, custom free, Minute. [*Ent. Book* 22, p. 131.]

May 9. Woolwich. 111. Chris. Pett to the Navy Comrs. The new mast for the Ann is finished. Francis Sparrow refused to tow it into Harwich, and is gone away with his smack, although with such a fair wind he might have got into port by night. Three and four inch oak plank wanted. [*Adm. Paper.*]

May 9. Cockpit. 112. Sir Wm. Clarke to the Navy Comrs. The Duke of Albemarle, having received letters from the fleet, desires the attendance of one of the Board by nine o'clock to-morrow. [*Adm. Paper.*]

May 9. Golden Lion, Woolwich. 113. Capt. Wm. Dale to the Navy Comrs. Being appointed to the Golden Lion, desires a warrant for Thos. Crowes to be master. [*Adm. Paper.*]

VOL. CXX.

1665.

May 9. Plymouth. 114. John Lanyon to the Navy Comrs. Has concluded with Thos. Teate for 10 tons of cordage at 44s. per cwt.; the money must be paid in two months. The Sorlings is off the hulk. Arrival of the Elizabeth and Eagle from Tangiers. Account of their engagement with two Dutch vessels off Scilly; one man was killed. [*Adm. Paper.*]

May 9. 115. Jacob Blackleach to the Navy Comrs. The three water ships are fully laden. [*Adm. Paper.*]

May 9. Chatham Dock. 116. Comr. Peter Pett to Sam. Pepys. Is obliged to send Mr. Lewsley up for his imprest money; he has been at the charge of 40*l.* a week in converting the Pluckley timber. Advises that a considerable sum be allowed him at once, to prevent further loss of time. [*Adm. Paper.*]

1665. VOL. CXXI. MAY 10–22, 1665.

May 10. Barber Surgeons' Hall. 1. Rich. Reynell to Thos. Hayter. Desires an order for the conveyance of several surgeons, mates, and barbers to the fleet. Hears that a surgeon is wanted for the Tiger, now at Portsmouth. One Pistoll was appointed three months since, his chest viewed, and himself sent to the ship; will learn whether his captain has given him leave to come up to town again. [*Adm. Paper.*] *Encloses,*

1. I. *Names of the 3 surgeons, 4 mates, and 4 barbers appointed to the fleet.*

May 10. 2. Thos. Lewsley [to the Navy Comrs.] Requests payment of his imprest bills; dares not appear where the timber is, without money to satisfy the workmen; urges the dispatch of warrants for land carriage. [*Adm. Paper.*]

May 10. 3. Capt. John Taylor to the Navy Comrs. Considers the proposals prefixed concerning the hire and freight of the Golden Falcon reasonable; both Mr. Wood and himself have a share in the vessel. The master cannot get men at the King's pay, and wants to know where to look for his money. With note [by Pepys] of Capt. Taylor's neglect in absenting himself from his ship, and of the consequent delay of the vessel. [*Adm. Paper.*]

May 10. Hill House. 4. Sir John Mennes to the Navy Comrs. Finds only two cables of 17 inches in the stores at Harwich, and great scarcity of Gottenburg masts. Comr. Pett is in London; has opened one of the packets sent to him in his absence, or should have known nothing of the Coventry, and provisions would have been still sent to Sheerness for her supply. Will dispatch the business of the Chest to-morrow. [*Adm. Paper.*]

Vol. CXXI.

1665.

May 10. Dover. 5. Thos. White to Sam. Pepys. Is glad to hear that more stores are ordered for Dover, the prices there being very high owing to the scarcity of the supply. Hears that the Duke of York's fleet rides before the Texel. With postscript on the 11th. Wants a press warrant, or else carpenters and pilots will not serve without ready money. The Paradox is beneaped in the harbour which is much grown up with muddy ooze. [*Adm. Paper.*]

May 10. 6. John Creed to Sam Pepys. Recommends Mr. Wright as master of the ship about to be taken on. [*Adm. Paper.*]

May 10. Yarmouth. 7. James Johnson to the Navy Commrs. Cannot reply about the Edgars' security till his return from the country. Requests a reply about a small parcel of shot he has for sale. [*Adm. Paper.*]

May 10. Cockpit. 8. Sir Wm. Clarke to Sam. Pepys. The Greyhound is ordered into Dover to victual; the Paul to ply between Calais and Winterton; the Blackamoor between Winterton and Flamborough; the Hector between Flamborough and Tynemouth; the Sorlings and two others which are coming from Ireland to ply in the Soundings, and call at Plymouth for provisions. [*Adm. Paper.*]

May 10. 9. Symond Emison to the Navy Commrs. Sends a list of 12 men on board the Kingfisher at Harwich. [*Adm. Paper.*]

May 10? 10. Account of the four rowing barges on the Thames, with the names of the masters and men on each, and the numbers of men pressed from them. [*Adm. Paper.*]

May 10. 11. Demand by the Victuallers for protection to the Cæsar Augustus and Amity, from Chatham to Hamburg, to fetch pipe staves, &c. [*Adm. Paper.*]

May 10. 12. Certificate by John Fortescue that four ships named have taken in their provisions. [*Adm. Paper.*]

May 10. Warrant for presentation of John Harding to the Rectory of Landilip, co. Cornwall. [*Ent. Book* 19, p. 45.]

May 10. Pass for Peter Dolyslagen and Abraham de Geldre, merchants, to embark for Flanders. [*Ent. Book* 22, p. 131.]

May 10. Warrant to Sir John Robinson to receive Lord Morley into the Tower as prisoner, for fighting contrary to law. Minute. [*Ent. Book* 22, p. 132.]

May 10. Pass from Lord Arlington for Jerome Henschcter with his wife into France. Minute. [*Ent. Book* 22, p. 133.]

[May 10.] [Whitehall.] 13. Proclamation confirming that of April 6th, for freedom from press of seamen in coal vessels; commending the conduct of the Lord Mayor and others in regulating the price of coals, &c., but permitting all coals brought in for the future to be sold without

1665. Vol. CXXI.

restraint of price, except those which are in the river, the owners of which, having refused submission to the price, are to be compelled to sell them at the price appointed. [*Two leaves.*]

May 10. Copy of the preceding. [*Printed. Proc. Coll., Charles II., p.* 183.]

May 10. Whitehall. 14. Proclamation forbidding all merchants of Hamburg and other aliens who have defeated the benefits granted to the company of Merchant Adventurers, to export any cloths or woollen commodities to the places limited by the Merchants' charter, and ordering strict searches, and punishment of offenders. [*Printed.*]

May 10. Duplicate of the above. [*Printed. Proc. Coll., Charles II., pp.* 184–5.]

May 10. Whitehall. 15. Petition of Sir Thos. Gower, Bart., to the King, for an order for payment to him of 2,230*l.* which he advanced without security to the late King, in his march from York against the rebels, although 1,200*l.* which he spent in raising dragoons was unpaid; being sheriff when his late Majesty was at York, he spent much money, and was forced by the rebels to pay large sums for things done in that office by command; all these losses, with the interest thereon, weigh down his small estate. With reference thereon to the Lord Treasurer, and his report, June 20, 1663, certifying the justness of the claim, though he is ever shy to admit payment of debts of the late King.

May [10?] 16. Earl of Peterborough to [Williamson]. The Duke has spoken very kindly to him, and promised to serve him, saying he should have what he pretended to there, but for a consequence to one whose behaviour made him unfit for it. The Duke of Buckingham and Earl of Sandwich are leaving soon; will then take his measures carefully; hopes soon to be at the first station near Harwich.

May 10. 17. Bond of John Wilson, of Berkeswell, co. Warwick, and two others, in 200*l.*, for his good behaviour, refraining from disturbance against government, and appearing before a principal secretary within 14 days.

May 10. Reference to the Attorney-General on the petition of Edm. Bostock, for a grant of several tenements in St. Andrew's parish, Holborn, formerly the estate of John Glassingham, and now escheated to the Crown. [*Ent. Book* 18, p. 151.]

May 11. Order on the petition of the King's Farriers for payment of their arrears, that Sir Edw. Griffin, treasurer of the chamber, pay them on sight of their bill, all that is due for salary and arrears, in the same proportion as is paid to His Majesty's other servants. [*Ent. Book* 18, p. 152.]

May 11. Pass for the Earl of Burlington to Ireland, with ten horses, custom free. Minute. [*Ent. Book* 22, *p.* 132.]

Vol. CXXI.

1665.

May 11. Leicester. 18. Willm. Loving and Willm. Frear to Robt. Lye. Loving went to Heather on Saturday, applied to Squire Merry, a deputy lieutenant, to show his pass, and was promised aid, if he needed it in the King's service; yet some inferior persons led him and Frear before Sir Verney Noel, who accused them of counterfeiting the King's and Lord Arlington's hand, and detained them. They beg letters for their release; there is contrivance to hinder them from the King's service. [*One and a half pages.*]

May 11. 19. Sir Phil. Warwick to Mr. Birch. He is to have the document written out fair, and carried to Mr. Williamson, informing him that the Lord Treasurer is satisfied therewith. Endorsed with the form of a grant to Jas. Hamilton and John Birch of 55 acres in Hyde Park, to be by them enclosed and planted with apples, they paying 5s. a year rent, and delivering half the apples for the King's household.

May 11. Whitehall. Pass for a French ship, Le Symbole de la Paix, from France to Hamburg, Norway, and the Baltic, and to return to any port of England, the goods which she imports being free, the Act of Navigation or any other notwithstanding. [*Ent. Book* 14, *f.* 59b, 60.]

May 11. Barber Surgeons' Hall. 20. Rich. Reynell to Thos. Hayter. Sends bills for the Swallow and the Sarah and Elizabeth, by Mr. Pistoll, surgeon of the Tiger, who will account to the Board for his absence from the ship. [*Adm. Paper.*]

May 11. Greenwich. 21. Capt. Phineas Pett to Sir John Mennes. Recommends John Clements as master of a ship, in room of Mark Peirce. [*Adm. Paper.*]

May 11. Dover. 22. Thos. White to the Navy Commrs. Dispatch of the Lily; repairs of the Paradox. Can get no men to work for want of a press warrant. Both carpenters and pilots require ready money. [*Adm. Paper.*]

May 11. Southwark. 23. Lieut. Martin Gardiner to Sam. Pepys. Sends the remaining 32 soldiers; desires an account of what ships they go on board, to satisfy the commissary on muster day. Corporal Bellows, sent above the required 8 men, is to be returned. [*Adm. Paper.*]

May 11. The Harp, Chester Water. 24. Capt. James Sharland to the Navy Commrs. Is ordered by the Lord Deputy of Ireland to convey vessels of trade between Chester and Dublin; is going with 24 sail, when the wind permits. [*Adm. Paper.*]

May 12. Victualling Office. 25. Denis Gauden to the Navy Commrs. Will endeavour to procure the 400 tuns of water cask above the 600 formerly ordered; fears it cannot be accomplished in time, without disappointing the supply of beer, on account of the scarcity of cask; wishes the water casks might be put into other hands, and be left in better capacity to serve in the brewing of beer. [*Adm. Paper.*]

Vol. CXXI.

1665.

May 12. Woolwich Ropeyard. 26. Wm. Bodham to the Navy Comrs. Sends an account of the hemp now in store; that served in by Capt. Cock is very inferior; wishes the remainder of his contract might be delivered at Chatham. Does not envy the Chathamites their good fortune in always getting the best, but would wish equal good to themselves. The coarser sorts are always the dearer bargains. With postscript on the 13th, complaining of a combination of merchants to defraud the Navy Office by selling to them at 100*l.* what they buy and sell among themselves at much smaller rates. [*Adm. Paper, two pages.*]

May 12. Deptford. 27. Thos. Harper to Sam. Pepys. Acknowledges a mistake in weighing Mr. Bodycott's cables, owing to the carelessness of the labourers in the too hasty handing out of the weights. [*Adm. Paper.*]

May 12. 28. List by Wm. Gilbert of 10 surgeons, barbers or mates, ready to go to the fleet; requests an order for their passage. [*Adm. Paper.*]

May 12. 29. Order from the Duke of Albemarle to Capt. Val. Tatnell, to repair to Norfolk and Suffolk for raising the 300 men required for the present service; they are to be sent to the fleet in any ships near to the places where they are pressed, or delivered to Sub-Comr. Taylor at Harwich, to be forwarded from time to time. [*Adm. Paper.*]

May 12. Cockpit. 30. Duke of Albemarle to the Navy Comrs. Has ordered a warrant to Capt. Valentine Tatnell for impressing 300 seamen in Norfolk and other parts; desires money for him for the business. [*Adm. Paper.*]

May 12. 31. Jacob Blackleech to the Navy Comrs. Account of the fitting up of the three water ships. [*Adm. Paper.*]

May 12. 32. Note from Jonas Shish to Wm. Ewest of the Navy Office, stating the dimensions and tonnage of ten vessels now bound out in the King's service. [*Adm. Paper.*]

May 12. Whitehall. 33. Petition of Dennis, wife of John Clayton, prisoner in the Gatehouse, to the King and Council, for the liberation of her husband, a poor tailor, who has been a prisoner twenty-two weeks for attending a private meeting; this is his first offence, and she and his family are ruined by having to pay 9*s.* a week for his chamber. With reference thereon to Lord Arlington, who is to order his release, if the allegations are found true.

May 12. Whitehall. Warrant to Viscount Mordaunt, to suspend William Taylour from all offices appertaining to the castle, forest, or honour of Windsor, to give notice to the tenants to pay no more rents to him, and to nominate receivers for the rents, &c. [*Ent. Book 22, p. 137.*]

May? 34. Petition of William Taylour, steward of Windsor Castle, to the King, that he may not be dispossessed of his office, from which

1665. VOL. CXXI.

he is suspended, and of the house belonging thereto, which his persecutors have sent him an order to quit, till his case has been heard by His Majesty's referees.

May 13. Whitehall. Warrants to the Lieutenant of the Tower to permit Peter Pryaulx and another to have access to Mr. Marchand, prisoner there, in presence of his keeper. Minute. [*Ent. Book* 22, *p.* 133.]

May 13. Warrant to Lord Ashley, treasurer of prizes, to pay to Henry Lord Arlington 1,200*l.*, out of prize money, for a very important and secret service. [*Ent. Book* 22, *p.* 133.]

May 13. Warrant for delivery of 30 tuns of wine to the Conde de Molina, the Spanish ambassador, duty free. [*Ent. Book* 22, *p.* 134.]

May 13. Pass for Abbé la Grange, with six couple of hounds, to France. Minute. [*Ent. Book* 22, *p.* 135.]

May 13. Whitehall. 35. Grant to Rich. Earl of Carbery, of the office of Constable of Ludlow Castle, and governor there, to act according to orders from the Duke of Albemarle, lord general. [*Damaged.*]

[May 13.] 36. Draft of the above.

May 13. Entry of the above. [*Ent. Book* 20, *p.* 61.]

May 13. Commission to Henry Herbert to be Lieutenant of a company of foot in Ludlow garrison, under the Earl of Carbery. [*Ent. Book* 20, *p.* 61.]

May 13. Whitehall. 37. Petition of Mary, widow of Rich. Dart, and Ann, widow of Jos. Batten, mariners, to the King, for relief and a livelihood; their husbands were grievously wounded, having their legs and arms shot off in the late fight with two Dutch ships, and died for want of an able surgeon and good medicaments. With order thereon to the Navy Commissioners to order the Treasurer of the Navy to make some provision for them.

May 13. Entry of the above order. [*Ent. Book* 18, *p.* 152.]

May 13. 38. Account of 19 conventicles held in London since the month began. With notice that a member of the House of Commons, whose name is not known but his person described, meets Strange and others at the Black Swan court, Old Change, and lets them know what is done or intended by Parliament; also that Calamy has come home and will hold a meeting at his own house, and Jenkins at Aldermary churchyard, &c.

May 13. Navy Office. 39. Warrant by the Navy Comrs. for arrest of Zachary Taylor, master of the Golden Falcon, for neglect of duty in dispatching the vessels with provisions to the fleet, and for not making use of the press warrant granted for supplying himself with men, or taking care, by his own attendance, to keep the men on board. Endorsed with note that it was not served, by reason of his sudden going. [*Adm. Paper.*]

Vol. CXXI.

1665.

May 13. 40. Sir Wm. Rider to Sam. Pepys. Requests a ship or two to convoy as far as the Sound the four vessels hired by him, now at Newcastle ready to sail for stores. [*Adm. Paper.*] *Encloses,*

40. i. *Account by Sir W. Rider and W. Cutler of the said ships appointed to bring home hemp, pitch, and tar from the Baltic.* *May 13, 1665.*

May 13. 41. Jonas Shish to the Navy Comrs. Recommends Robt. Withers, shipwright, for the survey of the new ship. [*Adm. Paper.*]

May 13. Dover. 42. Thos White to the Navy Comrs. The Paradox is tallowed and was ready to sail out of harbour, but by neglect of the men, is aground, and cannot be got off till the next high tide. "It was as near execution as the cup to the lip, which by carelessness and weakness of the hand, spills the drink in the bosom, which the mother with great care and cost had provided to cure the distemper upon the child." No damage is come to the ship, but the loss of time is to be regretted. Desires a press warrant both for pilots and workmen. [*Adm. Paper.*]

May 13. Lea. 43. Dan. Furzer to the Navy Comrs. Acknowledges an imprest of 200*l.* Has consulted with most of the "knowingest" smiths in Bristol about the quality of the forest iron; there is no better in England for all sorts of work. Will cause two anchors to be speedily made on trial. [*Adm. Paper.*]

May 13. Chatham. 44. Comr. Peter Pett to Sam. Pepys. Asks whether the masts for Dover are to be sent in the Augustine. The two great yards made for the Royal Katherine, lying now at Woolwich, are too big for her; it would be well to send them to Chatham to be kept in the wet dock. [*Adm. Paper.*]

May 13. 45. Capt. John Miller to Sir Wm. Batten. Offers for hire the Maidenhead, fitted to carry 40 pieces of ordnance. [*Adm. Paper.*]

May 13. Harwich. 46. Wm. Jones, junr. to the Navy Comrs. Has captured a Dutch fisherman, and delivered her into the hands of the Commissioners of Prizes. [*Adm. Paper.*]

May 13. Royal Charles. 47. Sir Wm. Coventry and Sir Wm. Penn to the Navy Comrs. Stores should be hastened to Harwich for repair of various ships in the Duke of York's squadron. The John and Katherine is out of stores, and must be supplied by her owners. [*Adm. Paper.*]

May 14. Royal Charles, off Lowestoft. 48. Sir Wm. Coventry to Sam. Pepys. The defect in the cables arises from the mixture of hemp. A prize is taken laden with hemp, which should be got in with speed. Has sent ships towards the Sound, in hopes of getting more of the like; a supply of cables and anchors will be seasonable, some having been lost in the late storm. Asks what proportion of beer will be allowed. The Leopard and Katherine have lost the foremasts and bowsprits. Recommends the

1665. VOL. CXXI.

practice adopted by merchants of "lowering their topmasts abaft the masts." An exact catalogue of wants shall be sent from the Gunfleet. [*Adm. Paper, two pages.*]

May 14. Harwich. 49. Sir Wm. Batten to Sam. Pepys. Desires payment of a bill of exchange received from the governor of the Chest to Sir Francis Clarke. Understands their Triparty ship is come in; wishes a bill of store got for his hogshead of high country white wine in her, to have it laid in his cellar. Has sent to Capt. Cock one of the Dutch handcuffs prepared for our men; they have several chains, and those engines are to go 100 on a chain. Hopes he will publish it at the coffee houses, where it will be spread like leprosy. [*Adm. Paper.*]

May 14. The Eagle, Spithead. 50. Capt. John Stanesby to the Navy Comrs. Engagement with two Dutch man-of-war off Scilly; the wind being high, could not carry his lower tier of guns. The enemy maintained their weather guns out, and kept within pistol shot till dark, when they escaped. Damage to the sails and rigging. Himself, the master, and corporal were wounded. Refers the Commissioners to Comr. Middleton's report.

May 14. 51. Capt. Jas. Sharland to the Navy Comrs. Account of the quality and condition of the Harp. The charge for lengthening her 10 feet will be 100*l.*, when she will carry 14 guns, and be in condition to fight any enemy of 16 or 18 pieces of ordnance. [*Adm. Paper.*]

May 14. 52. Post warrant from Lord Arlington for post horses and a guide from London to [Dover] and back, for the Abbé la Grange; with note from the Abbé, that in spite of his pass, he has been detained at Dover, from 8 p.m. to 11 a.m. of the 16th May.

May 14. Off Lowestoft, Suffolk. 53. Duke of York to Lord Arlington. Refers to Lord Falmouth for accounts of the fleet. Wants another supply of money for himself from the treasurer of the navy. Capt. Smith and his frigates have not joined the fleet, but several who were with him have brought in prizes. Hopes soon to take the sea again, if the victualling be ready at Harwich; if the Norway intelligence be true, hopes to give the King a good account of frigates sent there. [*Two pages.*]

May 14. Royal Charles. 54. Sir Wm. Coventry to Lord Arlington. Sir Thos. Clifford will give an account of the prizes, which is the best part of their present story, and Lord Falmouth of all other concerns. Hopes to-morrow to be at the Gunfleet, and to know what the victualler has done towards completing victuals to the end of August.

May 15. 55. Earl of Peterborough to [Williamson]. The fleet has come to Harwich. The Duke of Buckingham and Earl of Sandwich are returning; has not decided what to do, but will not be hasty. Would gladly exercise some other virtue besides patience.

VOL. CXXI.

1665.
May 15. Kidderminster. 56. Lord Windsor to Lord [Arlington]. Began before the King's letter came to keep some of the militia on duty. There are in Worcester 40 militia horse, a volunteer foot company of 200, and the clergy company of nearly 100. Will keep up a guard of 80 till the whole militia have done duty. Hopes soon to send an exact account of the two months' assessment; it will be 1,600*l.* and the expenses 400*l.* Has also received the King's orders of May 4, to collect a third month's assessment by 25th June, and has sent forth warrants accordingly. Has directed Major Wilde to convey John Knowles, with a party of horse, from Worcester to Whitehall. [*Two pages.*]

May 15. Recommendation to the Lord Treasurer of the petition of Abraham Dowcett for power to compound with the Farmers of Excise of Lincolnshire for 1,100*l.* arrears due from them, and for a grant of the same, in lieu of 1,700*l.* disbursed for His Majesty's service. [*Ent. Book* 18, *p.* 153.]

May 15. Reference to the Lord Treasurer on the petition of Major Greathead to be one of the Farmers of Excise for Suffolk, the King wishing to gratify the petitioner, on account of his services in discovering the late intended rebellion in the North. [*Ent. Book* 18, *p.* 162.]

May 15. Tower Wharf. 57. Giles Bond, master of the Harwich hoy, to Sam. Pepys. Has taken up from the London wreck a 9-inch hawser and 19 pieces of cable, but no guns at all. The weather is so bad that the divers have only been down three times. [*Adm. Paper.*]

May 15. Woolwich. 58. Chris. Pett to Sam. Pepys. Approves of Mr. Cooper as surveyor for the new ship at Blackwall, if his declining health will permit. Thinks another surveyor necessary for the ship building at Deptford. [*Adm. Paper.*]

May 15. 59. Capt. Wm. Badiley to the Navy Comrs. Proposes a chain to be made for the Henrietta's moorings, like that used by the Royal Katherine; in her last voyage, some ill-disposed person cut the cable at the anchor, and carried it away; if another should be laid it would be served in the same way. Certifies the death of Abram Goulstone, his assistant; desires a warrant appointing John Oliver in his stead. [*Adm. Paper.*]

May 15. Chatham. 60. Comr. Peter Pett to Sam. Pepys. Promises speedy dispatch of the galley. The Sovereign cannot be docked till a spring [tide]. Cannot spare seamen to carry the Blackcock into the Hope. [*Adm. Paper.*]

May 15. Dover. 61. Thos. White to the Navy Comrs. The Paradox is off the bank, her ballast, guns, &c., on board; she now rides in the road taking in victuals, waiting a fair wind to sail. The bank of beach is now taken away from hindering the ships. [*Adm. Paper.*]

VOL. CXXI.

1665.

May 15. 62. Memorandum that the four months' victualling, from April 1 to July 21, 1665, will be completed by the end of the week, for the ships now at Harwich and the six Gottenburg ships, if want of men and the winds hinder not; 2,000 tuns of beer a week might be dispatched, were empty casks returned from the fleet; 28,000 men consume 812 tuns per week, &c. [*Adm. Paper.*]

May 15. Bristol. 63. Sir John Knight to the Navy Comrs. Has given tickets and conduct money to 16 pressed seamen for Portsmouth; if a ship had been in Kingroad, 150 more might have been procured. There are two good ships fitting out for the service, the John and Mary, 300 tons burthen, and the Pearl of 260 tons. [*Adm. Paper.*] *Annexing,*

63. i. *List of 10 seamen, pressed since May 7, to appear at Portsmouth.* *Bristol, May 15, 1665.*

May 16. Cockpit. 64. Duke of Albemarle to the Navy Comrs. There will be 20 prizes sent into the Thames from the fleet; advises making use of the seamen sent with them in carrying down the victualling ships. [*Adm. Paper.*]

May 16. Cockpit. 65. Duke of Albemarle to the Navy Comrs. A supply of mast, cables, &c., must be sent to Harwich, to await the coming of the fleet, divers of the ships, especially the Fairfax, having been damaged in a storm. [*Adm. Paper.*]

May 16. Coleman Street. 66. Thos. Tyte to Sir Wm. Batten. Has received advice from Hamburg of five cables laden on board the Katherine, riding in Glucksstadt Road; the other two cables will be shipped in a day or two. The Dutch will watch the return of these vessels. [*Adm. Paper.*]

May 16. Plymouth. 67. John Lanyon to the Navy Comrs. Understands from the seamen that the conduct of Capts. Nixon and Stanesby, in their late engagement with two Dutch capers, was very foul; the night they left the Dutch, no lights were put out as formerly, and though in sight of them in the morning, they still kept on their way; the Eagle lay by some time, and both the enemy's ships plied on her, but finding the Elizabeth nearly out of sight, she also made sail; it is true the wind and sea were high, but there were no sufficient reasons for such endeavours to get from them. Will send account of the ten tons of cordage and Mr. Hacker's yarn. The Katherine, on her voyage from Jamaica, got upon the shoals off the coast of Florida; the long boat, with ten persons and gold and silver to the value of 600*l.*, was lost. The Sorlings has gone to sea, promising to recover what was amiss through long lying for orders. In expectation of the Dutch, the captain has torn down all his close cabins, and the men lie on deck. [*Copy. The original being sent to Coventry for the trial of Nixon and Stanesby. Two pages.*]

May 16. Warrant to Capt. Richard Chapman, John Hubberd, and Robert Wilson to apprehend John Pidgeon. Minute. [*Dom. Entry Book 22, p. 135.*]

Vol. CXXI.

1665.

May 16. Royal Charles, near the Gunfleet. 68. Sir Wm. Coventry to Lord Arlington. Besides what Sir George Downing writes of the Dutch resolution to come out, they hear that the Zealand fleet of 26 ships is gone into the Texel, so that the fleets are now joined and in considerable strength. Hopes to gather together the ships scattered by the late storm. Wishes more ships might have been set forth. The Duke of York has sent orders to stop the colliers going to Newcastle, apprehending danger for them, but not to take any men from them. They have stopped the packet boat, lest her return might give information of their arrival and numbers. [*Two pages.*]

May 16. 69. Sir Wm. Coventry to Williamson. If the commanders of the Little Mary and Paradox be found guilty, the Duke of York will be very severe, and he has written to that effect to the Duke of Albemarle.

May 16. Harwich. 70. Earl of Peterborough to Williamson. Has come to shore with the Duke's leave. He said the Dutch were joined and intend to come out to fight. Thinks he wishes this believed, to stop some whom despair of action draws away. Has little satisfaction and great mortifications on board. Under the rose, men begin to be sick in the fleet. Has had a letter from the Prince [Rupert], and will answer it when well enough. [*One and a half pages.*]

May 16. 71. Wm. Trollope to [Williamson?]. Has reached Casewick. There was likely to be a great conventicle held at Castle Bytham; some of the quality asked the minister for the use of the church, Dr. Winter, their minister, being licensed by the Bishop, but he was forewarned, and the meeting prevented, or it would have been of 200 or 300. There were many of quality from Rutlandshire. Will give Lord Campden notice of it. [*One and a half pages.*]

May 17. 72. Statement that by the charter of Chester, the mace and the sword, with the point erected, are to be carried before the mayor, except in presence of the King and his heirs, within the liberties of the city, and that this includes the cathedral, and was so decided in a contest in King James's time, and the now Judges have mediated for its continuance.

May 17. Whitehall. 73. Petition of Susan, widow of John Momford, and three other widows, to the King, for supply and subsistence. Their husbands, being mariners on the Milford frigate, were slain in the late engagement with the Dutch. With reference thereon to the Navy Commissioners to order them suitable relief, according to the general resolution for provision to be made for persons in that condition.

May 17. Entry of the above reference. [*Ent. Book* 18, p. 163.]

May 17. Warrant from Lord Arlington to a messenger to apprehend —— Izard, for contempt of the King's authority. [*Ent. Book* 22, p. 131.]

May 17. Warrant to the Sheriffs of the county palatine of Chester, for reprieve of Robert Calcott, convicted for the murder of Henry Bannaster, till further orders. [*Ent. Book* 22, p. 130.]

VOL. CXXI.

1665.

May 17? 74. Petition of Alice, wife of Robt. Calcott, to the King. Her husband was convicted at Chester great assizes for the death of Mr. Banaster, but reprieved till the 24th. Begs prolongation of the reprieve till His Majesty is more fully informed of the accident, that mercy may be extended to him.

May 17. Custom House, London. 75. Sir Jo. Wolstenholme to Lord Arlington. Sends seven letters taken from passengers who came to Harwich. The one to Fras. Clarke, a merchant of quality in the city, should be returned to him.

May 17. Whitehall. 76. The Lords Commissioners [for Prizes] to the Judges of the Court of Admiralty. Have received many complaints that the judges forbear to declare any goods contraband which are seized in ships trading with the Dutch, to the great discouragement of those who have taken particular commissions and armed themselves in this quarrel. State what goods are considered contraband; viz.,—naval commodities, provisions for support of life, and instruments of war. The King will in vain attempt to reduce his enemies if they enjoy unlimited supplies of these. Hope the forbearance has been rather from oversight, through stress of business, than misunderstanding of the King's declaration, which is conformable to the law of nations, and on which they are to proceed in future. [*Copy.*]

May 17. Harwich. 77. Sir Wm. Penn to the Navy Comrs. Progress of ships now in port for victualling and tallowing. Masts and boats wanted; also two cables for the Royal Charles. [*Adm. Paper.*]

May 17. The Exchange, Burlington Bay. 78. Wm. Gregory, commander, to Sam. Pepys. The ship was forced from her anchor by bad weather, and driven from the fleet, then lying off the Texel; Wentworth, the captain, being on board Prince Rupert at the time, was not able to get back. The Blackamoor, Maryland Merchant, and two fly boats also broke loose, leaving an anchor or more behind. Shall labour to return to the fleet after taking in fresh water. [*Adm. Paper.*]

May 17. Barber Surgeons' Hall. 79. Rich. Reynell to Sam. Pepys. Mr. Greenway, a surgeon in the last Dutch wars, was appointed surgeon to the Happy Entrance. His chest was viewed; believes him to be already gone, but will enquire. [*Adm. Paper.*]

May 17. Cockpit. 80. Duke of Albemarle to the Navy Comrs. Appoints Peter Brooke as surgeon of the Happy Entrance, on the non-appearance of Greenway. He is to be supplied with money for his chest, that he may not stay for medicines, but go down post to Portsmouth, as the ship is ready to sail. [*Adm. Paper.*]

May 18. Royal Charles, Gunfleet. 81. Sir Wm. Coventry to the Navy Comrs. Shall not attempt clearing as many ships as proposed at Harwich. Cables and anchors are greatly wanted. The merchant ships are generally unprovided with ground tackle, their anchors too light, and their cables, though of the number agreed on, too small, the owners thinking thus to evade the intent of the contract. The necessity has to be supplied

VOL. CXXI.

1665.

from the King's stores. Requests that such issues may be charged at full value to the owners. If the merchants at Hamburg had laden their ships before the coming of the convoy, and been able to sail within the 10 days limited, there would have been no danger to them. The water ship is to be returned with empty cask into the river to be refilled. Wishes the hospital ship were sent down. The men bringing up prizes are ordered into Harwich, for fear of their staying in London to spend their money; therefore the victualling ships cannot be sent down by them, as proposed by the Duke of Albemarle. [*Adm. Paper, three pages.*]

May 18. Cockpit. 82. Duke of Albemarle to the Navy Comrs. Desires an order to Mr. Gauden to supply the Giles ketch, bound for Tangiers, with victuals for 35 men. [*Adm. Paper.*]

May 18. Cockpit. 83. Duke of Albemarle to the Navy Comrs. Desires that Capts. Nixon and Stanesby, late commanders of the Elizabeth and Eagle, be sent as prisoners to the Fleet, to answer their neglect and cowardice in not taking the Dutch capers they engaged with. [*Adm. Paper.*]

May 18. 84. Certificate by Matthew Hayden, that the Mary commenced lading on the 11th instant. [*Adm. Paper.*]

May 18. 85. Robt. Mayors to the Navy Comrs. Survey of Mr. Andrews' timber lying at Taplow, Berks.; total, 85 loads already felled. [*Adm. Paper.*]

May 18. The Maryland, Burlington Bay. 86. Capt. Levy Green to [the Navy Comrs.]. His vessel broke loose from the fleet, leaving two anchors and four cables behind. Intends to call at the Humber for 20 sail of ships there bound for London, and hasten to the fleet. [*Adm. Paper.*]

May 18. Victualling Office. 87. Denis Gauden to the Navy Comrs. The victualling ships for the fleet cannot sail for want of men; sends a list of the number required on each vessel, 20 in all. [*Adm. Paper.*]

May 18. The Navy, off the Gunfleet. 88. Edw. Hyde to the Navy Comrs. Edw. Banks should have been entered as carpenter's mate in the pay book of the Expedition; the mistake will be a great loss to the poor man; begs it may be remedied on the request of Capt. Pyne. [*Adm. Paper.*] *Encloses,*

> 88. I. *Capt. Valentine Pyne to Edw. Hyde. Edw. Banks is to be entered as carpenter's mate of the Expedition; is sure the Navy Commissioners will not deny it.*
>
> *St. Andrew, May 8, 1665.*

May 18. Renewal of patent to the Trinity House, Deptford Strond, including the ballast and soil of the Thames, about which differences have arisen which are now ended, but leaving out purprestures, wastes, and encroachments on the river, which the King intends to grant to Sir Robt. Killigrew and Mr. Progers. [*Docquet.*]

May 18. Warrant to pay to Lord Arlington 2,000*l.*, for secret service, without account. [*Docquet.*]

VOL. CXXI.

1665.

May 18. Warrant to the Navy Comrs. to pay 2,000*l.* to Sir Allan Apsley, by command of Lord Admiral the Duke of York, to be employed by his direction. Minute. [*Ent. Book* 22, *p.* 136.]

May 18. Warrant to Sir Wm. Doyley to remove such Dutch prisoners at Ipswich as he thinks good to the common gaols at Colchester, co. Essex, and Bilborough, Woodbridge and Hadleigh, co. Suffolk, where the high sheriffs of the said counties will receive them into custody. [*Ent. Book* 22, *p.* 251.]

May 19. The King to the Mayor and Aldermen of Northampton. Recommends Thomas Eakens, a neighbour, and a person of constant loyalty and many sufferings, for the stewardship of the town, vacant by death of Wm. Rushton. [*Ent. Book* 17, *p.* 110.]

[May 19.] 89. Draft of the above.

May? 90. Petition of John Adams, one of His Majesty's watermen, to the King, for an order to the Governors of Sutton's Hospital, to admit his son to a Scholar's place; has a charge of eight small children.

May 19. Letter to the Master and Governors of Sutton's Hospital to receive John Adams into their school. Minute. [*Ent. Book* 17, *p.* 111.]

May 19. The King to the University of Cambridge. Recommends Sir Ellis Leighton for the degree of D.C.L., to encourage and render him more useful for service. [*Ent. Book* 19, *p.* 45.]

May? 91. Petition of Lieut.-Col. Thos. Duncan to Williamson, for a copy of a privy seal of July 1664, granting him a Reformado's place, duty free, in Hull, from which he has not yet received any benefit; will then be able to show the King and Duke of Albemarle that he has been slighted and wronged.

May 19. Letter recommending Lieut.-Col. Thos. Duncan to Hull. Minute. [*Ent. Book* 20, *p.* 62.]

May 19. Grant to Robt. Jocelyn, of Hyde Hall, co. Herts, of the dignity of a baronet. [*Docquet.*]

May 19. Grant to him of the usual discharge. [*Docquet.*]

May 19. Harwich. 92. Earl of Peterborough to [Williamson]. The bad weather has hindered the dispatch of provisions for the fleet; it could not sail for a fortnight, even if they knew the Hollanders were out. Is going on board to-morrow to compliment the Duchess; could not visit the Duke often when out, on account of the weather, being in another squadron, and at port he attends chiefly to business. Will have an enemy in this little man, but hopes not to be behind with him. As to [Williamson's] news of Guinea, hopes it will make a market ready for those who would sell their shares when the Hollanders are beaten. [*One and a half pages.*]

May 19. Bradford. 93. W. Hawksworth to Sir Thos. Gower. Rich. Walker, one questioned about the plot but dismissed on bail, was marched by

Vol. CXXI.

1665.

the constables, and several scandalous pamphlets and letters found in his portmanteau. Suspects that some of them came from David Lumly and Simeon Butler, two chief plotters who fled, but he will not confess, except that he had the pamphlet, "Murder will out," from Jos. Walley, a bookseller in London. The writer and Sir John Armitage thought fit to commit Walker as a disaffected person. [*Imperfect.*] *Encloses,*

93. I. *List of scandalous and seditious pamphlets and letters found on Rich. Walker, newly come from London, at Bradford.* *May 8, 1665.*

93. II. *Copy of the above.*

93. III. *J[ohn] T[aylor] to Willm. Hogg, shoemaker, Leeds. Will reward his kindness if the Lord spare his life; can only go out in evenings, for fear of arrest; John [Atkinson], the northern plotter, is again in the Tower; he is a stubborn fellow and will do the King no service, though reports to the contrary are raised by those who would have it so. Endorsed with notes that Taylor and Hogg were in correspondence with Atkinson, but some who witnessed against them were hanged, others are Quakers and will not swear.* *May 2, 1665.*

93. IV. *John T[aylor] to Hannah Booth, near Halifax. Encourages her to bear up under the troubles of this world, in hope of another. Advice on the education of her daughter. The King and Council are debating about toleration of popery; the popish party try hard to bring it about, and the French ambassador helps them. The English fleet went in a bravado to the mouth of the Texel, and spent 1,000l. in gunpowder, because it was the King's coronation day. The Dutch took the opportunity to bring in their Bourdeaux fleet of 80 sail, which had long lain on the French coast. Prodigies still continue; flames are seen in the heavens, &c. Endorsed with a note that the address is false; Walker will not confess from whom the letter came nor to whom it is sent, but it is supposed to be to Mrs. Marsden.* [*Two and a half pages.*] *May 2, 1665.*

93. V. —— *Jamson to Eliz. Jamson. Rejoices that she bears up well under her afflictions, and exhorts her to perseverance; begs her prayers; sends 20s. towards the loss by the second plunder. Endorsed with a note to prove that the letter must be from David Lumly, and that it was brought by Walker.*

93. VI. *Copy in the same handwriting as the above, of a letter written by an eminent godly presbyterian minister, banished from Scotland 27 years before, who had a strange prophetical spirit; he exhorts the godly to patience and strength in their sufferings, and foretells the return of the banished ones.* [*Three pages.*]

VOL. CXXI.

1665.

May 19. Whitehall. 94. Commission to Rich. Herbert to be Lieutenant in the foot company in Ludlow Castle under command of the Earl of Carbery.

May 19. Friday, 9 a.m. 95. Lord Chancellor Clarendon to Lord [Arlington]. Sends what he thinks fitting on the enclosed petition; without a severe execution, the law and government will fall into great contempt. Is so lame that he intends to rest a day, or he knows not what will become of him, but will come to council if there be any business of moment. Endorsed "Transportation of Quakers." *Encloses*,

95. I. *Reference of a petition to Lord Chief Justice Bridgeman and the Attorney General, who are to ascertain the petitioners' ability to go through their undertaking, and put it into such a way that the King may give all encouragement to the petitioners, and free the several prisons of so many tedious persons. [In Chancellor Clarendon's hand. Endorsed "Quakers."]*

May 19. Whitehall. Reference as above to the Lord Chief Justice Bridgeman and the Attorney General on the petition of Thos. Fraser and Rich. Baddeley, for a Dutch prize ship to transport the multitude of Quakers with whom the several gaols are filled, to their great inconvenience. [*Ent. Book* 18, p. 161.]

May 19. Westminster. 96. Patent granting to Sir Edmund Turner and George Carew, as assignees of the late Wm. Courteen, letters of reprisal on the subjects of the States General, to seize their goods and merchandise at sea, to the value of 151,612*l*., the value adjudged in the Admiralty Court of the ships Bona Esperanza and Henry Bonaventure. The said ships, belonging to the said Wm. Courteen, were seized near the Mauritius by the Dutch East India Company in 1643, and restitution often demanded in vain; the said letters of reprisal should hold good even should peace be concluded with the States General, till the said sum, and the expenses of its recovery be paid, but no damage be done to the persons of the States' subjects, unless in case of resistance. [*Two pages, printed.*]

May 19. Royal Charles, Gunfleet. 97. Sir Wm. Coventry to Lord Arlington. Sends letters; that directed for the Queen is intended for the Queen-Mother; four men-of-war are seen coming, which it is hoped are those left on the coast of Holland.

May 19. Royal Charles. 98. Sir Wm. Coventry to Williamson. The Duke of Albemarle is attending to convoys for coals. Is much surprized and many are indignant at the conduct of the captain of the Elizabeth; he was commended on account of his conduct in the late Dutch war by the Duke of Albemarle, who "hates a coward as ill as a toad." If there be a court-martial, neither he nor his companion, who followed his example, will find any favour, and it may make people take good heed to their actions. Forwards for Capt. Strode the Duke [of York]'s orders for levying the tax in the Cinque Ports. The weather is stormy. The Dutch joined on Friday, and could have come out on Saturday or Sunday, but not since. The colliers were ordered by the Duke

Vol. CXXI.

1665.

to stay at Harwich, but they disobeyed, though the convoy was ordered back to the fleet; so if they have bad success, they may thank themselves. Nixon and Stanesby have arrived, also the Marquis d'Humières. [*Two pages.*]

May 19. Grant to the three daughters of Sir William Brooke, Bart. viz., Dame Hill, wife of Sir William Boothby, Bart., co. Derby, Margaret Brooke, and Dame Frances, wife of Sir Thomas Whitmore, K.B., of the precedency of the daughters of a baron, although on account of the attainder of Hen. Brooke, Lord Cobham, and George Brooke, his brother and heir, the father of Sir William, the latter never became a baron. With note of a duplicate of the preceding grant, signed by the King the same day. [*Ent. Book* 22, *pp.* 138-9.]

May [19.] 99. Draft of the above. [*One and a half pages.*]

May 19. Order for a warrant to pay to Sir Wm. Boreman, keeper of the dwarf orchard at Greenwich, 589*l.* 17*s.* 8*d.* for keeping and planting 16 coppices and a dwarf orchard in Greenwich Park, and 140*l.* a year for gardeners' wages and other expenses. [*Ent. Book* 21, *pp.* 139-40.]

May 19. Licence to Jo. Packington and Dr. Yerbury, his tutor, to travel for three years. Minute. [*Ent. Book* 22, *p.* 140.]

May 19. Warrant for a grant to Thomas Offley of the office of groom porter. [*Ent. Book* 22, *p.* 140.]

May 19. Three warrants to deliver at Holy Island, convey, and receive at Windsor Castle Henry Martin, prisoner for the horrid murder of the late King. Minute. [*Ent. Book* 22, *p.* 149.]

May 19. Gravesend and Milton. 100. John Marlow, mayor of Gravesend, to the Navy Comrs. The town being a great receptacle and thoroughfare for all nations, desires some regulation for saving the seamen who man the tilt-boats from being impressed, that so the King's liege people and their goods may have safe passage to and from London. They might be manned with men too aged for the King's service. [*Adm. Paper.*]

May 19. Yarmouth. 101. James Johnson to the Navy Comrs. Expects five tons of cordage from Hamburg; proposes sending it to Deptford as before; asks if the frigate now building in the town is to be rigged there; can recommend a blockmaker and sailmaker for the service. Begs an answer touching his parcel of shot offered for sale, which "if not a commodity now," never will be. [*Adm. Paper.*]

May 19. Cockpit. 102. Duke of Albemarle to the Navy Comrs. Desires that proper allowance be granted to the widow of John Sawyer, mariner, slain in the Dutch war near Cadiz; or that she may petition the King and Council for relief. [*Adm. Paper.*]

May 19. Cockpit. 103. Duke of Albemarle to the Navy Comrs. Desires that the captain of the Golden Lion may be supplied with provisions, and the

1665. Vol. CXXI.

workmen hastened, that he may join the fleet. Is surprised at Capt. Pett's neglect in not coming down, although the Tiger is nearly ready. The Duke of York has sent his yacht to Greenwich to bring back two or three hogsheads of Thames water for his own use; orders must be given accordingly. Masts are wanted at Harwich. [*Adm. Paper.*]

May 20. 104. Warrant from the Navy Comrs. to the Clerks of the Store and Cheque at Deptford, to make out to John Stacy a bill for 30 tons of resin; the same to be charged as delivered to Mr. Mayors, purveyor, to be sent to Chatham. [*Adm. Paper.*]

May 20. 105. Notes of 24 boats now ready at Deptford, with the Navy Commissioners' warrant for washing and tallowing the Nonsuch ketch, and dispatching certain stores by her to the Prince Royal, as demanded by the Earl of Sandwich. [*Copy. Adm. Paper.*]

May 20. Ordnance Office. 106. Edw. Sherburne and two other Ordnance Officers to the Navy Comrs. The delay in furnishing the Tiger with guns and ammunition is caused by the endeavour to alter her former proportion, but that is now expressly forbidden by the King. Ask whether to supply the Hound, as it is reported that she is intended for a fireship. [*Adm. Paper.*]

May 20. Woolwich. 107. Wm. Bodham to Sam. Pepys. The 20 inch cable for the Prince will be ready this night. Understands that Mr. Colvin is discontented at his defective hemp being returned; has done his duty in the matter without prejudice; gives an account of its being examined and weighed, and the general opinion of its unfitness; begs that no complaints may be listened to; would do no corrupt act, though to gain an estate by it; reverences his superiors, but for the rest of the world, neither courts their favour nor fears their displeasure. [*Adm. Paper, two pages.*]

May 20. Woolwich. 108. Wm. Bodham to Sam. Pepys. Knows not how to get the two cables so suddenly ordered ready in time; all the men are dispersed in London, Deptford, and God knows where; will use all possible dispatch. [*Adm. Paper.*]

May 20. 109. Capt. Wm. Badiley to the Navy Comrs. Wishes the chain for mooring the Henrietta to be 89 fathoms, three links to a fathom; weight, 50 cwt. 2 qrs. 1 lb. [*Adm. Paper.*]

May 20. Chatham. 110. Philip Barrow to [the Navy Comrs.]. The clerk of the cheque refused to allow a labourer to carry his letter to the Commissioners. Employed a man on purpose, the business being pressing. Begs that notice may be taken of an insult which was never offered to any storekeeper before. [*Adm. Paper.*]

May 20. Chatham. 111. Philip Barrow to the Navy Comrs. Cannot dispatch the Augustine with masts and provisions to Dover, for want of hands, the men having orders from Mr. Lawrence to take up the galley

VOL. CXXI.

1665.

there is no warrant for so doing, although divers provisions are made, and things fetched out of the stores for that purpose, without his knowledge. [*Adm. Paper.*]

May 20. Hall End, near Lichfield. 112. Thos. Corbin to Thos. Hayter. Desires the settlement of his accounts for water dues and other disbursements in the carriage and converting of 643 loads of timber. [*Adm. Paper.*]

May 20. Royal Charles. 113. Duke of York to [Lord Arlington]. M. D'Humières has sailed for Dunkirk, much pleased with his kind usage; thanks those who have been so civil to him. Has long been of his lordship's opinion about the victualler, and once proposed a change to the King, but it was not done. Expects to-morrow to take in all the victuals ready, and will be at a stand unless more come speedily, and be obliged to use the wine and brandy of the prizes for beverage; it is want of drink that has forced this great fleet back. Capt. Smith has come in with his three ships and a prize. Expects Langborne daily, with the collier fleet. The sum named by his lordship will suffice for the present. [*Three pages.*]

May 20. Pass and protection for Anthony Carew, merchant of Ostend, to come and remain in England for two months. Minute. [*Ent. Book* 22, *p.* 147.]

May 21. Whitehall. Warrant from Lord Arlington to the Countess of Chesterfield, farmer of the Post Office, to pay 44*l.* to Thomas Parnell, for extraordinary services as postmaster to the Court. With note prefixed of his request for the same. [*Ent. Book* 22, *p.* 141.]

May 21. Sayes Court. 114. J. Evelyn to the Navy Comrs. Has been engaged in receiving the petitions of distressed widows. Sir John Lawson sent a list of about 50, whose conditions he particularly recommends. Several could not be admitted owing to their certificates being defective; the rest are ranked according to their merits and exigencies; is limited by his commission from granting more than 10*l.*, even to those judged worthy of the utmost bounty, but where pensions are expected, they are to be referred to the Board. [*Adm. Paper.*]

May 21. Portsmouth. 115. Capt. Phineas Pett to the Navy Comrs. The Tiger is completely rigged and victualled for three months; the cook-room being in the hold, a copper funnel for conveying away the smoke has to be made, which will delay her a few days. [*Adm. Paper.*]

May 21. Hall End, near Lichfield. 116. T. Corbin to Sam. Pepys. Has had many importunate letters from his brother, for procuring the bills he gave for the receipt of 460*l.*, ordered for him by the Board, to be disbursed in Sherwood Forest; hoped that all the timber lying at Bawtry would have been taken away, so as to make the account clear; finds Mr. Russell has sent down more, and it is mixed together; is already 40*l.* out of purse. Capt. Greene wishes to be again serviceable; he has felled 1,200 trees, and is confident as much more good timber can be found. Want of money only makes him go on slowly. [*Adm. Paper.*]

VOL. CXXI.

1665.

May 22. Cockpit. 117. Duke of Albemarle to the Navy Comrs. Orders that six able men be furnished from Trinity House as masters of victualling ships, to be in readiness to attend on all occasions. Hears many complaints from the Ordnance Comrs. of the misdemeanors of Mr. Salisbury, clerk of the survey; he must be removed and another appointed in his place. [*Adm. Paper.*]

May 22. Deptford. 118. Jonas Shish to the Navy Comrs. Conceives it convenient to place the main-top mast abaft the mainmast; has persuaded several merchant ships to adopt the plan; some would not, "because it was not the fashion." [*Adm. Paper.*]

May 22. Woolwich. 119. Wm. Acworth to the Navy Comrs. Account of anchors in store: 33 serviceable, 7 serviceable with repair. [*Adm. Paper.*]

May 22. Chatham. 120. Philip Barrow to the Navy Comrs. Account of the condition of 62 anchors in store; the mooring anchors are so placed that they cannot be judged of, either for weight or goodness. [*Adm. Paper.*]

May 22. Woolwich. 121. Chris. Pett to Sam. Pepys. Will appoint a fit person for the converting of Sir Wm. Warren's timber. Mr. Cooper has not yet returned from Aliceholt. Has taken a survey of the two ships, with Mr. Shish and the two persons intended for daily surveyors, in case Mr. Cooper does not accept the office. The complaint made by the captain of the Golden Lion to the Duke of Albemarle was only concerning his stores and provisions. The works will be completed by the end of the week. Timber wanted. [*Adm. Paper.*]

May 22. Woolwich. 122. Chris. Pett to Sam. Pepys. Mr. Cooper can survey the two new frigates building at Deptford and Blackwall. Sends his own survey, a copy of which should be given to the daily surveyor. Rear-Admiral Teddeman gives high commendation of the Royal Katherine, though many still raise clamours against her; he is in great want of a "carvell work pinnace" to row with nine oars; requests orders for the same. The captain of the Golden Lion plies hard to get men, and sets sentries over them to keep them on board. [*Adm. Paper.*] *Encloses,*

122. I. *Survey by C. Pett of the two ships building by Henry Johnson at Blackwall, and Wm. Castell at Deptford.*
Deptford, May 10, 1665.

May 22. Harwich. 123. Sir Wm. Batten to the Navy Comrs. Has not been idle in supplying the wants of the fleet, especially the merchant ships. Great want of masts. [*Adm. Paper.*]

May 22. Woolwich, 9 A.M. 124. Wm. Bodham to Sir John Mennes. Has received directions about the size of the cables for the Royal Charles; they will be ready by the afternoon. Asks in what vessel they are to go. [*Adm. Paper.*]

VOL. CXXI.

1665.

May 22 Woolwich, 4 a.m. 125. Wm. Rodham to Sam. Pepys. The great cable for the Royal Charles will be finished by the afternoon; wishes he had orders how to dispose of it; if not boated as soon as done, it will make a hole in another day's work. Riga and Quinsborough hemp wanted. [*Adm. Paper.*]

May 22 Chatham. 126. Comr. Peter Pett to [Sam. Pepys]. The Augustine, Harwich hoy, and Blackcock are ready to sail. Repairs of the Victory and galley. [*Adm. Paper.*]

May 22. 127. John Russell to the Navy Comrs. If Mr. Lister will undertake the land and water carriage, it will be a great help, as he has command of all the boatmen and porters. The greatest price given for millstones is 33s. 4d. per boat load. Hoys wanted. [*Adm. Paper.*] *Encloses,*

127. I. *Proposals of Thos. Lister, fee farmer of the manor and wharf of Bawtry, to the Navy Comrs., for the better ordering of timber lying on the wharf at Bawtry, and conveying it to Stockwith; for prevention of an accumulation of the timber on the wharf so as to leave room for other goods; for an allowance for loss and damage sustained by himself in conveying it at under rates; for preventing the carters' unlading timber in the high road and town, and for a protection to the watermen from pressing.* [2 pages.]

127. II. *Answers by John Russell to Mr. Lister's proposals: Has sent no more timber to Bawtry than what the waggons carried; and never attempted to stop his trade in millstones. Mr. Lister was not damaged by having to remove timber from the wharf. The carters unload at the back of the town, so that it is no disturbance to any one. A protection should be granted to the watermen, to save them from pressing.*

127. III. *Draft warrant forbidding timber to be brought to Bawtry until what already lies there be disposed of; waggons to be unloaded only at such places and such distances as Thos. Lister shall appoint; due allowance to be made to the said Lister for extra charges and freight, and waggons provided for him upon demand.* [2 pages.]

May 22. Royal Charles. 128. Sir W. Coventry to Lord [Arlington]. The Duke of York being at sea cannot give from time to time the orders needful to comply with the petition of the alum work farmers about convoy, but refers the case to the Duke of Albemarle, putting more ships under his direction than were formerly allotted to that service, that he may not have to make bricks without straw. Sends important letters, which cause the more regret about the stay of victuals preventing their going forth to seek the Dutch; could have met them better last voyage, as sickness and the great wages given by colliers have taken away many men; the colliers give 8*l.* or 9*l.* a voyage, which can be

VOL. CXXI.

1665.

taken in a month, and is equal to seven months' pay on the King's ships and without hazard. No fleet was ever sent out worse supplied with provisions as to quantity, nor better as to goodness. The Duke of York wants to know the King's pleasure whether a pass desired by Sir Bernard Gascoigne shall be granted. All are so fired by hearing that the Dutch are at sea as to be willing to go out with half the victuals intended. Hears that the Hamburg vessels are lost by delay in starting, the commander of the convoy waiting beyond the 10 days ordered him. [3 *pages*.]

May 22. Whitehall. The King to the Mayor and Aldermen of Coventry. Recommends them to offer William Bird and Richard Mury, both scholars in their free school, to the President and Fellows of St. John's College, Oxford, for the most capable to be chosen to a vacant scholarship there. [*Ent. Book* 14, p. 61.]

May 22. Whitehall. 129. Commission to Thos. Cheek to be Captain of a company of foot, lately commanded by Capt. Carey, in Col. John Russell's regiment of Guards.

May 22. Minute of the above. [*Ent. Book* 20, p. 62.]

May 22. Reference to the Lord Chancellor on the petition of John Earl of Clare, for some course to be taken to preserve an ancient family from ruin, through the ill condition of the estate of his son, Lord Clinton. [*Ent. Book* 18, p. 162.]

May 22. Kelden. 130. Sir A. Apsley to [Williamson]. Has written to his lord in behalf of Thos. Collins, falconer, who wishes to part with his place. *Encloses*,

130. I. *Sir A. Apsley to Lord Arlington. Requests favour in behalf of Fras. Young, to whom Mr. Collins wishes to part with his falconer's place. Is troubled about the Lord Chancellor's friend, not understanding his affair: quotes Pliny's advice for referring all doubtful matters to his lordship. Kelden, May* 22.

May 22. London. 131. List of 31 disaffected persons about the town, who meet at Gray's Inn Lane, Leadenhall Street, the Swan near Coleman Street, or Shoreditch.

May 22. London. 132. List of 17 seditious persons suspected to be in and about London, a few of whom are in the previous list.

VOL. CXXII. MAY 23–31, 1665.

1665.

May 23. Warrant to pay to Sir Edw. Carr and Edw. Halsall, equerries in ordinary to the Queen, 150*l.* each for board wages, and 30*l.* standing wages for one year and a half, ending Michaelmas, 1663. [*Docquet*.]

VOL. CXXII.

1665.
May 23. Presentation of John Harding to the Rectory of Landilp, co. Cornwall. [*Docquet.*]

May 23. Reference to the Lord Mayor, Aldermen, &c., of York, on the petition of George Finlawson, who served under the Earl of Tiviot and lost both his arms in battle, for recommendation to charity. [*Ent. Book* 18, *p.* 164.]

May 23. Royal Charles. 1. Sir Wm. Coventry to Lord Arlington. The Dutch packet has arrived without letters from Sir George Downing: fears they are stopped on the other side. Sends a letter from the Earl of Sandwich, and a printed paper from Sir Wm. Davidson. The Duke of York keeps a libellous picture about Holmes in Guinea.

May 23. 2. Sir Wm. Coventry to Sir Wm. Batten. Wishes Langley might be continued for the ketch at Wivenhoe, and the other appointed take the ketch at Deptford; guns and carriages for a ketch may be fitted out of the prize ships; sends a hoy for stores. The commander of the ketch at Wivenhoe refuses to give Langley possession, his commission being as captain, and Langley's only as master and commander. [*Adm. Paper.*]

May 23. Woolwich. 3. Wm. Bodham to Sam. Pepys. Has received Rundells' new estimate; proposes an interview with him before the Board. As to the hemp, sends Bowden, an indifferent witness, who has been been in the trade for 40 years, to give his opinion on the matter. The sight, touch, and smelling of the hemp will give sufficient information. [*Adm. Paper,* 2 *pages.*]

May 23. Ordnance Office. 4. Edw. Sherburne and two other Ordnance Officers to the Navy Comrs. The Merchants' Adventure and Providence, both of London, are ready laden with shot for Harwich, but cannot sail for want of men. [*Adm. Paper.*]

May 23. Plymouth. 5. John Lanyon to the Navy Comrs. Wants money for disbursements upon the several ships in port. Repairs needed for the Little Mary. The Paradox has arrived, and will send ashore some arms to be fixed. The Giles ketch, bound for Tangiers, is the only convoy appointed for the victualling ships; some other ship should see them safe out of the soundings, as several Dutch capers are abroad. A Newfoundland ship, the Reformation of Dartmouth, with 80 men, is taken. The prize ship, St. Mary of Amsterdam, would make a good convoy. [*Adm. Paper.*]

May 23. 6. Note by Wm. Foster of meat casks found amongst the ballast in the hold of the Unity prize. [*Adm. Paper.*]

May 23. London. 7. Wm. Breames to the Navy Comrs. Robt. Moulton, captain of the Centurion, being upon the coast of Holland, has seized a fly-boat and galliot hoy, laden with flax, potash, and other commodities; and in contempt of the Duke of York's order, has taken out 290 bundles of the flax and other goods, and disposed of one of the prize boats for his own advantage. [*Adm. Paper.*]

VOL. CXXII.

1665.

May 23. 8. Sir Wm. Coventry to Sam. Pepys. They are making all possible haste to get to sea and meet the Dutch. Must be content with less victuals than at first proposed; if three months dry and two months wet can be put on board, will sail forthwith. Casks must furnished for the John and Elizabeth hoy, sent to fill water in the river. [*Adm. Paper.*]

May 23. Chatham. 9. Comr. Peter Pett to Sam. Pepys. Has dispatched the hoy with the 10-inch cable and three pinnaces. The Augustine is ready to sail for Dover. Is offered a bargain of elm. [*Adm. Paper.*]

May 23. The Augustine, Chatham. 10. Capt. Rich. Teate to the Navy Comrs. Is ready to sail for Dover. Asks whether to go into the pier or remain in Dover Road. [*Adm. Paper.*]

May 23. Cockpit. 11. Sir Wm. Clarke to Sam. Pepys. The Duke will appoint a convoy for the Desire hoy to Portsmouth. [*Adm. Paper.*]

May 23. 12. List of 14 vessels taken up by Capt. Tatnell, but not employed. [*Adm. Paper.*]

May 24. 13. Certificate by the Masters and Wardens of Barber Surgeons' Hall of the goodness and reasonable price of a list provided by Mr. Selby, of drugs, instruments, &c., provided for Mr. Smart's chest, as surgeon of one of the hospital ships. [*Adm. Paper, 3½ pages.*]

May 24. 14. Like certificate for another surgeon's chest. [*Adm. Paper, 3½ pages.*]

May 24. 15. Account of cordage and other things recovered from the wreck of the London, since April 4th. [*Adm. Paper, 1½ pages.*]

May 24. Trinity House. 16. Nich. Hurleston, master, and four others of Trinity House, to the Navy Comrs. Will proceed with all diligence to provide six able persons as masters in the merchant ships hired for carrying provisions to the fleet. [*Adm. Paper.*]

May 24. Cockpit. 17. Duke of Albemarle to the Navy Comrs. Recommends Robt. Thorpe, sen., as master of a ship when opportunity offers. [*Adm. Paper.*]

May 24. Woolwich. 18. Wm. Bodham to Sam. Pepys. Has "ventilated" as much as possible Edw. Rundells' estimates; can but pronounce him a prevaricating knave; admires the audacious impudence of a bold mechanic who dares affront his superiors with such a piece of plain derision. His promise at first was to keep to the rates he set down; shows how, by altering the wording of the second contract, he has untied his hands; wishes to be confronted with him before the Board. Sends an abstract of the first estimates of Rundells and

Vol. CXXII.

1665.

Ellery, contrasted with Rundells' last. Endorsed with a breviate of the following estimates. [*Adm. Paper*, 1½ *pages*.] *Encloses*,

18. i–iii. *Estimates by Edw. Rundells, for a gallery from the old hemp loft to the street; total*, 15*l*. 1*s*.: *for repairing 38 feet of wharfing in the gunyard at Woolwich; total*, 18*l*. 2*s*. 4*d*.: *for altering and raising the shed at Woolwich ropeyard*, 25*l*. 18*s*.

Woolwich Ropeyard, May 6, 1665.

18. iv. *Enlarged estimates for the same works, the prices being* 27*l*. 5*s*., 22*l*. 16*s*. 3*d*., *and* 23*l*. 11*s*. 4*d*.

18. v. *Edw. Rundells to Sam. Pepys. Was unable to send the papers concerning the enlarged estimates sooner, having to meet Sir George Carteret about his fountain.*

Deptford, May 22, 1665.

18. vi. *Edw. Rundells' reasons why the estimates were afterwards enlarged.*

18. vii *Abstract of estimates for three pieces of work, two by Edw. Rundells and one by Robt. Ellery.*

18. viii. *Note by Sam. Pepys of the occasion and scope of the above papers; showing Rundells' knavery in making his estimate at the lowest rate, and then refusing to stand by it, his purpose being to make Robt. Ellery work at that rate.*

May 24. 19. Account by Thos. Harper of 39 anchors in store at Deptford, and of 28 more now received from Mr. Downing. [*Adm. Paper*.]

May 24. 20. Philip Tandy to Viscount Conway. Private affairs and accounts. Cannot get the creation money. No warrants are come out for the army, hence many of the soldiers mourn.

May 24. Royal Charles. 21. Sir Wm. Coventry to Lord Arlington. Hears that the Hamburg vessels still remain there. Hopes good luck to the fleet, but only fears about the men; no industry nor philosophy can preserve them, while they gain 8*l*. ready money more easily on board a collier than 23*s*. on the King's ships, for which they have to wait a year. The Duchess and her beautiful maids are departing, therefore long letters must not be expected from men under such a calamity; would vent their desperation on the Dutch, were not the victualler as cruel as the ladies. He is said to be there but does not appear, as his method is when he cannot give content. Many ships have been on short allowance, some have drunk water, and some been in danger of neither having beer nor water. [2 *pages*.]

May 24. 22. Petition of John Reyloffen to the King and Council, for liberty for himself and his son, a boy of 13, now prisoner in Chelsea College, to return home on equal exchange; was master of the King Solomon, serving Wm. Scott of Rouen, and only did what

1665. VOL. CXXII.

every master of a merchant ship is obliged to do, for preservation of its owners. *Amazing*,

22. I. *Wm. Scott to Reyloffen. Regrets the misfortune caused by the war, but will do his best for his liberation.* [*Dutch.*] *Rouen, April 25*, 1665.

May 24. Whitehall. Proclamation for further proroguing the Parliament which was appointed to meet June 21. [*Printed. Proc. Coll., Charles II.*, p. 186.]

May ? 23. Petition of the Governor and Company of Merchants trading to the Canary Islands to the King, for a proclamation in the usual form, declaring their incorporation as now granted by charter, several persons belonging to them still continuing the trade, on pretext that they are not bound to take notice of the charter till published by proclamation. [*Copy.*]

May 25. Whitehall. Proclamation for observance of the privileges granted to the Canary Islands' Company, forbidding others to intermeddle with their trade, as by so doing, the prices of those wines have been much enhanced in value, and the manufactures of England debased. [*Printed. Proc. Coll., Charles II.*, p. 187.]

May 25. Reference on the petition of John Patterson, attorney, to the Lord Chancellor, who is to consider how far errors of that nature are capable of pardon, the petitioner having ingenuously confessed his faults. [*Ent. Book* 18, p. 165.]

May 25. 24. Commission to John Howard to be Ensign to the King's own company of foot, in Col. John Russell's regiment of Guards.

May 25. Minute of the above. [*Ent. Book* 20, p. 62.]

May 25. Warrant for a grant to George Arnott, of fines due on lands and tenements in the duchy of Cornwall, amounting to 525*l.* [*Ent. Book* 22, pp. 142–3.]

[May 25.] 25. Draft of the above. [1½ *pages.*]

May 25. Warrant for a lease to James Hamilton, ranger of Hyde Park, and George Birch, auditor of excise, for 41 years, of 55 acres of land in the north-west corner of Hyde Park, on rental of 5s., on condition of their enclosing it, planting it with choice apple trees, and delivering one half of the produce for the King's household. [*Ent. Book* 22, pp. 144–5.]

May 25. Warrant for a release to Francis Phillips, from the covenant on which he holds the residue of a lease of Kempton Park, Middlesex, formerly granted to William Killigrew, on covenant of maintaining 300 deer there, and keeping up the parks. [*Ent. Book* 22, p. 150.]

May 25. Pass for Thomas Bromley, with five horses, sent by the King to the Prince of Orange, custom free. Minute. [*Ent. Book* 22, p. 151.]

Vol. CXXII.

1665.
May?   26. Petition of John Ogilby to the King, for a prohibition to any persons to reprint or counterfeit the sculpture of any of the following books, which he has printed at expense of 20 years' labour; viz., Virgil, Homer's Iliad and Odyssey, Æsop's Fables paraphrased, and the account of His Majesty's passing through London, and his coronation.

May 25. Whitehall.   27. Prohibition by the King to any person for 15 years to reprint or counterfeit the sculpture in certain works of John Ogilby, master of the revels in Ireland; viz., Virgil, Homer's Iliad, and Odyssey, Æsop's Fables, and His Majesty's entertainment in passing through London. [*Printed.*]

May 25.   Entry of the above. [*Ent. Book* 22, p. 151.]

May?   28. Jos. Walley to his Friends in Christ. Thanks for their kindness to him as a stranger. Thinks the duty of his dispensation is to stand still and see the salvation of God; regrets the spirit of division among God's people; begs their prayers; sends his brother William a concordance. Lives at Whitby, a cheesemonger's, at the Black Horse, Golden Lane. [3 *pages.*]

May 25.   Warrant for apprehending Joseph Walley with all his papers, at Whitby, a cheesemonger's, at the Black Horse, Golden Lane. Minute. [*Ent. Book* 22, p. 152.]

May 25.   The King to the Duke of Buckingham, [Lord Lieutenant of the West Riding of Yorkshire]. Having ordered the 3rd year's militia tax to be collected in Yorkshire before 24th June, and the time being short, directs him to employ Sir Fras Cobb, sheriff of the whole county, to raise and receive the same; an exact account thereof is to be sent to a Secretary of State. With note of like letters to Lords Delaryne and Fauconberg, for the other two ridings of Yorkshire. [*Ent. Book* 20, *pp.* 70-1.]

[May 25.]   29. Draft of the above. [*Imperfect.*]

May 25. Whitehall.   30. [Lord Arlington] to Lord Fauconberg. Enforces the King's letters on the raising of the militia tax. [*Damaged. Draft, altered into the form of a letter from the King.*]

May [25]. Whitehall.   31. The King to the [Mayor, &c.] of Newcastle. Requests assistance for Col. Edw. Villiers, governor of Tynemouth Castle, who is ordered to repair and fortify it, for security of the town and of trade, during the war with the United Provinces. Requests them,—especially as convoys are allowed for carrying on the coal trade, notwithstanding the occasions of the war,—to contribute thereto, after the example of London, which has given voluntary expressions of loyalty and affection to the public interests, and thus to ease the King of an expense not convenient in the great and pressing occasions of the war. [2 *pages.*]

May 25.   Entry of the above. [*Ent. Book* 17, p. 111.]

[May 25.]   32. Draft of the above. [2 *pages.*]

VOL. CXXII.

1665.

May 25. Portsmouth. 33. Capt. Phineas Pett to the Navy Comrs. Has all his gunner's stores on board; intends sailing the Tiger out to-morrow. [*Adm. Paper.*]

May 25. 34. List of the company of the prize ship Patriarch Isaac, manned with 15 able seamen; with certificate of her delivery to the Commissioners of Prizes, July 4, 1665. [*Adm. Paper.*]

May 25. The Coventry, Spithead. 35. Capt. Wm. Hill to Sam. Pepys. Has seized a ship coming from Amsterdam, L'Affection Renaissante; can obtain no order from the Duke of Albemarle whether to deliver her up again to the French, from whom he took her, or to the Commissioners of Prizes. She is square sterned, and carries 40 pieces of ordnance. Asks directions about Mrs. Pley's ships, still at Weymouth, which he is to convoy. Comr. Middleton will not give him orders to call there for them. [*Adm Paper.*]

May 25. Portsmouth. 36. Constance Pley to the Navy Comrs. The convoy is arrived, but so tied up in his orders that, although his course is to go out at the Needles, he will not step into Portland Road to take out their ships now ready to sail with him; he "clucks up all the ships along the coast like chickens, as far as Lyme and Topsham," but refuses to call at Portland for those which were chiefly intended; it will be like their last convoy, the King Ferdinando, which went about on the same errand, and lost the opportunity of serving them. Requests peremptory orders to the captain to call for the ships at Weymouth, and to see such as are bound to Chatham safe there before leaving them. [*Adm. Paper.*]

May 25. 37. Wm. Bodham to Sam. Pepys. Has received Mr. Moll's refused hemp according to order, but with regret, as giving occasion to maligners to cavil; has used the utmost circumspection in examining it. With Sam. Pepys' answer in shorthand, May 27. [*Adm. Paper, 2 pages.*]

May 25. 38. Report by Capt. John Proud and three others to the Navy Comrs., of their survey and valuation of 21 merchant ships hired into the service. [*Adm. Paper.*]

May 26. 39. Certificate that Jacob Copping and James Sherland were entered quartermasters on the Defence and changed into the Swallow; and request for payment of wages due to them by Capt. Thos. Rand, for service on board the former ship. [*Adm. Paper.*]

May 26. Harwich. 40. Sir Wm. Batten to the Navy Comrs. Is ignorant of Mr. Salisbury's crime; wishes not to countenance abuse of trust, but thinks he should be heard before his dismissal; every man is not born fit for a clerk of the survey, in these active times. Hopwood's hoy is not yet arrived. Pinnaces, oakum, and cordage wanted. [*Adm. Paper.*]

Vol. CXXII.

1665.

May 26. Gravesend 4 a.m. 41. Sir John Mennes to Sam. Pepys. Is prevented by contrary winds from sending off the victualling ships. Hopwood's hoy is returned without an anchor; it is strange that five great cables and goods to the value of 3,000*l.* should be put on board so rotten a vessel with so idle a master; requests that six able seamen be sent to carry her down. [*Adm. Paper.*]

May 26. Chatham. 42. Comr. Peter Pett to Sam. Pepys. Finds that Mr. Gregory is only guilty of indiscretion in forbidding the messenger to carry Mr. Barrow's letter; the other charge concerning the labourers is a mistake. As to the disputed priority of signing, both will give their reasons forthwith; they should agree well, but not too well, or the service may suffer, as it does in some places. Requests 618*l.* for 25 discharged shipwrights and 4 servants. Recommends Capt. Taylor's New England masts. Mr. Wild offers to contract for scuppers. [*Adm. Paper.*]

May 26. Chatham. 43. Comr. Peter Pett to Sam. Pepys. Will send the 25 pressed men to Deptford, but could well employ them in the many works now on hand. Fears the dispute between the clerk of the cheque and storekeeper will need the exercise of a higher power than his own to settle. [*Adm. Paper.*]

May 26. Woolwich. 44. Chris. Pett to Sam. Pepys. Objects to the plan of shifting the topmast abaft the mast for men-of-war; it may do for merchantmen, they having but little help, and not being so subject to labour in a sea gale; an experiment should be made of it on some of the smaller ships. Has sent the two captains of the Dutch prizes to wait on the Duke of Albemarle, and desired Anthony Deane to furnish Capt. Teddeman with a pinnace and awning. Great want of timber. [*Adm. Paper.*]

May 26. The Sorlings, Plymouth. 45. Capt. Jonathan Waltham to Sir Wm. Coventry. Has just arrived, disabled in an engagement with two Flushing men-of-war off Scilly, having two men killed and five wounded; could have secured them both with but one other ship's help. [*Adm. Paper.*]

May 26. Cockpit. 46. Sir Wm. Clarke to Sam. Pepys. Sends an order for 10 more soldiers for the Loyal Subject, out of Sir Chichester Wray's company. The Baltimore is to have 30 from Sir John Griffith's company. Lieut. Edwards is not to be employed any more until he has been heard for himself; he says he has impressed 200 men since May 10. Sends Capt. Pett's letter, which does not quadrate with Col. Middleton's. [*Adm. Paper.*] *Enclosed,*

46. i. *Capt. Phineas Pett to Sir Wm. Clarke. Forwardness of the Tiger. Intends sailing to-morrow; hopes when at Spithead to have some better account of men. Wishes for more particular instructions concerning the victuallers which he is to convoy to the fleet.*

Portsmouth, May 25, 1665.

VOL. CXXII.

1665.

May 26. Gravesend. 47. Fr. Hosier to the Navy Comrs. Has found out and examined the two waiters who are witnesses of the charge laid against Rich. Stringer, master's mate of the Merlin. [*Adm. Paper.*] *Encloses,*

47. I. *Deposition of Geo. Saunders. Paid Rich. Stringer 24s. for the discharge of Stephen Sampson, his boatswain, and David Dove, a boy; but the next day they were pressed again by the captain of the Merlin. May 22, 1665.*

47. II. *Deposition of Thos. Hall and Fras. Mawhood [King's waiters at Gravesend]. On 11th May, Rich. Stringer came on board the Brotherhood and pressed the boatswain and a boy. Mr. Saunders, master, thought to clear them, and offered 10s.; this was refused, and 15s. accepted. Were afterwards informed by Mr. Saunders that the sum did not satisfy Rich. Stringer, and that 10s. more had been given him. Gravesend, May 26, 1665.*

May 26. Royal Charles. 48. Duke of York to [Lord Arlington]. Thinks it too late to join any one with the victualler for this season, the time of year being past to make new provisions of flesh, but it should be done against next year or winter. Cannot judge whom it should be; that belongs to the Lord Treasurer and a committee of Council; will merely request Mr. Gauden to get what victuals he can for the present, and will then go and seek the Dutch, whose fleet is said to be on the west of the Dogger. A Dutch galliot is taken; thinks it was sent to fetch in things for the fleet, but the papers were chiefly thrown overboard: a private letter found makes the number of the Dutch fleet 112. Capt. Nixon is condemned to be shot; Capt. Stanesby is cleared. [*Begun on the 24th. 3½ pages.*]

May 26. Royal Charles. 49. Sir W. Coventry to [Lord Arlington]. For want of men, some ships will have to be left behind to man the rest. The Dutch fleet is variously reported at 100, 110, and 116, in the letters taken. Capt. Nixon is to be executed to-morrow. There is no evidence that Stanesby had sailed from the enemy, or deserted, till ordered by Nixon, who was his commander. A soldier is condemned to die for inciting the rest to mutiny, and to fall upon the seamen. Asks what is done towards encouraging private men-of-war. [*2 pages.*]

May 26. Reference to Sir Edw. Griffin, treasurer of the chamber, on the petition of Andrew Newport, for the allowance of 20s. a week, promised him on quitting his lodgings to Mdme. La Garde, but now run on two and a half years. [*Ent. Book 18, p. 166.*]

May 26. Reference to the Lord High Chancellor and the Attorney General on the petition of Lord Langdale, for determination about the change of the rectory of Holme, the college [St. John's, Cambridge] having accepted His Majesty's gracious offer. [*Ent. Book 18, p. 167.*]

VOL. CXXII.

1665.

May 26. Reference to the Commissioners of Prizes on the petition of Fras. Sandford, for a certain quantity of prize paper towards printing his collection of monuments. [*Ent. Book* 18, p. 168.]

May 26. Memorandum that John Knowles was committed to the Gatehouse for treasonable practices. Minute. [*Ent. Book* 22, p. 148.]

May 26. Warrant to Lord Ashley, treasurer for prizes, to pay to Arthur Earl of Anglesey 400*l.* out of prize money, for secret services, without account. [*Ent. Book* 22, p. 148.]

May 26. Warrant for a grant to Viel Vyvyan, in reversion after Sir Rich. Vivyan, Bart., his father, of the office of Captain of the Castle of St. Mawes, Cornwall. [*Ent. Book* 22, p. 148.]

May 26. Leeds. 50. John Bettam to Robt. Lye. The party are high in their expectations from the Dutch, and say the death of the 21 men at York does not discourage them from carrying on the work of God. A man much in their favour will become an intelligencer if he may not be made a witness, and may have 10*l.* in hand and a salary. Asks whether to engage him.

May 26. Whitehall. 51. Petition of Sir Thos. Strickland to the King, for the farm for 21 years of a halfpenny per gallon tax imposed by the present Parliament on Scottish salt, at the same rent which he now pays for it, as sub-farmer to the Farmers of Customs. The tax was chiefly promoted by him; it has encouraged English manufactures, and brought in a yearly revenue of 1,600*l.* With reference thereon to the Lord Treasurer to consider how the grant can be arranged, on expiration of the present farm of the customs; and his report, June 12, that the farmers do not object to the grant, but that he is no friend to minute farms [of customs].

May 26. Entry of the preceding reference. [*Ent. Book* 18, p. 106.]

May 26. Whitehall. 52. Petition of Sarah, relict of Capt. Willm. Pestle, to the King, for relief. Her husband was killed at the taking of the forts in the Isles of Cape Verd, in Major Holmes' late voyage to the coast of Guinea. With request thereon to the Navy Commissioners for an order to the Navy Treasurer to pay her 50*l.*, and make provision for her future subsistence.

May 26. Entry of the above reference. [*Ent. Book* 18, p. 168.]

May 26. Whitehall. 53. Petition of Oliver Cave and two others to the King, for pardon, because when in the company of Phineas and Thos. Hodgson, the said men stole 25*l.* from some country people, on the Borough bridge road, co. York. With reference thereon to the Attorney General.

May 26. Whitehall. 54. Petition of Capt. John Strode, lieutenant of Dover Castle, to the King, for as much as shall seem meet of the benefit of three Dutch prizes, the City of Rouen, laden with spices and calicoes, the Jacob, bound for Guinea, and the Golden Sun, laden with linseed, which are condemned in the Admiralty Court; they were got in at

VOL. CXXII.

1663.

his charge, he having fitted out two vessels from Dover for such services; had to give 20*l.* to the widow of one of the masters who was drowned in boarding. With reference thereon to the Commissioners for Prizes.

May 26. Entry of the above reference. [*Ent. Book* 18, *p.* 168.]

May 26. Note of the King's approbation of Roger Clavell and John Lawrence as Deputy Lieutenants of the Isle of Purbeck. Minute. [*Ent. Book* 20, *p.* 62.]

May 26. Grant to James Hyde, M.D., on surrender of Sir Thos. Clayton, of the office of Reader of Physic at Oxford; fee, 40*l.* a year. [*Docquet.*]

May 27. Grant to Anne Hume of all debts belonging to the King, by the forfeiture of John Gaisely, chandler, executed for murder in 1659. [*Docquet.*]

May 27. Warrant for conveying the Earl of Rochester prisoner to the Tower for high misdemeanors. Minute. [*Ent. Book* 22, *p.* 152.]

May 27. Warrant to Sir John Robinson to receive the Earl of Rochester prisoner. Minute. [*Ent. Book* 22, *p.* 152.]

May 27. Warrant requiring assistance in the search after divers armed men who aided the Earl of Rochester in taking by force of arms Mrs. Eliz. Mallet, without her consent, and carrying her from the city into the country; also aid for Sir John Warre in searching for the said Mrs. Mallet and restoring her to her friends. [*Ent. Book* 22, *p.* 153.]

May ? 55. Petition of the Earl of Rochester to the King, for restoration to favour; inadvertence, ignorance of law, and passion were the occasions of his offence; would rather have chosen ten thousand deaths than incurred His Majesty's displeasure.

May 27. Chatham. 56. Edw. Gregory to the Navy Comrs. Sends tickets for several shipwrights and calkers discharged by order of Comr. Pett, to be sent to Deptford. Has paid them conduct money. [*Adm. Paper.*]

May 27. Newcastle. 57. Capt. J. Lightfoot to the Navy Comrs. Will victual the Speedwell at as easy a rate as possible; sends a bill of exchange for 80*l.*, payable to Sir Wm. Batten. [*Adm. Paper.*]

May 27. 58. Sir Wm. Coventry to Sam. Pepys. As to the reputed embezzlement by Capt. Moulton, if any of the goods were between decks, they were prize to the seamen, and if in the great cabin, to the commander. Will endeavour to get Col. Middleton's business settled. The Bonadventure brings news that the Hamburg convoy and all the merchant ships are taken; it is a great loss. The fleet sails to Southwold Bay to-morrow. Money is much wanted for the slopsellers. The purser of the Loyal George does not appear; has put

VOL. CXXII.

1665.

another in his place. It is impossible to keep men on board when ships come in to clean; this might be obviated by having scrubbers or brushes made 16 or 18 inches long, of brass wire, a dozen or more to each ship, so that in calm weather the commanders could make their men put them upon long poles, and scrub to the very keel. Asks who is to bear the leakage of beer likely to take place, most of the casks being wood bound. Complains of the delay in victualling; but for that, Evertsen had not got into the Texel, nor the Hamburg convoy been lost. Wants some Laws of War to paste up in the ships. [*Adm. Paper, 4 pages.*]

May 27. Woolwich. 59. Capt. Wm. Dale to the Navy Comrs. Has received only 17 pressed men out of the 80 ordered from Capt. Taswell. Is hindered by weather from getting the guns on board. [*Adm. Paper.*]

May 27. Dover. 60. Thos. White to the Navy Comrs. Hears no news of the expected ship with provisions and stores. Requests payment of his accounts. [*Adm. Paper.*]

May 27. Coxpit. 61. Duke of Albemarle to the Navy Comrs. Desires that the water ships and victuallers be hastened away. [*Adm. Paper.*]

May 27. Harwich. 62. Sir Wm. Batten to the Navy Comrs. Is ordered not to leave Harwich while the fleet stays; three Gottenburg ships are come in. The Augustine must be hastened down with cables, and then remain as a store ship. Masts and broom much wanted. Capt. Nixon is condemned to be shot to death. [*Adm. Paper.*]

May 27. Bristol. 63. Sir Humph. Hooke, Sir Robt. Yeamans, and John Knight to Sir Wm. Batten. Received an imprest warrant for 400 men to be sent to London; little progress is made therein, no ships having arrived since the warrant came. Complain of Sir John Knight giving the men their conduct money, after they have received their imprest money. Went aboard all the vessels in Slangroad pill, Kingroad, &c.; find that the Mayor has given protection to 12 men upon the Providence of Glasgow. [*Adm. Paper.*] *Enclose*,

63. I. *Warrant of protection by John Lawford, mayor of Bristol, to 12 men on board the Providence of Glasgow, now in port. April 23, 1665. Endorsed with a note by Sir Robt. Yeamans to his father, promising to leave no means unattempted to serve the King, if no interruption be given to their employment.*

63. II. *List of 29 impressed seamen who have received their tickets and conduct money, and of 20 more who are impressed, but have not appeared.*

May 27. New Forest. 64. Thos. Eastwood to the Navy Comrs. Particulars of 1,400 loads of timber felled; desires an imprest of 200*l.* for land carriage. [*Adm. Paper.*]

VOL. CXXII.

1665.

May 27. Portsmouth. 65. Account of 69 anchors in store; with note [by Comr. Middleton,] that many of them are unservicable, and cannot be mended unless sent to London. [*Adm. Paper.*]

May 27. 66. Thos. Lewis to Thos. Haytor. Begs that the enclosed account may be presented to Mr. Pepys, to determine whether three vessels, hired by the ton as victualling ships, shall now be taken up by the month. Will get water-casks for one of the ships in the river. Wishes Mr. Pepys to be reminded of the certificate for the defective provisions put on shore at Tangiers. [*Adm. Paper.*] *Encloses.*

66. I. *Account by Thos. Lewis of eight hired victualling ships, four of which are returned from the fleet and relading, and three more returned with empty casks; more shipping is wanted to carry the remaining supply of beer.* *May 27, 1665.*

May 27. Cockpit. 67. Duke of Albemarle to the Navy Comrs. Capt. Perriman, of the Swallow, is to be "laid by the heels" for disobeying orders in refusing to release Thomas Gibbs and Henry Kitchin, impressed out of the Hope, contrary to proclamation. [*Adm. Paper.*] *Encloses,*

67. I. *Capt. John Perriman, commander of the Swallow, to the Duke of Albemarle. Answers the complaint made against him of impressing two men out of the Hope; Thos. Gibbs and Henry Kitchin were impressed by his mate between Gravesend and London; they had liberty the next day to go for their wages, when their master enticed them to decline the King's service; they were afterwards found ashore and pressed by Capt. Jas. Coleman of the Hound; they escaped from him, and came again on board the Swallow. With note, May 29, that the Duke consented to their remaining on board the Swallow.* *May 27, 1665.*

May 27. Redriff. 68. Capt. J. Perriman to Sam. Pepys. The two men pressed should be put on board the Hound, but they fear Capt. Coleman, and are willing to remain in the Swallow. Wishes the King knew of all the abuses offered to those that have orders to press; coal traders should be compelled not to exceed 3*l.* a voyage for each man; and west and north vessels should be bound to bring their coals to London, or many seamen will be drawn from the service. [*Adm. Paper.*]

May 28. 69. Jacob Blackleech to [the Navy Comrs.]. The water-ship Sarah and Elizabeth is returned from the fleet; 30 tons of new cask are sent on board the Swallow. [*Adm. Paper.*]

May 28. 70. Col. Reynes to Sam. Pepys. The convoys appointed for them are so clogged up with other orders as to be unable to perform what is desired. The captain of the Coventry refuses to call for ships which have waited a month in Portland Road, or to conduct any to Chatham when he returns, and yet is called a

Vol. CXXII.

1665.

convoy; begs that the name may be altered, or new orders given with all expedition; goods to the value of 10,000*l.* are ready at St. Malo. The report of a breach with France frightens the merchants, lest these goods should be seized. Begs an order for some vessel to make a trip over at once. [2 *pages.*]

May 28. Portsmouth. 71. Constance Pley to Sam. Pepys. Urges the necessity of hastening the St. Malo convoy; is troubled to think that so many goods lie waiting for transportation, and the Coventry, designed for a convoy, should remain there all this while. Begs an order to the captain to sail immediately, and call at Weymouth for the vessels waiting his conduct. *Encloses,*

> 71. i. [*George Pley, jun.*,] *to his mother, Constance Pley. Has* 10,000 *lbs. of hemp and other goods ready packed and marked, waiting only a convoy to set sail. Has drawn two bills of exchange. Private affairs. St. Malo, May* 23, 1665.

May 28. Royal Charles. 72. Sir Wm. Coventry to Williamson. The civilians must be consulted whether the alteration in letters of marque is to be done by new instructions or under the great seal, and if the Admiralty Court will not grant blank commissions, he must get as many drawn and engrossed as Lord Arlington thinks fit, there being neither time nor hands to do it in the fleet. Capt. Nixon's execution was prevented first by the storm, now by its being Sunday, and tomorrow will be the King's birthday. The Duke of Monmouth has arrived. Repines that they cannot sail after this storm, which may have scattered or damaged the Dutch.

May 28. Deal. 73. Jo. Carlisle to Williamson. The coast is clear; two supposed prizes are brought in. The Holland fleet is said to have gone northward, to meet De Ruyter, leaving 17 sail to guard their coasts.

May 29. Rotterdam. 74. W—— to ——. Is authorized to correspond with him. Mr. Oates came lately from England, and met Mr. Wiltshire secretly. Their friends in the west are in the best disposition, but do not think this a fitting time to make an offer to the [Holland] senate, or to make a gathering; first, because some of those at the helm, being in correspondence with Mr. Turner, might take advantage of what they offer, in order to advance the peace, which they earnestly seek underhand, notwithstanding their outward confidence; many of the [Holland] senate are in the Zauny interest, and wish their own fleet beaten; second, because the result of the French mediation and of an encounter between the two fleets must be waited for. It is said that the French and English Kings are combining to exterminate the Calvinist religion. C. B. is not in the least suspected of intelligence with the Court; he is of a great spirit and very ambitious, and a Dutchified Presbyterian, so that it is better to avoid intercourse with him. C. Sy. is very precipitate. Zealand and some other provinces, which are for the Prince of Orange's interest, speak of breaking off from Holland, and expect that the King, the Prince's uncle, will grant them all kinds of freedom of commerce with his dominions. [2 *pages.*]

Vol. CXXII.

1665.

May 29. King's Birthday. Royal Charles. 75. Earl of Falmouth to Lord Arlington. They sail to-morrow for Sole Bay, Sir George Downing's letter making them wish to be in deeper water. Hopes to meet the Dutch half seas over. Great skill will be necessary to get men. The decay by sickness and colliers is greater than could be imagined. Hopes soon to be the bringer of good news.

May 29. Royal Charles. 76. Sir Wm. Coventry to Lord Arlington. Capt. Langhorne has arrived with seven ships, and reports the taking of the Hamburg fleet, with the man-of-war their convoy; mistaking the Dutch fleet for the English, they fell into it. Will sail to-morrow for Southwold Bay, and there finish taking in victuals.

May 29. Chatham Dock. 77. Phineas Pett to the Navy Comrs. Forwardness of the Victory. Timber wanted; a considerable quantity can be supplied by Robt. Morecock of Chatham. [*Adm. Paper.*]

May 29. Chatham. 78. Edw. Gregory to the Navy Comrs. Denied the storekeeper a messenger to carry up a single letter, in virtue of the enclosed warrant, but did not refuse him labourers for shipping provisions; as to pre-eminency of signing, urges the undisputed custom of the yard, and the superiority of the office of clerk of the cheque, as shown by his being named first in all warrants, &c., his salary being higher than that of storekeeper, &c. [1¼ *pages.*] *Encloses*,

78. I. *Warrant from the Navy Comrs. to the Officers of the Yard at Chatham, to discontinue the employment of labourers for the carriage of letters, unless in cases of necessity.* [*Copy.*] *Navy Office, August* 21, 1662.

May 29. The Satisfaction, off Scarborough. 79. Capt. Edw. Grove to the Navy Comrs. Sailed for Flecckery and Mardow in Norway, with four other vessels, to seize or destroy the enemy's ships coming out of the Sound, or failing this, to go for Elsinore; received there from Sir Gilbert Talbot, Envoy Extraordinary to the King of Denmark, 8 convoys,—one a galliot hoy laden with shot and 36 pieces of brass and copper ordnance, as a present for the King. Has made all haste to return to the Gunfleet, notwithstanding bad weather. Saw no enemy. Asks where to find the fleet if already sailed. [*Adm. Paper.*]

May 29. Cockpit. 80. Sir Wm. Clarke to Sam. Pepys. Sends tickets for John Robinson, late surgeon of the Phœnix. Desires payment and some allowance for the loss of his chest. [*Adm. Paper.*]

May 29. 81. J. Uthwat to Thomas Hayter. Recommends John Hunt as master of the Black Dog galliot hoy in Deptford dry dock. [*Adm. Paper.*]

May 30. Harwich. 82. James Locke to the Navy Comrs. Desires a bill of imprest for present necessities on board the Bachelor ketch, hired for three months certain, and now to be continued. [*Adm. Paper.*]

Vol. CXXII.

1665.

May 30. Plymouth. 83. John Lanyon to the Navy Comrs. The damage sustained by the Sorlings in her late skirmish is repaired. Masts cannot be bought for money. The Mary is dispatched. The Giles ketch bound for Tangiers is in for repairs and victualling. Proposes the Monk as a watering boat for the port, until another be built. The eight tons of hearth pitch lying in the Prize Office would be useful. [*Adm. Paper.*]

May 30. Chatham. 84. Philip Barrow to the Navy Comrs. Justifies his own conduct in the late dispute with the clerk of the cheque; the signing above him will appear no offence by the enclosed reasons, once debated before the Board. Did not charge the clerk of the cheque with denying labourers to carry provisions on board some vessels; the obstruction met with was from the boatswain and his foreman. *Encloses,*

84. i. *Statement by Phil. Barrow of the grounds on which the storekeeper claims precedence in signing above the clerk of the cheque.* [*Four pages.*]

May 30. Cockpit. 85. Duke of Albemarle to the Navy Comrs. Desires that some of the prize ships which are to be appointed as provision ships may be for Harwich. The Truelove is to be victualled at Newcastle. [*Adm. Paper.*]

May 30. Harwich. 86. Sir Wm. Batten to the Navy Comrs. The victualling ships have arrived, after much loss from ill weather; of all the new boats sent, only four are brought in. Pinnaces, anchors, bowsprits, and masts are much wanted. The fleet is about to sail for Sole Bay. Lock's ketch, arrived from the Hamburg River, passed through the Dutch fleet off the Texel, and was chased by 15 of them. Carpenters and calkers wanted. Urges the immediate dispatch of stores, as the whole fleet depends upon Harwich. [*Adm. Paper, 2 pages.*]

May 30. Royal Charles. 87. Sir Wm. Coventry and Sir Wm. Penn to the Navy Comrs. Are under sail for the northward. Provisions wanted, especially beer; anticipate a battle with the Dutch; desire a sufficient supply of masts, yards, boats, &c., to be hastened to Harwich in case of need. [*Adm. Paper.*]

May 30. Portsmouth. 88. Hugh Salisbury to Sam. Pepys. Will hasten to London immediately upon notice of Sir Wm. Batten's arrival. [*Adm. Paper.*]

May 30. Woolwich. 89. Wm. Acworth to Sam. Pepys. Has taken the 80 cradles out of the Loyal Katherine; the 300 soldiers ordered for that ship refused at Greenwich to come on board until their arrears, amounting to 23s. 4d. a man, were paid; the arrears were promised at Woolwich, but only 120 came on board; many are gone away. [*Adm. Paper.*]

May 30. Victualling Office. 90. Certificate by Andrew Boult and John Milton of the neglect of three coopers named, pressed for service at the Victualling Office, in wilfully absenting themselves 10 or 14 days, and request for their punishment. [*Adm. Paper.*]

Vol. CXXII.

1665.

May 30. 91. Jacob Blackleech to [the Navy Comrs.] Account of water put on board three water ships. [*Adm. Paper.*]

May 30? 92. Petition of Thos. Old, of Deptford, mariner, to the Navy Comrs., to be admitted as master of one of the Flemish hoys now fitting out at Deptford; has served in a small vessel of his own ever since the King came to England. [*Adm. Paper.*] *Annexing*,

92. i. *Certificate by Capt. Wm. Badiley, and three others, of the fitness of Thos. Old to take charge of one of the galliot hoys.* May 25, 1665.

May 30. Warrant to Thomas Chiffinch to retain in his hands 250*l.* from moneys paid on composition by persons charged with goods, furniture, &c., of the late King, in reward for his zeal and industry in recovering the same. [*Ent. Book* 22, *p.* 182.]

May 30. Warrant to Thos. Chiffinch to pay to Colonel William Hawley and Thomas Beauchamp, his fellow commissioners, 250*l.*, for like services. [*Ent. Book* 22, *p.* 182.]

May 31. Royal Charles, Gunfleet. 93. Sir W. Coventry to Lord Arlington. The Dutch fleet will see their Hamburg prizes safe into the Texel and will then return to meet the English fleet. Delay of provisions is the mother of many mischiefs, and has lost the Hamburg ships, for if the fleet had been well victualled, it would have been at sea, and must have been beaten before the other could be taken, though that might have been safe, had it come within the 10 days prescribed. Thinks the King's ships are superior, a third rate being able to compare with Opdam's own ship, of whose guns they boast much, being 24 or 36 pounders. Comparison of the reported ordnance on the Dutch ships with that of the English, in favour of the latter. Sir George Downing's caution is observed, and no commander, with one exception, has any interest in his ship, nor have the owners even chosen the masters; thinks well of the commanders; there are only eight or ten of the good old commanders left on shore, and they either declined service or were unfit to be invited. The supply of ammunition is very complete; reasons why he thinks the suspicions of embezzlement of powder false. The Dutch packet boat brings no letters from Sir George Downing nor intelligence. Asks whither in this case it should still be allowed to come to Harwich, which—as being the place where stores are kept, preparations made, and whither the fleet must resort on its return,—is the most unfit for an enemy to be at; Woolwich or Chatham would be better, and Sir George Downing should be told to send his packets another way. It is resolved not to leave any ships behind for want of men, so those worst manned can ply the guns on one side. The Maryland Merchant, being defective, is left. [6 *pages.*]

May 31. Whitehall. 94. The King to the Earl of Bridgewater, lord lieutenant of Buckinghamshire. Has given directions that out of the militia money now raising for the third year, shall be paid the militia ex-

1665. Vol. CXXII.

penses and those for under officers, trophies, and 14 days' duty; the arrears of the two former years' tax are to be kept in a safe place. Thinks that in these distracted times, the Tower of London is the safest place, and requests him to send the money thither. [*Draft, signed.*]

May 31. Commission for James Howard to be Ensign to Col. Atkins, in Col. Russell's regiment. Minute. [*Ent. Book* 20, *p.* 62.]

May 31. Commission to Robt. Sydney to be Colonel of a regiment of foot. [*Ent. Book* 20, *p.* 63.]

May 31. Pass for Sir Thomas Higgons to go to France and return. Minute. [*Ent. Book* 22, *p.* 154.]

May ? 95. Petition of Thos. Ross to the King, for permission to nominate Rich. Pearson, now his deputy, as his successor in the place of Keeper of His Majesty's library, to which he was appointed 22nd Aug. 1661; is now at service in the fleet, and uncertain of subsistence for his family if he should die.

May 31. Whitehall. 96. Warrant for a grant to Rich. Pearson, in reversion after Thos. Ross, of the office of Keeper of the King's libraries; salary 200*l.* a year.

May 31. Entry of the above. [*Ent. Book* 22, *p.* 154.]

May 31. Order for a warrant for erection and incorporation of a Scottish hospital in Westminster, to be under 41 Scots as governors, with licence to purchase in mortmain lands not exceeding 500*l.* a year. [*Ent. Book* 22, *p.* 155.]

May 31. Pass for a vessel called the St. Pierre of Bayonne, employed by merchants of that place, to go to France and return. Minute. [*Ent. Book* 22, *p.* 157.]

May 31. Pass for George Porter, employed by the Queen-Mother, to go to France. Minute. [*Ent. Book* 22, *p.* 157.]

May 31. Privy seal for 200*l.* to George Porter, gentleman of the privy chamber to the Queen Consort, for his expenses on his journey to France. Minute. [*Ent. Book* 22, *p.* 157.]

May 31. Pass for the St. Peter of St. Malo, belonging to French merchants, to go to Dantzic and Riga, without touching at any port within the United Provinces. [*Ent. Book* 22, *p.* 158.]

May 31. Warrant to pay to Sir Edw. Turner, Attorney General to the Duke of York, 2,000*l.*, as the King's free gift. [*Docquet.*]

May 31. Warrant to pay to Sir Willm. Boreman, keeper of the dwarf orchard at Greenwich, 589*l.* 17*s.* 8*d.*, for keeping Greenwich Park, with 16 coppices and the orchard, for three years past, and building the garden house, and to allow him 148*l.* yearly, for paying gardeners and other services. [*Docquet.*]

Vol. CXXII.

1665.
May 31. Warrant to allow on the account of Farmers of Customs all moneys which have been or may be remitted for five years, from Feb. 18, 1664, on imposts of the growth and production of Jamaica. [*Docquet.*]

May 31. Grant to Thos. Offley, gentleman of the privy chamber, of the office of Groom-porter, in place of Sir Rich. Hubart, deceased. [*Docquet.*]

May 31. Warrant to pay to Stephen Fox 3,000*l.*, for secret service, without account. [*Docquet.*]

May 31. Warrant for delivery of 30 tuns of wine, half French and half Spanish, custom free, to the Count de Molina, ambassador extraordinary from the King of Spain, and for defalcation to be made for the same to the Farmers of Customs. [*Docquet.*]

May 31. Grant to Edw. Halsall of 225*l.*, the King's moiety of 450*l.*, forfeited by Connistant Cant, of Lynn Regis, for embarking wool to Guernsey, not entered in the Custom House, with power to compound and sue for the same. [*Docquet.*]

May 31. Warrant to pay to George Arnott 525*l.*, being fines and sums due from George Ward and others to the Receiver of the duchy of Cornwall, with power to recover the same, and to receive them from the Exchequer, in case they have been paid in. [*Docquet.*]

May 31. Dover. 97. Thos. White to the Navy Comrs. The Augustine is arrived from Chatham with stores. [*Adm. Paper.*]

May 31. Gravesend. 98. Fr. Hosier to Sam. Pepys. Found such disorder on board the Loyal Katherine that there was great difficulty in mustering the seamen; many of the men were too drunk to appear, and the master absent on shore; begs excuse if anything be wanting in the muster-book. The serjeants for Gravesend soldiers have carried money down to pay the men their arrears. Asks if it be necessary to muster victuallers or ammunition ships. Cannot be sure of letting none pass Gravesend without muster, as they may pass in the night, on Sunday, or in a gale of wind. [*Adm. Paper.*]

May 31. Gravesend. 99. Note of the arrival into port of the Merlin with 81 men, and the Cygnet with 46 men, giving good attendance on board. [*Adm. Paper.*]

May 31. Chatham. 100. Comr. Peter Pett to Sam. Pepys. Complains of the master of the Black Cock going away to London and losing the opportunity of a fair wind to sail to Blackwall, after being furnished with men on purpose; begs that Sir Wm. Warren may be informed of his neglect. [*Adm. Paper.*]

May 31. Shipwrights' Hall. 101. Masters, Wardens, &c., of the Shipwrights' Company to the Navy Comrs. Have received the copy of contract made with Wm. Castall and Hen. Johnson, for building two ships, and nominate the master, two wardens, and three assistants, to overlook the work. [*Adm. Paper, 12 signatures.*]

Vol. CXXII.

1665.

May 31. 102. Geo. Phenney, owner of the William and John, to [the Navy Comrs.] Recommends Geo. Wescott and John Clarke as boatswain and carpenter. [*Adm. Paper.*]

May 31. Newstead. 103. John Russell to the Navy Comrs. Finds Lord Byron's timber in Newstead Woods good and fit for the service. Arrangements for transporting it to London; boys wanted. [*Adm. Paper.*] *Encloses,*

103. I. *Proposal by Lord Byron for the delivery of 2,000 loads of timber at certain prices.*

May? 104. Petition of John Burrowes, Navy slopseller, to the Navy Comrs., to be indemnified for the loss of clothes, value 512*l.* 3*s.* 7*d.*, in the wreck of the Hopewell. They were delivered to Mr. Tooker according to directions from the Board, and shipped on his responsibility, the petitioner refusing to be answerable for any hazard. [*Adm. Paper.*] *Annexing,*

104. I. *Affidavit of Luke Noon, servant to John Burrowes, that at the special importunity of Mr. Tooker, messenger of the Navy Commissioners, clothes, shoes, and bedding, to the value of 512l. 3s. 7d., were delivered on board the Hopewell, going with provisions for the fleet, 2d May, 1665.*
May 30, 1665.

104. II. *Deposition by Alexander Harwood, one of the company of the Hopewell of Lynn, that the said vessel, employed as a victualler, and lost through damages sustained by ill-usage from the master of the Resolution, had on board at the time of her sinking the packs of clothes, shoes, &c., sent by John Burrowes.*

104. III. *Certificate by Richard Beckford, that in the late Dutch wars he received 25l. for 47l. worth of clothes lost in the Mary Rose.* *May* 31, 1665.

May. 105. Petition of John Burrowes to the Navy Comrs., to the same effect, urging payment in consideration of losses of more than 1,000*l.* in several other ships.

May? 106. Petition of Sir John Lowther, Bart., to the King. By the cunning practice of some Commissioners for enquiring after derelict lands, his salt houses and staythes at Whitehaven were said to be within high-water mark, and his petition thereon for a grant of the premises for corroboration of title was referred to the Lord Treasurer and Lord Ashley; begs that no other grant of the premises may pass till their report be made.

May? 107. Petition of the Company of Skinners, London, to the King and Council, for a hearing of the dispute between them and the feltmakers, who have entered a caveat against the solicited confirmation of their charters, on the ground that the cutting and clipping of skins and furs belongs to them. [*See June* 23, *infra.*]

VOL. CXXII.

1665.
May.
Whitehall.

108. Pass for the St. Nicholas, laden with oils, &c., at St. Malo, to go to Holland and Gottenburg and return, on certificate that she belongs solely to merchants of France. [*Draft*, 1½ *pages*.]

May.

109. Memoranda [by Williamson, from the Signet books], of warrants, grants, &c., passed during the month, the uncalendared entries of which are:—

Note that moneys paid out or assigned on the revenues of the duchy of Cornwall are to be allowed by the auditor of the duchy, on the receiver's accounts.

Order for the money for the Royal aid to be brought up in specie in carts well guarded, to be hired by Sir Hen. Vernon, Sir Wm. Doyley, and Robt. Scawen, with power to allow fitting salaries therefor.

May?

110. Warrant to issue from the Tower stores 30 barrels of powder, 2 hogsheads of flints, and other arms, formerly directed for the Admiral's regiment, to be delivered to Sir Chas. Littleton, Major. [*Draft*.]

May?

111. The King to Katherine Lady Mohun, Boconnock, Cornwall. Wishes her speedily to give up to her son, Lord Mohun, the deeds and writings touching his estate, which she detains in spite of a decree of Chancery. He is going to sea with the Duke of York, and wishes to settle his estate before he goes. [*Draft*.]

May.

112. Henry Planchy to Lord [Arlington]. Throws himself on the compassion of a peer, one of the chief ornaments of the age. Has never been a villain, but has led an ill life, and put some little slurs on merchants or women to supply his wants, but so cleverly that the law could not take hold of him; yet sees men worse than himself preferred. Begs for some livelihood, without which he will be obliged to return to his former life. [*Partly in Spanish*; 3 *pages*.]

May.

113. C. Bowerman to the Navy Comrs. After sending down ballast, according to order, to the St. Paul and Marmaduke, finds them already ballasted by Smyth the boatswain. Complains that by this practice he not only loses the benefit of that for which so great a rent is paid, but is liable to pay considerable sums for the lighters and hoys employed. Begs redress, and that Smyth may be compelled to make good his losses. [*Adm. Paper*.] *Encloses*,

113. I. *John Lewes' account for ballast; total*, 15 *tons* 3 *qrs*. 9 *lbs*.

May.

114. Ellis Osborne, master of the Sarah and Elizabeth, [to the Navy Comrs.] Recommends Robt. Johns as his boatswain. [*Adm. Paper*.]

May.

115. Fr. Barham, Mr. Johnson's partner, to [the Navy Comrs.] Requests an order to keep some shipwrights employed on the new ship building in the East India yard; also a warrant to press barges and hoys for the service. [*Adm. Paper*.]

Vol. CXXII.

1665.

May 1 116. Shorthand notes by Sam. Pepys, endorsed "Several papers relating to the masts bought of Mr. Wood." [*Adm. Paper.*] *Enclosing,*]

116. i. *Tender of deals, timber, cant spars, &c., by Caleb Veren* *February* 23, 1665.

116. ii. *Tender of* 40 *pieces of elm timber, at* 55*s. per load, by Edw. Buckley.* *February* 23, 1665.

116. iii. *Tender of* 80 *loads of dram timber, at* 55*s. per load, by Edmund Lee.* *February* 23, 1665.

116. iv. *Tender of deals, timber, and masts, by Mr. Wood and Mr. Graves.*

116. v. *Comparison of some of the above tenders.* *February* 23, 1665.

116. vi. *Survey and report of Edw. Gray's masts. May* 26, 1665.

116. vii. *Tender of masts, timber, and deals, by Caleb Veren and Robt. Walker.*

116 viii. *Account of masts tendered by Veren and Walker; with note by Robt. Mayors of their good condition.*

116. ix. *Account of old masts contracted for with Mr. Wood; with comparison of tenders made by Warren, Veren, and Gray, and abstract of the case by Pepys.*

May. 117. Names of three masters of lighters employed to transport timber out of Essex for building the Loyal London, and of 15 shipwrights engaged on the work, for whom protections are wanted. [*Adm. Paper.*]

May ? 118. Account of the dimensions of eight ships taken up for the service, from Jan. to April. [*Adm. Paper.*]

May. 119. Similar account by John Fortescue and Jonas Shish of the dimensions of 13 ships. [*Adm. Paper.*]

May ? 120. Reasons why a proclamation should be issued on the patent granted to Col. [Edw.] Gray, [Thos.] Killigrew, and others for licensing pedlars and petty chapmen; that otherwise no public notice would be taken of them; that the conveniences of licensing industrious and honest pedlars, and suppressing rogues will be many; as preventing the dispersion of Quakers' and other sectaries' books; stopping robberies and murders by rogues who wander on pretence of selling wares, and supply those who live remote from market towns; none are to be licensed without a certificate of good conduct from a justice of peace, and a recognizance for good behaviour. [*Patent granted May* 3, 1665.]

May. 121. Request by Lord Holles, ambassador extraordinary to France, for a privy seal for payment of 400*l.* expenses, due 29th April 1665, in addition to 800*l.* ordered him 27 June last.

VOL. CXXII.

1665.

May ? 122. Statement that Dr. Paul, Bishop of Oxford, being possessed of the rectory of Chinner, had, before his accession to the bishopric, obtained from the Archbishop [of Canterbury] a dispensation to retain it, confirmed by the King; the presentation to cures void by promotion belongs to the King, who, on the death of Dr. Paul, claims the right of presentation, which is denied by the patron.

May ? 123. Proposal of expedients for prevention of the plague, showing that the infection greatly spreads by the present attempts at concealment, and by not shutting up a house till some one in it dies, as many persons may have visited the house and spread the infection in the interim; but if it were published that every infected person shall have medical attendance, &c., and payment for loss of time, persons would not conceal their misfortune, and 40 houses thus provided might prevent the infection of 10,000. With proposal that a stock may be raised, physicians appointed, and commissioners accountable to the King bejoined with the physician for their management.

May ? 124. Petition of Sir Charles Berkeley, treasurer of the household, to the King, for the estate of John Somerset, of Wells, value 100*l.* a year, and forfeit to the Crown for want of a lawful heir.

VOL. CXXIII. JUNE 1–9, 1665.

1665.

June 1. Ribston. 1. W. Hawksworth to Sir Thos. Gower. Had Jos. Walley been taken, something material would have been discovered, as he is a great factor for the sectaries; the books and letters must be kept for the assizes; will send copies of them. R. Walker is fast in prison.

[June 1.] 2. Petition of poor Capt. Tom Man to the King, to sign a warrant for payment of his debts, as promised to the Duke of Buckingham in his behalf.

June 1. Reference of the above petition to the Lord Chancellor, His Majesty compassionating the petitioner, because of the unreasonable obstinacy and refractoriness of the creditors. [*Ent. Book* 18, *p.* 109.]

June 1. Warrant for a grant to Fras. Young, on surrender of Thos. Collins, of the office of one of the King's falconers; fee, 44*l.* a year. Minute. [*Ent. Book* 22, *p.* 154.]

[June 1.] 3. Grant of the above office to Fras. Young.

[June 1.] 4. Note that the Commissioners of Prizes being requested to furnish the Queen-Mother with the prize ship Orange Tree, lying at Rye, to carry over her horses, it was thought better for the ship to be given to the Queen and equipped at her expense, so that their lordships desire a warrant accordingly.

Vol. CXXIII.

1665.

June 1. Warrant to the Commissioners for Prizes to deliver the ship Orange Tree, now lying in the port of Rye, to persons appointed to receive it as a gift to the Queen-Mother. [*Ent. Book* 22, *p.* 155]

[June 1.] 5. Draft of the above.

June 1. Southwold Bay, 11 P.M. 6. Sir Wm. Coventry to Lord Arlington. A fleet, so numerous that it must be the Dutch, is discovered four or five leagues off; they are preparing to sail, and now want neither health nor victuals. Men are being taken from a great fleet of 150 colliers which has arrived. Hopes a glorious victory to-morrow.

June 1. 7. Petition of John Athey and three other Coopers to the Navy Comrs., for discharge from imprisonment, and leave to repair to their work, being pressed for the Victualling Office, Tower Hill; acknowledge their fault in neglect of punctual attendance by "incident of a too common frailty," but crave mercy and release for a first offence. With note of a warrant for their release. [*Adm. Paper.*]

June 1? 8. Petition of Mary Tuck to the Navy Comrs., for acceptance of bail for her husband, James Tuck, waterman, detained in custody for having ignorantly bought certain brass shives from the boatswain and carpenter of a Dutch prize, and sold them again, not knowing they were the King's goods. [*Adm. Paper.*]

June 1. 9. Jacob Blackleech to the Navy Comrs. Account of the water on board three water ships. [*Adm. Paper.*]

June 1. 10. Report by Capt. John Proud to the Navy Comrs. of the condition of the Loyal Subject and Baltimore, and of anchors, cables, &c., required. [*Adm. Paper,* 1½ *pages.*]

June 1. Wapping. 11. Sir Wm. Warren to the Navy Comrs. As the state of the fleet now is, expecting a fight with the Hollanders, cannot see how convoy is to be allowed for the vessels freighted to fetch masts from New England. From this day demurrage must begin; the western coast, since Capt. Nixon eschewed fighting, is too dangerous to venture without a convoy. [*Adm. Paper.*]

June 1. Deptford. 12. Jonas Shish to the Navy Comrs. Intends putting the 16 shipwrights from Chatham on the two hoys now in dry dock, to give them all possible dispatch. Has not yet received the large elm timber from Mr. Blackborow. [*Adm. Paper.*]

June 1. Harwich. 13. Sir Wm. Batten to the Navy Comrs. The Admiral Trump prize is most fit for a store ship; the fleet now rides in Sole Bay; has with much trouble got the Gottenburg ships and victuallers out of harbour; they are a company of cross-grained knaves. Is plagued with the seamen running away; has found 40 in the town and sent them to the fleet. Cordage and oars wanted. The Dutch fleet still lies off the Texel. Two ketches are dispatched

1665. Vol. CXXIII.

to London for ammunition and victuals, and as much water as they can carry. Three ships of wine and brandy are sent to the fleet. [*Adm. Paper*, 1½ *pages*.]

June 2. Yarmouth. 14. James Johnson to the Navy Comrs. Fears a disappointment in the cordage expected from Hamburg, as it is confidently reported that the fleet is taken by the Dutch. The sailmaker will work at London rates; the blockmaker demands more. [*Adm. Paper*.]

June 2. Victualling Office. 15. Thos. Lewis to the Navy Comrs. Requires shipping for conveying 200 tuns of beer to the fleet, more than the vessels now in the river can take in. [*Adm. Paper*.]

June 2. Plymouth. 16. John Lanyon to the Navy Comrs. Dispatch of the Sorlings and other vessels. Arrival of the Foresight from Tangiers. Masts wanted. Proposes the Mary of Amsterdam prize, as a convoy. [*Adm. Paper*.]

June 2. Lambeth House. 17. M. Smyth to Sir Wm. Coventry. Is commanded by the Archbishop of Canterbury to give notice of the appointment of Morgan Godwin, student of Christ Church, Oxford, and Bachelor of Arts, as Chaplain of the Baltimore. [*Adm. Paper*.]

June 2. Woolwich. 18. Chris. Pett to the Navy Comrs. Can make no progress with the new ships, for want of oaken plank and moulding timber. Entreats that Sir Wm. Warren and Mr. Castell may be quickened in sending in their timber from Guildford; begs leave to go into Essex for three days on business. [*Adm. Paper*.]

June 2. Cockpit. 19. Duke of Albemarle to the Navy Comrs. Desires prize ships to be appointed at Harwich for the keeping of victuals, Mr. Gauden complaining of want of room; asks what vessels are suitable for the purpose. The Fox is to be provided with stores and men. [*Adm. Paper*.]

June 2. Cockpit. 20. Duke of Albemarle to the Navy Comrs. A speedy engagement being expected with the Dutch, masts and all things needful for ships after a fight must be hastened to Harwich. [*Adm. Paper*.]

June 2. Harwich. 21. Sir Wm. Batten to the Navy Comrs. The Dutch fleet being descried off Sole Bay, the Duke of York, with great alacrity, weighed anchor and stood off to them; nothing can have hindered an engagement except calms. As many men as can be picked up are dispatched to the fleet. Begs that stores of all sorts, but especially masts and small rigging, may be hastened down. [*Adm. Paper*.]

June 2. Harwich. 22. Sir Wm. Batten to the King. A victualler just arrived left the fleet last night off Sole Bay, the Dutch fleet only four miles distant; great shots are heard like thunder at a distance. The Leopard is got out of harbour, and with a merchant ship sent to

Vol. CXXIII.

1665.

the fleet, and hopes to send another ship to-morrow, besides which the fleet consists of 95 vessels. The victual and ammunition ships are returned into harbour.

June 2. Royal Charles, off Southwold, 4 P.M.

23. Sir Wm. Coventry to Lord [Arlington]. On seeing the Dutch, who kept to windward, put to sail, and wrought during the ebb, but anchored during the flood. The Dutch have done much the same, but keeping the wind, are now three leagues distant. Had the Dutch been eager to attack they might have done so; they keep close and in good order, and seem 100 or 110 sail. The King's fleet is courageous and the sick men get upon their legs; extraordinary accidents have hindered Nixon's execution; viz., a storm detaining the orders; Sunday and the King's birthday intervening, and then the fleet in motion; these things have been much noticed, and the Duke is giving him leave to fight, to redeem his fault. Begs the Portsmouth ships may be hastened, but ordered to work warily when they leave the Downs, lest they fall in with the enemy; the colliers only escaped by the fleet being come out of the sands. Edw. Montague is violently sick, and is to be sent on shore. All are eager to engage, especially the volunteers, whose beds, cabins, and even tables are down, so that there is scarce means to eat or sleep till the business is over. Thinks the Crown too big a ship for Tangiers; a less would do as well. A large Dutch ship, supposed by some to be a flag ship, has blown up. With postscript of compliment from the Earl of Falmouth. [2 *pages*.]

June 2. Warrant for a grant to Thos. Lockey of the prebend in Christ Church, Oxford, void by death of Dr. Creed, with clause of revocation, in case of appointment of any other than Dr. Rich. Allestree, who is already a prebendary, to the Divinity professorship, to which that prebend is usually annexed. [*Ent. Book* 19, p. 46.]

June 2. Licence for Ch. Bayley to see R. Bayley in the Tower. Minute. [*Ent. Book* 22, p. 157.]

June 2. Pass for Madame De Fiennes, with eight horses, to France. Minute. [*Ent. Book* 22, p. 157.]

[June 2.] Pass for Mons. De l'Amignon, with ten horses, to France. Minute. [*Ent. Book* 22, p. 157.]

June 2. Pass for 10 horses for Madame De Fiennes to France, custom free. Minute. [*Ent. Book* 22, p. 158.]

[June 2.] Pass for Mons. De l'Amignon, with eight horses, free of custom. [*Ent. Book* 22, p. 158.]

June 2. Passport for the Clarity, belonging to Capt. Cascade, merchant of Cadiz, which has been to Amsterdam to recover goods injuriously detained by the Hollanders, to go to Cadiz. [*Ent. Book* 22, p. 158.]

VOL. CXXIII.

1665.

June 2. Whitehall. 24. Pass for the ship Santa Maria, built near Amsterdam, but belonging to the subjects of the King of Spain, to go to Ostend; to be in force for two months. [*Copy.*]

[June 2.] Entry of the above. [*Ent. Book* 22, *p.* 159.]

June 2. Whitehall. 25. Petition of Major Alexander Marchant *alias* De St. Michell, of near Baugé in Anjou, to the King, for the sole exercise of his invention of a mode of keeping water in ponds clean and sweet, and fit for horses to drink, though farriers and others falsely maintain that stinking water is good for horses; also of another invention of moulding ornamental bricks for buildings, instead of carving them. With reference thereon to the Attorney General, and his report in favour of the petition, provided the inventions are really new.

June 3. Doctors' Commons. 26. Dr. Jenkins to Williamson. Sends a supplement to the draft [about prize bonds], judging by the recognizances that the 3rd article is against breaking bulk, and the 4th limits the number of the King's subjects to be employed. Asks on what terms the King stands with the customers [farmers of customs] thereon. They, as well as the Commissioners of the Duke of York's tenths, are concerned to oppose the effecting of the King's pleasure therein.

June 3. Warrant to the Keeper of the Gatehouse to seize Joseph Welley. Minute. [*Ent. Book* 22, *p.* 160.]

June 3. Deal. 27. Ri. Watts to [Williamson]. The fleets have undoubtedly been engaged, broadsides having been heard without intermission. Thinks the fight was about seven leagues off the North Foreland. The Truelove has gone to join the fleet with 130 soldiers. Thinks the English are boarding the enemy, because there is no intermission.

June 3. 28. List of 22 Dutch prizes taken in the fight, with the number of guns on each, varying from 81 to 18.

June 3. 29. Similar list of prizes, giving notes of the ships by which they were severally taken.

June 3. [Harwich.] 30. Sir Wm. Batten to Sam. Pepys. Has sent news of the fleet to the King and Duke of Albemarle. The thundering of guns continues. Has written to Sir Wm. Doyley at Ipswich, to remove such sick men as may endure it, and make way for the wounded. Intends doing the same himself. Urgent need of small cordage, masts, and oars; 190 soldiers are sent by the Maryland to the fleet. [*Adm. Paper.*]

June 3. Dover. 31. Capt. Rich. Testo and Thos. White to the Navy Comrs. Cannot ship the small cordage, sails, &c., for Harwich before to-morrow. The cables must be sent afterwards.

June 3. Bristol. 32. Sir John Knight to the Navy Comrs. Complains of Sir Robert Cann, Sir Robert Yeamans, and John Knight having neg-

VOL. CXXIII.

1665.

lected to give accounts to the mayor of the number of men impressed, thereby encouraging dishonesty among the seamen in taking press and conduct money. The Duke of Albemarle has ordered all impressed men on board the George frigate, but that ship not being yet in port, knows not what to do to prevent their running away. Has imprisoned one runaway, Sam. Brown; sends a note found upon him. Has procured only nine seamen. [*Adm. Paper.*] *Encloses,*

32. I. *Certificate by Capt. John Andrews, commander of the Lizard, by order of Comr. Sir Wm. Pett [Penn?] of free leave granted to Sam. Brown, carpenter of the Lizard, to go to Bristol for necessary things belonging to him.* [*Copy.*] *Portsmouth, May 28,* 1665.

32. II. *List of nine seamen pressed and sent to London to appear before the Board.*

June 2. 33. Jacob Blackleech to the Navy Comrs. Account of water on board three water ships. [*Adm. Paper.*]

June 3. Rinsale. 34. Robt. Cookin to Sam. Pepys. Has made an inspection of several ships attending the coast; the stores are very bare. Many things are not to be had for money. Is troubled to see ships going about from place to place to borrow powder from the forts. Has supplied several barrels at 5*l.* per barrel. If the Commissioners have any account of repairs of ships in the harbour, they will see their loss in not buying the hulk. Will take no less than 100*l.* for her; she is worth that for breaking up. [*Adm. Paper, 2 pages.*]

June 4. 35. J. B., surgeon's mate on the Convertine, to Thos. Hollier. Mr. Hawkins being dead, has acted single handed during the late engagement with the enemy. It is the captain's pleasure to name him surgeon of the ship; requests a warrant and an able mate. Signed by Capt. John Pearse. [*Adm. Paper.*]

June 4. Dover. 36. Thos. White to the Navy Comrs. The Augustine is dispatched to Harwich with sails, cordage, &c. A victualler under her convoy also carries 13 of the biggest sails. [*Adm. Paper.*]

June 4. Royal Charles. 37. Sir Wm. Coventry and Sir Wm. Penn to the Navy Comrs. A good quantity of masts, yards, and all other stores must be sent immediately to the Downs. Engaged yesterday with the Dutch; they began to stand away at 3 p.m.; chased them all the rest of the day and all night; 20 considerable ships are destroyed and taken; we have only lost the Great Charity. The Earl of Marlborough, Rear-Admiral Sansum, and Capt. Kirby are slain, and Sir John Lawson wounded. [*Adm. Paper.*]

June 4. Chatham. 38. Comr. Peter Pett to Sam. Pepys. Has ordered seven masts from 22 to 28 hands, to be chosen out for Harwich; the last either of New England or Gottenburg that can be supplied of those

VOL. CXXIII.

1665.

dimensions. Mr. Shorter's ship will carry the provisions to Harwich with 20 hawsers for standing rigging. Five cables, of 17 inches, are closed to-day, by beginning at 3 or 4 a.m. [*Adm. Paper.*]

June 4. Chatham. 39. Comr. Peter Pett to Sam. Pepys. Eight of the 24 cables will be shipped to-morrow, 9 more on Monday, the rest on Saturday. Pinnaces, masts, and other provisions for Harwich will be ready shortly. Dares not send them without convoy. Requests orders. [*Adm. Paper.*]

June 4. Commission for Robt. Warden to be Lieutenant to the Duke of York's troop of Guards, whereof Louis De Duras, Marquis of Blanquefort, is captain. [*Ent. Book* 20, *p.* 71.]

June 4. Warrant empowering the Trustees of the Queen-Mother to grant to Lord Arlington the remainder of her lease of 99 years of the demesne lands in Holdenby, co. Northampton, and Havering, co. Essex. [*Ent. Book* 22, *pp.* 163-4.]

June 4. Before the Texel. 40. Duke of York to Lord Arlington. Hastens the bearer to inform the King that God has blessed his fleet with victory; refers to the bearer for particulars, and begs that all stores, especially ammunition, may be sent down. Poor Lord Falmouth is killed, as also Lords Marlborough, Portland, and Muskerry, and Mr. Boyle. One ship taken from the Dutch in the last war was lost the first pass; has taken 20 or 30 of theirs. [2 *pages.*]

June 4. Royal Charles. 41. Sir Wm. Coventry to [Lord Arlington]. Have pursued the victory to the Texel, as far as the draught of water and state of the ships permit. The victory has been very glorious, and the greatest defeat the Dutch ever received, yet it has cost many men and commanders; Lord Falmouth with Lord Muskerry and Mr. Boyle were killed at one shot. Dare not stand too near shore, because the rigging of many ships is too much damaged for them to get off, if the wind blows toward shore; also the enemy's fleet, being close to shore, may at any time go in to refit, and so be ready the first, as they have many ships in port ready fitted, and great merchantmen, and having plenty of money, can probably procure men by great wages. The fight lasted from break of day to dark, but more ships would have been taken had the day been longer; they got away in the night, and were close under their own shore before overtaken; Opdam's ship is blown up; Trump, Cortenaer, Stillengwerth, and Schram, their commanders, are said to be dead; Trump's vice-admiral's ship and six or seven more were burned, one after it had been taken, lest it should be recovered. The Charity is lost. The four Norway ships joined our fleet during the fight, and young Eversen, who was lately released, repaired to theirs with his father's ship and two more. Rear-Admiral Sansum, Capt. Kirby of the Breda, and Capt. Ableson of the Guinea are killed. Many Dutch commanders showed great courage, but the English did better, only some deserve punishment. Apologises for his imperfect relation, having had little sleep lately. Sir John Lawson is hurt in the knee, but it is hoped there is no danger.

VOL. CXXIII.

1665.

Prince Rupert and Lord Sandwich behaved eminently well, and Sir Wm. Penn so well that those who were most unsatisfied with him before are full of his commendations. The Duke is safe, though he was so near the noble persons killed by that fatal shot that his clothes were besmeared with their blood. When Sir John Lawson was hurt, his care for the service was such that he sent for another commander. The Duke sent Capt. Jordan, who did excellent service. [4 pages.]

June 4. Deal. 42. J[ohn] C[arlisle] to Williamson. An engagement with the Dutch began on Friday, 20 leagues east of the North Foreland, and a second on Saturday, which still continues, for the guns sound like broadsides. The report is that the Hollanders are worsted, and our fleet in pursuit.

June 4. Deal. 43. Ri. Watts to [Williamson]. There was a hot dispute past nine last night, for half an hour, when they sailed northward on a chase. The seamen think the Dutch were worsted and have made for their own coasts.

June 5. Yarmouth. 44. Rich. Burges to Williamson. The engagement was at break of day on Saturday. The Dutch fired the first gun; Prince Rupert's squadron gave the first attack with undaunted courage; the whole fleet engaged, and till 10 a.m. it was hard to say which had the better; then the Duke of York and Sir John Lawson bore down and sunk two Dutch ships; the Leopard ran into the thickest of the fight, and for an hour could not be seen for smoke; then nine Dutch ships ran away, Capt. Berkeley pursuing them with six; the rest made for the Texel, but our fleet forced them northward. Thirteen Dutch ships are said to be sunk, and one blown up. The bells are ringing and colours flying, which displeases some in the town who are friends to the Dutch, and have grown impudent through the negligence of the King's friends. One said the Duke of York deserted the engagement and went ashore disguised, and that he hoped the Dutch would beat, and then down would go the bishops.

June 5. 45. Morgan Lodge to Williamson. There are two of the King's ships, six merchant ships, and ten victuallers bound for Harwich in the Downs; guns have been heard, but no vessel has come from the fleet. News from London reports that 60 Dutch ships are sunk, burnt, and taken, and Opdam taken alive.

June 5? 46. Lord Arlington to the Lord Mayor of London. The King having been in expectation ever since the guns were heard on Saturday, wishes the account which he has just received of his fleet to be sent to the city, to avoid mis-reports. The Dutch, induced by the preceding foul weather and reports of our unreadiness, appeared on the coasts June 1st, just when the colliery fleet coming up, provided ours with their only lack,—that of men; which when the Dutch perceived, they stood off, being 110 sail and 10 fireships; on the 3rd, his Royal Highness having got to windward of them, the

Vol. CXXIII.

1665.

engagement began, their whole fleet passing and firing at every ship, and the fire returned, which was repeated several times, till, at 1 p.m., weary of fighting at a distance, we divided their fleet; Opdam's ship blew up; a pell-mell conflict ensued, when the Dutch fleet was driven into the Texel or Maes, 30 ships being burnt or taken, and Trump and many of their admirals and officers killed, with 8,000 seamen. On our side one ship was lost, and Lords Marlborough, Portland, Falmouth, and others killed, three by one shot close to the Duke of York, whom God has preserved to be the instrument of so signal a success. Two papers. [*Draft, 3½ pages.*]

June 5. Warrant to the Keeper of Newgate to discharge Jo. Francis Pollet and John Lewis, natives of Germany, on bond before the Recorder of London to go beyond seas. [*Ent. Book* 22, *p.* 160.]

June 5. Order for a warrant authorizing the Barons of the Exchequer to examine the accounts of Thomas Earl of Cleveland, relative to his mortgaged estates in the manors of Stepney and Hackney, and make a final order therein. He had a permission to redeem his mortgaged lands, if it could be done within seven years, but they have descended to Rich. Blackwell, a collector of prize goods during the usurpation, and are extended for debts due by him; but his debts to the Crown having been granted to the Earl of Crawford and others, they extend the lands, and thereby obstruct any settlement. [*Ent. Book* 22, *pp.* 161–2.]

June 5. The King to the Earl of Suffolk. The militia tax is now raising for the third year, and as the Tower of London is the safest place to keep it in these distracted times, wishes what is still unexpended of the first two years' tax to be sent thither, being delivered by the high sheriffs of each county to that of the adjoining county, till it arrives at the Tower, and so with the moneys levied for the third year. With note of 27 similar letters to counties and towns named. [*Ent. Book* 20, *pp.* 64-5.]

June 5. 47. Draft of the above letter as addressed to the Lord Lieutenants of Derbyshire, Staffordshire, and Shropshire. [*Imperfect.*]

June 5. Whitehall. The King to the Earl of Bridgewater. Similar letter, ordering him to send up the arrears of the first two years' militia tax within his lieutenancy to the Tower. [*Ent. Book* 20, *p.* 66.]

June 5. 48. Earl of Bridgewater to [Lord Arlington]. Was ordered by the King's letters of 31st December to put the [militia] money levied in Buckinghamshire for the first two years into a trunk, to be sent to the Governor of Windsor Castle; was ordered May 4th to raise the third year's assessment, and the former directions about the first two years' taxes were renewed; will have all ready about Midsummer; the King's letter of May 31st orders the payment of the first two years' money into the Tower, leaving the former directions to be proceeded in for the third year. Asks further directions thereon.

Vol. CXXIII.

1665.
June 5. London. Sir And. Riccard, governor of the Levant Company, to Morgan Read, consul at Leghorn. Capt. Rand sends a letter to Signor Milenet for release of the captive Turk, who is to be sent home to Smyrna. [*Levant Papers, Vol. V., p. 113.*]

June 5. Cockpit. 49. Sir Wm. Clarke to Sam. Pepys. Recommends Capt. Wm. Martin for command of the new ketch at Deptford. [*Adm. Paper.*]

June 5. Dover. 50. Thos. White to the Navy Comrs. Proposes the White Dove prize ship for carrying great masts to Harwich; dares not put more on board the Augustine, for fear of grounding her. Entreats that no ship above a fifth-rate be sent in until the harbour be mended. [*Adm. Paper.*]

June 5. Chatham. 51. Comr. Peter Pett to Sam. Pepys. Account of provisions shipped away to the fleet. Hopes Morecock's timber may be hastened in, also Mr. Shorter's, master [*Adm. Paper.*]

June 5. Harwich. 52. Sir Wm. Batten to the Navy Comrs. Arrival of a victualler from the fleet; masts and small stores received; cordage and great masts demanded with all possible speed. Death of Lieut. Minns of the Lion. [*Adm. Paper.*] *Encloses,*

52. I. *Information of Geo. Long, commander of the Friendship victualler. Left the fleet lying eight or nine leagues off the coast of Holland in good condition after the engagement. One ship damaged, the Duke and all commanders well. The fleet charged three times through the enemy; eight or nine Dutch vessels were burnt. When he left the guns were still firing.*

52. II. *Draft of the above, adding that Long found a flag and ensign floating, and brought them ashore.*
Harwich, June 5, 1665.

52. III. *Note of the flag and ensign, taken from the Dutch Admiral's ship, being sent to the King.*

June 5. 53. J. Uthwat to Sam. Pepys. Sends a list of useful sizes for laying the French yarn lately contracted for. [*Adm. Paper.*]

June 5. Whitehall. 54. John Birtby to Sam. Pepys. Has six letters ready written to the justices of various counties, for hastening the carriage of timber, but not knowing the general superscription, nor whether to apply them to some particular person, sends them with flying seals for inspection, to be directed as required. With note of their delivery, June 10th, to Mr. Langrack and Mr. Morehouse. [*Adm. Paper.*] *Encloses,*

54. I. *Form of superscription to Sir John Norton on sending warrants for the Justices of Hampshire.*

54. II. *Names of four Justices in Essex to be put in warrants for land carriage.*

Vol. CXXIII.

1665.

June 5. Deptford. 55. Thos. Cowley to Sam. Pepys. Sends the names of 35 shipwrights and 15 calkers picked out for Harwich; they clamoured for money before they left, but agreed to send up a messenger about it. The Chatham men await payment at Deptford. [*Adm. Paper.*] *Encloses,*

55. I. *List of the shipwrights and calkers sent to Harwich.* *June 6, 1665.*

June 5. 56. Capt. Geo. Cock to Sam. Pepys. Is ordered to provide 10 cases of old linen to be sent to Sir Wm. Doyley at Ipswich for the use of the wounded seamen. Asks how it is to be forwarded. [*Adm. Paper.*]

June 5. Deptford. 57. Thos. Harper to Sam. Pepys. Is dispatching a raft of masts and a small anchor to the fleet. The Indian Merchant will be laden next week with cables, small cordage, sails, &c.; 10,000 yards of Noyals canvas, half the stock in the store, is ready also to be sent, but can hardly be needful unless sailmakers are settled there. [*Adm. Paper, 2 pages.*]

June 5. Waltham Forest. 58. John Morehouse to Sam. Pepys. After much trouble, has obtained warrants from the justices of peace in Essex for the carriage of timber to Barking. [*Adm. Paper.*]

June 5. Victualling Office. 59. Certificate, by Thos. Lewis of the Sparrow pink taking in a lading of beer on the 7th of April last. [*Adm. Paper.*]

June 6. Portsmouth. 60. Account by Ben Johnson of 65,091 yards of Noyals canvas, delivered out of the stores, shipped on board the Golden Buss for London. [*Adm. Paper.*]

June 6. Portsmouth. 61. St. John Steventon to Sam. Pepys. Wants another bill of imprest, the 1,000*l.* last granted being more than expended. Sends account of money paid for board wages, broom, hemp, building, &c.; total, 1,072*l.* 17*s.* 3*d.*, and of money due to the masons, 432*l.* [*Adm. Paper.*]

June 6. Harwich. 62. Sir Wm. Batten to the Navy Commrs. Has received news from Yarmouth of 20 or 30 Dutch vessels destroyed, and the enemy chased to the northward of the Texel. Hopes to have a good account of their whole fleet. [*Adm. Paper.*]

June 6. 63. Sir Wm. Coventry to the Navy Commrs. Out of the 200 men expected to be taken from the merchant ships for the Sovereign, only 70 can be had. Desires expedition in procuring others as soon as possible. [*Adm. Paper.*]

June 6. Portsmouth. 64. Constance Pley to Sam. Pepys. Complains of the Captain of the Coventry for sailing away without carrying even a letter. It is feared that he will be stopped in France for his severe doings towards (not to say plundering of) the French ship he brought in with him. Earnestly begs convoy for her goods home by the next ship, that stops in there, lest they be seized for his doings. [*Adm. Paper.*]

VOL. CXXIII.

1665.

June 6. Golden Lion. 65. Capt. Wm. Dale to the Navy Comrs. Is ordered to sail. Waits for men, boatswain's stores, and a surgeon. [*Adm. Paper.*]

June 6. Plymouth. 66. John Lanyon to the Navy Comrs. Can find but 20 good and bad masts in the town. Will secure some of the best, lest they be taken up for the prize ships now repairing. Water boats shall be fitted. Pitch and rosin is to be shipped for London on the St. Maria. Arrival of the Pearl from Ireland. [*Adm. Paper.*]

June 6. Harwich. 67. Sir Wm. Batten to the Navy Comrs. Expects the fleet suddenly back. Asks whether to remain at Harwich. Is sending 150 recovered soldiers and seamen to the fleet, by Zachary Taylor and Bond's ships, which, though the worst in London, are the best there, for they delivered all their provisions before the fleet went, and the rest little till its return. Small stores and pinnaces received from Deptford. Masts, oars bowsprits, &c., wanted. Gives a list of six prizes fitted for store ships. Supposes the Board to have heard of the taking of the Great Charity by the Dutch, and the base usage of the men, who were thrown into a boat, wounded and well alike, and their oars taken from them. [2 *pages.*] *Encloses,*

67. I. *Sir Wm. Coventry to Sir Wm. Batten. The enemy persist in keeping to windward, so that it is impossible to engage them; cannot exactly tell their number; judges them to be about* 100; *thinks they decline to engage until nearer their own coast, or they expect more strength.*

Royal Charles, off Southwold, June 2, 1665.

June 6. Warrant for John Wilton, messenger, to take Thomas Smallwood into custody. Minute. [*Ent Book* 22, *p.* 161.]

June 6. Warrant to Sir John Robinson to receive Col. Rich prisoner into the Tower. Minute. [*Ent. Book* 22, *p.* 165.]

June 6. 68. J[ohn] C[larke to James Hickes. The Greyhound frigate has brought in two Dutch and one Hamburg prize, which all pretend to be bound for Dunkirk. Some Zante vessels for London came in also. Arrival of other vessels.

June 6. 69. Mor. Lodge to Williamson. There are one King's ship and three merchant ships in the Downs. There is a report that our fleet has arrived at the Gunfleet, that they have destroyed 50 or 60 Dutch ships, and brought in Opdam with them.

June 7. Whitehall. 70. Order in Council that the proclamation for better regulating the lotteries in Great Britain and Ireland be forthwith printed and published.

June 7. Whitehall. 71. The King to the Vice-Chancellor of Cambridge. Requests the degree of D.D., without performance of the usual exercises, for James Meale, formerly of that University, but debarred from taking his degree by the iniquity of the late times.

June 7. Minute of the above. [*Ent. Book* 19, *p.* 10.]

VOL. CXXIII.

1665.
June 7. Warrant for a grant to Lady Wentworth, widow of Thos. Lord Wentworth, of a pension of 600*l.* a year. [*Ent. Book* 22, p. 96.]

June ? 72. Petition of Philadelphia Wentworth to the King, that the pension of 600*l.* a year granted her may be paid not from the Exchequer, where she will have great expense and endless solicitation, but from the Customs, of which she has hitherto found the benefit. It is her only support; there is no benefit to be had for herself or child out of that which has only the name of the Earl of Cleveland's estate.

June ? 73. Philadelphia Lady Wentworth to Williamson. Asks if Lord Arlington has done anything in her business. The truth is she is starving.

June 7. Pass for the ship Nuestro Signor del Pueblo, from Bruges in Flanders to Spain and back. [*Ent. Book* 22, p. 165.]

June 7. Warrant to Sir Philip Honeywood to deliver the brandy remaining in his custody to Humphry Taylor, Robert Castle, and Michael Clipsham, contractors for the purchase at 20*l.* a tun, the highest price yet offered, of all brandy condemned in the Admiralty Court. The value of the seamen's share, being what is found between decks, shall be paid by Lord Ashley to Thos. Chicheley for their use. [*Ent. Book* 22, p. 166.]

June 7. Similar warrant to Mr. Stockdale to deliver seamen's brandy to the contractors. Minute. [*Ent. Book* 22, p. 167.]

[June 7.] Warrant to the High Sheriff of Kent to allow Dutch prisoners to be received into the gaols of Canterbury, Rochester, and Maidstone, and if these be not sufficient, to provide other places for them, and to aid John Evelyn, to whom the service is entrusted, in providing sufficient guards for their safe keeping. [*Ent. Book* 22, p. 167.]

June 7. 74. Draft of the above.

June 7. Grant to Colonel William Legg of the value of the lop and top of the timber trees ordered to be felled for the navy in the forests of Alice Holt and Woolmer, co. Hants, for repair of the lodges there. [*Ent. Book* 22, pp. 167-8.]

June 7. 75. Draft of the above.

June 7. Warrant for creating Robert Duckenfield, of Duckenfield Hall, county palatine of Chester, a baronet. Minute. [*Ent. Book* 22, p. 168.]

June 7. 76. Thos. Lewis to Thos. Hayter. Sends the names of five masters of vessels who consented to go by the ton, but hearing of

Vol. CXXIII.

1665.

others being taken up by the month, refuse to serve except on the same terms. [*Adm. Paper.*] *Annexing,*

76. I., II. *Lists of five ships taken up as victuallers for the fleet, and of the number of men for each to be supplied by press warrants. Two papers.* *June 5 and 6, 1665.*

June 7. Cockpit. 77. Duke of Albemarle to the Navy Comrs. Expected the Loyal Subject to have been in a more forward state than it is; desires them to enquire where the fault is. [*Adm. Paper.*] *Encloses,*

77. I. *Capt. John Fortescue to the Duke of Albemarle. Justifies himself from the charge of neglect of orders in not dispatching the Loyal Subject for Harwich. States the condition of the ship when the order was received: a mere outside, newly launched out of the carpenter's hands, without masts or rooms: shows the impossibility of setting sail. The pilot is now on board, expecting to get the ship away the first opportunity.* [1½ pages.]

June 7. Chatham. 78. Comr. Peter Pett to Sam. Pepys. Two hoys of provisions are sent to Harwich, and another ship is lading; is at a loss for news of the fleet. [*Adm. Paper.*]

June 7. Deptford. 79. Thos. Cowley to Sir John Mennes. Has given notice to 25 Chatham shipwrights to have their tools and clothes ready to be shipped away for Harwich; they expect their conduct money. Can hear of no vessel ready to sail away at once, except an open hoy. [*Adm. Paper.*]

June 7. Harwich. 80. Sir Wm. Batten to the Navy Comrs. Does not approve of sending masts in the Gottenburg ships; proposes the use of rafts, with anchors and hawsers to moor them. Arrival of two rafts, as also the Augustine and Tiger. Has now above 8,000 tuns of victuals in the harbour, awaiting the Duke of York's orders. Great masts, small cordage, oars, &c., are still wanted; has three sailmakers at work. Recommends Wm. Martin for the ketch at Deptford. [*Adm. Paper, 2 pages.*]

June 7. Dover. 81. Thos. White to the Navy Comrs. Asks the command of the White Dove to carry stores to the fleet, not as being weary of his present occupation, but desiring to be in action. Begs orders to take possession of the ship, and will get volunteers to work with him. [*Adm. Paper.*]

June 7. Woolwich. 82. Chris. Pett to the Navy Comrs. Mr. Morehouse's timber in Waltham Forest is very fit for the service in hand. Carriages are ordered for the dispatch thereof, after some opposition from the justices. The works of the Unity are in good progress. Oak plank and spruce deals wanted. [*Adm. Paper.*]

Vol. CXXIII.

1665.
June 7.
The Dartmouth, Bay of Dublin.

83. Capt. Rich. Booth to Sam. Pepys. Since his arrival from the West Indies, has been cruizing between Strangford, the Isle of Man, and Holyhead, by order of the Lord Deputy [of Ireland] to clear the coast of privateers. Is now to transport Sir Paul Davis's lady, Sir John Percival and his lady, with servants, to Chester Water; and thence ply on the north coast of Ireland, there being a rumour of two or three capers seen. Requests payment of a bill of 224*l.* for victualling the frigate; has already been at great charges for impressing above 200 seamen, and buying and repairing cask, &c., at his own expense, of which no mention is made in the account. [*Adm. Paper.*]

June 8.

84. Thos. Lewis to Thos. Hayter. Sends Sage Lawson, master of the Adventure, taken up as a victualler, for inserting in his contract of the number of men required to sail her. [*Adm. Paper.*]

June 8.

85. Bond of Joseph Dobyns for the appearance of Robt. Bennet, seaman, to serve in the Elizabeth, now at Harwich. [*Adm. Paper.*]

June 8.
Portsmouth.

86. John Timbrell and Edw. Sylvester, anchorsmiths, to the Navy Comrs. Asks permission to buy of the Commissioners for Prizes some iron contained in the two prize ships Wheel of Fortune and White Eagle. [*Adm. Paper.*]

June 8.
Sole Bay.

87. Sir Wm. Coventry to Sam. Pepys. Most of the fleet is safely anchored in Sole Bay. Some ships are not yet arrived. Has no reason to fear for their safety, but rather that they are clogged with prizes. Is not one of those who think the war has been so fatal that the enemy will not come out again. It is certain they have ships and money enough. Men are wanted, but where there is plenty of money, there are men enough who will sell either soul or body. Masts, yards, fishes, &c., wanted by every ship in the fleet. Has sent for Capt. Taylor to survey all defects, and resolve where to dispose each ship. Sir Wm. Penn is unwell. The volunteers are going for London. [*Adm. Paper, 2 pages.*]

June 8.
Harwich.

88. Sir Wm. Batten to the Navy Comrs. Will unload the Augustine and send her up for masts. Bowsprits, cordage, and blocks must be sent down forthwith. Could procure them at Yarmouth but in regard of the sickness, has no mind to anything from that port. Expects the fleet to-morrow. Hears that 75 of the enemy's ships have been taken, burnt, and sunk, and not a flag ship is left. Opdam and many other commanders are slain. Four lords were killed on board the Duke [of York's] ship. [*Adm. Paper.*]

June 8.
Woolwich.

89. Wm. Acworth to the Navy Comrs. Complains of the neglect of the boatswain of the Golden Lion in not getting all his stores on board before sailing. Sends account of cables and other provisions prepared for him. [*Adm. Paper.*]

June 8.
Cockpit.

90. Duke of Albemarle to the Navy Comrs. All stores ready for the refitting and furnishing of the fleet are to be sent to the Hope until further orders. [*Adm. Paper.*]

Vol. CXXIII.

1665.

June 8. Royal Charles. 91. Sir Wm. Coventry to Lord [Arlington]. The fleet is to anchor in Southwold Bay, to have its condition surveyed, and thence to proceed to the Downs or elsewhere, as the King's service requires. Asks intelligence about the Dutch, especially their East India fleet, and their preparations for coming out again. The Duke wishes a permission to come to London for a few days to be sent to him at Harwich. *Encloses,*

91. I. *Detailed account of the proceedings of the Royal Charles, from its setting sail from the Gunfleet, May 30, 9 a.m., to its arrival off the Texel, June 4, giving the state of the wind, proceedings of the Dutch fleet, &c.* [1½ pages.]

June 8. Perth. 92. William Rayne to St. Browne. Thanks for the good news of last post. Wants a bill of mortality weekly. Death of three persons near, from drinking poisoned ale, at an alehouse.

June 8. Sunderland. 93. Wm. Ettrick to Hum. Pibus, Newcastle. Discharge of ordnance has been heard all night; some say 100 pieces have been discharged, and that flashes have been seen far off at sea, to the east and south-east.

June 8. Plymouth. 94. Dan. Grosse to Williamson. Arrival of ships. Many guns are said to have been heard from the eastward. Two Dutch men-of-war have taken a London ship laden with sugars and oils, value 12,000*l.*; it was in company of the Nightingale, which is much shattered. The Dutch ships are 12 leagues off, and it is feared they will do damage on their return. The news of the victory over the Dutch was welcomed with guns, bell-ringing, &c. Asks for his commission.]

June 9. [Plymouth.] 95. J[ohn] C[larke] to James Hickes. Capture of the Elizabeth and Sarah of London, from Oporto, by two Dutch men-of-war, after six hours' fight.

June 9. Newcastle. 96. Rich. Forster to James Hickes. Report of firing being heard as it were broadsides. Sent off a man on horseback to Sunderland to enquire. All are filled with joy at the rout of the Dutch.

June 9. 97. Sir Wm. Batten to the Navy Comrs. Begs that masts, cordage, and oars may be hastened down. [*Adm. Paper.*] *Encloses,*

97. I. *Sir Wm. Coventry to Sir Wm. Batten. The Duke of York is coming to Southwold Bay to survey the fleet. Desires that Comr. Taylor and the master shipwright may be sent to help in the survey; if he (Sir William) be still at Harwich, his presence also will be welcome. Supplies must be hastened. The Dutch have received a greater blow than ever they had before, with but little loss to the fleet. Sir Wm. Penn has the gout, and Sir John Lawson a hurt in the knee.* [Two pages.]

Royal Charles, June 8, 1665.

Vol. CXXIII.

1665.

June 9. Galleons Reach. 98. James Blake, of the Constant Ann, to the Navy Comrs. Is at anchor, waiting for the ships' carpenters, who were to be put on board by Mr. Cowley of Deptford. Only eight have yet arrived, but there are the chests and tools of several more. [*Adm. Paper.*]

June 9. Plymouth. 99. John Lanyon to the Navy Comrs. The few masts to be obtained in the town, though old and not good, are very dear. Has ordered the shipwright to secure such as may be of service. Account of the capture of Capt. Peter Westlake's ship by Dutch men-of-war. Escape of the Nightingale, much shattered. It is thought that Capt. Westlake's men gave up their ship, being of all nations, and but few English. [*Adm. Paper.*]

June 9. Plymouth. 100. Thos. Yeabsly and John Lanyon to Sam. Pepys. Arrival of the Nightingale after an engagement with two Dutch men-of-war. Loss of Capt. Peter Westlake's ship, laden with sugar and oils. Advice from Tangiers of several Dutch vessels ranging the seas in those parts. Beg that a thorough convoy may be appointed for ships trading thither. [*Adm. Paper.*]

June 9. 101. Jacob Blackleech to the Navy Comrs. Account of water on three water ships. [*Adm. Paper.*]

June 9. Royal Charles. 102. Sir Wm. Coventry to Mr. White, master of the Maryland Merchant. He is to receive, victual, and carry to Blackwall 300 Dutch prisoners, giving notice on arrival to the Commissioners for Prisoners and the Navy Commissioners. He is to keep company with such ships as are going into the river, for better security. [*Adm. Paper.*]

Vol. CXXIV. June 10–21, 1665.

1665.

June 10. 1. Sir Wm. Coventry to the Navy Comrs. The Duke of York, with the advice of the Council of War, resolves to keep the fleet where it is, to take in victuals and stores. All things necessary must be hastened down. [*Adm. Paper.*]

June 10. The Resolution. 2–4. Certificates by Capt. Wm. Kempthorne, that a butt of beer was staved in hoisting it on board; also that 5½ tons of cask and 57 iron hoops were cut for gun tubs spent in extra uses in time of fight, or lost; also that 28 pieces of beef were given for Rear-Admiral Sansum's ship, and 105 lost in the fight, &c. Three papers. [*Adm. Paper.*]

June 10. Chatham. 5. Comr. Peter Pett to Sam. Pepys. Almost all the masts are in, and the cables ready to be dispatched. The Victory and other ships go on apace. [*Adm. Paper.*]

June 10. Woolwich. 6. Chris. Pett to the Navy Comrs. The Fox and Merlin are ready to take in provisions. [*Adm. Paper.*]

Vol. CXXIV.

1665.

June 10. Chatham Ropeyard. 7. John Owen to the Navy Comrs. More hemp is wanted; only 100 tons remain in store. [*Adm. Paper.*]

June 10. Bristol. 8. Sir Hump. Hooke, Sir Robt. Yeamans, and John Knight to the Navy Comrs. Promise not to interrupt others employed, like themselves, in impressing seamen. Have taken two from a Plymouth ship. The men ordered on board the George expect to be billeted until she arrives, but are told that there is work enough to employ them till then, so that they should not be a needless charge. [*Adm. Paper.*]

June 10. Bristol. 9. Sir John Knight to the Navy Comrs. The Pearl is about to sail into King Road; requires the purser's bond. Mr. Morgan, the collector, will not promise when the 400*l.* ordered by them shall be paid. Requests three months' provisions for the ship at Bristol, the rest to be taken in at Milford. Recommends the purchase of a large Swedish ship, of 500 tons burthen, belonging to John Peterson, offered under peculiar circumstances for 800*l.*, fitted for a man-of-war; it carries 40 pieces of ordnance, is large and spacious, and worth at least 2,000*l.* [*Adm. Paper, 2 pages.*]

June 10? 10. Capt. John Blake to Thos. Haytor. Requires 100 tickets for the use of the ship Hilversom. [*Adm. Paper.*]

June 10. 11. Jacob Blackleach to the Navy Comrs. Account of water ships. [*Adm. Paper.*]

June 10. Warrant for dispensing with the second article in a commission for letters of marque against the States of the United Provinces,—ordering the entering of bonds for bringing all prizes taken into some port of England or Ireland,—as it proves inconvenient and hazardous; therefore all commissions are to be issued or renewed without this clause. [*Ent. Book 22, pp. 168–9.*]

June [10.] 12, 13. Two drafts of the above.

June 10. Edinburgh. 14. Rob. Mein to Hen. Muddiman. The fast for the success of the navy was solemnly kept, and even the fanatics, who do not go to church at other times, were seen there then. Bells are tolled and guns fired at Berwick for a defeat over the Dutch, but the certain news of it has not reached Edinburgh. Rob. Craill's wife is committed close prisoner and none allowed to see her, because she will not confess the writer of some intercepted seditious letter, sent to her husband in Holland.

June 10. Edinburgh. 15. Proclamation appointing Thursday, July 13th, as a day of special thanksgiving throughout the realm of Scotland, for the victory gained by the Duke of York over the Dutch fleet. [*Printed.*]

June 10. Southwold Bay. 16. Sir Wm. Coventry to Lord Arlington. There were thoughts of carrying the fleet into the Downs, but that place is thought better, considering its state, and the stores already at Harwich. Only those

1665. Vol. CXXIV.

ships whose defects require it will go into port. The prizes do not appear as many as were expected. There are only eight men-of-war there; one is said to be gone into the river.

June 10. Westminster. Warrant to John Lord Robartes, keeper of the privy seal, to draw up letters for the Great Seal in form given, confirming the charter of the borough of Ripon, nominating Walter Strickland as mayor, Rich. Etherington, recorder, and Edw. Hodgson as town clerk. With proviso for all officers to take the Oaths of Allegiance and Supremacy, and reservation to the King of the approbation of the town clerk in future. [*Latin. Case B, Charles II., No. 5.*]

June 10. Docquet of the above.

June 10. Deal. 17. Willm. Smith to Williamson. Twenty French vessels, bound for London and Yarmouth, have sailed through the Downs. Arrival of other vessels.

June 10. Newcastle. 18. Rich. Forster to James Hickes. The country is now convinced of the happy success of His Majesty's navy; 100 ships in port wait a confirmation of it before they sail. The Blackamoor has had a shrewd fight with a Dutch caper, and is much shattered.

June 10. Chester. 19. Sir Geoffrey Shakerley to Williamson. Is in great hopes that the enemy is beaten, but wants to know to what extent, and with what loss on the English side. Hopes all news may be to the honour and happiness of the kingdoms.

June 10. Hull. 20. —— to James Hickes. A Yarmouth ketch which came from the fleet on Tuesday, affirms that the English have taken 30 Holland men-of-war, fired and sunk 27, and are still in pursuit; from Scarborough comes news of a total rout.

June 10. Knighton. 21. R. Dillington to Williamson. Some of the crew of a small French vessel, tried to land on the south of the island, to buy bread, but a file of musketeers on guard conveyed them to Sandham Castle. Thinks they wanted to sound the most convenient landing places. Wishes there were a better defence against any sudden attempt; the militia is numerous, but in no excellent order. Rumours of the Dutch being beaten.

June 10. Careby. 22. Jo. Hatcher to Williamson. Thanks for his weekly news, and especially for that of the glorious victory over their ambitious, usurping neighbours.

June 10. Landguard Fort. 23. Edw. Suckley to James Hickes. On the 9th, the Duke of York with all his fleet came to Sole Bay, where they are at anchor, with 15 Dutch ships taken, and 2,000 prisoners; 35 sail are sunk or taken. Opdam, Trump, and Eversen, and other commanders killed. On our side, Lords Fitzharbert and Falmouth and two other lords are killed.

June 10. Doncaster. 24. Leo. Williams to Robt. Lee [*alias* Lord Arlington]. Finding that his friends knew of his proceedings, pretended to have come

VOL. CXXIV.

1665.

in and made his peace with Sir Roger Langley, within the time of the proclamation, but to have done no man wrong, and to be the same as formerly; on finding that they treated him as before, went to Squire Merry, a deputy-lieutenant of Leicestershire, to show his pass and prevent trouble, but got into trouble. Went thence to Durham, first visiting the Bishop, and told his friends there the same tale. Though their hopes are great, they have no inclination to plot. Some persons have fallen off from them, and more would do so were it not for shame.

June 10? 25. James Hickes to [Williamson]. All are dissatisfied with last Friday's relation of the success of the fleet. There is no account of the Duke of York's singular encounter with Opdam, whose ship was sunk, though two other Dutch flag ships, and several others tried to sink the Duke's ship and to kill him. Nor is a word said of Prince Rupert, though the seamen said none excelled him in valour and success: he received the charge of their fleet, not discharging again till close to, and then firing through and through the enemy with great success. The Earl of Sandwich, Sir John Lawson, Major Smith, Lord Marlborough, Major Holmes, and several others should also be reported for their valour.

June 10. London. 26. "Second narrative of the signal victory which it pleased Almighty God to bestow upon His Majesty's navy," 3 June 1665, giving details of the proceedings of the fleet from May 30, and of the battle, particularly of the attack by the Duke of York on Opdam's ship. The enemy have 23 or 24 ships destroyed or taken, and about 8,000 men killed. [*Quarto, 16 pages, printed.*]

June 11. Dover. 27. J[ohn] C[arlisle] to Williamson. Thanks for the good news. Capt. Wagger fought with three Hollanders, ran two ashore, and sunk one. There is a rumour that eight Holland men-of-war have taken five of our merchant ships off the Land's End. Longs to hear the success of the pursuit of the Dutch; the French at Calais did not credit the victory.

June 11. Tuesday. 28. And. King to Williamson. Sends an account of the defeat of the Spaniards by the King of Portugal. Wishes quarters near the Court for dispatch; will keep his man in London.

June 11. Royal Charles, Southwold Bay. 29. Sir Wm. Coventry to Lord [Arlington]. Surveyors are on board to inquire into the damages, and to put all things in a way of dispatch. They are anxious to be out to meet with the Dutch East India fleet. Laments greatly the loss of Lord Falmouth. [*2 pages.*]

June 11. Royal Charles. 30. Sir Wm. Coventry and Sir Wm. Penn to the Navy Commrs. The Duke has ordered the Royal Oak, Mary, and St. George to Sheerness, for repairs; more than ordinary care must be used in their dispatch; Commr. Pett is to be on the place, to forward the work and keep the men on board. [*Adm. Paper.*]

VOL. CXXIV.

1665.

June 12. Chatham. 31. Comr. Peter Pett to Sam. Pepys. Promises care in the re-fitting of the Royal Oak, Mary, and St. George, and seeing their men kept on board; masts and yards will be needed. [*Adm. Paper.*]

June 12. Chatham. 32. Comr. Peter Pett to Lord Brouncker, Navy Comr. Has had frequent contests with the Board about their dependance upon one single person for a supply of Gottenburg masts, and the hazard to which it would expose the service in time of engagement; the late demand for Gottenburg masts at Harwich has drained the stores so dry that a further supply is impossible, and the repairs of the Royal Oak, Mary, and St. George cannot be proceeded upon. All the masts that can be got in the river should be seized and bought. [*Adm. Paper.*]

June 12. Chatham. 33. Comr. Peter Pett to Sam. Pepys. The flyboat laden with stores for Harwich is ready to sail, but the master has not yet appeared; he must be hastened down; begs consideration for Hayward, a poor country fellow, to whom 200*l.* or 300*l.* are due for good and cheap bargains of timber, that he come not into the goldsmiths' hands, or their high rates would undo him. [*Adm. Paper.*]

June 12. Woolwich. 34. Chris. Pett and Wm. Acworth to the Navy Comrs. Demand for plank, masts, and other stores. [*Adm. Paper.*]

June 12. Southwold Bay. 35. Capt. Phineas Pett to Sam. Pepys. Was unable, before leaving with the fleet, to settle the victualling of the several yachts under his command; requests that John Rogers may indent for the Henrietta, and Lisingham for the Katherine yacht. [*Adm. Paper.*]

June 12. Leghorn. 36. Thos. Clutterbuck to the [Navy Comrs.]. Earnestly entreats the settlement of his victualling account for 1,300*l.* 9s. 6*d.*; would have waited personally on the Board but is terrified by the violent heat from undertaking such a journey. Has made many disbursements for the service, not relating to victualling, for which he also begs consideration. [*Adm. Paper,* 1½ *pages.*]

June 12. Chatham Ropeyard. 37. John Owen and Robt. Sliter to the Navy Comrs. The cordage demanded will take 300 tons of yarn; the hemp in store will only make 140 tons. [*Adm. Paper.*]

June 12. Norwich. 38. Willm. Nowell to Henry Muddiman. The Mayor of Norwich caused all the bells to be rung for the victory over the Dutch, and the trained bands in arms gave several volleys and acclamations, drums beating, colours flying, &c.; the city waits played first on the leads of the Guildhall, and then on the market cross. The Fairfax, supposed to be lost, has joined the fleet. The Hollanders make the people believe that they have got the victory, and that Opdam and Van Trump are in pursuit of the English.

June 12. The Prince, Sole Bay. 39. Earl of Sandwich to Lord [Arlington]. The victory will be of great consequence to the King's affairs, if rightly improved. Bewails the sad fate of Lord Falmouth, whose generosity cannot

VOL. CXXIV.

1665.

enough be valued. The Duke being in London will tell all that is of importance. [2 pages.]

June 12. Whitehall. 40. Warrant for a grant to Elizabeth Countess of Guildford of waste grounds and lands in several hundreds of Norfolk, which shall be found by inquisition to belong to the Crown, or have been left by the sea, and of all enclosures or buildings thereon, for 31 years, on rental of one fourth of the profits; with power to issue commissions, &c., to recover the same. [Copy.]

June 12. Falmouth. 41. Rich. Kingston to James Hickes. Longs for particulars of the victory. Two Hamburghers were brought in, on suspicion of being Hollanders. There are Dutch capers between the coast and Scilly.

June 12. Chester. 42. T—— T—— to Henry Muddiman. The news of the victory filled the city with gladness; guns were fired, bells rung, and there was a bonfire before almost every house; it will bring not only honour and benefit to King and kingdom, but be an antidote to those who thirsted for change. A Dutch caper anchored in Chester Water, but Capt. Rooth of the Dartmouth, being in Dawpool, has gone to look after him.

June 12. Yarmouth. 43. Rich. Bower to Williamson. Ships pass to and fro daily from the port without convoy; 13 Dutch ships have got safe into Flushing. Many Ostenders were in the Dutch fleet; 15 died of the plague at Yarmouth last week.

June 12. 44. Examination of Henry Brandriffe before Lord Arlington. Denies being with the Dutch ambassador, or meeting in company with any discontented seditious persons, unless accidentally in the street.

June 12/22. Chelsea. Ambassador Van Gogh to the States General. Differing accounts of the late fight. Preparations for setting the fleet to sea again. The lord mayor and aldermen have been to congratulate the King on the victory, and to promise to stand by him, if need be, against France, with which the commonalty are more incensed than with the States; when they rejoiced in the city over the victory, they fell upon Lord Cominge's house. Several foreign ministers have also congratulated the victory; 43 died of the plague and 16 of the spotted fever last week; 24 vessels with navy stores have arrived within 16 days. [Holland Corresp., 22 June, 1665.]

June 12. Licence to Francisco Macedo, a Teneriffe merchant,—who imported Canary wine into London, and with the proceeds bought an English ship, the St. Ann,—that it may be navigated to Teneriffe by strangers. [Ent. Book 14, p. 62.]

June 12. Warrant for a grant to John Crisp, Thomas Crisp, and Nicholas Crisp, in reversion after Sir John Wolstenholme, jun., of the office of Collectors of tonnage and poundage in the port of London, on surrender of a similar patent to Sir Nicholas Crisp, Thos. Crisp, and Hen. Clarke. [Ent. Book 22, p. 235.]

VOL. CXXIV.

1665.

June 12. Commission for Thos. Check to be Captain of Sir Edw. Broughton's company. Minute. [*Ent. Book* 20, *p.* 67.]

June 13. Whitehall. 45. Blank commission for a major and captain in a regiment of horse.

June 13. Grant to Robt. Duckenfield, jun., of Duckenfield, co. Chester, of the dignity of a baronet. [*Docquet.*]

June 13. Grant to the same of the usual discharge. [*Docquet.*]

June 13. Order—on the petition of Thos. Killigrew for a proportion of the lands, co. Herts, formerly belonging to Sir Thos. Hyde, Bart., but escheated to the Crown,—that on the death of the said Sir Thomas, the petitioner shall have a writ of estate on the lands, and when he has entitled the King thereto, his further pleasure shall be known. [*Ent. Book* 16, *p.* 170.]

June 13. Warrant to John Wilson to search for Henry Brandrith, *alias* Brandriffe, and seize him with his papers. Minute. [*Ent. Book* 22, *p.* 170.]

June 13. Warrant for Sir Thos. Ingram to affix the seals of the duchy of Lancaster to the grant made to the trustees of the Queen-Mother of the manor and lordship of Knaresborough, &c., co. York, during her life, and for two years after her decease. [*Ent. Book* 22, *p.* 171.]

June 13. Pass for horses to be embarked by Lord Arundel, master of horse to the Queen. Minute. [*Ent. Book* 22, *p.* 171.]

[June 13.] Representation of such rents and dues out of prizes as are considered, by the Commissioners for collecting the perquisites of Lord High Admiral the Duke of York in this time of hostility, to belong to him. [*Ent. Book* 22, *p.* 172.]

June 13. Dunwich. 46. Prince Rupert to Lord [Arlington]. His greatest joy is to have been a small instrument in chastising so high an insolency as that of the Dutch; hopes to continue so till they are brought to their duty, which will be an easy task if the time is not lingered out. Is on the lee through a small mistake of the surgeon's, and writes in bed. [2 *pages.*]

June 13. Royal Charles, Southwold Bay. 47. Sir Wm. Coventry to Lord Arlington. The sea there causing delay in refitting the ships, some are to be sent to Ousley Bay, the Rolling Grounds, Harwich, and the buoy of the Nore, to be in smoother water. The Duke is sailing for London. Capt. Holmes asked to be rear-admiral of the white squadron, in place of Sansum who was killed, but the Duke gave the place to Capt. Harman, on which Holmes delivered up his commission, which the Duke received, and put Capt. Langhorne in his stead. [2 *pages.*]

June 13. Plymouth. 48. J. C[larke] to James Hickes. Two ships sent to convoy vessels from Morlaix have arrived, with one of Plymouth, two of Lyme, and two of London, which they are convoying to those ports.

VOL. CXXIV.

1665.

June 13. Newcastle. 49. Rich. Forster to James Hickes. The news of the victory was received with bonfires and ringing of bells, but the fanatics hang their heads, which makes people suspect they wished better to the Dutch than to their own country. Forty ships have come in, and bring tidings of two Dutch vessels being taken by two ships of the blue squadron. Two men-of-war will convoy the Newcastle fleet, which will be 150 sail.

June 13. Dartmouth. 50. G. S—— to Williamson. The news of the victory caused a day of great rejoicing: the guns from the castle, the town, and the ships have fired 150 shots, and bonfires were made on the quays. There are Dutch capers under French colours near; wishes some frigates to clear the coast of them to Land's End. Two Dartmouth vessels have arrived from St. Malo, bringing the men from a Newfoundland ship which was taken by a Dutch caper. At St. Malo, they were rejoicing in a report that the English fleet had been beaten by the Dutch.

June 13. 51. Jacob Blackleech to the Navy Comrs. Account of water sent on board two water ships; with note that he was directed by the Board to desist. [*Adm. Paper.*]

June 13. Cockpit. 52. Duke of Albemarle to the Navy Comrs. Desires supplies for repair of the Nightingale at Plymouth; masts and other stores should be sent there for the ships in those parts. [*Adm. Paper.*] *Encloses,*

52. I. *Carpenter and boatswain's report of damage sustained by the Nightingale, in an engagement with two Dutch privateers. The Nightingale, June 9, 1665.*

June 13. Royal Charles. 53. Sir Wm. Coventry and Sir Wm. Penn to the Navy Comrs. The Duke of York has left as many ships in Ousley Bay, the Rolling Grounds, and Harwich, as will take up all hands and stores provided for their repair; first and second rate ships are ordered to the Nore; masts, yards, boats, &c., must be furnished with all speed. [*Adm. Paper.*]

June 13. Royal Katherine, Sole Bay. 54. Capt. Thos. Teddeman to the Navy Comrs. Benjamin Phillips, pressed into the Royal Katherine, was made a midshipman at the request of Isaac Wooden, under whom he had formerly served in New England; gave him leave to go to London, upon bond to return; seeing it is the desire of the Board to employ him to fetch masts, has returned his bond. *Encloses,*

54. I. *Bond of Ben. Phillips in 50l., to return to his ship within eight days. April 10, 1665.*

June 13. Victualling Office. 55. Thos. Lewis to the Navy Comrs. The decision about the victualling at Leghorn was made too late to provide flesh in that country for this year, and it was therefore ordered to be supplied from home; the William and Mary was laden with 100 tons of beef and

1665. VOL. CXXIV.

pork for Leghorn; but when ready to sail and a convoy demanded, orders were received from the King for her not to proceed, but for the provisions to be used for service at home. [*Adm. Paper.*]

June 13. 56. Thos. Lewis to Sam. Pepys. Begs employment for Robt. Whynlard as a joiner at Deptford. [*Adm. Paper.*]

June 13. 57. List of 10 ships provided by Sir Wm. Rider and Wm. Cutler, ready at London and Newcastle to sail for the Sound, to fetch naval provisions. [*Adm. Paper.*]

June 13? 58. List of 18 prize ships at Portsmouth, Harwich, and in the Thames, proposed to be fitted up as water ships and victuallers. [*Adm. Paper.*]

June 13. The Ruby, Erith. 59. Capt. Wm. Jennings to the Navy Comrs. Requests orders for the disposal of his prize ship and 100 prisoners. [*Adm Paper.*]

June 13. 60. List of 38 Dutch prisoners victualled on board the Resolution by order of Rear-Admiral Sansum; certified by Capt. Wm. Kempthorne. [*Adm. Paper.*]

June 14. Harwich. 61. Sir Wm. Batten to the Navy Comrs. Has been with Capt. Taylor and Anthony Deane, taking survey of the defects of the fleet. Account of stores wanted. Desires that the shipwrights may be paid once a quarter; is commanded to stay at Harwich until the fleet be refitted; must have money, having borrowed as much as he can get; thinks the Augustine and Admiral Trump will be sufficient for storeships, and the Friezland to be fitted for Capt. Teale; is informed the States have hanged 10 of their captains; the Duke of York had good reason to serve some of his so; had all the captains done as they ought, not 10 of the enemy's ships would have escaped. [*Adm. Paper, 2 pages.*]

June 14. Cockpit. 62. Sir Wm. Clarke to Sam. Pepys. The Olive Branch and Friends' Adventure, bound to Stockholm for pitch and tar for the service, desire five pressed men for each out of the Vine ketch. [*Adm. Paper.*]

June 14. Ordnance Office. 63. Edw. Sherburne, Rich. Marsh, and Fras. Nicholls to the Navy Comrs. Desire an order for four men to serve on board the Prudent Housewife, laden with powder. [*Adm. Paper.*]

June 14. 64. James Watkin [of the Joseph hospital ship], to Capt. George Erwin. Desires warrants for a boatswain, gunner, and carpenter. [*Adm. Paper.*]

June 14. Edinburgh. 65. Capt. J. Lightfoot to the Navy Comrs. Has victualled the Speedwell for three months, almost within the stated price, though at the dearest time of the year; has drawn a bill of 80*l.* on Sir Wm. Batten and James Stanfield, and provided 208*l.* for victuals, payable

VOL. CXXIV.

1665.

to John Lindsey, goldsmith, of Lombard Street; the whole city is overjoyed at the happy news of the great victory over the Dutch; a supply of clothes is wanted for the men. [*Adm. Paper.*]

June 14. Edinburgh. 66. Capt. J. Lightfoot to Sam. Pepys. Requests punctual payment of two bills of exchange for 80*l.*, and 378*l.*, for three months' victualling of the Speedwell. [*Adm. Paper.*]

June 14. London. 67. Jacob Blackleech to the Navy Comrs. Account of water put on board two water ships. [*Adm. Paper.*]

June 14. Falmouth. 68. Rich. Kingston to James Hickes. Two Irishmen from France report that the King of France has issued a proclamation that whoever is known to buy any sort of goods taken from the English by the Hollanders shall immediately be hanged, and therefore an English prize brought by the Dutch into Brest was taken and sunk, ship and goods. Another lies there, but no one dares to buy her.

[June 14.] [Whitehall.] Proclamation appointing June 20 to be kept in London and Westminster, and July 4 in other places, as a day of thanksgiving for the late victory at sea, and of supplication for further assistance. [*Printed. Proc. Coll., Charles II., p.* 188.]

June 14. Whitehall. Proclamation forbidding the holding of Barnwell Fair, near Cambridge, usually kept on 24 June, for this year, for fear of spreading the present contagion, declaring that the persons interested in the profits of the fair shall not be prejudiced by this restraint. [*Printed. Proc. Coll., p.* 189.]

June 15. Landguard Fort. 69. Edw. Suckley to James Hickes. The Duke and Prince Rupert have sailed for London with part of the fleet; 20 sail are ordered for Harwich and are coming in, bringing several prizes. None of the fleet are much damaged. There are 800 men killed and 500 wounded. The Dutch have lost 8,000 or 9,000, besides prisoners.

June 14. Reference to the Lord Privy Seal, Lord Lauderdale, and Lord Ashley, on the petition of Robt. Turner, a frequent solicitor, but the nature of whose complaint is long and intricate. [*Ent. Book* 18, *p.* 170.]

June 15. Harwich. 70. Rich. Marbury to [Williamson]. Hopes they have almost done for the Dutch, having sunk or burnt 32 of their best ships: Opdam was blown up in his ship, and but three of all his men saved. Had the wind been easterly, most of their ships would have been spoiled. They have but two admirals returned to Holland, of all their flag ships.

June 15. Whitehall. 71. Order for a warrant to pay to Edw. Wood 200*l.*, for acceptable service in foreign parts.

June 15. Amsterdam. 72. Sir Willm. Davidson to Lord Arlington. Sends a letter from a person in Rotterdam, who has promised to discover a plot for a rising in the west and north of England, to be aided from Holland.

VOL. CXXIV.

1665.

The informer is much in favour with the rulers in Holland, and is son to one of the King's judges who was quartered. Has promised him a large sum for his secret. There are in Holland 160 English officers, fugitives, and disaffected persons, who are meeting at Leyden, and the informer with them. The ringleaders are Major General Desborough, Col. Ludlow, and Col. Faris; this latter is to be sent to England; all the Flanders packet boats should be examined, as he intends to come that way under another name. Gives names of others of the party. The victory is God's own work. Admirals Opdam, Cortenaer, and Evertsen are gone, but Trump is come into the Texel with 30 or 40 ships, and they flatter themselves with a great victory. *Encloses,*

72. I. *Thos. Corney to Thos. Kempe, merchant of London. Business details. The loss on the Dutch side has put the workmen to a stand, and they fear a league designed by the States with the Spaniards. Particulars of the fight. Opdam was killed and his ship blown up; the Orange sunk, and the fleet shamefully pursued by the English into their harbours. John Evertsen, Admiral of Zealand, and six or eight more are to be tried for their lives, for running away, and will assuredly be hanged. Trump is to be Admiral, and will be at sea in 14 days, to secure the Cadiz and East India fleet, if they can get men. A drummer was thrown into the water at Leyden, because he did not use the Prince* [*of Orange's*] *name. The men taken from the English convoy were put on Dutch ships, and forced to fight against their country. An Englishman has been killed in the town for speaking for the English.* [2 *pages.*] *Amsterdam, June* $\frac{9}{19}$, 1665.

June 15. 73. Declaration to Drs. John Exton and L. Jenkins, judges of the Admiralty Court, of the King's appointment of Sir Ellis Leighton, D.C.L., as one of the King's counsellors in the said court.

[June 15.] 74. Draft of the above.

June 15. Entry of the above. [*Ent. Book* 22, *p.* 162.]

June 15. Warrant for a grant to William Bulmer, in reward for his loyal sufferings and losses, of the forfeited estate of the manor and lands at Hurthwaite, co. York, value 45*l.* 6*s.* a year, and the personal estate, value 10*l.*, late belonging to George Denham, attainted of high treason. [*Ent. Book* 22, *p.* 173.]

June 15. Whitehall. The King to the Farmers of Customs. Although the transportation of horses is contrary to law, and daily refused to the most considerable men of France, yet understands that it is daily done by connivance, to the prejudice of the service and defrauding of customs. None are to pass in future without licence under his hand and that of the Duke of Albemarle, master of the horse. [*Ent. Book* 14, *ff.* 62 *b*, 63.]

Vol. CXXIV.

1665.
June 15. Warrant to pay to Henry Harris, yeoman of the revels on surrender of John Carey, 13*l.* 6*s.* 8*d.* a year for board wages, 18*l.* for house rent, and 1*s.* a day additional allowance. [*Docquet.*]

June 15. Young Prince, Harwich. 75. Capt. John Chappell to the Navy Comrs. Wants a surgeon, purser, and seamen. Is almost ready, but has no provisions on board. [*Adm. Paper.*]

June 15. Cockpit. 76. Duke of Albemarle to Capt. Val. Tatnell. He is to proceed with impressing seamen, and the Ordnance Officers are to be supplied with pressed men for the store ships going to the fleet. [*Adm. Paper.*]

June 15. Cockpit. 77. Sir Wm. Clarke to Sam. Pepys. The master of the ketch at Calais is to stay there, until orders for her restoration are received from Ambassador Holles. [*Adm. Paper.*]

June 15. Loyal Katherine, hospital ship, Harwich. 78. Hugh Rider, surgeon, to Sam. Pepys. Being six days detained by contrary winds, has expended all the lines received for the wounded on the hospital ship; requests a speedy supply, and four more assistants. The men are injured by the ship's being small and crowded, and many must perish unless allowed cooks to dress their victuals. With note from Capt. J. Pearse, Royal Charles, June 9, desiring that provisions named be furnished forthwith for the hospital ship. [*Adm. Paper.*] *Enclosing,*

78. i. *Invoice by Hugh Rider, of necessaries wanting in the Loyal Katherine, hospital ship.*
Buoy of the Nore, June, 1665.

June 15. 79. Thos. Cowley to Sir John Mennes. Sends a list of the men discharged from Chatham to be sent to Harwich; most of their clothes and tools were shipped in the Constant John, the men were too stubborn and refractory, after receiving their conduct money, to give account what way they intended to take. [*Adm. Paper.*]

June 16. 80. Thos. Cowley to Sam. Pepys. Sixteen shipwrights and ten calkers are pressed for Harwich; they make great clamours for conduct money and wages. Requests an order for their tickets to be made out, to quiet them; unless they have conduct money, they will come up to trouble the Commissioners. [*Adm. Paper.*]

June 16. Woolwich. 81. Chris. Pett to the Navy Comrs. Has masts, yards, bowsprits, &c., ready to send away to the fleet, as soon as ships can be provided to take them; wants a smack to carry down an assistant with 20 shipwrights, and a store of oars and small iron work. Complains of an obstruction in the shipping of timber at Barking, because the townsmen will have it shipped from the common wharf, which is low, inconvenient, and out of repair, in order to get the benefit of the wharfing, although there is another wharf very convenient. [*Adm. Paper.*]

VOL. CXXIV.

1665.

June 16. The Hound, Buoy of the Nore. 82. Capt. James Coleman to [Sam. Pepys]. Has not received the men pressed for him out of the merchant ships; had eight from Capt. Tatnell, but none of them fit for labour; begs that the masters may be forced to pay in their wages to the Navy Comrs., until they appear. [*Adm. Paper.*]

June 16. The Norwich, Gravesend. 83. Capt. John Wetwyng to Sir John Mennes. Complains of the neglect and disobliging manner of his purser, Peter Myles; begs that another may be appointed. [*Adm. Paper.*]

June 16. Plymouth. 84. Thos. Yeabsly to Sam. Pepys. The management of Tangiers' affairs will, in future, pass chiefly through his hands, Mr. Lanyon having passed his year's account. Can go no further in the contract, which is hard at best, without money. Want of more frequent convoys may prejudice the service. Proposes to obtain 2,000*l.* or 3,000*l.* through the Commissioners for Prizes. The Maria prize might be fitted up as a constant convoy for Tangiers. [*Adm. Paper.*]

June 16. Dover. 85. Thos. White to the Navy Comrs. Has bought up 300 feet of plank for which ready money must be paid; was unable to obtain any until "ready money opened the gate;" 300 feet more is to be had at 3½*d.* per foot; if the price be not too high, will take it in store while it can be had. Is sorry his last letter gave offence; his desire was, not to slight his duty at Dover, but to do some service in time of action; wants cables and cordage. [*Adm. Paper.*]

June 16. 86. John Knight, serjeant-surgeon, to the Navy Comrs. Gives a list of ten surgeons and ten mates impressed for the service and sent to Harwich, but afterwards returned to London. With note that the Commissioners for sick and wounded sent them back, having provided others before. [*Adm. Paper.*]

June 16. 87. List of sixteen shipwrights and ten calkers pressed by Mr. Shish at Deptford, to be sent to Harwich. [*Adm. Paper.*]

June 16. 88. Certificate by the Churchwardens of St. Mary Overy's, Southwark, that Sam. Fell, a poor man, impressed at the age of 40, has never been to sea, and has a wife and four children who will be left to the parish charge if he is taken, and request that he be allowed to remain free. [*Adm. Paper.*]

June 16. Ordnance Office. 89. Edw. Sherburne and Fra. Nicholls to the Navy Comrs. The Prudent Housewife of Sandwich, laden with powder for the fleet, is delayed by the pressing of two of her men; begs an order for their release, and for two more in lieu of two pressed before. [*Adm. Paper.*]

June 16. Plymouth. 90. John Lanyon to the Navy Comrs. Can find no trees in the town to be depended on as masts; must have some sent from Portsmouth or London. Progress of the Nightingale's repairs.

VOL. CXXIV.

1665.

Difficulty of procuring powder. Dutch capers continue numerous on the coast; three or four fourth-rate ships are wanted to deal with them. [*Adm. Paper.*]

June 16. Plymouth. 91. Thos. Yeabsly and John Lanyon to Sam. Pepys. Long to know the determination of the Board touching the dispute of the agent with the officers and soldiers at Tangiers. The war is a great disappointment to the advantage they hoped for by their contract, having lost 500*l.* for want of payment, owing to the present rise in corn. Are willing to resign it to Sir Thos. Ingram. Two men-of-war lie before the harbour; no ship can stir forth. If the Nightingale be appointed thorough convoy, can dispatch two ships forthwith with provisions for the garrison. [*Adm. Paper.*] *Encloses,*

91. I. *Thos. Yeabsly and John Lanyon to [Mr. Creed]. Request convoy for two ships laden with provisions for Tangiers, compelled to lie on demurrage, owing to the danger of the seas, and two men-of-war before the harbour: the Nightingale might do the business.* [*Copy.*]

June 16. Warrant to pay to Sir George Carteret, treasurer of the navy, 102,000*l* on account, or to assign the same on the receivers of the Royal aid. [*Docquet.*]

[June 16.] 92. Petition of Alice, the miserable wife of Major Robert Calcott, to the King, not to be diverted by uncharitable addresses from his intended mercy to her husband, if he find that he neither gave the occasion of the quarrel, nor was guilty of any unhandsome circumstance relating to it, he having served His Majesty in his greatest straits.

June 16. Reference of the above petition to Sir Job. Charleton, chief justice of Chester, and Mr. Millard, who sat upon the trial. [*Ent. Book*, 18, p. 171.]

June 16. Whitehall. 93. Petition of Elizabeth Countess of Guildford to the King, to issue commissions to enquire into corn and other mills built over channels of the sea, marsh grounds lying within high-water mark, commons, waste grounds, houses, &c., encroached, concealed, or detained from the King, in several hundreds of Norfolk; and for leases of such as shall by inquisition be found to belong to the Crown; with reference thereon to the Lord Treasurer.

June 16. Entry of the above reference, cancelled, with a second reference, June 19, to the Lord Treasurer and Chancellor of the Exchequer to issue commissions of enquiry as desired, and do what is needful for the prosecution, granting leases to the petitioner when the King's right to the premises is cleared. [*Ent. Book* 18, *pp.* 172, 173.]

June [16]. 94. Copy of the latter reference. With note that Sir Paul Neile and Sir Herb. Lunsford had a similar reference on their petition

Vol. CXXIV.

1665.

for lands in Suffolk, dated 30 Aug., 1664, the petition being only for a commission for an inquisition to entitle the King to the said lands.

June 16. Order on the petition of John Rudstone, aged 74, for some provision in his old age that he be allowed a dead pay in the garrison of Hull, and that the Lord General give orders accordingly. [*Ent. Book* 18, *p.* 172.]

June 16. 95. Note that 60 sail of small vessels have passed the Isle [of Wight ?] eastward.

June 16. Yarmouth. 96. Rich Bower to Williamson. There have passed 150 sail under convoy of the Blackamoor, and 100 sail of laden colliers, under two convoys, northward. Thirty have died of the plague; it will increase until there are cleansing houses, which the people do not like to build, on account of the charge. Infected families are put altogether, and then after the month return to the town. The poor make sad lamentations, being deprived of the charity and trade of the inhabitants, who are fled, so that it is like a country village. Is glad the fleet has left Southwold Bay, for many people of the town flocked to see their relations on board, pretending to have come from some other country town. Hopes the fleet may have received no prejudice.

June 16. London. 97. Tho. Knapton, of Dorchester, to Samuel Jolly, at Lord Arlington's lodgings, Whitehall. Thinks that the Sheriff of Dorsetshire, who has slighted the King's letters, and not appeared before Council, though sent for, should be fined for selling his offices. Will make good his charge, if required. *Annexing,*

97. i. *Statement that Robt. Swayne, sheriff of Dorsetshire, would not permit Renaldo Knapton to continue gaoler of Dorsetshire, though recommended by the King, without payment of 40l.; that he sold the office of county clerk to Thos. Delacourt for 13l. 6s. 8d., and that of under sheriff to Hen. Backway, which offices no sheriff ought to sell.*

June 17. 98. —— —— to Lord Arlington. There is nothing on foot worth coming to see his lordship about, only undigested overtures of fugitives across the water; but the party are all quiet now. The business in Scotland is shrunk to nothing; but perhaps the state of affairs may soon encourage those in Holland and Scotland to resume their tumultuous councils.

June 17. Poole. 99. William Skutt to Williamson. Thanks for his good news. The fishermen see ships pass daily; a fleet of 30 sail is standing eastward, supposed to be a French fleet bound for Newhaven, with salt.

June 17. 100. List of 83 ships which cleared at Newcastle during the past week.

VOL. CXXIV.

1665.

June 17. Newcastle. 101. Rich. Forster to James Hickes. The Hector has taken a galliot hoy, which did much mischief on the coast and sunk five small ships. Particulars of the capture; she has many cables and one anchor on board, and 100*l.* in money.

June 17. Commission for Henry Howard to be ensign to Capt. Witherington's company at Berwick. Minute. [*Ent. Book* 20, *p.* 67.]

June [17.] Commission for Sir Fras. Mackworth to be Captain of the company lately commanded by Capt. Carey. Minute. [*Ent. Book* 22, p. 67.]

June 17. Warrant to Percival Stanney to discharge Mayhoe. Minute. [*Ent. Book* 22, *p.* 174.]

June 17. Warrant to Sir William Doyley and the High Sheriffs of Essex and Suffolk to remove the Dutch prisoners from Ipswich to the gaols of Colchester, Bilborough, Woodbridge, and Hadleigh, where they are to be received and safely kept. [*Ent. Book* 22, *p.* 174.]

June 17. Warrant empowering three Justices of Peace in the several divisions of London and Westminster to purchase ground for erection of pest houses, in order to stay the spreading of the plague, to have the said houses built, and to buy any byeways or passages for more convenient access to the same. [*Ent. Book* 22, *pp.* 174–5.]

June 17. 102. Petition of Sir Thos. Strickland to the King, for a lease at 1,800*l.* a year or less, of the farm of the ½*d.* per gallon lately imposed on Scotch salt, of which he is now sub-farmer, in compensation for the loyalty of his family.

June 17. Warrant for a lease to Sir Thomas Strickland, of Thornton Bridge, co. York, for 21 years, of all duties payable on salt imported from beyond seas or Scotland, to begin from Michaelmas 1667; rent, 1,800*l.* [*Ent. Book* 22, *p.* 176.]

June 17. Warrant to —— Dixon to discharge Henry Brandriffe. [*Ent. Book* 22, *p.* 176.]

June 17. Whitehall. 103. Petition of Gervase Price to the King, for an order for insertion of his name in the new establishment of the household, as keeper of the private armory, as previously granted, whereon Mr. Fox cut off his former allowances, but now he hears his name is not inserted in the new establishment, and his ancient allowance of 16*d.* a day and a nag's livery is also left out. With order thereon for him to have 100*l.* a year as keeper of the armory, and his other allowances continued.

June 17. Entry of the above order, the date altered to July 21, Hampton Court. [*Ent. Book* 18, *p.* 171.]

June 17. 104. Capt. Thos. Strickland to the Navy Comrs. Begs the release of Charles Frigs, pressed while unlading a prize ship of flax; he is unfitted for service by want of sight. [*Adm. Paper.*]

VOL. CXXIV.

1665.

June 17. Gravesend. 105. Fr. Hosier to Sam. Pepys. Account of five of the King's ships at Gravesend. Will show the order received to the victuallers as they come down. [*Adm. Paper.*]

June 17. Deptford. 106. Jonas Shish to the Navy Comrs. Arrival of the Ruby; if care be not taken to get out her provisions, guns, and ballast, the benefit of the spring [tide] will be lost in docking her. [*Adm. Paper.*]

June 17. Chatham. 107. Comr. Peter Pett to Sam. Pepys. Has put the Charles, Prince, and flag ships in a way of repair; the Mary and Triumph must be docked as soon as masts, shipwrights, and calkers can be sent down. [*Adm. Paper.*] *Encloses,*

107. I. *Phin. Pett and Joseph Lawrence to Sam. Pepys. Want 100 shipwrights for the speedy dispatch of ships now in dock.* *Chatham Dock, June* 17, 1665.

June 17. Sheerness. 108. Phin. Pett to the Navy Comrs. The damage sustained by the St. George cannot be repaired without bringing her into dock. [*Adm. Paper.*]

June 17. 109. Capt. John Proud to the Navy Comrs. Progress of the Loyal Subject. List of stores required for her completion; carpenters wanted. [*Adm. Paper.*]

June 17. Navy Office. 110. Navy Comrs. to the Officers of Ordnance. Ask whether anything is expected from them with reference to the Loyal Subject's guns, that nothing may be wanted for her dispatch. With reply by the Officers of Ordnance that they will supply 42 guns for the Loyal Subject, but the wants of the fleet prevent their sending six more, as asked for by the owners. [*Adm. Paper.*]

June 18. 111. John Shish to the Navy Comrs. Repairs of the Ruby; 50 shipwrights and calkers are sent to Harwich; desires a warrant to press 40 more in their room. [*Adm. Paper.*]

June 18. Chatham. 112. Comr. Peter Pett to Sam. Pepys. Begs an order for pressing 60 calkers at Deptford and Woolwich. [*Adm. Paper.*]

June 18. Chatham. 113. Comr. Peter Pett to Sam. Pepys. The Triumph, Mary, and Resolution will be launched speedily; requests victuals for them; also that the shipwrights and calkers demanded may be sent down. Sailmakers and glaziers are much wanted. [*Adm. Paper.*] *Encloses,*

113. I. *John Smith to [Comr. Pett]. Great want of six sailmakers for the repair of sails at Chatham.* *June* 18, 1665.

June 18. Hull. 114. Luke Whittington to James Hickes. Hears from Burlington that the Eagle has taken a Holland private man-of-war. Arrival of ships.

Vol. CXXIV.

1665.

June 18. Plymouth. 115. Dr. Grosse to Williamson. Several capers are cruising about and taking soundings. Arrival of a ship from Virginia and others.

June 19. Plymouth. 116. J. Clarke to James Hickes. Arrival of vessels. A private man-of-war has brought in a ship of 300 tons, with passengers and household goods from Amsterdam, bound westward.

June 19. Isle of Wight. 117. Col. Walter Slingsby to Williamson. The company of the Greyhound being sickly gives cause to idle people to suspect the sickness, but there is no such matter. A house in Southampton has been shut up on suspicion of the plague, but the physicians and surgeons say that is not the case.

June 19. 118. [Jas. Hickes to Williamson]. A Dutch caper has taken two Liverpool vessels on the coast between England and Dublin; the Dartmouth would have taken her, but is windbound. Sir Phil. Frowde's orders about some letters going out on Saturday night have been observed.

June 19. Commissions for Willm. Harwood to be Ensign and Thos. Stradling Lieutenant to Capt. Barker's company in Portsmouth. Minute. [*Ent. Book* 20, p. 67.]

June 19. Commission to Sir Willm. Berkeley to be Lieut.-Governor of the town and garrison of Portsmouth. [*Ent. Book* 20, p. 68.]

June 19. Commission for Sir Willm. Berkeley to be Captain to the company of foot in the garrison of Portsmouth, commanded by the Earl of Falmouth, deceased. Minute. [*Ent. Book* 20, p. 68.]

June 19. Warrant to pay to Sir George Carteret, treasurer of the navy, 20,000*l*., to be issued on bills of imprest made by the Navy Commissioners to Capt. George Cock, for relief of the sick and wounded, and prisoners taken at sea. [*Docquet.*]

June 19. Licence to erect a hospital or workhouse at Westminster, to be called the Scottish hospital of King Charles II., for the relief of poor artificers and orphans of that nation, inhabiting London and Westminster, eight Scots to be governors, and one elected master yearly. [*Docquet.*]

June 19. Grant to Lady Wentworth, widow of Thos. Lord Wentworth, of an annuity of 600*l*. [*Docquet.*]

June 19. Grant to the Trustees of the Queen-Mother of approbation and confirmation of certain leases by them made to sundry persons named, of the manor, mansion house and park of Eltham, the rents to be paid to her for life, and afterwards to revert to the Crown. [*Ent. Book* 17, pp. 112-4.]

June 19. Whitehall. Warrant for a grant to Sir John Lowther, Bart., of the messuages, &c., at St. Bees, Cumberland, now in tenure of Thos. Jackson and

1665. VOL. CXXIV.

10 others, with the salt houses, pier or quay, and all lands, &c., between high and low water mark, belonging to the manor, for ever. [*Ent. Book* 22, *p.* 177.]

[June 19.] 119. Draft of the preceding.

June 19. Warrant from Lord Arlington to the Lieutenant of the Tower to discharge the Earl of Rochester, on sufficient security to surrender to a Secretary of State, the first day of Michaelmas Term. [*Ent. Book* 22, *p.* 178.]

June 19. Warrant for erecting an office for the Keeper of the King's libraries, fee, 200*l.* a year; and grant thereof to Thomas Rosse, with reversion to Richard Pearson. [*Ent. Book* 22, *pp.* 178–9.]

June 19. London. Sir And. Riccard, governor of the Levant Company, to Gilbert Searle, merchant at Leghorn. Hearing of Consul Read's death, sends a copy of Capt. Rand's letter to Signor Arena Milenet, for release of the captive Turk whom Rand brought from Spain, and intended to sell as a slave, which might have been of great danger to the Turkey trade; he is to send the Turk to Smyrna. [*Levant Papers, Vol.* v., *p.* 113.]

June 19. 120. Sir Wm. Coventry to the Navy Comrs. Desires that the complements of men to be allowed to each prize ship be established, and the victualler ordered to furnish them accordingly. [*Adm. Paper.*]

June 19. Dover. 121. Thos. White to the Navy Comrs. Can supply cordage for Capt. Seymour of the Pearl, but at the cost of 4*s.* per cwt. more than in London. Asks whether to make a 14-inch cable landed there into ropes for her. The Lily is tallowed and ready for victualling; requests a bill of imprest for timber and plank furnished to the Pearl on his own credit. [*Adm. Paper.*]

June 19. The Baltimore. 122. Capt. Charles Wylde to the Navy Comrs. Is near Gravesend, and so miserably manned that there is no venturing to sea; out of 100 pressed men, not 30 are seamen, the rest boys, weavers, cobblers, any that have been picked up in the street; could not get a man from five colliers, the fleet having taken their men; begs some able seamen forthwith. The cook is a fellow not fitting for his place; is obliged to hire a soldier to dress the men's food. [*Adm. Paper.*]

June 19. 123. List of 31 calkers pressed for the dockyard at Chatham by Dan. Boutwell. With duplicate of the former part of the list. [*Adm. Paper*, 1½ *pages.*]

June 19? 124. List of seven seamen pressed by Thos. Elmes, who have not yet appeared.

June 19. Woolwich. 125. Chris. Pett to the Navy Comrs. Has dispatched a hoy of provisions, with 20 shipwrights and calkers, to assist in the repairs of the fleet at the Nore. Prince Rupert is pleased to command a new pinnace of 10 oars to be speedily built for his own use, and a similar one is ordered for Rear-Admiral Teddeman; asks to have the making of them both; shall only want four large wainscots sent

Vol. CXXIV.

1665.

down, and will dispatch them in eight days; can spare about 50 shipwrights and calkers for Chatham, if no more of the maimed ships come in to be repaired. Tender of plank by Edw. Hulbert, of Horseydown. [*Adm. Paper.*]

June 20. 126. Sir Wm. Coventry to Sam. Pepys. Gives the names of the eight prize ships made men-of-war; begs that all remaining stores may be hastened to the fleet; the Sovereign goes into dock to-morrow; the Triumph, Resolution, and Mary are ready to victual; will endeavour to get the Commissioners' order for fitting the Hare lying at Aldborough. [*Adm. Paper.*]

June 20. 127. List of the above-named eight prizes, with the number of guns in each. With request by Sam. Pepys to [Coventry?] that the number of men fit for each ship be decided on, that orders may be dispatched to the victualler. [*Adm. Paper.*]

June 20. 128. John Brooke and Jas. Norman to [Sam. Pepys]. Request six more sailmakers for Chatham. [*Adm. Paper.*]

June 20. Plymouth. 129. John Lanyon to the Navy Comrs. The Nightingale is fitted, and only waiting for powder; has borrowed some of Sir John Skelton and agreed to pay him in specie; promises care in the disposal of pitch to the various ships under repair; requests settlement of his accounts, being much out of purse already. [*Adm. Paper.*]

June 20. Chatham. 130. Comr. Peter Pett to Sam. Pepys. Has put all hands to work for the dispatch of the fleet at the Nore; victuals to be sent down to 16 ships mentioned; is glad of Mr. Uthwat's provision of cordage, but thinks all such things should be sent direct to Chatham, to be disposed of as occasion requires; shipwrights, calkers, and six sailmakers are wanted. [*Adm. Paper.*]

June 20. 131. Warrant from the Navy Comrs. to Mr. Harper, storekeeper at Deptford, to receive into the stores the cordage brought from the wreck of the London. [*Adm. Paper.*]

June 20. Warrant for a grant to Sir John Robinson of the reversion of a lease of certain tenements, wharfs, &c., in the parishes of St. Peter's ad Vincula within the Tower, and All Hallows, Barking, formerly granted to Henry Timberlake and Robert Bradbury, and then to Sir Robert Aston, with proviso of demolition of any buildings thereon that may be prejudicial to the Tower. [*Ent. Book* 22, p. 180.]

[June 20.] 132. Draft of the above. [2½ *pages.*]

June 20. Warrant for a patent to Charles Hildyard of his invention of making blue paper used by sugar bakers and others, an art not hitherto known in England. [*Ent. Book* 22, p. 181.]

June 20. [Rome.] 133. Sir Bernard Gascoigne to [Williamson]. Wants a pass for a ship of his from Holland. The Archduke of Inspruck, the last of the family, died of pain in his foot, after an illness of seven hours.

VOL. CXXIV.

1665.

From Spain it is reported that the Emperor is to renounce his rights as the Queen of France has done. Hopes the news from Holland, of their taking 10 Hamburg ships, laden with goods for the navy, is false. Sends the Foglietta from Rome.

June? Pass for a ship laden for the sole risk and account of Sir Bernard Gascoigne. Minute. [*Ent. Book* 22, p. 160.]

June 20. 134. J. I. [John Ironmonger] to Sir Thos. Gower. The designers hardly dare trust one another; London is the place, and all depended on the success of the Dutch, and hopes from France; they were dead on news of the victory, but build much on the increase of the plague. Sends a copy of a letter from Holland. *Affixing,*

134. I. *L. T. M. and W. to* [*Ironmonger*]. *Exhort the godly to constancy; though the beginning be dangerous, the end will be glorious. Hope those who try to ruin their trade will not succeed, in spite of the ill practices of the new company, the head and masters of which must be cut off, even at the risk of life. It is said the French will declare for the Dutch, and none can resist them joined.*

June 20. Landguard Point Fort. 135. Edw. Sackley to James Hickes. There are nine good Dutch men-of-war, some of 50 or 60 guns, brought to Harwich, four sent to London, and four or five more said to be at Ousley Bay. There are 2,500 Dutch prisoners taken, and they confess they have lost 10,000; they say the States will hang 17 or 18 captains for running away. It is reported that the French will furnish them with 30,000 men. If some of the English captains had their desert, they would be badly off, for 24 were questioned, but only Capt. Hyde of the Sapphire put out.

June 20. Plymouth. 136. J. Clarke to James Hickes. Two frigates have arrived with a vessel from Lisbon, which waits for convoy, the frigates having put to sea again.

June 20. Newcastle. 137. Rich. Forster to James Hickes. The coal vessels are going to and fro without convoy; 600 or 700 great shots are reported to have been heard off the Lincolnshire coast. Wants a Holland Current every week, as well as the English paper.

June 20. Harwich. 138. Fra. Newby and Rich. Marbury to [Williamson]. The Dutch are fitting out their fleet with all expedition; they are choosing land commanders, as many of the sea commanders have had to run for it. Evertsen hardly escaped with his life from the people, and is in prison with the usual punishment of pumping. The English ships are fitting out with all expedition.

June 20. Dover. 139. J[ohn] C[arlisle] to Williamson. The Emperor is said to be marching into Flanders with 8,000 men; the Hollanders are hastening for a second engagement. There is no sickness in the place. A prize has been sent in.

VOL. CXXIV.

1665.
June 21. Exeter House. 140. Lord Ashley to Lord Arlington. There is a privy seal for payment of 4*l.* a day to the Lord Privy Seal for diet, so that his lordship only needs a letter to the Lord Treasurer for the arrears.

June 21. Westminster. 141. Commission to the Lord Chancellor, Lord Treasurer, and numerous others, to prorogue the present Parliament to the 1st day of August next, ordering the obedience thereto of all concerned. [*Latin. Two pages, copy.*]

June ? 142. Request of the Royal Fishing Company to Lord Arlington, to obtain a proclamation suppressing all lotteries except such as are granted to them; to obtain the recall of the King's letter to the Mayor of Norwich about lotteries, and an emendation in the patent of the company.

June 21. Whitehall. Proclamation forbidding any persons to use or exercise lotteries in Great Britain or Ireland, except Sir Ant. Desmarces, Bart., Louis Marquis Blanquefort de Duras, Jos. Williamson, Lawrence Dupuy, and Rich. Baddeley, to whom the sole right of managing them is granted, in order to raise a stock for the Royal Fishing Company. [*Printed. Proc. Coll., Charles II., pp.* 190–1.]

June 21. Newhall. 143. Duke of Albemarle to Lord Arlington. All that come from court so urge on him to induce the King to give the privy purse to the Earl of Bath, that he thinks his reputation concerned in the success of the request, and will be much troubled to be denied; the Earl is his near kinsman, very faithful to His Majesty, and fit for the employment.

June 21. The King to the High Sheriff of Surrey. Sir Nich. Stoughton, late high sheriff, having paid over to him the surplus of the month's assessment for the militia, and he hesitating to pay it over without a special warrant, commands him to pay the same forthwith to Sir John Robinson, lieutenant of the Tower, any former orders to the lord lieutenant or deputy lieutenant notwithstanding. [*Ent. Book* 20, p. 69.]

June 21. The King to [the Master of the Rolls?] A grant was made to Lord Colepeper of the nomination to the next vacancy in the Six Clerks' Office in Chancery, but not entered before a letter of later date in behalf of Silius Titus. To avoid dispute, orders that Lord Colepeper should have the first nomination. [*Ent. Book* 17, p. 115.]

[June 21.] 144. Draft of the above.

June 21. Whitehall. The King to the Archbishop of Canterbury. Many complaints being made of the bad management of hospitals, he is to issue his mandate to the several Bishops, to give in speedily their certificates on instructions sent therewith, in order to effect redress of the same. [*Ent. Book* 14, p. 63.]

June 21. The King to the Master and Senior Fellows of Trinity College, Cambridge. Grants a dispensation to William Robson, M.A.,

VOL. CXXIV.

1665.

chaplain of their college and chaplain of the navy, to be absent beyond seas, for recovery of his health. [*Ent. Book* 14, p. 65.]

June 21. Warrant to John Sumpner, messenger, Daniel Gotherson, and Peter Shepherd, to search for Charles Hildyard, his wife Joan, Elizabeth, wife of Tobias Barne, and Major Danborne, and to bring away all the King's concealed goods. Minute. [*Ent. Book* 22, p. 181.]

June 21. Warrant to the Commissioners of Ordnance to admit Jonas Moore, assistant surveyor, as the duties of the surveyor at this present conjuncture are of great importance; salary, 150*l*. a year. [*Ent. Book* 22, p. 183.]

[June 21.] 145, 146. Two drafts of the above.

June 21. Warrant to [Lord Ashley,] treasurer for prizes, to pay 2,000*l*. to George Cock, treasurer for the sick and wounded, for their service. [*Ent. Book* 22, p. 184.]

June? 147. Petition of Grace, widow of Capt. Willm. Pestle, to the King, for some allowance, her husband being slain at Guinea, at the taking of Goree, under Major Holmes.

June 21. Warrant to the Navy Comrs. to pay 50*l*. to Sarah [Grace], widow of Capt. William Pestle, slain in a voyage to Guinea under Capt. Robt. Holmes. [*Ent. Book* 22, p. 184.]

June [21]. 148, 149. Two drafts of the above.

June? 150. Petition of Sir John Evelyn to the King, for liberty to enclose the highway leading from West Tudderley, co. Hants, to West Dean, co. Wilts, on condition of opening another as convenient to passengers. *Annexing*,

150. I. *Inquisition of Ad quod damnum, pronouncing that a grant to Sir John Evelyn, of a highway in the parish of West Dean, co. Wilts, leading from West Tudderley to White parish, co. Hants, will be in no way prejudicial to the King or his subjects, provided he lay out a sufficient road in its stead. With the writ for the above inquisition, dated 16 Feb. 1665, prefixed.* [*Latin, six leaves.*]
West Dean, March 31.

June 21. Warrant for a license to Sir John Evelyn to enclose a highway in the parish of West Dean, co. Wilts, he making another highway through his grounds instead. [*Ent. Book* 22, p. 185.]

June 21. Warrant for creating Peter Tirrell, of Hanslape and Castlethorp, co. Bucks, a baronet. Minute. [*Ent. Book* 22, p. 199.]

June 21. 151. Capt. Geo. Erwin to the Navy Comrs. The Abigail received 30 tons of water cask on board at Deptford. [*Adm. Paper.*]

VOL. CXXIV.

1665.

June 21. Newhall. 152. Duke of Albemarle to the Navy Comrs. Sends an order to the Lieutenant of the Tower to assist Capt. Geo. Erwin with two files of men, which will do the work. [*Adm. Paper.*]

June 21. 153. Report by Mr. Tooker,—sent down the river by the Navy Comrs., to enquire what ships are employed to carry victuals, water, &c., to order the laying of cordage at Woolwich, and the dispatch of ironwork,—of the execution of his orders. [*Adm. Paper, 2 pages.*]

June 21. 154. Certificate by Chris. Pett and two others that Wm. Castell's ship is ready for the second payment, according to contract. [*Adm. Paper.*]

June 21. Chatham. 155. Comr. Peter Pett to Sam. Pepys. Only six of the pressed men have yet appeared. Wishes Capt. Boddilaw, master attendant of Woolwich, to be sent down. Particulars of ships. All hands are turned to the dispatch of the fleet. [*Adm. Paper.*]

June 21. 156. Certificate from the Masters and Wardens of Barber Surgeons' Hall of bills of free gift and imprest received for furnishing the chest of Wm. Downs, surgeon of the Resolution, and of his subsequent removal into the Swiftsure; also of the appointment of Robt. Peirse from the Swiftsure to the Resolution, without free gift or imprest money. [*Adm. Paper.*]

June 21. Chatham. 157. Comr. Peter Pett to Sam. Pepys. If expected to answer the present emergency, more care must be taken in sending down shipwrights. Desires victuals for 23 ships mentioned. [*Adm. Paper.*]

VOL. CXXV. JUNE 22-30, 1665.

1665.

June 22. Deptford. 1. Jonas Shish and two others to the Navy Comrs. Account of repairs needed to the clerk of the survey's house, in the yard at Deptford; estimate of charge, 12*l.* [*Adm. Paper.*]

June 22. 2. Sir Wm. Coventry to Sam. Pepys. The commander and most of the companies of the Maryland and John and Katherine are removed into two prize ships. Asks where the vessels are to be kept, till it is decided whether to use them further or pay them off. [*Adm. Paper.*]

June 22. 3. Account of extra light money and other money due on board the Royal Sovereign since January 1st; total, 17*l.* [*Adm. Paper.*]

June 22. 4. Walter Lemingham and Thos. Crowe to Sam. Pepys. Request warrants for two months' sea victuals for the Katherine and Henrietta yachts. [*Adm. Paper.*]

VOL. CXXV.

1665.

June 22. Custom House. 5. John Lawson to Sam. Pepys. Employs many carpenters at the Custom House wharf, to repair the lighters in use there. Four of them are pressed, much to the prejudice of his business. Begs release of Wm. Fleming, one of the men. [*Adm. Paper.*]

June 22. 6. Account by Chris. Pett and Jonas Shish of masts delivered into the stores at Deptford, by Wm. Wood and Mr. Gray, June 17–22. [*Adm. Paper, 5 pages.*] *Annexing,*

6. I–IV. *Four papers of memoranda relating to the above masts.*

June 22. 7. Note that the Earl of Shrewsbury's grant of 800 acres of fen [land] is dated July 23, 1664, and entered in the signet office June 22, 1665. [*Damaged.*]

June 22. Landguard Point Fort. 8. Edw. Suckley to James Hickes. In a few days, 30 frigates will go northwards to meet De Ruyter's fleet, though 20 sail of Dutchmen are going to bring him home. A few Dutch capers are on the coast to snap up colliers, and took one which was retaken with the Dutch caper, but not one of our men that they will give account of.

June 22. St. John's College. 9. Certificate by Dr. Peter Gunning, master, and seven Fellows of St. John's, Cambridge, to the good conduct of Thos. Smoult, for seven years student there. [*Latin.*]

June 22. 10. Report by Attorney General Palmer, on the petition of [Oliver Cave, John Holbrook, and Edw. Green,] that they were not proved guilty in reference to the highway robbery committed in their company, for which Phineas and Thos. Hodgson were executed last summer assizes at York, and that they are therefore capable of pardon.

June 22. Whitehall. 11. Petition of Philip Wilde, of Wolley, co. Derby, to the King, to be included in the general pardon, being too poor to pay the fees of a particular pardon. Was condemned for high treason at the last Derby assizes, through his inadvertency. With reference thereon to Baron Turner, and his report in favour of the petitioner, as being deranged, not only by the least drinking, but at certain seasons of the moon.

June 22. Entry of the above reference. [*Ent. Book* 18, p. 175.]

June 22. Reference to the Solicitor General on the petition of Erasmus Smith, for security by a clause in the new bill, in reference to five free schools which he wishes to make, but finds that the lapsed money is assigned upon the lands designed for the same. [*Ent. Book* 18, p. 175.]

June 23. Reference on the petition of Peter Bar and other French Merchants to the Commissioners for Prizes, who are to release the ship, and order all just right done to the petitioners who had a pass from the ambassador at Paris. [*Ent. Book* 18, p. 175.]

VOL. CXXV.

1665.

June 23. Reference to the Attorney General, on the petition of Sir Thos. Orby, for the mastership of St. John Baptist's Hospital, Bedford. [*Ent. Book* 18, *p.* 176.]

June 23. Reference to the Lord Treasurer, on the petition of Wm. May, for a grant of the estate of Thos. Oates. [*Ent. Book* 18, *p.* 176.]

June 23. Newcastle. 12. Rich. Forster to James Hickes. Particulars of small vessels captured or threatened. All the town wishes that they had two or three good sailing frigates to clear their coasts, and that Capt. John Wetwyng, of the Norwich, were one of those appointed.

June 23. 13. Folding sheet, endorsed "letters that were intercepted by Sir Thos. Gower."

June 23. Gatehouse. 14. John Knowles to Lord Arlington. Begs a speedy trial or release from his miserable restraint, which he has suffered most patiently, as knowing that governors are obliged to be jealous in times of danger. Protests his innocence; has always been a faithful and obedient subject, and careful to incite others to be the same, and detests all faction and sedition.

June 23. London. 15. Leo. Williams to Lord Arlington. All is quiet, there being little hopes from the difference with other nations. They would rather comply if they could for shame. Thinks if he saw Atkinson, he could say something to him that would make him confess what he knows of particular persons.

June 23. Warrant for the insertion of a proviso for John Payne to have his arrears due to him as a 1649 officer in full, although he was obliged to accept some small allowance in Cromwell's time. Minute. [*Ent. Book* 22, *p.* 198.]

June 23. Commissions for Lieut. Patrick Vaus to be Quartermaster and Marshal, Gervase Rouse, Adjutant, and James Perrie, Surgeon [in the Holland regiment]. [*Ent. Book* 20, *p.* 77.]

June 23. Whitehall. Proclamation forbidding the holding of St. James' fair at Bristol on 25 July, for fear of spreading the present contagion. [*Printed. Proc. Coll., Charles II., p.* 192.]

June 23. 16. John Rowley to Lord Arlington. The attorney of the Skinners' Company, who drew up their petition about their differences with the felt makers, presented it, unknown to the company; it is referred to his lordship to decide whether to bring it before Council; thinks that to avoid a concourse of people, in this time of sickness, it would be better to refer the case to the Lord Chancellor or Attorney General; the company will understand as they ought to do their obligations to his lordship.

June 23? Friday. Worcester House. 17. Lord Chancellor Clarendon to Lord Arlington. The King before he left was so sorry for the poor controller, who is more troubled for his creditors than for want of his own wealth, that he resolves to give him 5,000*l.*, settled on some fund for the next year;

VOL. CXXV.

1665.

he chooses the warrant to be in his own name, and relies on his lordship's friendship to get it dispatched. It should be done on the ground of sums advanced by him for the King's service.

June 23. 18. Wm. Howe, muster-master, to Sam. Pepys. Sends muster books of most of the ships in the Earl of Sandwich's squadron; endeavoured to call over the whole after the engagement, but was prevented by some being sent into harbour. [*Adm. Paper.*]

June 23. Woolwich. 19. Chris. Pett to the Navy Comrs. Gives an account of a mutiny amongst the labourers in the yard, through the example of William Watkins, one of the lately-pressed men, who refuses to return to ordinary hours and daily wages, now that the press of work and allowance of tides are at an end; requests that some severe course may be taken to bring them to their duty; has paid off and dispatched for Chatham 30 shipwrights and calkers, with provisions of all sorts. *Enclosing,*

19. I. *List of* 11 *shipwrights absenting themselves from work.* [*Adm. Paper.*]

June 23. Chatham. 20. Comr. Peter Pett to Sam. Pepys. Denis Gauden must be hastened in sending down agents for disposal of beer and victuals to the fleet. The service is much retarded and many seamen lost by the absence of commanders from their ships; some shipwrights and calkers have arrived; boats wanted. [*Adm. Paper.*]

June 23. Chatham Ropeyard. 21. John Owen to the Navy Comrs. Reminds them that there are not 100 tons of hemp in store. [*Adm. Paper.*]

June 24. 22. John Tooker to the Navy Comrs. Finds from the brokers that 40 pairs of old sheets for the fleet will cost 18*l.* or 19*l.*; beds with mats, 15*l.*; the rest of the goods 20*l.*; requires 60*l.* advanced on account to pay for the goods. [*Adm. Paper.*]

June 24. Ordnance Office. 23. Edw. Sherburne and Ric. Marsh to the Navy Comrs. The Owners' Endeavour is laden with ammunition for the fleet; want an order for the clothes of two men now on board her, formerly pressed out of the Sarah and Elizabeth. [*Adm. Paper.*]

June 24. 24. Phin. Pett to [Sam. Pepys]. Account of masts wanting for the dispatch of the fleet, and for a supply at Chatham. [*Adm. Paper.*]

June 24. 25, 26. Account of press warrants granted for five ships belonging to Sir Wm. Rider, with a memorandum relating to the same. Two papers.

June 24. 27. Sir Wm. Coventry to Sir Wm. Batten. If the Admiral Trump prize be desired for a storeship, it is time to obtain the necessary orders; proposes the Black Spread Eagle as a fire ship; water ships must be hastened to the fleet. [*Adm. Paper.*]

VOL. CXXV.

1665.

June 24. Chatham. 28. Comr. Peter Pett to Sam. Pepys. All sorts of persons have been set to refit the fleet; masts are still the great want; is sorry the last demand caused ill feeling; has no wish to quarrel, but must once more desire to know what supply is in view, in case of another engagement. Sailmakers are wanted; particulars of ships. [*Adm. Paper*, 2 *pages*.]

June 24. Bristol. 29. Sir John Knight to the Navy Comrs. Has agreed for the Pearl to be fitted up as a man-of-war, and carry 32 pieces of ordnance, at the rate of 115*l*. per month, two months paid in advance. Requests orders for the supply of victuals and ammunition, and that an ensign and pennant be hastened down; proposes Walter Morgan as commander; asks whether the Resolution, a smaller ship of 20 guns, shall be hired also. [*Adm. Paper*, 2 *pages*.]

June 24. Whitehall. 30. Warrant for a grant to Edward Griffin of the reversion of the office of Treasurer of the Chamber, after his father, Sir Edw. Griffin. [*Copy*, 1½ *pages*.]

June 24.] 31. Draft of the above. [*Imperfect*.]

June 24. Entry of the above. [*Ent. Book* 22, *p.* 193.]

June ? 32. Request that Williamson would obtain passes for horses for M. De Longueville, governor of Fescamp, and M. Bourlon de Plailly. [*French*.]

June 24. Whitehall. 33. Pass for six horses to France for M. Bourlon de Plailly.

June 24. Minute of the above. [*Ent. Book* 22, *p.* 194.]

June 24. Whitehall. 34. Warrant for creating Richard Gething a Baronet, and for discharge of the usual payments.

June 24. Minute of the above. [*Ent. Book* 22, *p.* 194.]

June 24. Whitehall. 35. Pass for six horses to France, for the Sieur De Longueville, governor of Feschamp.

June 24. Minute of the above. [*Ent. Book* 22, *p.* 194.]

June 24. Pass for seven horses for the Sieur De Monlovet. Minute. [*Ent. Book* 22, *p.* 194.]

June 24. Warrant for creating Abel Barker, of Hambleton, co. Rutland, a Baronet. Minute. [*Ent. Book* 29, *p.* 194.]

[June 24.] 36. Warrant to pay 58*l*. 8*s*. to Richard Royston for stationery, &c., for Lord Arlington, from 31 Oct. 1662 to 7 Feb. 1665.

June 24. Minute of the above. [*Ent. Book* 22, *p.* 194.]

June 24. Warrant for a pardon to Oliver Cave, Joseph Holbrook, and Edward Green, condemned to death at York assizes, because when

1665. Vol. CXXV.

in drink, they were enticed to accompany Thos. and Phineas Hodgson, highwaymen, in a robbery for which both are executed. [*Ent. Book* 22, *pp.* 196–198.]

June 24. Whitehall. 37. Pass for the Sieur De Lionne, with one horse, to France.

June 24. Minute of the above. [*Ent. Book* 22, *p.* 201.]

June 24. Hull. 38. L. Whittington to James Hickes. Three collier vessels and a ship laden with salt have been taken by a Zealand privateer; report of 30 Holland men-of-war gone northwards.

June 24. 39. Estimate of the establishment of the Holland regiment under Col. Robt. Sydney, beginning from 24th June 1665; total yearly expense, 10,504*l.* 8*s.* 8*d.*

June 24. Yarmouth. 40. Rich. Bower to Williamson. There are great fears that the colliers will suffer for want of convoys; if they receive a blow, many will be beaten from the trade; 50 or 60 have just sailed; those from the south come into the road, and when they have lost several south winds and are weary of riding, they go forward without fear or wit; three vessels were lately taken by a Dutch man-of-war; 20 sail are at anchor, waiting to go northward. There have 20 persons died of the plague, being a decrease of 10 since last week.

June 24. Whitehall. 41. Commission to Louis Marquis of Blanquefort to be Captain of the Duke of York's Guards.

June 25. The Sarah pink, Hole Haven. 42. Lambart Wood to the Navy Comrs. Has no great number of men impressed, to show his diligence in the service, having lent so many to assist other ships; asks an indemnity for pressing men out of colliers; has seen other officers do it; could do it well because, riding without colours, he is not mistrusted. Asks how to dispose of 10 men at present on board. [*Adm. Paper.*]

June 25. The Baltimore, Downs. 43. John Clarke, cook, to Sam. Pepys. Begs to be continued in his employment; protests against the false accusation of the purser and captain that he is "no cook at all;" can have the hands of all the ship's company for the wholesome dressing of their meat. [*Adm. Paper.*]

June 26. Chatham. 44. Capt. Mart. Carslake to the Navy Comrs. Requests a master for his ship Charles the Fifth, prize; has 54 soldiers and 30 seamen on board, but most of them lent; knows not when or where to get more. [*Adm. Paper.*]

June 26. Chatham. 45. Comr. Peter Pett to Sam. Pepys. Cannot answer expectation in the timely repair of the fleet, for want of hands; the few shipwrights scraped together are on extra duty day and night, until quite tired; entreats more men to be hastened down with the master of attendance, who is much needed. Progress of ships; great expense of masts and yards. [*Adm. Paper.*]

Vol. CXXV.

1665.

June 26. Bristol. 46. Dan. Furzer to the Navy Comrs. Progress of the ship building at Compill; requests money and an order to fell trees in the Lea Baly for plank. Mr. Bayly's ship must be surveyed. Offered 3*l*. a load for 3-inch plank at Chepstow, but 5*s*. a load more is asked. Wants 300*l*. or 400*l*., having paid for four or five tons of good iron ware. [*Adm. Paper*, 1½ *pages*.]

June 26. Bristol. 47. Sir John Knight to the Navy Comrs. The Pearl frigate is hired for 6 months certain and 12 uncertain, at 115*l*. a month. Asks what ammunition and stores are to be provided for her; can procure no other square-sterned ship in the city. [*Adm. Paper*.]

June 26. Deal. 48. Ric. Watts to Williamson. Account of vessels in the Downs. Mr. Carlisle is too ill to write.

June 26. Whitehall. 49. Jos. Williamson to [Roger] L'Estrange. Lord Arlington wishes the preceding narrative to be inserted in the next four news books, for the public benefit. *Prefixes*,

49. I. *Statement by Lord Arlington that the Council, in their care to prevent the spreading of infection, have ordered the Justices of Middlesex to treat with James Augier for remedies to stop the plague and disinfect houses; the experiment being made in the house of Jonas Charles, of Newton Street, St. Giles-in-the-Fields, and other infected houses, and no persons have died of the plague in those houses since. Therefore the said Augier's certificates from abroad having been further examined and approved, the justices wish to advertise the public where his remedies may be obtained, and give six addresses where they are sold, promising a fuller narrative of the experiments made with them.*

June 26. Newport, Isle of Wight. 50. [Col. Walter Slingsby] to Williamson. There are four vessels in Cowes, bound for the West Indies, including 15 volunteer couples going to Jamaica. The small-pox is in the town and is turning to the worst of spotted fevers; as the plague is in Southampton, the gentlemen wish the post to be sent by Portsmouth. The fanatics meet frequently, the neighbouring justices being remiss. Waits to undertake a general rendezvous of the island companies on the 10th, and will then hasten to London. Loses many opportunities by that empty employment.

June 26. 51. Sir Henry Widdrington and Sir Robt. Delaval to Lord Bennet. Have put Wm. Coulson, of Northumberland, in gaol for words spoken a year ago, and have taken good security for appearance of the informer to answer why he concealed the matter so long. Request directions of the Council. *Enclose*,

51. I. *Information of Wm. Carnes, of Jesmond, Northumberland. Was in company last Lammas with his landlord, Wm. Coulson, of Jesmond, and was praising Monk's quiet bringing in of the King without blood spilling,*

1665. VOL. CXXV.

when Coulson called Monk a traitor, and said it had cost him 15l. to get a pardon, because he set his hand to the late King's death; that he hoped to see His Majesty go the same way as his father, and that his chief intriguers would be the first to put him out again.

June 26? 52. Estimate by the Navy Comrs. of the expense of building a masthouse at Sheerness; total, 691l. 2s.

June 26. London. Levant Company to [the Earl of Winchelsea]. In spite of the remarkable and glorious victory over the Dutch, they have taken several men-of-war in the Straits; are soliciting a convoy for their own four general ships, now lading at Smyrna, which are therefore not to depart without convoy, but will be allowed a demurrage. [*Levant Papers, Vol.* v., p. 114.]

June 26. London. Levant Company to Consul Cave. The ships are to remain there [at Smyrna] till the arrival of a convoy. [*Levant Papers, Vol.* v., p. 115.]

June 26. Reference to Lord Admiral the Duke of York on the petition of Hen. Bruncard, for liberty to erect a double lighthouse at Holyhead. [*Ent. Book* 18, p. 177.]

[June 27.] 53. Warrant for discharge to the Attorney General for acknowledging satisfaction on certain judgments already obtained in the Court of King's Bench against William Scarborough and John Ireton, for plate, jewels, &c., belonging to the late King, or for any other similar judgments that may be obtained. With note by the Attorney General that this privy seal is necessary to enable him to acknowledge satisfaction on these judgments.

June 27. Entry of the above. [*Ent. Book* 22, p. 199.]

June 27. Warrant to pay to Edward Backwell, 1,750l., for secret service, without account. [*Ent. Book* 22, p. 200.]

June 27. Pass for twenty packs or bales for the use of Mons. de Cominge. Minute. [*Ent. Book* 22, p. 205.]

June 27. Pass for six horses to France, for the Sieurs De St. Quentin and Baillon, custom free. Minute. [*Ent. Book* 22, p. 206.]

June? 54. Request for passports for the Esperance of Calais, which brought over the Duke of Verneuil's baggage, without payment of the 5s. per ton duty; for another vessel to take back the said baggage, and for six horses which the Duke sends to France.

June 27. Pass for the domestics and baggage of the Duke of Verneuil to France. Minute. [*Ent. Book* 22, p. 206.]

June 27. Pass for the ship Esperance, free of custom, and particularly of the tonnage on French ships. Minute. [*Ent. Book* 22, p. 206.]

Vol. CXXV.

1665.

June 27. Warrant to pay to Henry Progers 200*l.*, for re-building a house in the Mews, held by him as one of the King's equerries. Minute. [*Ent. Book* 22, p. 211.]

[June 27.] 55. Draft of the above.

June 27. 56. Warrant from Attorney General Palmer to Mr. Farrington, clerk of assize for co. Derby, to make copies of the indictment of Phil. Wilde, convicted of high treason. *Annexing*,

56. I. *Certificate by A. Farrington that Phil. Wilde, of Wolley, co. Derby, was convicted of high treason before Sir Chris. Turner and other justices, for endeavouring to enlist soldiers to levy war against the King, and was adjudged to be hanged, drawn, and quartered.*

June 27. Warrant to Sir Chris. Turner to insert into the general pardon Philip Wilde, who was sentenced to death at the Derby assizes for high treason, in endeavouring to list soldiers and wage war against the King. Minute. [*Ent. Book* 22, p. 211.]

June 27. 57. Warrant for a grant to Elizabeth, widow of Col. John Poyer, of recognizances entered into by several persons for certain sums of money, on proviso that 1,399*l.* 13*s.* 5½*d.*, unpaid upon an assignment long since made to the band of gentlemen pensioners, be first discharged. *Annexing*,

57. I. *List of* 17 *persons holding the above recognizances, the total value being* 3,000*l.*

June 27. Entry of the above. [*Ent. Book* 22, pp. 211–2.]

June 27. 58. Sir Wm. Coventry to Sir Willm. Clarke. Requests him to obtain the Lord General's consent for James Pearse to be surgeon in part of the Duke of York's regiment, now to be divided. His Royal Highness has consented, having observed his care and diligence in the fleet.

June 27. Royal Charles, buoy of the Nore. 59. Capt. John Cox to Thos. Ross, gentleman to the Duke of Monmouth. Gives details of the first expedition against the Dutch, from the anchoring off the Texel, April 23d, to the 28th. Thinks there was too much fear of wind and weather shown, and that otherwise the whole Dutch fleet that came round England and Scotland, which was 28 sail, might have been intercepted; but the fleet stood so far off the shore of Holland that they slipped in. [2¼ *pages.*]

June 27. The King to the Earl of Northampton [lord lieutenant of Warwickshire]. Finding that inconveniences arise in transmitting the moneys raised on the militia from one high sheriff to another till paid into the Tower, orders that such sums as are unpaid be sent to a certain town, and there delivered to Thos. Chicheley, who is appointed to transmit the same to the Tower. With note of like letters to the Lord Lieutenants of cos. Nottingham, Lincoln, Northampton, Worcester, and Warwick. [*Ent. Book* 20, pp. 71–2.]

VOL. CXXV.

1665.

June 27. The King to [the Lord Lieutenants of Bedfordshire and seven other counties]. Similar letter, but directing them to transmit the money to the Tower by the best and speediest way they can, the charges of carriage to be paid by them. [*Ent. Book* 20, *pp.* 73–4.]

[June 27.] 60. Draft of the two preceding letters.

June 27. Similar letters sent to the Lord Lieutenants of cos. Derby, Stafford, and Salop; they are to pay the moneys to Thos. Chicheley. [*Ent. Book* 20, *pp.* 74–5.]

June 27. Minutes of commissions in the Holland regiment of foot, as follow:—

Robt. Sydney, Colonel Captain of a company.
Thos. Howard, Lieutenant-Colonel and Captain.
Bruce, Major and Captain.
Ogle, Henry Pomeroy, and Bap. Alcocke, Captains.
Wildehore, Captain Lieutenant to the Colonel's company.
Griffin, Lieutenant to the Lieut.-Col.'s company.
Williamson, Lieutenant to the Major.
Risley, Lieutenant to Capt. Ogle.
Barnes, Lieutenant to Capt. Pomeroy.
Sterling, Lieutenant to Capt. Alcocke.
Myles, Ensign to Col. Sidney.
Boulton, Ensign to Lieut.-Col. Howard.
Saul, Ensign to Bruce.
Manley, Ensign to Capt. Ogle.
Barnes (altered to Phettiplace), Ensign to Pomeroy.
Phettiplace, Ensign to Alcocke. [*Ent. Book* 20, *p.* 76.]

[June.] 61. Draft of the above, with several differences.

June [27]. 62. List of the officers of Col. Sydney's regiment, slightly differing from the above, and adding the names of Lieut. Pat. Vaux as Quartermaster and Marshal and Lieut. Gervase Rowse, Adjutant. With note that of the officers who left their places in Holland, Lieuts. Thos. Honywood, —— Sterling, and Rob. Moore, and Ensigns Phil. Phettiplace and Thos. Preston are to be paid by Mr. Fox, at 3s. a day each to the lieutenants, and 2s. 6d. to the ensigns.

June 27. Grant to Col. William Legg, lieutenant of the forests of Alice-holt and Woolmer, of the whole produce and benefit of all tops, lops, &c., of timber trees felled in the said forests for the use of the navy, to be employed in reparation of the fences. [*Docquet.*]

June 27. Warrant to suspend payment to the King of 2,967*l.* 9*s.* 4½*d.*, balance due to him of 6,248*l.* 7*s.* 1*d.*, to be paid from the arrears of Excise, until a sum due therefrom to Prince Rupert is paid. [*See Feb.* 16, *ante. Ent. Book* 17, *p.* 117.]

June 27. Portsmouth. 63. Comr. Thos. Middleton to Sam. Pepys. Departure of ships. Dares not send to view the cordage at Southampton, as the plague is in the town, and eight houses are shut up; has forbidden the

VOL. CXXV.

1665.

carpenters who live there to go home; these already gone shall not be re-admitted into the yard. Much timber is to be had in the forest, but the carters refuse to bring it down for want of money. Particulars of ships. Wants two galliots for carrying timber. There is such distress among the ropemakers that they buy and eat the offal formerly given to the dogs. Discovery of deal boards supposed to be embezzled. [*Adm. Paper, 3 pages, damaged.*]

June 27. 64. Jonas Shish to the Navy Comrs. Will launch the Ruby and fit the Dutch ship Bull for present service. Is forced to take 12 shipwrights off from work, to unlade a hoy of Suffolk plank just arrived. The Colchester is almost ready to take in victuals. [*Adm. Paper.*]

June 27. Chatham. 65. Capt. Mart. Carslake to the Navy Comrs. Recommends Michael Davidson as master for the prize ship Charles V. [*Adm. Paper.*]

June 27. Tangiers. 66. Lord Belasyse to the Navy Comrs. Begs payment to Thos. Andrews and Company for provisions supplied by his lordship to the Crown frigate, in great necessity; also of 4l. 7s. paid for landing the said provisions. [*Adm. Paper.*]

June 27. Portsmouth. 67. St. J. Steventon to the Navy Comrs. Sends tickets for discharged shipwrights and calkers; 5s. each conduct money has been paid them. [*Adm. Paper.*]

June 27. 68. Sir Wm. Coventry to the Navy Comrs. The King Ferdinando is to be continued in the service; the late unhealthiness of the ship is conceived to have arisen from the leakage of beer upon her ballast, which is to be shifted, and her men, if sufficiently recovered, to be sent down to other ships in the fleet; desires the purser's account of provisions lost while the vessel was aground. [*Adm. Paper.*]

June 28. 69. Sir Wm. Coventry to Sam. Pepys. The King intends the John and Katherine and the Maryland to be set forth again; thinks a little punishment would be well bestowed upon Watkins (the mutinous shipwright) notwithstanding his return, that others may not think to neglect the King's service at pleasure; the Greyhound may venture without convoy, if the fleet remain upon the coast; the ships mentioned by Sir John Knight will be too small. [*Adm. Paper, 2 pages, damaged.*]

1665? June 28. 70. Sir Wm. Coventry to Capt. Val. Tatnell. Twenty pressed men are to be delivered to Capt. Trafford, besides those reserved for the Sovereign. [*Adm. Paper.*]

1665, June 28. Ordnance Office. 71. Edw. Sherburne to Sam. Pepys. Desires instructions concerning 20 tons of junk required for the supply of the fleet. [*Adm. Paper.*]

VOL. CXXV.

1663.

June 28. Whitehall. Order on the petition of Percy Lord Powis, that Sir Edw. Walker, clerk of the Council, with Baron Spilman, or some other bencher of Gray's Inn, look over the papers of Rees Vaughan, and deliver those of any kind belonging to his lordship to his solicitor or agent, taking a receipt for the same. [*Ent. Book* 18, *p.* 178.]

June 28? Order on the petition of Dr. Hugh Chamberlain—for a patent for making ships to sail with two points by the help of the wind—that when he has effected what he offers, he shall have the sole exercise of his invention, with any further advantages he may deserve. [*Ent. Book* 18, *p.* 179.]

June 28. 72. Estimate of the expense of an establishment for a company of foot under Major Benj. Henshaw, to be added to the garrison in the Isle of Jersey; total, 1,610*l.* 4*s.* yearly.

June 28. 73. Estimate of the expense of an establishment of 40 private soldiers, to be added to John Lord Frescheville's troop, in the Earl of Oxford's regiment; total yearly cost, 1,820*l.*

June 28. Whitehall. 74. Order in Council for renewal and printing of the proclamation of 18th November 1661, requiring all officers or soldiers that served under the late usurped powers to depart from London and Westminster, and not to come within 20 miles thereof before 1st November next.

June 28. Whitehall. Proclamation ordering all cashiered soldiers of the late usurped powers, who have not special licence, to depart from London and Westminster on or before 30th June, and not to return before 1st November. [*Printed. Proc. Coll., Charles II., p.* 193.]

June 28. Somerset House. 75. Will of the Queen[-Mother], disposing of her goods and the revenues given her by the King, for two years after her decease, for payment of her servants and other debts, as stated; and for legacies to Abbot Montague, Sir Hen. Wood, her Capuchins and others; leaving the Duke of York, Lord Chancellor, Earl of St. Alban's, and others executors. [*French, two pages, copy.*]

June 28. Warrant to the Lord Mayor, Deputy Lieutenants, and Militia Comrs. of London and Westminster, to continue to the College of Physicians their ancient privilege of exemption from keeping watch and ward, and from bearing or providing arms. [*Ent. Book* 14, *p.* 64.]

June 28. Whitehall. 76. The King to [the Mayor, &c., of Lichfield]. Recommends John Rogerson, who was loyal during the rebellion, and is skilful in the law, to be Town Clerk, on the death or surrender of John Hill, the present clerk.

June 28. Entry of the above. [*Ent. Book* 17, *p.* 116.]

June 28? 77. Memorial presented by Sir John Shaw to Lord Arlington, for an order to pay to him 1,900*l.*, which he has advanced without sufficient warrant for seven quarters' pension for the late Lord Wentworth, since the stay of pensions 31st August 1663, and also for his funeral expenses.

Vol. CXXV.

1665.

June 28. Warrant to allow to Sir John Shaw 2,000*l.*, which he has paid on a verbal order to the late Lord Wentworth or his executors, out of the pension allowed him of 1,000*l.* a year, notwithstanding the general stay of pensions. [*Ent. Book* 17, p. 118.]

June 28. 78. Pass for Leonard Gray to go to France.

June 28. Minute of the above. [*Ent. Book* 22, p. 200.]

June 28. Warrant to the Commissioners for Prizes to deliver to Sir Thomas Clifford the prize Patriarch Isaac, now at Harwich, in reward for his constant service in the disposal of ships, preventing embezzlements, &c. [*Ent. Book* 22, p. 201.]

June 28. The King to the Attorney General. Finds that in previous charters to Totness, no grant is made of the nomination and election of recorder, steward, and town clerk; they are therefore to be omitted in the confirmation of the charter. [*Ent. Book* 22, p. 202.]

June 28. Whitehall. 79. Pass for the Earl of Lincoln to travel for a year.

June 28. Entry of the above. [*Ent. Book* 22, p. 203.]

June 28. Order for release of the St. Nicholas of Hamburg, taken at sea by a private man-of-war and brought into Rye. [*Ent. Book* 22, p. 206.]

June 28. Pass for the ship L'escu de France, laden with brandy belonging to Ant. Houcquart, a Nantes merchant, and to Wm. Pletts, of Dunkirk, from Nantes to Dunkirk. [*Ent. Book* 22, p. 206.]

June 28. Similar pass, *mutatis mutandis*, for the ship St. Jean Evangelist, laden at Bordeaux with brandy, and belonging to the same Pletts. Minute. [*Ent. Book* 22, p. 207.]

June 28. Memorandum of release of [Thos.] Smallwood from John Wilson. Minute. [*Ent. Book* 22, p. 208.]

June 28. Whitehall. Warrant to the Commissioners for Prizes, permitting two instead of four of their number to form a quorum, on account of the necessities of removal, provided that Lord Arlington or Lord Ashley be one of them, and that all warrants for issue of money be signed by four. [*Ent. Book* 22, p. 208.]

June 29. Order to Lord Ashley to pay for M. De la Favolière 50*l.*, out of moneys arising from sale of prizes, &c. Minute. [*Ent. Book* 22, p. 210.]

June 29. Warrant to Sir William Humble, Bart., to reprieve [John] Lacey, sentenced to death for killing Thos. Ellis. Minute. [*Ent. Book* 22, p. 217.]

June 28. 80. Warrant for a grant to John Barefoot of the rent of 1,000 marks a year, reserved on a lease for 21 years to Edw. Gray and five others, of the office of licensing pedlars and petty chapmen, reserving 100 marks yearly to the Crown. With note from Lord Ashley

1665. VOL. CXXV.

to the Attorney General, Exeter House, 28 April, 1660, that the King wishes this warrant to pass.

June 28. Entry of the above. [*Ent. Book* 22, *p.* 227.]

[June 28.] 81. Draft of the above.

June 29. Grant of reprieve to John Lacey, indicted at the Kingston assizes for feloniously killing Thomas Ellis; directed to Sir Walter Plumer, high sheriff of Surrey. [*Ent. Book* 22, *p.* 200.]

June 29. Commission to the Ordnance Commrs. to provide ships for carrying ammunition and other stores on board the ships of the navy. [*Docquet.*]

June 29. Confirmation to Sir John Lowther, Bart., of several tenements in the parish of St. Bees, Cumberland, and the lands between high and low water mark belonging or adjoining to his manor of St. Bees. [*Docquet.*]

June 29. Order on the petition of Jane wife of Browne Whorwood for her husband to be called before His Majesty, &c.,—that the Lord Chancellor take care that the decree made thereon in Chancery be carried into effect, and that the petitioner receive the full advantage of the agreement made with her husband. [*Ent. Book* 18, *p.* 179.]

June 29. Reference to the Attorney General on the petition of Major Harland. [*Ent. Book* 18, *p.* 180.]

June 29. Portsmouth. 82. Comr. Thos. Middleton to Sam. Pepys. Progress and dispatch of ships; 45 carpenters are to be discharged; the ropemakers have discharged themselves for want of money, and gone into the country to make hay. Asks how many sorts of sails shall be made. [*Adm. Paper*, 1½ *pages*.]

June 29. Portsmouth. 83. Comr. Thos. Middleton to Sam. Pepys. Hears that the blockmakers and joiners have gone away and refuse to work any longer without money; the sawyers say they must do the same. [*Adm. Paper.*]

June 29. Portsmouth. 84. Comr. Thos. Middleton to Sam. Pepys. Is sorry to hear of the death of Sir John Lawson. [*Adm. Paper.*]

June 29. Gravesend. 85. Fr. Hosier to Sam. Pepys. Has mustered all the ships of the fleet at the Nore, except the Royal Charles, Henry, Lion, and Fairfax. Complains of obstructions in the performance of his duty. [*Adm. Paper.*] *Encloses,*

85. I. *Fr. Hosier to Sam. Pepys. Gives an account of the muster of 14 ships riding below the buoy of the Nore. Asks whether any further mustering is required for them.*

June 30. Deptford. 86. Thos. Cowley to Sam. Pepys. Fifty shipwrights can be spared, but some work will stand still; the 20 men borrowed from Mr. Castell's yard can go also. The Ruby will speedily be launched, and the Bull prize taken in hand. [*Adm. Paper.*]

Vol. CXXV.

1665.

June 30. Cockpit. 87. Duke of Albemarle to the Navy Comrs. Requests their attendance at the Cockpit, to advise upon several things in relation to the navy, during the absence of the Duke of York. [*Adm. Paper.*]

June 30. Woolwich. 88. Chris. Pett to the Navy Comrs. Elias Long and Geo. Trundell, two of the accomplices in Wm. Watkin's mutiny, have not yet returned; begs they may be made severe examples to the rest; five of the last pressed men ran away. Can spare 30 shipwrights, but only one calker amongst them; if more be taken, the works of the two new ships must lie still. Timber wanted. [*Adm. Paper.*]

June 30. [Woolwich.] 89. Wm. Sheldon to the Navy Comrs. There are now 110 shipwrights and 10 calkers employed; 30 can be spared for the present necessity; requests orders for sending them down. [*Adm. Paper.*]

June 30. Woolwich. 90. Wm. Acworth to the Navy Comrs. Account of prize goods received into the stores. [*Adm. Paper.*]

June 30. Chatham. 91. Comr. Peter Pett to Sam. Pepys. Is daily expecting provisions from London for dispatch of the fleet. List of things in urgent demand. With note by Sir George Carteret that these demands be hastened down forthwith, not forgetting the providing of hemp. [*Adm. Paper.*]

June 30. Edwinstow, Sherwood. 92. John Russell to the Navy Comrs. Has dispatched the Love hoy laden with timber for Harwich; more hoys are wanted; begs that the land carriage may be stopped till after harvest. Wants money. [*Adm. Paper.*]

June 30. Plymouth. 93. John Lanyon to the Navy Comrs. Only the Hawk and Giles ketches are now in port. Has received news of three Dutch men-of-war and thirteen merchant ships having besieged Tangiers. The Portuguese have again beaten the Spaniard. Sixteen Dutch ships are off Cape Clear; some think that this may be De Ruyter, but others think he has gone northward, having been encountered off Newfoundland by some fishing ships just returned. [*Adm. Paper.*]

June 30. Deptford. 94. Jonas Shish to the Navy Comrs. Account of repairs needed for the Dutch prize ship Bull, with estimate of the expense; total, 285*l.* [*Adm. Paper.*]

June 30. Reference to the Judges of the Admiralty on the petition of Don Villa Viciosa concerning the ship Jacob, the documents relating to the ship to be meanwhile restored to the owners. [*Ent. Book* 18, p. 180.]

June 30. 95. Sir Lionel Tollemache to Williamson. The King, wishing the writer to surrender his interest in the New park to Sir Dan. Harvey, orders Sir Rob. Long to pay him 250*l.*, and also engages to satisfy all persons employed by him in providing meat for the deer, or doing other work.

Vol. CXXV.

1665.

June 30. Whitehall. 96. Sir Hugh Pollard, comptroller of the household, to Lord Arlington. Begs his lordship to dispatch his part of the business. Is infinitely concerned in it.

June 30. 97. M. De Monthrun to Lord Arlington. Has not time to take leave. Has received full powers to pursue the affair relative to Desfontaines and Hoyau the goldsmith, both prisoners for having poisoned Fontenay, who are suspected of having [jewels, &c.] belonging to the late King. [*French, damaged.*]

97. I. *Extract from numerous depositions against Mathurine Desfontaines and Rob. Hoyau, to prove their complicity in poisoning Fontenay, late esquire of His Britannic Majesty, and taking possession of the jewels belonging to the late King which he left behind him. With statement of the impropriety of leaving an affair of state, which their recovery is, to private arbitrage, as proposed, one of the arbitrators being a friend of Hoyau, and of the importance of its being properly taken up. Also a list of the said jewels, made by Hoyau, which has been shown to all the jewellers in Paris.* [4½ *pages.*]

June 30. Grant to Abraham Dowcet of 1,230*l.* due to the King from the late farmers of excise for Lincolnshire. [*Docquet.*]

June 30. Grant to Sir John Evelyn of liberty to enclose a common highway leading from West Tudderley, co. Hants, by Whiteparish, to West Deane, co. Wilts, he making a way as convenient through his own land. [*Docquet.*]

June [30]. Passport for the St. Nicholas, belonging to French merchants, and laden with oils, &c., to proceed from St. Malo to Gottenburg, and return thence laden with deals, pitch, &c. [*Ent. Book* 22, *p.* 156.]

[June.] 98. Petition of Wm. Herd to the King, to call for his petition, delivered three weeks before, informing that Thos. Prengrave, baker of Westminster, said that at sea His Majesty had lost sixteen ships and the Dutch only four; that he had not fought in the last engagement but was reserving himself, as the French intended to land whilst His Majesty's fleet was engaged, to make their way to Whitehall, and to destroy the King and royal family, root and branch; that he had a mare on which Ludlow escaped, after being in his house when search was made for him; that he was in constant intelligence with Ludlow's younger brother, and that Goffe and Whalley were with him.

June Whitehall. 99. Pass for Sir George Hamilton, Bart., employed on the King's special affairs, to pass and repass and continue in London and Westminster and elsewhere as he thinks fitting, without molestation.

VOL. CXXV.

1665.

June Whitehall. 100. Pass for Lady Mary Hamilton, who is returning to Ireland, to go from London or Westminster to West Chester, Holyhead, or whence she thinks fit to transport herself.

June? 101. Warrant to [the Treasurer of the Navy?] to order payment of the wages due to certain shipwrights at Deptford, who have been discharged for refusing to work, whereby their wages are suspended.

June. Privy seal authorizing the Barons of the Exchequer to take an account of Blackwall and others' interest, in the manors of Stepney and Hackney, mortgaged by the Earl of Cleveland, notwithstanding the saving of the King's rights in an Act of Parliament obtained by the said Earl, for the benefit of redemption. [*Docquet.*]

June. Warrant to pay to Sir George Carteret 917*l.* monthly, for 150 soldiers added to each of the six companies in the Duke of York's regiment, and 2,500*l.* for recruiting soldiers for that regiment, at 20*s.* a man, in place of those gone to sea. [*Docquet.*]

June. Warrant to pay to Stephen Fox 1,484*l.* 5*s.* 4*d.*, for the arrears of Guernsey garrison, to 4th November last; also 241*l.* 10*s.* 4*d.* monthly, for Capt. Sheldon's company newly added to the garrison, and 500*l.* for fortifications in the island. [*Docquet.*]

June. Warrant to strike tallies in anticipation out of the rent for the Customs of 390,000*l.* for the payment of 9,437*l.* 7*s.* 4*d.* to Sir John Jacob, being the remainder of 15,728*l.* 18*s.* 10*d.* due to him, to be paid at the rate of 1,572*l.* 17*s.* 10½*d.* yearly. [*Docquet.*]

June. Like Warrant to strike tallies for payment of 7,200*l.* to Sir John Wolstenholme, being balance of a debt of 12,000*l.*, to be paid by 1,200*l.* a year. [*Docquet.*]

June. Warrant to pay to Col. Willm. Legg 14,045*l.* 9*s.* 1½*d.*, for ordnance and powder for 33 ships, and for the hire of ten ships. [*Docquet.*]

June. Grant to Sir Thos. Strickland of the customs on salt imported from foreign parts, or from Scotland into England, for 21 years, from Michaelmas 1667, on rent of 1,800*l.* [*Docquet.*]

June.? 102. M. De Sannier to the King. Entreats his compassion for a poor stranger, who has been nine months prisoner in Canterbury, only for exercising his trade of comb making; this is against the privilege of Queen Elizabeth, who allowed two men of each vocation in that town, and he is the only one in the neighbourhood; was obliged to leave London 13 years ago, and take a bond of 100*l.* not to exercise his vocation, and is now in gaol for payment of the bond. [*See Council Register, August 21, 1668.*]

Vol. CXXV.

1665.
June.
Chertsey Hav. 103. John Langrack to Sam. Pepys. The barges employed for carriage of timber have been taken by Mr. Blackbery for his own purposes; 500 loads of timber are lying on the wharf. Sir John Norton desires to speak with the Board concerning land carriage; has taken up another barge, and entreats protection for it. [*Adm. Paper.*] *Encloses,*

103. I. *Names of the eight men employed upon the King's Head barge, in carrying timber from Chertsey wharf to Woolwich and Deptford.*

June. 104. Philip Barrow and Jas. Norman to the Navy Comrs. Desire a speedy supply of oil, oars, and other stores for Chatham; 12 pinnaces and yauls wanted for the fleet. With note, by Comr. Peter Pett, requesting dispatch of the above-mentioned provisions. [*Adm. Paper.*]

June. 105. Account of press warrants granted 7th June to six water ships and victuallers. [*Adm. Paper.*]

June. 106. Note of three ships freighted by Sir Wm. Rider, according to contract, requiring press warrants. [*Adm. Paper.*]

June? 107. Note of the patents for the erection of lighthouses; viz., that of Dungeness, Kent, to Sir Edw. Howard, with a reversion to George Marsh, May, 1664; to Sir Wm. Batten, for a lighthouse at Harwich, December, 1664; to Hen. Bruncard, for one at Milford Haven, April, 1665; a grant for one at Hampton Cliff, co. Norfolk, for vessels between Lynn Regis and Boston; to Edw. Villiers for one at Tynemouth, June, 1665.

June? 108. Account by John Pawlett of 16 letters delivered to William Stone or his wife, from 30th August, 1664, to 18th June, 1665, the postage paid, but the letters not delivered in London. With note that there are others which he cannot at present come at. Endorsed, "Weymouth postmaster."

[June.] 109. Examination of Joseph Walley. Was in Yorkshire last July, and visited one Waite there; sold Bibles in London to R. Walker, and sent a letter by him to Wm. Marshall and others in York. Had the books which he dispersed from Martin Grocer, in Newgate prison, and he had them from another prisoner.

[June.] Certificate by the Secretaries of State that the allowances due to the Countess of Chesterfield, as defalcation from her rent of the post office, on account of dispatch of letters to and from the Duke of Ormond, Lord Lieutenant of Ireland, Earl of Ossory, lord deputy, Duke of Albemarle, the general of the forces in Scotland, the members of Parliament during the session, and the Commissioners of Prizes, with the sums paid to Thos. Parnell, postmaster at Court, amount in all to 2,037*l.* 11*s.* 11*d.* [*Ent. Book* 18, *pp.* 181–2.]

VOL. CXXV.

1665. June. Lists sent by Morgan Lodge to Williamson of King's and merchants' ships in the Downs during the month, and the state of the wind:—

No.	Date.	King's.	Merchants'.	Wind.
110.	June 6	2	9	S.W.
111.	" 13	4	7	S.W.
112.	" 14	4	7	S.W.
113.	" 15	2	5	S.W.
114.	" 16	2	5	S.E.
115.	" 17	2	0	N.E.
116.	" 21	4	1	S.W.
117.	" 22	4	1	S.W.
118.	" 24	5	3	S.W.
119.	" 26	6	3	S.W.

VOL. CXXVI. JULY 1-15, 1665.

1665. July 1. Preston. 1. Sir Willm. Lowther to Sir Phil. Warwick. Sends Sir John Armitage's letter, and that of White to Sir John, but not to be shown, as they were privately written. Some speedy course should be taken, as these persons grow to such a height. In taking them, they proceeded on the Act for suppressing conventicles. Humbled a drunken Presbyterian, who was as high as if Lambert were at the head of 20,000 men. Has advised that the prisoners should not be released, since that would make them more insolent. The difficulty is occasioned by the assembly's being in a chapel, and the Bishop and his officers having neglected to send a certificate, as the Act of Uniformity requires, that this preaching nonconformist might have been imprisoned. Wants directions from some fit person. The second payment for his division is paid in to the Receiver General. Hopes the fleet will be kept free from infection, and sent to sea soon, as the [Dutch] East India fleet is daily expected. If their privateers go three or four together, English men-of-war should not be hazarded, and the merchants required not to hazard their estates, and thus encourage the enemies. *Encloses,*

1. 2. *Sir John Armitage to Sir Willm. Lowther. There have been 24 persons brought before himself and other justices, for being at an assembly at Shadwell of 300 or 400; they would not promise not to do the same again, but were insolent and high, and threaten an action for false*

1665. Vol. CXXVI.

imprisonment, because the Act does not name churches nor chapels. They are encouraged by a justice of peace in the West Riding. *Kirklees, June 26.*

I. II. *Fras. White to Sir John Armitage, Bart. The Shadwellers threaten to sue, because the Act does not name churches nor chapels, yet meetings there are the more dangerous, and if these prisoners be liberated, it will make them more audacious. Knows no reason why an unlawful assembly should not as well be held on a moor or heath, otherwise it would be easy to avoid the Act.* [*Copy.*] *June 26.*

July 1. Commissions for Sir James Smith to be Lieutenant-Colonel and Jo. Miller Major of the Lord General's regiment of foot. Minutes. [*Ent. Book* 20, *p.* 81.]

[July] 1. Warrant to the Duke of York to order the Navy Treasurer to pay to Prince Rupert 2,000*l.* as the King's free gift. [*Ent. Book* 17, p. 119.]

July 1. London. 2. Sir Wm. Warren to the Navy Comrs. Reminds them of his two ships lying at demurrage below Gravesend, waiting for convoy to New England to fetch masts. Entreats haste, as the year spends and winter begins betimes in New England. [*Adm. Paper.*]

July 1. Blackamoor pink, off Cromer. 3. Capt. John Barton to the Navy Comrs. Is ordered to victual at Hull; wishes to clean and tallow there also. Wants carpenter's stores. Has found his lost boat. *Encloses,*

3. I. *Account, by Capt. Barton, of carpenter's stores required for the Blackamoor.* *June 1, 1665.*

July 1. Bristol. 4. Fr. Baylie to the Navy Comrs. Progress of the fourth-rate ship in building. [*Adm. Paper.*]

July 1. Royal Charles. 5. Sir Wm. Coventry to Sam. Pepys. Sir Wm. Rider and others sending ships to the Sound are to hasten them to Southwold Bay, to accompany the fleet, until a convoy can be appointed. [*Adm. Paper.*]

July 1. Harwich. 6. Capt. John Hubbard to the Navy Comrs. Is ready to take in victuals. Wants a master and lieutenant. [*Adm. Paper.*]

July 1. Weymouth. 7. Geo. Pley to the Navy Comrs. Arrival of the Barbadoes fleet, with news of the destruction of ships and plantations in Newfoundland by De Ruyter, who, after victualling his fleet from the English ships, departed homewards by the north of England. The Coventry and Lizard are detained by contrary winds.

July 1. Bristol. 8. Sir John Knight to the Navy Comrs. Sends the articles of agreement for the hire of the Pearl, to be signed and sealed by the Commissioners. Has received no orders from the victuallers or Officers of Ordnance. Names his captain and crew. The owners

VOL. CXXVI.

1665.

of the Pearl demand their two months' advance pay, and 100*l.* will be needed for gunners' stores and other materials. Can procure no other square-sterned vessel at present. Wishes to be advised when the colours are sent, as all goods from London are prohibited entrance into the city. Five more Bristol ships are taken, whereby the King loses 2,000*l.* customs, and the citizens 30,000*l.*; hardly a ship there escapes. Sends names of prisoners at Middleburg to be exchanged. Asks what provision is made for seamen's widows. [*Adm. Paper, 2 pages.*]

July 2. Portsmouth. 9. Comr. Thos. Middleton to Sam. Pepys. Particulars of ships in readiness to sail. The sickness increases at Southampton; booths are built outside the town for the sick to be carried into. The ropemakers, blockmakers, and joiners have left; if money be not had, matters must stand as they are. Is sorry the two galliots have been taken away to serve at Chatham; would not be so indiscreet as to deliver a vessel without orders. Hopes to get the Greyhound soon out of harbour. Complains of the men being very unruly; is obliged "to carry a broad axe in one hand and a plane in the other to make all smooth," or there would be no dealings with them. [*Adm. Paper, 3 pages, damaged.*]

July 2. Chatham. 10. Sir Wm. Coventry to Sam. Pepys. The Duke has returned with the King to Hampton Court. Hears from Sir G. Carteret of the mutiny amongst the Portsmouth ropemakers; he has written for money to pay them, and thinks all should be paid, except the mutineers. Has left orders for the Gottenburg ships, when unladen, to be hastened to the fleet at Southwold Bay. Is at Chatham to help the dispatch of things; an anchor must be sent forthwith for the Prince Royal; such a ship, especially with the Earl of Sandwich's presence, may be of infinite moment. Sir Wm. Rider's ships must be sent to join the fleet; beer is wanted without delay. Are again undone by the victualler; 700 tuns of beer are lacking, and some must follow the fleet in fitting ships. [*Adm. Paper, 2 pages.*]

July 2. Chatham, 12 P.M. 11. Sir Wm. Coventry to Lord Arlington. The King left the fleet to-night for London, and wishes Lord Sandwich to meet him at Hampton Court to-morrow. His Majesty proposed to Prince Rupert to share the command of the fleet with Lord Sandwich by joint commission; but the Prince disliking it is to accompany him to Hampton Court to come to a resolution; for this reason the King wishes the Lord Chancellor to be there, and the Lord Chamberlain to provide lodgings for the Prince. Some of the great ships have sailed to-day, others go to-morrow, so that the King's visit has not been useless for the dispatch of the fleet. [*2 pages.*]

July 2. Plymouth. 12. John Lanyon to the Navy Comrs. Arrival of the Happy Entrance; repairs needed for a leakage. [*Adm. Paper.*]

July 2/12. Chelsea. Ambassador Van Gogh to the States General. Fears that as the plague increases, the Dutch prisoners at Chelsea College and else-

1665. Vol. CXXVI.

where will take service under the English, as those who have done so bring home money in their pockets and accounts of their good entertainment. The prisons at Colchester and elsewhere can hardly contain them, they are so numerous. The Privy Council removes from Whitehall to St. James's, on account of the increase of plague, and the Admiralty Court to Winchester. Great numbers of London merchants and shopkeepers are retiring to the country. The foreign ministers are gone to Hampton Court. The fleet is preparing. There is a doubt whether the Duke of York will go to sea. Prince Rupert will probably stay at home, because there is some difference about command between him, as vice-admiral only of a squadron, and the Earl of Sandwich as vice-admiral of England. [*Holland Corresp.*, 13 *July*, 1665.]

July 3. Chester. 13. Sir Geoffry Shakerley to Williamson. Great strictness is observed in keeping out strangers suspected to bring in the sickness, but the pest of disobedience and nonconformity continues rife. A conventicle of 100 persons was assembled at the house of Dr. Thos. Harrison, late chaplain to Harry Cromwell; broke open the house, and, though many escaped, some were taken hidden under beds or in closets, &c., and 30 or 40 brought before the mayor. The chief were examined, and paid their money to escape imprisonment, this being their first conviction, as Harrison himself, Edw. Bradshaw, and Peter Lee, late aldermen, Major Jas. Jolly, and others. These are not Anabaptists, but of the first and worst stamp of sectarism, and therefore require the more severity. The parties are so linked together in the city that it will be difficult to surprise them, unless it be by a special commission for their punishment, directed to those of no affinity with them. Some of them threaten to complain of the writer for breaking down the door and disturbing them. [1½ pages.]

July 3. Hampton Court. Warrant for a demise from Sir Hugh Cholmeley and four others to the Crown, of certain alum works and mines erected on the ground of Sir Hugh Cholmeley or Sir William Cholmeley, deceased, in the parish of Whitby, co. York, for 21 years, on rent of 1,300*l.*, with clause of re-entry in case of non-payment of rent. [*Ent. Book* 14, *p.* 70.]

July 3. Young Lion, Lynn. 14. Capt. Michael Young to Sir Wm. Coventry. Is detained at Lynn for repairs. All the beer on board stinks; requests the discharge of his account in victualling men taken in at Harwich. [*Adm. Paper.*] *Encloses*,

14. I. *List by Capt. Young of 16 passengers taken on board the Young Lion by order of Sir Wm. Batten, and victualled from the 6th to the 14th June,* 1665.

July 3. 15. Edw. Gregory to Sam. Pepys. Sends papers to be laid before the Board. Attests the truth of the certificate, and entreats extra allowance for Walter Dyer. Requests a shipwright's pay for Bernard Eales, an assistant of his own, in consideration of industry

VOL. CXXVI.

1665.

and diligence displayed in the present urgent business. [*Adm. Paper.*] *Encloses,*

15. I. *Phin. Pett and two others to the Navy Comrs. Certify the care and diligence of Walter Dyer, clerk to the Clerk of the Cheque at Chatham, in extra service during the last 12 months; recommend an increase of his salary, which is now 20l.* *July 3, 1665.*

15. II. *Petition of Walter Dyer to the Navy Comrs., for an allowance of shipwright's pay for his constant attendance, day and night, and several sabbath days' extra service, in mustering men, &c.*

July 3. Cockpit. 16. Duke of Albemarle to the Navy Comrs. Desires payment to the wives and relatives of such seamen as were upon the first muster of the Westergate. [*Adm. Paper.*] *Encloses,*

16. I. *Petition of the Widows, Mothers, and Creditors of the men lately belonging to the Westergate, to the Duke of Albemarle, for a general payment of wages due, certain accounts being received of the loss of the vessel.*

July 3. Chatham. 17. W. Howe to Sam. Pepys. Sends an important letter to be enclosed to Mr. Shepley and forwarded securely and speedily to Lady Pickering. [*Adm. Paper.*]

July 3. Guildford. 18. T. Dalmahoy to Sam. Pepys. Requests a warrant to distrain upon John Wilkins, bargeman, for obstinately refusing to carry timber without double rates. [*Adm. Paper.*]

July 3. Ordnance Office. 19. Edw. Sherburne and two other Ordnance Officers to the Navy Comrs. Ask whether the Golden Phœnix, Castle frigate, and Blackamoor, are to be continued in the service, before complying with the Blackamoor gunner's demand for five pieces of ordnance to replace those broken in the last engagement; the owners should either make good broken ordnance, or, in case of dismissal, return the stores furnished. [*Adm. Paper.*]

July 3. Bristol. 20. Sir John Knight to the Navy Comrs. Complains of the small proportion of victuals allowed for the Pearl, only one month's provision for 140 men; great part of it will be spent before the ship puts to sea; requests a better supply and money for furnishing other materials, to be received from the collector of customs at Bristol. [*Adm. Paper.*]

July 4. 21. Capt. John Perriman of the Swallow to Sam. Pepys. Sends account of grievances to be redressed; is sorry to receive evil thoughts when his utmost endeavour is to promote the service. Wants a pilot. His wood and candles are expended. Will disburse no more money until assured how it is to be paid. [*Adm. Paper.*] *Encloses,*

21. I. *List by Capt. Perriman of grievances arising from scanty allowance, and want of money on board the Swallow.*

Vol. CXXVI.

1665.
July 4. 22. Wm. Castell to the Navy Comrs. Has not received due payments for building the new third-rate ship; cannot therefore proceed with the work according to expectation. [*Adm. Paper.*]

July 4. Portsmouth. 23. Comr. Thos. Middleton to Sam. Pepys. The mutinous ropemakers have returned to their work. Cannot get the Greyhound out of port for want of wind; shall be exceeding glad to see Sir John Mennes, especially if he bring "an olive branch in his mouth;" hopes at his coming to discover the ringleader of the late disturbance. English twine is tendered at 13*d.* per lb. [*Adm. Paper, 2 pages.*]

July 4. Godalming. 4 a.m. 24. Sir John Mennes to the Navy Comrs. Is hastening to Portsmouth with the resolution of not paying the mutinous ropemakers; is glad his authority is strengthened by the joint opinion of the Board. [*Adm. Paper.*]

July 4. 25. Robt. Southwell to Sam. Pepys. The order for the Hare was delivered into Sir Wm. Coventry's own hands; as another original cannot be easily obtained, sends an attested copy. [*Adm. Paper.*]

July 4. Plymouth. 26. John Lanyon to the Navy Comrs. Leakage of the Happy Entrance caused by bad calking; thinks her overcharged with guns and men. The St. Maria prize would make a better vessel for the commander of the squadron. Four French ships are brought into port. [*Adm. Paper.*]

July 4. Navy Office. 27. Warrant from the Navy Comrs. to the Clerks of the Store and Cheque at Deptford, to receive the canvas and deals sent up from Portsmouth, out of the prize ship Harderine. [*Adm. Paper.*]

July 4. Marmaduke, Sole Bay. 28. Certificate by John Best, captain, and two others, that Patrick Routh has served in the Marmaduke since 27th March last, and was in the engagement with the Dutch. [*Adm. Paper.*] *Annexing,*

28. i. *Certificate by John Cooke and four others of Pat. Routh's engagement in the service of the Commonwealth, and of his being wounded in fight with the Hollanders.*
Nightingale, near Dublin, December 14, 1653.

28. ii. *Certificate by John Price that Patrick Routh was paid his quarterly pension of* 5*l.* 4*s. till* 24*th December last, but not since.* *June* 16, 1660.

July? 29. Petition of John Banister to the King, for payment of the increased allowance of 600*l.* a year promised to the 12 violinists over whom he is director, to encourage their practisings and particular attendance on His Majesty.

July 4. Hampton Court. Warrant to Sir Edward Griffin, treasurer of the chamber, to pay 350*l.* to Jo. Banister, master of the particular band of violins and

Vol. CXXVI.

1665.

six of the band, for their charges in attendance on the King in his journeys this summer. [*Ent. Book* 14, *p.* 63.]

July 4. Christ's College. 30. Dr. Thos. Fuller to Williamson. Has no benefit by the King's letter, the scrupulous doctors thinking they cannot do it without His Majesty's hand to it. Suspects that somebody is keeping back the original for Mr. Beale, as he speaks of having two letters, in one of which Fuller's name is joined with his. Will try to discover where the miscarriage lies.

July 4. Lincoln's Inn. 31. Willm. Coward to Williamson. Has obtained the Duke of Ormond's report on Capt. Hall's petition, and hopes the order will easily be effected, on the certificate both of the lord lieutenant and his deputies. Begs dispatch if the King come to town to-morrow; if not, will wait on him at Hampton Court; is obliged to stay in this contagious town for the order. Endorsed "Mr. Hall's debt."

July 5. Grant to [Edw.] Griffin, in reversion after his father, Sir Edw. Griffin, of the office of Treasurer of the Chamber. [*Docquet.*]

July 5. Chatham. 32. Jas. Norman to Sir Wm. Batten. The fleet is almost all dispatched. Account of provisions still wanting as store for six months, in case of no engagement. A flyboat with deals has arrived. [*Adm. Paper.*]

July 5. The Crown, Malaga Road. 33. Capt. Chas. Wager to Sir Wm. Coventry. Left Tangiers on the 16th June, and has since been cruising on the Spanish shore. The Dutch Smyrna fleet, of 17 men-of-war and six merchant ships, left the port June 30. They vapour much, but in vain, and strike high at the King's Crown. Intends following them as far as Tangiers. Hopes a squadron of ships may be there to salute them. Ten sail might destroy them. They are poorly manned and likely to be worse, as at all ports their men run from them. [*Adm. Paper.*]

July 5. Royal Charles, Sole Bay. 34. Sir Wm. Penn to the Navy Comrs. Is under sail with a fleet of 20 ships. Great want of men. The Good Hope pink must be sent with water immediately. [*Adm. Paper.*]

July 5. S.P.W. Portsmouth Yard. 35. Sir John Mennes to the Navy Comrs. Cannot discover the ringleaders of the mutiny of the ropemakers; knows not how to punish; to stop their pay destroys all their hopes of credit, and must bring the works to a standstill. Will pay the rest of the yard to-morrow, as far as the money holds out, but it will only pay three quarters out of the five due; this causes a difficulty in settling with shipwrights who have served only the last two quarters, and would thus receive nothing. [*Adm. Paper.*] *Encloses,*

35. I. *Petition of the Shipwrights, Caulkers, &c., of the dockyard at Portsmouth to the Navy Comrs., for a supply of money to set them free from their creditors, and in a condition to provide for themselves and families.*

VOL. CXXVI.

1665.
July 5. Dover. 36. Thos. White to the Navy Comrs. The Pearl and Little Mary await orders to tallow and victual. [*Adm. Paper.*]

July 5. St. James's. 37. Sir Wm. Coventry to Sam. Pepys. Judges the prizes at Chatham to be all fourth-rate ships, except the Hilversom which may be a third-rate. Wishes the Ordnance Officers would provide tobacco stalks for the use of gunners; else where service comes, for want of stalks, the cables and cordage must be cut. [*Adm. Paper.*]

July 5. 38. Sir Wm. Coventry to [Pepys]. The surveyor's agents can best inform as to the quantity of old canvas in store; as to new standards, thinks only Union flags should be used in future, it being solemnly resolved, when Prince Rupert went to Guinea, that none but he should carry the standard in the King's absence. If the ropemakers universally throw up their work, corporal punishment ought to be inflicted by inprisonment.

July 6. 39. Sir Wm. Coventry to Sam. Pepys. Masters wanted for various ships; begs that men of courage as well as skill may be selected. Hopes there will soon be a meeting of the Commissioners for Tangiers. Water ships must be hastened to Southwold Bay. Victualling required for the Sovereign and Sta. Maria. [*Adm. Paper.*]

July 5. 40. Certificate by Geo. Erwin of the want of extra men on board the Golden Falcon. [*Adm. Paper.*]

July 6. Portsmouth. 41. Comr. Thos. Middleton to Sam. Pepys. The sickness increases at Southampton. Great care is taken to prevent any communication with other towns. Portsmouth was never in a better condition of health. If money be not procured, much damage will accrue to the service. The Greyhound is dispatched to the fleet. Stores of hemp, pitch, and tar received. [*Adm. Paper.*]

July 6. Portsmouth. 42. Sir John Mennes to the Navy Comrs. Thinks the late desertion of the ropemakers rather a necessity from the hardness of the times than from any desire of quitting the service. The plague increases at Southampton; the poor will not suffer the rich to quit the town and leave them to starve. Complaints from Col. Reymes and Mr. Pley of the negligence and delay of Capt. Hill, sent to convoy merchant ships from St. Malo; 1,200*l.* of the King's goods are waiting to sail, for want of vessels; they fear plunder by the French, and an edict is coming forth to prevent commerce with England during the plague. Mr. Pley laments the starving condition of the seamen set on shore by the Dutch at St. Malo; many of the merchants have relieved them as far as possible, and would send them over to Portsmouth, upon assurance of being repaid for such service. Money wanted. [*Adm. Paper, 1½ pages.*]

July 6. Scarborough. 43. Col. Edw. Villiers to Williamson. Is visiting Lord Suffolk, but will return to his garrison on Monday, and gladly receive Lord Arlington's commands. A private man-of-war has brought in a Dutch

VOL. CXXVI.

1665.

prize bound for Norway, laden with brandy, wine, and hops. A great fleet of colliers has passed southward, under convoy of the Truelove.

July 6. St. James's. Proclamation appointing July 12 to be kept as a general fast for stay of the plague now visiting London and Westminster, and threatening to spread; and thenceforward the first Wednesday in every month, till the plague is withdrawn. Collections to be made on these fast days, for relief of the poor visited by the plague. [*Printed. Proc. Coll., Charles II., pp.* 194-5.]

[July 6.] London. 44. "A form of Common Prayer; together with an order for fasting for the averting of God's heavy visitation upon many places of this realm. The fast to be observed within the cities of London and Westminster, and places adjacent, on Wednesday the twelfth of this instant July, and both there and in all parts of this realm on the first Wednesday in every month; and the prayers to be read on Wednesday in every week during the visitation." Containing forms for morning and evening prayer, and also an "Exhortation fit for the time." [*Printed, 80 pages.*]

July 6. 45. Arise Evans to Lord Bennet. Was troubled at his refusing to give him more money, because he had cozened him about his book called "Light to the Jews," showing the cause of the plague, and the way to prevent it. Never saw it in print till 1664, but wrote it in 1655 and 1656, and being unable then to get it printed, wrote out many copies of it, and gave them away. It may have been printed in 1650 and many times since, as that is the date upon it; those gentlemen who saw and read it in print seven or eight years ago cannot swear it is verbatim the same book. Men have had experience of the truth of his prophesyings. God is angry with the unbelieving questioning of the book, and sent forth a blazing star and a plague, and did not appear so much against the Dutch as he would have done; but there was a victory, because the King believed the book. He who laid a wager against it is become like the lord who opposed Elisha's good tidings. Sword, famine, and plague are only sent for national sin; hopes the King and Council will now see and repent the sin.

July 7. Commission for —— Henshaw to be Captain of a company of foot in the Isle of Jersey, and —— Gladstone his Lieutenant. [*Ent. Book* 20, *p.* 77.]

July 7. Note of the King's approval of Wm. Basset to be Deputy Lieutenant of Glamorganshire, in place of Sir Rich. Bassett; Walter Vaughan, of Pembrokeshire, in place of Geo. Hayward; and Rich. Wynne, of Denbighshire, in place of Wm. Wynne. The Earl of Carbery is to issue out their deputations accordingly. [*Ent. Book* 20, *p.* 77.]

[July 7.] 46. Petition of John Knowles, prisoner in the Gatehouse, Westminster, to the King, for release. Though accused by none, has been confined six weeks, since May 20 on suspicion of treasonable

VOL. CXXVI.

1665.

practices, on account of papers found about collecting money for relief of the Polanders, which he did not know to be unlawful, and thought them objects of pity.

July 7. Warrant for a patent to Major Alexander Merchant, *alias* St. Michael, of his inventions of a new way of keeping water in ponds sweet and wholesome, with little or no mud at the bottom; and also of the moulding of bricks in anyform for ornament of buildings. [*Ent. Book* 22, p. 215.]

July ? 47. Petition of Rich. Hodgkinson, stationer, to Lord Arlington for a privy seal for payment of 674*l*. 13*s*. 1*d*., due for stationers' wares furnished to the House of Commons by the King's command. *Annexing*,

47. I. *Account by Rich. Hodgkinson, of stationery delivered to the House of Commons, from* 6 *Aug.* 1661 *to* 27 *July* 1663, *and* 16 *and* 22 *March* 1665; *total sum due*, 674*l*. 13*s*. 1*d*. [23 *pages*.]

July 7. Order for a warrant to pay to Richard Hodgkinson, stationer, 674*l*. 13*s*. 1*d*., for paper, &c., furnished to the House of Commons from Aug. 1661 to March 1665. [*Ent. Book* 22, p. 216.]

July 7. Warrant for a grant to Sir Robert Vyner, on surrender of Thos. Lisle, of the place of Water Bailiff and Keeper of the prison of Dover. [*Ent. Book* 22, p. 216.]

July 7. Privy seal for 20,000*l*. to the Duke of York as the King's free gift, towards the supply of his particular occasions. Minute. [*Ent. Book* 22, p. 217.]

July 7. 48. Certificate by Robt. Woodward purser, of the discharge of the William and Mary hoy from attending on the Swiftsure. [*Adm. Paper.*]

July 7. Chatham. 49. Comr. Peter Pett to Sam. Pepys. Account of the breaking of a block strap on board the Sovereign; several men were hurt, one killed; there are only 30 tons of hemp in store; reed and broom wanted. [*Adm. Paper.*]

July 7. 50. Sir Wm. Coventry to the Navy Comrs. Is sending orders to Southwold Bay for convoying such ships as are ready, for Gottenburg and the Sound. Wishes they could have orders overland to be ready; delay may be prejudicial; 700 tuns of beer are wanting, besides that for the prize ships, so that 500 tuns is a poor supply; the want of a purser for the Mars is through mistake, two having been appointed to another ship; is glad Comr. Taylor has recommended one; the Phenix, Blackamoor, and Castle are ordered to the Downs. Men must be sent to Chatham for the Sovereign. [*Adm. Paper.*]

Vol. CXXVI.

1865.

July 8. Greenwich. 51. Dan. Morgan to the Navy Comrs. Desires a warrant for Rowland Anderson to be boatswain of the John and Abigail, the former boatswain being killed in the late engagement. [*Adm. Paper.*]

July 8. 52. Request by Mr. Castell for protection for the master and crew of the Providence, when fetching plank from Rye for the building of a frigate in Deptford yard. [*Adm. Paper.*]

July 8. 53. Jonas Shish to the Navy Comrs. The fire-ship Providence is in the wet dock, and joiners' stores on board, but no one to look after them; begs that some one may be appointed. The new ketch is ready to launch. [*Adm. Paper.*]

July 8. Hampton Court. 54. Sir Wm. Coventry to Sam. Pepys. Hears that James Johnson can furnish cordage by way of Dunkirk; he must be written to; expects difficulty in procuring men for the Sovereign. The Ruby and Black Bull must be hastened to the fleet. [*Adm. Paper.*]

July 8. Young Prince, Harwich. 55. Capt. John Chappell to the Navy Comrs. Requests payment of the wages due to Hugh Gleg, for service in the Lizard, to Mrs. Butler, his late widow. [*Adm. Paper.*]

July 8. Chatham. 56. Comr. Peter Pett to Sam. Pepys. Progress of the Sovereign's repairs; 100 watermen and 200 soldiers wanted. With business notes [by Pepys]. [*Adm. Paper.*]

July 8. Ordnance Office. 57. Officers of Ordnance to the Navy Comrs. Approve the expedient proposed to have the 4,000*l.* assigned to the Ordnance Office at Portsmouth paid in London by Sir George Carteret, but cannot yet tell whether the money has been paid there. [*Adm. Paper.*]

July 8. The Augustine, Harwich. 58. Capt. Rich. Teale to the Navy Comrs. Cannot get lighters to commence unlading; 24 of his best seamen are taken away by order of Sir Wm. Penn; thinks the Friezland a better ship for service than the Triumph; the Augustine is so old as to be hardly fit to sail to Portsmouth; proposes leaving her at Harwich, as a store ship. [*Adm. Paper.*]

July 8. Portsmouth. 59. Sir John Mennes to the Navy Comrs. An officer from the Ordnance Office is at Winchester, to solicit the justices who are met at the assizes to procure money for the present necessity; cannot discover the ringleaders of the ropemaker's revolt; all profess proper humility and that nothing but actual want of bread would have made them forsake their work; is convinced that they deserve commiseration rather than punishment, being in such great need and all things so dear; is paying himself 1*s.* a night for hay for one horse, and 4*s.* a bushel for oats, ready money; what must they have to give for victuals, who go upon trust! There are 300 tons of hemp in store. [*Adm. Paper.*]

July 8. 60. Petition of Wm. Bowden and two other Ropemakers of Woolwich to the Navy Comrs., for allowance or exchange in goods for certain cuttings and rakings found in a parcel of groundtows

1665. VOL. CXXVI.

bought by them for 14l. per ton. With reference thereon to Wm. Ikelham; his report, 22 July, that the petitioners had hard measure in having the cuttings and rakings forced upon them, but that he cannot tell the quantity or the loss sustained; order by the Navy Comrs., August 8, that the petitioners make oath of their pretended damages; and their certificate, Aug. 10, that they have received five tons of cuttings and rakings, only worth 4l. a ton. [*Adm. Paper.*]

July 8. Pass for six horses to France for the Duke of Luxembourg, free of custom. [*Ent. Book* 22, *p.* 217.]

July 8. Hampton Court. The King to the Farmers of Customs. Orders,—on complaint that several Dutch prisoners have broken prison and escaped beyond seas,—that no vessel be permitted to sail out of any port with Dutchmen on board, unless they have passes from His Majesty, the Privy Council, one of the Secretaries of State, or one of the Commissioners for sick and wounded. Minute. With note of a like order on July 11th, that passes from the Dukes of York and Albemarle are to be allowed in like cases accordingly. [*Ent. Book* 14, *p.* 85.]

July 8. The King to Sir Wm. Doyley at Harwich. Has sent 1,000l. and will send more; the Navy Treasurer can do nothing, having paid 80,000l. in three weeks. He may lend Dutch prisoners, on security of re-delivery, to manufacturers in their own trades, to captains to help to rig prizes, and to colliers, merchantmen, and fishermen. Minute. [*Ent. Book* 14, *p.* 65.]

July 9. Portsmouth. 61. Comr. Thos. Middleton to Sam. Pepys. Sends the appraisement of the St. Lawrence and Young King, with account of money disbursed in fitting them as timber ships; total, 316l. [*Adm. Paper.*]

July 9. Portsmouth. 62. Sir John Mennes to the Navy Comrs. Hopes soon to be relieved by a supply of money; wishes to ease the yard from the unnecessary charge of useless pressed men from sundry places, who without board wages can get no credit, are put to hard shifts, and cause all manner of disorder; Col. Reymes and Mrs. Pley will have the English seamen sent with as much care and thrift as possible; the convoy and vessels have started from Weymouth; has encouraged them to bring over the 500 bales of Noyals canvas formerly treated for; Capt. Pett sailed yesterday; no other vessel in the harbour is ready; 20 joiners are discharged. [*Adm. Paper.*]

July 10. Deptford. 63. Jonas Shish to Sam. Pepys. The Ruby can be at Gravesend in a day or two. Will get the Dutch ship Bull on shore for repairs, as soon as she can be cleared. [*Adm. Paper.*]

July 10. Gravesend. 64. Capt. Valentine Tatnell to the Navy Comrs. Has left 50 seamen with Comr. Pett for the Sovereign, and sent 24 others to Chatham. Has captured on board Capt. Cox's ship the waterman who killed a Navy lieutenant at Temple Stairs; he confesses the fact, and is now left in the hands of the Governor at Gravesend, to await the King's pleasure. [*Adm. Paper.*]

VOL. CXXVI.

1665.

July 10. Chatham Hill. 65. Sir Wm. Batten to Sam. Pepys. Junk is wanted for the St. George and the prize ships; requests that tobacco stalks may be hastened down. [*Adm. Paper.*]

July 10. Blackwall. 66. Wm. Cooper to Sam. Pepys. Will remedy the defective timbers put into his new third-rate ship. *Encloses,*

66. I. *Christ. Pett and two others to the Navy Commrs. Report of the survey of the third-rate ship building at Blackwall, with account of defects in the timbers which are to be remedied.* *Blackwall, July 8, 1665.*

July 10. Post House, Lea. 67. Dan. Furzer to the Navy Commrs. Requests an immediate supply of money, and an order for survey of the new ship building at Bristol. Wishes an answer about the tender of plank at Chepstow. Complains of abuses committed in the forest by cutting and spoiling the timber; one case is in the hands of the justices, but they judge it not business for them to decide without the sanction of the Board. [*Adm. Paper, 1½ pages.*] *Encloses,*

67. I. *John Barrows and William Morgan, justices of peace for Gloucestershire, to the Navy Commrs. Send examinations concerning two pieces of timber wilfully cut and spoiled in the Forest of Dean. Annexing,* *July 1, 1665.*

67. II. *Examination of John Morgan, of Alvington. His son, Wm. Morgan, and a servant did, with a saw, cut in two places two pieces of timber in Dean Forest, but carried none away from the place.* *Lydney, July 6, 1665.*

67. III. *Examination of Thos. Dunning, of Lydney, and Walter Werin, of Flaxley. The said pieces of timber were sealed with the King's seal, and intended for a ship in building at Conpill; warned John Morgan not to meddle therewith; saw William Morgan squaring the timber by his father's command.* *Lydney, July 8, 1665.*

July 10. The King to Wm. Whitmore, high sheriff of Essex. He is to pay immediately to Sir Wm. Doyley, treasurer of sick and wounded soldiers and Dutch prisoners, 620*l.* 4*s.* 3*d.* out of the Norfolk assessments for the militia, and 101*l.* 19*s.* 11*d.*, out of the same for Norwich, now in his hands for transmission to the Tower of London. [*Ent. Book* 20, p. 78.]

July 10. Cockpit. 68. Statement of an information that Chas. Mitchell, Thos. Roberts, and Art. Crispin have taken money from watermen impressed for the King's service, and fit to serve, and have discharged them; giving names of witnesses to prove the same. With reference of the case by the Duke of Albemarle to the Navy Commrs. [*Adm. Paper.*] *Annexing,*

68. I., II. *Memoranda relating to the above-named witnesses.*

68. III. *List of 15 witnesses of the Watermen's Company.*

Vol. CXXVI.

1665.

68. IV.–VII. *Four certificates, signed by Thos. Lowe, clerk of the Watermen's Company, of substitutes being allowed by the company to be found, by persons impressed for the King's service.* Oct. 10–16, 1664.

July 10? 69. Shorthand memoranda of [Sam. Pepys] found with and belonging to the same subject. [*Adm. Paper.*]

July 10? 70. Petition of Edmund Wyndham, His Majesty's servant, to the King, for a grant of such money as may be recovered in a suit depending in the Admiralty Court, about logwood, value 2,000*l.*, taken before the Restoration, which he hopes to prove was fraudulently claimed by London merchants, to deceive His Majesty. Wants thereby to satisfy his debts incurred in the public service.

[July 10.] 71. Note that in any grant to Col. Wyndham of the proceeds of the logwood in the Peahen, a proviso should be added that no discharge of the security be allowed to the prejudice of the King, without the privity of Sir Rob. Wiseman, advocate general.

July 10. Hampton Court. 72. Grant to Edmund Wyndham, gentleman of the privy chamber, of such moneys as shall be adjudged by the High Court of Admiralty to belong to the King, out of a prize of logwood taken in the Peahen, claimed by Simon Delbow, Rob. Wilmot, and other English merchants, and sold on their security to be responsible for its true value. [1½ *pages.*]

July 10. Entry of the above. [*Ent. Book* 22, *p.* 222.]

July 10. Warrant to pay to Sir Hugh Pollard, Bart., comptroller of the household, 5,000*l.* due to him by the late and present King. [*Docquet.*]

July 10. 73. E. Countess of Dysart to Williamson. Did not understand his message by her sister Allington, and will not understand his promise of a visit to-morrow, unless he will take an ill dinner with her, when he shall be most welcome.

July 11. Naseby. 74. Dr. Thos. Fuller to Williamson. The King's letter on his behalf is said to be sent to Dr. Widdrington, but the Doctor denies it; has therefore taken his degree with the ordinary exercises. Begs aid in detecting the fraud, also delay in the business of Newark; the incumbent is his friend, will resign as may best serve his end, and thinks he [Fuller] will be acceptable to the town. Will not leave till the danger of the sickness is over.

July 11. South latitude 54·30, Texel. 75. Earl of Sandwich to Lord [Arlington]. This morning was the first fair day that friends could visit him, and Sir Thos. Clifford has come to his ship. The fleet has been hastened away, though having 3,500 fewer men than the former. Hopes the men will be sent from Sole Bay. Is trying to get into his appointed station, and will do his utmost to serve and please the King. [2 *pages.*]

Vol. CXXVI.

1665.

July 11. Goring House. 76. Leonard Williams and John Betteson to Robt. Lye, Hampton Court. Dawson, one of the two named by them as entrusted to buy and gather arms, is taken by Capt. Thomas. Will acquaint his honour further if sent for. Are to be addressed at Capt. Thomas's, Hatton Garden, and he will let them know, they being a little remote on account of the sickness.

July 11. Tuesday. 77. J. Bulteel to ——. "My lord" approves of the paper, but it should be shown to a Secretary of State. Reminds him of the old gentlewoman who desires a passage in his ship. Endorsed [by Williamson] "The dispatch for Bruges." [2 pages.]

July 11. The King to Sir William Doyley. He is to get certificates under the hands of Dutch officers at Ipswich and Colchester as to their good usage, and to send attested lists of the prices of provisions. He may dispose of what prisoners he pleases, to work in harvest between now and Michaelmas. Minute. [*Ent. Book* 14, *p.* 66.]

July 11. Hampton Court. The King to the Lord Treasurer and Lord Ashley. Hears it is probable that coals may be found in Windsor Forest, which would be a great security to London, and save inconvenience through interruption in bringing coals from Newcastle. They are therefore to prepare a grant to Henry Hyde, Lord Cornbury, Sir George Carteret, and six others, of the sole digging of coals in the said forest, on their paying a rental of 6*d.* for every chaldron of coals that they raise. With memorandum that to the grant was added a similar licence to dig for coals in any of the King's lands, within 12 miles of Windsor, Oatlands, and Bagshot. [*Ent. Book* 14, *p.* 66.]

July 11. Chatham. 78. Comr. Peter Pett to Sam. Pepys. Several vessels are dispatched from Sheerness for Sole Bay, under convoy of the Convertine. Progress of the Sovereign's repairs, and forwardness of other ships. [*Adm. Paper.*]

July 11. Chatham. 79. Sir Wm. Batten to Sam. Pepys. The Sovereign is careened; four tons of tobacco stalks wanted. Asks what is to be done with the Gift; if sent out again, her men should have six months' pay. [*Adm. Paper.*]

July 11. Portsmouth. 80. Comr. Thos. Middleton to Sam. Pepys. Particulars of stores; account of goods on board the prize ship King David; has leave from the Commissioners of Prizes to land them, if warrant can be procured. [*Adm. Paper.*]

July 11. Portsmouth. 81. Comr. Thos. Middleton to Sam. Pepys. Has just received news of four Dutch capers lying off the Channel. [*Adm. Paper.*]

July 11. Southwold. 82. John Parker to Sir Wm. Rider. There are five vessels detained at Sole Bay for want of convoy. Having lost sight of Sir Thos. Allin's ships in a wind, they were obliged to put back; requests vessels to take them on. [*Adm. Paper.*]

VOL. CXXVI.

1665
July 11. 83. Sir Wm. Coventry to the Navy Comrs. Asks what victuals may be expected from Hull and Newcastle for supply of the fleet. The masters of the Gottenburg ships are negligent in their business, for but three of them have arrived at Southwold Bay. [*Adm. Paper.*]

July 11. Hampton Court. 84. Sir Wm. Coventry to the Navy Comrs. Some of the Gottenburg ships are gone with Sir Thos. Allin, to await the rest at Tynemouth; knows not where the others are, nor how to procure convoy for them; begs payment of contingent money to Comr. Taylor, to encourage his dispatch of ships at Harwich. Two New England ships, if now ready, may have convoy through the Soundings; suggests that a smack be employed to gather the sick and wounded when recovered, and carry them to the fleet. [*Adm. Paper.*]

July 11. Ordnance Office. 85. Ordnance Officers to the Navy Comrs. Certify that Walter Perry passed his accounts for the gunner's stores on board the Ruby. [*Adm. Paper.*]

July 12. Rome. 86. Ode addressed by Dr. Jacobus Albanus Ghibbesius to Joseph Kent, a visitor at Rome, on occasion of the victory gained by James Duke of York over the Hollanders. [*Latin, printed; he was poet laureate of the Emperor Leopold.*]

July 12. Edinburgh. 87. Proclamation by the Council of Scotland, that on account of the prevalence of the plague in London and other towns in England, all trade or intercourse with the places infected be suspended till 1st Nov., or till the prohibition be removed; that all ships now at sea, laden with goods from any of the said places, perform quarantine, and that all goods passing by land be stayed on the Borders till they have licence to pass, or submit to any trial required; and that all goods privately brought in be forfeited; charging all civil officers to enforce these regulations. [*Printed, 2 sheets.*]

July 12. Whitehall. 88. Order to Sir Edward Griffin to pay 20*l.* to the gentlemen of the chapel, in lieu of three deer annually given them by His Majesty. Endorsed, "Received of Mr. John Goodgroom, 11*l.* in Christmas quarter 1665, Wm. Child."

July 12. Minute of the above. [*Ent. Book 22, p. 227.*]

July 12. 89. John Tooker to [Sam. Pepys]. Certifies that the commanders of the Constant John, Swallow, and Sarah and Elizabeth were not on board their respective ships on Tuesday the 11th inst. at 9 o'clock p.m., by which neglect the opportunity for sailing was lost; the non-attendance of the Constant John's pilot is urged as the cause of its delay. A jack is wanted for the Recovery. List of ships undelivered of their empty cask and corrupt beer. The Hopewell is ready to take in water cask. [*Adm. Paper.*]

July 12. Chatham. 90. Comr. Peter Pett to Sam. Pepys. The Sovereign is ready to take in victuals. [*Adm. Paper.*]

VOL. CXXVI.

1665.

July 12. Hampton Court. 91. Warrant to the Board of Greencloth to pay full board wages to the officers of state and household servants, according to a book signed in 1662, until their allowance of diet decreed by the late establishment be restored, and also to continue the allowance of 4s. a day to the poor, provided the said allowances do not exceed the 100,000*l*. a year assigned for the use of the house; when the diets are restored, abatements are to be made to prevent the exceeding of the said sum. Endorsed, "Sir Herbert Price."

July 12. Hampton Court. 92. The King to [the Wardens, &c. of the Mint]. The office of assay master in the Mint being vacant by death of John Woodward, and absence of Thos. Woodward his father, who, if alive, is at some plantation on York River in Virginia, John Brattle is to exercise the office during the absence of Thos. Woodward, with a fitting allowance; but as he is at present employed by the Goldsmiths' Company, they are to permit him to assist the company, as far as can be done without neglect to the service, until some person is found in his place. [*Copy.*]

July 13. Dover. 93. Jo. Carlisle to Williamson. Saw Lord Aubigny aboard the French shallop ordered for him and his train, and thinks he got over to Calais in four hours. Has hired a vessel to carry his horses, but the Custom House have recent orders to allow no horses to pass without the Duke of Albemarle's hand to the warrant. Sends a man for it.

July 13. St. Alban Hall. 94. Dr. T. Lamplugh to Williamson. Thanks for a present of wine; will remember him at the opening of every bottle.

July 13. Warrant to pay to Edw. Backwell 1,750*l*., for secret service, without account. [*Docquet.*]

July 13. Grant of pardon to Oliver Cave and two others, for a robbery and felony on Willm. Webster, for which two persons have been executed. [*Docquet.*]

July 13. Warrant to pay to the Duke of York 20,000*l*. as the King's free gift, for supply of his own particular occasions. [*Docquet.*]

July 13. Warrant to pay to Rich. Hodgkinson, stationer, 674*l*. 13*s*. 1*d*., for paper, &c., for the House of Commons, from 6 Aug. 1661 to 10 March 1665. [*Docquet.*]

July 13. Portsmouth. 95. Comr. Thos. Middleton to Sam. Pepys. Sir John Mennes is much troubled at there being no news nor appearance of money for the present great want. The Elizabeth is at Spithead, with four butts of stinking beer on board. The ships going to convoy the East Indiamen from Ireland await a favourable wind. [*Adm. Paper.*]

July 13. Gravesend. 96. Fr. Hosier to Sam. Pepys. Account of the muster of nine ships. Was obliged to leave the Joseph, hired to take in sick and wounded, unmustered, through the opposition of the master. The seamen on board the Zebulon, bound for Tangiers, complain of

VOL. CXXVI.

1665.

short diet, no hammocks to lie on, and great want of clothes; the men say they will be hanged rather than go to sea, and several refused to give in their names to be mustered. [*Adm. Paper.*]

July 14. London. 97. Certificate by Geo. Smith, owner of the Hopewell pink, that John Burrows is master thereof instead of Elias Hind. [*Adm. Paper.*]

July 14. Dover. 98. Thos. White to the Navy Comrs. Repairs of the Little Mary. [*Adm. Paper.*]

July 14. The St. George, Chatham. 99. Lieut. Stephen Pyend to Sam. Pepys. Is ready to sail for Sheerness; hopes to find provisions ready. Wants 100 seamen, having 12 slain and 50 wounded in the fight, and 100 fallen sick and sent ashore. Begs a supply of junk or tobacco stalks. [*Adm. Paper.*]

July 14. Portsmouth. 100. Sir John Mennes to the Navy Comrs. Requests orders to Capt. Fleetwood to pay in the money promised by the Ordnance Officers. Has sent to the Isle of Wight and twice to Winchester about it. Money must be had to pay off the rest of the yard; the men grow impatient at the delay and not without reason. Begs that the necessary orders may be sent express, to stop the "bawlings and impatience of these people, especially of their wives, whose tongues are as foul as the daughters of Billingsgate." [*Adm. Paper.*]

July 14. Blackamoor pink, Hull. 101. Capt. John Barton to the Navy Comrs. Asks leave to be cleaned and victualled at Hull. Has taken a Dutch privateer, a galliot hoy of four guns, the best sailer in Holland. [*Adm. Paper.*]

July 14. 102. Robert Mayors to the Navy Comrs. Report of Mr. Rich's Christians and dram deals. [*Adm. Paper.*]

July 14? 103. Request by the Duke of Verneuil to Lord Arlington, for passes for his carriage, horses, servants, and baggage to go to France, before he follows the Court to Hampton Court. [*French.*]

July 14. Grant to Fras. Burdett, of Burthwaite, co. York, of the dignity of a Baronet. [*Docquet.*]

July 14. Grant to him of discharge of 1,095*l.* usually paid for that dignity. [*Docquet.*]

July 14. Warrant to pay to Adrian May 1,200*l.*, for levelling, planting and other works directed by the King in and about Greenwich Park. [*Docquet.*]

July 14. The Prince, near Flamborough. 104. Earl of Sandwich to Lord Arlington. Has no news beyond what Sir Thos. Clifford's account or his own letter to Sir Wm. Coventry will give.

July 14. Squire Bennet's house, Pall Mall. 105. Thos. Bancks to Williamson. The Admiralty Judges have cleared the Milkmaid, belonging to himself and his brothers of Hamburg, but their adversary appeals to the Lords at Syon House; has petitioned them, and begs his influence.

Vol. CXXVI.

1665.

July 14. Letter to the Lord Treasurer for 10,000l. to be paid to Stephen Fox, out of the Dunkirk money. Minute. [*Ent. Book* 17, *p.* 119.]

July 14. Whitehall. 106. Warrant to the Commissioners for Prizes to release, at suit of the French West India Company, three ships of Dieppe, the Jonas, Hercules, and Florimant, laden with goods for Barbary and Martinique, which will spoil, if they wait the usual forms of the Admiralty Court.

July 14. Entry of the above. [*Ent. Book* 22, *p.* 225.]

July 14. Warrant for delivery of a leash of fat bucks to Sir William Hickes, Bart. [*Ent. Book* 22, *p.* 226.]

July 14. Hampton [Court]. Warrant to Sir William Doyley to deliver 400 of the fittest Dutch prisoners to be set to work at Portsmouth, following the Duke of Albemarle's instructions for their transmission. [*Ent. Book* 22, *p.* 220.]

July 15. Bridekirk. 107. Geo. Williamson to Joseph Williamson. Has arrived there with his brother Curwen, who is willing to take the place of an ensign, quartermaster of horse, or any other thought fitting.

July 15. 108. Order in the Admiralty Court, in the case of the King *v.* Rich. Batson; a petition of Batson to the King was read, showing that he purchased prize goods 11 years before, for which, after allowance for payments and defalcations, 73l. only was due, but was sued in the said court, for 610l. and 30l. costs; sentence was given against him, in the absence of his witnesses, and he taken prisoner, whereon he pleaded for another trial, and release meanwhile, on depositing the money. He had a reference July 14, 1665, to the Admiralty Judges, who on the money being paid in, decreed his release from prison. [*Latin, 3 pages.*]

July 15. Orchard-Portman. 109. Two Deputy Lieutenants of Somersetshire to Lord Arlington. Having notice of a great conventicle, got some servants, broke open the doors, and took 60 men and as many women; sent the men to the sessions, where they were convicted and some paid, others went to gaol. Among them are 11 ministers living in or near Taunton, and there are as many more who preach up and down, and are so close in their meetings that they cannot be heard of till over; the head layman is Mr. Malleck, a man of fortune, who keeps a non-conforming minister in his house. With note thereon [by Lord Chancellor Clarendon] that every minister taken should be proceeded against severely; those too wary to be taken at conventicles should be watched, and imprisoned, or bound over to good behaviour; if two or three of the head people be sent to gaol, it is well. Also that any doubtful person taking a minister into his house should be bound to good behaviour.

July 15. Broadcourt. 110. Sir Brian Broughton to Williamson. Can get nothing from the clerk of the peace but the record of past years. Finds 20 Presbyterians convicted last sessions. Hears of none dead of the plague in that or the neighbouring counties.

VOL. CXXVI.

1665.

July 15. Hampton Court. Warrant to the Master of the Great Wardrobe to pay the bills of the tradesmen and artificers for the wardrobe, and allowances for servants, for the year ending Michaelmas 1663; total, 17,318l. 11s. 8d. [*Docquet.*]

July 15. Warrant to John Viscount Mordaunt, constable of Windsor Forest, to allow no woods to be felled there, on account of the destruction of woods in the late rebellion; the receiver is to allow to divers officers of the castle 5s. for each load of wood that they used to receive from the forest. [*Ent. Book* 14, *p.* 66.]

July 15. Navy Office, Seething Lane. 111. Sir Wm. Warren to the Navy Comrs. Entreats once more for a convoy for the Blackcock and Neptune, freighted by him to fetch masts from New England. Asks whether they will pay 200l., the insurance of the Lady, homeward bound, laden with masts for the King from New England, or run the risk. By contract it should have returned with the Newfoundland convoy, but none has been sent this year. [*Adm. Paper.*]

July 15. Bristol. 112. Sir John Knight to the Navy Comrs. Mr. Gauden's agent has no orders to furnish the ship [Pearl] with two months' more provisions as desired; must dispatch her to Milford, though it may prove destructive to her intended service. Will forbear freighting any more ships. Had the Pearl two months' more provisions, she might set sail directly to meet the capers and clear the coast. Asks if she is to be accounted a fourth or fifth-rate ship. [*Adm. Paper.*]

July 15. 113. Nath. Webb to the Navy Comrs. The master appointed for the Young Prince has not appeared. Begs an order to act in his stead. [*Adm. Paper.*]

VOL. CXXVII. JULY 16–31. 1665.

1665.

July 16. 1. Denis Gauden to the Navy Comrs. Has six months' victuals for 1,000 men now ready at Newcastle, and the same quantity at Hull; also 100 tuns of beer at each port. Is providing more on notice that ships may put into those ports to victual. The provisions remaining in the victualling ships at Harwich must be disposed of. [*Adm. Paper,* 1½ *pages.*]

July 16. 2. Denis Gauden to the Navy Comrs. Will furnish with all possible speed the account of the victuals each ship was supplied with at Sheerness, the Nore, Ousely Bay, Harwich, and the Rolling Grounds. [*Adm. Paper.*]

July 16. London. 3. Warrant by Sir Wm. Batten authorizing Thos. Heath, fisherman of Woolwich, to have and enjoy the sole fishing of Ham Creek, with power to seize any of the King's embezzled goods there. [*Adm. Paper.*]

Vol. CXXVII.

1665.

July 16. Portsmouth. 4. Comr. Thos. Middleton to Sam. Pepys. Particulars of prize goods landed. The Loyal Subject and Maryland Merchant set sail for Ireland, to convoy the East India ships thence to London. Dispatch of the Elizabeth; her beer is defective. [*Adm. Paper.*]

July 16. Ipswich. 5. J. Knight to Williamson. Begs performance of his promise. Sir Wm. Doyley has arrived well furnished, and gives life to the dying affairs of the King in that place. An honest old Trojan cavalier will have it that De Ruyter is taken. Wishes it may prove true, and be the cause of another thanksgiving. [2 *pages.*]

July 16. 6. Hen. Carter to Viscount Conway. Private business. Trade is very dead and money scarce.

July 17. Chester. 7. Sir Geoffry Shakerley to Williamson. Thanks for Lord Arlington's letter in the King's name, to encourage what he does against Nonconformists. Not being a justice of peace of the city, required the help of some justices, who committed the persons, but much favoured them in their fines. Will be vigilant to prevent clandestine meetings. The city and county are cautious in their watches not to suffer persons from infected places to come into the city, but the country fills space with passengers and strangers, many of whom will be forced to lie in the fields.

July 17. Tower. 8. Capt. G. Wharton to Col. Willm. Legg. Sends for alteration a warrant to Lord Lindsey, Lord Lieutenant of Lincolnshire, to pay the militia money to Mr. Chicheley, as meanwhile Sir John Buck, late high sheriff, brought it to town, and has already paid in 4,438*l*. Begs a warrant authorising Sir John to do what he has already done.

July 17. Monday. Putney. 9. Sir Rich. Ford to Williamson. Reminds him of his promise to dine with him. Hopes a day is assigned for hearing, either by the King or Council, of his petition and the proposals of the tin farmers. What they desire will be more for the King's interest than their own; all their advantage will be to lose only their time and labour, and come off with their principal stock.

July 17. Near Flamborough Head. 10. Earl of Sandwich to the King. Has obeyed his orders, in accommodating Lord Rochester as well as he can. Sir Thos. Allin has joined them, and by advice of the Council of War, the fleet has sailed for the Naze in Norway. Is sustained under his present weight by the blessing that rests on His Majesty's affairs. [2 *pages.*]

July 17. Kingston. 11. Simon De Petkum [Danish resident] to Sir Geo. Carteret. Tender of dram timber. Is informed by late letters from [Denmark] of the permission granted to the English to import masts of 20 palms from Norway, formerly forbidden. Recommends Peter Rich, merchant, as agent for supply of the same. [*French. Adm. Paper,* 1½ *pages.*]

July 17. 12. J. Smyther, accountant general of the Post Office, to John Earl of Lauderdale, Secretary of State for Scotland. The Scots

1665. VOL. CXCVII.

mail of 28 June last was opened, or the strap cut and letters taken out, near Berwick: hears that this is sometimes done by the governor or garrison of Berwick; begs a warrant against it. Asks his influence to obtain allowance for extra expenses sent to and from Scotland; also that a trial intended at Newcastle against Thos. Swan, postmaster, and his servants, for pressing a horse, in obedience to his lordship's post-warrant, may be stopped; such warrants will not be obeyed, unless the King's servants are protected against the fury of those who take advantage of the short penning of the Act of Parliament for the Post Office, and weary them out with vexatious suits for doing their duty. [2 *pages*]

July 17. Woolwich Ropeyard. 13. Wm. Bodham to Sam. Pepys. Entreats consideration for the state of the wharf. Edw. Rundell's estimate is only an audacious mockery, which he will not stand to, but suffers the wharf to be ruined for want of repair, while he beats off others from undertaking it. Begs it may be taken in hand by some one, or the next tide will throw down the crane. [*Adm. Paper.*]

July 17. Chatham Hill. 14. Sir Wm. Batten to the Navy Comrs. No ships are gone to the Hope, except the Zealand prize, to fetch men and take in provisions. Other vessels will soon follow. A press warrant is wanted for the Clove Tree; 80 calkers are to be discharged. Has sent two furnaces and a great kettle to Harwich. Requests orders that no contracts be made in Chatham, except for trivial things. Has advised the Mayor of Gravesend to get the assistance of the soldiery against the men of Owen Coys, a privateer, to examine their commissions, if they have any; if not, to lay them by the heels. [*Adm. Paper.*] *Encloses*,

14. I. *John Marlow, mayor of Gravesend, to Thos. Wilson, Navy clerk at Chatham. Complains of the disturbance caused by privateers' men coming on shore and assuming to themselves the power of impressing seamen belonging to the King's ships; they threaten to draw upon the constable and other gentlemen, and use abusive language to the officers of the corporation. Desires the advice of the Board. Has secured several Dutchmen who were to be transported by those privateers. Gravesend, July 15, 1665.*

July 17. Portsmouth. 15. Col. Bullen Reymes and Constance Pley to the Navy Comrs. Are forced to renew their demand for money. Have bought goods to the value of 10,000*l.* Entreat an imprest of 3,000*l.* on a bill to be discounted on the arrival of the said goods. [*Adm. Paper.*]

July 17. Dover. 16. Thos. White to Sam. Pepys. Has obtained the signature of Robt. Wickenden, clerk and registrar of Dover Castle, to the roll; the Paradox is sent in to clean by the Duke of Albemarle. [*Adm. Paper.*]

July 17. Bristol. 17. Dan. Furzer to the Navy Comrs. Has inspected Mr. Baylie's new ship now in building; begs that some one may be appointed to

VOL. CXXVII.

1665.

overlook the work, his own business not permitting the constant attendance needful. Has received 100*l.* from Mr. Morgan, but wants a further supply. [*Adm. Paper.*]

July 17. Portsmouth. 18. Comr. Thos. Middleton to Sam. Pepys. Want of money is a great inconvenience to the service. Arrival of the Unity, 102 butts of bad beer were thrown overboard, only five left on board till fresh supplies can be obtained. The men begin to fall sick, and would have been poisoned had she gone to sea with that beer. [*Adm. Paper.*]

July 17. Hayes Court. 19. J. Evelyn to the Navy Comrs. Is ordered to report what sick and wounded are fit to be totally discharged. Edw. Walker, of the Plymouth, is judged by the Commissioners totally unfit for service, being of a consumptive and ill habit. [*Adm. Paper.*]

July 17. Portsmouth. 20. Sir John Mennes to the Navy Comrs. Is much troubled at Mr. Fenn's dilatory answer about sending money; has long since signified that 4,000*l.* was the sum needed to complete the pay; is tired out with the vexatious delay and clamours of unsatisfied people, yet fears to stir till all is done, lest at the King's coming, he should be troubled with sad petitions from a crew of tumultuous women, who threaten as much. [*Adm. Paper.*]

July 17. Portsmouth. 21. Sir John Mennes to the Navy Comrs. Has sent Capt. Fleetwood and others to the Isle of Wight to bring over the 4,000*l.* there ready; understands that the money is lent by the Ordnance Officers to Sir Geo. Carteret, to be repaid by him in London. Desires an order to have the money paid, and power, if required, to assure repayment in London, on bills signed by himself at Portsmouth, for the receipt of the full value. Particulars of ships in harbour; has found out a way to secure the ropemakers from playing such pranks again, by denying payment of the letters of attorney of all runaways, and leaving strict orders that all pressed men forsaking work without leave shall be pricked "runaways," their wages lost, and they prosecuted. Mr. Pley is likely to get off if money can be sent, as ships from Weymouth are still admitted at St. Malo's, though not those from London. The money has just arrived. [*Adm. Paper.*]

July 17. Hampton Court. 22. Sir Wm. Coventry to Sam. Pepys. A surgeon is wanted for the Young Prince prize at Harwich. [*Adm. Paper.*]

July 18. Cockpit. 23. Duke of Albemarle to the Navy Comrs. Desires a master for the Maryland Merchant. Capt. Taylor has abused the warrant granted him for the carriage of Lord Petre's timber; he ought to have carried his own, and when Comr. Pett uses the carts, they clash with one another. If such orders be granted the country will complain of it; begs that Parsons, secured by the Mayor of Gravesend, may be sent to the fleet to be tried. [*Adm. Paper.*] *Encloses*,

23. I. *Note to Mr. Pepys for Parsons, now in prison at Gravesend, for running away from the service, to be sent to the fleet, and delivered to the Earl of Sandwich.*

VOL. CXXVII.

1665.

July 18. Chertsey. 24. John Langrack to Sam. Pepys. Entreats his interest with Sir Geo. Askew for the release of his brother, James Langrack, pressed into the *Henry*, where he is without clothes or acquaintance, after having for 16 years served as master's mate in other vessels. [*Adm. Paper.*]

July 18. Woolwich Ropeyard. 25. Wm. Bodham to Sam. Pepys. Urges the necessity of repairing the wharf where hemp is taken up; account of hemp in store; progress of the works. [*Adm. Paper.*]

July 18. Camphill. 26. Dan. Furzer to the Navy Comrs. Thinks 3*l*. per load a fair price for Mr. Blackborow's plank; 3*l*. 5*s*. would not buy such another parcel in those parts; advises that 240 or 250 loads be immediately contracted for. [*Adm. Paper.*]

July 18. Barber Surgeons' Hall. 27. Rich. Reynell to Thos. Hayter. Surgeons are wanted for the *Yarmouth* and *John and Thomas*; begs that bills for their appointment may be obtained from the Commissioners. [*Adm. Paper.*] *Encloses*,

27. I. *Capt. Hen. Dawes to Mr. Thickness, master warden of Surgeons' Hall. Notifies the death of his surgeon; requests that another may be supplied immediately.*
John and Thomas, Harwich, June 26, 1665.

27. II. *Capt. Thos. Ayliffe to the Masters and Wardens of Surgeons' Hall. Begs that Robt. Nash, late surgeon of the Greyhound, now put on board as surgeon of the Yarmouth, may have the allowance for a fourth-rate ship.*
The Yarmouth, off Harwich, July 11, 1665.

July 18. Portsmouth. 28. Sir John Mennes to the Navy Comrs. Money must be hastened down, or orders sent to receive what is already told out. The shipwrights have commenced new murmurings. Particulars of ships arriving and dispatched. The sickness is much less at Southampton. Longs to return; will take heed hereafter how to go about business without better prospect of the issue. [*Adm. Paper.*]

July [18?] Tower, Tuesday. 29. J. Fenn to Sam. Pepys. The 4,000*l*. to be paid at Portsmouth by the Ordnance Officers cannot be disposed of until the next post. Sir John Mennes should know this. [*Adm. Paper.*]

July 18. Blackwall. 30. Henry Johnson and Fr. Barham to the Navy Comrs. Demand their first payment of money due upon contract for building a third-rate frigate; have received only 250*l*. out of 1,750*l*. promised; if not complied with, must discharge the men and give up the work. [*Adm. Paper.*]

July 18. Hampton Court. 31. Commission to Col. [John] Legge to be Major of the Admiral's regiment, lately commanded by Sir Wm. Killigrew, whereof Sir Chichester Wray is colonel.

July 18. Minute of the above. [*Ent. Book* 20, *p.* 79.]

Vol. CXXVII.

1665.

July 18. Hampton Court. 32. Commission to Sir John Griffin to be Captain of a company in the Admiral's regiment, whereof Sir Christopher Wray, Bart., is colonel.

July 18. Minute of the above. [*Ent. Book* 20, *p.* 79.]

July 18. Minutes of commissions for the Admiral's regiment of foot, as follow:—

Sir Chichester Wray, Bart., Colonel, in the same form as Sir Wm. Killigrew, and also Captain.
Sir Chas. Littleton, Lieutenant-Colonel and Captain.
Nath. Dorrell and Thos. Bennet, Captains.
Martin Gardiner, Captain-Lieutenant, and Fras. Hoblin, Ensign, to the Colonel.
Edw. Talbot, Lieutenant, and John Snelling, Ensign to the Lieut.-Colonel.
Chas. Cole, Lieutenant, and —— Hume, Ensign, to the Major.
[Godfrey] Dennis, Lieutenant, and —— Ingram, Ensign, to Sir Jo. Griffin.
—— Steward, Lieutenant, and —— Thompson, Ensign, to Dorrell.
Phil. Bickerstaffe, Lieutenant, and —— Carey, Ensign, to Capt. Bennett. [*Ent. Book* 20, *pp.* 79, 80.]

July 18. The King to the Earl of Lindsey, lord lieutenant of Lincolnshire. Finds that the militia moneys for the county, which were ordered to be paid over from sheriff to sheriff of counties, till they reached the Tower, are already brought up to London, by Sir John Buck, Bart., late high sheriff. Requests an immediate order to him to pay the same to Sir John Robinson, lieutenant of the Tower. [*Ent. Book* 20, *pp.* 80–81.]

July 18 Durham. 33. Dr. Guy Carleton to [Williamson]. The persons who wish to make it clear that Sir Hen. Vane's personal estate belongs to the King, wish the Commissioners to return their depositions upon their inquisition, and then the adverse party to make their defence before the Lord Chancellor and others in London, and have a jury there. The reason is that most of the estate is unjustly seized by the Bishop of Durham, and as he nominates sheriffs and coroner, they are his creatures, and the adverse party fear a packed jury. Ant. Pearsons, the great quaker, is under sheriff, and has great dependance on the Bishop. If the case were in London, the witnesses would neither be overawed nor tampered with. There are seven houses shut up with the plague in Sunderland, one in Wearmouth, and one in Durham, where there is great fear because of the resort of persons from London; now strict watch is kept, and no suspected persons are allowed to enter. The fanatics and nonconformists still meet. Great clamour is caused by the cruel treatment of John Ellerington by Sir Hen. Witherington's son and servant;

1665. Vol. CXXVII.

they surprised him into a place where they arrested him on an action of trespass, refused bail, and because he would not deny Sir Henry's being at a meeting in Muggleswick Park, where the plotters took an oath of secrecy, sent him to Morpeth gaol, and had him put in the dungeon, kept without food some days, and not allowed to see his friends. [2 *pages.*]

[July 18.] Tuesday. 34. Countess of Dysart to Williamson. There have been unreasonable delays in her affair. Begs a positive answer, the thing being only what is usual. Wants some assurance, not in general terms, but so positive that she may know Lord Arlington's real mind. Will drop the addition she desired, if that be the obstruction. [1½ *pages.*]

July 18. Warrant to the Lieutenant of the Tower to release Colonel Nathaniel Rich. Minute. [*Ent. Book* 22, *p.* 227.]

July 18. Memorandum for committing William Roe to the custody of Thomas Dixon. [*Ent. Book* 22, *p.* 228.]

July 18. Sec. Morice to Sir William Doyley. He is to suffer none to speak with the Dutch prisoners, except in presence of one who understands the language; and to have special care of one Lunice of Flushing who was endeavouring to make his escape. Minute. [*Ent. Book* 14, *p.* 67.]

July 19. Hampton Court. 35. Sir Wm Coventry to Sam. Pepys. The Princess, Yarmouth, and Oxford are appointed as convoys to the ships bound for Gottenburg and the Sound; the Eaglet ketch is to remain at Harwich as a packet boat. It will be time enough to consider of return convoy for the Gottenburg ships after their arrival. Asks what victuals Mr. Gauden has in readiness at Hull and Newcastle, and what proportion the fleet went out with. [*Adm. Paper.*]

July 19. Trinity House. 36. Wardens, &c., of Trinity House to the Navy Comrs. Consider either Capt. Wm. Badiley or Capt. John Proud qualified to undertake the charge of master of the Royal Sovereign. [*Adm. Paper.*]

July 19. Chepstow. 37. Robt. Ems to Thos Sherley, Cornhill, London. Hears that he has offered plank to the Commissioners at 3*l.* per load, so that Mr. Furzer is blamed for asking 3*l.* 5*s.* Has advised Furzer to write and say that the owners can get 3*l.* 5*s.* for all 2 and 3-inch plank, well seasoned. [*Adm. Paper.*]

July 20. 38. Account by Mr. Tooker of five victualling ships, lying in the river for want of provisions for lading. [*Adm. Paper.*]

July 20. Hampton Court. 39. Sir Geo. Carteret to [Sam. Pepys]. It is necessary to secure what French canvas can be had with all imaginable speed. Mr. Harbin and other French merchants in London must be sent for, and no time lost in getting goods over from St. Malo. [*Adm. Paper.*]

Vol. CXXVII.

1665.

July 20. Portsmouth. 40. Sir John Mennes to the Navy Comrs. Is glad there is some hope of his dispatch; were ready money payments made, the King would save the third penny in all his works. Want of iron; desires an order for all that is in the prize ships to be sent in. Expects hourly the goods from St. Malo. Particulars of Col. Norton's timber. *Paper.*]

July 20. London. 41. Capt. Val. Tatnell to the Navy Comrs. Requests new warrants for apprehending runaways, and persons pressing without due authority; also orders to search any private men-of-war for runaway seamen. [*Adm. Paper.*]

July 20. Norwich. 42. James Johnson to the Navy Comrs. Messrs. Edgars' frigate proceeds well; the second payment is due. Wishes an answer to the proposals of the sailmaker and blockmaker for supply of the frigate. Has hopes of some cordage from Zealand. [*Adm. Paper.*]

July 20. 43. List of 20 bargemen for whom protections from impress have been issued. [*Adm. Paper.*]

July 20. Hampton Court. Warrant to Robert Child and William Bowles, masters of toils, to remove 25 brace of fallow deer, with their fawns, from the New Forest to places in Woolmer Forest, appointed by Col. Legg. [*Ent. Book* 22, *p.* 231.]

July 20. Eggleston. 44. Christopher Sanderson to Williamson. The party are doing nothing in those parts, but expect something done in the south. Major Beake, who was captain of Oliver's life guard, should be secured. He is desperately engaged. One of the three informers professes to be pricked in his conscience, and though, to avoid suspicion, he must still attend at Court, he will tell them anything that concerns them. The fanatics rejoice in the increase of the plague, and hope it will go through the kingdom.

July 20. Ipswich. 45. Jo. Knight to Henry Muddiman. There is a noise of guns, more like salutes than an engagement. Hopes De Ruyter or some other good thing has fallen into the hands of the English, and that if their fleet has sheltered in Norway, ours will pull them thence by force. The King of Denmark would take satisfaction for the affront or a share in the prey. The French will probably bring the Duke of Beaufort's fleet into the Channel, but we shall have 20 ships to confront them. There is yet no appearance of pestilence. [2 *pages.*]

July 20. 46. Minutes of commissions renewed for Officers in Sir Chichester Wray's regiment, and of an order to the Navy Treasurer to pay 2,000*l.* to Prince Rupert.

July 21. Haigh. 47. Sir Roger Bradshaigh to Williamson. Is glad to hear of the court being removed from the contagion in London. Confines to their own houses, for a month, all persons who come from London, and those who entertain them. At the sessions, two were convicted

1665. Vol. CXXVII.

for the second time, and one for the first time, of conventicles; but the stubborn Anabaptists, refusing to pay the 10s. fine, are sent to gaol for only two months. Thinks the third offence will quit the place of them, and many more by the same trap. At the thanksgiving at Bolton for the victory, the godly, counterfeiting excessive joy, took too much, and five of them fell on the clerk of the church and killed him, for which they are sent to gaol. One of the Barbadoes fleet, just returned richly laden, was burnt by an accident, through the drunkenness of the sailors: it belonged to Mr. Blundell of Ince, an ancient gentleman of good estate in the county. [2 pages.]

July 21. Hampton Court. 48. The King to the [the Fellows of Eton College]. Recommends Dr. Rich. Allestree, professor of Divinity at Oxford, to the place of Provost of that college, void by death of Dr. Meredith.

July 21. Entries of the above. [*Ent. Books* 19, *p.* 47; *and* 21, *pp.* 148-9.]

July 21. [Hampton Court.] Warrant empowering Hen. Lord Arlington and John Lord Berkeley, who are to be postmasters-general on expiration of the two years still remaining of the lease to the late Dan. O'Neale, to make contracts with foreign postmasters for supplying the defects in intercourse with foreign countries, and for the better carrying out of that office. [*Ent. Book* 22, *pp.* 231-2.]

[July 21.] 49. Draft of the above. [1½ *pages.*]

July 21. Bethnal Green. 50. Capt. John Hesilgrave to Sir John Mennes. Requests that his Lewes frigate may be freighted as a victualler for Tangiers, in order that she may sail thence to Turkey, where he has assurance of a full lading homewards. [*Adm. Paper*, 1½ *pages.*]

July 21. Plymouth. 51. John Lanyon to the Navy Comrs. Asks payment of money due to Dan. Harker for yarn, and Thos. Teate for cordage; total, 921*l.* 14*s.* 8*d.* [*Adm. Paper.*]

July 21. Barber Surgeons' Hall. 52. Rich. Reynell to Sam. Pepys. A surgeon has been long since appointed for the Young Prince; his pretence of stay is, want of conveyance for himself and chest to Harwich. [*Adm. Paper.*]

July 21. Chatham. 53. Comr. Peter Pett to Sam. Pepys. Sends a plan of the quantity of ground and manner of contrivance for the alterations at Sheerness; and an estimate of the charge. No more boats need be sent down, they are in no way fit for service. [*Adm. Paper.*] *Encloses,*

53. i. *Plan of the proposed dockyard at Sheerness.*

July 21. Dover. 54. Thos. White to the Navy Comrs. Dispatch of the Paradox. [*Adm. Paper.*]

Vol. CXXVII.

1665.

July 21. Kinsale. 55. Capt. Wm. Crispin to the Navy Comrs. The Dartmouth was called away before the laying of her cable. Account of money due to himself and his surgeon. Sends report of the sick and wounded. Arrival of the Baltimore and Loyal Subject. There is less noise of the Dutch capers at present. [*Adm. Paper*, 1½ *pages*.] *Encloses*,

55. i. *Certificates by John Godnuffe, surgeon, and Wm. Penn, clerk of the cheque, of the number of sick and wounded landed in Kinsale from the Dartmouth and Little Gift, and provided for. Names of those since dead, and of others returned cured, verified by Wm. Broadbeare, surgeon of the said town.* *Kinsale*, 1 *July* 1665.

55. ii. *List of the sick and wounded received at Kinsale from April 21 to July 18, with account for their quarters, 35l. 5s. 5½d., and burial charges, 2l. 19s. 1½d.*

July 21. Deptford. 56. Wardens, &c., of Trinity House to the Navy Comrs. Being requested to nominate one of their brotherhood as master of the Royal Sovereign; present for choice Capt. Simon Nicholls and Capt. Joseph Dobbins; and for the Maryland Merchant, John Hunton or Mr. Fleming, both of Redriff. [*Adm. Paper*.]

July 22. Woolwich. 57. Chris. Pett to the Navy Comrs. Repairs needed for the hulk and the Welcome; timber and treenails wanted. It is time to contract with the joiner and carver for the works of the new fourth-rate frigate. [*Adm. Paper*.]

July 22. Gravesend. 58. Fr. Hosier to the Navy Comrs. The Zealand musters 130 men; has stores and ammunition on board, and waits orders to sail. Muster of the Ruby, Merlin, and Fox. [*Adm. Paper*.]

July 22. 59. Statement of Thos. Smart and two others to the Navy Comrs., of the abuse of trust carried on by Arth. Crispin and five other rulers of the Watermen's Company, in receiving and converting for their own use sums of money for the release of able pressed seamen, and request that they may be deposed from all rule in the company. [*Adm. Paper*.]

July 22. Victualling Office. 60. John Bowles to Sam. Pepys. Account of beer and dry provisions dispatched to the Sovereign and several other ships. [*Adm. Paper*.]

July 22. Hampton Court. Warrants to Sir William Doyley to deliver up Sieur Cunaeus; to ——— to receive Cunaeus and convey him to the Tower; and to the Lieutenant of the Tower to receive and keep him close prisoner. Minutes. [*Ent. Book* 22, p. 233.]

July 22. 61. ——— ——— to Lord Arlington. There is a general disposition to quietness, and to improve the liberty allowed, in praying for removal of the plague. At the meetings, there is a sense expressed of the Lord's displeasure for the sins of the people, but no reflections

Vol. CXXVII.

1665.

on the government. If the King heard their earnest prayers for God's mercy and favour, and their deep contrition for their own sins and those of the land, he would not think them unworthy of the prudent indulgence which he declares for. There is no cause for fear unless some desperate Commonwealth men avail themselves of the present distress of the poor to excite tumults; but they can do little, the town being so emptied of those from whom they hope assistance. The Dutch refuse to countenance any faction against government, because none can assure them of any united interest on which they can rely to make disturbance. The party could move in Scotland, but are too much discouraged both from Holland and England. [1½ *pages.*]

July 23. Cockpit. 62. Order from the Duke of Albemarle to Capt. Bennet, of Col. Russell's regiment, to march to Salisbury, quartering his troops in convenient places not occupied by the horse guards or the attendants at court, taking care that the soldiers conduct themselves civilly, and pay for what they have.

July 23. Dover. 63. Jo. Carlisle to Williamson. His servant Osborne came in time, and has sailed for Dunkirk; hopes he will pass clear, though they are stricter there than at Calais. There is a rumour of De Ruyter's fleet being taken. The town is free from the plague, which is wonderful, since it is a general place of reception. Lords Aubigny and Berkeley went to Calais last week, and were with some difficulty suffered to enter.

July 23. Portsmouth. 64. Constance Fley to Sam. Pepys. Is hourly expecting the ships from St. Malo; was obliged to leave London without signing the last contract; has since done so in presence of Sir John Mennes. Hears nothing from Mr. Fenn about his readiness to pay the bill of 1,000*l.* drawn on him for sailcloth and cordage served in. Will manage by her son's interest to keep up the French trade, though the expected breach should take place. [*Adm. Paper.*]

July 23. Portsmouth. 65. Col. Bullen Reymes to Sam. Pepys. Thanks for his bill accepted, and for promise of timely payment. Will deliver the canvas last contracted for by Christmas, if ready money be furnished, and if the King will run the risk of all enemies. As the report goes of a fall out with the French, their goods may be seized in the cellars of St. Malo. [*Adm. Paper.*]

July 23. Plymouth Fort. 66. Sir John Skelton to Sam. Pepys. Six weeks' victuals are put on board the Sta. Maria; she will sail in a few days. [*Adm. Paper.*]

July 24. Chatham. 67. Commr. Peter Pett to Sam. Pepys. Will put in execution the new careening wheel for ships; it has been practised with success at Harwich. Proposes a prize ship as second hulk for Sheerness. Has power by his patent of office to contract for provisions, and thought by expressions in former letters that he had the consent of the Board also; wished therefore to deal with Mr. Cole thinking his provisions as reasonable as any that can be bought. If his supply be stopped, some other must be procured immediately, or all the men discharged. [*Adm. Paper.* 1½ *pages.*]

Vol. CXXVII.

1665.

July 24. Norwich. 68. James Johnson to the Navy Commrs. Recommends three persons competent to undertake the survey of the new frigate now building at Yarmouth; the second payment is due to MM. Edgar. [*Adm. Paper.*]

July 24. Bristol. 69. Fra. Baylie to the Navy Commrs. Has been unable to find time to furnish the draft of his ship now building, by reason of the continual trouble in getting timber and other goods necessary for dispatch of the work. [*Adm. Paper.*]

July 24. Warrant to pay to Lady Cornwallis, widow of Charles Lord Cornwallis, such parts of the arrears of her pension of 900*l.* a year as were due before Michaelmas, 1663, when all such pensions were stayed. [*Ent. Book* 22, p. 234.]

[July 24.] 70. Draft of the above.

July 24. / Aug. 3. Chelsea. Ambassador Van Gogh to [the States General]. Both great and mean fly the city on account of the plague, and many Netherlanders desire their passes, there being no manner of trade left, nor conversation, either at Court or on the Exchange. The Court of Scotland has interdicted all trade [with England] for three months, and imposes quarantine on such ships as have not been long on the way. The King and Duke of York go on Thursday from Hampton Court to Portsmouth for three or four days, and thence to Salisbury, whither the Queen and Duchess are already gone. The Archbishop of Dublin is chosen to supply the place of the Lord Chancellor of Scotland, deceased. [*Holland Corresp., Aug.* 7, 1665.]

July ? 71. Petition of Thos. Smoult, M.A., to the King, for letters for his election to the fellowship now void in St. John's College, Cambridge, denied him by the late master, because of the loyalty of his family.

July 24. The King to the Masters and Senior Fellows of St. John's College, Cambridge. Recommends Thos. Smoult, M.A. of that university, on account of his orthodox learning and sobriety, to a vacant fellowship in the college. [*Ent. Book* 19, *p.* 47.]

July 24. Ham. 72. E. Countess of Dysart to [Williamson]. Thanks both him and Lord Arlington that her business approaches a conclusion. The names of the grantees are wanted. Wishes the 10 acres within her walls to be passed solely to her, all the rest of the lease to her sisters equally with her.

July 24. Carlisle. 73. Sir W. Clarke to Williamson. Requests him to send the commissions for Sir Jas. Smith to be Lieut.-Colonel, and Major John Miller, Major in the Duke of Albemarle's regiment of Guards. The fees are paid to Mr. Godolphin.

July 24. Wanstead. 74. John Lawson to Sir Willm. Coventry. Sends the part of the will which concerns the pension. Her ladyship hopes his respect

VOL. CXXVII.

1665

for her late husband will encourage his kindness to the fatherless. *Encloses,*

74. I. *Clause from Sir John Lawson's will, dated April 19, 1665, requesting that the pension of 300l. a year settled upon him for life, and which was promised to his daughters if he died in the service, should be either divided equally between Elizabeth and Anna Lawson, or left to Anna for her to give a share to Elizabeth; with note of Lady Lawson's wish for it to be so effected.*

July? 75. Wm. Frisell to [Lord Arlington]. Is sent by the Countess of Chesterfield to end the differences between the postmasters of France and Flanders, and quicken and improve intelligence from beyond seas. As her grant is nearly out, offers to him or to her successor, if they will obtain him a pension of 300l. a year from the post office, to settle a correspondence in all the maritime places of Spain and Italy; this is to be independent of any arrangement about the letters of Holland and Zealand. Has served and suffered 33 years, and has increased the revenue of the office more thousands than he asks hundreds. [1½ *pages.*]

July 24. Hampton Court. 76. Lords Arlington and Berkeley to M. De Nouveau. Mr. O'Neale being dead and his wife having only two years left of the lease of the post office, they are appointed reversioners, with order to remedy inconveniences in the late treaties with O'Neale. Request him to give credence to Mr. Frisell, sent to ascertain the means of rendering the former treaties reciprocally useful to both nations. [*French.*]

[July 24.] 77. Draft of the above.

July 24. 78. Lords Arlington and Berkeley to the Conte de Taxis. To the same effect. Mr. O'Neale had agreed for the Holland letters to come by way of Flanders, if it could be done with the same expedition, but this has not been punctually performed. Send Frisell to converse with him about this and the transport of letters for Italy by Switzerland. [*French, 2 pages.*]

July 24. 79. Draft of the above.

July 24? 80. Memorial for Mr. Williamson, to dispatch Mr. Frisell with all haste; for a pass for horses to France for Sir Phil. Frowde; for Mr. Boles to send letters requiring haste to the postmaster, Charing Cross, others to the post office; for a messenger always to attend, to go between Goring House and the Post Office.

July 24. Hampton Court. Order,—on the petition of the Farmers of the pre-emption and coinage of tin,—that the petitioners propose what they have to offer in this matter to the Council Board. [*Ent. Book* 18, *p.* 185.]

July 25. 81. L. W. [Leonard Williams] to Lord [Arlington]. Gathers enough from the female kind and others to prevent insurrections, which might arise from the city being so left; they dare not plot, being

Vol. CXXVII.

1665.

fearful of trespass; those who have religion flee the city as well as others, for fear of the plague. Atkinson wishes much to see the writer on His Majesty's service; asks whether he is to see him.

July 25. Navy Office. 82. Sir Wm. Batten to Williamson. Begs his assistance with Lord Arlington on his petition. Sends him a present of sturgeon. *Encloses,*

82. i. *Petition of Sir William Batten to the King, for a grant of the fly boat Arion, taken on the coast of Guinea, in compensation for his loss of the 10th part of the Constant Warwick, in 1648, of which he was deprived for remaining with His Majesty in Holland.*

July 25. Hampton Court. Warrant to the Judges of North Wales and Sheriff of Anglesea to reprieve John Griffith, of Croydavey, co. Anglesea, convicted at Beaumaris assizes, Sept. 5, 1662, of manslaughter, from the penalty of being burnt in the hand, or any other punishment, until further pleasure. [*Ent. Book* 14, *pp.* 67-8.]

July 25. Hampton Court. Warrant to Lord Ashley to pay to Doctor Jenkins, judge of the Admiralty Court, 300*l.* a year out of money for sale of prizes, for his constant attendance and service. [*Ent. Book* 22, *p.* 233.]

July 25. Warrant to Sir William Doyley to release Hendrick Van Baid, son of Hendrick Van Reid. Minute. [*Ent. Book* 22, *p.* 234.]

July 25. 83. Notes of grants, dating 25 July, 1665, to Sir John Robinson, of reversion of all those houses, &c., near the Tower, formerly granted by King James to [Sir Roger Aston], and to Hen. Timberlake and Rob. Bradbury.

July 25. 84. R. Manley to Lord [Arlington]. Is there [in Holland] on the King's service, but some wrong has been done him in his absence, by preferment of others to his prejudice, which to men of his profession is a sensible disgrace. The pensioner De Witt ordered him to be gone, but he excused himself on the privilege of the embassy. Has been employed 20 years in fortification, and had hopes of preferment given him by the Lord General, but is prejudiced by absence in this respect as well as the other.

July 25. 85. Petition of Wm. Cole, surgeon of the Paradox, to the Navy Comrs., for recruit of his medicine chest after 14 months' attendance. Signed by Capt. Leo Guy and two others. [*Adm. Paper.*]

July 26. Cockpit. 86. Duke of Albemarle to the Navy Comrs. Certain ships are to be furnished with necessaries and hastened to the Gunfleet. A mainmast may be had at Plymouth for the Sorlings. [*Adm. Paper.*] *Encloses,*

86. i. *List of 12 ships ordered for the Gunfleet.*

July 26. Woolwich. 87. W. B. [Wm. Bodham] to Thos. Hayter. Wants 300 feet of refuse shaken oak plank to repair the floor of the ropehouse. Repairs needed for the wharf at the gun yard. [*Adm. Paper.*]

VOL. CXXVII.

1665.

July 26. The Zealand, Hope. 88. Capt. John Whately to Sir Wm. Coventry. Is ready to sail. Waits for water and water cask from London. Wants 18 of his company, but expects to pick some up in the way. [*Adm. Paper.*]

July 26. 89. Denis Gauden to the Navy Comrs. Sends a list of 18 victualling ships hired by the month, with the tonnage and number of men on each. Wishes some of them continued to carry the remaining provisions to the fleet. [*Adm. Paper.*]

July 26. Hampton Court. 90. Petition of James Riddell, of Leith, Scotland, to the King, for redress for a damage of above 4,000 rixdollars, because his ship was seized in Leith Road by a Dover privateer, who, notwithstanding an order from the Lord Commissioner for Scotland for its restoration, carried it off to Holy Island, pillaged it, and then left it to the mercy of a Dutch vessel, which came and took it as prize to Holland. With reference thereon to the Court of Admiralty.

July 26. Hampton Court. The King to [the Dean and Chapter of Canterbury]. Requests on behalf of Elis. Turner and Elis. Bargave, poor widows whose husbands lost much by their loyalty, the renewal of a lease of a house which, being built within the Cathedral precincts, the lease cannot be renewed without his dispensation. [*Ent. Book* 17, *p.* 120.]

[July 26.] 91. Draft of the above.

July 26. Warrant for discharge of the Abraham's Offering, which in her voyage from Bayonne to Hamburg, was taken by Capt. Knight of Dover and brought into Rye, but proves to belong truly to Hamburghers. [*Ent. Book* 22, *p.* 236.]

July 26. Warrant to Sir William Doyley, Comr. for sick and wounded prisoners, to release Capt. Adrian Van Reda, on bond for his appearance when demanded. [*Ent. Book* 22, *p.* 237.]

July 26. Whitehall. 92. Warrant to Sir Edward Griffin to pay to Richard Royston, the King's stationer, 58*l.* 8*s.* for paper, &c., furnished to Lord Arlington, from December 21, 1662, to February 7, 1665.

July 26. Entry of the above, giving the sum as 8*l.* 8*s.* [*Ent. Book* 22, *p.* 237.]

July? 93. Petition of George Paul to the King, for a grant of 324*l.*, public money not disposed of nor accounted for, remaining in the hands of —— Browne, formerly a captain in Cromwell's own regiment.

July 26. Hampton Court. Warrant for a grant to George Paul of 324*l.* remaining in the hands of —— Browne not accounted for, with power to recover the same. [*Ent. Book* 22, *p.* 238.]

July 26. Hampton Court. Warrant to the Sheriff of Surrey to order the transportation to Jamaica of John Lacey, condemned for murder at Kingston assizes. Minute. [*Ent. Book* 22, *p.* 239.]

July? 94. Petition of Charles Gifford to the King, for the place of Assay Master in the Tower, for which he has obtained consent of

VOL. CXXVII.

1665.

the wife of Thos. Woodward, now in the Tower, notwithstanding the allegation that he is unfit for it, being a gentleman not a tradesman. The place was formerly held by a gentleman, who had a deputy.

July 26. Hampton Court. 95. Warrant to the Officers of the Mint to admit Charles Gifford to the place of Assay Master of the Mint, void by death of John Woodward, he having the consent of the wife of Thos. Woodward.

July 26. Entry of the above. [*Ent. Book* 22, *p.* 239.]

July [26]. 96. Draft of the above.

July 26. Pass for Colonel Richard Talbot to Ireland, with eight horses. Minute. [*Ent. Book* 22, *p.* 240.]

July 26. Pass for Mr. Frisell, with two horses. Minute. [*Ent. Book* 22, p. 240.]

July 26. Pass for the Earl of Carlingford, with eight horses. Minute. [*Ent. Book* 22, *p.* 240.]

July 26. Pass for Oundeloes. Minute. [*Ent. Book* 22, *p.* 240.]

July 26. Hampton Court. Proclamation ordering the Exchequer to be removed to Nonsuch, on account of the increase of the plague in Westminster. [*Printed. Proc. Coll., Charles II., p.* 196.]

June 26. Minute of the above. [*Ent. Book* 22, *p.* 240.]

[July 26.] 97. Draft of the above. [*Three sheets.*]

July ? 98. Request on behalf of the Countess of Dysart, wife of Sir Lionel Tollemache, and her sisters, daughters of the late Earl of Dysart, for a grant to Sir Lionel of certain lands in Petersham and Ham, on rent of 4*d.* per acre; also for a lease in reversion of the demesne lands of the said manor, at the ancient rent of 16*l.* 9*s.* With the heading of a letter [to the Lord Treasurer] thereon.

July 26. Hampton Court. 99. Warrant for a grant to Sir Lionel Tollemache of 75 acres of land in the manors of Petersham and Ham, co. Surrey, and also of a lease in reversion of the demesne lands there. [1½ *pages.*]

July 26. Entry of the above. [*Ent. Book* 22, *p.* 241.]

July 26. The King to Sir John Robinson. Ordered him previously to pay to the Lieutenant of Ordnance such sums as were placed in his hands by the several sheriffs, of the arrears of the month's assessment for the militia, but on account of pressing occasions, now orders him first to pay 20,000*l.* to Sir George Carteret. [*Ent. Book* 22, 242.]

July [26.] 100. Draft of the above.

July 26 101. Charles Duke of Richmond and Lenox to Williamson. Thanks for his care in procuring his pass; hopes it will be allowed custom free. Will be that night at Dover, and only waits his answer.

Vol. CXXVII.

1665.

July 26. Cockpit. 102. Sir Wm. Clarke to Williamson. The Duke of Albemarle wishes an order for Col. Gilby, deputy governor of Hull, to have a prize ship to fetch coals from Newcastle for the garrison; begs that it may be the Salt house of Middleburg, which is condemned and appraised. The plague increases; 326 have been buried in St. Giles', 200 in St. Martin's, 142 in Westminster, and 104 in Holborn, since the last bill.

July 27. 103. Order [by the Comrs. for Tangiers] that the Tiger, freighted by the contractors for victualling Tangiers, be dispatched before the rest of the ships now lying at Plymouth, the King bearing the risk of any enemy; the rest are to wait a convoy, the contractors doing all in their power to preserve the provisions from damage. [*Copy.*]

July 27. Hampton Court. 104. Order from Lord Steward the Duke of Ormond to the Officers of Greencloth, to allow to Sir Herbert Price the rights, privileges, and allowances which belong to his place as Master of the Household.

July 27. Note for Thos. Evernden to be Almsman in Canterbury. [*Ent. Book* 19, *p.* 48.]

July 27. Portsmouth. 105. Constance Pley to Sir John Mennes. Has received good news from France; the barks are safely laden, only waiting for other ships to sail for England. Entreats money or credit with Alderman Backwell to pay bills of exchange. [*Adm. Paper.*]

July 27. Deal. 106. Mor. Lodge, postmaster, to Sam. Pepys. Has caused the instructions for Capt. Neales to be delivered. [*Adm. Paper.*]

July 27. Portsmouth. 107. Comr. Thos. Middleton to Sam. Pepys. An order for the delivery of iron from the prize ships will be welcome to the smith. The Unity has set sail. The King and Duke of York are expected. There is much fear lest their followers should bring the plague into the town, which is much pestered with soldiers and seamen, and their wives and children. [*Adm. Paper.*]

July 27. 108. Capt. John Proud and Edw. Stevens to the Navy Comrs. Survey and appraisement of the Baltimore, Joseph, and Loyal Subject. [*Adm. Paper.*]

July 27. Downs. 109. Capt. Rich. Neales to the Duke of Albemarle. Intends to set sail as soon as wind and weather permit; hopes to be at Calais by 1st August. Has ordered the Golden Phoenix to convoy the New England men into the Soundings, and the Truelove hoy to Spithead. [*Adm. Paper.*]

July 28. Wivenhoe ketch, North Shields. 110. Capt. Wm. Berry to Sir Wm. Batten. Particulars of his late voyage, to the north of Scotland, in search of the Dutch fleet. Encountered 11 Dutch men-of-war off North Shetland, and was chased and within shot for seven hours. Capture of a galliot hoy, with eight Dutch pilots for their East India fleet; is in port for repairs. [*Adm. Paper.*]

Vol. CXXVII.

1665.

July 28. Ludlow Castle. 111. Greg. Flavell to Williamson. It is Henry not Richard Herbert whom Lord [Carbery] recommends as his lieutenant in the garrison; requests that the commission may be rectified.

July 28. 112. Sir Willm. Fleetwood to Williamson. Hopes for his company, as he is so near. Sends him half a buck.

July 29. Thistleworth. 113. Col. Dan. O'Brien to Williamson. Wants a meeting with him. Also a post warrant for three horses and a guide from Salisbury to Holyhead, for they will hardly let anybody from those parts pass through Chester, except on the King's service.

July 29. Ordnance Office. 114. Estimate by the Ordnance Officers of materials not in store which would be required for a train of artillery of 24 pieces of ordnance, given according to an order of the Duke of Albemarle of the 27th instant; total, 5,140*l.* 2*s.* 6*d.* [*Five sheets.*]

July 29. Dover. 115. Thos. White to Sam. Pepys. Acknowledges the favour received from the Earl of Sandwich and others, which "as a sweet posie so freshly refresheth me, that it draweth from me all the thankfulness I can express;" regrets the zealous passion that made him crave employment at sea. Is willing to spend his whole time in service at the port. Requests a supply of stores. Arrival of the Cygnet for repairs and victualling. [*Adm. Paper.*]

July 29. Cockpit. 116. Duke of Albemarle to the Navy Comrs. Desires a warrant for Capt. Sadd of the John and Katherine, or any other captains coming into the river to impress watermen, unless the rulers of the watermen will do it better. [*Adm. Paper.*]

July 28. Clapham. 117. Denis Gauden to Sam. Pepys. The Duke of York's instructions shall be fully complied with, unless the 11 ships named have sailed. Sends an account of their victualling at London, Chatham, and Harwich, that it may be seen what ships are short. [*Adm. Paper.*]

July 29. 118. Sir Wm Rider and Wm. Cutler to the Navy Comrs. Complain of the delay in appointing a convoy for the ships hired to transport stores from the Baltic; if the goods come not in time, no blame can be imputed to the contractors. Three ships laden with tar, pitch, &c., lie in the Sound, ready for a return convoy; ask whether they shall be insured; think it better to run the hazard of the seas than pay so great a premium.

July 29. Convertine, Burlington Bay. 119. Capt. John Pearse to Sir Wm. Coventry. The provision ketch and water ship under his convoy are leaky, and cannot proceed. Capts Blake and Perriman are stopped for want of victuals; manages to supply them, by putting his own passengers and soldiers on board the fire ships bound to the fleet. Wishes firm ships and willing men were provided for victuallers. Report of the collier fleet and other vessels met with. [*Adm. Paper.*]

July 30. Chatham. 120. Comr. Peter Pett to Sam. Pepys. Is about to discharge the joiners; their bills amounting to 300*l.* must be passed. [*Adm. Paper.*]

VOL. CXXVII.

1665.

July 30. Hull. 121. Wm. Blaydes to the Navy Commrs. Requests payment of his bill of 20*l.* 1*s.* 2*d.* for repairing and victualling the Blackamoor, at the governor and captain's request. Arrival of the Delft frigate. Offers cordage at 30*s.* per cwt. [*Adm. Paper.*]

July 30. Deal. 122. Thos. Warren to [Sam. Pepys]. Finds all the ships in good equipage, and the men in health. Begs that provisions may be ready for the soldiers at Plymouth. The purser of the Fox will attend Mr. Gauden to make up his accounts. [*Adm. Paper.*]

July 31. 123. Petition of the Boatswain, Gunner, and Carpenter of the yacht Henry to the King, for the same allowance of fifth-rate wages as allowed in the Katharine; are poor men, and cannot maintain their families with sixth-rate pay. With order thereon granting the petition. [*Copy.*]

[July 31.] 124. Similar petition to the same effect.

July 31. Grant to Sir Thos. Peyton, Bart., of Knowlton, Kent, and others, of the Rectory of East Church, Isle of Sheppey, forfeited by attainder of Sir Michael Lindsey, in trust for Robt. Wilkinson, present vicar, and the future vicars of Knowlton. [*Docquet.*]

July 31. Putney. 125. Sir Rich. Ford and John Buckworth to Williamson. Thanks for his interest in the tin farmers' case; Lord Ashley promises to promote the hearing of the cause, when offered to Council. Beg to have warning that they may be in waiting. [1½ *pages.*]

July 31. Chester. 126. Col. Ro. Werden to Williamson. Thanks for the weekly paper; entreats its continuance. Is ill of the gout. Begs that the enclosed may be sent to the Duke's back stairs.

July 31. Cockpit. 127. Duke of Albemarle to the Navy Commrs. The remaining ships for the Gunfleet must be hastened away. If the owners of the King Ferdinando will not set her out, some other merchant ship must be hired at the same rate, and the men transferred. [*Adm. Paper.*]

July 31. 128. Sir Wm. Batten to Sam. Pepys. Has sent money to Chatham, with orders to fit the Great Gift for sea, instead of the King Ferdinando. All possible haste is required for the 12 ships. [*Adm. Paper.*]

July 31. Coxpill. 129. Dan. Furzer to the Navy Commrs. Urges the necessity of a constant survey on the building of Mr. Baylie's new ship; unserviceable timber is still used, though on pretence of being only put up for the present. Begs an order for planks of certain thickness to be used. The land carriage of timber gets on very unhandsomely, and requires speedy redress. Wants money. [*Adm. Paper.*]

July 31. 130. Agreement between Cuthbert Atkinson, shipmaster of Newcastle-upon-Tyne, and Humphrey Pybus, merchant of Newcastle, on

Vol. CXXVII.

1665.

behalf of Edw. Dering, merchant of London, for hire by the latter, for 200*l.*, of the Promise, to fetch goods from Hamburg, whither she is going, freighted by the former; 440*l.* to be paid by either party, on breach of covenant. [*Adm. Paper.*] *Annexing,*

130. i. *Memoranda of three other ships hired by Humphrey Pybus, on behalf of Edw. Dering, for conveyance of goods from Hamburg to London.* *July 27, 1665.*

July 31. Fleet. 131. Roger Rymer to the Navy Comrs. Requests payment of 60*l.* 15*s.*, drawn on Nicholas Buckeridge, merchant, for supply of victuals to the William, on her homeward journey from St. Helena. [*Adm. Paper.*]

[July.] Sec. Morice to the Farmers of Customs. They are privately, as from themselves, to caution all English merchants to withdraw their goods from France, and send no more till they see how things will settle. With note of the like advice to the Mayor of Plymouth for Western merchants. Minute. [*Ent. Book* 14, *p.* 67.]

[July.] Orders to Sir William Doyley to free Lieut. Mauregnault, upon the ambassador's parole. Minute. [*Ent. Book* 14, *p.* 67.]

[July.] Order for Mr. Turner to see Mr. Cannus at Colchester, or any other prisoner. Minute. [*Ent. Book* 14, *p.* 67.]

July. 132. Memoranda [by Williamson, from the Signet books,] of warrants, grants, &c., passed during the month, the uncalendared portions of which are as follow:—

Note that the King incorporated the feoffees of the 12,000*l.* left by Humph. Cheetham, for erecting a hospital and library in Manchester, as governors of the hospital and library of Manchester, founded by Humph. Cheetham, with permission to use a common seal, make laws, and purchase lands in mortmain.

Grant to Laurence Hyde, in soccage, of Killingworth manor, with mines, advowsons, &c.

Note that the King pays for the stationery used in Parliament, on a bill signed by the clerk of Parliament.

Note that by the farm of 1665, the excise of London and Westminster was advanced in value 22,000*l.* a year.

July? 133. Sam. Pomfret to Mr. Haines. Wishes to see him about the papers coming from Oxford, whither he is going.

July? 134. —— Haines to Sam. Pomfret. Cannot obey his summons, not having received it till six at night. Wishes him a good journey to Oxford, and sends service to his friends at Christ Church. Has lost his credit, and neither the Bishop of London nor his relatives will help him to preferment at Cambridge; will therefore be forced to accept the post, but wishes it were a better one than serving-man or valet-de-chambre.

VOL. CXXVII.

1665.
July. Gatehouse, Westminster. 135. John Knowles to the Duke of Albemarle. Has lain in deplorable condition two months, on the misinformation of some. Is conscious of no evil against government and has always hated seditious practices. Entreats release on bail, especially considering the present contagious disease.

July? 136. [Lord Arlington] to the Bishop of London. The King is informed that many ministers and lecturers having been absent from their posts during this time of contagion, nonconformists have thrust themselves into their pulpits, to preach sedition, and doctrines contrary to the Church; His Majesty wishes him to prevent such mischiefs to Church and State.

July. 137. Wm. Wood and 4 other Members of the Shipwrights' Company to the Navy Comrs. There is great scarcity of shipwrights, because many able shipwrights are impressed to serve as mariners and seamen. Beg an examination into this abuse, that the men may be restored to their proper calling. [*Adm. Paper.*]

July? Salisbury. 138. List, sent by the Earl of Sandwich, of the fleet as divided into three squadrons,—32 ships headed by the Prince; 32 by the Royal Charles, and 27 by the Royal James.

July? 139. List of the division of the fleet into squadrons, under the Duke of York, Prince Rupert, and the Earl of Sandwich; with the fire ships, and the subdivisions of the Duke's squadron, under the admiral, vice-admiral, and rear-admiral.

July? 140. Similar list, with slight differences, giving the total 135 vessels.

July? 141. Draft of the above.

VOL. CXXVIII. AUGUST 1–10, 1665.

1665.
Aug. 1. Leicester. 1. Sir Wm. Coventry to Lord [Arlington]. The Duke of York is well, but has not been without alarms. At St. Alban's, one of his pages fell ill with fever and vomiting, and the innkeeper, thinking it the plague, was about sending him without leave to the pesthouse; he is now better. The magistrates of Leicester waited on the Duke at his arrival. Lords Devonshire and Bridgewater waited on him at St. Alban's. In his journey, the Earl of Kent, and Lords Bedford, Maynard, and Lucas met him, near Woburn, an excellent and capacious house, where he lodged and was well treated by Lord Bedford; there several gentlemen attended him. Towards Northampton, the sheriff of Buckinghamshire, with Sir Wm. Tyringham and others, met him; also in Northamptonshire, the sheriff, who made a good speech, with some gentlemen. There Lord Sunderland invited him to his house near Northampton; he declined, but dined there yesterday, and supped at Lady Thomond's. The magistrates of Northampton met and attended him through the town, also Lords

VOL. CXXVIII.

1665.

Northampton, Peterborough, and Thomond. The Duke declined an invitation to breakfast at Lord Banbury's, but his lordship stopped the coach as it passed, and being again refused, laid hold of his Highness' leg, and pulled so hard that he had almost drawn off his shoe. This rhetoric, with the trouble he expressed, induced their Royal Highnesses to go in, where a table was prepared with sweetmeats and fruit. He was importunate with the Duchess to see his lady, who was lying in, but as she was not ready to be seen, the Duchess broke loose, with a promise to see her on her return. Lords Westmoreland and Exeter sent excuses that they could not come in time. At the entrance to Leicester, the Duke was met by Sir G. Villiers and other gentlemen, and by the magistrates. Their Highnesses have dined and been well treated at Mr. Griffin's, where came the Duke and Duchess of Buckingham, Lords Cardigan, Rockingham, Brudenell, the Attorney General, and other gentlemen of those parts. Lady Yerbury's sisters, Mrs. Jennings and Mrs. Temple, have impaired their beauty by heat and swelling in the face; thinks this a providence to preserve those who approach them frequently from danger. [*Four pages.*]

Aug. 1. Boston. 2. Dan. Rhodes, mayor of Boston, to Lord Arlington. Sends an information, and requests directions thereon. *Encloses,*

2. I. *Information of Rich. Hole, of Fosdike, and Nath. Smith, of Boston. Heard Rich. Davis blame Mr. Berridge, rector of Algarkirk and Fosdike, for preaching against the late King's death, and call him a maker of strife among neighbours, fitter to be hanged than to preach. He also spoke ill of other gentlemen of the county. July 29, 1665.*

Aug. 1. Sir Rob. Holt's, Aston, near Birmingham. 3. Geo. Brereton to Williamson. Thanks for his help in obtaining him employment in the army. Hears that Ostend is likely to be ours, and then there will be employment for many gentlemen.

Aug. 1. Commission for —— Watts to be Lieutenant to a company of foot in the Isle of Guernsey. [*Ent. Book 20, p. 81.*]

Aug. 1. 4. Memorandum from the Journals of Parliament of messages sent from the King to the two houses, between Feb. 18, 1663, and Aug. 1, 1665.

[Aug.] 1. The Coventry, Portsmouth. 5. Capt. Wm. Hill to Sam. Pepys. Understands that Col. Reymes and Capt. Pley have prejudiced his reputation with the Board. Begs an examination of himself with all the officers and masters of the ships under his charge. [*Adm. Paper.*]

Aug. 1. The Crown, Malaga. 6. Capt. Charles Wager to Sir Geo. Carteret. Requests payment of bills drawn for supply of victuals. Is much harassed by the Holland fleet thereabouts of 20 sail. Longs for the relief of a squadron's arrival. [*Adm. Paper.*]

Aug. 1. Plymouth. 7. John Lanyon to the Navy Commrs. Can supply a mast for the Sorlings. The captain complains of her mainshrouds, sails, &c. [*Adm. Paper.*]

Vol. CXXVIII.

1665.
Aug. 1. 8. Estimate of officers and seamen's wages due upon 18 ships named; total, 24,960*l.* [*Adm. Paper.*]

Aug. 1. [Portsmouth.] 9. Col. B. Reymes and Partners to Sam. Pepys. Safe arrival of ships from St. Malo; had they reached St. Malo three days later, they must have performed quarantine. All further commerce is prohibited there during the plague, and for six months after. Cannot therefore perform the contract within the time. Offer hemp and rope yarn at a reasonable rate. Would scorn to raise the price in a "nick of scarcity." Must have money for goods already delivered, 10,000*l.* being due. "Did the Parliament give so much money towards the Dutch war, and shall not sailcloth and cordage be paid for till the contractors be undone for providing it?" The King left that morning, and was to dine at Salisbury; he slept last night in his pleasure boat, intending to have gone to the Isle of Wight, but altering his mind, came back in the evening. He was at Major Holmes's, but would not see the Major, because he had not seen and pacified the Duke of York. Will leave no stone unturned to continue the supply of goods from St. Malo. [*Adm. Paper,* 2½ *pages.*]

Aug. 1. Portsmouth. 10. Comr. Thos. Middleton to Sam. Pepys. Can prove that one fourth of the expense of naval business might be saved, the work better done, and all men better pleased. The King reached Portsmouth at 9 last night, and left at 4 o'clock in the morning. Arrival of the St. Malo fleet. The Coventry and Lizard are in port. [*Adm. Paper.*]

Aug. 1. Chatham. 11. Comr. Peter Pett to Sam. Pepys. The Sovereign is moored at the buoy of the Nore. Victuals and ammunition must be hastened down. She waits but to complete her number of men. [*Adm. Paper.*]

Aug. 2. Plymouth. 12. John Lanyon to the Navy Comrs. Answers the objections lately made to his accounts; begs consideration thereon, having acted for the best according to his understanding. Requests payment of money due. [*Adm. Paper,* 1½ *pages.*]

Aug. 2. Salisbury. The King to the Officers of Greencloth. Notwithstanding the care taken to prevent the unnecessary flocking of persons to that city, it is still encumbered with numbers of useless persons. They are to order a list to be given in of servants employed at Court, that their numbers may be reduced, if too great, and that others who shelter themselves on plea of service may be dismissed. [*Ent. Book* 22, *p.* 243.]

Aug. 2. 13. Draft of the above.

Aug. 2. Salisbury. Similar order to the Lord Chamberlain, to take a list of the servants, &c., about Court. Minute. [*Ent. Book* 22, *p.* 243.]

Aug. 2. Salisbury. Pass for a vessel, called Our Lady of Olivera, from Lisbon to Amsterdam, laden with oils, sugar, tobacco, and salt. Minute. [*Ent. Book* 22, *p.* 244.]

Vol. CXXVIII.

1665.

Aug. 2. Like pass for the St. Lorenzo, bound and laden as the preceding. Minute. [*Ent. Book* 22, *p.* 211.]

Aug. 2. Order for a warrant to pay to Robert Child and William Bowles, masters of the tents and toils, 1,322*l.*, for furnishing waggons, tents, toils, &c. [*Ent. Book* 22, *p.* 281.]

Aug. 2. Sheen. 14. Col. Dan. O'Brien to Williamson. Asks leave to wait on him on the journey into Northamptonshire. Hopes to come on the 11th, but is going with his parchment, till he sees the great seal affixed to it.

Aug. 3. 15. ——— to ———. Thos. Corney thinks that by means of Wm. Scott he can discover all actions of the discontented party, both there [in Holland] and in England, but he is filled with untruths by Scott, Col. Bampfield, and Lord Nieuport, late ambassador in England; they plotted together and took Corney prisoner and had his papers searched; Oudart, who corresponded with Corney, was also taken and his papers; the latter will die, but Corney will be spared. Sandes Temple, lieutenant of the Charity, was called in on pretence of giving bail, and taken close prisoner: he is a person much admired by the Dutch, as a stout man, and a perfect Englishman. The States will soon issue a declaration that they mean no wrong to the good people of England, nor to the liberty of any Christian, but are against such as seek to destroy Christian liberty. Will get Temple out of prison, if possible, and then go to the Hague, and report what happens. With additional note that Mr. Temple was liberated 27 July / 6 Aug. on bail of 1,000 rixdollars. Long John has given Wm. Scott a place of 1,000 dollars a year in the Hague. Capt. Wilkinson cannot be liberated, because no one will be his security. [1¼ *pages.*]

Aug. 3. Deptford. 16. Seven Masters, &c. of Trinity House to the Navy Commrs. Nominate Capt. Dobbins and John Brooke, master attendant at Chatham, as fit persons for the command of the Royal Sovereign. [*Adm. Paper, copy.*] *Prefixing,*

16. i. *Similar letters, dated respectively July 21 and 20, recommending Capts. Simon Nichols or Jas. Dobbins, and Capts. Hen. Sheeres or Gilbert Crane, to the command of the said ship.* [*Copies.*]

Aug. 3. Cowpit. 17. Sir Wm. Clarke to Sam. Pepys. Desires letters of recommendation in behalf of Jonathan Bedford to be purser of the new galliot hoy. [*Adm. Paper.*]

Aug. 3. Deptford. 18. Capt. Wm. Badiley and two others to the Navy Commrs. Want an anchor and other provisions for the Deptford ketch. [*Adm. Paper.*]

Aug. 3. Portsmouth. 19. Constance Pley to Sir John Mennes. Complains of the non-payment of bills drawn upon Mr. Fenn for goods delivered; a poor requital for all her tedious waitings, great risk, and care;

entreats a speedy supply; has not had a penny for the last six weeks, even for necessary food, but what was borrowed; is fain to draw 300*l.* upon her son, which is a hard measure, but "necessity hath no law." [*Adm. Paper*, 1½ *pages*.] *Encloses*,

19. I. *List of bills of exchange which Rich. Fuller has accepted for Col. Reymes from George Pley and others, due from Aug.* 1 *to Aug.* 27, 1665; *total*, 3,036*l.* 16*s.* 7*d.*

Aug. 3. Dover. 20. Thos. White to Sam. Pepys. Has waited upon Lord Hinchinbroke, who had just landed, with the offer to furnish him with what money might be required; he only wanted the changing of 70*l.* in French gold. A merchant changed him some at 16*s.* 2*d.* the piece. [*Adm. Paper.*]

Aug. 4. 21. Request for a protection for Thos. Oak, master of the Orange Tree of Rye, and six men, in bringing up timber for Sir Wm. Warren. [*Adm. Paper.*]

Aug. 4. The Hardwin, Chatham. 22. John Coudre to the Navy Comrs. Has delivered the hemp; is ready to sail; has only 12 days' victuals on board. [*Adm. Paper.*]

Aug. 4. Cobham. 23. Capt. Geo. Erwin to Thos. Hayter. Is unable, from serious illness, to attend the Navy Comrs. [*Adm. Paper.*]

Aug. 4. Plymouth. 24. John Lanyon to the Navy Comrs. Has provided a mainmast for the Sorlings; defects in her gunner's stores; requests the settlement of his accounts.

Aug. 4. 25. Jas. Norman to Sam. Pepys. Desires the assistance of a servant at shipwright's pay, in this time of extra service; in case of sickness, none would be acquainted with his books and papers, and method of carrying on business. [*Adm. Paper.*] *Encloses*,

25. I. *Memorandum of sums advanced on imprest to Mr. Gregory and others.*

Aug. 4. Clapham. 26. Thos. Lewis to Sam. Pepys. The Sovereign's supply of victuals is dispatched; has been waiting a meeting of the Board to render a victualling account. [*Adm. Paper.*]

Aug. 4. Norwich. 27. James Johnson to the Navy Comrs. Mr. Dunne will survey the new frigate now building at Yarmouth, but having removed his family two miles from the town, to avoid the plague, cannot be so constantly with the carpenters as might be wished; if this be not satisfactory, Robt. Michelson, alderman, is a man of ability to inspect the work, unless the plague spreading make him also leave the town. Messrs. Edgar promise the certificate required. [*Adm. Paper.*]

Aug. 4. Cockpit. 28. Petition of John Geraldine, master of the Sta. Maria of Ostend, to the Duke of Albemarle, for reimbursement of damage sustained through Capt. Wm. Hill; with reference thereon to the

Vol. CXXVIII.

1665.

Navy Comrs, that Capt. Hill's pay may be stopped until full satisfaction be given. [*Adm Paper.*] *Annexing*,

28. I. *Inventory of goods and furniture embezzled from the Sta. Maria by Capt. Wm. Hill. Endorsed with the survey of the said vessel taken, July 28, by Hen. Fearmer and John Beresford, stating that John Geraldine's demands are reasonable, and the things lost material to the vessel. With note by Col. Edmund Wyndham, Aug. 1, that the above survey has been made according to orders from the Navy Comrs.* [1½ *pages.*]

Aug. 4. Warrant to the Earl of Southampton, Lord Lieutenant of Hampshire, to order the felling of 500 loads of timber in the New Forest for fortification of Portsmouth garrison; to be chosen by John Moody master gunner. [*Ent. Book* 17, *p.* 122.]

Aug. 4. Salisbury. Warrant from Lord Arlington for Col. John Breman to have his liberty for six months, in addition to two months which he has already had, surrendering himself at the end of that time, and meanwhile giving an account of himself to Sir John Lewknor, a deputy lieutenant of Sussex. With note of a pass for Col. John Breman. [*Ent. Book* 22, *p.* 244.]

Aug 4. 29. Petition of Jane, relict of Sir John Lawson, to the King, for payment of a pension of 500*l.* to be divided equally between her daughters, His Majesty having promised that in case her husband died in the engagement with the Dutch, her daughters should have the pension.

Aug. 4. Warrant for grants to Elizabeth and Ann, daughters of the late Sir John Lawson, of a pension of 250*l.* a year each. [*Ent. Book* 22, *p.* 245.]

Aug. 4. Salisbury. Warrant appointing John Fox clerk of the market to the King's household, so long as Thos. Howard, to whom the same office was granted for life, neglects to exercise it. [*Ent. Book* 22, *pp.* 245–7.]

Aug 4. Edinburgh. 30. "Act of the convention of estates of the Kingdom of Scotland, for a free and voluntary offer of taxation to His Majesty." [11 *pages, printed. Also printed in Acts of Parliament of Scotland, Vol. VII., pp.* 530–535.]

Aug. 4. Putney. 31. Sir Rich. Ford to Williamson. Enquires after his welfare by his son and son-in-law, who are going to Salisbury. Begs him to hasten the summons for the writer and Mr. Buckworth to attend him.

Aug. 4. Dover. 32. Jo. Carlisle to Williamson. The town is free from infection. One house was visited, and five died, but none since. There is a flying report that De Ruyter and his whole fleet are taken. Last week 18 French ships were restored, and not a penny to the storekeeper, who in the last war had 40*s.* for every ship. Lord Hinchinbroke, the Earl of Sandwich's son, has landed from France

Vol. CXXVIII.

1665.

Aug. 4. Salisbury. 33. Warrant to the Officers of the Mint to admit Chas. Gifford to the place of Assay Master, he having first obtained the consent of the wife of Thos. Woodward, any former order to the contrary notwithstanding.

Aug. 5. Hampstead. 34. Sir Philip Frowde to Williamson. Is sorry for the accident at Fiskerton. Hopes the remove need be no further than Wilton. Knows not how to help him on the other side the river, but on this side, will take care that his letters are aired at Hounslow. Sends a memorial how the post is managed, to avoid passage through London.

Aug. 5. Tadcaster. 35. Sir Wm. Coventry to Lord Arlington. They have been in continual motion, but end with nothing, except augmentation of the greatness of the Duke of York's reception, caused by his lordship's letters. In Nottinghamshire all the gentry and Lord Ogle met him, and near Nottingham seven troops of horse, chiefly volunteers, were drawn up, one or two of which attended him to Yorkshire, but he dismissed the rest for fear of being burdensome to the gentlemen. On the borders of Yorkshire, the sheriff and four troops of horse met him; they were also dismissed. Lord Fauconberg met him at Doncaster, but is gone to York to meet him again with the gentlemen of that part of the country. The Duke and Duchess of Newcastle met them between Nottingham and Rufford, and attended them to Rufford. Hopes good news from the fleet, which has fair winds to carry it northward. [2 *pages.*]

Aug. 5. Cockpit. 36. Duke of Albemarle to the Navy Comrs. Wishes persons to be appointed to impress seamen for the supply of the Sovereign and other ships going out to the fleet. There should be an impress of watermen above the bridge towards Chelsea, as some of those formerly impressed have come back again. [*Adm. Paper.*]

Aug. 5. [Deptford.] 37. Certificate by John Tooker and two others, that the Sarah and Elizabeth returned to Deptford to repair a leakage; her lading of water was dispersed amongst several ships wanting a supply, but some was nasty, being put into unwashed beer casks, and some leaked out for want of care in hooping. [*Adm. Paper.*]

Aug. 5. Clapham. 38. Thos. Lewis to Sam. Pepys. Certifies that Thos. Hunter, lately pressed on board the John and Katherine, has for two months past been employed by Mr. Gauden in the dispatch of victualling ships to the fleet. [*Adm. Paper.*]

Aug. 5. 39. Wm. Davies to the Navy Comrs. Recommends an able gunner for the Mereland Merchant. [*Adm. Paper.*]

Aug. 5. Cockpit. 40. Sir Wm. Clarke to Sam. Pepys. The fleet is upon the coast of Norway, and expected back upon the Dogger Sands with the first fair wind. The Duke of Albemarle has no dispatches to send; all letters are left with the postmaster at Harwich. [*Adm. Paper.*]

Aug. 5. Tadcaster. 41. Sir Wm. Coventry to the Navy Comrs. The water ships bound for the fleet, under convoy of the Convertine, are short of vic-

Vol. CXXVIII.

1665.

tuals, and one too leaky to proceed. The purveyor of Sherwood Forest complains that his bill of imprest is yet unpaid. Vessels must be hired for the carriage of timber. [*Adm. Paper.*]

Aug. 5. Ordnance Office. 42. Edw. Sherburn, Fras. Nicholls, and Rich. Marsh to Sam. Pepys. Desire an order for six weeks' victuals for Giles Bond, master of the Harwich hoy, and his 24 men, engaged upon the recovery of the London wreck. [*Adm. Paper.*]

Aug. 5. St. George, Gunfleet. 43. Capt. John Coppin to the Navy Comrs. Has mustered his men to the number of 254, but never went to sea with such men before; had it not been for 160 seamen from other ships' companies, dared not have ventured so low as the Gunfleet. If these are taken away, will be incapable of any service, having many sick on board; has no ketch nor smack for use, and only eight weeks' provision. [*Adm. Paper.*]

Aug. 6. Portsmouth. 44. St. John Stevenlon to Sir John Mennes. Requests speedy payment of his last bill of imprest for 800*l*., to meet the pressing necessities of the ropemakers and other workmen. [*Adm. Paper.*]

Aug. 6. Portsmouth. 45. Comr. Thos. Middleton to Sam. Pepys. The two pleasure boats are cleaned; progress of other ships in harbour; more care should be taken by the Ordnance Officers to supply wads for guns; is obliged to take up old moorings to make oakum spun yarn; the St. Malo fleet is nearly unladen; Portsmouth is at present free from the plague, though fevers and small-pox abound; dreads the appearance of the fatal distemper amongst so crowded and miserably poor a population; it were well to consider beforehand what must be done in case of necessity; account of money due; requests speedy payment to the poor Frenchman for his rosin. [*Adm. Paper, 2 pages.*]

[Aug. 7.] [Salisbury.] 46. Proclamation forbidding the holding of Bartholomew Smithfield, or any other fair within 50 miles of London, also of Stourbridge fair, near Cambridge, lest the conflux of people should spread the infection already dispersed in many parts of the kingdom. [*5 sheets.*]

Aug. 7. Copy of the above. [*Printed. Proc. Coll., Charles II.*, p. 197.]

Aug. 7. Sarum. Warrant to the Prize Comrs. for release of the Mairewine of Dieppe, coming from Martinique, and brought into Falmouth as a prize, because of the Dutch mariners therein. The said vessel belongs to French subjects, and has 21 Frenchmen on board. [*Ent. Book* 22, *p.* 247.]

Aug. 7. Like release for the ship Carolus. Minute. [*Ent. Book* 22 *p.* 247.]

Aug. 7. Knowlton. 47. Sir Thos. Peyton to Williamson. Asks aid for Wm. Webb, who has a business with Lord Arlington. He lives in London, but in a part free from infection. At Canterbury four houses were shut

1665. Vol. CXXVIII.

up, but are all open again; only one person died there last week. The danger is over at Dover, the infected family being removed to the hills. In one country parish, the minister's house is infected, but as it stands alone, they hope to prevent its spreading. In harvest time it is difficult, without good watches, to keep the people in order. That one parish of St. Giles', London, has done all the mischief.

Aug. 7. York. 48. Sir W. Coventry to Williamson. The place is in good health, and the justices of the peace very careful, but some parts of the country are infected. The nobility and gentry are much pleased with the Duke of York's coming into those parts, and have received him with as much respect as the short warning would allow. Sends an answer to the Spanish agent Don Antonio de Villa Viciosa. Is sorry the plague threatens Salisbury, but from the small increase in London, hopes the worst is past.

Aug. 7. York. 49. Earl of Peterborough to [Williamson]. The short notice prevented all the gentlemen from going to meet the Duke of York; joined him with his wife near Northampton, at Clarence House, where they slept, and dined next day at Althorp; thence to Billing, Leicester, Nottingham, and thither, without any disaster. Cannot tell what entertainments winter can bring; intends to renew the sports long laid aside, as they are in the inclinations of the Prince. [2 *pages*.]

Aug. 7. Ipswich. 50. J. Knight to Williamson. There is a terrible alarm because Wm. Huggard, surgeon and comptroller of customs, pronounced that the death of two persons has been from the plague. Was entreated by the bailiffs to see whether it was true, that town being the place whence most of the navy provisions are dispatched; sent two experienced surgeons to view the bodies, who declared that it was not the plague. Huggard has a great hatred to the corporation, and will do anything against them, and others join him. The Mayor of Hadleigh, a town nine miles thence, is engaged against Sir Wm. Doyley, and set a guard on the marshal's house, because, since 18th July, 6 out of 150 Dutch prisoners had died; viewed one of the bodies and found no cause of suspicion; they are grieved to have the Dutch prisoners put upon them, and private animosities everywhere perplex the King's business. Ipswich has an ill name, but her present rulers are sober and disinterested. There are Col. Legg and Capt. Dorell's foot companies in the town. The latter captain quarrels with the bailiffs, because they have not waited upon him at his lodging, which they say they are not bound to do. The town is overburdened, having 1,600 sick and wounded, 300 Dutch prisoners, the two companies, and a concourse from the fleet, when it is at Harwich or in the roads. [3 *pages*.]

Aug. 7. Dover. 51. Jo. Carlisle to Williamson. One Desborough has been seized with Lord Arlington's pass, on suspicion of debt. He says he cares neither for the King nor the mayor, and his wife is riding post to

VOL. CXXVIII.

1665.

Court to complain to the King. Thinks he is a dangerous person, going to join his fellow rebels in Holland, and should be nipped in the bud. The town is in good health, and Canterbury is now pretty free.

Aug. 7. Dover. 52. Nath. Desborough to Lord Arlington. Was going by his orders to France, but hearing that the French King had issued a proclamation forbidding the landing of any English in his dominions, went to Dover, and hired a vessel to carry him to Holland, when the Mayor of Dover seized and imprisoned him, and took his money and papers, contemning the King's passport; requests his lordship's order for his release.

Aug. 7. York. 53. Sir Wm. Coventry to Lord Arlington. Is sorry to hear his lordship's fear that the plague is gone with the Court to Sarum. Finds no evidence of any plot at York, beyond what the Lord General mentioned in London. The seizure of Wilkinson in Hull will do good. Some think that the rescue of Danvers in Cheapside shows a bad disposition in the vulgar, and proves him to be engaged in some plot. Hopes it proceeded rather from the neglect of his keepers than the great strength of his rescuers. The rabble should not find themselves successful in such attempts, and some should be punished for it when the plague is abated. Is glad the prorogation of Parliament was attended by more than 40, to secure it from doubts, though the judges think it was not necessary. The Duke's reception into York was the most honourable of the whole journey; besides the lords and gentlemen attending him, and the King's troops of horse and foot, there were two regiments of trained bands, the Duke of Buckingham's and Sir Thos. Slingsby's, the latter in red coats lined with green; also the Lord Mayor and Aldermen on horseback, in their habits, who, beside the speeches, presented the Duke with 100 pieces and the Duchess with 50. At Tadcaster, the Duke was visited by the Archbishop of York, and by Lord Fairfax, who was full of professions of loyalty, and he is thought to be a man who does not make professions contrary to his thoughts; he has good interest in those parts, so that if he attend the Duke when anything happens, there need be no fear. It is said that Trump thinks 80 ships enough to fight the English fleet, though 110 could not do it before. De Witt's condition requires a success. The Deputy Lieutenants are soon to meet the Duke, with an account of the state of things there. If the French Ambassador leave, and De Beaufort's fleet come, it will look suspicious. Sir Wm. Swan's proposals of interrupting the trade over the Watt could only be carried on by privateers, there being too little water there for the King's ships. Lord Langdale, the high sheriff, and other gentlemen have attended the Duke, and say they apprehend great danger from the Howden fair, lest tradesmen bringing goods from London should scatter infection thereby, the shopkeepers of the neighbouring towns usually buying their goods; they wish a proclamation to prohibit this fair, as was done with those at Bristol and Stourbridge. Suggests whether, during the infection, justices of the peace might not have

Vol. CXXVIII.

1665.

the power to prohibit fairs. Will conceal the death of the groom's wife at Sarum, lest the people, who are very apprehensive, should fear the like consequence from the Duke of York's coming there. [5 *pages*.]

Aug. 7. Portsmouth. 54. Comr. Thos. Middleton to Sam. Pepys. Has taken some pains to inquire into Capt. Hill's business. Can answer for his carefulness and diligence in dispatch of his vessel, after bringing in the French prize ship; no one knows what has become of his purser; is glad the Frenchman's rosin is approved, and speedy payment promised. Would rather have nothing to do with Mr. Stanley's contract at present, judging it unsafe to receive goods from Southampton for fear of contagion. Portsmouth is still free from plague; small pox abounds, but few die of it. The May Bell is dispatched to fetch timber from the New Forest. [*Adm. Paper*, 2½ *pages*.] *Encloses*,

54. i. *Declaration from masters of eight vessels under convoy of Capt. Hill to St. Malo, testifying to his having used all possible care and diligence in the voyage, and to his being delayed at Weymouth by contrary winds and bad weather.* [*Copies*, 2 *pages*.] *Aug.* 7, 1665.

Aug. 7. Chatham. 55. Comr. Peter Pett to Sam. Pepys. A ketch is wanted for the Sovereign; it would be a work of mercy to get money for Mr. Barrow's bill of imprest, for paying the oakum pickers. [*Adm. Paper*.]

Aug. 7. Dover. 56. Thos. White to the Navy Comrs. Upon urgent request and in a case of great danger, has supplied a cable from the store house to one of the King of Portugal's ships, on payment of 101*l*. 5*s*. till it be replaced; will answer to the King for the money. Account of stores required. [*Adm. Paper*.]

Aug. 8. 57. John Geraldine to the Navy Comrs. Has orders from the Duke of Albemarle for the stopping of Capt. Hill's pay, which is granted to himself for wrongs sustained; begs assistance, and some of the money paid forthwith. [*Adm. Paper*.]

Aug. 8. Hole Haven. 58. John Stepwell to the Navy Comrs. Begs release from serving on board the Sarah pink, being pressed as foremast man, and detained since July 29; is serving on board the Expedition, and was in the last engagement with the Dutch, but was permitted to return on business. [*Adm. Paper*.]

Aug. 8. Kinsale. 59. Capt. Wm. Crispin to the Navy Comrs. Requests payment of his bills; Rob. Southwell, deputy vice-admiral, offers money upon order from the Board; has declined giving account of the sick and wounded to the Lord Deputy and Council. The Constantinople East Indiaman and a frigate were chased into Castlehaven by three Dutch capers, and fetched thence by the Loyal Subject and two other ships. [*Adm. Paper*.]

Vol. CXXVIII.

1665.

Aug. 8. Deptford. 60. Jonas Shish to the Navy Comrs. Estimate of repairs needed for the Swallow ketch; total, 85*l.* Two boys are to be launched this week. [*Adm. Paper.*]

Aug. 8. The Coventry. Portsmouth. 61. Capt. Wm. Hill to Sam. Pepys. Refers to the examination taken in writing of all the officers and masters of ships under his convoy to St. Malo, to show the unjustness of the accusations brought against him, that he did not keep his ship's company in good order. [*Adm. Paper.*]

Aug. 8. York. 62. Sir Wm. Coventry to Lord Arlington. Wants the blank commissions sending; the militia of the West Riding is very unsettled, and wanting officers; the Lord Lieutenant is away, and ready to take offence if anything be done in his sphere, but ceremonies must not be stuck at. Thinks the King should consider how soon to raise more troops, as many loose people out of employment would be glad to take arms for him, but would also go to his enemies when they appear. Suggests whether the Lord General has troops enough in London, now that most of the substantial men and officers have left the town; unless they could be got back or new ones created, the companies would be rather dangerous than useful; troops might be sent thither from the West, or the King move towards London, for in case of a hurly-burly, London must be kept, at any expense and hazard, or the loss of it would lose all. Somebody should be ready to take the Lord General's place, in case of accident this sickly time. Asks how far the Presbyterians are supposed to be engaged, and whether persons are to be secured of whom there is no good assurance, or only those against whom there are informations or violent suspicions. The Lord General thinks the fanatics rely on Scotland. Asks whether the Duke of York could hold any correspondence with persons there. [3 *pages.*]

Aug. 8. Salisbury. Warrant to apprehend —— Ireton and convey him safe prisoner to the Tower, for dangerous and seditious practices. [*Ent. Book* 22, p. 249.]

Aug 8. Warrant to Sir John Robinson to receive the above —— Ireton and keep him close prisoner. [*Ent. Book* 22, *p.* 249.]

Aug. 8. Salisbury. Warrant to the Lord Mayor of London to publish a proclamation prohibiting the keeping of Bartholomew and Stourbridge fairs, although time did not permit it to be directed as usual by writ under the great seal. [*Ent. Book* 22, *p.* 250.]

Aug. 8. Privy seal for 5,140*l.* 2*s.* 6*d.* to Colonel William Legg, for materials, &c., to attend a mounting train of artillery, of 24 pieces. Minute. [*Ent. Book* 22, *p.* 250.]

Aug. 8. Salisbury. The King to the Lord General. Alderman Backwell being in great straits for the second payment he has to make for the service in Flanders, as much tin is to be transmitted to him as will raise

VOL. CXXVIII.

1665.

the sum. Has authorized him and Sir George Carteret to treat with the tin farmers for 500 tons of tin, to be speedily transported under good convoy; but if on consulting with Alderman Backwell, this plan of the tin seems insufficient, then without further difficulty, he is to dispose for that purpose of the 10,000*l.* assigned for pay of the Guards, not doubting that before that comes due, other ways will be found for supplying it; the payment in Flanders is of such importance that some means must be found of providing for it. [*Ent. Book* 17, *pp.* 122–3.]

[Aug. 8.] 63. Draft of the above.

Aug. 8. Salisbury. The King to the Farmers of tin. Having determined to raise money beyond seas by sale of tin, has authorised the Duke of Albemarle and Sir George Carteret to treat with them for sale or deposit of 500 tons on good security for their forbearance. The occasion being pressing, admits of no return nor reply. [*Ent. Book* 17, *p.* 124.]

[Aug. 8.] 64. Draft of the above.

[Aug. 8.] 65. Another draft partially cancelled and with considerable variations.

Aug. 8. Salisbury. The King to the Lord General and Sir George Carteret. Authorizes them to treat with the farmers of tin for the sale or deposit for a year of 500 tons of tin, to be sent to Flanders and sold to meet the second payment which Alderman Backwell has to make there. They are to agree with the farmers as best they can, giving tallies on the Royal aid to secure repayment, to conclude the contract at once, the pressing importance of the service admitting no delay, and to have vessels and convoys ready to transmit the tin to Ostend. [*Ent. Book* 17, *p.* 125.]

Aug. 8. 66. Draft of the above.

Aug. 8. London. 67. Capt. George Cock to Williamson. Hopes he got his wine, and Mr. Chiffinch his sturgeon. Cannot send the list he desires; lives in the greatest ignorance. Is troubled with De Ruyter's fleet getting into Holland; he might as easily have been taken as the Hamburg fleet saved. Is afraid of tricks.

Aug. 8. Windsor. 68. W. Bowles to Williamson. Begs him to get the King's signature to a warrant, that of the Lord Chamberlain being mislaid; his brother will wait on him with the fees.

Aug. 8. 69. P—— to Lord Arlington. Finds a general purpose at meetings in the county to rise on opportunity. The Dutch officers at Colchester say the Dutch will either beat us or make us weary of war. Heard that two Dutch captains and a lieutenant had escaped; hoped they were retaken, but the persons found proved to be only three private seamen. The Dutch officers have some friends near to guide them to a place of safety. Sir Chichester Wray used the

1665. Vol. CXXVIII.

writer roughly, and was hardly persuaded not to secure him; thinks all will be quiet, unless after harvest, when the poor have spent their money; if ill success at sea happen, trade being stopped by the sickness, they may be wrought on to make disturbances. [2 pages.]

Aug. 9. Wherwell. 70. Willm. Stanley to Col. Willm. Legg. A tax, for relief of Southampton, is laid by the neighbouring justices on the neighbouring parishes, but the remoter justices refuse to collect or distrain for it. There should be a letter from a Secretary of State or the Council to the Justices, to levy the tax quickly, and the mayor of Salisbury should have a copy of it.

Aug. 9. York. 71. Dr. Willm. Quatremaine to Williamson. Their Highnesses [the Duke and Duchess of York] are in good health. Begs an account of his health, being anxious about him when at a distance.

Aug. 9. Salisbury. 72. Commission to Sir Wm. Berkeley, governor, and Sir Phil. Honeywood, deputy governor of Portsmouth, and five others, to erect fortifications there, according to an approved draft, purchasing ground, entering into contracts for the work, &c. [1½ pages.]

[Aug. 9.] 73. Draft of the above. *Annexing,*

73. i. *Instructions to the Commissioners for fortifying Portsmouth. They are to see that the fortifications be made according to a plan by Sir Bernard De Gomme; to divide the counterscarp and give a portion to each Commissioner to attend to; to give the Dutch prisoners 3d. a day, in addition to the allowance of 8d., to work extra hours, &c.* [3 pages.]

Aug. 9. Bagshot. 74. Anne Desborough to Lord Arlington. Is led by duty to her King and passion for her husband to ride post from Dover to obtain an order for his release, and is impatient to return to Dover, where she left him a prisoner.

Aug. 9. York. 75. Sir Wm. Coventry to Lord Arlington. Thinks the French willing to have anything on foot which may look like mediation, and yet not be so. The King might give them that pretence of being quiet, and through them ask higher terms than he would take, but not let them know his true price, as they only intend to disturb the market. The distractions in Spain might be made use of, if there were tools on the place fit to work with. Sends reports of the fleet, but hopes soon to have more authentic reports that the East India ships are taken, to recompense De Ruyter's getting in. [2 pages.] *Encloses,*

75. i. *Hen. Brabant to Sir Wm. Coventry. A Dutch privateer brought into the port affirms that, on July 27, 90 sail of the fleet were off the Naze; 15 were sent after 11 Hollanders, supposed to be the East India fleet, and the rest went for North Bergen, to find out the Dutch merchant-*

Vol. CXXVIII.

1665.

men and De Ruyter; also that four prizes have been carried into the Firth in Scotland. There are nine ships at Newcastle, levied by Mr. Dering for the King's service at Hamburg, waiting a convoy. [1½ *pages.*]

Newcastle, Aug. 8, 1665.

Aug. 9. Barber Surgeons' Hall. 76. Certificate by Rich. Reynell of free gift and imprest money paid to James Burleigh, surgeon of the Great Gift, on July 14, 1664. [*Adm. Paper.*]

Aug. 9. Portsmouth. 77. St. John Steventon to Sam. Pepys. Is referred by the treasurer at Salisbury to Anthony Stevens, for payment of the last imprest for 100*l.* [*Adm. Paper.*]

Aug. 9. Edwinstow. 78. John Russell to the Navy Comrs. Has dispatched the Love hoy, laden with timber from Stockwith. More hoys are needed. Great want of money. Has not received the promised imprest of 200*l.* [*Adm. Paper.*] *Encloses,*

78. i. *Bill of lading for timber brought in the Love hoy from Sherwood to Harwich; total, 61 loads.* *Aug. 9, 1665.*

Aug. 10. Sarah pink. Hole Haven. 79. John Stapwell to the Navy Comrs. Begs discharge from his servitude as foremast man; has been master of the Ruby, but left it through the cruelty of the commander. [*Adm. Paper.*]

Aug. 10. Bethnal Green. 80. Sam. Heron to Sam. Pepys. Would have brought the enclosed personally but for ill health. [*Adm. Paper.*] *Encloses,*

80. i. [*Sir William Rider*] *to John Fenn. Has been obliged to raise money from his own estate for payment of bills due for the supply of hemp, tar, &c. If in future the ships return dead freight for want of money, shall take no blame upon himself.* *Cantis, Essex, Aug. 10, 1665.*

Aug. 10. Deal. 81. Thos. Warren to Sam. Pepys. Requires six weeks' provisions for 203 soldiers. Waits fair weather to sail to Plymouth. [*Adm. Paper.*]

Aug. 10. Woolwich Ropeyard. 82. Report by Peter Russell, master of the ropeyard, of the hemp and yarn offered by Mr. Bushell, Robt. Hooker, and Capt. Askew. [*Adm. Paper.*]

Aug. 10? 83. Petition of the pressed Shipwrights at Chatham dock to the Navy Comrs., for payment of their 15 weeks' arrears of board wages for relief of their great necessities in this hot and sickly season; are far from their homes, and no credit is to be obtained. [*Adm. Paper.*]

Aug. 10. Cockpit. 84. Duke of Albemarle to the Navy Comrs. Names 12 ships to be hastened out to the Gunfleet. Asks when they will be ready, and what men are wanted. [*Adm. Paper.*]

Aug. 10. Portsmouth. 85. Comr. Thos. Middleton to Sam. Pepys. Departure of the Lizard. The Coventry is still in port; her beer has nearly poisoned one man who, being thirsty, took a draught of it. One galliot is at

Vol. CXXVIII.

1665.

Spithead, the other at Greenwich. It is strange that Weymouth cannot afford them victuals. They might have been in the Downs by this time, had they not touched at Portsmouth for provisions. All the families in the dockyard are still in health. Fever and small-pox are in the town. Is sorry to hear of De Ruyter's safe arrival in Holland. The new house will not be fit to live in this winter. [*Adm. Paper, 2 pages.*]

Aug. 10. Portsmouth. 86. Comr. Thos. Middleton to Sam. Pepys. Asks the intention of the Board concerning the new house building. Intends not to reside in Portsmouth if possible, though if commanded by the King to live under water, would endeavour to do it. Complains of his discomfort ever since coming to Portsmouth. Nine people are packed to sleep in a room 10 ft. by 12 ft. There are 26 in family in the mayor's house, nine of whom are small children. What comfort can a man have in such a condition? Knows not what to resolve, to stay "packed like herrings in a barrel" or risk the moist air of a new house and cost of furnishing. Is resolved not to make Portsmouth his habitation, but will stay in his employment as long as the war continues. [*Adm. Paper, 1½ pages.*]

Aug 10. 87. Col. Reymes to Sam. Pepys. If Mr. Fenn will pay the bills already drawn on him, and foreign bills as they come due, he shall be troubled no more for a month. Has news of a London vessel laden with more goods from St. Malo; desires that the Coventry may be sent as convoy. Hopes to obtain permission from our ambassador [in France] to freight six barks more, and so complete the contract. Asks whether there be sufficient need of the commodities to run the risk, as the extraordinary charges at this time eat out all the profit. [*Adm. Paper, 1½ pages.*]

Aug. 10/20. Chelsea. Ambassador Van Gogh to [the States General]. The King has gone from Salisbury to Wilton. There is great fear of insurrections in both kingdoms, as proved by the seizure of many considerable persons, Lieut.-Gen. Hepburn, and Major-Gen. Montgomery in Scotland, and Capt. Spencer, and divers others. The Scots have granted a tax for five years, to promote the war against the Dutch. The English fleet is northward; the Hamburg fleet dares not stir from Harwich. The plague increases at Yarmouth, and at London 4,030 are dead, of whom 2,817 died of the infection. [*Holland Corresp., Aug. 20, 1665.*]

Aug. 10. The King to the Justices of the Peace for Middlesex. Is most careful for relief of his subjects and prevention of the spreading of infection; diligent circumspection must be used to prevent removals of goods or persons from London and Westminster and the neighbourhood, to other towns and villages; also to suppress disorders in persons who, though of infected families, refuse to remain shut up, and to hinder persons removing goods, &c., up and down the Thames. They are to take great care to enforce order in these points, and on refusal or neglect, to commit the offenders to Newgate,

VOL. CXXVIII.

1665.

to be severely proceeded against next sessions. In the respective towns and parishes, searchers, nurses, &c., are to be appointed, and no lodger nor tenant to be admitted, without permission of two justices of peace. [*Ent. Book* 17, p. 126.]

[Aug. 10.] 88. Draft of the preceding. [1½ *pages*.]

Aug. 10. Cockpit. 89. Sir Wm. Clarke to Williamson. Sends the enclosed from the Earl of Carbery. Fanatics are taken daily, which will prevent their plots.

Aug. 10. Whitehaven. 90. Sir John Lowther to Williamson. Thanks for favours. Finds the country free from sickness; the Quakers multiply, though some are under the lash, yet for want of the executive part, transportation, little good is done. The tax comes in more cheerfully than usual in those remote places. Lord Carlisle has lately come, but given no hopes of a man-of-war to scour those seas. The shipping of the place was detained two months in harbour by a Dutch caper, but they have heard nothing of him lately.

Aug. 10. 91. List sent by Mor. Lodge to Williamson of ships in the Downs; three King's ships, nine merchant ships, the wind south-west, blowing hard.

VOL. CXXIX. AUG. 11–22, 1665.

1665.

Aug. 11. Custom House, London. 1. The Customs' Comrs. to Lord Arlington. Request a tally for the 1,500*l.* delivered him by Sir Nich. Crisp, as they are to have interest for it. Send a duplicate of a former letter about horses to be transported to Ireland, the King wishing to show respect to the Lords who are going there. *Enclose*,

1. I. *Form of a warrant for a tally on the farmers of customs for 1,500l., advanced by them on July 27, to be allowed from their next half-year's rent.* [1½ *pages*.] *Aug.* 1665.

Aug. 11. Chester Castle. 2. Alexander Rigby to Williamson. Sir Geoffrey Shakerley will be absent three weeks in Yorkshire, and wishes correspondence to be carried on with the writer meanwhile.

Aug. 11. Bethnal Green. 3. Sam. Heron to Sam. Pepys. Requests orders for receipt at Woolwich of 80 barrels of tar and 33 of pitch, arrived from Hull. [*Adm. Paper*.]

Aug. 11. Chatham. 4. Comr. Pett to [Sam. Pepys]. Regrets the misunderstanding about bills for provisions served in by contracts made without the Navy Comrs.' privity; will make no more such if they will save him harmless in case of want of provisions. Has received orders for the Sheerness business; sends the master shipwright's opinion

1665. Vol. CXXIX.

on the subject. A ketch is wanted for the Sovereign. [*Adm. Paper.*] *Encloses*,

4. I. *Phin. Pett and Jas. Lawrence to Comr. Pett. Have seriously considered the works to be performed at Sheerness; recommend the house carpenter's work to be performed "by great with His Majesty's materials;" the workmanship, with sawyer's work, will be worth 330l.* *Chatham Dock, Aug. 11.*

4. II. *Estimate by Thos. Tunbridge of house carpenter's work in making a yard and conveniences at Sheerness; total, 335l.* *Chatham Dock, Aug. 10.*

Aug. 11. Ordnance Office. 5. Edw. Sherburne and Jonas Moore to the Navy Comrs. A considerable proportion of gunners' stores is sent down to Plymouth; will supply fitting provisions for the Sorlings, and extra guns for the Great Gift. [*Adm. Paper.*]

Aug. 11. Chatham. 6. Edw. Gregory, clerk of the cheque, to Sir John Mennes and Sam. Pepys. Returns thanks on behalf of the governors for care taken in the Chest's concerns; has drawn bills upon Woodcott and Colville, to complete the sum of 1,000l. due to him; begs that the tally may be transmitted by a sure hand. [*Adm. Paper.*]

Aug. 11. Plymouth Fort. 7. Sir John Skelton to Sam. Pepys. The Barbadoes ships sailed six weeks since; three East Indiamen have arrived; will go on board them to-morrow, and impress as many men as possible. [*Adm. Paper.*]

Aug. 11. 8. Statement by Capt. Val. Tatnell of men and stores required for the Bull and Mereland Merchant. [*Adm. Paper.*]

Aug. 12. Cockpit. 9. Sir Wm. Clarke to Sam. Pepys. Encloses the petition of widow Rogers, sent from Comr. Pett. Asks what can be done in it. [*Adm. Paper.*]

Aug. 12. The Colchester, Burlington Bay. 10. Captain of the Colchester ketch to Sir Wm. Batten. Capture of several suspected vessels; damage sustained; waits orders to put in at Harwich or Sole Bay. [*Adm. Paper.*]

Aug. 12. York. 11. Sir Wm. Coventry to Lord Arlington. On the alarm from the Lord General, the Duke of York wrote to the Duke of Newcastle, Lords Darby and Carlisle, the Bishop of Durham, and the Deputy Lieutenants of Northumberland, to be watchful, and will order them to secure the dangerous men in their lieutenancies. An express from Scotland reports that Major-General Monroe, Holborne, and Montgomery are clapped up; a body of horse from Yorkshire might soon be sent to support the King's authority there. The Duke of York goes to Hull on Wednesday till Friday. There seems no intention of any evil attempts speedily. The fanatics' chief design is London, with an eye to Scotland, and assistance from the Dutch, who are providing for transport of men and provisions, in case their fleet conquer the King's. [2 *pages.*]

VOL. CXXIX.

665.

Aug. 12. Isle of Wight. 12. Col. Walter Slingsby to Williamson. Sir Wm. Lisle died of malignant fever. As he was newly arrived, a false report spread that it was the plague, though the doctor assures that it was not.

Aug. 12. Salisbury. 13. Declaration of the King's pleasure that his household servants and officers shall be admitted according to seniority in the new establishment, unless there be some exception to any, and the supernumeraries re-admitted on any vacancy; this order is to be observed, notwithstanding the list of servants made on dissolution of the household, 29th Sept. 1663, provided those admitted do not exceed the appointed number. [*Copy.*]

Aug. 12. Dover. 14. Jo. Carlisle to Williamson. The town is free from plague, though one house is shut up in it, one at Sandwich, one at Eastry, one at the Earl of Winchelsea's Park, one at Westwell, and seven at Canterbury, but only a few are dead. Hears that De Ruyter is to be general, next expedition. Four prizes are sent in by privateers belonging to the harbour. A conventicle of 300 or 400 fanatics was held, and some are bound over to the next sessions, but the parson, Mr. Nicholls, escaped. A foot company lies waiting to go to Jersey, under Capt. Gladson. Capt. Desborough still continues prisoner.

Aug. 12. York. 15. Earl of Peterborough to [Williamson]. Thinks it very useful for a court sometimes to grace that province. It will give power over an army to entertain the brethren of the Kirk, if they should desire to disport, and will balance London, and make it court the Crown more, when it finds another town able to receive the Court. The city is nobly situated on a river surrounded with pleasant meadows, has abundant provisions, and the men are of excellent temper, the gentlemen very zealous for the government. Proceeds cautiously in a court where there are few who do not esteem themselves lowered by his admittance. The Duke is very obliging, and promises to assist him in reference to two new regiments that are to be raised. Cannot work well with the buffoon who is placed with him in the bedchamber, though several of his qualities give him interest at court. [3 *pages.*]

Aug. 12. Putney. 16. Sir Rich. Ford and John Duckworth to Williamson. Thanks him for his care about the tin business. Hope the next proof of it before Council will be with good effect; though the selling of 500 tons to the King will not benefit them, as they will have to wait long for their money, they will agree to it, on security for payment. The Bergen fleet think they have discovered the Dutch East India ships: that would be a booty that would pay for the powder and shot of a twelvemonths' war.

[Aug. 13.] Sunday, St. Giles's. 17. Sir Thos. Ogle to Williamson. Would have come to Salisbury, but the sickness being there, dares not, for those of Poole, where his company is, scruple to receive any from infected places; encloses an important letter which he intended to bring.

Aug. 13. Portsmouth. 18. W. B. [Sir Wm. Berkeley] to Williamson. The fortifications are proceeding. The Dutch prisoners sent from London to work will

VOL. CXXIX.

1665.

be carried to Portsea Castle, till provision is made for them. The town is free from sickness except agues. The fanatics are quiet. The Coventry, which has convoyed vessels from St. Malo, is fitted again to return to the same port. [1½ *pages.*]

Aug. 13. York. 19. Sir Wm. Coventry to Lord Arlington. Guns were heard off Landguard Point: probably De Witt would not go into port with the Dutch men-of-war till the merchantmen were safe, and this might lead to an engagement. Hears that Sir George Downing has landed [in England], but hopes care is taken for intelligence from Holland, without which nothing can be done as it ought. Thinks the Dutch will come to an agreement with the Bishop of Munster. The Duke of York has not yet decided on his journey, not knowing when the King removes. All there are healthy. Fears Oxford will not escape in such a concourse of people, the neighbouring villages being infected. Care should be taken to prevent goods and winter clothes being sent from London. Wishes, if the war continue, that the Algiers Consul, who would make a good commander for a man-of-war, might be sent for. [2 *pages.*]

Aug. 13. Plymouth Fort. 20. Sir John Skelton to Sam. Pepys. The three East Indiamen have set sail, notwithstanding their promises, so could not take the master's engagement to remain a day and night. Hopes this notice will be in time to secure the seamen on their arrival in London. [*Adm. Paper.*]

Aug. 13. Portsmouth. 21. Comr. Thos. Middleton to Sam. Pepys. Will see what can be done with the tobacco stalks as wadding for guns. Why the Commissioners should trouble themselves with what properly concerns the officers of Ordnance is a mystery; would not himself assist them with a pound of junk, had he "as much as would cover the whole dockyard and reach a mile perpendicular;" let them take pains to buy it, and look after their own business. Will obey orders about payment of 150*l.*, for the rosin and freight of goods sent out; they are already 600*l.* in debt there, so that the 800*l.* will soon be gone. Asserts Capt. Hill's civility and diligence; his purser is to blame. Begs that the two galliots may be provisioned at Weymouth. The gunner of the Coventry was found selling the King's powder at Weymouth. [*Adm. Paper,* 2½ *pages.*]

Aug. 13. The Coventry, Spithead. 22. Capt. Wm. Hill to Sam. Pepys. Is thankful that Comr. Middleton has removed the bad opinion entertained of himself by the Navy Comrs., merely at the suggestion of Col. Reymes. It is a sad thing to be condemned without a hearing. Hopes Sir Wm. Coventry will be satisfied that he is not guilty of what was laid to his charge. [*Adm. Paper.*]

Aug. 14. The Ullen. 23. John Shorter to Sam. Pepys. Has advice from Norway of a considerable fleet arrived off Bergen. Knows not what they are, nor whence they come. [*Adm. Paper.*]

Aug. 14. Norwich. 24. James Johnson to the Navy Comrs. Has commissioned Thos. Dunne to procure a draft from Messrs. Edgar, and sign certificates for payment. [*Adm. Paper.*]

Vol. CXXIX.

1665.

Aug. 14. Cobham. 25. Capt. Geo. Erwin to Sam. Pepys. Has been ill a week and unable to wait upon him. [*Adm. Paper.*]

Aug. 14. York. 26. Sir Wm. Coventry to Lord Arlington. The yachts sent out for news to the fleet could not find it. Regrets the breaking out of the plague at Salisbury. It is more dangerous in little towns, where there is less means of avoiding it than in London, especially when every house is full whilst the Court is there. The Duke is to be feasted by the city to-morrow, and then goes to Hull, the Duchess remaining at York, which is still free from plague; it does not spread in the country places, because of strict means taken for separation. At Beverley it did not go beyond the family first infected. Sends the Duke's directions about Mr. Lye, though against his Highness' ordinary rule about affairs there, to Dr. Gorges, now his agent in Ireland; the Duke has discharged his commissioners there, who injured him on pretence of his own letters of recommendation, and appointed Dr. Gorges instead, on recommendation of the Lord Chancellor. [2 *pages.*]

Aug. 14. London. 27. James Hickes to Williamson. Has written to the postmaster at Huntingdon to dispatch Williamson's letters, airing them over vinegar before he sends them. The post office is so fumed, morning and night, that they can hardly see each other, but had the contagion been catching by letters, they had been dead long ago. Hopes to be preserved in their important public work from the stroke of the destroying angel. Will give, as he orders, 5*l.* on his behalf, to the poor of St. Martin's-in-the-Fields, but knows not where to get it in this time, where all doubt ever seeing each other again. The sickness increases. Their gains are so small that they will not at the year's end clear 10*l.* of their salaries.

Aug. 14. Chester. 28. Col. Ro. Werden to [Williamson]. Sends a letter from Mr. Povey. Is ordered from York to attend the King, with 100 horse of the Guards, at Salisbury.

Aug. 14. York. 29. Sir W. Coventry to Williamson. Is sorry for the apprehension that the plague follows the Court. The increase in London makes all hopes rest on the approaching season, without which no place would be kept free. Thinks the fanatics will attempt nothing, as the Duke has secured some of the most dangerous in those parts. Hopes yesterday's storm will not have scattered the fleet. The Duke will be feasted to-morrow by the city, and goes next day to Hull, returning on Friday.

Aug. 15. Portsmouth. 30. Capt. Andrew Newport to Williamson. Mr. Halsall fears fanatic troubles, and asks what prisoners have been released from Portsmouth for 12 months. It was lately said at a private meeting that a friend, released from Portsmouth through the governor, would look after Portsmouth. It is thought this must be Col. Rich, who was prisoner there 12 months, released through Lord Falmouth, then sent prisoner to the Tower, and now released thence. Has known Rich many years, but he always professes peaceable principles. There are many sectaries in the place who wish for a change. [2 *pages.*]

Vol. CXXIX.

1665.

Aug. 15. Newmarket. 31. Jo. Man to Williamson. These parts are peaceable and healthful.

Aug. 15. Salisbury. Warrant to Sir Arthur Slingsby, Bart., and Capt. John Paris, commander of the True Blue, to make full restitution to Zederick Constantine of goods, as coaches, horses, &c., sent from the French King and others to the King and Queen of Poland, and plundered by them on private letters of marque, and for the latter to appear before Council to answer for such a misdemeanor. [*Ent. Book* 17, *pp.* 128–9.]

Aug. 15. Salisbury. The King to the Navy Comrs. The great increase of infection about London and Westminster makes it inconvenient for that office, which at this time is of great concern, to continue longer there; it is therefore to be removed to such rooms in the manor house at Greenwich as shall be appointed by Sir John Denham, there to continue during pleasure. [*Ent. Book* 17, *p.* 129.]

Aug. 15. Salisbury. Warrant for creating Sir William Oglander, of Nunwell in the Isle of Wight, a baronet. Minute. [*Ent. Book* 22, *p.* 232.]

Aug. 15. Salisbury. Warrant to the Ordnance Officers to deliver to John Viscount Mordaunt, Constable of Windsor Castle, 100 firelocks, bandoliers, pikes, and swords, and 500 cases of pistols, carbines, and saddles, to be kept in the magazine there. [*Ent. Book* 22, *p.* 232.]

Aug. 15. Warrant to the Farmers of Customs to suffer the shipping of 350 barrels of gunpowder, for the use of the King of Portugal, on payment of customs. [*Ent. Book* 22, *p.* 233.]

Aug. 15. Pass for the Hope of Konigsberg, laden with barley at Amsterdam or Emden, and bound for Lisbon. Minute. [*Ent. Book* 22, *p.* 25.]

Aug. 15. The King to the Lord Lieutenants of counties. Hoped that the spreading contagion at home, whilst he is employing arms and treasure in defence of trade, would have quelled the restless spirit of faction; but finding the implacable malice of his enemies still tending to confusion and blood, exhorts them to be extraordinarily watchful over all persons of seditious temper; to imprison those who give ground for suspicion, and cause others to give security for good conduct, on any jealousy of a commotion; also orders them to assemble the volunteer troops, or part of the militia, but so as not to burden the people during harvest, and see them provided with powder, match, bullet, &c. [*Ent. Book* 20, *pp.* 82–3.]

[Aug. 15.] List of the names of the Lord Lieutenants in England and Wales. [*Ent. Book* 20, *pp.* 83–5.]

Aug. 15. Cockpit. 32. Duke of Albemarle to the Navy Comrs. Under the present difficulty of getting money, the expenses of the navy must be contracted as much as possible, not to exceed 25,000*l.* per week ready money. The Navy Treasurer has gone to Court. Desires another gunner for the Golden Phoenix, the former one having embezzled the stores. The

Vol. CXXIX.

1665.

Welcome is to be repaired and rigged ready for service. A quantity of provisions must be ready at Harwich. [*Adm. Paper.*] *Encloses,*

32. I. *Capt. Rich. Neales to the Duke of Albemarle. Discovery of embezzlements carried on by the gunner of the Golden Phœnix, with the connivance of all the officers except the captain and master.* *Downs, Aug.* 11, 1665.

32. II. *John Stapleton to Sir Wm. Clarke. Craves a hearing in regard to the charges laid against him, in the discharge of his duties when on board the Golden Phœnix.* *Blackamoor, Downs, Aug.* 11, 1665.

Aug. 15. Plymouth. 33. John Lanyon to the Navy Comrs. Dispatch of the Sorlings; the captain is removed upon an information of the Farmers of Customs, and a son of Sir John Skelton's appointed instead. The Nightingale and Elizabeth are under repairs. [*Adm. Paper.*]

Aug. 15. The Elizabeth, Plymouth. 34. Capt. Robt. Robinson to the Navy Comrs. Particulars of the cleaning and repairs of various ships. [*Adm. Paper.*]

Aug. 15. Woolwich. 35. Chris. Pett to the Navy Comrs. Plank and deals are wanted. It has pleased God to send the infection of the plague into the town, and two houses are already visited; fears it will be very mortal; will take every care to prevent it spreading to the yard. [*Adm. Paper.*]

Aug. 15. Chatham. 36. Comr. Peter Pett to Sam. Pepys. Proposes the fitting up of the St. Maria prize at Sheerness, and sending the Happy Entrance there also. Recommends Mr. Punnett's smack to be hired for the Sovereign; awaits an answer about the Sheerness business; Alderman Meynell must be treated with beforehand about the ground which is needed, and which he claims. [*Adm. Paper.*] *Enclosed,*

36. I. *Note of the burden of the Mayflower hoy, Thos. Punnett, master, hired for the use of the Sovereign: 90 tons.*

Aug. 15. Portsmouth. 37. Comr. Thos. Middleton to Sam. Pepys. The Coventry waits a fair wind to sail to St. Malo, to fetch thence a ship laden with goods on account of Col. Bullen Reymes; 500 Dutchmen are received into Porchester Castle, many of them very sick. [*Adm. Paper.*]

Aug. 16. Cockpit. 38. Duke of Albemarle to Sam. Pepys. A bill of 1,000*l.* payable at Cadiz will be required for Capt. John Hubbard, of the Hilversom; asks whether such a sum will be answered there; begs the Commissioners may not be informed to whom it is to be paid as yet. [*Adm. Paper.*]

Aug. 16. Passport for the Santa Maria, built at Amsterdam for merchants of Ostend and Bruges, subjects to the King of Spain, to pass to Ostend, provided she carry no goods belonging to persons in hostility with the King. [*Ent. Book* 22, *p.* 253.]

Aug. 16. Salisbury. Pass for —— Mangle to go to Ireland. Minute. [*Ent. Book* 22, *p.* 254.]

Vol. CXXIX.

1665.

Aug. 16. Antwerp. 39. Sir Martin Noel to Williamson. Begs that his papers may be kept private; more use may be made of them than would at present be judged, till they are put into form as propositions to his Majesty, and they will be to his honour and profit; has trusted the business in Lord Compton's hands.

Aug. 16. Salisbury. The King to the Duke of Ormond, lord lieutenant of Somersetshire. The Deputy Lieutenants complain that they cannot without great hazard and trouble pay to the Lieutenant of the Tower the balance unexpended of the militia money for the first two years; it is therefore to be paid to Sir Phil. Honeywood, deputy governor of Portsmouth, notwithstanding the former orders to the contrary. [*Ent. Book* 17, *p.* 130.]

Aug. 16. Sarum. Reference to Sir Thos. Ingram, chancellor of Lancaster, on the petition of Col. Edw. Vernon. [*Ent. Book* 18, *p.* 185.]

Aug. 16. York. 40. Sir Wm. Coventry to Lord [Arlington]. An Ostender reports that 18 or 19 days ago the fleet was before Bergen, and Capt. Teddeman, with 20 ships and 2 fire-ships, going in to take 50 Dutch ships. Lord Fairfax attended the Duke of York to the Lord Mayor's feast yesterday, and on a little conversation with him, overcame his ordinary difficulty in speaking, and discoursed rationally and pleasantly. The gentlemen of the county much noticed his pleasure at his Royal Highness' good usage, which it is not hard for the Duke to afford to a man of courage so eminent. Believes that in spite of his lordship's infirmities, he would get on horseback to serve the King. The Duke told him in confidence that he had heard of designs on foot, and should call on him for assistance if needful, to which he made a good reply; he is a man of honour and of his word. [2 *pages*.]

Aug. 17. Hull. 41. Duke of York to Lord Arlington. Has received a short account of the engagement at Bergen from Sir Thos. Teddeman, who refers for a full account to Sir Thos. Clifford's letters to his lordship. Is just going about the town to view the fortifications, which he fears to find but ill ones, and will give an account of them from York. [2 *pages*.]

Aug. 17. Hull. 42. Sir Wm. Coventry to Lord Arlington. Sends Sir Thos. Clifford's and other accounts relating to the engagement at Bergen. Thinks Teddeman's squadron is at Sole Bay by this time, as four or five of his ships were much shattered; the rest will only want men and victuals; the loss of six commanders and 400 men in so short a time shows that there lacked neither danger nor courage. The consequences of the dishonour of the repulse are not so great as the discouragement that it will give to the rest of the fleet, especially during the absence from them of so considerable a number of their body, now that the Dutch fleet is abroad. Wishes Lord Sandwich were on the coast, that the ships from the Gunfleet might join him, and they might then meet De Witt, convoying the fleet from Bergen. As the Duke of York is so far removed

1665. VOL. CXXIX.

from King and Council, directions should be sent to the Duke of Albemarle. The Duke was met on his arrival in the East Riding by two troops of the trained band horse, well armed, and a very numerous assemblage of the gentlemen of the riding. The Mayor of Hull, besides a speech, presented him with a purse of 50*l.* in gold, and invited him to a dinner in the town to-morrow. [2 *pages.*]

Aug. 17. London. 43. Capt. George Cock to Williamson. Sends letters to Lord Arlington and the Lord Chamberlain, about the sick, wounded, and prisoners, who must starve ignominiously in the streets, unless money be sent for them. The Commons of England would resent it the next sessions. The last two supplies have been sent to Sir Wm. Doyley, who is only a commissioner, instead of to himself as receiver. Hopes the destruction of the East India fleet, and preservation from tricks.

Aug. 17. Letter Office, London. 44. James Hickes to Williamson. Sends expresses to Sir W. Coventry on Mondays, Wednesdays, and Fridays, but cannot send Williamson's letters then, because of Mr. Muddiman's taking abstracts of them; this detains his letters much, and there are express orders that those for the Duke and Coventry be sent express.

Aug. 17. Carlisle. 45. Sir John Lowther to Williamson. Two Dutch capers have taken a vessel of Whitehaven and two of Liverpool. Begs some remedy, the trade of the county being almost ruined. The suspected persons of the two counties are being secured by the Duke of York's orders. Is going to him with Lord Carlisle. His own business of dereliction lies with the privy seal. Hears that Williamson has been at Oxford.

Aug. 17. 46. H. M[uddiman to Williamson]. Sends the foreign letters, not knowing how it might be taken at Court were he to view them. Those inland contain nothing remarkable, except mention of conventicles, and that the Colchester ketch has taken two prizes on the Norway coast, and had a hot dispute with a Dutch caper. A pickeroon took two barks on the coast of Chester, set the men ashore, but will carry away the owners unless they pay 300*l.* ransom.

[Aug.?] 17. Conway. 47. Viscount Bulkeley to Viscount Conway. The Deputy Lieutenants caused no restraint to be made on the lead, but apprehending false play, had written to inform his lordship that his agent was taking down the lead and other materials belonging to the castle. It was hard to make them believe that the fort was to be abolished, but being assured that it was so, they acquiesce in his lordship's directions. Will buy six or seven tons from him, if he may have it reasonably. [2 *pages.*]

Aug. 17. London. 48. Edward Dering to the Navy Comrs. Represents the high charge for demurrage that will be incurred upon certain ships, hired

VOL. CXXIX.

1665.

according to contract for the importation of plank from Hamburg, which have been some time ready to sail, as soon as convoy can be appointed. [*Adm. Paper.*]

Aug. 17. Portsmouth. 49. Comr. Thos. Middleton to Sam. Pepys. There is great distress among the workmen in the yard. Many from Southampton and London are forced, by the too common distemper, to live at Portsmouth for the time; no board wages are allowed them, and their last payments were used for former debts. Turned out of doors by their landlords, they perish more like dogs than men, and though giving attendance and answering their call, are unable to work. Knows not how to act; so many workmen employed and so little work done, can but bring a reflection upon what he esteems above all outward things, "a thing called reputation." There are none of the evils attending the King's service but what may be cured, "if a plaister be rightly applied." Only pay these poor men board wages, and 200 will do as much work as 300 at the present time. [*Adm. Paper, 2½ pages.*]

Aug. 18. Chatham. 50. Philip Barrow to Sam. Pepys. Entreats a bill of imprest for settling the clamorous demands of the oakum pickers. Provisions wanted. [*Adm. Paper.*]

Aug. 18. The Elizabeth, Plymouth. 51. Capt. Robt. Robinson to the Navy Comrs. Is detained by contrary winds. Particulars of other ships in harbour. [*Adm. Paper.*]

Aug. 18. Woolwich. 52. Chris. Pett and three others to the Navy Comrs. Estimate of the charge for cutting through the bank, for the convenience of carrying timber into the ballast pit intended to be laid in Woolwich Dockyard; total, 667*l.* 15*s.* [*Adm. Paper, 2 pages.*]

Aug. 18. Norwich. 53. James Johnson to the Navy Comrs. Mr. Dunne promises requisite care in surveying the new frigate now building at Yarmouth. A small vessel of pitch and tar from Stockholm is speedily expected. [*Adm. Paper.*]

Aug. 18. Yarmouth. 54. Thos. Pupplett and Nath. Ashby, bailiffs of Yarmouth, to the Navy Comrs. Notify the damage sustained by the Mayflower smack, driven aground in a storm. Ask orders concerning the same. It will cost 40*l.* to fit her for sea again. [*Adm. Paper.*]

Aug. 18. Portsmouth. 55. Comr. Thos. Middleton to Sam. Pepys. Notes the vessels arived from the Downs; repairs needed; promises a further account of what has been done about Sir Wm. Warren's timber. [*Adm. Paper.*]

Aug. 18. Portsmouth. 56. Comr. Thos. Middleton to Sam. Pepys. Arrival of the Coventry, much damaged by bad weather; doubts whether it be worth the charge to set her to sea again. [*Adm. Paper.*]

Aug. 18. Dover. 57. Jo. Carlisle to Williamson. Has sent Mr. Desborough to Ostend, but was obliged to engage to pay his debt on bond, amount-

VOL. CXXIX.

1665.

ing in all to 26*l*., unless it prove to be paid, as he says it is. Had he known Desborough's business, would not have detained him a tide. Report says that we have taken six of the Dutch East India fleet, sunk two, and three have got to Bergen in Norway. There is little or no infection about. The Duke of Lenox is at the castle, and very careful about the prizes brought in by his privateers; one is worth 4,000*l*. Does not hear that the King's tenths or the Duke's fifteenths are looked after.

Aug. 18. 58. H. M. [Hen. Muddiman] to Williamson. Items from news letters, viz.:—

Deal, August 16.—A prize is brought in from the Texel; the East India fleet has sailed. The Dutch fleet is said to be 90 sail, with 16 fire-ships, and 12 galliots.

Landguard fort, August 19.—Three prizes are brought into the harbour, and our ships still in the Gunfleet.

Yarmouth, August 18.—The Milford frigate has taken a Dutch prize, but falling in with the Dutch fleet, had difficulty in making her escape; 80 have died in the town since Friday night.

Dartmouth, August 17.—A Morlaix vessel was not suffered to come in, for fear of the sickness. The Dutch privateers are busy about the Land's End, and have taken two small vessels of that harbour, bound for Newfoundland for dried fish.

Aug. 18. York. 59. Earl of Peterborough to [Williamson]. The Duke of York has left great marks of his vigilance and industry at Hull, and in all other parts of the provinces. The news of the enterprise of Bergen, gives occasion to wish that something more useful may be heard from the fleet; there would have been a great clamour if a lord of the King's party had had no better success than this old seaman. The Duke of Buckingham is expected this week, and Mr. Bronker, who is to bring word what will be the intentions of the commissions. The plague is an infinite interruption to the whole trade of the nation. Wishes a better managed war or a peace, for the sake of the Guinea trade. Sir Thos. Clifford, who was in the late action, will give particulars. [Edw.] Montague had the happy part to die in it. [2 *pages*.]

Aug. 19. York. 60. Fras. Lord Hawley to [Williamson]. They are kindly used in the county, and the Duke is pleased with the North. He was well received in Hull. Will not remove his troop from the country during his Highness' stay, unless on orders from Salisbury, for there is some apprehension of the fanatics.

Aug. 19. Lysnare. 61. Robt. Conway to Viscount Conway. Sir Hen. Conway greatly injures him by detaining from him 54*l*. of his rents, &c., in spite of engagements to the contrary. Begs assistance in this trouble. If brotherly kindness do not prompt it, begs that Sir Henry will return the money, and submit to arbitration as to the

1665 VOL. CXXIX.

additional revenue, which Sir Henry pretends to be in his free gift. Wants a commission to be Sir George Rawdon's quartermaster. [1½ pages.]

Aug. 19. Chichester. 62. John Breman to Lord Arlington. Sir John Lewknor was friendly to him on hearing a good account of him, but by his lordship's order, has now remanded him into custody; would perish rather than abuse the King's favour and his solemn engagements. Begs only to be restrained to his own house, on security for his appearance, the rather because of the mighty spreading of the disease.

Aug. 19. Fulham. 63. Humphrey, Bishop of London, to Lord Arlington. Thanks for his warning of disorders that may arise if ejected ministers are allowed to occupy the vacant pulpits; the sober clergy remain. Has refused some that offered to supply vacancies, suspecting them to be of the factious party, though they promised conformity. Most of his officers have deserted him and gone into the country, but cannot learn that any nonconformists have invaded the pulpit. Many of those who never attended divine service are now present. The greatest danger is from the distress of the poor. Has made collections for them, and consults with the Lord General about distribution of the money. [2 pages.]

Aug. 19. Salisbury. The King to the Duke of Ormond, [lord lieutenant of Somersetshire]. Having considered since his letter of the 16th, that the deputy lieutenants should have part of the militia money for Somersetshire, to supply emergencies, orders him to retain one moiety, disposing of the other according to former orders. [*Ent. Book* 17, *p.* 130.]

Aug. 19. York. 64. Sir Wm. Coventry to Lord Arlington. Lord Sandwich is on the coast, and going into Sole Bay, being short of provisions, especially beer. The success of the summer and quiet of the winter will depend upon a quick dispatch of provisions, that the fleet may go out and meet the Dutch coming home. The Duke of York has sent from Hull two prize ships, laden with wine and dry provisions for 600 men for six months. The Dutch say they have taken a man-of-war of 36 guns; fears it is the Fountain. It is determined, even amongst the most disaffected there, to be quiet, unless encouraged by any invasion, or a success at London. [2 *pages.*]

Aug. 19. Cockpit. 65. Duke of Albemarle to the Navy Comrs. A supply of provisions must be sent forthwith to the Gunfleet, and thence convoyed to Southwold Bay. Ammunition is wanted also, and as many men as can be obtained. [*Adm. Paper.*]

Aug. 19. Dover. 66. Thos. White to the Navy Comrs. Difficulty of procuring a pilot for the Castle frigate, employed to carry out a company of foot soldiers to Guernsey; what the governor, and the mayor, and the master of Trinity House failed to do, money has accomplished; has

1665. VOL. CXXIX.

engaged a man for the service on promising to be his paymaster, and threatening him with prison if he refused. Begs pardon for so unusual a proceeding. [*Adm. Paper.*]

Aug. 19. Bristol. 67. Dan. Furzer to the Navy Comrs. Has received the bill of imprest for 300*l.*, but no order how or where it is to be supplied. [*Adm. Paper.*]

Aug. 19. Bristol. 68. Dan. Furzer to Thos. Hayter. Instead of a bill of exchange from the Farmers of Customs for 300*l.*, to be paid at Bristol, has received a bill, signed by three Commissioners, to the [Navy] Treasurer, without any directions; entreats counsel therein. Hears nothing from the Commissioners about appointing a surveyor for Mr. Bayly's ship. [*Adm. Paper, 1½ pages.*] *Encloses,*

68. I. *Bill of imprest on the Navy Treasurer for 300l. for Dan. Furzer, signed by Lord Brouncker, Sir John Mennes, and Sam. Pepys.* [*Copy.*]

Aug. 19. 69. Abstract of the several sorts of workmen employed in Chatham Dockyard; total, 800. [*Adm. Paper.*]

Aug. 19. 70. Robt. Stockdale to Sam. Pepys. Has desired Mr. Baker to present the bill of the hemp delivered at Woolwich, and to receive warrants for the money. [*Adm. Paper.*]

Aug. 19. 71. Certificate by John Springfield, high constable, and three others, that a report stating that bribes were received by the men employed by Capt. Taylor about Engerstone in converting and carrying timber from the grounds belonging to Lord Petre, to acquit the town of Burntwood of the carriage thereof, is false and abominable; and that a poor fellow, calling himself Robin the Devil, made the above false charge, and is willing to ask forgiveness on his knees. [*Adm. Paper.*]

Aug. 19. Downs. 72. Capt. Rich. Neales to the Navy Comrs. Will endeavour to find a man capable of supplying the place of gunner in the Golden Phœnix. [*Adm. Paper.*]

Aug. 19. Harwich. 73. Comr. John Taylor to the Navy Comrs. Has many supernumerary men, some returned from the hospitals, but not cured. Proposes that all who wish to leave or are unfit for service be discharged from pay and diet, by means of a certificate, and that when the ship to which they belonged is paid off, such wages as by the ship's books appear due be made over to them or their assigns. [*Adm. Paper.*]

Aug. 20. Portsmouth. 74. Constance Pley to Sam. Pepys. Sends her London agent's letter, to show how Mr. Hornby, Alderman Backwell's servant, has hindered the receipt of the 4,000*l.* so faithfully promised by Mr. Fenn. They have already delivered 13,000*l.* worth of goods; entreats the payment of bills as they fall due; can apprehend

Vol. CXXIX.

1665.

nothing but an approaching ruin, unless speedy relief be granted; 6,000*l.* owing is wanted this month and next. Must end her days in sorrow for meddling with this affair, and bringing in Col. Reymes and other friends to suffer with her. [*Adm. Paper.*] *Encloses,*

74. i. *Richard Fuller to Mrs. Constance Pley. Might as well "press money" from a stone as from Hornby and Mr. Fenn; requests positive orders to them both, under cover to himself. Not one merchant in a hundred is left in the city; every day looks like Sunday. Has a great deal of money owing, but cannot get in a penny, nor sell any goods. London, Aug. 17, 1665.*

Aug. 20. Portsmouth. 75. Thos. Warren to Sam. Pepys. Is detained by contrary winds; requests a supply of provisions for the soldiers. [*Adm. Paper.*]

Aug. 20. Portsmouth. 76. Comr. Thos. Middleton to Sam. Pepys. Sends for approval Sir Wm. Warren's contract for oak timber. Thirty tons of rosin have arrived. A bargain of hemp is to be sold in the town; dares not buy it unless ready money be provided. Repairs of the Coventry; proposes the Maybell to attend her as convoy for the St. Malo ships. The Merlin frigate is said to be defective. All ships sent from the Thames seem as though the carpenters had known nothing of their work; the Fox is leaky, and must come on shore; promises speedy repairs for all. [*Adm. Paper, 2½ pages.*]

Aug. 20. York. 77. Sir Wm. Coventry to Lord [Arlington]. There seems no intention of a rising. The escape of one of the suspicious persons seized may be only through the guilt or folly of a single man. Refers for further information to Sir Thos. Clifford. Wishes the Dane would take the wealth at Bergen, if he will not give the English any of it. [*2 pages.*]

Aug. 20. Salisbury. Warrant to the Commissioners for Prizes speedily to release, without prosecution in the Admiralty Court, the Harty Van Clere and Comtie de la Marq, vessels belonging to the Marquis of Brandenburg, which, being Dutch built, are taken a second time after a former discharge, on their return from Spain, laden with salt. [*Ent. Book 22, p. 255.*]

Aug. 20. Salisbury. 78. Jo. Swaddell to Williamson. Particulars of letters received. Lord Carlingford is dispatching for Germany. The King has desisted from any further thoughts of removing to Wilton. Lord Arlington promises to consider of Mr. Gregory's business.

Aug. 20. Salisbury. 79. Robt. Lye to [Williamson]. Lord [Arlington] solicits the grant made to him of John Fitzgerald's estate, which they had so much trouble to find in London; sends him some private letters, which have not been read. Is glad the miscarriage at Bergen was not worse; the Dutch fleet might have met ours in that shattered condition. [*2 pages.*] *Encloses,*

79. i. *News letter. The Earl of Sandwich, being on the Norway coast, ordered Sir Thos. Teddeman with 20 ships to*

VOL. CXXIX.

1665.

attack 80 Dutch merchant ships in Bergen harbour; six convoyers had so placed themselves that only four or five of the ships could be reached at once. The Governor of Bergen fired on our ships, and placed 100 pieces of ordnance and two regiments of foot on the rocks to attack them, but they got clear without the loss of a ship, only 300 men killed or wounded, five or six captains among them. The fleet has gone to Sole Bay to repair losses, and be ready to encounter the Dutch fleet, which is gone northward. *Salisbury, Aug.* 19.

Aug. 21. 80. H[en.] M[uddiman] to Williamson. The town is full of the news from Bergen; 112 killed and 309 wounded. Teddeman's brigade have got into Burlington Bay, and the Earl of Sandwich has joined them.

Aug. 21. Salisbury. 81. Commission to John Lord Frecheville, captain of a troop of horse in the Earl of Oxford's regiment, to take the command of two troops of horse and several companies of foot, which are aggregated in those quarters, to prevent the dangerous attempts of seditious conventicles; obeying the orders of the Lord Lieutenants or Secretaries of State, of the Duke of York whilst he remains in those parts, or of the Duke of Albemarle.

Aug. 21. Chester. 82. Jo. Corrance to Viscount Conway. Private business. Commends his nephew, John Melton, for some business required by his lordship.

Aug. 21. Salisbury. The King to the Bailiffs of Yarmouth. Is much troubled to hear of the continuance of sickness in the town, and the sufferings of the people. Has ordered the Bishop of Norwich to do his utmost for relief of the poor, and to promote benevolence by collections on fast days. Fears that by the withdrawal of persons of condition, the place may not be so well watched as it ought to be, and the day of election of magistrates being at hand, dispenses with such formalities as cannot be observed, and recommends Robt. Nicholson and Wm. Bateman as bailiffs for the ensuing year. [*Ent. Book* 17, p. 138.]

Aug. 21. Purford, Surrey. 83. Robt. Parkhurst to Sir Willm. Batten. Understands that Wm. Castell is commissioned to take up any barges required for the conveyance of timber upon Guilford River; particulars of a controversy between Henry Prescot, Mr. Castell's deputy, and tenant to the owners of the land through which the river passes, and Radcliffe, bargemaster, who claims the King's interests in the river. Mr. Prescot is favoured by himself, Sir Geo. Askew, Mr. Delmahoy, a lieutenant of the county, and other gentlemen proprietors. Begs assistance for him. [*Adm. Paper*, 2 *pages.*]

Aug. 21. The William, Downs. 84. Capt. Wm. Basse to the Navy Commrs. Particulars of his voyage from St. Helena; report of ships trading thither since last October; has the scurvy on board from want of water and provisions; was obliged to put in at Fiall Road for supplies. [*Adm. Paper*, 2 *pages.*]

Vol. CXXIX.

1665.

Aug. 21. Dover Road. 85. Roger Rymer, purser of the William, to Thos. Hayter. Has arrived in the Downs, in company with the John and Margaret and five East Indiamen; wants provisions; took up a bill of exchange for victualling his ship at Fiall. [*Adm. Paper.*]

Aug. 21. Chatham. 86. Comr. Peter Pett to Samuel Pepys. Arrival of the Sapphire; repairs needed; complains of the small quantity of cordage in store; is stopped for want of hemp at a time when men are well able to work, and so great a fleet is abroad; entreats a speedy supply. [*Adm. Paper.*]

Aug. 21. Chatham Dock. 87. Phin. Pett to the Navy Comrs. Has received a verbal order from Comr. Pett to stop the works at Sheerness; asks further direction; if continued, recommends that work be "performed by the great rather than by the day." [*Adm. Paper.*]

Aug. 21. The Hound, Southwold Bay. 88. Capt. Jas. Coleman to Sam. Pepys. Went with Sir Thos. Teddeman to North Bergen, to attempt taking the Dutch East India ships and other merchantmen, 50 sail in all. Teddeman, with 22 men-of-war and two fire-ships, sailed from the fleet July 30th, and reached Bergen August 1st, at 3 p.m. The Dutch ships were lying one on another, incapable of execution, but all the afternoon was spent in treating with the Dane; meanwhile the Dutch got four ships athwart the harbour; could, if permitted, have driven across their hawsers into the harbour, before they were ready to fire, and then the ships might have been taken without loss of English blood. The fight began August 2d, at 5 a.m., and lasted two and a half hours, the castles and forts plying fast upon them. Teddeman is a brave man, but spent too long in treating with the Dane, who proved very treacherous. The killed and wounded amount to 357, including six captains. Asks an appointment to the command of any small man-of-war. [*Adm. Paper, 3 pages.*]

Aug. 21. Clapham. 89. Thos. Lewis to Thos. Hayter. Returns the book of the William and Mary. Cannot allow, without orders, the number of supernumeraries borne upon her. Knows not when her victualling began or ended. [*Adm. Paper.*]

Aug. 22. 90. Sam. Heron to Samuel Pepys. Asks a protection for two of Sir Wm. Rider's watermen. [*Adm. Paper.*]

Aug. 22. Plymouth. 91. John Lanyon to the Navy Comrs. The Elizabeth and Nightingale are dispatched. Account of disbursements thereupon, as also on the Sorlings; total, 307*l*. 18*s*. 8*d*. [*Adm. Paper.*]

Aug. 22. Portsmouth. 92. John Tippetts to Thos. Hayter. Can say nothing concerning the price of Col. Norton's timber. His statement was that the Commissioners had agreed for 46s. the ton. Refused to fill up the bill without an order. [*Adm. Paper.*]

Aug. 22. Cockpit. 93. Sir Willm. Clarke to Sam. Pepys. Recommends Thos. Caswell, as purser for the Constant Warwick; the last purser will not be continued, as he has not made up his accounts for the last voyage. [*Adm. Paper.*]

VOL. CXXIX.

1665.

Aug. 22. The Loyal Subject, Downs. 94. Capt. John Fortescue to Sir John Mennes. Has completed the East India Company's directions, by convoying their fleet into the Downs. Wants a surgeon, surgeon's mate, and supply of provisions. [*Adm. Paper.*]

Aug. 22. 95. Report by John Conny that the medicine chest on board the Happy Entrance may well serve for six months longer. [*Adm. Paper.*]

Aug. 22. Portsmouth. 96. Constance Pley to the Navy Comrs. Encloses the fourth bill for provisions lately delivered into the stores. Requests a receipt. Asks what they will give for her yarn and hemp. [*Adm. Paper.*]

Aug. 22. London. 97. Capt. George Cock to Williamson. Sends a letter for brave Jack Fenn, at Mr. Vice-Chamberlain's lodgings.

Aug. 22. Portsmouth. 98. And. Newport to Williamson. A great fleet has been seen to the eastward of the Isle of Wight. Hopes it is not M. Beaufort coming to pay a visit. Vavasour Powell, a Welsh prophet there, says the Dutch will beat the next encounter.

Aug. 22. 99. H[en.] M[uddiman] to Williamson. The conventicles are hotly pursued, and the brethren prosecuted according to the strictness of the law. The Royal Sovereign has suffered a little in the late storm, and five of the Dutch ships have been much shattered. Two Dutch capers are haunting the coasts about Whitehaven. Five of our East India ships, with three convoys, have come safe into the river. At Salisbury, a man died suddenly, and it was suspected of the plague. The King passing by the inn, which was shut up on account of the farrier's death, made a stand, and called to ask the people if they were all well. They said "All well," when he assured them they should want nothing, and he would consider the losses they sustained by their confinement. The Dutch Ambassador wrote to Sir Chas. Cotterel that he and all his family were well, and he wished leave to go to Court, but would not go without it. The commissions for levying 36 companies of foot, and as many horse, are for the most part sent to the Duke of York at York, with blanks for the names. The Tower Officers are ordered to have three ships' lading of arms, both for horse and foot, ready at an hour's warning. [3 *pages.*]

VOL. CXXX. [AUGUST 22], 1665.

1665.

[Aug. 22.] Sarum. Blank commissions, as follow:—

1–3. Three for Colonels to be Captains in their own regiments.

4–9. Six for Marshals.

10–15. Six for Chaplains of horse regiments.

16–20. Five for Chaplains for foot regiments.

VOL. CXXX.

1665 ?
[Aug. 22.] Blank commissions, as follow :—

Ferm. 21. One for a Colonel to be Captain in his own regiment.

22–50. Twenty-nine for Captains of horse.

51. One for a Lieutenant of horse.

52–56. Five for Adjutants of foot.

1665.
[Aug. 22.] Blank commissions, as follow :—

57–61. Five for Colonels of horse regiments.

62–64. Three for Colonels to be Captains.

65–69. Five for Majors to be Captains of horse.

70–96. Twenty-seven for Captains of foot companies.

1665 ?
[Aug. 22.] 97. Blank commission for a Colonel to be Captain of horse.

[Aug. 22.] 98. Blank commission for a Colonel to be Captain of foot.

[Aug. 22.] 99. Blank commission for a Captain. [*Unfinished.*]

VOL. CXXXI. AUGUST 23–31, 1665.

1665.
Aug. 23. Letter Office, London. 1. James Hickes to Williamson. Did not receive the note, &c., named by him to obtain 10*l.* from Sir Rob. Vyner, but will attend to his wishes.

Aug. 23. Cockpit. 2. Duke of Albemarle to the Navy Comrs. Wants cordage, hemp, and Gottenburg masts for Comr. Pett. [*Adm. Paper.*] *Encloses,*

> 2. I. *Comr. Peter Pett to the Duke of Albemarle. The Sapphire is ordered in for repairs. Arrival of the Happy Entrance. Great want of hemp, cordage, and Gottenburg masts. Chatham, August* 21, 1665.

Aug. 23. 3. Warrant by Rear-Admiral Jo. Harman, authorizing the masters of the Anne and East India Merchant to survey the defective beer on board the Resolution. Endorsed with certificate, by Roger Granger and John Cholmeley, the said masters, that they have found seven butts of stinking beer. [*Adm. Paper.*]

Aug. 23. Custom House. 4. Sir John Wostenholme and J. Harrison, farmers of customs, to the Navy Comrs. Request orders for the discharge of John Earle, lately pressed, though in their service. [*Adm. Paper.*]

Aug. 24. Portsmouth. 5. Thos. Eastwood to the Navy Comrs. Particulars of timber in the New Forest ready to be transported for Portsmouth; the whole charge for felling, converting, and land and water carriage amounts to 800*l.* Requests a bill of imprest for part of the amount. [*Adm. Paper.*]

VOL. CXXXI.

1665.

Aug. 24. Cockpit. 6. Sir Wm. Clarke to Sam. Pepys. Capt. Hubbard and the rest that were in the Gunfleet have joined the fleet in Southwold Bay. [*Adm. Paper.*]

Aug. 24. Chatham. 7. Comr. Peter Pett to Sam. Pepys. If the Happy Entrance be converted into a fire-ship, it would be well to discharge the surgeon and other unnecessary persons. The captain of the Galley frigate wishes to have Bartholomew Taylor as master. Demand for provisions from Mr. Barrow. Fears the sickness will spread in Chatham, for two houses are shut up. [*Adm. Paper.*] *Encloses,*

7. I. *Certificate, by Capt. Thos. Blackman, of the fitness of Bart. Taylor to go as master in the Galley frigate.*

Aug. 24. The Elizabeth. 8. Capt. Robt. Robinson to the Navy Comrs. Has captured a French frigate laden with oil, wool, &c. The Turks have taken a West India galleon worth 20 millions of dollars. Repairs of ships. [*Adm. Paper.*]

Aug. 24. Portsmouth. 9. Constance Pley to the Navy Comrs. Presents her 5th bill in part of the goods brought by the Lizard and Coventry; desires favorable usage as to abatements; asks what can be allowed for the hemp and yarn, and what further quantities of cloth, hemp, &c., are required. [*Adm. Paper.*]

Aug. 24. Portsmouth. 10. Comr. Thos. Middleton to Sam. Pepys. Has bought two tons of English hemp at 37*s.* per cwt.; more is offered at the same price, but dares not venture to buy it without an order; arrival of the Lizard at Spithead; has ordered Capt. Andrews to St. Malo, to convoy the merchant ships, owing to the disaster befallen the Coventry. [*Adm. Paper.*]

Aug. 24. Salisbury. The King to the [Earl of Suffolk], Lord Lieutenant [of Suffolk], and the Deputy Lieutenants of Suffolk and Essex. Sir William Doyley having represented the necessities of the sick and wounded and Dutch prisoners in those counties, and being disappointed of payments for their relief, they are to pay to him for the said persons part of the sum raised upon a single month's assessment on the Militia Act, leaving a proportionable sum in their own hands for the expense of the militia. [*Ent. Book* 17, p. 132.]

Aug. 24. London. 11. Capt. George Cock to Williamson. There has been some fault at Bergen, if the Exchange or coffee houses are to be believed. Begs Lord Arlington to remember the sick and wounded, or he will be reproached next Parliament for his neglect.

Aug. 25. Mortlake. 12. Dr. Hugh Chamberlain to Williamson. Thinks the great mortality might have been prevented, had his proposals been accepted. The author of navigating with all winds has sent a draught of his invention, to be shown to none except by the King's command; he has 20 ways of performing it, and can make a ship, by help of the wind, sail within two points, if not full against the wind; he is

1665.

VOL. CXXXI.

very anxious for a patent before it be discovered, lest there be delays and objections; he objects to a wording in the declaration which might oblige him to build a large trial vessel at his own charge, whereas he only wishes to make a model or to alter a ship at the King's charge; if approved, he will alter as many as His Majesty thinks fit. Is authorised to offer Williamson and Lord Arlington a present from the first fruits. [2 *pages*.]

Aug. 25. Rotherfield. 13. Sir H. Bennet to Lord Arlington. Entreats him to beg the King not to be offended that Dr. Hinton stays at his house to attend his wife in a desperate disease; he can be with him in a few hours if needed. Is anxious to serve His Majesty. Is sending a warrant to examine two saddlers—who are making more saddles than they have done these seven years,—as to whom they are for.

Aug. 23. 9 P.M. 14. Earl of Sandwich to [the Duke of Albemarle]. Has received 250 recruits; those from Hull are good men, but the new-raised men or rather boys are so unserviceable that he put them to shore again, rather than pester and increase the sickness of the fleet; it would be a waste of the King's money to receive them into any regiment. There are sharp diseases among the men; many are put ashore sick daily, and the fleet is very badly manned. Has sent a yacht for the Sovereign. Has dry provisions for six weeks, but liquor only for three. Hopes care will be taken to provide for such ships as continue in service, and to pay off the great ships, to save charge. [2 *pages*.]

Aug. 25. Barrowden. 15. Sir Heneage Finch to Lord Conway. Is anxious about his lordship's [wife] and his sister [Lady Conway's] health, in this melancholy time of dispersion. Begs him to apologize to Lord Orrery for his not taking leave of him. [*Damaged*.]

Aug. 25. Warrant to apprehend George Webb. Minute. [*Ent. Book* 22, *p.* 256.]

Aug. 25. Privy seal for 10,000*l*. to the privy purse. Minute. [*Ent. Book* 22, *p.* 257.]

Aug. 25. Warrant for all forfeitures, &c., to be paid to B. May, keeper of the privy purse. Minute. [*Ent. Book* 22, *p.* 257.]

[Aug. 25.] Pass for Howard of Arundel, with four horses, to Germany. Minute. [*Ent. Book* 22, *p.* 257.]

Aug. 25. Warrant for exchange of 14 Dutch prisoners in the garrison of Plymouth for as many English, who are to be released, with a list of both annexed. [*Ent. Book* 22, *p.* 257.]

Aug. 25. Deptford. 16. Elizabeth Russell to the Navy Comrs. Her husband cannot get exchange for his money in the north; begs them to send it by the boys now ready to sail; the country is fearful of receiving anything from London. [*Adm. Paper*.]

VOL. CXXXI.

1665.

Aug. 25. Clapham. 17. Thos. Lewis to Thos. Hayter. Sends sea-books of the Prosperous, Sea Venture, and Fortune; their bills for freight should not be delivered until their victualling accounts are settled. [*Adm. Paper.*]

Aug. 25. Bethnal Green. 18. Sam. Heron, servant of Sir Wm. Rider, to Sam. Pepys. Account of pitch, tar, hemp, &c., received. Asks directions where to deliver them. [*Adm. Paper.*]

Aug. 25. Chatham. 19. Comr. Peter Pett to Sam. Pepys. Has stopped the progress of the works at Sheerness, to prevent the King's paying the same thing twice, it not being concluded whether to go on by the day or by the great; promises a plan of Sheerness, and his own thoughts in the business. [*Adm. Paper.*]

Aug. 25. Blackwall. 20. Wm. Cooper to Sam. Pepys. Progress of the ships building by Mr. Johnson and Mr. Castell; desires a survey of them. [*Adm. Paper.*]

Aug. 25. Plymouth. 21. John Lanyon to the Navy Comrs. Repairs of ships. Damage sustained by the Sorlings in chasing three French vessels. [*Adm. Paper.*]

Aug. 26. Bethnal Green. 22. Sam Heron to Sam. Pepys. Sir Wm. Rider is willing to make over a third of the wire in the warehouse at the Hall to Sir Geo. Carteret. [*Adm. Paper.*]

Aug. 26. Bristol. 23. Dan. Furzer to Thos. Hayter. Is much disappointed at receiving no bill from the Farmers of Customs; is resolved not to go near the labourers until furnished with money to satisfy them; never received any command to appoint a surveyor for Mr. Bayly's ship; was obliged to put Isebum Holland on the business for his own credit's sake. [*Adm. Paper,* $1\frac{1}{4}$ *pages.*]

Aug. 26. Harwich. 24. Sir Wm. Batten to the Navy Comrs. The greatest obstacle in the dispatch of the fleet is want of drink. Sir Thos. Allin is dangerously ill at Lowestoft. Ships are sent into dock, others ready to sail; tickets wanted. [*Adm. Paper.*]

Aug. 26. Portsmouth. 25. Thos. Warren to Sam. Pepys. Requests five weeks' provision for the soldiers; the Zebulon is too much broken to proceed on her voyage; has bought two new ships of 200 tons burthen. [*Adm. Paper.*]

Aug. 26. Loyal Subject, Downs. 26. Capt. John Fortescue to Sam. Pepys. Is ordered to join the fleet at Southwold Bay. Entreats attention to his request for a surgeon and surgeon's mate. [*Adm. Paper.*]

Aug. 26. 27. Capt. Val. Tatnell to Lord Brouncker. Lieut. Peter Edwards refused to obey the Commissioners' orders to come ashore at Greenwich, and put his men on board the Vine ketch. Compelled him to go on board the ketch, and he now complains to the Duke of Albemarle about it. Fearing his Grace is offended, prays that he may be informed of the truth of the matter. The command of the

Vol. CXXXI.

1665.

Constant Warwick, formally promised him by the Duke, is ordered to another. [*Adm. Paper.*]

Aug. 26. Hull. 28. Wm. Blaydes to the Navy Comrs. Can find no one having occasion for money in London. Asks payment of his disbursements for ballasting and repairs of ships; total, 27*l.* 12*s.* 4*d.* Cordage can be supplied for ready money. The Governor, Col. Gilby, has prize money in hand, if he had but orders to pay it. Arrival of the Little Lion. With postscript, August 28, that Sir Wm. Coventry has written to order her cleaning. [*Adm. Paper.*]

Aug. 26. 29. Account by Mr. Stephens of money disbursed, giving the Navy Comrs.' orders for the distribution of the same. [*Adm. Paper, 4 pages.*] *Annexing,*

29. i. *Another paper of accounts relative to Mr. Stephens' payments of money.* [3 *pages.*]

Aug. 26. York. 30. Sir Wm. Coventry to Lord Arlington. Hopes not to need the blank commissions sent, as the most intelligent men say that there will be no great danger of risings, now that the most dangerous men are secured. It is clear from Sir George Downing's letter that Beuningen may go into Holland, to concert some matters not fit to be written. Quotes a passage in cypher sent him by Downing which cannot be read by his key. [Decyphered by Lord Arlington, "I pray that an eye be on Van Gogh, that he slip not away privately, till I be hence."] In the pocket of Hen. Darcey, who was secured, was found a scheme of a seditious book, which he tore, but it has been put together again. On Thursday their Royal Highnesses had a fine entertainment at Lord Fauconberg's, and to-day are to be feasted at Sir Thos. Slingsby's. The guards are doubled, and all fitting precautions taken there, and at Hull and Scarborough, for these two days, but "if London do not lead the dance in this distracted time, the country will not stir." The Duke has received the King's letter, and is dispatching orders for securing dangerous people in the Cinque Ports. The Duke of Buckingham is expected next week; the Duchess is at her father's [Lord Fairfax], six miles off. [3 *pages.*]

Aug. 26. 31. H[en.] M[uddiman] to Williamson. All is quiet in Scotland. The forts in Shetland progress. Major-General Monroe is sent prisoner to Edinburgh Castle. The fleet is now judged to be 100 sail, and will be ready for sea in a few days. Adm. Allin is ill at Lowestoft. Several persons have been seized in London, and Col. Duckenfield is sent to the Tower; 22 ships from the East country, laden with hemp, pitch, &c., have arrived lately. A fort is building at Queenborough, for security of the river. The Duke of Ormond, lord lieutenant, is settling the militia at Bristol, the city entertaining him at their own charge. The Danish resident does not come to Court, pretending to have no account of the affair at Bergen, but to think it an affront offered. The Lord Chancellor has been at Christchurch, to view the rivers making navigable. [2½ *pages.*]

VOL. CXXXI.

1665.

[Aug. 27.] 32. Petition of Erasmus De Brewer, subject of Spain, to the King, for release of his ship, the St. Francis, seized on when driven by weather into Fowey Bay, Cornwall, and there detained by the Vice Admiral's deputies, in spite of orders by the High Court of Admiralty, &c., for its release, and for restoration of all the goods embezzled therefrom.

Aug. 27. Salisbury. Proclamation forbidding the holding of Holden or Howden fair, near York, lest the infection should be carried into those parts of the country which are yet free, and especially forbidding any inhabitants of London or Westminster to repair thither, or to any fairs in Yorkshire, till the infection ceases. [*Printed. Proc. Coll., Charles II., p.* 198.]

Aug. 27. Salisbury. The King to Thomas Woodall, surgeon. The public service requiring the residence of one of the King's surgeons in Westminster, during this time of infection, he is to repair thither, for so long as the Duke of Albemarle thinks fit, but shall not in his absence be prejudiced as to his place of surgeon of the Guards. [*Ent. Book* 22, *p.* 250.]

Aug. 27. Salisbury. 33. Jo. Swaddell to [Williamson]. Particulars of letters. All are in good health, and no talk of removing. The Exchequer is ordered to pay 17,500*l.* to Mr. Pepys for Tangiers. Lord Carlingford has his final dispatch, and Mr. Loving goes as his secretary. Mr. Chiffinch cannot send Williamson a buck, the King having refused them to Lord Craven, Col. Legg, and others. Sir Thos. Clifford is to go for Denmark. [2 *pages.*]

Aug. 27. 34. Jo. Swaddell to Hen. Muddiman. Similar to the preceding letter, adding the following paragraphs from letters:—

Eggleston: Capt. Gower, coming to consult the Bishop of Durham on some lawsuits, was sent to gaol.

Rotterdam, August 18: there is great rejoicing for the success at Bergen. They have given the Governor 30,000 dollars for the service done the Dutch fleet.

Portsmouth, August 22: Major Holmes saw a great fleet pass east of Sandham Fort, Isle of Wight.

Hamburg: Amb. Borod is returned to give an account of his negotiations at Moscow. A fast was kept by order of the States General at the Texel on the $\frac{8}{18}$.

The Hague: the Dutch fleet went out, 90 sail, 12 fire-ships, and 6 frigates; it waited for De Ruyter till the $\frac{7}{17}$.

Isle of Wight: several frigates have been blown back by the storm, and the fanatics are very confident.

The King will send to know the intentions of the King of Denmark about Bergen, to see whether he may be persuaded to make himself richer by keeping what he has in charge.

Aug. 27. Salisbury. 35. Robt. Lye to Williamson. Lord Arlington promises to let him know when he must return. Cannot find the grant of Fitz-

VOL. CXXXI.

1665.

gerald's lands, but his lordship keeps his humour about it. Sir Thos. Clifford, who was at Bergen, says Sir Gilbert Talbot's advice came five days after the attack; the Governor then desired another attempt, but the wind did not serve. Sir Thomas is returning, and wants the Governor to take all the things to himself, but fears the Dutch fleet will have been before him and brought them off. [2 *pages.*]

Aug. 27. [Conway.] 36. W. Milward to Lord Conway. Has been at Sir Heneage Conway's. Has tried to settle the dispute between his lordship and Sir Rob. Williams. Proceedings in taking down Conway Castle. Thinks it would be better to sell the lead there at 12*l.* or 13*l.* a ton, than send it over to Ireland. Has been questioned as to the right to pull down the castle. [3 *pages, damaged.*]

Aug. 27. Portsmouth. 37. Constance Pley to the Navy Comrs. Entreats attention to her request for some person to be appointed to correspond with them. Encloses the 9th bill for part of the goods lately brought by the Coventry and Lizard from St. Malo. [*Adm. Paper.*]

Aug. 27. Loyal Subject, The Downs. 38. Capt. John Fortescue to Sam. Pepys. Has been to Dover about the victualling of his own and other ships. Will hasten to Southwold Bay to join the fleet. Begs that a surgeon and his mate may be provided immediately; has much sickness on board. [*Adm. Paper.*]

Aug. 27. The Bendish. 39. Capt. Abraham Houlditch to Sir Wm. Clarke. Has arrived at the Hope in the hired ship Bendish, much disabled in a late engagement at Bergen; requests speedy orders for her repairs; by order of Comr. Taylor, delivered into the Royal Sovereign what men they liked to take. [*Adm. Paper.*]

Aug. 27. Portsmouth. 40. Comr. Thos. Middleton to Sam. Pepys. Has bought a parcel of oak timber, on condition of its approval by the Board. Sends the purveyor's report of it. Requests speedy directions, that orders may be given for marking such as shall be reserved for special purposes. [*Adm. Paper.*] *Encloses,*

40. I. *Purveyor's report of the fitness and good quality of Mr. John Pemble's parcel of oak timber. August 15, 1665.*

40. II. *Contract between John Pemble and Comr. Thos. Middleton for 1,500 loads of oak timber, at 42s. per load. With note of its approval by the Navy Comrs., August 29.* [2 *pages.*] *Portsmouth, August 17, 1665.*

Aug 27. Portsmouth. 41. Comr. Thos. Middleton to Sam. Pepys. The Dutch prisoners confined in Porchester Castle refuse to work, on the plea that they are servants of the States of Holland, and their wives would get no relief from their masters if they worked for the King of England; there is much sickness in the town, but few deaths. The Coventry is new rigged. The vessel that brought the rosin came direct from France, and was never near Southampton. Particulars of storms, in

VOL. CXXXI.

1665.

purchasing, ready money must be paid. Report of ships in dock. Has been obliged to hire men out of the Henrietta pleasure boat to help to rig the Portsmouth and Warwick; had much to do to persuade them to work for 5s. a week; would have put two or three of them in prison but for consideration of their necessities and hard living. [*Adm. Paper, 2 pages.*]

Aug. 28. Prince Royal, Southwold Bay. 42. Wm. Howe to Sam. Pepys. Is ordered to pay 10*l.* to the boatswain of the Dolphin; Sir George Carteret has put the contingencies of the fleet into his hands; all warrants must therefore be directed to him. [*Adm. Paper.*]

Aug. 28. Kinsale. 43. Capt. Wm. Crispin to the Navy Comrs. Begs a supply of money by imprest, until his accounts can be settled; the money to be paid to Lady Penn, on his account. [*Adm. Paper.*]

Aug. 28. Portsmouth. 44. Comr. Thos. Middleton to Sam. Pepys. Begs advice upon a troublesome business concerning a bond for 300*l.*, entered into with Sir James Draper, six years ago, for two men, Lutton and Wetherdon; had, in security, a parcel of goods of greater value; part of the goods were afterwards sold for 272*l.*, leaving 28*l.*, still due, besides interest. Upon Lutton's death, a bill in Chancery was filed for 300*l.*, for goods said to have been received; got clear of that; another subpœna was sent after six months' time; had Wetherdon to prove that Lutton had no part nor interest in the goods; had another subpœna at Portsmouth; took off the order at considerable cost, and has spent much money in the business; cannot manage his defence at so great a distance; thinks of petitioning the Duke of York about it, or writing to Sir Wm. Coventry, that no proceedings may be taken until he can come to London. [*Adm. Paper, 3 pages.*]

Aug. 28. Unicorn, Southwold Bay. 45. Capt. Henry Teddeman to the Navy Comrs. Complains of the negligence of the master of the Amity ketch, sent out to wait upon the Unicorn; he took 12 days to go and return to and from London with the Earl of Peterborough's things, and to fetch water, after the engagement in Southwold Bay of 14 June; is now fain to send ashore for candles, which this master is to bring. An anchor and cable were lost by the ketch off the coast of Holland. [*Adm. Paper.*]

Aug. 28. York. 46. Sir Wm. Coventry to Lord Arlington. Is confident Lord Sandwich will do what he can to get out to sea, the King and Duke having both pressed it. All is quiet, and order is taken for being in readiness without burdening the country, except to keep together for a few days the troops drawn together to receive the Duke of York in the North Riding. Thinks his lordship's kinsman had better not press his suit, the Duke being engaged for the place, in case Mr. Montague should succeed. Thinks the French court is playing fine and disguising its intentions, in order to prevent the resolutions which might be taken thereon. Havens, an able shipwright bred under Chris. Pett, went into Holland for nonconformity, and the Dutch offered him the building of two ships; he has hitherto declined, and desires to return to England if he might have

VOL. CXXXI.

1665.

liberty of conscience. Requests to know the King's pleasure therein. Sends a paper found in Mr. Darley's pocket, and asks how far it makes him liable to law. [2 *pages*.]

Aug. 28. York. 47. Dr. Will Quatremaine to Williamson. Begs a line to know how he is. They are all in good health.

Aug. 28. Salisbury. 48. Proclamation forbidding the holding of Wayhill fair, co. Hants, for fear of spreading the infection to parts of the land which are still free.

Aug. 29. Warrant to pay to Geoffry Banister, musician in ordinary for the violin, 46*l.* 12*s.* 8*d.* quarterly for life, from Michaelmas 1663. [*Docquet*.]

Aug. 29. 49. H. M[uddiman] to Williamson. Sir Thos. Allin has been ill, but is past danger. Hopes the fleet will sail on Monday, they desire nothing more than another engagement. Major Hollis, who took the Dutch ship, is to have the command of the Breda. At Deal it is feared that the plague has crept into the Loyal Subject. Capt. Fortescue, the commander, and six men have died suddenly. The King of Bantam has sent His Majesty a silver tobacco box, worth 1,000*l.* A lady from the Indies, married to Mr. Chambers, has come over in the fleet, and is to have a portion of 500,000*l.* The French ambassadors, at least M. Courtin, are daily in conference with the Lord Chancellor and Lord Arlington. The Elector of Brandenburg is discontented, because his ships are liable to be condemned by the Admiralty Court for carrying Dutchmen. A public prohibition is made to hinder any coming to the King to be touched for the evil, unless presented by the peculiar officers. Sweden has made four new field marshals. Holland is in great joy for their preservation at Bergen, and the Governor there has been presented with 3,000 rixdollars. The States met only to declare some propositions made to them by the French. [2 *pages*.]

Aug. 29. Letter Office, London. 50. James Hickes to Williamson. The Lord General has sent two men to the Gatehouse and also two to the Tower, viz., Major Butler, who exercised all imaginable afflictions on the King's subjects in Northamptonshire, and Major Nich. Kelk, of Burchin Lane, London, formerly an officer in Scotland.

Aug. 29. Salisbury. 51. Jo. Swaddell to Williamson. Wants notice of his return, to prepare his room. The King talks of removing in a fortnight. The place is cold and moist, and he does not sleep well there. He will go to Marlborough for three or four weeks. Lady Anderson is dead, and supposed to be of the sickness.

Aug. 29. Salisbury. 52. T. Rosse to Williamson. The English were very brave at Bergen, though shrewdly beaten. The fleet is in Sole Bay. Hears that their quick return was because the provisions are bad. Those sick who are put on shore are not well accommodated, so that complaints are universal from sea and land. The fanatics are very busy and in high hopes. Sir Wm. Armorer surprised a waggon

Vol. CXXXI.

1665.

with 20 barrels of powder, going through Reading to Malmsbury, and is following up the scent. A conventicle of 60 was broken up at Camberwell, and several substantial citizens taken. Dr. Hen. Wilkinson, M.A. of Oxford, was holding forth to them. There are several candidates for the place of Mr. Montague [master of the horse to the Queen], who after behaving very bravely, was shot at Bergen, but his good-faced brother will carry it, being recommended by the Queen, on whom the King says he will impose nobody: his deserts are such that no man could express them, and though the ladies may not be in love with his face, he will be in love with it himself. Hopes Williamson will not stay long in that rheumatic country, for Hannibal lost an eye among fens. [2 *pages*.]

Aug. 29. 53. Examination of Wm. Andrews of Bulford, before Lord Arlington. Called George Webb a knave for fighting against the King, on which Webb said he would do it again to-morrow. Knows little of Spinage and Pleadwell.

Aug. 29. 54. Examination of George Webb, servant of Mr. Poore, before Lord Arlington. Served in Col. Norton's regiment in the late rebellion. Is a kinsman of Andrews, but was a witness in a trial against him. Had no dispute with any of the King's Guards, but when they were fishing in the ponds of his master, proffered them a dish of fish to be quiet, which they refused, and said they would have their sport. Formerly served Spinage, but has had no communication with him lately.

Aug. 29. 55. Sir Wm. Clarke to Sir John Mennes. Begs an order for the release of his groom and coachman, Wm. Falkner, lately pressed into the service upon his arrival from the East Indies. [*Adm. Paper*, 2 *pages*.]

Aug. 29. 56. Thos. Lewis to the Navy Comrs. One month's extra supply of dry provision was sent to the fleet during May and June last, to prevent want through the extraordinary expense made by supernumeraries borne upon several ships. Mr. Gauden requests a warrant for the said provisions and further orders. [*Adm. Paper*.]

Aug. 29. Deptford. 57. Chris. Pett and seven other members of the Shipwrights Company to the Navy Comrs. Report that the two third-rate frigates, building by Wm. Castell at Deptford and Henry Johnson at Blackwall, are answerable to contract. [*Adm. Paper*.]

Aug. 29. Canons, Essex. 58. Sir Wm. Rider to Sam. Pepys. Though still lame, was yesterday at Woolwich, on board the Coronation, lately arrived from India. Met Sir John Mennes there. Dispatched a supply of hemp to Chatham. Six ships at Stockholm laden with pitch and tar await convoy from the Sound. If Sir Geo. Carteret will appoint a person to receive his share of the wine, will remove his own to another place. It is hardly a time to remove goods of value within the city of London, when people drop down dead at the scale. [*Adm. Paper*, 1½ *pages*.]

Vol. CXXXI.

1665.

Aug. 29. The Bendish. 59. Capt. Abraham Houlditch to the Navy Comrs. Repairs needed for the Bendish; 29 of her choicest men were taken up by the Sovereign, according to order, and 32 soldiers put on board in their room; has now 125 men on board, and 16 sick on shore. [*Adm. Paper.*]

Aug. 29. Custom House. 60. Sir John Wostenholme to Sam. Pepys. Desires an order for release of Robt. Mott, a boatman employed by the Farmers of Customs, lately pressed while in the execution of his duties; caution should be given to the press-masters not to attempt to disturb so great a branch of the King's revenue by a similar proceeding. [*Adm. Paper.*]

Aug. 29. Portsmouth. 61. Comr. Thos. Middleton to Sam. Pepys. The payment of board wages to the poor workmen will revive their drooping spirits and do good service. Cannot procure hemp and yarn without ready money. Particulars of ships. Complains of the London shipwrights doing their business at a strange rate. Not one of their ships but is out of order when it comes to Portsmouth. Repairs of the Merlin and Fox. [*Adm. Paper.*]

Aug. 29. Portsmouth. 62. St. J. Steventon to Sam. Pepys. Sends account of money disbursed, with blank bill of imprest, to be filled in at pleasure, for board wages; the weekly charge amounts to 34*l.* for 136 men; requests immediate payment. *Encloses,*

62. I. *Account by St. J. Steventon of disbursements on an imprest of 800l. for board wages, contracts, timber, &c.; total,* 778*l.* 15*s.* 10*d.*; *also of money still owing; total,* 431*l.* 3*s.* 9*d.* 29 *Aug.*, 1665.

Aug. 29. Portsmouth. 63. St. J. Steventon to Sir John Mennes. Sends account of his disbursements. Has forwarded a blank bill of imprest to Mr. Pepys to be filled; hopes to get it paid by the Treasurer, who is now at Salisbury, out of the royal aid of the county. [*Adm. Paper.*] *Encloses,*

63. I. *Account of disbursements on an imprest of* 800*l.*, *as above.* 29 *Aug.*, 1665.

Aug. 30. Cockpit. 64. Duke of Albemarle to the Navy Comrs. Hears of a mast at Plymouth which will serve the Sorlings; desires their order for it. [*Adm. Paper.*]

Aug. 30. Wanstead. 65. Joshua Child to the Navy Comrs. Hears that his English masts are accepted, except a few of the largest; urges the acceptance of the whole parcel; ordered them solely for the King's service; large masts are difficult to obtain; cannot without detriment leave out any of them. The number of those disliked is but five; begs they may be all taken, lest he suffer too severely for buying before contracting. [*Adm. Paper,* 1½ *pages.*]

Aug. 30. Chatham Dock. 66. Phin. Pett to the Navy Comrs. The Assistance is launched, and the Diamond docked for repairs; sheathing nails wanted. [*Adm. Paper.*]

VOL. CXXXI.

1665.

Aug. 30. London. 67. J. Bence, secretary to the Royal Company, to Sam. Pepys. Complains that no watermen can be found to go down the river on board the company's ships, for fear of being pressed; requests a warrant for protection of them. [*Adm. Paper.*]

Aug. 30. Woolwich. 68. Wm. Couper to the Navy Comrs. Mr. Castell has removed the defective timber from his new ship building at Deptford, and no fault is found by the surveyors in the performance of the work. [*Adm. Paper.*]

Aug. 30. Surgeons' Hall. 69. Thos. Hollier, warden, to the Navy Comrs. Has received a demand from Hugh Rider, master surgeon of the Loyal Katherine, for a speedy supply of necessary medicaments for 260 sick and wounded discharged at Harwich. [*Adm. Paper.*]

Aug. 30. Portsmouth. 70. Comr. Thos. Middleton to Sam. Pepys. Expects the purveyor shortly, to mark out such timber in the New Forest as is ready for service. Is sorry the Maybell is sent for timber; she was intended for St. Malo. "There is a remedy for all things but death." She shall have quick dispatch in unloading, and still go under convoy of the Fox or Merlin. Will consider with Mr. Tippetts about the business of the mast-maker. The ketch will be launched in about 14 days, and may well carry 12 guns. Employs the men out of the Henrietta pleasure boat, at 5s. a day, in re-fitting the Warwick; promises she shall be a pattern for all the King's officers to look upon. Has appointed a boatswain for the ketch. The company of the Fox swear they will not go beyond the Land's End in her, for she will drown them all; defective state of the vessel. [*Adm. Paper, 8 pages.*]

Aug. 30. Portsmouth. 71. Comr. Thos. Middleton to Sam. Pepys. Cannot imagine that his present house was built only for himself; is content with a good bed to lie on, a hammock to sleep in, two or three stools and chairs, and a few platters for meat. Supposes accommodation will be expected for any of the Commissioners, when they come down; if not, begs that no further expense may be incurred. [*Adm. Paper.*]

Aug. 30. Salisbury. Proclamation proroguing the Parliament summoned for Westminster for Oct. 3, to meet at Oxford on Oct. 9, on weighty and urgent affairs; the increase of the plague being so dreadful, and the infection so generally dispersed in London and Westminster that they cannot meet there. [*Printed. Proc. Coll. Charles II., p. 200.*]

Aug. 30. York. 72. Sir Wm. Coventry to Lord [Arlington]. No one who knows what has passed in the fleet can deny that the victualling has not been as it ought to be, either as to time or quantity. This caused the loss of the Hamburg fleet, and the meeting of De Witt may depend upon it. It is a matter which should be considered of now, since at Michaelmas, provision of victuals begins. Had Mr. Gauden died, all would have stood still; where he was in person, he usually gave good dispatch, but he could not be in all places. Proposes that

VOL. CXXXI.

1665.

other contractors be joined with him, whose skill, activity, and credit may keep the stores full. It would be a saving if contractors undertook the several ports. The Yorkshire gentlemen offer to supply for 5d. what now costs 6d. The victualling was at a cheaper rate when the King first returned than it now is. The victualler's agents had not in store the victuals which they pretended to have. The quantity required to be in store the last reign, when fleets were small, will not suffice now that the fleet consists of near 30,000 men. [3 pages.]

Aug. 30. York. 73. Sir Wm. Coventry to Lord [Arlington]. Capt. Strode, of Dover, has written of the folly of a man calling himself Sir Wm. Lloyd, who seems to be mad; but none should play with kings in matters of such moment, without exemplary punishment, to frighten other fools from talking of the King. Wants an answer about Howden fair, and tidings of his brother Henry. Mr. Darley owns a paper sent to be his own, but says it was written in Cromwell's time, which is very improbable; he has always been an ill-principled man. Sir Wm. Doyley complains of want of money, and the business under his care is of consequence.

Aug. 30. Deal. 74. Earl of Carlingford to Lord Arlington. Is ready to start. Mr. Solicitor [General] with his wife and family have come to recommend their son, who will accompany him to Vienna. Will send his eldest son to receive the King's commands for Ireland. Kent is exposed to danger, by the militia being in the hands of unskilful persons. Dover might be burnt without opposition. Recommends Sir Arthur Slingsby, an active and loyal man, for employment therein.

Aug. 30. Salisbury. The King to the Sheriff of Leicestershire. Danvers, long since charged with high treason, and summoned by proclamation for trial, was lately apprehended, but has escaped. He is to enquire about a good estate which Danvers is said to have, in manors, lands, &c., in the county, inventory his goods, and put them into responsible hands till Danvers' prosecution; meanwhile the farmers and tenants are to retain the rents. [Ent. Book 17, pp. 133–4.]

Aug. 30. Warrant to Baptist May, keeper of the privy purse, to pay to Capt. Fras. Berkeley 100l. out of every 1,000l. paid in as fines and forfeitures on prohibited goods. [Ent. Book 22, p. 266.]

Aug. 30. 75. Earl of Sandwich to Lord [Arlington]. Is sailing with the fleet, all in good condition, and hopes success; has but little liquor. His brother, Sir George Carteret, will inform of what things are needed against their return.

Aug. 30. Chester. 76. Jo. Corranne to Lord Conway. Note of courtesy.

Aug. 30. Letter Office, London. 77. James Hickes to [Williamson]. There is some doubt of the sickness at Hull and Newcastle. The fleet in Sole Bay was to put to sea last night; 117 died at Yarmouth last week, 86 of whom were

1665. Vol. CXXXI.

of plague. Major Swallow, Mr. Money, a minister, and others have been secured at Norwich.

Aug. 31. 78. James Hickes to Williamson, at the Earl of Peterborough's, Drayton, Northamptonshire. An express came from the Earl of Sandwich, on board the Prince, to the Duke of Albemarle. The fleet numbers 112 brave ships; the Royal Sovereign is with them. Has paid the 5*l.* to the Churchwardens of St. Martin's parish.

Aug. 31. 79. H. M[uddiman] to Williamson. Mr. Reid supposes that the reason of Sir Bern. Gascoigne's receiving no letters in three weeks is that Italy fears infection from letters from England. Items from letters;—

Dover, August 28: five ships are brought in, but it is thought four will prove French.

Deal, August 28: two houses are shut up on suspicion of the plague. Those who died in the Loyal Subject died from calenture.

Yarmouth, August 28: three vessels have been taken near. Two Dutch vessels will damage the colliers who venture without convoy, unless the Little Mary can prevent.

Sir Thos. Clifford will go to Sweden as well as Denmark. A plot is discovered in Holland to surprise Arnheim for the Bishop of Munster, and severely punished; they are dismayed there at the removal of Sir George Downing, without whom they have small hopes of accommodation. [2 *pages.*]

Aug. 31. Salisbury. 80. Robt. Lye to Williamson. Lord [Arlington] wishes his return as soon as convenient, since the Court will not remove to Oxford for a month yet. His lordship thanks him for his care about an apartment for him at Oxford.

Aug. 31. Harwich. 81. Comr. John Taylor to the Navy Comrs. The Unity ketch is unfit to be continued in the service; has ordered her delivery to the owners. [*Adm. Paper.*]

Aug. 31. Purford. 82. Robt. Parkhurst to Sir Wm. Batten. Represents the opposition met with by Henry Prescot from Radcliffe, a bargemaster, in reference to the carriage of timber. [*Duplicate of his letter to Pepys of August* 21. *Adm. Paper,* 2 *pages.*] *Encloses,*

82. I. *Petition of Francis Lucas, deputy to Capt. John Taylor, employed in building the London frigate, to the Navy Comrs., to prevent the great inconvenience caused through the bargemen's refusing to carry timber, by empowering Henry Prescot to impress vessels for the carriage of timber; has 80 loads upon Woodbridge wharf, ready for the building of the London frigate, but can get no conveyance for it.*

82. II. *Form of a warrant from the Navy Comrs. authorizing Henry Prescot to take up all barges, boats, &c., necessary for transporting from Woodbridge Wharf, Guildford River, to Deptford, 80 loads of timber for the London frigate.*

Vol. CXXXI.

1665.

Aug. 31. Chatham Dock. 83. Jno. Lawrence to the Navy Commrs. Capt. Blackman is appointed commander of the fifth-rate frigate now building. Sends the dimensions and number of guns required. [*Adm. Paper.*]

Aug. 31. Harwich. 84. Sir Wm. Batten to the Navy Commrs. Departure of the fleet; the Sovereign, Bell, and other ships in company make it a much gallanter show than formerly. The Prudent Mary and Guernsey are left behind for repairs. The ketches are all gone; 500*l.* is wanted to pay the shipwrights. Small pox is prevalent in the town. [*Adm. Paper.*]

Aug. Salisbury. 85. Pass for the St. Mary Magdalena, bound for Ostend, brought into Portsmouth by the Katherine, but restored as belonging to subjects of the King of France.

Aug. Minute of the above. [*Ent. Book* 22, *p.* 279.]

Aug. Memoranda [by Williamson from the Signet books] of warrants, &c., passed during the month; viz.:—

Grant to Sir Lionel Tollemache of the Rangership of the new park, near Richmond.

Grant to the King's trumpeters of 20*l.* a year out of the Treasury chamber. [*Domestic Corresp., July* 1665, *No.* 132.]

Aug? 86. Warrant for alteration of the commissions drawn up for captains and other officers of foot, wherein instead of their being assigned to regiments to be appointed, the particular regiment in which they are to serve shall be mentioned. [*Draft.*]

Aug. Portsmouth. 87. Comr. Thos. Middleton to [Sam. Pepys]. Has bought 12 tons of rosin lately brought into port by a French vessel, at 9*l.* 10*s.* per ton; has promised ready money for it; begs it may be paid, so as not to lose credit with the people. The French yarn proves better than any yet sent to Portsmouth. A cable is wanted for the Lizard. [*Adm. Paper.*]

Aug. Sarum. 88. "Declaration of a person who is seemingly of this confede-"racie, on purpose to do His Majesty and country service." Major Dale, *alias* White, formerly escaped from the Tower, came to New Sarum six weeks ago, and told Mr. Parker, a baker, of a great plot in hand, which Buffet was promoting in the west. Their design is to seize the Tower and magazine, and the King's Guards at Whitehall; 2,000 are to attack the Tower, with help of the prisoners and such of their attendants as are of that party; 10,000 are ready at an hour's call in the West; they will seize the King's Guards if he be there, and use their arms. Major Dale visits Bristol, Taunton, Glastonbury, and Cornwall; Buffet is usually in Cornwall. Account of other plotters; Rich. Edwards, formerly accused of treason but released on bail, has forfeited his recognizance, and gone to Ireland to promote the design there.

VOL. CXXXI.

1665.
Aug. ? 89. Case of John Davis, late of Acton. He spent 20,000*l.* for the King's service in his peregrinations; on 20 Dec. 1662, he was sent to the Tower, by warrant of Sec. Bennet, his papers searched, but being only on private business, they were restored; his imprisonment was very close. He was compelled to pay 3*l.* weekly to [Sir John Robinson], the lieutenant of the Tower, who converted to his own use the 3*l.* allowed for him by the King, and other contributions of Sir Hen. Bennet. Davis threatened to take the benefit of the law, and sue the lieutenant for false imprisonment; after 54 weeks' restraint, Sir John told him he had the King's orders to send him away, but would not tell him where; Davis replied that this was acting contrary to law, which he was sure the King would not do if he knew it, and threatened to make him answer to Parliament; a file of musketeers forced him out of the Tower; he was conveyed by Ensign Boddiley, on the Katherine yacht, to the Essex frigate, to be sent to Tangiers, on purpose that if there he whistled a discontented note, or sung a melancholy tune, a court martial might dispatch him as a mutineer. He is treated with great inhumanity in the voyage, being in a cabin too narrow to hold him, and without sheets or clothes to keep him warm. With marginal notes, aggravating the conduct of Sir John Robinson, and of the King, who himself signed the warrants and went on board the yacht to give directions about him. Endorsed, "John Davis's case; found by Mr. L'Estrange with Bagshaw, then prisoner in the Tower, upon the 30th of January, 1665." [2 *pages.*]

VOL. CXXXII. SEPTEMBER 1–15, 1665.

1665.
Sept. 1. Letter Office. 1. James Hickes to Williamson. Will attend to his commands, and inform Mr. Muddiman thereof.

Sept. 1. 2. Examination of John Rede, of Porton. Has seen no discontented people lately. Was imprisoned in the Tower in 1661; was governor of Poole during the rebellion, and will not say whether he is sorry for it. Knows Pleadwell, but has not seen him for two years, nor Spineage for nine months; cannot remember when he was at a parish church; will not say whether people resort to his house in greater numbers than the Act allows. Has not heard from London during the infection, nor from Poole, except about a private debt. Was at Mr. Fines' house five or six months ago; knows nothing of an intended rebellion. Has not heard of Col. Booth nor others named for 12 months; does not know Major Dale, *alias* White, nor Mr. Webb; has no correspondence in Taunton nor Glastonbury. Saw Capt. Spineage lately, but he said nothing of a plot, and is a quiet honest man. [1 *page.*]

Sept. 1. Plymouth. 3. John Lanyon to Sam. Pepys. Repairs of the Sorlings. Not another mast is left in store. The Unity and Richmond are in port. [*Adm. Paper.*]

Vol. CXXXII.

1665.
Sept. 1.
Plymouth Fort.

4. Sir John Skelton to Sam. Pepys. The Barbadoes fleet did not anchor in the harbour, so there was no opportunity to impress the seamen. Masts and ropes are wanted. [*Adm. Paper.*]

Sept. 1.
Chatham.

5. Comr. Peter Pett to the Navy Comrs. Thinks the ground staked out for a yard near the graving place at Sheerness will be most fit for a single or double dry dock, to contain nearly an acre and a half of ground. The platform should stand upon the Ness Point and will conveniently hold 26 pieces of ordnance. Will not be hasty to proceed until an engineer be sent down to advise about the fort. Hopes Alderman Meynell may be found reasonable in his demands of rent. Purposes putting the ropemakers upon a day and a half, now that the hemp is arrived. Has removed 20 of the Bendish's men to the Gift, the rest to the Sta. Maria. The sickness increases very much in Rochester and Chatham. [*Adm. Paper, 2 pages.*] *Encloses,*

5. I. *Estimate by Phin. Pett and two others of the charge for altering the yard at Sheerness; total, 694l. 2s.*
Chatham, July 20, 1665.

Sept. 1.
Chatham.

6. Capt. Thos. Elliot to the Navy Comrs. Requests an order for two months' provisions for 180 men, on board his ship the Sapphire. Cannot conveniently stow more. The gratis and impress moneys are due to the surgeon. [*Adm. Paper.*]

Sept. 1.
Norwich.

7. James Johnson to the Navy Comrs. The ship with pitch and tar has not yet arrived. Thos. Dunne reports well of the ship building by Messrs. Edgar. The second and third payments are almost due. Cordage is offered at 52s. 6d. per cwt. [*Adm. Paper.*]

Sept. 2.
Bristol.

8. Dan. Furzer to the Navy Comrs. Mr. Morgan, the collector for the Farmers of Customs, can now furnish money for the service. Begs that a considerable sum may be ordered. Hopes they may be spared amidst so many thousands that fall. [*Adm. Paper.*]

Sept. 2.
Harwich.

9. Sir Wm. Batten to the Navy Comrs. Has sent the Happy Return and Bonaventure, with the hospital and victualling ships, to join the fleet. The Norwich is gone to Copenhagen with Sir Thos. Clifford. Has paid up the yard. Expects money from Ipswich for the ordinary. The plague has appeared. Sir Thos. Allin and Sir Jeremy Smith both lie sick at Lowestoft. [*Adm. Paper.*]

Sept. 2.
York.

10. Duke of York to Lord Arlington. All is quiet there. Hears that there is likely soon to be a breach with France. No time should be lost in making sure of Spain, before entering into war with France. Begs him to remind the King that before the time for declaration of victuals comes, some men, diligent and able in purse, should be joined with the victualler, it being too great a trust and too much for any one man's purse. [3 *pages.*]

Sept. 2.
York.

11. Sir Wm. Coventry to Lord Arlington. Thinks Sir Thos. Clifford the fittest man to send to Copenhagen, and hopes he may

VOL. CXXXII.

1665.

arrive in time. Regrets the absence of so considerable a man from Parliament, where there will be a great change, by death, promotions, or absences, since the last meeting. His (Coventry's) brother should know, if recalled, what he is to trust to. Thinks the successor designed for him a fitting man, if he can be spared from the business in hand in Parliament, where he may be the most useful member in the house. Hopes the fleet is at sea, but unless the victualler send supplies, they cannot remain long, so that if De Witt stay any time in Norway, they will be obliged to come back, and lose the opportunity. Nothing will be effectual with the victualler, unless he be quickened by King and Council. It would be a charitable work to reimburse consuls abroad for relief given to English seamen, but it must be provided for otherwise than through the Navy Treasury, which is only concerned with men actually in service, and is already burdened by the sick and wounded and by the Admiral's regiment. Their Royal Highnesses go to-morrow after prayers to Lady Burlington's, and return on Tuesday. All continues quiet. Asks when the King goes to Oxford. [3 *pages.*]

Sept. 2. Warrant permitting John Lord Kingston to export to Ireland 2,000 ozs. of wrought plate. Minute. [*Ent. Book* 22, p. 258.]

[Sept. 2.] 12. Warrant to the Ordnance Comrs. to deliver up 4,000 muskets, 2,000 pikes, and 300 barrels of powder, to be sent to the Council of Scotland at Edinburgh, and paid for at the usual rates by that Kingdom. [*Draft.*] *Annexing,*

12. I. *Memoranda relative to the above warrant; the arms to be lodged in Edinburgh Castle.*

Sept. 2. Entry of the above warrant, with variations. [*Ent. Book* 22, p. 250.]

Sept. 2. Newcastle. 13. Sir John Marley to Lord Chancellor Clarendon and Lord Arlington. Sir James Clavering and himself, with several others, have endeavoured to settle the government of the town for the King's service, and have tried to persuade the corporation to choose a suitable mayor; Sir Fras. Liddell, the present mayor, Sir Nich. Cole, who never comes to the town except to make disturbance, and others wish to choose Mr. Maddison, who is the more unfit in these times of danger, because the mayor is a deputy lieutenant, and a commissioner for the royal aid. They plead that it is his turn, but formerly, the person thought fittest was elected. The ill-affected party are high and vigilant. They concealed the resignation by Sir Fras. Bowes of his alderman's place till they had got most of the votes for Thos. Davison, to strengthen their faction, but the plot was discovered, and Bowes' resignation was not accepted. Sir Jas. Clavering is fittest to be mayor, and Capt. Brabant alderman. The King's letters to the town thereon would do good. If things fall out otherwise, nothing but a governor and a strong garrison can prevent Newcastle being delivered into the enemy's hands. Sends a list of persons committed to prison for the plot.

Vol. CXXXII.

1665.
Sept. 3.
Portsmouth.

14. Comr. Thos. Middleton to Sam. Pepys. Mr. Askew promises to look after the law business; cannot stop the proceedings at common law, the case being in chancery; is sure that nothing can be proved against him but by suborning of false witnesses; it is too true that the plague is at Newport, brought over by a certain knight who had an estate there, and sickened and died at his lodgings; the master of the house thought it quinsy, and threatened the mayor for shutting up the house, but two women took the infection, and died from merely changing and airing the sheets of his bed; the poor gentleman was obliged to bury the bodies himself in his own garden; sheep and goats since put in the house are all dead; the plague increases at Southampton. Arrival of the Paradox with a ship of pitch and tar from Harwich; particulars of ships; is very careful that none of the men come on shore, for fear of infection; cannot procure the yarn under 48s. per cwt.; one ton and a half of cordage is served in by Col. Reymes. [*Adm. Paper, 3 pages.*] *Encloses*,

14. i. *Comr. Thos. Middleton to Sam. Pepys. Knows not how to dispose of the fleet when their summer work is done; fears that either Chatham, Woolwich, or Deptford may be dangerous, in consideration of the men and women going to and from London and carrying the infection; it will not do to keep them constantly on board ship; recreation is as refreshing as food. Proposes the Isle of Wight, as a fitting place to send them to; the men can have liberty to go on shore by turns, from time to time, and cannot run away because it is an island; they would be within two hours' sail of Portsmouth harbour, in case of necessity, and as safe there with two anchors as at Spithead with three; there would be good quarters for the sick and wounded; houses enough stand empty at East Cowes to accommodate 1,000 men. Postscript. Has just heard that the plague has broken out at Newport.* [3 pages.]

Sept. 3.
Clapham.

15. Thos. Lewis to the Navy Comrs. Was prevented attending the Board through the illness of one of his family; must forbear to do so until the issue is known. Ten ships are now in the river, and a daily charge to the King, and no provision made for their lading. [*Adm. Paper.*]

Sept. 3.
Portsmouth.

16. Constance Pley to Sam. Pepys. Pleads the goodness that has never failed her, as the most powerful argument to prevail for the acceptance and payment of three bills, amounting to 15,000*l.*, for Noyals canvas and other stores lately delivered. Has news from France that Beaufort has arrived at Belle Isle, with 14 men-of-war, and that many regiments of infantry and cavalry are on the march into Normandy and the Low Countries. [*Adm. Paper.*]

Sept. 3.
Portsmouth.

17. Constance Pley to the Navy Comrs. Has come to an end in measuring the goods lately arrived from St. Malo; encloses the

1665. VOL. CXXXII.

seventh and last bill; particulars of goods delivered. Is deeply in debt; beseeches speedy reimbursement for the great sums expended, that the reputation of her husband and Col. Reymes, who were drawn into the business by her advice, be not shipwrecked; the total amount owing is 17,234*l.*; the credits lately sent by Mr. Fenn upon the customs of the ports have not turned to advantage. [*Adm. Paper, 2 pages.*]

Sept. 3. Portsmouth. 18. Col. B. Reymes to the Navy Comrs. Finds men at the docks measuring Noyals canvas, sent in by Mr. Browne and Le Taxer as patterns, to outvie that furnished by himself and Mrs. Pley; hears "that it is the same the French King uses for his own ships, and prohibited to any other to buy;" has had it viewed and compared with theirs by Comr. Middleton, who pronounces it not a jot better; would fain know what is asked for this much commended ware, and whether, upon a nick of time, 900 ballets can be supplied at once, as at present by himself and Mrs. Pley; calls to mind the large sums still owing, at least 20,000*l.* If the Parliament's gift was not to buy sailcloth and cordage, what was it for? Would have been aground long since, but for his woman partner. Offers them eight ballets of canvas, the last to be had from France, at 20*d.* per ell, though others offer large prices for it. [*Adm. Paper, 3 pages.*]

Sept. 3. Salisbury. 19. Jo. Creed to Sam. Pepys. The two Tangiers victualling ships await Sir Wm. Warren's ships at Plymouth. Asks where Sir Wm. Warren is all this time. There is good news from Tangiers; corn and wine were sent in by the King of Portugal, upon the report of a siege. [*Adm. Paper.*]

Sept. 4. Norwich. 20. James Johnson to the Navy Comrs. Directions for the second and third payments due to Messrs. Edgar for the new ship now building; no fault is found with the work. [*Adm. Paper.*]

Sept. 4. Chatham. 21. Comr. Peter Pett to Sam. Pepys. Asks whether the joiner's and carver's work for the Victory is to be done by contract, and if so, whether the parties should come up to contract with the Board or should contract with him. The Sta. Maria is ready for her provisions and men. [*Adm. Paper.*] *Encloses,*

21. I. *Estimate by Phin. Pett and Jas. Lawrence of joiner's work needed for the new fifth-rate frigate; total,* 25*l.* *Chatham Dock, Aug.* 31, 1665.

21. II. *Similar estimate for carved work; total,* 28*l.* *Chatham Dock, Aug.* 31, 1665.

21. III. *Phin. Pett and Jas. Lawrence to Comr. Pett (?) Advise the joiner's work and the carved work for the Victory and third-rate frigate to be performed by the great and not by the day; estimate for the Victory,* 150*l.* *for each; for the third-rate frigate,* 100*l.* *each. Chatham Dock, Sept.* 4.

Vol. CXXXII.

1665.
Sept. 4. 22. Account by John Tooker, of the names and times of arrival of 23 hired ships, August 11 to September 4. [*Adm. Paper.*]

Sept. ? 23. Petition of John Walters to the King, for maintenance till he can be appointed to a company as promised, having been long out of employment, and knowing no other means of livelihood.

Sept. 4. Commission for Capt. John Walters to be Captain of the company lately commanded by Capt. John Munson, now at Berwick. Minute. [*Ent. Book* 20, *p.* 86.]

Sept. 4. Northwich. 24. P. Leicester and five other Deputy Lieutenants [of Cheshire] to Sir Geoffrey Shakerley. Dr. Thos. Harrison and two others of Chester, and Mr. Blackwell, of Bidston, are to be secured and kept prisoners, and security taken for the peaceable demeanour of Mr. Jolly and nine others. [*Copy.*]

Sept. 5. Shillingham, near Plymouth. 25. John Wakefield to Williamson. Thanks for his expressing his wishes to Mr. Beeby at Oxford, that the writer might attend the ambassador to Germany as chaplain. Will gladly do so, and would take with him the son of Fras. Buller, with whom he now is, and who for ingenuity and handsome carriage has not his fellow in England.

Sept. 5. The Prince, 38 leagues from the Texel. 26. Earl of Sandwich to the King. They were little damaged by a storm between the coast of Holland and Yarmouth sands. On Sept. 3, discovered seven or eight ships ahead; sent some frigates in chase and took the whole, being two of the richest Dutch East Indiamen, a Straits' man, and four men-of-war. The Dutch fleet was scattered by the late storm, the main body being only about 80 sail. [*2 pages.*]

Sept. 5. The Prince, 30 leagues from the Texel. 27. Earl of Sandwich to Lord Arlington. Similar to the preceding. They have taken 1,300 Dutch prisoners. The Hector, a fifth-rate frigate, is sunk. Hopes with good weather to be soon up with the body of the Dutch fleet. [*2 pages.*] *Encloses,*

27. I. *List of 10 prizes taken from the Dutch Sept.* 3 *and* 4, *with the names of the English ships by which they were captured.*

27. II. *Similar list, noting that the Hector is the only English ship lost.*

Sept. 5. 28. H. M[uddiman] to Williamson. At Fisherton, near Salisbury, one is dead, suspected to be of the plague, so that a removal of the Court is talked of. The King will visit several places in the county before he goes to Oxford. The Queen will stay out a fortnight, and then go with him. A league is talked of between Spain and Portugal. The Lord General daily sends discontented people to the Tower. A party of robbers, feigning a warrant from him, gained admittance to Sir Walter Walker's, a noted civilian, to

1665. Vol. CXXXII.

search for fanatics, and carried away money and jewels worth 2,000*l.* Items from news letters:—

Deal, Sept. 4: Seven sail of ships have arrived, three bring from Guinea, belonging to the Royal Company, and four more are in the Channel.

Yarmouth, Sept. 4: A Danish ship reports that the Dutch fleet is returned, and Tromp has only six ships with him; 110 died during the week there, 100 being of the plague.

Florence, Aug. 25: The Pope is in trouble, because the University of Paris, in conformity to the opinions of the Sorbonnists, has voted against his infallibility.

The burials this week have been 8,252: 6,978 of the plague, being an increase of 758. The parishes infected are 118. One man was pronounced by the searchers to be dead of the plague, but not being buried the same day, the next day he came to life. Despairs of finding in the Paper Office several treaties wanted by Lord Arlington, they being in some private reserve. [3 *pages.*]

Sept. 5. 29. William Milward to Lord Conway. Opposition of the magistrates of Conway to his demolishing the castle, as ordered by his lordship. They try to frighten the workmen employed, and threaten to prevent the lead and timber being carried away. Is employing a skilful man from Beaumaris, who values the materials at 100*l.* and will charge 50*l.* for taking it down, the work being dangerous; will sell it at the best rate he can. The lieutenants of the county have written to the King about his demolishing the castle. [2 *pages.*]

Sept. 5. Prison. 30. J. Rede to Lord Arlington. Wishes to recant every syllable in his examination, not consistent with one willing to submit to the present government, and to pray for the governors. Is no plotter and will not disturb government. Thanks for his liberation, and begs to suggest a plan to prevent the necessity of restraining persons of their liberty for conscience' sake. Some are taken for plotting at conventicles to stir up insurrections, the very name of which he abhors, yet knows many good people, who do not think it right to attend their parish church nor will be compelled by persecution; men should not be allowed to attack these at their devotions and take them to prison, except by warrant. Begs that while God's hand is stretched over the country in pestilence, those that pray may not be hindered from meeting, nor disturbed in their devotions, &c. [3 *pages.*]

Sept. 5. Portsmouth. 31. Comr. Thos. Middleton to Sam. Pepys. Requires 50*l.* for furnishing his new house; promises to send an inventory of things purchased. If more than that sum be laid out, will pay it himself. Has found a convenient place in the Isle of Wight for ships to haul ashore. One of the prizes in Cowes Creek can be made a storehouse. Has much trouble with the Fox's crew; the ship may proceed with safety; everything has been done to strengthen her. The repairs of the Paradox are completed. [*Adm. Paper, 2 pages.*]

Vol. CXXXII.

1665.

Sept. 5. Portsmouth. 32. Comr. Thos. Middleton to Sam. Pepys. Has sufficient canvas in store to supply double the quantity ordered. Great want of masts and boats. The great lighter cannot be launched till the next spring tide. Thinks supplies might as easily be sent from London as elsewhere. [*Adm. Paper*, 1½ *pages*.]

Sept. 5. Portsmouth. 33. Constance Pley to Sam. Pepys. Returns thanks for the payment of 2,000*l*. to Mr. Fuller, and for promise of consideration on her own affairs. [*Adm. Paper*.]

Sept. 5. Guildford. 34. T. Dalmahoy to Sam. Pepys. Would have distrained upon Wilkins, the bargeman who refused to obey the Commissioners' warrant concerning the carriage of timber to Deptford and Woolwich, but for their order first to demand treble the freight of the barges, according to the Act. Sends Henry Prescot, tenant of the river near Guildford, to make complaint. [*Adm. Paper*, 2 *pages*.]

Sept. 6. Bethnal Green. 35. Sam. Heron to Sam. Pepys. There are nine lasts of pitch arrived; desires orders for its receipt [at Deptford, on account of Sir Wm. Rider and Co.] [*Adm. Paper*.]

Sept. 6. Bristol. 36. Sir John Knight to the Navy Comrs. Has not been able to send the account for fitting up the Pearl, from press of business. The George frigate's six months' hire is almost expired; asks whether she is to be continued in the service. There are 20 ships ready to sail for Virginia, and others for Barbadoes; requests orders for their convoy, and advice concerning the exchange of prisoners with the Dutch. [*Adm. Paper*.]

Sept. 6. York. 37. Sir Wm. Coventry to Lord Arlington. They were at Lady Burlington's on Sunday, and returned to keep the fast. Hopes Sir Thos. Clifford's journey to Sweden will release his (Coventry's) brother, as it would seem a distrust of his brother's capacity to join another with him when he has done all to the King's satisfaction. The Duke of York has been in such constant diversions, whilst abroad, that he could not be spoken to on Capt. Coningsby's petition, but his ship is not vacant; the command has been disposed of by Lord Sandwich. Is glad wine is sent from Portsmouth to the fleet. Has long foreseen that the victualling was not in the right method, but was not believed, and did not wish to obstruct the service by quarrels. There will be reproach if the fleet return without doing anything, which must be, unless they have extraordinary good luck in meeting with the Dutch soon. Beaufort's fleet coming into these seas should be thought of, and Portsmouth, as the nearest place, plentifully provided with victuals for the fleet in the winter. Asks whether, for prevention of plots on foot, the prisoners in those parts are to be continued in custody, or released on bail. The Swedish ship must be restored, as ordered in Council, on the Swedish resident's memorial; but if the affirmation of a resident is allowed as a proof of a free ship, there will be few prizes, and few privateers will arm and risk money and lives, then to have their hopes frustrated by an order of Council, without a trial. Has a very bad opinion of priva-

Vol. CXXXII.

1665.

teers, and never shares in them, but when a man is tempted by letters of marque to lay out his money, it implies a promise that he may proceed legally against what he seizes. If it be intended, as some say, to lay aside the great fleet, and carry on the war by privateers, they should have better encouragement. [4 *pages*.]

Sept. 6. Salisbury. Order for a warrant to the Officers of the Exchequer to allow in the accounts of Sir George Carteret, treasurer of the navy, 2,073*l*., which he has paid for interest at 6 per cent. on moneys borrowed, and 1,404*l*. 6*s*. 8*d*. paid by him for navy service, by the King's special direction. [*Ent. Book* 22, *pp.* 259–261.]

Sept. 6. Bockingham. 38. Lu. Wilkes to Williamson. Private news. The plague is strongly dispersed, and takes whole families. Will meet the Lord Chamberlain at Oxford to-morrow.

Sept. 6. Warwick Castle. 39. List by Lord Brooke of 15 suspected persons secured, and four intended to be secured, in his lieutenancy of Staffordshire.

Sept. 7. Soam, Chenvey parish. 40. W. Ball to Williamson. Sends particulars of a house and lands offered for sale. Offers services if he proceed further therein.

Sept. 7. Letter Office. 41. James Hickes to Williamson. Sends his letters, as ordered, by way of Northampton.

Sept. 7. The King to the Mayor and Aldermen of Bristol. Is displeased with the efforts of the disaffected to disturb the quiet of the city. The election of officers approaching, recommends them to choose persons of discretion and fidelity, and especially to choose the mayor from the court of aldermen, not the common council, lest the choice should fall on one disqualified. [*Ent. Book* 17, *p.* 134.]

Sept. 7. Warrant for immediate completion of the demolishing the works at Poole, levelling the fences, ramparts, &c. [*Ent. Book* 17, *p.* 135.]

Sept. 7. Warrant to [Col. Reymes ?] for the stranger prisoners in his custody to be delivered to Captain Fran Rodarigo de Segora, master of a Portuguese frigate, to be sent for the use of the King of Portugal. [*Ent. Book* 22, *p.* 261.]

Sept. 7. Warrant to the Commissioners for Prizes to sell the Springer of Huisden to Andrew Newport. [*Ent. Book* 22, *p.* 262.]

Sept. 7. Pass for William and Barth. Bertelels to France. Minute. [*Ent. Book* 22, *p.* 263.]

Sept. 7. Congé d'élire to the Dean and Chapter of Bangor to elect a bishop in place of Dr. Roberts deceased, and recommendation of Dr. Rob. Price, now Bishop of Ferns in Ireland. Minute. [*Ent. Book* 19, *p.* 49.]

VOL. CXXXII.

1665.
Sept. 7.
Portsmouth.

42. Comr. Thos. Middleton to Sam. Pepys. The Barbary ships are at Spithead. The Fox may well perform her voyage; her company very troublesome. In the order to supply wine to the fleet from the prize ships, Comr. Taylor is named to assist; thinks this is a mistake, and that the order was intended for himself; has acted accordingly. Asks whether ships shall be hired for the service. Recommends the May Bell. [*Adm. Paper*, 1½ *pages.*] *Encloses*,

42. I. *Petition of the Officers and Seamen of the Fox to Comr. Thos. Middleton, for a just survey of the ship, that she may be ordered to remain in the English Channel, and the crew removed into some other vessel, she being unfit for the voyage designed for her.*

Sept. 7.
Woolwich Ropeyard.

43. Wm. Bodham to the Navy Comrs. Good hemp is wanted; has only 13 tons of Riga and Quinborough in store. [*Adm. Paper.*]

Sept. 7.
Barber Surgeons' Hall.

44. Certificate by Rich. Reynell of free gift and imprest money due to Peter Noxon, surgeon of the Little Gift. [*Adm. Paper.*]

Sept. 8.
The Blackamoor, Bridlington Bay.

45. Capt. John Barton to the Navy Comrs. Requests a speedy supply of provisions, and carpenter's and gunner's stores. [*Adm. Paper.*]

Sept. 8.
Compill.

46. Dan. Furzer to the Navy Comrs. Has received a bill of credit for 400*l.* from the Farmers of Customs. Mr. Bayley's ship is much hindered for want of suitable timber. Has left Isebarn Holland to overlook the works. The great hindrance in his own business is still land carriage. [*Adm. Paper.*]

Sept. 8.
Woolwich.

47. Chris. Pett to the Navy Conys. Recommends a parcel of 300 Dram deals and 150 spars, offered by Rich. Smith, boatswain of the dockyard. [*Adm. Paper.*]

Sept. 8.

The King to [the Dean and Chapter of Winchester]. Dispenses with the absence of Dr. Thos. Gumble, whose attendance on the Duke of Albemarle and others in and about London prevents his residence at Winchester, as bound by statute. [*Ent. Books* 19, *p.* 49; *and* 21, *p.* 149.]

Sept. 8.

Presentation of —— Greenwood to the vicarage of Dewsbury, diocese of York. Minute. [*Ent. Book* 19, *p.* 50.]

Sept. 8.

Warrant to Col. Reymes to deliver up all his French, Swedish, and Danish prisoners to Captain Francisco Roderigo de Segora, to be transported for service to the King of Portugal, on sufficient security that they will not serve against the English. [*Ent. Book* 22, *p.* 202.]

Sept. 8.
Salisbury.

48. Warrant to Charles Lord Gerard to quarter the Horse Guards in Abingdon, Faringdon, and villages adjacent, in Berkshire, for

1665. VOL. CXXXII.

more convenient attendance whilst the King is in Oxford; the constables to assist in quartering them, and the men to behave civilly and pay for what they get.

Sept. 8. Entry of the preceding. [*Ent. Book* 22, *p.* 263.]

Sept. 8. Privy seal for 700*l.* to Sir Charles Cotterel, whereof 400*l.* to be paid Dr. Patricio Muledy and 300*l.* to Dr. Bernardo de Salinas, as the King's gratuity. Minute. [*Ent. Book* 22, *p.* 205.]

Sept. 8. Salisbury. Warrant to the Commissioners for Prizes to deliver to Col. Gilby a vessel called the Salthouse of Middleburg, condemned as a prize, as the King's free gift. [*Ent. Book* 22, *p.* 260.]

Sept. 8. York. 49. Sir Wm. Coventry to Lord [Arlington]. Forwards the good news just received from the Earl of Sandwich. Hopes the Earl may meet with more of the Dutch fleet which is so dispersed, though our ill-provided fleet keeps together. Unless a much greater blow is given the Dutch, De Witt, who conducted the fleet himself and might otherwise have been satisfied with the honour of carrying home the East India fleet safe, will try to get out the fleet again, if it be but for bravado, when the French may help them, as the vent of their wines will be concerned. Therefore we should always be in readiness to meet them, should the French join, as it will be the best husbandry in the end to do the thing effectually. The trade in the Straits and Guinea should also be thought of, and above all, next year's victualling business well settled. [3 *pages.*] *Encloses*,

49. I. *List of* 13 *Dutch prizes taken and one set on fire, Sept.* 3 *and* 4, *including the Phœnix and Slothany, East India merchants, the English loss being only the Hector. Sept.* 4, 1665.

Sept. 8. York. 50. Earl of Peterborough to [Williamson]. Hopes to be marching for Oxford on the 20th. Thinks the Dutch will not offer our fleet the chance of another victory. Major Holmes is blamed as causing the war and the embarrassment of the Guinea trade. The Prince is not out of his difficulties. Mr. Vernatti does not send him wherewith to satisfy the little lord; he must seek more in Lombard Street, and his mistress will not allow him to approach; he has written to engage the Duke of York for a commission to a person unknown to himself (the writer) to be his captain lieutenant. [1½ *pages.*]

Sept. 9. 51. Examination of John Wright of Madderwall, co. Stafford. Knows not where his master, Col. Danvers, is. Has not heard from him since July, but has sent him money. Has twice received books from his brother, Chas. Danvers, the last parcel being on the death of John James, condemned for treasonable words.

Sept. 9. 52. H. M[uddiman] to Williamson. Items from news letters:—
Salisbury, Sept. 7: The Lord Chancellor and Lord Chamberlain have left for Oxford. The King is going to hunt at Lord Ashley's. The suspected houses are still

1665. VOL. CXXXII.

shut up, but it is thought the disease was spotted fever. There are rumours of war with France, that King sending forces towards Flanders and the borders, and being himself incognito at Calais.

Ipswich, Sept. 7: The fleet is still on the Dogger Sands; the Diamond is repaired and has rejoined it; passage of ships.

Plymouth, Sept. 6: There are 20 sail ready for the first wind.

Amsterdam, Sept. $\frac{4}{14}$: The new fleet proceeds earnestly. The Bishop of Munster is marching with several regiments, and it is feared there is a movement of Roman Catholics, but the French King assures the States that if he cannot prevail in his attempts at mediation, he will declare for them.

The French Gazette records a fight between the Duke of Beaufort and the Barbary pirates. Half of Constantinople is burnt and great part of the seraglio. [2½ pages.]

Sept. 9. Letter Office, London. 53. James Hickes to Williamson. Will send his next letters to Oxford. Our fleet of 109 brave ships waits, on the Dogger Bank, the return of the Holland fleet and merchant ships from Bergen.

[Sept. 9.] 54. Note for Abel Barker, of Hambleton, co. Rutland, to be made a baronet.

Sept. 9. Warrant for quartering 120 of the Guards in such towns and villages in Dorsetshire as are most convenient for attendance on the King, till he returns to Sarum. [*Ent. Book* 22, p. 287.]

Sept. 9. Reference to the Lord Treasurer and Chancellor of the Exchequer on the petition of Edw. Manning for satisfaction for cutting the river from Langley (?) to Hampton Court, ordering him payment for the same, and also for improving the banks and bridges, keeping it clean, &c. [*Ent. Book* 18, p. 186.]

Sept. 9. Cockpit. 55. Duke of Albemarle to the Navy Comrs. In regard to the uncertainty of Lord Hanibal Sestade's coming to Calais, the King's yacht must wait further orders at Dover. [*Adm. Paper.*]

Sept. 9. St. Maria, Sheerness. 56. John Page, purser, to Thos. Hayter. Has received a warrant from the Duke of Albemarle for the Sta. Maria, but in consequence of the plague having driven so many thousands out of London, cannot find his usual securities. Asks if they can be dispensed with for the present. [*Adm. Paper.*]

Sept. 9. Plymouth. 57. John Lanyon to the Navy Comrs. Account of his disbursements upon the Unity, Richmond and Sorlings; total, 185*l.* 7*s.* 1*d.* Asks permission to employ an experienced seaman to attend personally to the dispatch and regulate the demands of ships. [*Adm. Paper.*]

Sept. 9. Navy Office. 58. Cancelled warrant from the Navy Comrs. for payment to Wm. Wood and John Williams of 800*l.* for the William, to complete its six months' hire as a man-of-war. [*Adm. Paper.*]

Vol. CXXXII.

1665.
Sept. 9. Greenwich. 59. Navy Comrs. to the Storekeeper and Clerk of the Cheque at Deptford. Mr. Haile's white and tarred lines being provided by contract, must not be refused, but must be forthwith received and disposed of, according to the warrant of 29th August, although they have the like quantity in store. [*Adm. Paper.*]

Sept. 10. The Unity, Spithead. 60. Capt. Thos. Trafford to the Navy Comrs. Capture of suspected vessels; one a Flemish flyboat with 75 Frenchmen on board, come from Cape Verd, laden with hides, elephants' teeth, wax, &c. Has brought their papers for further examination by the Commissioner at Portsmouth. [*Adm. Paper,* 1½ *pages.*]

Sept. 10. Portsmouth. 61. Comr. Thos. Middleton to Sam. Pepys. One man is dead from going into an infected house at Newport; as to other consequences, is confident the place is as good as can be for the accommodation of sick and wounded. There are sufficient empty houses at East Cowes to contain 1,000 men. The dockyard and town continue healthy. [*Adm. Paper.*]

Sept. 10. Portsmouth. 62. Comr. Thos. Middleton to Sam. Pepys. Considers the last parcel of canvas very dear at 20s. per ell. Has written to Sir Wm. Coventry about his chancery business. Particulars of yarn tendered. The Fox and Merlin sailed to Spithead. Has inquired into the business of the man complained of, and finds he is an idle person and was not punished as was reported, but only put in bilboes. A ship has arrived at Cowes from Barbadoes, laden with sugar, sent as a present to the King from Lord Willoughby, being part of the 4½ per cent. customs in Barbadoes. The captain is unable to venture further without another cable, and there is not one to be procured in the island. Has lent from the stores a 12-inch cable made of French yarn, upon condition of an English made one of 100 fathoms being returned. Begs pardon for taking such a step without orders. [*Adm. Paper,* 3 *pages.*] *Encloses,*

62. i. *Certificate by Capt. Henry Osgood and Thos. Warren, that Matthew Brandwood, for drinking and pilfering brandy on board the Fox, was put in the bilbors.*
September 7, 1665.

62. ii. *Bond in* 500*l., by Capt. John Parry, to deliver a new* 12*-inch cable made in England, of* 100 *fathoms length, in lieu of one borrowed from the stores at Portsmouth, for the use of the Royal Catherine of Barbadoes.*
September 7, 1665.

Sept. 10. Commission for Arthur Broughton to be Lieutenant to Sir Fras. Mackworth's company. [*Ent. Book* 20, *p.* 87.]

Sept. 10. Salisbury. Warrant to Sir Phil. Honeywood to pay the 2,000*l.* delivered to him by the deputy lieutenants of Somersetshire to Col. Bullen Reymes, commissioner for sick and wounded and Dutch prisoners, to be employed for their maintenance. [*Ent. Book* 22, *p.* 267.]

VOL. CXXXII.

1665.

Sept. 10. Salisbury. Warrant to Sir Art. Slingsby to restore the French galliot Crown, and all things taken out of her by his people, notwithstanding any pretence of Dutch mariners or colours, she being the private property of the King of France. [*Ent. Book* 22, *p.* 268.]

Sept. 10. Salisbury. Warrant to the Board of Greencloth to allow to John Forbes and James Roche, supernumerary pages of the back stairs to the Queen Consort, 3s. a day in lieu of diet, and to her confessor and a lay brother 12s. a day instead of their ancient diet, to be paid by the Cofferer of the Household from the 100*l.* (*sic*) allowed for the yearly charge of household, chamber, and stable. [*Ent. Book* 22, *p.* 268.]

Sept. 10. Pass for the ship *La Theresa*, being for the use of the King of Portugal, to go to Amsterdam. Minute. [*Ent. Book* 22, *p.* 270.]

Sept. 10. York. 63. Earl of Peterborough to Williamson, addressed in mistake to Penelope Countess of Peterborough. The Dutch vessels taken by the Earl of Sandwich's fleet will bring 200,000*l.* to the King, beside the prey to officers, which is very seasonable. The Duke of York is invited, as he returns, to the Duke of Newcastle's, where a great entertainment is expected. Hopes to be at Oxford on the 20th.

Sept. 11. York. 64. Duke of York to Lord Arlington. Is glad the King's distemper is over, and hopes the change of air will prevent that or any other kind of pains. Has seen his lordship's letter and the Vice-Chamberlain's [Sir G. Carteret] to Coventry, and finds there will be money to pay off some of the great ships, but it must first be resolved that this is reasonable, the Dutch should first set the example, or they may make a bravado, and try to regain in winter the reputation they lost in summer. The French also might do mischief, if they saw us not masters of the sea. Wishes he could see the King about this affair and the disposal of the fleet which, from the short supply of victuals, must soon return; the season of the year will make Sole Bay unfit for a fleet to ride in; the Downs or Portsmouth will be the fittest places, but the victualler and Lord Sandwich should be consulted. Directions should either be sent to Lord Sandwich how to dispose of it, or it should be left to him, but with a hint of M. De Beaufort's coming into the Channel, and of the need to be masters of that, and to maintain the honour gotten, which will require a considerable strength kept together. Has said more than he intended in a case of so much importance. Begs for his letter to be shown to the King and Mr. Vice-Chamberlain, and asks when His Majesty will be at Oxford, that he may join him there. [5 *pages.*]

Sept. 11. York. 65. Sir Wm. Coventry to Lord Arlington. Thinks Lord Sandwich's success will provoke De Witt to do his utmost to bring the fleet out again this year. The Duke of York's absence from the King is inconvenient at this juncture when, to form a resolution, all the circumstances of foreign business should be thoroughly

VOL. CXXXII.

1665.

debated. Wishes that to save time, His Majesty would consult whom he thinks best, and send orders to Lord Sandwich, as time presses; this may be not according to form, but accidents may happen by delay. Mr. Vice-Chamberlain gives no results of the debates before the King, but asks the Duke's opinion before concluding. Hardly thinks De Beaufort can be at Belle Isle, so soon after his victory at Algiers. Writing to Scarborough about complaints made as to the Swedish prizes, Sir Jordan Crosland says that he has a share in the caper which has been adjudged a prize in the Admiralty Court, and duties paid thereon. Asks whether the sentence should be reviewed, or the ordinary course left of appeal to delegates. The Duke is willing to recommend Capt. Coningsby to Lord Sandwich, for the next vacancy in a fifth-rate frigate. [3 pages.] *Encloses,*

65. I. *Sir George Carteret to Sir Wm. Coventry. The victualler has played his part so ill that the fleet can neither keep the sea long, nor will there be provisions at Harwich on its return to send out the whole body again. The Duke of York should consider its disposal for winter. Hopes soon to have money to pay off six or seven of the largest ships, but can do no more, as there is no mart in London; all are away from their business. Has paid 210,000l. since August last, 80,000l. being to the dockyards, and yet more is called for, as in these perilous times, people will give no credit, even for meat and drink. Is much straitened, having assigned money five or six quarters beforehand. The King is very sensible of the failings of the victualler, especially as he has been paid 270,000l. in ready money for this year's service. Hopes good use will be made of the offers of the northern gentlemen. His Majesty thinks that new contractors should be joined with Mr. Gauden, and undertakers be employed in the several ports, but there is no time before Michaelmas for people to provide casks, &c. The King has sent orders to Portsmouth for as much wine as possible to be shipped for Harwich.* [*Copy.*]
Salisbury, September 7, 1665.

Sept. 11. Billing.

66. T. Feltham (?) to [Williamson]. Sends an important dispatch but hopes it will not prevent his writing to-morrow to my lady, now at Northampton. My Lord and Lady are earnestly wished for and will be very welcome.

Sept. 11. Flower, Northamptonshire.

67. Examination of Willm. Goffe. Particulars of his recent journeyings and proceedings; subsists on an estate in money, and his business as a solicitor; converses with no disaffected persons, nor has heard of any plots to disturb the peace. His musket belongs to him as a militiaman, and the colours found in his barn he used in the North with Lambert, during the usurpation. [1½ pages.]

VOL. CXXXII.

1665. Sept. 11. 68. Petition of William Goffe, prisoner in the common gaol of Northampton, to John Earl of Exeter, lord lieutenant of the county, for release on bail, as granted to others in prison on suspicion, having already taken the Oath of Allegiance and given surety for his loyalty.

Sept. 11. 69. L[eonard] W[illiams] to the Duke of Albemarle. Wants some money, his small salary being in arrears, and he at great expense. Will acquaint his Grace with anything of concernment.

Sept. 11. 70. Receipt and discharge by Hugh Walker, yeoman, of Over Brayles, and Elizabeth his wife, for 200*l.* from Charles Bentley of Little Kington, both co. Warwick.

Sept. 11. Warrant to Sir John Talbot, in marching 100 men to the Isle of Wight, to quarter them on their way, they paying their quarters, &c. [*Ent. Book* 22, *p.* 269.]

Sept. 11. Warrant to the Officers of Customs to permit a piece of silk stuff to be landed for Mons. Courtin, and brought to Salisbury or elsewhere. [*Ent. Book* 22, *p.* 270.]

Sept. 11. Warrant to Sir John Talbot to march 100 of the Guards now attending at Salisbury to Hurst Castle, and thence to the Isle of Wight, to assist Lord Colepeper, observing his directions. [*Ent. Book* 22, *p.* 270.]

[Sept. 11.] [Salisbury.] 71. Petition of Juliana Coningsby to the King, for a reward as often promised for her services; attended His Majesty when Jane Lane left him at Col. Wyndham's at Trent, to Charmouth, Burford, &c., and the vessel promised by Capt. Elesdon failing, back to Trent, and thence to Broad Hempson, the happy place of his transportation.

Sept. 11. Order on the above petition for grant to the petitioner of a pension of 200*l.* a year. [*Ent. Book* 16, *p.* 166.]

Sept. 11. Portsmouth. 72. Thos. Eastwood to Sam. Pepys. Returns a bill signed, to be delivered to Mr. Stephens, and paid by him to Mr. Colville, goldsmith in Lombard Street, on a bill of exchange payable at Winchester. [*Adm. Paper.*]

Sept. 11. York. 73. Sir Wm. Coventry to Sam. Pepys. Believes there have been some embezzlements of provisions in the fleet, yet cannot take the whole blame off Mr. Gauden. The supplies have been very short and very slow. It is of no use sending victuals now that the fleet has changed its station in pursuit of the scattered Dutch. Urges dispatch in the building of ships, as by the spring, the Dutch will have the best fleet they ever yet had, and it will be necessary to make good provision to meet them. Is glad to hear all are yet well at the office, and that the yards have escaped in this very great contagion. [*Adm. Paper*, 2 *pages.*]

Vol. CXXXII.

1665.

Sept. 12. Portsmouth. 74. Comr. Thos. Middleton to Sam. Pepys. Particulars of ships ready to sail. Asks about convoy for the Paradox. Arrival of the Unity with two French ships and an Ostender. Letters for Amsterdam and a Dutch ensign were found on board. [*Adm. Paper,* 1½ *pages.*]

Sept. 12. The Dartmouth, Waterford River. 75. Capt. Rich. Rooth to the Navy Comrs. Is commanded to clean and tallow his frigate at Kinsale. Is greatly in want of cables and other cordage. [*Adm. Paper.*]

Sept. 12. Deptford. 76. Jonas Shish and two others to [the Navy Comrs.] Give a list of 16 mastmakers and shipwrights pressed at Deptford and Harwich; of eight pressed men who have absented themselves, and of nine who did not appear. The sum spent in pressing and boat hire is 2*l.* 2*s.* 8*d.* [*Adm. Paper.*]

Sept. 12. Chatham. 77. Comr. Peter Pett to Sam. Pepys. Is rejoiced to hear of the late success of the fleet. Progress of ships in dock. Great want of plank. There is a sad cry amongst the joiners for the 500*l.* promised them twelve months past. [*Adm. Paper.*] *Encloses,*

77. i. *Phin. Pett to [Comr. Pett]. Thinks the plank tendered by John Fean, of Fenerton, Suffolk, very good and suitable for the works of the Victory and other ships now in hand.* *Chatham Dock, September* 12, 1665.

Sept. 12. Barber Surgeons' Hall. 78. Rich. Reynell to Sam. Pepys. Exculpates himself from the charge of neglect, in reference to the dispatch of a warrant for a surgeon for the Loyal Subject. [*Adm. Paper.*]

Sept. 12. Plymouth. 79. James Kember, master of the Richmond, to the Navy Comrs. Complains of gross mistusage from the captain of the Richmond, who beat him, and hearing that he intended to desert, turned his servants, instruments, and apparel out of the ship. Will hasten to London with Capt. Pett, to make further representations.

Sept. ? 80. James Kember, master of the Richmond, to the Navy Comrs. Entreats to be appointed to the new fourth-rate frigate now building in the forest near Bristol; begs that if ever the least cause of complaint be found against him he may be made an example to all the world.

Sept. ? 81. James Kember, master of the Richmond, to Sir John Mennes. Is utterly undone, not having a farthing in the world. Has served for two years as master, mate, and gunner, without ever receiving one farthing. Hopes never to see salvation if he is not innocent of that for which he has suffered. Begs to be appointed to the St. David, or else to have liberty to lay down his present employment, and go as pilot to Leghorn or elsewhere. [*Adm. Paper.*]

Sept. ? 82. James Kember, master of the Richmond, to Sir John Mennes. There is a vacancy for a master on board the St. Patrick; begs a warrant for it, in consideration of past services and promises.

VOL. CXXXII.

1665.

Sept. 12. Sole Bay. 83. Earl of Sandwich to the King. On Sept. 9, met with 18 sail of Hollanders, and has taken most of them; four are men-of-war, some merchantmen, and some ships of victuals and munition for their fleet. Two vessels set themselves on fire. Capt. Lambert is killed; has taken 1,000 prisoners. Has just met Bancker with 40 sail, standing for the Texel, but durst not attack him, being but eight or nine leagues off their coast, the weather thick, and a storm rising. Has come to anchor with 80 ships, the Sovereign, the two East India prizes, and several other prizes. Refers for particulars to Lord Rochester, who was present, and showed himself brave, industrious, and of useful parts. [3 *pages*.]

Sept. 12. Sole Bay. 84. Earl of Sandwich to Lord Arlington. Is glad his short voyage has not proved unprosperous. Refers him to his letter to the King and Lord Rochester's relation.

Sept. 12? 85. —— to Lord Arlington. Gives an account of the fleet since it left Sole Bay, August 30. The Dutch fleet being much dispersed by a great storm on August 31, four men-of-war, two East India ships, and 12 Straits' vessels were taken September 3, and September 9, four more men-of-war, two West India ships, and 12 fly boats; 20 more vessels were seen and chased, but escaped on account of the weather. The Hector is lost, with most of her crew, and her captain, a gallant man, who had brought in the Vice-Admiral of the East India fleet. Capts. Lambert and Langborne have also fallen. The fleet returned to Sole Bay on the 11th. Expects the Duke will now have all the great ships laid up. [2 *pages*.]

Sept. [12?] Salisbury. 86. Prince Rupert to Lord [Arlington]. Sends an account of the condition of the fort of Goree in Guinea. The writer says it is victualled only for two months, and that there is a design to drive the English from the river of Gambia, to which the Portuguese offer their assistance; he also mentions some English shipping as having come in and brought ill news. Supposes it was of the last battle.

Sept. 13. Cockpit. 87. Duke of Albemarle to the Navy Comrs. Desires the stoppage of all payments due to Mr. Stockdale, for the sale of hemp and other Dutch goods, alleged to be the property of the seamen, till it is ascertained how he came by the said goods. [*Adm. Paper.*]

Sept. 13. Whitehall. 88. Ed. Grey to the Navy Comrs. Entreats the payment of arrears due to Robt. Atkins and John Blake, now set on shore sick and unfit for service, and their recommendation to some hospital. [*Adm. Paper.*]

Sept. 13. 89. Capt. Wm. Badiley to [the Navy Comrs.] Two lighters were sent into the Hope on the 5th of January last, to remove ballast from the Royal Katherine, but by reason of her fulness of provisions, and the ice in the river, it was the 23d before she was discharged. [*Adm. Paper.*]

Sept. 14. Woolwich. 90. Chris. Pett to the Navy Comrs. There are 300 dry dram deals tendered by Rich. Smith, boatswain, with 150 small spars, for any reasonable price. [*Adm. Paper.*]

Vol. CXXXIII.

1665.

Sept. 14. Dover. 91. Thos. White to the Navy Comrs. Damage sustained by the Lily in a storm. Repairs needed. [*Adm. Paper.*]

Sept. 14. Newcastle. 92. Attestation of Robt. Bulman, notary of Newcastle, that nine ships named were hired by Humphrey Pibus, merchant of Newcastle, on behalf of Edw. Dering, merchant of London, for the importing of goods from Hamburg to London, Chatham, &c.; that they were ready to sail on 7th August, and that from August 16th, they have been on demurrage, waiting for a convoy, whereby there has become due to them 783*l.* [*Adm. Paper.*]

Sept. 14. Wilton. 93. [Dr. Leoline] Jenkins to [Williamson]. Sends a letter for Sir Ellis Leighton, who has left Winchester. The Dutch ambassador went supperless to bed, either angry with his *maître d'hotel*, who had provided him but a slender supper, or mortified by the bells and bonfires made in imitation of Salisbury. M. Courtin, who came last night, is much comforted.

Sept. 14. 94. Willm. Milward to Lord Conway. Sends an account of the weight and quantity of lead [taken from Conway Castle], and will try to get a vessel to carry it away, lest it be stolen. Sir Henry Conway wants four or five tons, which he says were promised him by his lordship. There are very few offers for the timber, but some of the gentry will come to look at it when the assizes are over.

Sept. 14. St. Giles's. The King to Lord Treas. Southampton. Having promised his lordship to admit Mr. Vernon to the Customer's place at Chester, directs a fiat for him for that place, void by Mr. Smith's death. [*Ent. Book* 22, *p.* 273.]

Sept. 15. Salisbury. The King to the Mayor and Aldermen of Oxford. Requests them to give a free and fair reception to the judges and other officers of the Admiralty Court, which is ordered to be kept in the Common Hall of that city, and to all persons who shall have occasion to repair to the said court. [*Ent. Book* 22, *p.* 271.]

Sept. 15. Warrant to the Commissioners of Prizes to release the St. John and Charity of Rouen, brought into Plymouth as prizes, but belonging to the French farmers of salt. [*Ent. Book* 22, *p.* 274.]

Sept. 15. Harlow, Essex. 95. Sir Wm. Warren to Pepys. Entreats his interest in obtaining payment for six months' freight due for the Sarah victualler. Wishes to hear the success of the last encounter with the Dutch. Hopes the hemp ship is well on her way by this time; her detention has run up at least 500*l.* in freight by the month. [*Adm. Paper.*]

Sept. 15. 96. Examination of Stephen Jew, fisherman of Rochester, before Comr. Peter Pett. Was engaged by Joseph Webb, of Eastgate, house carpenter, to get as many of the King's masts as possible, upon promise of reward. Has procured several which were hauled into Mr. Bellamy's yard, and since cut into quarters and boards; was paid 10*s.* for the first, but has received nothing since. [*Adm. Paper.*]

VOL. CXXXII.

1665.
Sept. 15.

97. Information of Thos. Bellamy, brewer, of Rochester. Agreed with Joseph Webb, two months past, to build a brewhouse for 16*l.* or for 30 barrels of strong beer. Found him sawing good fir timber; asked where he had it; was answered that he had bought it with his money honestly. [*Adm. Paper.*]

VOL. CXXXIII. SEPTEMBER 16–30, 1665.

1665.
Sept. 16. Wanstead.

1. Jos. Child to Thos. Hayter. Is to have the highest price in their books for masts served in, this being the dearest time that ever was. Wishes the amount of imprest determined. [*Adm. Paper.*]

Sept. 16.

2. Fr. Hosier to Sam. Pepys. Desires orders for the mustering of the fleet now at the buoy of the Nore. The musters do good by preventing the pursers from bearing men for a longer time than they are really belonging to the ships; an order will be needed, as the fleet is beyond the bounds of his warrant. [*Adm. Paper.*]

Sept. 16. Navy Office, Greenwich.

3. Warrant from the Navy Commrs. to the Clerks of the Store and Cheque at Deptford, to make out John Lewin's bill for the 36 hammocks by him delivered on board the Royal Charles. With the boatswain's receipt annexed, dated Nov. 5, 1664. [*Adm. Paper.*]

Sept. 16. Salisbury.

Warrant for the removal of the Admiralty Court to the Guild or Common Hall, Oxford, till the King's further pleasure. [*Ent. Book* 22, *p.* 271.]

Sept. 16. Weymouth.

Commission for Sir Thos. Ogle to be Major in the Holland regiment, in place of Major Bruce deceased. Minute. [*Ent. Book* 20, *p.* 86.]

Sept. 16. Weymouth.

Commission for Roger Manley to be Captain to the company whereof Sir Thos. Ogle was captain; and blank commission for an ensign to Capt. Manley. [*Ent. Book* 20, *p.* 80.]

Sept. 16. York.

4. Sir Wm. Coventry to Lord Arlington. Thinks the general postmaster could trace by whom it is that packets have been opened, as was formerly done about one to the Lord General, which came safe to Ware and left Royston broken. Shooting has been heard, and good news is hoped of the fleet, for had it been ill, ships enough would have appeared to publish their own shame. The Duke will leave on Tuesday week, to join the King at Oxford. Fears a thin meeting of Parliament, through apprehension of the plague, or guessing that the business they go about will not be very popular. Being somewhat of a merchant, goes out of his place to make a proposal about the East India prizes; if long unladen, they will be subject to much damage and embezzlement, and few Prize Commrs. are in town to take care of them. Thinks they should be sent to the East India Company's storehouses, and the goods sold

1665. Vol. CXXXIII.

with the company's goods, at the next general sale by the candle, the company advancing the King money at 6 per cent., which they can easily do, as they daily take up money at 4 and 5 per cent.; they will do this to avoid the spoiling of their markets by the King's goods being sold at low rates. Directions are wanted about the prisoners. The Deputy Lieutenants of Lincolnshire have secured Col. King, and refused him bail; he appeals to the Lord Lieutenant, and sends to demand his *habeas corpus*. The Duke wishes the King to consider the case, for the consequence of Col. King's proceedings will be the bringing to trial the validity of His Majesty's instructions to the lieutenants. [4 *pages*.]

Sept. 17. York. 5 Earl of Peterborough to [Williamson]. Sir Hen. Belasyse has arrived from the Earl of Sandwich, with news of the ships lately taken, and has much satisfied this court, though they are concerned for the loss of such eminent officers. The journey holds for Tuesday, and it is more than time; the Parliament men should be quickened with a more than ordinary intimation of the King's pleasure that they should attend, or there will be a thin house, and what is to be done should not seem to be acted by a few. Rejoices in the decrease of the plague, and hopes it will soon bring the Court to London. [2 *pages*.]

Sept. 17. Portsmouth. 6. Comr. Thos. Middleton to Sam. Pepys. The Maybell is nearly laden. Has received orders from the Duke of Albemarle not to send wine to the fleet while in Sole Bay; recommends a parcel of French yarn offered at 48s. per cwt.; has heard nothing of the hemp merchants lately. Men dread to be paid at London, even upon the promise of ready money; they would rather give three months' time and be paid in Portsmouth, the reasons for this are "not fit to be communicated to paper." Has agreed with the mastmaster for 10*l*. per annum. The plank served in is only fit for lighters and hoys; repairs are needed for Capt. Pett's ship; wishes to defer them until the Warwick is completed. [*Adm. Paper*, 3½ *pages*.]

Sept. 18. Tower. 7. Jonas Moore to Sam. Pepys. Omitted to give a particular account of stores and guns provided for several ships, owing to the exigency of the time; the gunfounder will give the full value for broken masts from Deptford and elsewhere, to make formers for the guns. [*Adm. Paper*.]

Sept. 18. St. Malo. 8. Thos. Browne to the Navy Comrs. It is useless to dispatch the vessels for hemp and ballets, there being no admittance on any shore for ships from England, Scotland, or Ireland, on pain of death, until the plague abates. Is sorry for the interdiction, since lying so long will damnify the commodity; proposes that some of it be spun into yarn. Asks whether to buy up Noyals canvas; there being no trade, all canvas will fall and can be bought cheaply. [*Adm. Paper*.]

Sept. 18. Weymouth. Warrant for recall of Sir John Talbot and his men from the Isle of Wight, to join the regiment at Oxford. Minute. [*Ent. Book* 22, p. 273.]

Vol. CXXXIII.

1665.

Sept. 18. Weymouth. Warrant to Sir Thomas Ogle, captain of a foot company in the Holland regiment, to send forty of his company to relieve the same number of Capt. Alcock's company in the Isle of Portland. Minute. [*Ent. Book* 22, p. 273.]

Sept. 18. Weymouth. Warrant to the Commanding Officer of the part of Capt. Alcock's company at Portland, on arrival of part of the Holland regiment, to take his men to the Isle of Wight. [*Ent. Book* 22, p. 273.]

Sept. 18. York. 9. Duke of York to Lord Arlington. There was general rejoicing at Lord Sandwich's having lighted on another parcel of Dutch ships, and at his good success in taking what he did, though he did not come up with the great body of their fleet. What was done is much beyond expectation, the fleet being so slenderly victualled. The business now is to keep such a strength together as will maintain the honour and advantage obtained this summer. Mr. Coventry has sent proposals about the fleet; approves his suggestions as to the landsmen. [2 *pages*.]

Sept. 18. York. 10. Sir Wm. Coventry to Lord Arlington. Hears that Lord Rochester has gone to tell the King the success of the fleet. Is sorry their necessities drove them home, as they might have met with a third portion of the Dutch divided fleet. Wonders what De Witt will make of the business. Thinks Portsmouth the most fitting place for the body of the fleet. Sends a copy of his letter to the Lord-General on its disposal, &c. The Duke of York does not disapprove the proposals, but as they are to be amended or rejected, they should be presented in his own (Coventry's) name. Hopes the decrease of the plague will continue, and people take heart again, and the members attend Parliament, to which they are not much inclined as yet. [2 *pages*.] *Encloses*,

10. I. *Sir Wm. Coventry* [*to the Duke of Albemarle*]. *The fleet being returned, its disposal for the winter should be thought of. Suggests dispatching a squadron to Guinea. Thinks the landsmen should be sent to shore, where they can be kept at half the cost, as they would contract diseases by a winter at sea, and if quartered in the Isle of Wight or on the Western coast, they would be a security if there should be a breach with France. The victualling and merchant ships should be paid off, and the prize ships fitted out to use instead, in the spring. If the two East India ships would make good men-of-war, they should not be sold. The ketches should be paid off, but the masters and mates,—most of whom are good pilots for the North,—and the men, should be put on board the King's ships. Cannot say how far the great ships should be discharged, for though the last rencontre was better than could have been expected from a fleet so ill-provided, the Dutch have ships ready to add to their fleet, and might come out suddenly. A few good sailing vessels on the back of Ireland would do service in intercepting their merchantmen, but*

VOL. CXXXIII.

1665.

it should be speedily, as their Smyrna ships are preparing to come home by Scotland. They have convoys, so resistance may be expected. The Merchant Adventurers' ships and those of Hull must be convoyed to Hamburg, and the Gottenburg ships convoyed back with masts, without which next summer's war could not be carried on. The more ships are laid up at Portsmouth the better, that a body of the fleet may be kept together. [Copy. 3 *pages*.] *Sept.* 18, 1665.

Sept. 19. Weymouth. Warrant to pay to Hugh May, paymaster of the works, 600*l*., from the sale of prize ships and goods, for works and buildings directed by the King. [*Ent. Book* 22, *p.* 274.]

Sept. 19. Like warrant for 1,000*l.* to Hugh May, towards carrying on a building at Greenwich, directed by the King. Minute. [*Ent. Book* 22, *p.* 274.]

Sept. 19. Salisbury. Warrant to Lord Lovelace, lord lieutenant of Berkshire, to convey Captains Sharp and Hand to Windsor Castle, to be there detained prisoners for treasonable practices. [*Ent. Book* 22, *p.* 272.]

Sept. 19. Salisbury. Warrant to Lord Mordaunt, constable of Windsor Castle, to receive into custody Captains Sharp and Hand, and detain them prisoners for seditious and treasonable practices. [*Domestic Corresp.*, 1664, *Aug.* 15.]

Sept. 19. Minute of the above. [*Ent. Book* 22, *p.* 272.]

Sept. 19. Egglestone. 11. Christopher Sanderson to Williamson. Capt. Gower has been providentially secured; he came into the country to order the work in the southern part. Dares not let any one speak with him in prison, for fear of discovery. Complains of the laxity of the Bishop [of Durham] in not convicting John Cock, agent for Lady Vane at Raby Castle, who was brought before him. Has incurred much malice, and for rubbing up some of those about the Bishop, had nearly been put out of the commission of peace, though almost equal to the others in extraction and estate, and inferior to none in loyalty. Details several slights put upon him in being left out of office. Particulars of his private quarrel with John Morland, clerk of the crown and assize in the county. He is a temporizing Presbyterian, and a friend of John Joplin the plotter. There is no intention of any action in the county, but if the news of the Dutch success be true, they hope the coasts will be infested with Dutch ships; then there will be no commerce, and no money stirring, and the people will be prepared for action. They rejoice that the plague is so violent in London, as the King would otherwise have been more violent against them. Has just received the good news of the great blow to the Dutch. [2½ *pages*.]

Sept. 19. Flushing. 12. Nath. Hatly to Lord [Arlington]. Has gained acquaintance with John Everson. The De Witts are still at sea. The Hollanders show great animosity to England. Ludlow is in England, and

Vol. CXXXIII.

1665.

insurrections are expected. Sir George Downing is reported to have run away 10,000*l.* in debt. Two Dutch East India ships have come into the Texel, where Van Trump is cruising with 60 men-of-war; the rest of their fleet, with De Witt and De Ruyter, and the merchant ships are dispersed in a violent tempest.

Sept. 19. Wanstead. 13. Jos. Child to the Navy Comrs. Will take care to provide the additional three masts required; offers those of and under 25 inches diameter at the same rate as the last New England masts served in. [*Adm. Paper.*] *Encloses,*

13. i. *Note by Jos. Child of the rate of prices formerly given for masts of certain dimensions; from 23l. for those of 20 inches diameter, to 33l. for those of 25.*
Wanstead, September 19, 1665.

Sept. 19. Harwich. 14. Comr. John Taylor to the Navy Comrs. Has received orders for victualling 23 ships named. Asks what to do about the fire-ships not included in the list; if any are to be fitted, it should be known at once. Black oakum is wanted. [*Adm. Paper.*]

Sept. 19. 15. Capt. Thos. Blackman to Sir Wm. Clarke. Requests a warrant for James Shackmapell to serve as boatswain in the Little Victory. [*Adm. Paper.*]

Sept. 20. Deal. 16. Tim. Gardner to the Earl of Sandwich. As deputy to the Commissioners for sick and wounded, has received, from the Royal Katherine hospital ship, 256 seamen and soldiers, to be put into healthful quarters on shore. Sandwich is already infected with the plague. Requests orders to the Justices of the county to appoint some place in the healthful country towns adjacent. [*Adm. Paper.*]

Sept. 20. Norwich. 17. James Johnson to the Navy Comrs. Requests, on behalf of Messrs. Edgar, that the second and third payments due for the new ship in building may be made payable through Robt. Bendish, treasurer of the county. A parcel of ropes has arrived from Holland; 32*s.* 6*d.* per cwt. is demanded for them. Dares not give that price without orders. [*Adm. Paper.*]

Sept. 20. Salisbury. 18. J. Swaddell to [Williamson]. Expecting his arrival, has failed to write to him. The King comes to Salisbury on Monday, and goes thence to Oxford, sleeping at Lord Seymour's. There was a sad fire at Weymouth, after the King's arrival, which burned down 35 houses. Mr. Godolphin does not wish to go to Oxford, and therefore wishes Williamson to be there. [2 *pages.*]

Sept. 20. Salisbury. 19. W. G[odolphin] to Williamson. Would like a month's time in Cornwall. Hopes Williamson will get good accommodation in Oxford, by going before the Court. Wishes him to secure a private stable for them to join of.

VOL. CXXXIII.

1665.

Sept. 20. York. 20. Sir Wm. Coventry to Lord Arlington. The Duke [of York] leaves on Saturday next, and hopes to be at Oxford on Monday. The Duchess will journey by the stages formerly agreed on. Lord Hollis mentions a strange proceeding against M. Bailleul, going with the Duke of York's commission.

Sept. 21. Salisbury. Proclamation forbidding the holding of Wantage fair, co. Bucks, for fear of spreading the infection to parts of the country still free. [*Printed. Proc. Coll., Charles II.*, p. 201.]

Sept. 21. Pass, directed to Capt. Davis, commander of the George frigate, to transport Sir John Perrivale's lady, Mrs. Southwell, and Col. Piggot to Ireland. Minute. [*Ent. Book* 22, *p.* 275.]

[Sept. 21.] Warrant to Capt. Thomas Howard to march his company from Sarum to Oxford, quartering them in inns, alehouses, &c., not taken up by the Horse Guards or officers attending the King. [*Ent. Book* 22, *p.* 275.]

[Sept. 21.] Like warrants to Capts. Bennet and Clerk, Col. Grey, Sir John Talbot and Col. Paston. Minute. [*Ent. Book* 22, *p.* 275.]

Sept. 21. Cockpit. 21. Duke of Albemarle to the Navy Comrs. Desires that Capt. Basset, with his ship William, may be paid off, if there is money to do it; if not, that he be kept on petty warrant till there is money. [*Adm. Paper.*]

Sept. 21. Chatham. 22. Comr. Peter Pett to Sam. Pepys. There are 50 calkers wanted for the repairs of ships sent in by the Earl of Sandwich. Sends up the master calker to press such as are fitted for the service from Woolwich and Deptford. Plank is wanted for the Victory; if the Commissioners will not buy, nor suffer others to buy, it were better to discharge the men at once, as it is impossible to continue the works. Masts are also wanted. There are sad cries of poor sick seamen perishing daily in the streets for want of quarters, hundreds more being sent on shore than those parts can receive, unless the Commissioners for the sick and wounded enlarge their quarters. [*Adm. Paper*, 1½ *pages.*]

Sept. 21. Woolwich Ropeyard. 23. Wm. Bodham to James Pugh. Gives a list of five carpenters whose wages are due; requests tickets for them. [*Adm. Paper.*]

Sept. 22. Deptford. 24. Certificate by Chris. Pett and Jonas Shish of the third payment due to Wm. Castell for the ship building at Deptford. [*Adm. Paper.*]

Sept. 22. The King to the Mayor and Aldermen of Newcastle. The unquiet spirit of the disaffected leads them to create new troubles, during a war likely to produce so much public advantage, and blessed with such results. To prevent the success of their malice there, urges the electing of a good and sufficient mayor, for preservation of the peace of a place of so much consequence. [*Ent. Book* 17, *p.* 136.]

VOL. CXXXIII.

1665. Sept. 22. Warrant from Lord Arlington to Robert Oyde, serjeant-at-arms, to take into custody Samuel Farmer, for treasonable practices, and be ready to bring him before King and Council next week. [*Ent. Book* 22, *p.* 275.]

Sept. 1. 25. Petition of Samuel Farmer to the King and Council, for a speedy hearing and trial, and if no proofs appear against him, for a discharge; his many sufferings for loyalty are now continued by Lord Willoughby of Parham, who imprisoned him at Barbadoes, hurried him on ship board, without trial, and exiled him from his family to England, where he has to beg or borrow bread, and is under custody of a serjeant-at-arms.

Sept. 22. Pass for a Hamburg ship to Lisbon, laden with gunpowder, barley, and cloves. Minute. [*Ent. Book* 22, *p.* 276.]

Sept. 22. Warrant for discharge of Albert Mathyson and Adrian Van Roden, Dutch prisoners now in Chelsea College, in exchange for Capt. Robert Wilkinson and Capt. Thomas Gardiner, prisoners in Holland. [*Ent. Book* 22, *p.* 276.]

Sept. 22. 26. Petition of Jonadab Holloway, gunmaker in the Tower, to the King, for the place of chief gunsmith, void by death of George Fisher. Followed the late King to Oxford with 14 able workmen, and stayed four years, till the surrender of the place, expending several sums never repaid him.

Sept. 23. Greenwich. 27. Earl of Sandwich to the King. Had decided to distribute the fleet before receiving His Majesty's orders to keep it together at the Nore; thought it necessary to consult with the Lord General thereon, and letters being very dilatory, went up to London to see him, and took to the Cockpit the Navy Comrs. and Mr. Evelyn, commissioner for the sick and wounded. The Lord General will give an account of their resolution. Has sent two frigates to Holland to gain information of what they are doing, and is fitting up 20 or 30 ships to sail when they return, and to take charge of the convoys to Hamburg, and bring in homeward bound ships. Has sent off to Portsmouth ships which cannot be repaired elsewhere, finding too much provision required when the fleet remains together; the frigates can take in recruits at Dover, and then return to the fleet. The rest of the fleet will remain at the Nore. Has been obliged to sell or pawn goods for the necessities of sick and wounded prisoners, and to pay the sailors short allowance, the seamen having borne with alacrity great extremities, though some of them have perished. Has ordered Sir Jos. Jordan to put himself on board one East Indiaman, and command all the prizes to Erith, to prevent embezzlement, and Capt. Kempthorne to command the other East Indiaman. Has ordered Lord Brouncker and Sir John Mennes to go and remain on board the East Indiamen, and see the goods delivered into the warehouses. Will return to the fleet to-morrow. [3 *pages.*]

Vol. CXXXIII.

1665.

Sept. 23. Sayes Court. 28. J. Evelyn to Sam. Pepys. Begs that the sick prisoners at Woolwich may be ordered to Gravesend, where they can be well guarded and taken care of. No less than 3,000*l.* out of the 5,000*l.* ordered by Lord Ashley is diverted for other purposes from Oxford. Is in despair with indignation at the misery and confusion all will be in at Chatham and Gravesend, for want of the promised supply. They threaten to expose the sick in the streets. [*Adm. Paper.*]

Sept. 23. Kewlanton, Sherwood. 29. John Russell to the Navy Comrs. Dispatch of the Love hoy laden with timber. More hoys are wanted. Is providing plank. Wants money. [*Adm. Paper.*] *Encloses*,

29. I. *Bill of lading for the Love hoy, to be delivered at Harwich.*

Sept. 23. Royal Charles. 30. Sir Wm. Penn to the Navy Comrs. The two East India ships are dispatched, and may be in London by this time. There is great need of fresh meat, the fleet being very sickly. Animals might be killed on board the hulk at Sheerness, so as to save the hides and tallow, or on a ship in the fleet reserved for the purpose. Hopes [the victualler] will comply with the proposal. [*Adm. Paper.*]

Sept. 24. Portsmouth. 31. Comr. Thos. Middleton to Sam. Pepys. Repairs needed for the Lizard. Has supplied the Tiger with the main-mast appointed for the Warwick; 140 bales of canvas have arrived, and are landed on account of Col. Reymes. Masts, spars, and deals are wanted. [*Adm. Paper.*] *Encloses*,

31. I. *Thos. Brown to Comr. Middleton. Accounts for some of the French hemp being damaged from its lying so long waiting for vessels to fetch it. All English vessels are forbidden, under pain of death, to enter the French ports until the plague abates. Asks tidings of goods sent to Sir Geo. Carteret. St. Malo, Sept. 18, 1665.*

31. II. *John Harris to Comr. Middleton. Bespoke part of the last parcel of yarn for his own occasions. Understands Comr. Middleton is offended at its being used for bolt ropes. Has not consulted profit in it, but thinks it fine and good, and goods are not now at the market for men to pick and choose. All trade is out of order on account of the sickness; 7,163 are dead of the plague. Would not wrong the King, not knowing how soon he may go the way of all the earth. London, September 21, 1665.*

Sept. 24. Portsmouth. 32. Comr. Thos. Middleton to John Harris, sailmaker. Answer to the above. Has sent all particulars of the matter to the Navy Comrs. [*Adm. Paper.*]

Sept. 24. Greenwich. 33. Earl of Sandwich to Lord Arlington. Thanks for his kindness. Refers to his letter to the King for information.

Sept. 24. Oxford. 34. Wm. Godolphin to [Williamson]. Their Majesties arrived at Oxford in safety last night.

Vol. CXXXIII.

1665.
Sept. 24. Order to the Commissioners for Prizes to discharge the ship Bergière, belonging to the French East India Company. Minute. [*Ent. Book* 22, *p.* 279.]

Sept. 25. Marshal's House, Leicester. 35. Clement Nedham to Gervase Price, serjeant trumpeter. Reminds him of having entertained him after his distress at Worcester, and begs help. Was taken prisoner a month ago with many others, and brought to Leicester, and is still detained with a few more who were in arms; the deputy lieutenants refuse to dismiss him on bond, as they have done the others, professing to have received special directions from Lord Arlington to detain him. Thinks the Earl of Stamford, with whom he had a lawsuit a few years ago, has prejudiced the Council against him. Begs a letter from Lord Arlington to the deputy lieutenants in his behalf, and on that of Dr. Wilkinson, his fellow prisoner, a man of great learning and gravity, and unsuspected of arms or plots.

Sept. 25. Horton. 36. Katherine Countess of Chesterfield to Williamson. Asks him to remind Lord Arlington of the lease of the French tonnage, which she fears John Ashburnham and Sir George Carteret will get from her. Has petitioned the King about it.

Sept. 25. The Cygnet, Downs. 37. Capt. Roger Jones to the Navy Comrs. Has safely arrived from Ostend after a dangerous voyage; sustained much damage, and has only one anchor and cable left to trust to; was forbidden to enter the harbour of Ostend, and stood out amongst the piles, the outmost ship. The pressed men run away at every port, through want of clothes. Requests orders for repairs, victualling, and supplies. [*Adm. Paper.*]

Sept. 26. Portsmouth. 38. Comr. Thos. Middleton to Sam. Pepys. Much extra work is occasioned by the return of the fleet into the river; though never idle, is glad to be better employed, if only to keep off the scurvy. Has ordered Mr. Salisbury to deliver his hemp at 46s. per cwt. Shall endeavour to prevent the use of Mr. Harris's yarn, unless appointed for the King's service. The mastmaker is thankful for his 10*l.* per annum. Particulars of stores. Captain Pett is still earnest for a forecastle, but he will have none made at Portsmouth. [*Adm. Paper, 1¼ pages.*]

Sept. 26. 39. Capt. Lambert Wood to the Navy Comrs. Has brought the Sarah pink from Hole Haven to Deptford. If not required any more, asks when and where to give up his accounts for provisions and transport of impressed men, how to dispose of his crew, and where to bestow the empty casks, &c. [*Adm. Paper.*]

Sept. 26. London. 40. Thos. Papillon to Sam. Pepys. Requests an answer to the enclosed letter concerning yarn offered. [*Adm. Paper.*] *Encloses,*

40. I. *Thos. Papillon to the Navy Comrs. Has been offered 46s. per cwt. by Comr. Middleton, for the parcel of French yarn lately landed; the price fixed was 48s., and*

1665. VOL. CXXXIII.

he acknowledges it is the best he has ever seen; begs to be allowed something more, as the commodity deserves it. At the rate of 47s. for the ordinary sort, and 52s. for the finest, will undertake to procure a further supply forthwith. London, Sept. 26, 1665.

Sept. 26. Oxford. Proclamation postponing the fast to be held on the first Wednesday of November from November 1, which being All Saints' Day, is a festival, to November 8; to be held thenceforward on the first Wednesdays monthly; also exhorting to cheerful contributions for the poor visited with sickness. [*Printed. Proc. Coll., Charles II.*, p. 202.]

Sept. 26. Oxford. Proclamation adjourning the trials in all causes in the courts at Westminster, from Michaelmas term to the octaves of St. Martin [Nov. 10], and removing the courts from Westminster to Oxford, on account of the plague; also continuing the Exchequer at Nonsuch; with proviso that all persons owing money into the Exchequer, at the said term, pay it in at Oxford, notwithstanding the adjournment of the term, on penalty of prosecution. [*Printed. Proc. Coll.*, p. 203.]

Sept. 26. St. James's Palace. 41. N. Le Fevre to Williamson. States particulars of the illness of a female servant at Goring House: does not think there is any infection of pestilence, and hopes soon to recover her. Asks if Lord [Arlington] or his house have need of any remedies before the writer starts for Oxford. [*French.*]

Sept. 26. 42. H. Muddiman to Williamson. Sends a list of letters enclosed. Mr. Bowers, of Yarmouth, wants to command a fifth-rate frigate now building there.

Sept. 26. London. 43. Alderman J. Bence to Williamson. Sends his petition on the [African] Company's business, and a copy of the counsel's advice. Capt. Heath, of the Barbadoes, brings word that our people are safe at Cape Coast Castle, and at Ardra have a quantity of blacks on their hands, and want shipping to take them off. The blacks are wary of the Dutch, and had the English a fleet there, they might easily have all again. Wishes the King to be moved in it.

Sept. 26. 44. Speech, in verse, addressed to the King, Queen, and Duke of York, at her Majesty's entrance into her court royal at Merton College.

Sept. 27. Commission for Ferdinando Littleton to be Lieutenant to Lord Frescheville's troop, in the room of Sir Thos. Carnaby, who was suddenly stabbed by one Harland. [*Ent. Book* 20, p. 87.]

Sept. 27. Commission for Edw. Andrews to be Quartermaster to Sir W. Blakeston. [*Ent. Book* 26, p. 87.]

Sept. 27. Letter Office, London. 45. James Hickes to Williamson. All are in health at Newcastle and Hull, but the sickness is hot at Harwich: in London it is abated 1,500. If Summers come not, he should be made an ex-

Vol. CXXXIII.

1665.

ample of for his pride and carelessness. Has established a postmaster at Brackley, between Oxford and Towcester, for the King's concerns to Ireland and those parts, and will instruct the postmaster in Chester to enclose all letters to Towcester. The burials have decreased 1,873 during the week.

Sept. 27. Warrant to Robert Gyde, serjeant-at-arms, to go to Coventry, take into custody the Mayor and —— Alsop, for high misdemeanours, and bring them before the Privy Council. [*Ent. Book* 22, p. 277.]

Sept. 27. Warrant to Lord Ashley to pay to the Treasurer of the Navy, out of money for the sale of prizes 10,000*l.*, to relieve the distress of the sick and wounded and Dutch prisoners, and 5,000*l.* to make up the short allowances of seamen whilst abroad. [*Ent. Book* 22, p. 278.]

Sept. 27. Cockpit. 46. Duke of Albemarle to the Navy Comrs. Wishes two of the most convenient prize ships to be unladen, and prepared for the reception of the Dutch prisoners, under care of the Commissioners for the sick and wounded. The King and Duke of York approve the selling or pawning prize goods to the value of 10,000*l.*; urges speed and circumspection in the matter; the money must be raised to supply the wants of prisoners; petty warrants for victuals are to be issued in the meantime; Mr. Pepys is desired to send notice of these orders to Lord Brouncker and Sir John Mennes, if they are gone on board the prizes. [*Adm. Paper.*]

Sept. 27. Cockpit. 47. Duke of Albemarle to the Navy Comrs. The victualler must be hastened in providing supplies. [*Adm. Paper.*]

Sept. 27. Ordnance Office. 48. Edw. Sherburne to the Navy Comrs. Orders are issued for receiving guns and stores from the discharged ships. All things are in readiness for the new ketch at Portsmouth; four barrels of gunpowder have been seized at Dartmouth, supposed to be embezzled from the King's stores. [*Adm. Paper.*]

Sept. 28. 49. Denis Gauden to Pepys. Sends the accounts. Will spare no care in His Majesty's service. [*Adm. Paper.*] *Encloses*,

49. I. *Account by Denis Gauden of dry provisions now in store for* 168 *days, at London for* 2,400 *men, Harwich* 1,000, *Dover* 600, *and Portsmouth* 1,200. *Sept.* 28, 1665.

Sept. 28. The Bishopsgate [?]. 50. Lord Brouncker and Sir John Mennes to the Navy Comrs. Have taken means to secure all goods remaining upon the East India ships at Erith from embezzlement; tarpaulin, padlocks, and oakum are required to secure them. The Smyrna and Straits' ships have not yet arrived; have selected the Gold-hand and Prince William prize ships to convey the prisoners down to Gravesend, there to observe the orders of the Commissioners for sick and wounded; the Eaglet ketch is to act as guard ship to them; provisions of all sorts are wanted for the ships there. List of 22 ships now there. With postscript by Lord Brouncker to Sam. Pepys, acknowledging the receipt of three letters from the Navy Comrs. since writing the

VOL. CXXXIII.

1665.

above; the 10,000*l.*'s worth of goods ordered can only be disposed of from one of the East India prizes, for there is nothing of value in any other prize.

Sept. 28? 51. Lord Brouncker to Sam. Pepys. Requests the payment of 72*l.* due to Mr. Searles, who serves cordage from Ipswich.

Sept. 28. Chatham Dock. 52. Capt. Phin. Pett, master shipwright, to the Navy Comrs. Good oaken plank is offered at a reasonable rate; it is much wanted for carrying on the works of the Victory and new third-rate ship; account of ships launched, cleaned, and docked; masts are wanted. [*Adm. Paper.*]

Sept. 28. Portsmouth. 53. Comr. Thos. Middleton to Sam. Pepys. Repairs needed for the Blackamoor and Francis; the latter is a merchant ship; asks whether it be fit to employ the King's men to repair a merchant ship, and let his own ships want those hands so made use of, or whether it were not better to discharge her as insufficient for service, and turn the men over to other ships where they are more wanted. [*Adm. Paper.*]

Sept. 28. Tower, 8 P.M. 54. Capt. G. Cock to Williamson. Writes a second time that day, hoping to hear from him, though his boat lies at Tower Stairs to take him to Greenwich. With postscript by Sir John Robinson, that Aldermen Hanson and Hooker, honest and loyal men, are that day chosen sheriffs, and that Sir Thos. Bludworth is to be elected lord mayor.

Sept. 28. Newcastle-on-Tyne. 55. Examination of Robt. Andrew, of Newcastle-upon-Tyne, before Sir Fras. Liddell, mayor, and five other justices of peace. Acknowledges that he deserves the sentence of death, but promises, if he may be pardoned, to discover the most notorious coiners in the northern parts. Ant. and Wm. Wilson, pardoned coiners, have discovered some, but concealed others. Gives details of the transactions of numerous coiners, in 1662 and 1663.

Sept. 28. The King to the Board of Greencloth. They are to dispense with the attendance of Sir Winston Churchill, one of the clerk controllers of the household, he being appointed a commissioner for carrying into effect a bill for the better settlement of Ireland. [*Ent. Book* 17, *p.* 147.]

Sept. 28. Oxford. Warrant to the Officers of Greencloth to pay full allowances of board wages in lieu of diet to the two Secretaries of State for the year 1663–1664, notwithstanding the suspension of 25 Aug. 1663. [*Ent. Book* 22, *p.* 228.]

Sept. 28. Similar warrant for the Duke of Albemarle's allowance for board wages. Minute. [*Ent. Book* 22, *p.* 288.]

Sept.? 56. Petition of the Gate Porters to the King, for consideration: attend continually night and day, maintaining five servants, but have only the ancient fees, 5*l.* a year, the board wages given to them in lieu of diet being taken away.

VOL. CXXXIII.

1665.

Sept. 28. Warrant to the Board of Greencloth to allow full board wages in lieu of diet to the porters of the gate for the year ending 30th of September 1664, on account of their constant attendance. [*Ent. Book* 22, *p.* 291.]

Sept. 29. Pass for the St. Maria, built near Amsterdam for Ostend merchants, to Ostend. Minute. [*Ent. Book* 22, *p.* 280.]

Sept. 29. Warrant to the Board of Greencloth to pay to Mrs. Lesmby 103*l.*, for distilled cordial waters and sweetmeats for the King's use. [*Ent. Book* 22, *p.* 281.]

Sept. 29. Woolwich. 57. Chris. Pett to the Navy Comrs. Account of ships ready to launch. Has received orders for the speedy fitting of the Pearl. Another Dutch prize is expected. Masts wanted. The plague increases in the town and many of the workmen are dead; fears soon to be disabled from carrying on the works. Wishes a pest-house might be erected for receiving the workmen of the yard, and strict orders given for all infected families to be kept in and shut up. [*Adm. Paper.*]

Sept. 29. Sayes Court. 58. J. Evelyn to Sam. Pepys. A letter was left at his house by two captains, during his absence, only repeating former orders about the conveyance of sick men; supposes it was written to pacify their importunity, and quicken the raising of money to be assigned. The bearer, a surgeon, will give account of the extreme misery of seamen and prisoners for want of bread. [*Adm. Paper.*]

Sept. 29. London. 59. James Watkins, master of the Joseph hospital ship, to Thos. Hayter. Is sick of the gout and unable to attend the Commissioners. Account of his proceedings in gathering the sick and wounded from various ships in the fleet. Damage sustained in a storm. The ship is unfit for sea this winter. If continued in the employment, must have time to fit her again; would be glad of her discharge, as no owners will contract to set her out. [*Adm. Paper,* 1½ *pages.*]

Sept. 29. Dover. 60. Thos. White to Sam. Pepys. Hastens his quarter's accounts, thinking some of the frigates may be called in. A well grounded peace and healthful season would make glad the hearts of men. Has been a great time out of money, and has daily disbursements. [*Adm. Paper.*] *Encloses,*

60. I. *Account by Thos. White of sums due to him for salary, repairs of ships, &c., from June 1st to Sept. 29th* 1665; *total* 190*l.* 12*s.* 1*d.*, *of which he is to make good* 101*l.* 6*s.* *for a cable.* [1½ *pages.*]

Sept. 30. Hamburg. 61. Invoice of goods shipped on board the St. John Baptist prize, on account of the French West India Company. [*Adm. Paper,* 7 *pages. French.*]

Sept. 30. Hamburg. 62. Translation of the above. [*Adm. Paper,* 7 *pages.*]

VOL. CXXXIII.

1665.
Sept. 30. 10 P.M. Sayes Court.

63. J. Evelyn to Sam. Pepys. Is occupied in sending orders for quartering the extra sick men obtruded upon Woolwich and the adjacent places. Cannot procure a guard for the prisoners, or any who will undertake to govern the affair. Cares not for censure if he discharge his conscience, and has neither been sluggish nor "indiligent." Is not of so slavish a nature as to be tied to impossibilities and servitude. Cannot work miracles, nor sell like a merchant, but can discharge his trust; is ready (in acknowledgement of deficiencies) to resign his post to greater talent. [*Adm. Paper.*] *Encloses,*

63. I. *J. Evelyn, vice-chamberlain, to [Sir George Carteret]. Is obliged to use importunity for the relief of necessities which nothing but a considerable supply of money will alleviate. Has now 5,000 sick, wounded, and prisoners, dying for want of bread and shelter. This barbarous exposure must needs redound to the King's great dishonour, and to the consequence of losing the hearts of his people. The pittance promised will be spent before received. Entreats speedy aid, or deliverance from the unspeakable servitude of his charge.* [*Copy.*]

Sayes Court, Sept. 30, 1665

Sept. 30. Weymouth.

64. Capt. Geo. Pley to the Navy Comrs. Cannot obtain the money promised from the ports of Bristol and Weymouth. Is much hindered in carrying on the manufacture of English sail-cloth and cordage. Is advised by Sir Geo Carteret to draw a bill on the Navy Comrs. Has received 200*l.* from the customer at Lyme, on a bill to Sir Nicholas Crisp. Has submitted English and French sailcloth for comparison to the King, who agrees that the English does "far surpass the French in goodness, and the selvage better," desiring that by all means the manufacture be encouraged. The Lizard has arrived from St. Malo, with 200 bales of Noyals and Vittry canvas. [*Adm. Paper.*]

Sept.?

65. Petition of John Avery, soldier, to the King, for three years' arrears of pay due to him for service in Ireland, whence he was called in February 1665, to serve against the Dutch; lost his leg on June 3, and now lies in St. Thomas Hospital, Southwark; begs also for the pay due to sick and wounded soldiers there.

Sept.?

66. Petition of John Willoughby, mayor, and other Merchants of Bristol, adventurers to Virginia, to the King, for a convoy to be sent to Virginia to escort back 24 ships which they have sent thither, a far greater number than they intended, but that the trade from London and other places is obstructed by the plague; these ships produce a large revenue in customs, and supply many mariners, but the Dutch are making great preparations to surprise them in their way homewards. Signed by John Willoughby, mayor, and 20 others.

VOL. CXXXIII.

1665.
Sept. ? 67. Petition of Captain John Casy to the King. Details his past services, for which on a former petition he obtained a reference to the late Lord Fitzharding, ordering him to be made equal to his fellow officers if his statements were true, but has yet received nothing; prays payment of his arrears from the privy purse, or he and his family must perish.

Sept. ? 68. Petition of Abraham Chapman, late of Amsterdam, to the King. On the declaring of war with the States General, resolved to remove to England, and procured a protection, 10 Aug.; notwithstanding which, two chests of buff skins, sent by him to Middleburg to be shipped for Ostend, and thence for London, were carried with the ship into Dunkirk, by a French vessel. Requests redress.

Sept. ? 69. Petition of the two Clerks of the Carriages and all the Carttakers to the King, for a warrant for allowance to them of boardwages for the year from Michaelmas 1663 to 1664, as granted to several servants, notwithstanding the order of suspension.

Sept. ? 70. Similar petition, to the same effect.

Sept. ? 71. Petition of Francis Crake, the King's footman, to the Queen, to obtain his release from the porter's lodge, where he lies at a cost of 5s. a day; was committed for asking the falconer for five dead partridges, bringing them to Salisbury, and intending to eat them unless inquired for; served Her Majesty ever since her arrival till Christmas last, when he entered the King's service, and did nothing worthy of displeasure.

Sept. ? 72. Petition of Hugh Fisher, trumpeter in ordinary, to the King, for a recommendation to the Duke of Albemarle, master of the horse, to allow him to remain in a house in the Mews, Charing Cross, which he purchased from Sir Wm. Armorer; a maid servant was visited with sickness, but is now recovered, yet his house was shut up a whole month; has been at a great charge in cleansing it, but the surveyor of stables threatens to turn out his family.

Sept. ? 73. Petition of His Majesty's Gondoliers to the King, for speedy payment of their arrears of wages, being dismissed the service, and for some consideration for their expenses; were at great charge last year, in bringing their wives and families from Venice, and will be at as much in returning thither; fear being stayed in Flanders, on account of the sickness here, if they do not get passage before the 40 days limited are expired.

Sept. ? 74. Petition of Col. Edward Grey, on behalf of himself and the Earl of Arran, to the King, for stay of a lease ordered to pass by immediate warrant to the Earl of Carlingford and Sir Edw. Green, of lands left by the sea in Cumberland; the petitioners were the first discoverers, having made a return of the lands on a commission, and having a prior grant.

75. Petition of Richard Gwynne and Arthur Crispin, watermen, to the King, for permission to return home, to preserve themselves

Vol. CXXXIII.

1665.

and families, at least during this great visitation; were informed against for obstructing the impress of watermen, sent to prison seven days, and then to sea on board the Bull, which is now returned home.

Sept.? 76. Petition of James Halsall, cup-bearer, to the King, for reversion after —— Crisp, son of Sir Nich. Crisp, of the office of Collector of Customs outward in the port of London.

Sept.? 77. Petition of Major Henshaw to the King, for allowance from the contingent money for the clothes which he provided for some of his company, ordered on board the Charles, who were slain in the engagement; in the haste they were thrown overboard in their new clothes, so that he had to raise and clothe 100 more; also for allowances for those who ran away or were accidentally left behind, and therefore have no tickets, and for a second drummer.

Sept.? 78. Petition of Patrick Melvin to the King, for a grant of the estates, value 300*l.*, of Nich. Gronne, of Southampton Buildings, who hanged himself. Was the last person sent by the Marquis of Montrose to His Majesty at Breda. Served in the Scotch Guard in France, and then at Tangiers.

Sept.? 79. Petition of Willm. Miller to the King, for an audience; having received no answer to many petitions, is forced to remain with his family lying at death's door, in Lambeth, where they are in hourly danger of the raging pestilence. Is sure his requests would be granted, were His Majesty informed of his loyal endeavours towards the Restoration.

Sept.? 80. Petition of Edward Phillipps, barber to the household, to the King, for relief. A stranger, supposed to be visited with the sickness, ran into his tent in his absence, whereon the tent and all his goods and instruments of livelihood were burnt, he confined, and his servants sent away, according to the orders for preservation of the Court, so that he lost his trade and is utterly ruined.

Sept.? 81. Petition of the Ropemakers at Portsmouth Dockyard to the King, for payment of their arrears, to save them from utter ruin. For want of ready money they have to give 1*s.* 6*d.* for what is worth 1*s.*; their creditors threaten them with prison, and other places being visited, they are brought into terror of destruction.

Sept.? 82. Petition of Lieut. Darby Riordan to Lord Arlington, for employment. Served during the King's travels abroad; was enlisted into the Foot Guards as a reformed officer, but is now reduced to insupportable misery, by the loss of Lord Muskerry.

Sept. 83. Petition of Capt. John Sherman to the King, for an ensign's place in His Majesty's own company, if Mr. Stradling, now ensign, be promoted to the place bestowed on the death of Lord Wentworth on Capt. Barker. Served the late King till the disbanding at Truro; then as captain of a private man-of-war till commissions were recalled; was taken prisoner at Colchester, and

Vol. CXXXIII.

1665.

kept two years; then served in Scotland and Flanders, and his bail was imprisoned and forced by Cromwell to pay 1,000*l.* for his acting against the then government.

Sept.? 84. Petition of Capt. Anthony Stampe to the King, for command of the next vacant company in the new levies; is an old tried officer, and has suffered much for the Crown.

Sept.? 85. Petition of Christopher Tart to the King, for a command in the army now raising. Served the late King in the rebellion as captain-lieutenant, and His Majesty in his maritime affairs in Normandy, and in the present war with the Dutch.

Sept.? 86. Petition of Rice Vaughan, prisoner in the Tower, to the King and Council, for release on security for good conduct, an allowance for maintenance, and leave to walk on the leads with his keeper. Has been in prison since May 25, and not allowed to take air since the increase of the sickness. Has had to sell his household goods for support, and has little left beside his practice.

Sept.? 87. Petition of Eliz., widow of James Wheeler, to the King, to obtain her payment of 23*l.*, due to her husband as master of the ship Diligence, for conveying goods from Deptford to Portsmouth. The [Navy] Comrs. cannot pay her, because her bill is above 20*l.* Her husband went volunteer in the Ruby as master's mate, and was slain in the last engagement, 2 June.

Sept. 88. Petition of Col. Stephen White to the King, for a small sum of money to cover his nakedness; has received no allowance for 17 months.

Sept.? 89. Petition of the Workmen of the Privy Gardens, for money to maintain themselves; being scattered abroad by reason of the sickness, cannot be trusted as formerly.

Sept.? 90. Petition of the Grand Juries of Yorkshire to the House of Commons, that no Scotch and Irish cattle may be allowed to be brought into those parts, between June and February. The multitude daily brought in glut the markets, so that farmer and grazier cannot sell their cattle at cost price, and much coin is carried out of the kingdom.

Sept.? 91. Commission [from the Sub-commissioners of Prizes in the port of London] to —— Key and Hen. Rumbold to act as storehouse keepers for prize goods in that port. [*Draft.*]

Sept.? 92. Warrant to pay to Col. W. Legg, Lieut. of Ordnance, 3,140*l.* 2*s.* 0*d.* for munitions, materials, &c., for a train of 24 pieces of artillery. Minute. [*Draft.*]

Sept.? 93. Warrant to pay from the 250,000*l.* advanced on the farm of the chimney money 60,000*l.* to the Victualler of the Navy; 90,000*l.* to the Treasurer of the Navy for wages of seamen and workmen in the yards and docks; 50,000*l.* to Edw. Backwell, in part of a debt

1665. Vol. CXXIII.

due from the King to him, and the remaining 50,000*l.* to Sir G. Carteret, Treasurer of the Navy, to be transmitted to the Bishop of Munster, in part also of a debt due to him. [*Draft.*]

Sept. ? 94. Warrant from Lord Arlington to all Magistrates, &c., to permit the bearers, domestic servants of the Conde de Molina, Spanish Ambassador, who have been for many weeks at Court, where there is no infection of sickness, to go to his house for goods and furniture, which he requires for his accommodation at Oxford. [*Draft.*]

Sept. Memoranda [by Williamson from the Signet books] of warrants, &c., passed during the month, the uncalendared portions of which are as follow :—

Note that fines and forfeitures upon prohibited and uncustomed goods are ordered to be paid into the privy purse, excepting the double customs granted out of them to the Farmers of Customs.

Privy seal to Sir G. Carteret to pay interest half-yearly on such moneys as he has taken up or shall take up for the naval expedition.

Grant to Sir W. Killigrew of a pension of 500*l.* a year out of the excise of London and Middlesex.

[*Domestic Corresp., July* 1665, *Vol.* CXXVII, *No.* 132.]

Sept. 95. Chris. Battars, gunner of the Santa Maria, to [Sam. Pepys]. Has not money to complete the necessary fittings of the ship. Begs to be allowed part of his pay before going to sea, and an order for staff to build a cabin. Has lain upon deck ever since he belonged to the ship. [*Adm. Paper.*] *Encloses,*

95. I. *Chris. Battars to Sam. Pepys. Desires a port rope for the Sta. Maria.*

Sept. 96. Constance Pley to Sir John Mennes. Sends the seventh bill completing last year's parcel of French goods, amounting in all to 17,234*l.* Has drawn bills for 15,000*l.* Trusts to him as the father of her hopes and chiefest patron, to further her interests with the rest of the Commissioners. [*Adm. Paper.*]

Sept. Sarum. 97. —— to the King. James Hely, of Castle Street, Salisbury, a captain under the usurped powers, and chief stickler and governor there, is a dangerous person, and is constantly abroad, a month at a time; when he returns, 40 or 50 nonconformists flock to him for intelligence.

Sept. ? 98. M. De la Fabvolière, engineer, to the King. Has been a year in his service without assured employment or pension, and being reduced to great necessity, begs to be fixed in his service or pension. [*French.*]

Vol. CXXIII.

1665.
Sept. ? 99. Rob. Marsham to ———. Went to Fritwell to visit Sir Sam. Danvers, when they both, with Pope Danvers and Mr. Jackman, went to an alehouse to drink. Particulars of a fray between the two latter, in which the writer parted them, but the next morning Danvers and Jackman fought a duel, and the latter was slain. Danvers is found guilty of wilful murder at the coroner's inquest, but nothing was done against himself.

Sept. ? 100. Jane Rokeby and Mary Phillips to the Duke of Albemarle. Have waited by his advice on the Secretary of State, to procure the release of Sam. Goodwin, prisoner in the Tower, and were referred to the Council. Entreat him to effect their request when presented, without Goodwin's taking the Oath of Allegiance.

[Sept.] 101. Account by the Officers of Works of the charges for repairing the King's house at Nonsuch since August 1; total, 455*l.* 7*s.* 1½*d.* With notes for a warrant to Mr. May, paymaster of the works, to pay 305*l.*, 105*l.* having been received already, and also 300*l.* for repair of the Duke of Monmouth's lodgings near the Cockpit.

Sept. 102. List of 11 persons in Leicestershire, Derbyshire, Cheshire, Staffordshire, Wales, and Ireland, who have been engaged in this business.

Sept. 103. List of nine persons secured at Newcastle, and of three that are fled. The writer thinks that more ought to be apprehended, but there is greater danger from the partiality of friends than from enemies.

Sept. ? 104. Request by George Browne and Col. Thos. Culpepper, the King's gunfounders, that the undertakers, to whom by Act of Parliament the making of the River Medway is consigned, will take care that the branch from Broadford Bridge to Yealding may be done at once, as very needful for the transport of the ordnance, which is to be ready by April 1, the roads being almost impassable.

Sept. Lists sent by Morgan Lodge to Williamson of ships in the Downs during the month, viz.:—

	Date.	King's.	Merchants'.	Wind.
105.	Sept. 22	3	4	N.W.
106.	23	6	7	W.
107.	24	6	7	—

GENERAL INDEX.

A.

B.

C.

D.

F.

G

H.

I.

J.

K.

L.

M.

N.

P.

M.

R.

S.

U

V.

W

Y.

ERRATA.

Page. No.

12, 63, Margin, *for* Woolwich, *read* Harwich.

34, 65, *for* Thos. Ayliffe, *read* Capt. Thos.

89, 23, and p. 91, No. 91, *for* Metal, *read* Main.

104, 87, *for* Ansas, *read* Arras.

107, dele the third entry from the bottom.

110, 7th entry from the top, *for* Wiska, *read* Wilkes.

122, 4th entry from the bottom, *for* treasurer of prize goods, *read* treasurer of moneys arising from the sale of prize ships and goods.

129, 4th entry from the top, *for* Fane, *read* Farr.

132, 7, *after* burgesses, *read* of Hertford.

153, 183, last line, *for* pensions, *read* board wages.

179, 118, margin, *for* Norwich, *read* Harwich.

194, 95, *for* Lesley, *read* Lesley.

208, 141, dele the whole entry.

241, 83–84, *for* Leghorn and Lisbon, *read* Lisbourne.

279, 70, dele the entry.

280, 74, *for* is on board, *read* is ordered on board.

299, 10. n., *for* Ansley, *read* Ansley.

329, 60, *for* Wm. Turner, *read* Dr. Wm.

338, 67. n., *for* Fras. Liddell, *read* Sir Fras.

436, 4th entry from the bottom, *for* Sir Robert Anson, *read* Sir Roger.

437, 184. n., *for* L. T. M. and W., *read* L. T. and M. W.

LIST OF WORKS

PUBLISHED

By the late Record and State Paper Commissioners, or under the Direction of the Right Honourable the Master of the Rolls, which may be purchased of Messrs. Longman and Co., London; Messrs. J. H. and J. Parker, Oxford and London; Messrs. Macmillan and Co., Cambridge and London; Messrs. A. and C. Black, Edinburgh; and Mr. A. Thom, Dublin.

PUBLIC RECORDS AND STATE PAPERS.

ROTULORUM ORIGINALIUM IN CURIA SCACCARII ABBREVIATIO. Henry III.—Edward III. *Edited by* HENRY PLAYFORD, Esq. 2 vols. folio (1805—1810). *Price* 25*s*. boards, or 12*s*. 6*d*. each.

CALENDARIUM INQUISITIONUM POST MORTEM SIVE ESCAETARUM. Henry III.—Richard III. *Edited by* JOHN CALEY and JOHN BAYLEY, Esqrs. Vols. 2, 3, and 4, folio (1806—1808; 1821—1828), boards: vols. 2 and 3, *price* 21*s*. each; vol. 4, *price* 24*s*.

LIBRORUM MANUSCRIPTORUM BIBLIOTHECÆ HARLEIANÆ CATALOGUS. Vol. 4. *Edited by* The Rev. T. H. HORNE, (1812), folio, boards. *Price* 18*s*.

ABBREVIATIO PLACITORUM, Richard I.—Edward II. *Edited by* The Right Hon. GEORGE ROSE and W. ILLINGWORTH, Esq. 1 vol. folio (1811), boards. *Price* 18*s*.

LIBRI CENSUALIS vocati DOMESDAY-BOOK, INDICES. *Edited by* Sir HENRY ELLIS. Small folio (1816), boards (Domesday-Book, vol. 3). *Price* 21*s*.

LIBRI CENSUALIS vocati DOMESDAY-BOOK, ADDITAMENTA EX CODIC. ANTIQUISS. *Edited by* Sir HENRY ELLIS. Small folio (1816), boards (Domesday-Book, vol. 4). *Price* 21*s*.

STATUTES OF THE REALM, large folio. Vols. 4 (in 2 parts), 7, 8, 9, 10, and 11, including 2 vols. of Indices (1819—1828). *Edited by* Sir T. E. TOMLINS, JOHN RAITHBY, JOHN CALEY, and WM. ELLIOTT, Esqrs. *Price* 31*s*. 6*d*. each, except the Alphabetical and Chronological Indices, *price* 30*s*. each.

VALOR ECCLESIASTICUS, temp. Henry VIII., Auctoritate Regia institutus. *Edited by* JOHN CALEY, Esq., and the Rev. JOSEPH HUNTER. Vols. 3 to 6, folio (1810, &c.), boards. *Price* 25s. each.

*** The Introduction is also published in 8vo., cloth. *Price* 2s. 6d.

ROTULI SCOTIÆ IN TURRI LONDINENSI ET IN DOMO CAPITULARI WESTMONASTERIENSI ASSERVATI. 19 Edward I.—Henry VIII. *Edited by* DAVID MACPHERSON, JOHN CALEY, and W. ILLINGWORTH, Esqrs., and the Rev. T. H. HORNE. 2 vols. folio (1814—1819), boards. *Price* 42s.

"FŒDERA, CONVENTIONES, LITTERÆ," &c.; or, Rymer's Fœdera, A.D. 1066—1391. New Edition, Vol. 2, Part 2, and Vol. 3, Parts 1 and 2, folio (1821—1830). *Edited by* JOHN CALEY and FRED. HOLBROOKE, Esqrs. *Price* 21s. each Part.

DUCATUS LANCASTRIÆ CALENDARIUM INQUISITIONUM POST MORTEM, &c. Part 3, Calendar to the Pleadings, &c., Henry VII.—Ph. and Mary; and Calendar to the Pleadings, 1—13 Elizabeth. Part 4, Calendar to Pleadings to end of Elizabeth. (1827—1834.) *Edited by* R. J. HARPER, JOHN CALEY, and WM. MINCHIN, Esqrs. Folio, boards, Part 3 (or Vol. 2) *price* 31s. 6d.; and Part 4 (or Vol. 3), *price* 21s.

CALENDARS OF THE PROCEEDINGS IN CHANCERY IN THE REIGN OF QUEEN ELIZABETH; to which are prefixed, Examples of earlier Proceedings in that Court from Richard II. to Elizabeth, from the originals in the Tower. *Edited by* JOHN BAYLEY, Esq. Vols. 2 and 3 (1830—1832), folio, boards, *price* 21s. each.

PARLIAMENTARY WRITS AND WRITS OF MILITARY SUMMONS, together with the Records and Muniments relating to the Suit and Service due and performed to the King's High Court of Parliament and the Councils of the Realm. Edward I., II. *Edited by* SIR FRANCIS PALGRAVE. (1830—1834). Folio, boards, Vol. 2, Division 1, Edward II., *price* 21s.; Vol. 2, Division 2, *price* 21s.; Vol. 2, Division 3, *price* 42s.

ROTULI LITTERARUM CLAUSARUM IN TURRI LONDINENSI ASSERVATI. 2 vols. folio (1833—1844). The first volume, 1204—1224. The second volume, 1224—1227. *Edited by* THOMAS DUFFUS HARDY, Esq. *Price* 81s., cloth; or separately, Vol. 1, *price* 63s.; Vol. 2, *price* 18s.

PROCEEDINGS AND ORDINANCES OF THE PRIVY COUNCIL OF ENGLAND, 10 Richard II.—33 Henry VIII. *Edited by* Sir N. HARRIS NICOLAS. 7 vols. royal 8vo. (1834—1837), cloth 98s.; or separately, *price* 14s. each.

ROTULI LITTERARUM PATENTIUM IN TURRI LONDINENSI ASSERVATI, A.D. 1201—1216. *Edited by* THOMAS DUFFUS HARDY, Esq. 1 vol. folio (1835), cloth. *Price* 31s. 6d.

*** The Introduction is also published in 8vo., cloth. *Price* 9s.

ROTULI CURIÆ REGIS. Rolls and Records of the Court held before the King's Justiciars or Justices. 6 Richard I.—1 John. *Edited by* SIR FRANCIS PALGRAVE. 2 vols. royal 8vo. (1835), cloth. *Price* 28s.

ROTULI NORMANNIÆ IN TURRI LONDINENSI ASSERVATI, A.D. 1200—1205; also, from 1417 to 1418. *Edited by* THOMAS DUFFUS HARDY, Esq. 1 vol. royal 8vo. (1835), cloth. *Price* 12s. 6d.

ROTULI DE OBLATIS ET FINIBUS IN TURRI LONDINENSI ASSERVATI, tempore Regis Johannis. *Edited by* THOMAS DUFFUS HARDY, Esq. 1 vol. royal 8vo. (1835), cloth. *Price* 18s.

EXCERPTA E ROTULIS FINIUM IN TURRI LONDINENSI ASSERVATIS. Henry III., 1216—1272. *Edited by* CHARLES ROBERTS, Esq. 2 vols. royal 8vo. (1835, 1836), cloth, *price* 32s.; or separately, Vol. 1, *price* 14s.; Vol. 2, *price* 18s.

FINES SIVE PEDES FINIUM SIVE FINALES CONCORDIÆ IN CURIA DOMINI REGIS. 7 Richard I.—16 John (1195—1214). *Edited by* the Rev. JOSEPH HUNTER. In Counties. 2 vols. royal 8vo. (1835—1844), cloth, *price* 11s.; or separately, Vol. 1, *price* 8s. 6d.; Vol. 2, *price* 2s. 6d.

ANCIENT KALENDARS AND INVENTORIES OF THE TREASURY OF HIS MAJESTY'S EXCHEQUER; together with Documents illustrating the History of that Repository. *Edited by* Sir FRANCIS PALGRAVE. 3 vols. royal 8vo. (1836), cloth. *Price* 42s.

DOCUMENTS AND RECORDS illustrating the History of Scotland, and the Transactions between the Crowns of Scotland and England; preserved in the Treasury of Her Majesty's Exchequer. *Edited by* Sir FRANCIS PALGRAVE. 1 vol. royal 8vo. (1837), cloth. *Price* 18s.

ROTULI CHARTARUM IN TURRI LONDINENSI ASSERVATI, A.D. 1199—1216. *Edited by* THOMAS DUFFUS HARDY, Esq. 1 vol. folio (1837), cloth. *Price* 30s.

REGISTRUM vulgariter nuncupatum "The Record of Caernarvon," e codice MS. Harleiano, 696, descriptum. *Edited by* SIR HENRY ELLIS. 1 vol. folio (1838), cloth. *Price* 31s. 6d.

REPORTS OF THE PROCEEDINGS OF THE RECORD COMMISSIONERS, 1800 to 1819, 2 vols., folio, boards: *Price* 5l. 5s. Report of their Proceedings, 1831 to 1837, 1 vol., folio, boards: *Price* 8s.

ANCIENT LAWS AND INSTITUTES OF ENGLAND; comprising Laws enacted under the Anglo-Saxon Kings, from Æthelbirht to Cnut, with an English Translation of the Saxon; the Laws called Edward the Confessor's; the Laws of William the Conqueror, and those ascribed to Henry the First; also Monumenta Ecclesiastica Anglicana, from the 7th to the 10th century; and the Ancient Latin Version of the Anglo-Saxon Laws; with a compendious Glossary, &c. *Edited by* BENJAMIN THORPE, Esq. 1 vol. folio (1840), cloth. *Price* 40s.

—— 2 vols. royal 8vo. cloth. *Price* 30s.

ANCIENT LAWS AND INSTITUTES OF WALES; comprising Laws supposed to be enacted by Howel the Good; modified by subsequent Regulations under the Native Princes, prior to the Conquest by Edward the First; and anomalous Laws, consisting principally of Institutions which, by the Statute of Ruddlan, were admitted to continue in force. With an English Translation of the Welsh Text. To which are added, a few Latin Transcripts, containing Digests of the

Welsh Laws, principally of the Dimetian Code. With Indices and Glossary. *Edited by* Aneurin Owen, Esq. 1 vol. folio (1841), cloth. *Price* 44s.

—— 2 vols. royal 8vo. cloth. *Price* 36s.

Rotuli de Liberate ac de Misis et Praestitis, Regnante Johanne. *Edited by* Thomas Duffus Hardy, Esq. 1 vol. royal 8vo. (1844), cloth. *Price* 6s.

The Great Rolls of the Pipe for the Second, Third, and Fourth Years of the Reign of King Henry the Second, 1155—1158. *Edited by* the Rev. Joseph Hunter. 1 vol. royal 8vo. (1844), cloth. *Price* 4s. 6d.

The Great Roll of the Pipe for the First Year of the Reign of King Richard the First, 1189—1190. *Edited by* the Rev. Joseph Hunter. 1 vol. royal 8vo. (1844), cloth. *Price* 6s.

Documents Illustrative of English History in the 13th and 14th centuries, selected from the Records in the Exchequer. *Edited by* Henry Cole, Esq. 1 vol. fcp. folio (1844), cloth. *Price* 45s. 6d.

Modus Tenendi Parliamentum. An Ancient Treatise on the Mode of holding the Parliament in England. *Edited by* Thomas Duffus Hardy, Esq. 1 vol. 8vo. (1846), cloth. *Price* 2s. 6d.

Monumenta Historica Britannica, or, Materials for the History of Britain from the earliest period. Vol. 1, extending to the Norman Conquest. Prepared, and illustrated with Notes, by the late Henry Petrie, Esq., F.S.A., Keeper of the Records in the Tower of London, assisted by the Rev. John Sharpe, Rector of Castle Eaton, Wilts. Finally completed for publication, and with an Introduction, by Thomas Duffus Hardy, Esq., Assistant Keeper of Records. (Printed by command of Her Majesty.) Folio (1848). *Price* 42s.

Registrum Magni Sigilli Regum Scotorum in Archivis Publicis asservatum. A.D. 1306—1424. *Edited by* Thomas Thomson, Esq. Folio (1814). *Price* 15s.

The Acts of the Parliaments of Scotland. 11 vols. folio (1814—1844). Vol. 1, *Edited by* Thomas Thomson and Cosmo Innes, Esqrs. *Price* 42s. Also, Vols. 4, 7, 8, 9, 10, 11; *price* 10s. 6d. each.

The Acts of the Lords Auditors of Causes and Complaints. A.D., 1466—1494. *Edited by* Thomas Thomson, Esq. Folio (1839). *Price* 10s. 6d.

The Acts of the Lords of Council in Civil Causes. A.D. 1478—1495. *Edited by* Thomas Thomson, Esq. Folio (1839). *Price* 10s. 6d.

Issue Roll of Thomas de Brantingham, Bishop of Exeter, Lord High Treasurer of England, containing Payments out of His Majesty's Revenue, 44 Edward III., 1370. *Edited by* Frederick Devon, Esq. 1 vol. 4to. (1835), cloth. *Price* 35s.

—— Royal 8vo. cloth. *Price* 25s.

ISSUES OF THE EXCHEQUER, containing similar matter to the above, James I.; extracted from the Pell Records. *Edited by* FREDERICK DEVON, Esq. 1 vol. 4to. (1836), cloth. *Price* 30s.

—— Royal 8vo. cloth. *Price* 21s.

ISSUES OF THE EXCHEQUER, containing similar matter to the above, Henry III.—Henry VI.; extracted from the Pell Records. *Edited by* FREDERICK DEVON, Esq. 1 vol. 4to. (1837), cloth. *Price* 40s.

—— Royal 8vo. cloth. *Price* 30s.

NOTES OF MATERIALS FOR THE HISTORY OF PUBLIC DEPARTMENTS. By F. S. THOMAS, Esq. Demy folio (1846). *Price* 10s.

HANDBOOK TO THE PUBLIC RECORDS. By F. S. THOMAS, Esq. Royal 8vo. (1853.) *Price* 12s.

STATE PAPERS DURING THE REIGN OF HENRY THE EIGHTH. 11 vols. 4to., cloth, (1830—1852), with Indices of Persons and Places. *Price* 5*l.* 15*s.* 6*d.*; or separately, *price* 10*s.* 6*d.* each.

Vol. I.—Domestic Correspondence.
Vols. II. & III.—Correspondence relating to Ireland.
Vols. IV. & V.—Correspondence relating to Scotland.
Vols. VI. to XI.—Correspondence between England and Foreign Courts.

HISTORICAL NOTES RELATIVE TO THE HISTORY OF ENGLAND; from the Accession of Henry VIII. to the Death of Queen Anne (1509—1714). Designed as a Book of instant Reference for ascertaining the Dates of Events mentioned in History and Manuscripts. The Name of every Person and Event mentioned in History within the above period is placed in Alphabetical and Chronological Order, and the Authority whence taken is given in each case, whether from Printed History or from Manuscripts. By F. S. THOMAS, Esq., Secretary of the Public Record Office. 3 vols. 8vo. (1856.) *Price* 40s.

CALENDARS OF STATE PAPERS.

[Imperial 8vo. *Price* 15s. each Volume.]

Calendar of State Papers, Domestic Series, of the Reigns of Edward VI., Mary, and Elizabeth, 1547–1580, preserved in Her Majesty's Public Record Office. *Edited by* Robert Lemon, Esq., F.S.A. 1856.

Calendar of State Papers, Domestic Series, of the Reign of James I., preserved in Her Majesty's Public Record Office. *Edited by* Mary Anne Everett Green. 1857–1859.

Vol. I.—1603–1610.
Vol. II.—1611–1618.
Vol. III.—1619–1623.
Vol. IV.—1623–1625, with Addenda.

Calendar of State Papers, Domestic Series, of the Reign of Charles I., preserved in Her Majesty's Public Record Office. *Edited by* John Bruce, Esq., V.P.S.A. 1858–1862.

Vol. I.—1625–1626.
Vol. II.—1627–1628.
Vol. III.—1628–1629.
Vol. IV.—1629–1631.
Vol. V.—1631–1633.

Calendar of State Papers, Domestic Series, of the Reign of Charles II., preserved in Her Majesty's Public Record Office. *Edited by* Mary Anne Everett Green. 1860–1863.

Vol. I.—1660–1661.
Vol. II.—1661–1662.
Vol. III.—1663–1664.
Vol. IV.—1664–1665.

Calendar of State Papers relating to Scotland, preserved in Her Majesty's Public Record Office. *Edited by* Markham John Thorpe, Esq., of St. Edmund Hall, Oxford. 1858.

Vol. I., the Scottish Series, of the Reigns of Henry VIII., Edward VI., Mary, and Elizabeth, 1509–1589.
Vol. II., the Scottish Series, of the Reign of Elizabeth, 1589–1603; an Appendix to the Scottish Series, 1543–1592; and the State Papers relating to Mary Queen of Scots during her Detention in England, 1568–1587.

Calendar of State Papers relating to Ireland, preserved in Her Majesty's Public Record Office. *Edited by* H. C. Hamilton, Esq. 1860.

Vol. I.—1509–1573.

Calendar of State Papers, Colonial Series, preserved in Her Majesty's Public Record Office, and elsewhere. *Edited by* W. Noël Sainsbury, Esq. 1860–1862.

Vol. I.—America and West Indies, 1574–1660.
Vol. II.—East Indies, China, and Japan, 1513–1616.

Calendar of State Papers, Foreign Series, of the Reign of Edward VI. *Edited by* W. B. Turnbull, Esq., of Lincoln's Inn, Barrister-at-Law, and Correspondant du Comité Impérial des Travaux Historiques et des Sociétés Savants de France. 1861.

Calendar of State Papers, Foreign Series, of the Reign of Mary. *Edited by* W. B. Turnbull, Esq., of Lincoln's Inn, Barrister-at-Law, and Correspondant du Comité Impérial des Travaux Historiques et des Sociétés Savants de France. 1861.

Calendar of Letters and Papers, Foreign and Domestic, of the Reign of Henry VIII., preserved in the Public Record Office, the British Museum, &c. *Edited by* J. S. Brewer, M.A., Professor of English Literature, King's College, London. 1862.

Vol. I.—1509–1514.

Calendar of Letters, Despatches, and State Papers, relating to the Negotiations between England and Spain, preserved in the Archives at Simancas, and elsewhere. *Edited by* G. A. Bergenroth.

Vol. I.—Hen. VII.—1485–1509.

In the Press.

Calendar of State Papers relating to Ireland, preserved in Her Majesty's Public Record Office. *Edited by* H. C. Hamilton, Esq. Vol. II.

Calendar of Letters and Papers, Foreign and Domestic, of the Reign of Henry VIII., preserved in Her Majesty's Public Record Office, the British Museum, &c. *Edited by* J. S. Brewer, M.A., Professor of English Literature, King's College, London. Vol. II.

Calendar of State Papers, Domestic Series, of the Reign of Charles II., preserved in Her Majesty's Public Record Office. *Edited by* Mary Anne Everett Green. Vol. V.

Calendar of State Papers, Domestic Series, of the Reign of Elizabeth (continued), preserved in Her Majesty's Public Record Office. *Edited by* Robert Lemon, Esq., F.S.A.

Calendar of State Papers, Domestic Series, of the Reign of Charles I., preserved in Her Majesty's Public Record Office. *Edited by* John Bruce, Esq., F.S.A. Vol. VI.

Calendar of State Papers, Foreign Series, of the Reign of Elizabeth. *Edited by* the Rev. J. Stevenson, M.A., of University College, Durham.

In Progress.

Calendar of State Papers relating to England, preserved in the Archives of Venice, &c. *Edited by* Rawdon Brown, Esq.

Calendar of Letters, Despatches, and State Papers relating to the Negotiations between England and Spain, preserved in the Archives at Simancas, and elsewhere. *Edited by* G. A. Bergenroth. Vol. II. Henry VIII.

Calendar of State Papers, Colonial Series, preserved in Her Majesty's Public Record Office, and elsewhere. *Edited by* W. Noël Sainsbury, Esq. Vol. III. East Indies, China, and Japan.

THE CHRONICLES AND MEMORIALS OF GREAT BRITAIN AND IRELAND DURING THE MIDDLE AGES.

[ROYAL 8vo. *Price* 10s. each Volume or Part.]

1. THE CHRONICLE OF ENGLAND, by JOHN CAPGRAVE. *Edited by* the Rev. F. C. HINGESTON, M.A., of Exeter College, Oxford.

2. CHRONICON MONASTERII DE ABINGDON. Vols. I. and II. *Edited by* the Rev. J. STEVENSON, M.A., of University College, Durham, and Vicar of Leighton Buzzard.

3. LIVES OF EDWARD THE CONFESSOR. I.—La Estoire de Seint Aedward le Rei. II.—Vita Beati Edvardi Regis et Confessoris. III.—Vita Æduuardi Regis qui apud Westmonasterium requiescit. *Edited by* H. R. LUARD, M.A., Fellow and Assistant Tutor of Trinity College, Cambridge.

4. MONUMENTA FRANCISCANA; scilicet, I.—Thomas de Eccleston de Adventu Fratrum Minorum in Angliam. II.—Adæ de Marisco Epistolæ. III.—Registrum Fratrum Minorum Londoniæ. *Edited by* J. S. BREWER, M.A., Professor of English Literature, King's College, London.

5. FASCICULI ZIZANIORUM MAGISTRI JOHANNIS WYCLIF CUM TRITICO. Ascribed to THOMAS NETTER, of WALDEN, Provincial of the Carmelite Order in England, and Confessor to King Henry the Fifth. *Edited by* the Rev. W. W. SHIRLEY, M.A., Tutor and late Fellow of Wadham College, Oxford.

6. THE BUIK OF THE CRONICLIS OF SCOTLAND; or, A Metrical Version of the History of Hector Boece; by WILLIAM STEWART. Vols. I., II., and III. *Edited by* W. B. TURNBULL, Esq., of Lincoln's Inn, Barrister-at-Law.

7. JOHANNIS CAPGRAVE LIBER DE ILLUSTRIBUS HENRICIS. *Edited by* the Rev. F. C. HINGESTON, M.A., of Exeter College, Oxford.

8. HISTORIA MONASTERII S. AUGUSTINI CANTUARIENSIS, by THOMAS OF ELMHAM, formerly Monk and Treasurer of that Foundation. *Edited by* C. HARDWICK, M.A., Fellow of St. Catharine's Hall, and Christian Advocate in the University of Cambridge.

9. EULOGIUM (HISTORIARUM SIVE TEMPORIS), Chronicon ab Orbe condito usque ad Annum Domini 1366; a Monacho quodam Malmesbiriensi exaratum. Vols. I. and II. *Edited by* F. S. HAYDON, Esq., B.A.

10. MEMORIALS OF KING HENRY THE SEVENTH: Bernardi Andreæ Tholosatis Vita Regis Henrici Septimi; necnon alia quædam ad eundem Regem spectantia. *Edited by* JAMES GAIRDNER, Esq.

11. Memorials of Henry the Fifth. I.—Vita Henrici Quinti, Roberto Redmanno auctore. II.—Versus Rhythmici in laudem Regis Henrici Quinti. III.—Elmhami Liber Metricus de Henrico V. *Edited by* C. A. Cole, Esq.

12. Munimenta Gildhallæ Londoniensis; Liber Albus, Liber Custumarum, et Liber Horn, in archivis Gildhallæ asservati. Vol. I., Liber Albus. Vol. II. (in Two Parts), Liber Custumarum. Vol. III., Translation of the Anglo-Norman Passages in Liber Albus, Glossaries, Appendices, and Index. *Edited by* H. T. Riley, Esq., M.A., Barrister-at-Law.

13. Chronica Johannis de Oxenedes. *Edited by* Sir H. Ellis, K.H.

14. A Collection of Political Poems and Songs relating to English History, from the Accession of Edward III. to the Reign of Henry VIII. Vols. I. and II. *Edited by* T. Wright, Esq., M.A.

15. The "Opus Tertium," "Opus Minus," &c., of Roger Bacon. *Edited by* J. S. Brewer, M.A., Professor of English Literature, King's College, London.

16. Bartholomæi de Cotton, Monachi Norwicensis, Historia Anglicana (A.D. 449—1298). *Edited by* H. R. Luard, M.A., Fellow and Assistant Tutor of Trinity College, Cambridge.

17. Brut y Tywysogion; or, The Chronicle of the Princes of Wales. *Edited by* the Rev. J. Williams ab Ithel.

18. A Collection of Royal and Historical Letters during the Reign of Henry IV. Vol. I. *Edited by* the Rev. F. C. Hingeston, M.A., of Exeter College, Oxford.

19. The Repressor of over much Blaming of the Clergy. By Reginald Pecock, sometime Bishop of Chichester. Vols. I. and II. *Edited by* C. Babington, D.D., Fellow of St. John's College, Cambridge.

20. Annales Cambriæ. *Edited by* the Rev. J. Williams ab Ithel.

21. The Works of Giraldus Cambrensis. Vols. I. and II. *Edited by* J. S. Brewer, M.A., Professor of English Literature, King's College, London.

22. Letters and Papers illustrative of the Wars of the English in France during the Reign of Henry the Sixth, King of England. Vol. I. *Edited by* the Rev. J. Stevenson, M.A., of University College, Durham, and Vicar of Leighton Buzzard.

23. The Anglo-Saxon Chronicle, according to the several Original Authorities. Vol. I., Original Texts. Vol. II., Translation. *Edited by* B. Thorpe, Esq., Member of the Royal Academy of Sciences at Munich, and of the Society of Netherlandish Literature at Leyden.

24. Letters and Papers illustrative of the Reigns of Richard III. and Henry VII. Vol. I. *Edited by* James Gairdner, Esq.

25. Letters of Bishop Grosseteste, illustrative of the Social Condition of his Time. *Edited by* H. R. Luard, M.A., Fellow and Assistant Tutor of Trinity College, Cambridge.

26. Descriptive Catalogue of Manuscripts relating to the History of Great Britain and Ireland. Vol. I. (in Two Parts); Anterior to the Norman Invasion. *By* T. Duffus Hardy, Esq., Deputy Keeper of the Public Records.

27. ROYAL AND OTHER HISTORICAL LETTERS ILLUSTRATIVE OF THE REIGN OF HENRY III., from the Originals in the Public Record Office. Vol. I., 1216–1235. *Selected and edited by* the Rev. W. W. SHIRLEY, Tutor and late Fellow of Wadham College, Oxford.

28. THE SAINT ALBANS' CHRONICLES:—THE ENGLISH HISTORY OF THOMAS WALSINGHAM, MONK OF SAINT ALBANS. Vol. I. 1272–1381. *Edited by* HENRY THOMAS RILEY, Esq., M.A., Barrister-at-Law.

29. CHRONICON ABBATIÆ EVESHAMENSIS, AUCTORIBUS DOMINICO PRIORE EVESHAMIÆ ET THOMA DE MARLEBERGE ABBATE, A FUNDATIONE AD ANNUM 1213, UNA CUM CONTINUATIONE AD ANNUM 1418. *Edited by* the Rev. W. D. MACRAY, M.A., Bodleian Library, Oxford.

30. RICARDI DE CIRENCESTRIA SPECULUM HISTORIALE DE GESTIS REGUM ANGLIÆ. A.D. 447—1066. *Edited by* J. E. B. MAYOR, M.A., Fellow and Assistant Tutor of St. John's College, Cambridge. Vol. I.—447–871.

In the Press.

RICARDI DE CIRENCESTRIA SPECULUM HISTORIALE DE GESTIS REGUM ANGLIÆ. Vol. II. 872–1066. *Edited by* J. E. B. MAYOR, M.A., Fellow and Assistant Tutor of St. John's College, Cambridge.

LE LIVERE DE REIS DE BRITTANIE. *Edited by* J. GLOVER, M.A., Chaplain of Trinity College, Cambridge.

RECUEIL DES CRONIQUES ET ANCHIENNES ISTORIES DE LA GRANT BRETAIGNE A PRESENT NOMME ENGLETERRE, par JEHAN DE WAURIN. *Edited by* W. HARDY, Esq.

THE WARS OF THE DANES IN IRELAND: written in the Irish language. *Edited by* the Rev. J. H. TODD, D.D., Librarian of the University of Dublin.

A COLLECTION OF SAGAS AND OTHER HISTORICAL DOCUMENTS relating to the Settlements and Descents of the Northmen on the British Isles. *Edited by* GEORGE W. DASENT, Esq., D.C.L. Oxon.

A COLLECTION OF ROYAL AND HISTORICAL LETTERS DURING THE REIGN OF HENRY IV. Vol. II. *Edited by* the Rev. F. C. HINGESTON, M.A., of Exeter College, Oxford.

EULOGIUM (HISTORIARUM SIVE TEMPORIS), Chronicon ab Orbe condito usque ad Annum Domini 1366; a Monacho quodam Malmesbiriensi exaratum. Vol. III. *Edited by* F. S. HAYDON, Esq., B.A.

LETTERS AND PAPERS ILLUSTRATIVE OF THE WARS OF THE ENGLISH IN FRANCE DURING THE REIGN OF HENRY THE SIXTH, KING OF ENGLAND. Vol. II. *Edited by* the Rev. J. STEVENSON, M.A., of University College, Durham.

POLYCHRONICON RANULPHI HIGDENI, with Trevisa's Translation. *Edited by* C. BABINGTON, B.D., Fellow of St. John's College, Cambridge.

LETTERS AND PAPERS ILLUSTRATIVE OF THE REIGNS OF RICHARD III. AND HENRY VII. Vol. II. *Edited by* JAMES GAIRDNER, Esq.

Official Correspondence of Thomas Bekynton, Secretary to Henry VI., with other Letters and Documents. *Edited by* the Rev. George Williams, B.D., Senior Fellow of King's College, Cambridge.

The Works of Giraldus Cambrensis. Vol. III. *Edited by* J. S. Brewer, M.A., Professor of English Literature, King's College, London.

Royal and other Historical Letters illustrative of the Reign of Henry III., from the Originals in the Public Record Office. Vol. II. *Selected and edited by* the Rev. W. W. Shirley, Tutor and late Fellow of Wadham College, Oxford.

Original Documents illustrative of Academical and Clerical Life and Studies at Oxford between the Reigns of Henry III. and Henry VII. *Edited by* the Rev. H. Anstey, M.A.

The History and Cartulary of St. Peter's Monastery at Gloucester. *Edited by* W. H. Hart, Esq., F.S.A.; Membre correspondant de la Société des Antiquaires de Normandie.

Year Books of the Reign of Edward the First. *Edited and translated by* Alfred John Horwood, Esq., of the Middle Temple, Barrister-at-Law.

The Saint Albans' Chronicles:—The English History of Thomas Walsingham, Monk of Saint Albans. Vol. II. *Edited by* Henry Thomas Riley, Esq., M.A., Barrister-at-Law.

Roll of the Privy Council of Ireland, 16 Richard II. *Edited by* the Rev. James Graves.

Chronicles and Memorials of the Reign of Richard the First. Vol. I. Ricardi Regis Iter Hierosolymitanum. *Edited by the* Rev. William Stubbs, M.A., Vicar of Navestock, Essex.

Annals of Tewkesbury, Dunstaple, Waverley, Margan, and Burton. *Edited by* Henry Richards Luard, M.A., Fellow and Assistant Tutor of Trinity College, and Registrary of the University, Cambridge.

In Progress.

Historia Minor Matthæi Paris. *Edited by* Sir F. Madden, K.H., Keeper of the Department of Manuscripts, British Museum.

Descriptive Catalogue of Manuscripts relating to the History of Great Britain and Ireland. Vol. II. *By* T. Duffus Hardy, Esq., Deputy Keeper of the Public Records.

March 1863.

LONDON:
Printed by George E. Eyre and William Spottiswoode,
Printers to the Queen's most Excellent Majesty.
For Her Majesty's Stationery Office.

www.ingramcontent.com/pod-product-compliance
Lightning Source LLC
Chambersburg PA
CBHW021927110726
47901CB00003B/743

* 9 7 8 3 7 4 2 8 3 0 7 1 5 *